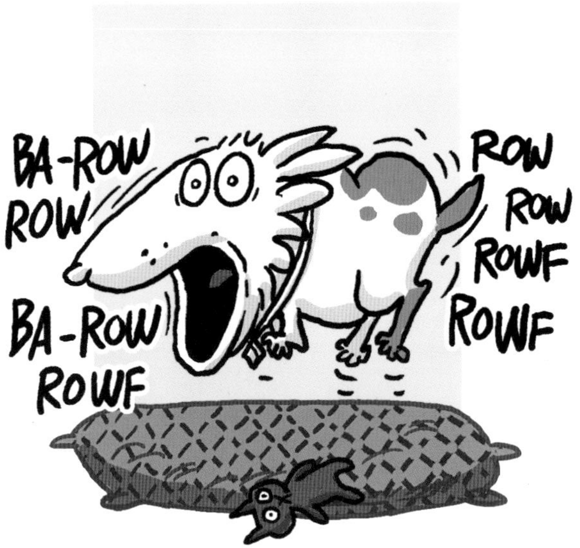
BA-ROW
ROW
BA-ROW
ROWF
ROW
ROW
ROWF
ROWF

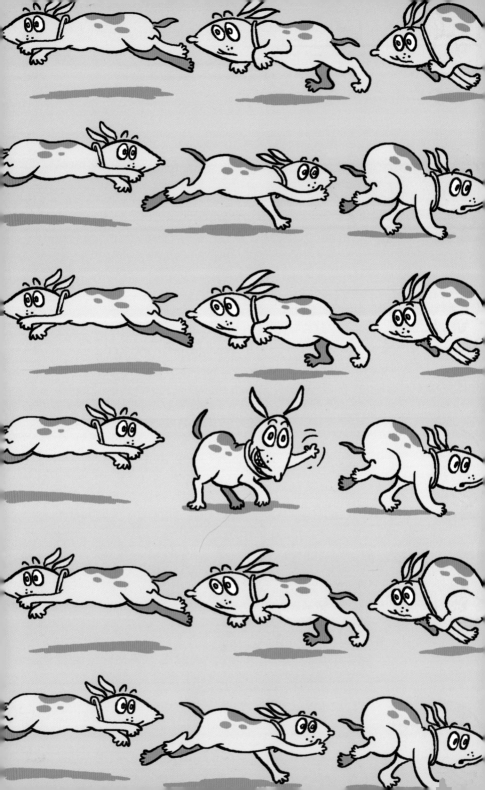

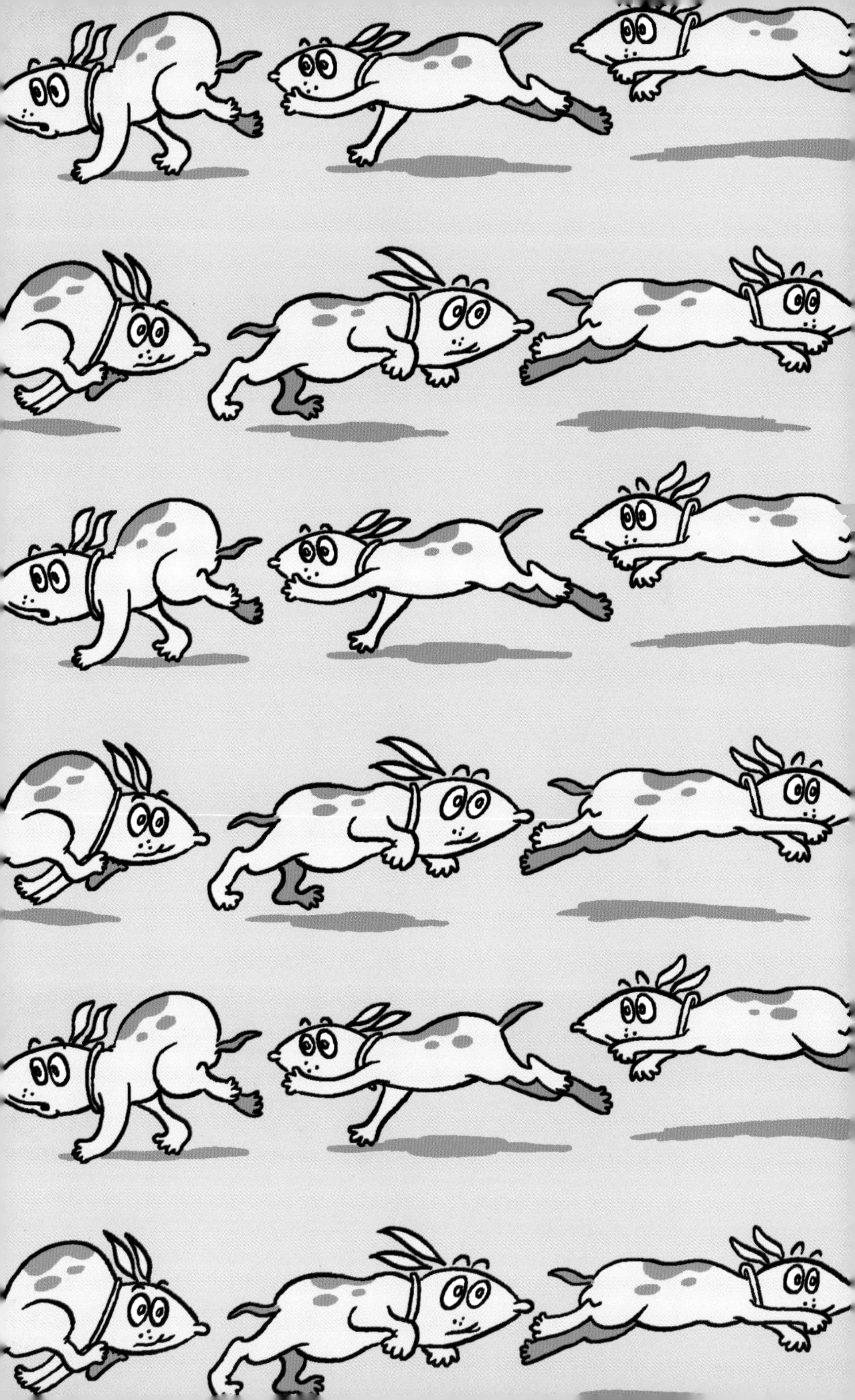

THE EXPETS

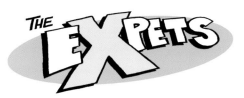

THE EX PETS

MARK TATULLI

A CAITLYN DLOUHY BOOK

ATHENEUM BOOKS FOR YOUNG READERS

NEW YORK LONDON TORONTO SYDNEY NEW DELHI

A
atheneum

ATHENEUM BOOKS FOR YOUNG READERS

An imprint of Simon & Schuster Children's Publishing Division

1230 Avenue of the Americas, New York, New York 10020

ATHENEUM BOOKS FOR YOUNG READERS is a registered trademark of Simon & Schuster, Inc. Atheneum logo is a trademark of Simon & Schuster, Inc.

Simon & Schuster: Celebrating 100 Years of Publishing in 2024

For information about special discounts for bulk purchases, please contact Simon & Schuster Special Sales at 1-866-506-1949 or business@simonandschuster.com.

The Simon & Schuster Speakers Bureau can bring authors to your live event. For more information or to book an event, contact the Simon & Schuster Speakers Bureau at 1-866-248-3049 or visit our website at www.simonspeakers.com.

Interior design by Rebecca Syracuse

The text for this book was hand-lettered.

The illustrations for this book were rendered digitally.

Manufactured in China

1223 SCP

First Edition

2 4 6 8 10 9 7 5 3 1

Library of Congress Cataloging-in-Publication Data

Names: Tatulli, Mark, author.

Title: The eXpets / Mark Tatulli.

Description: New York : Atheneum Books for Young Readers, 2024– | Audience: Ages 7–12 | Audience: Grades 4–6 | Summary: "This is a story of a pet dog named Bosco who discovers he has special skills and is asked to join the eXpets and saved the world's kittens from an evil mastermind"— Provided by publisher.

Identifiers: LCCN 2022058011 | ISBN 9781665914871 (v. 1 ; hardcover) | ISBN 9781665914895 (v. 1 ; ebook)

Subjects: CYAC: Graphic novels. | Pets—Fiction. | Ability—Fiction. | Superheroes—Fiction. | Humorous stories. | LCGFT: Funny animal comics. | Superhero comics. | Graphic novels.

Classification: LCC PZ7.7.T377 Ex 2023 | DDC 741.5/973—dc23/eng/20230214

LC record available at https://lccn.loc.gov/2022058011

TO
ANDRE, FELLINI, TWO DAYS,
MIMI, BELLA, HENRY,
GUINNESS, JOLLY, SAMMY,
AND ALL THE OTHER CREATURES
WHO GRACIOUSLY SHARED
THEIR LIVES WITH ME.

YOU INSPIRED ME TO MAKE THIS
BOOK, AND SO MUCH MORE!

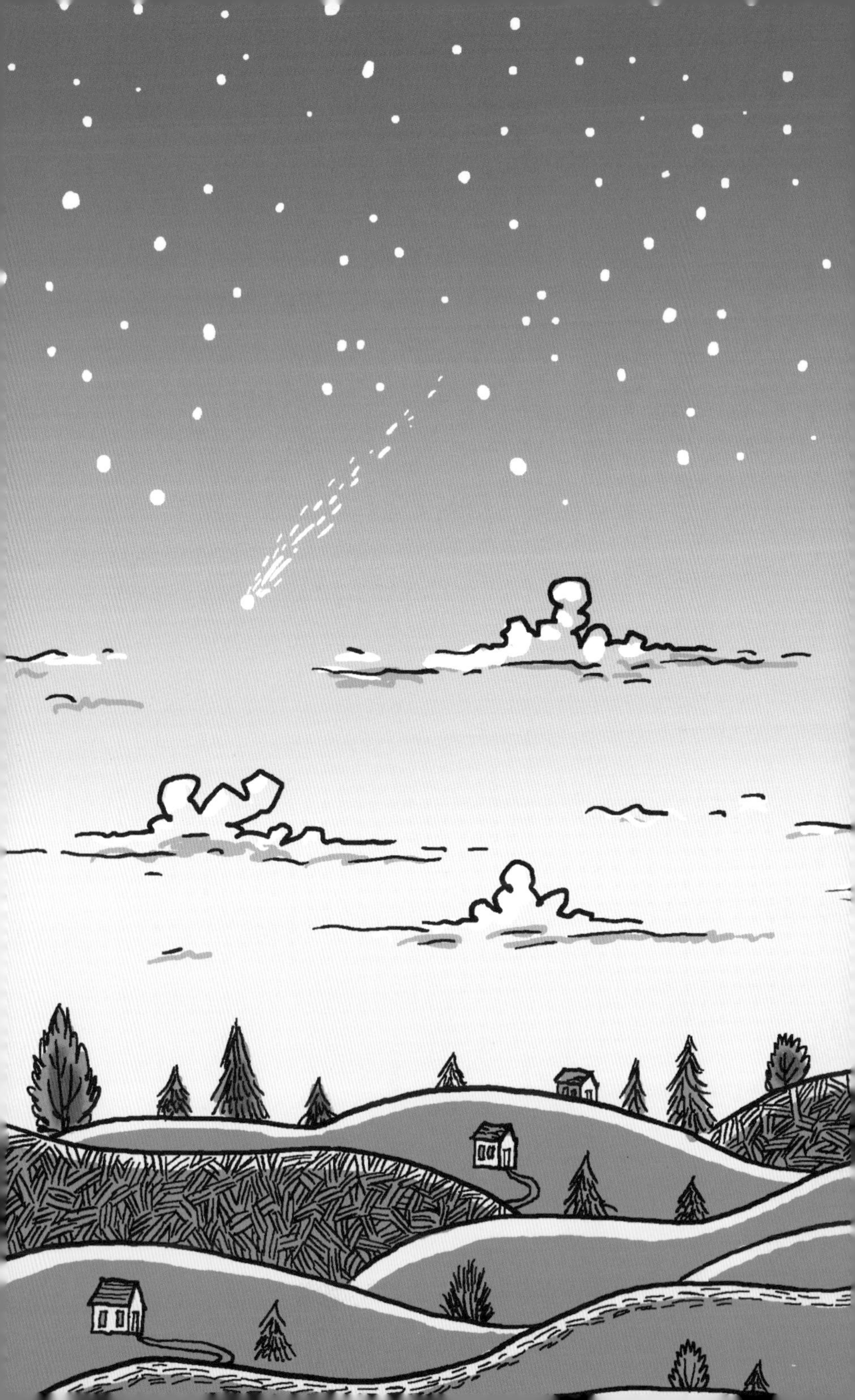

PART 1: A CALL TO ACTION

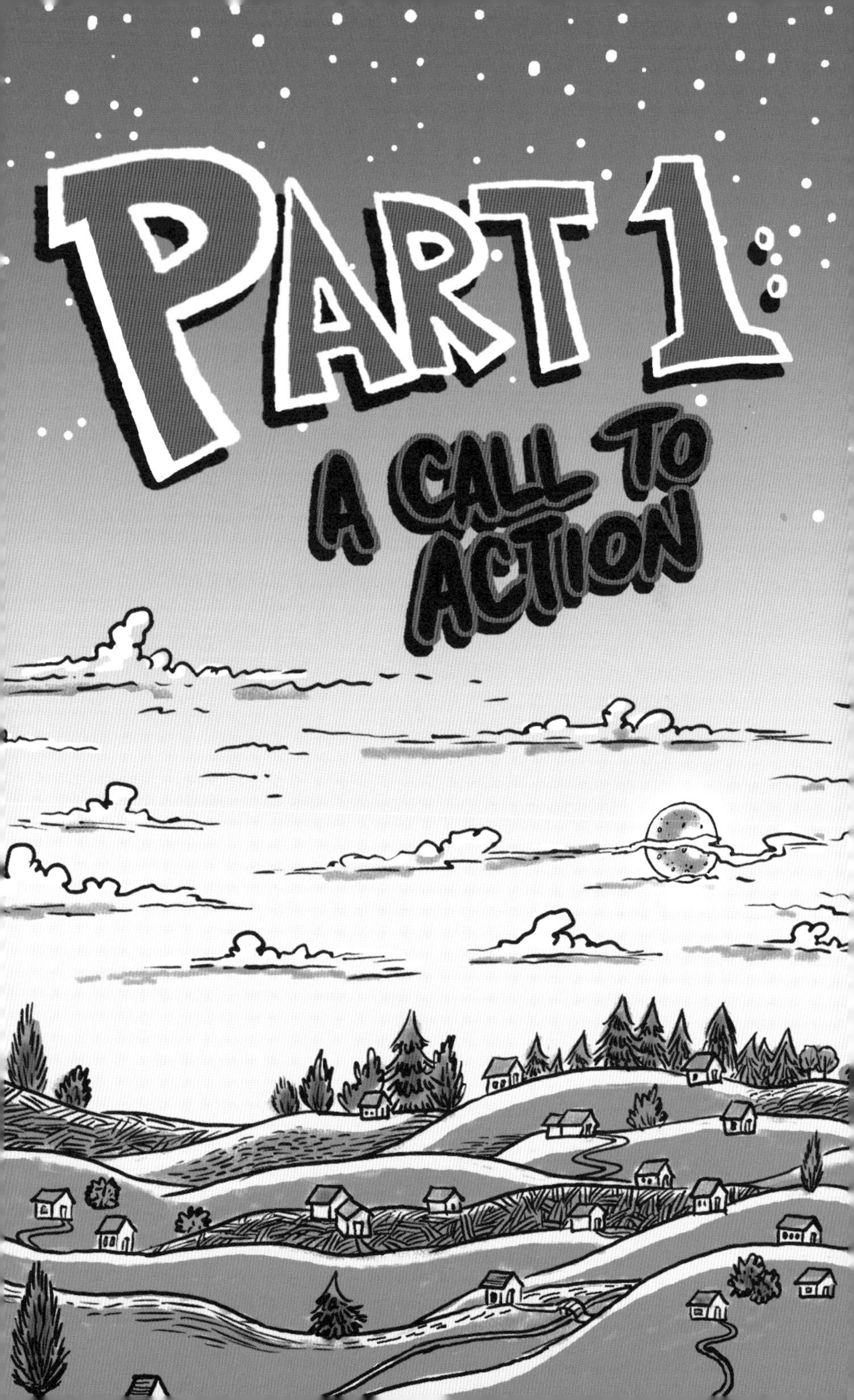

CHAPTER 1

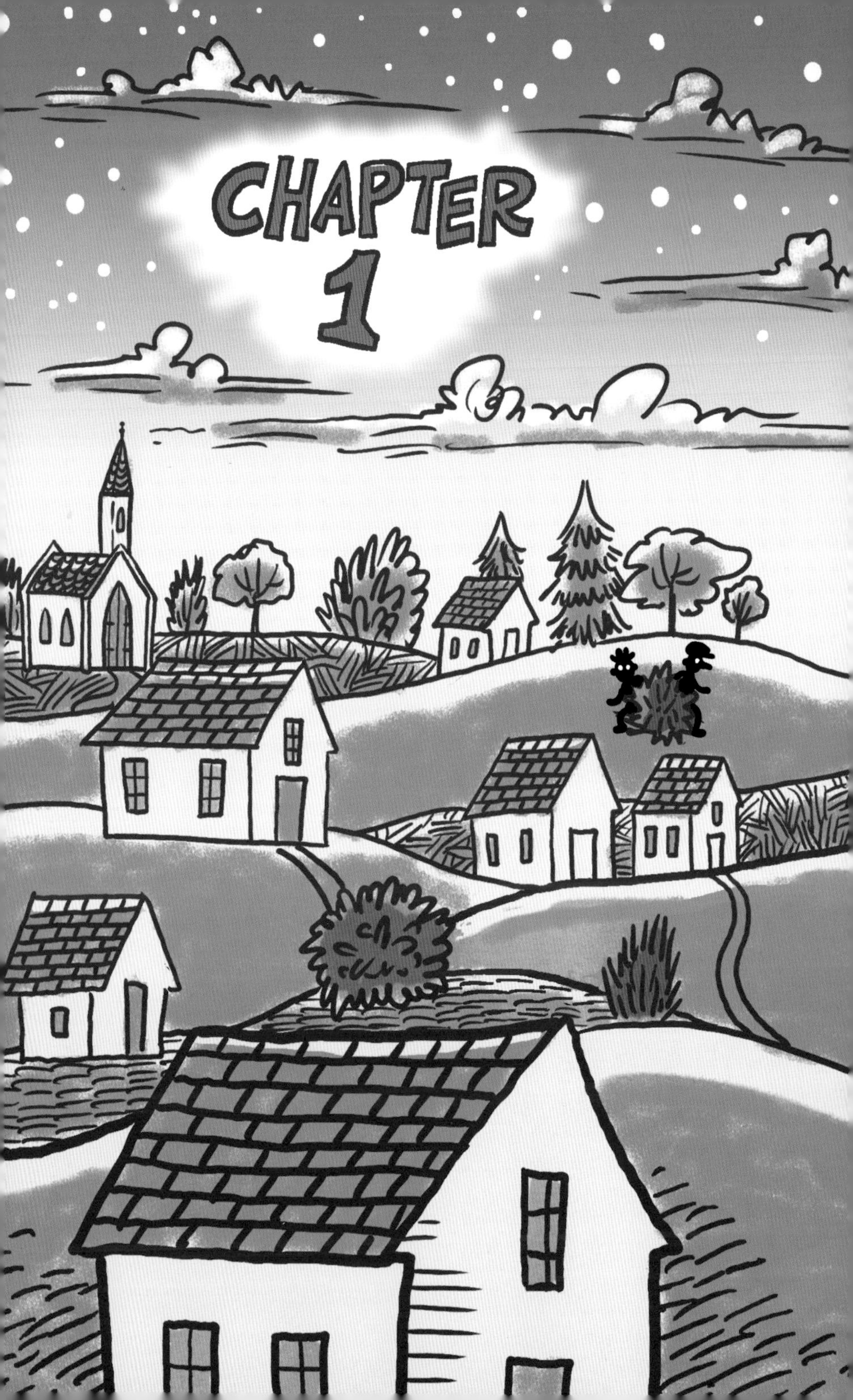

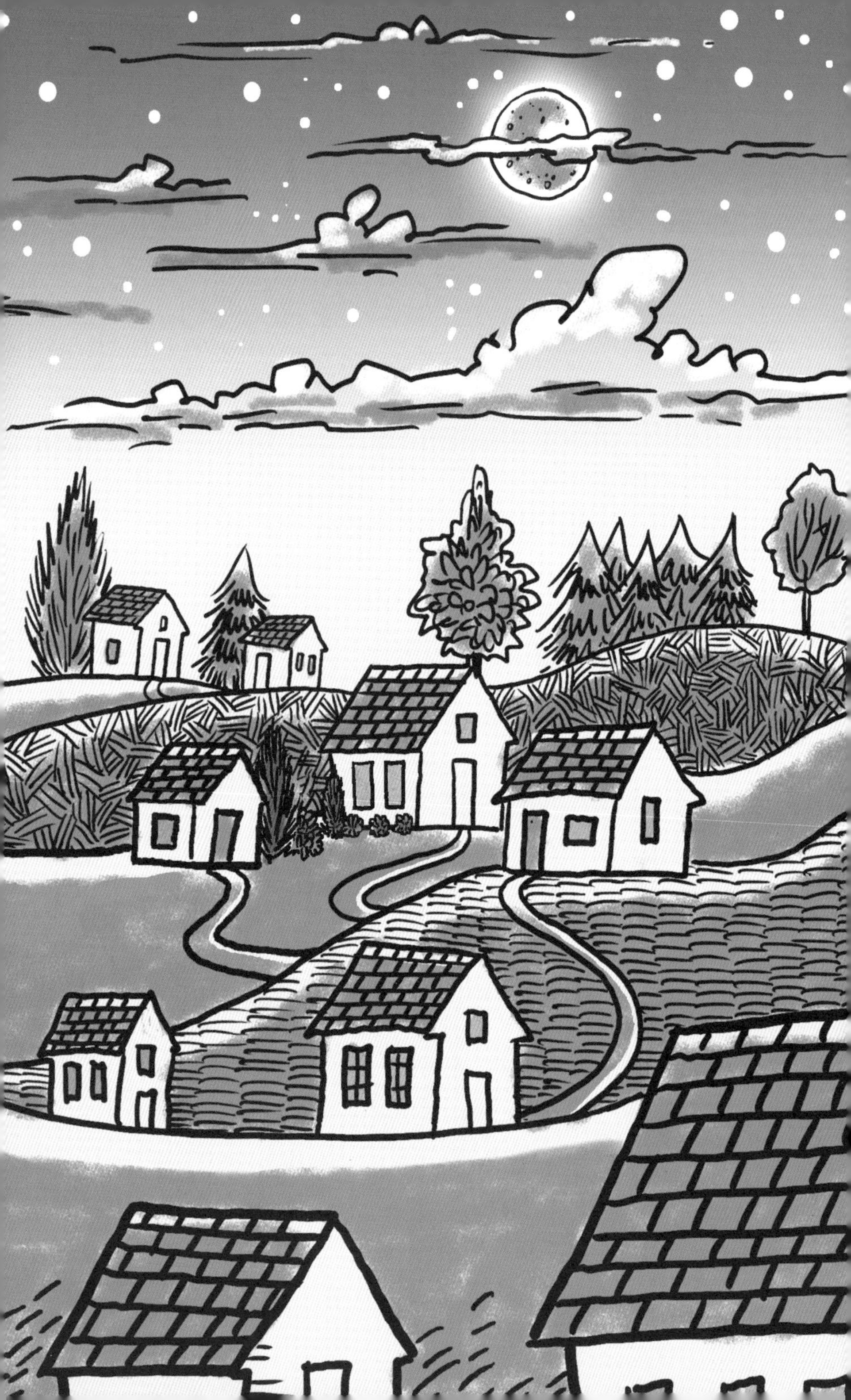

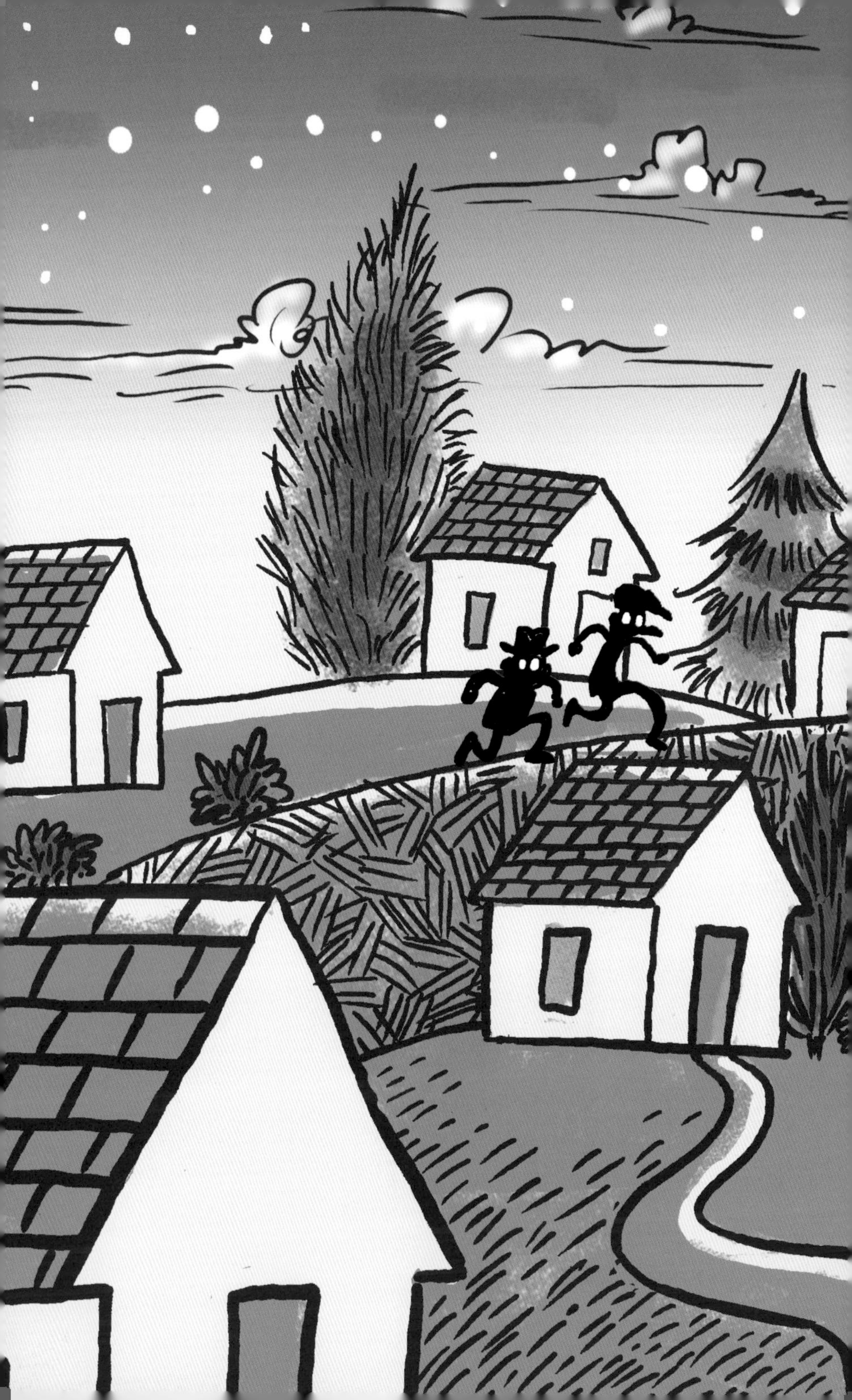

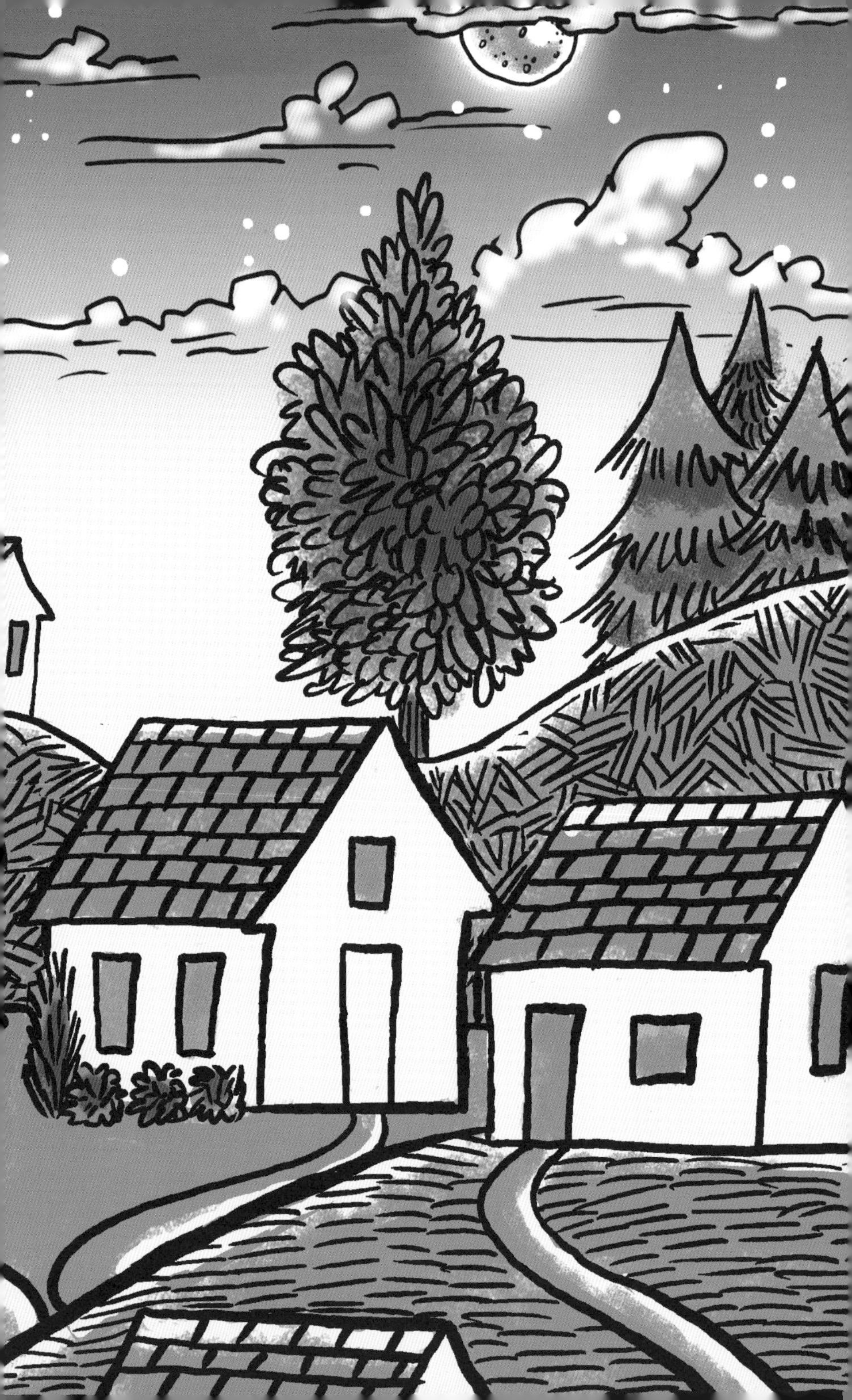

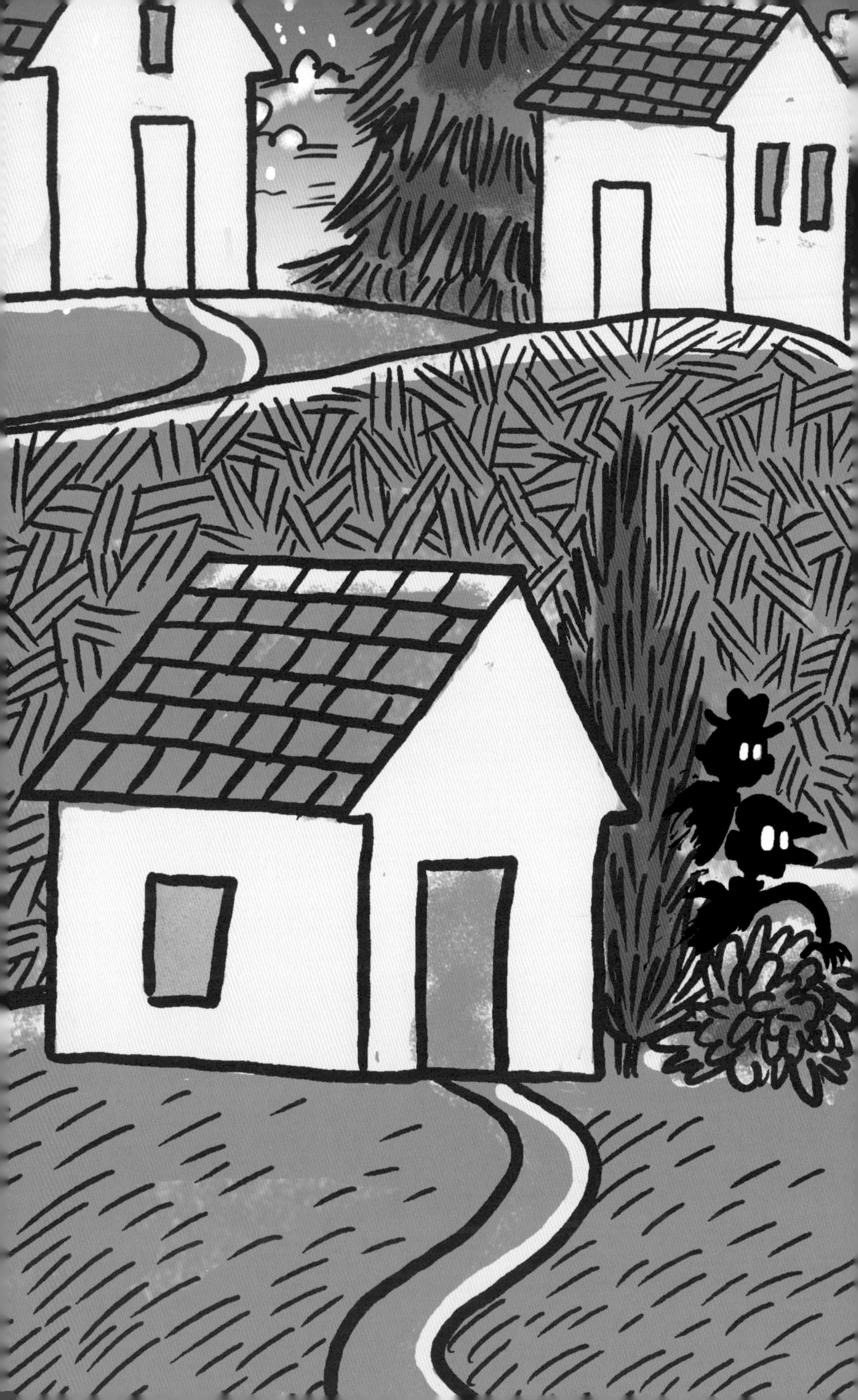

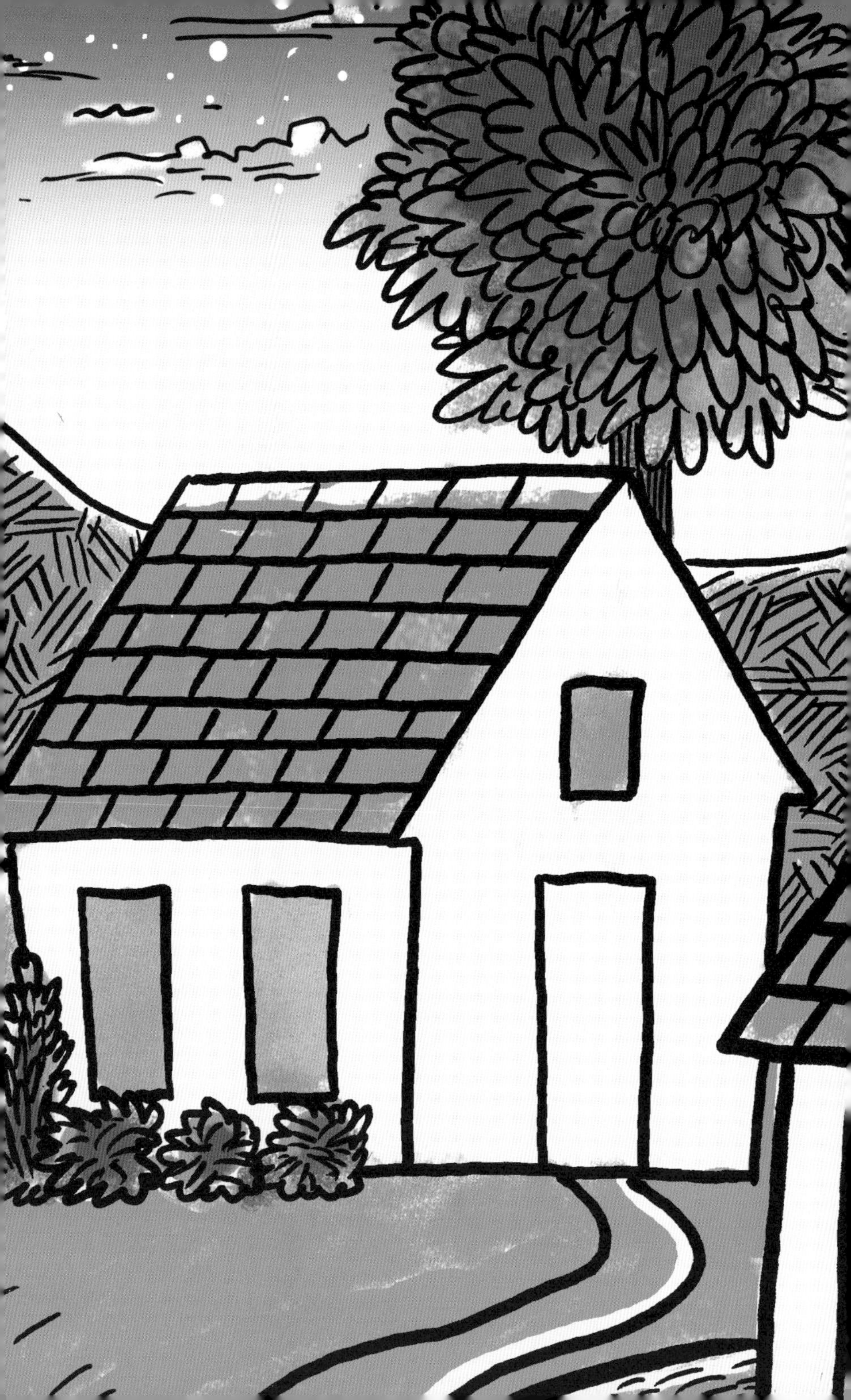

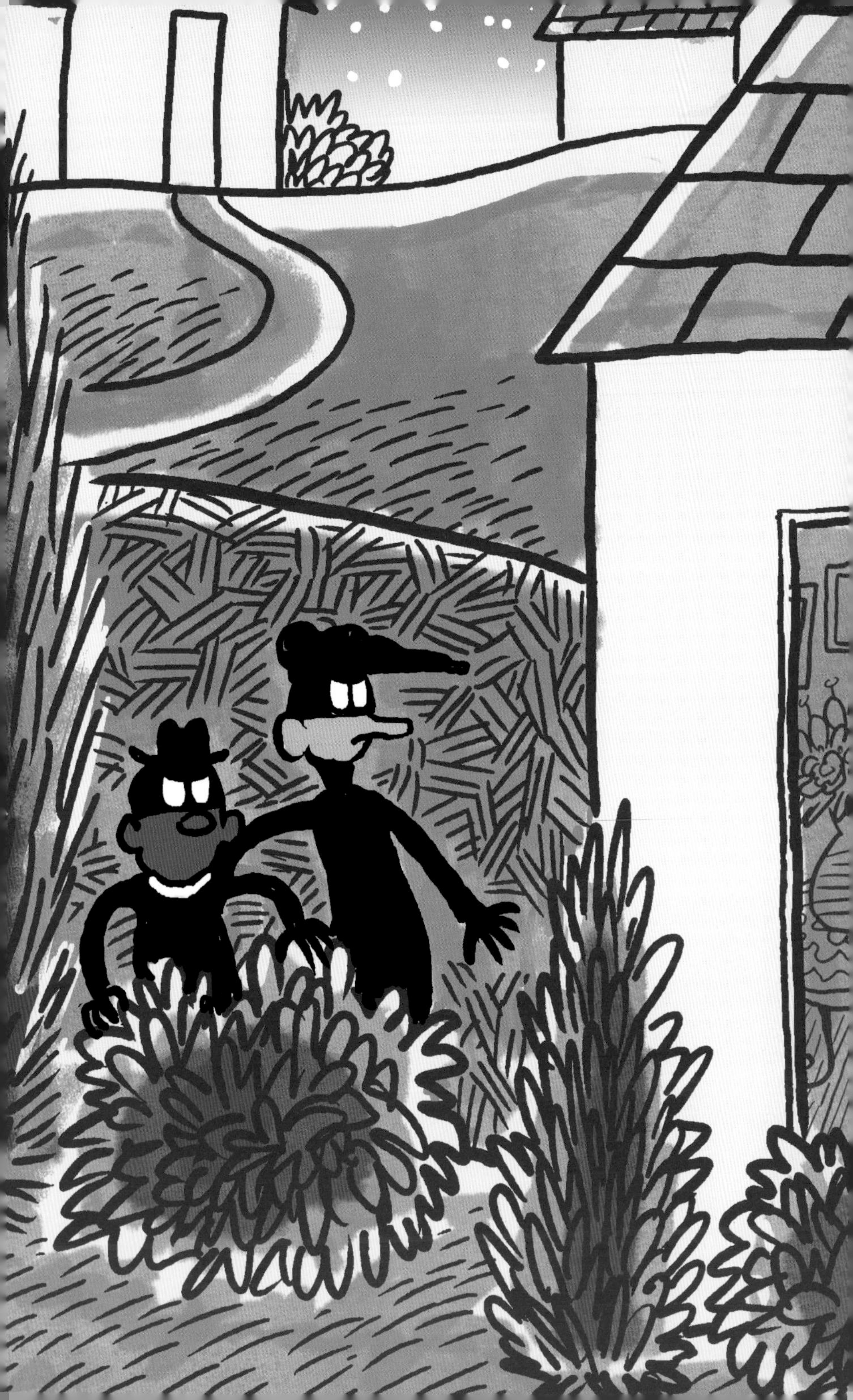

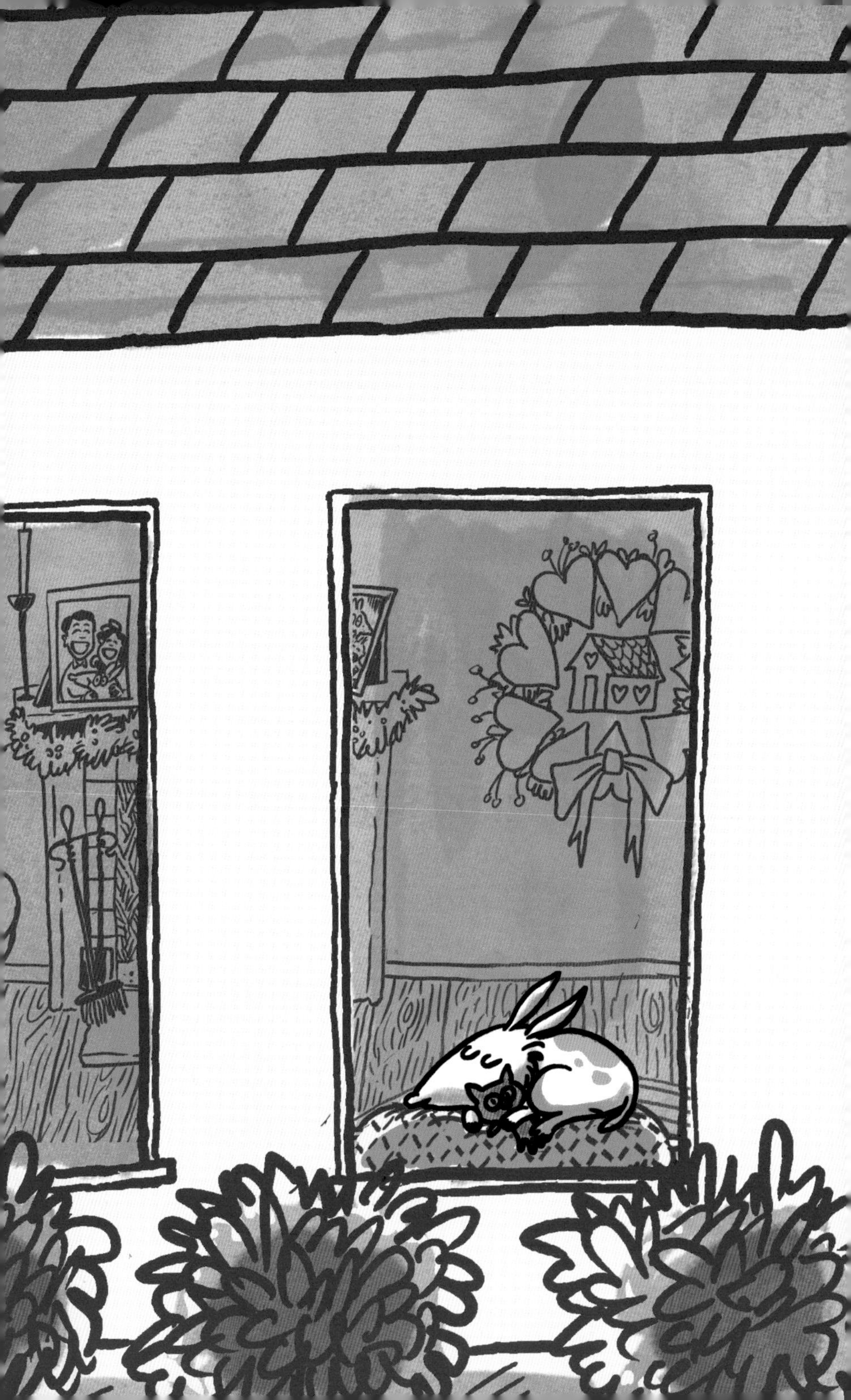

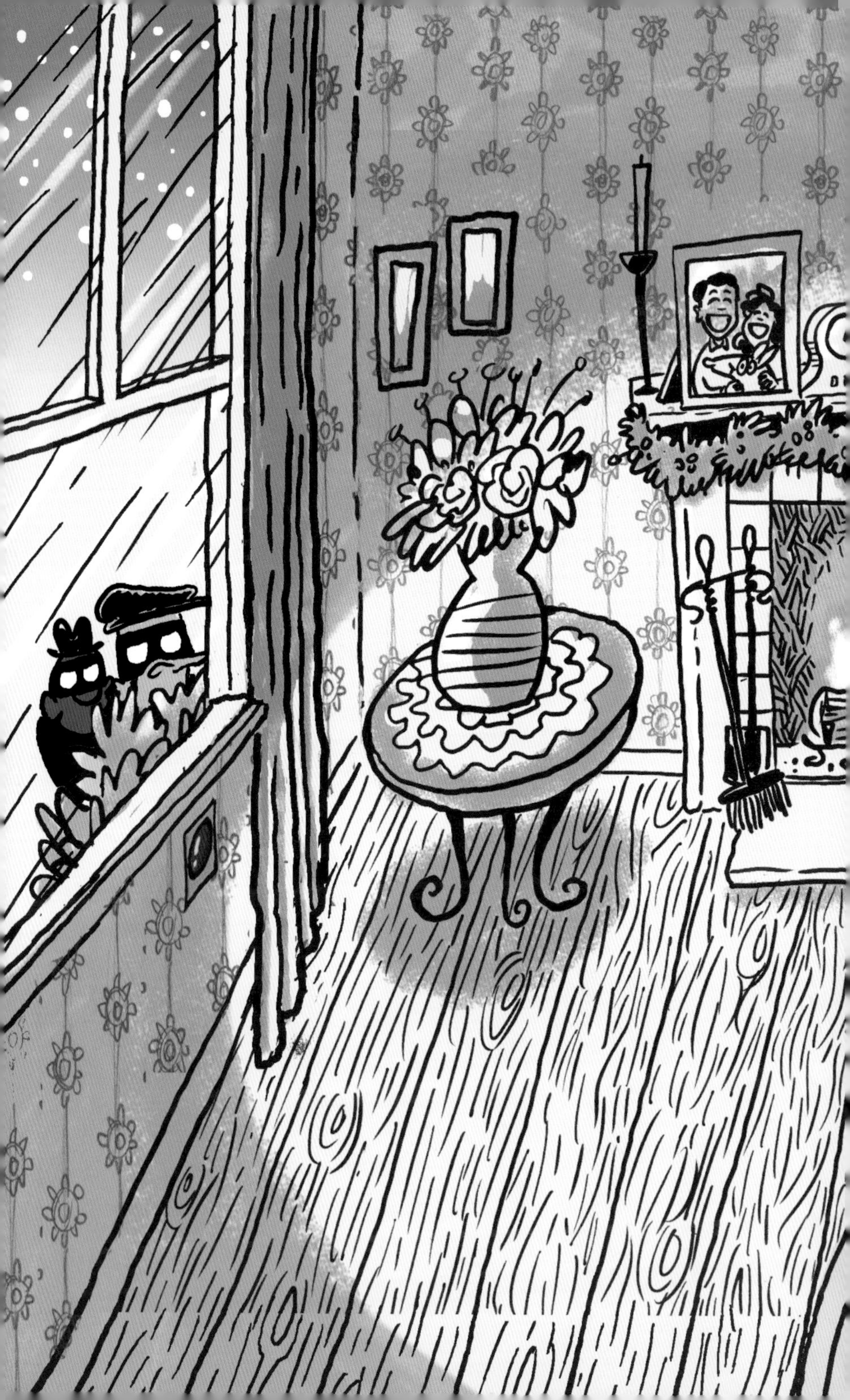

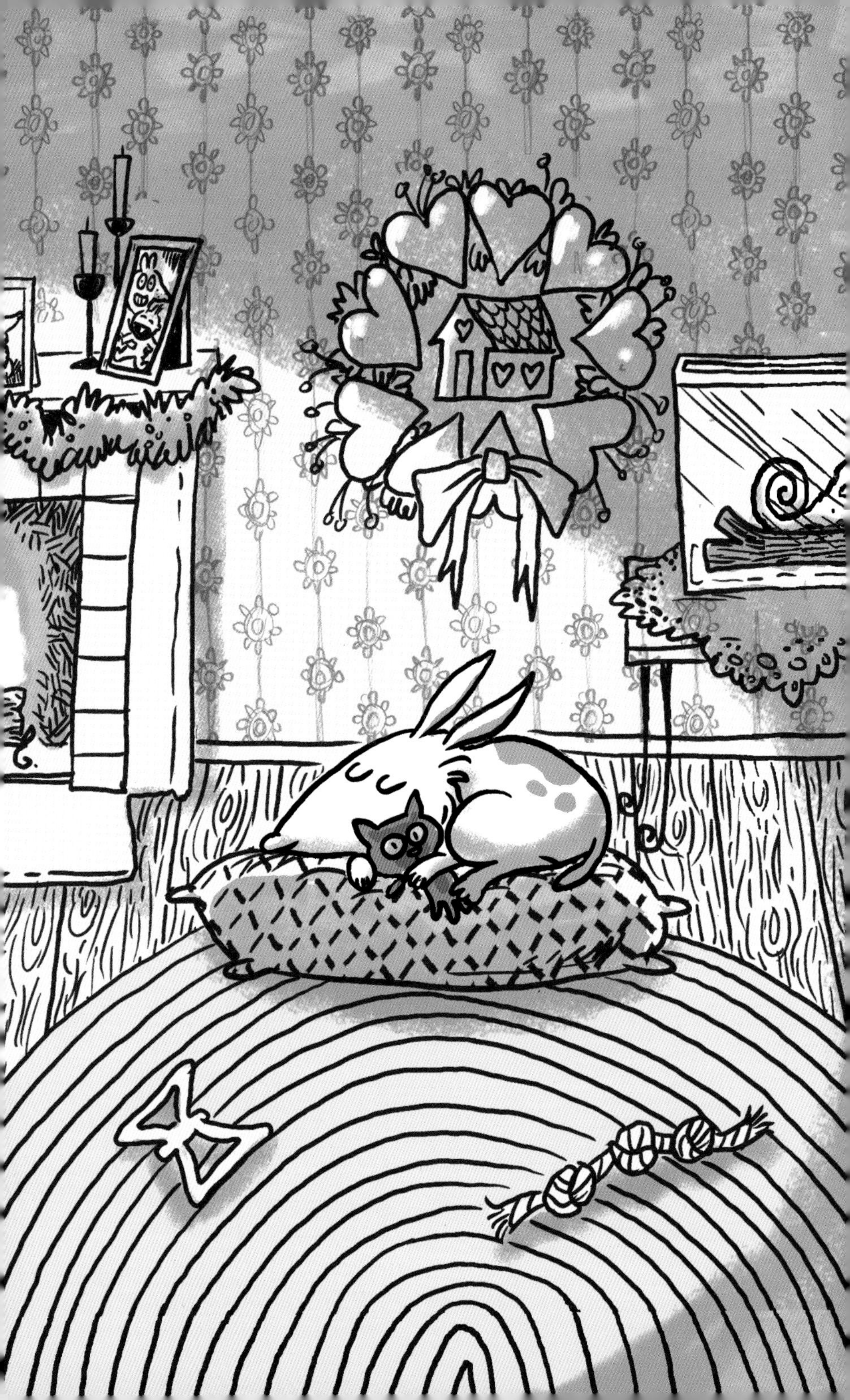

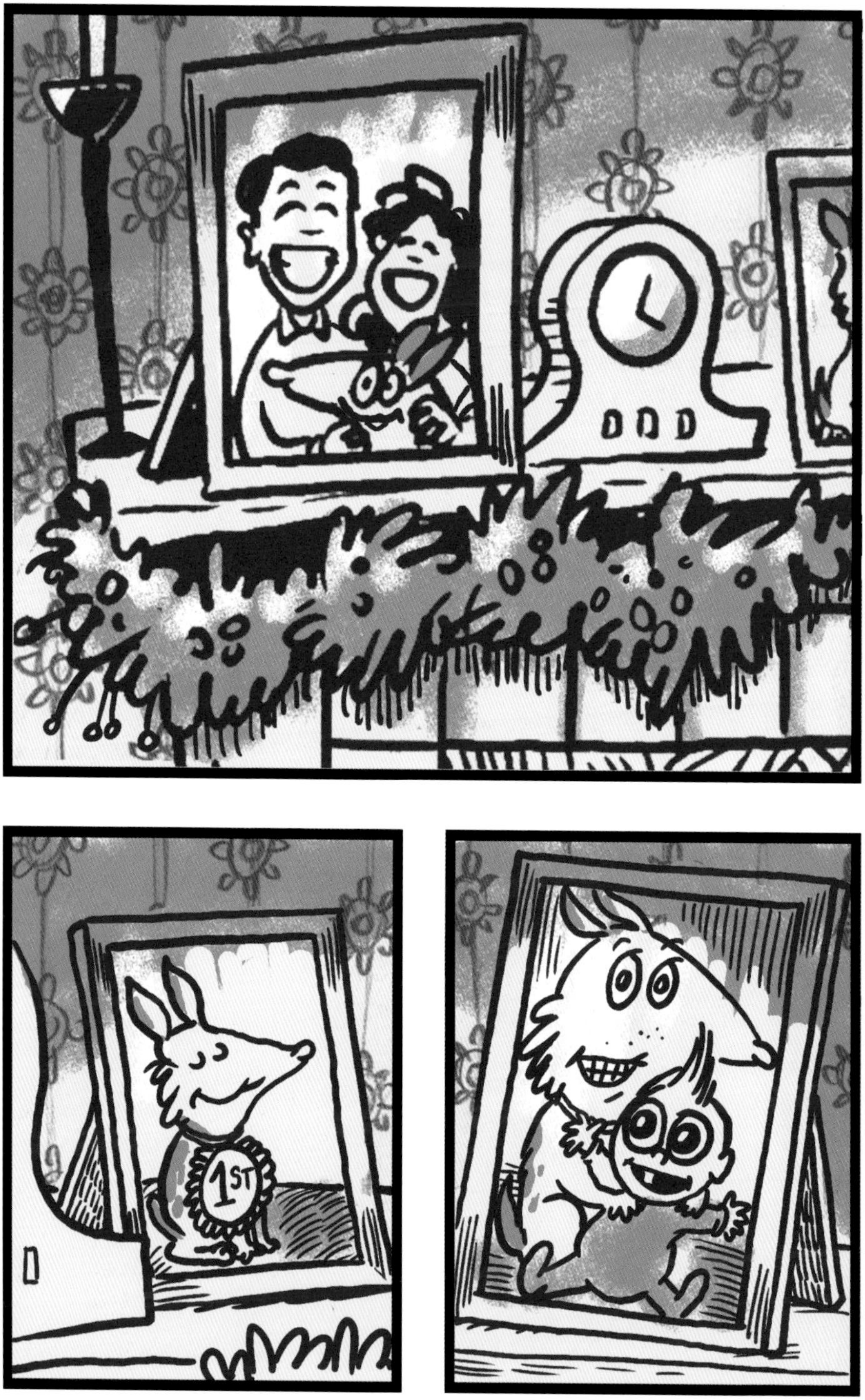
1ST

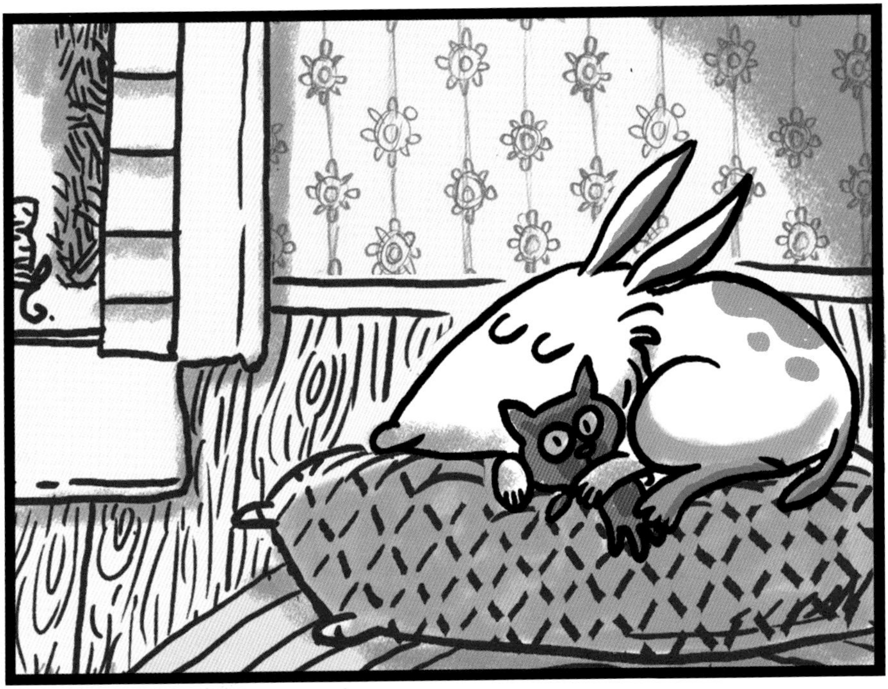

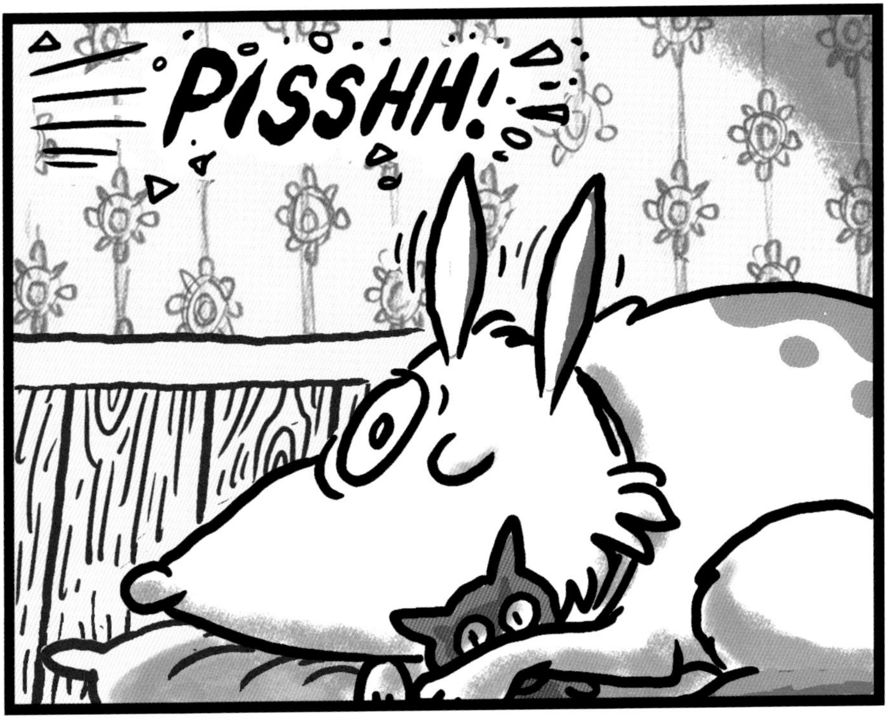
PISSHH!

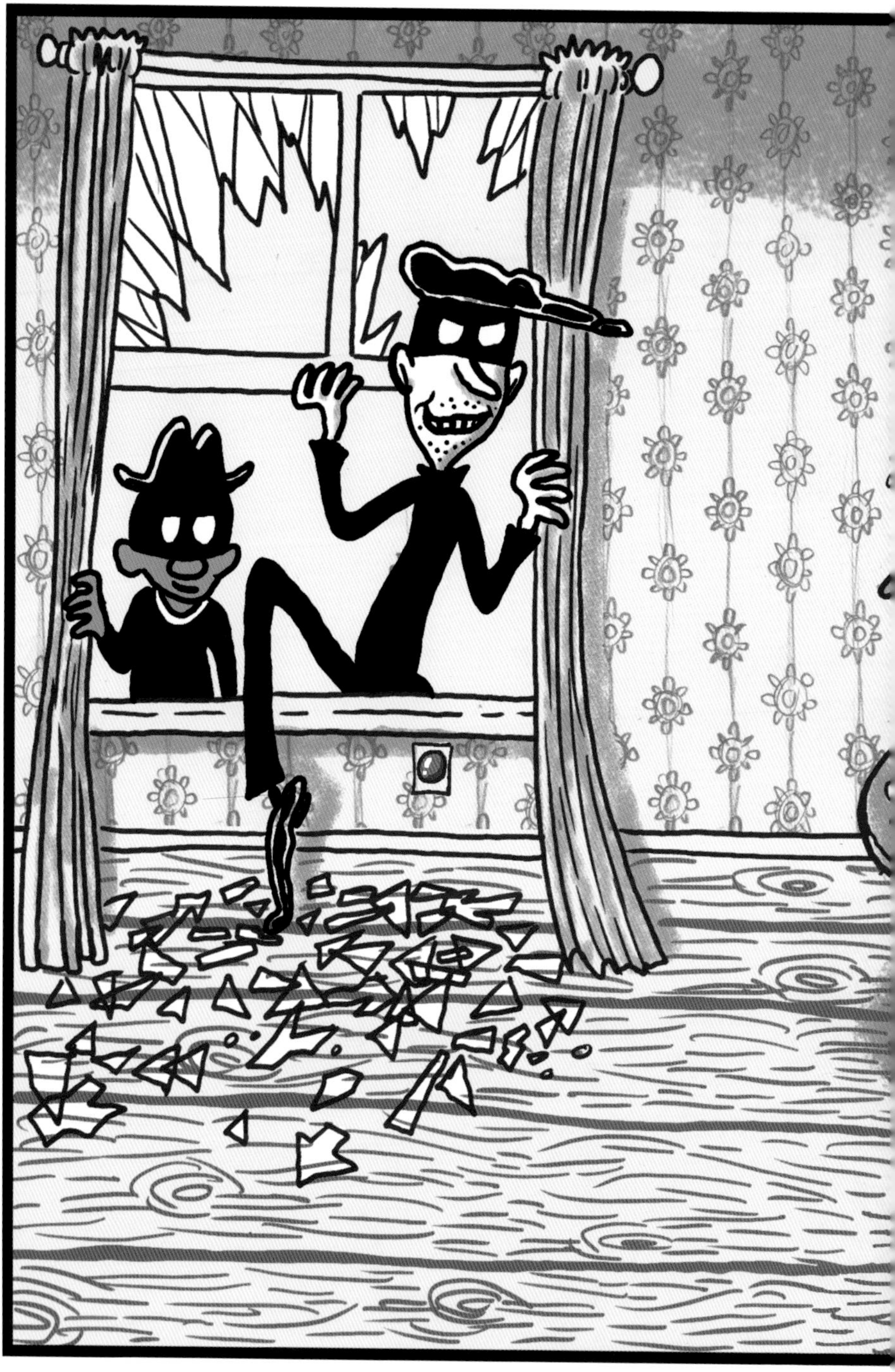

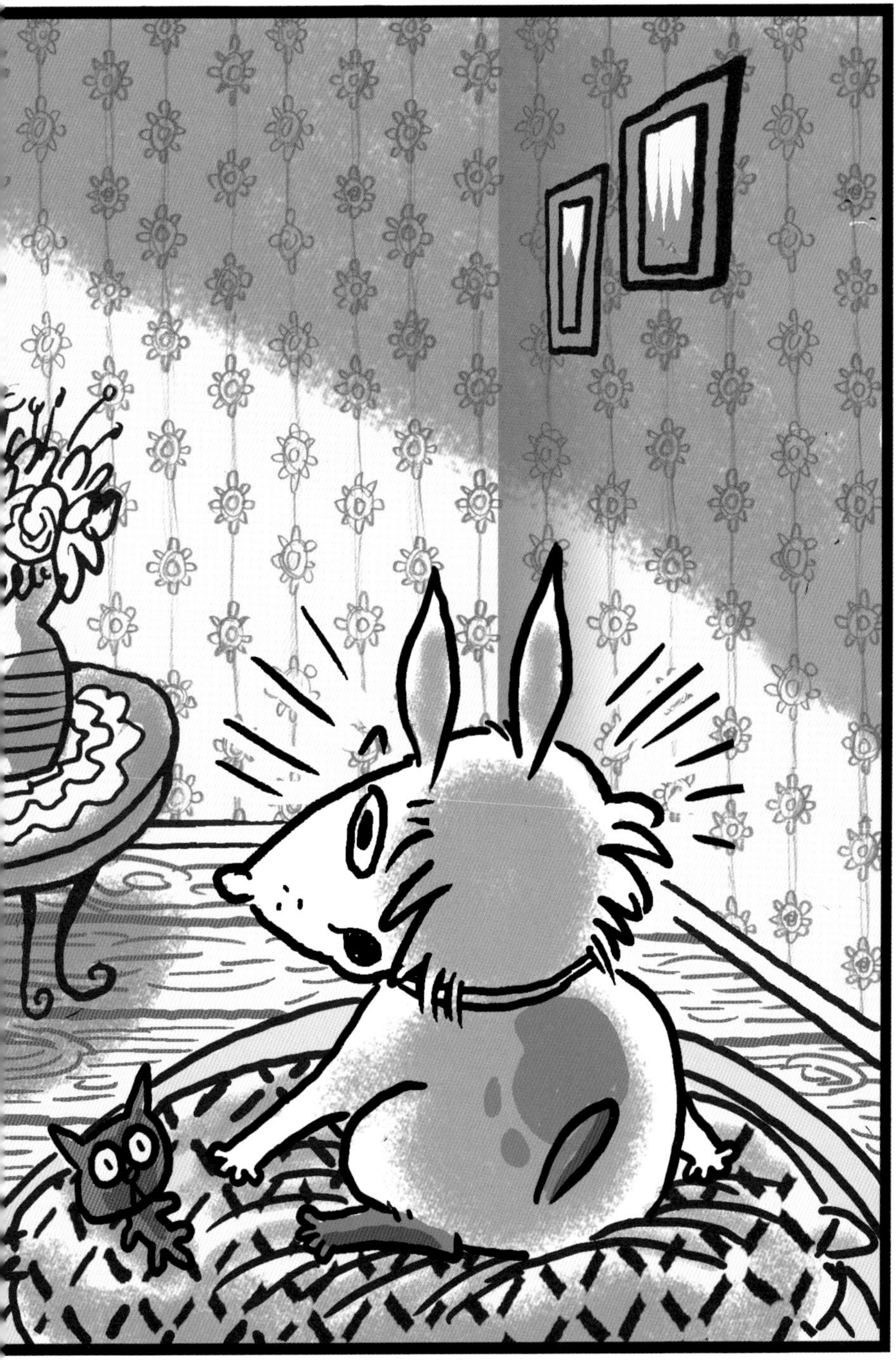

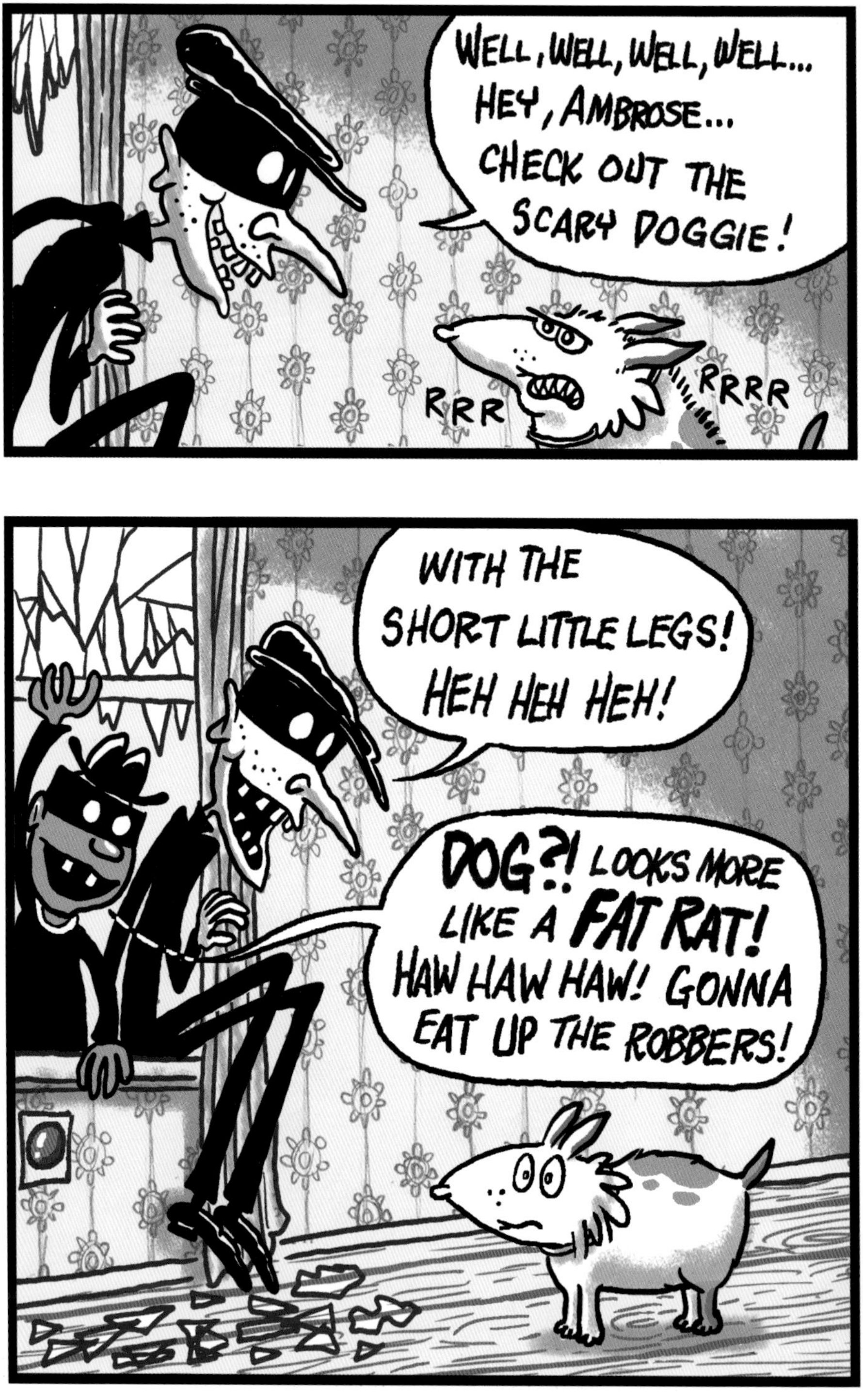
WELL, WELL, WELL, WELL... HEY, AMBROSE... CHECK OUT THE SCARY DOGGIE!
RRR
RRRR
WITH THE SHORT LITTLE LEGS! HEH HEH HEH!
DOG?! LOOKS MORE LIKE A FAT RAT! HAW HAW HAW! GONNA EAT UP THE ROBBERS!

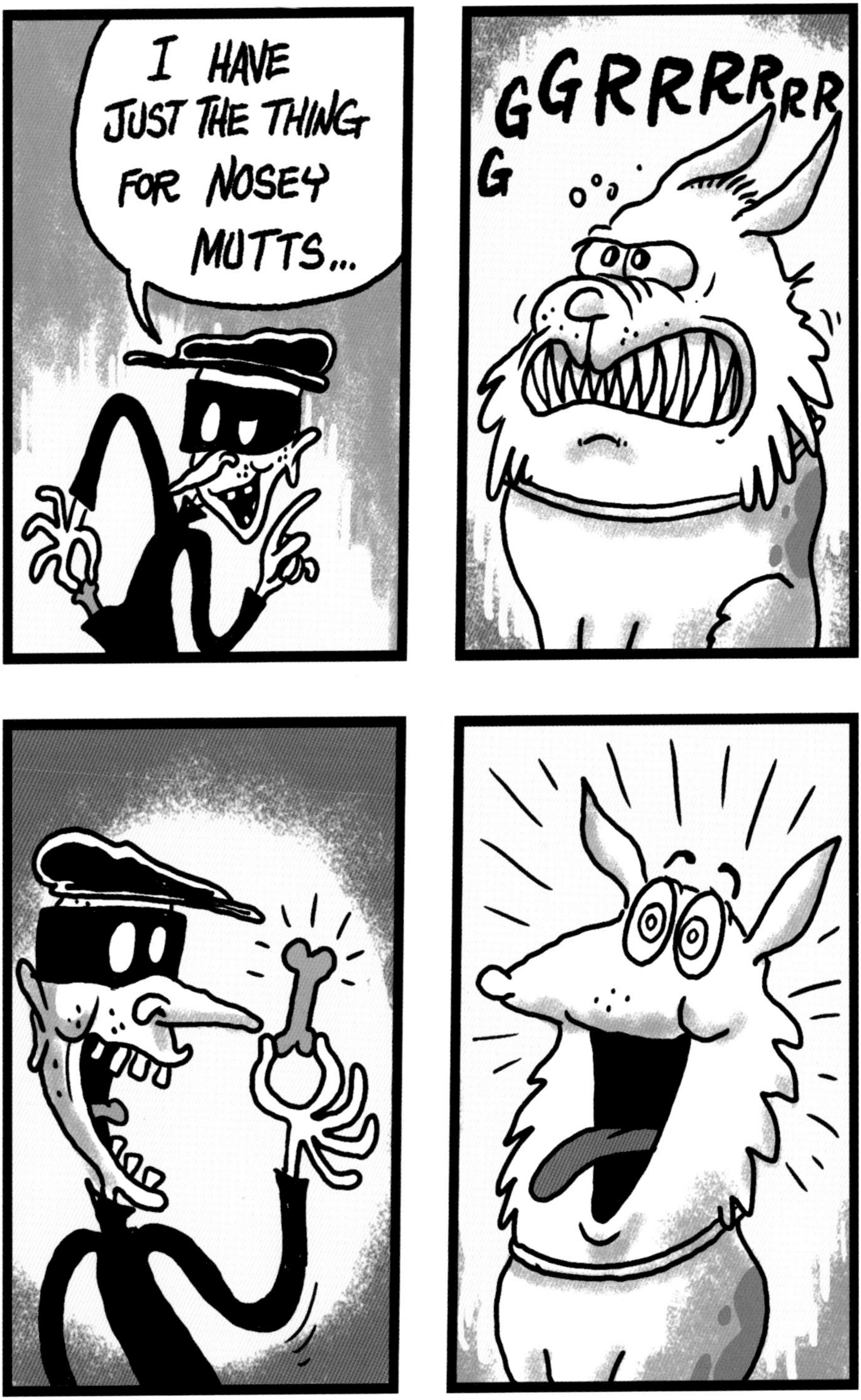
I HAVE JUST THE THING FOR NOSEY MUTTS...
GGGRRRRRRR

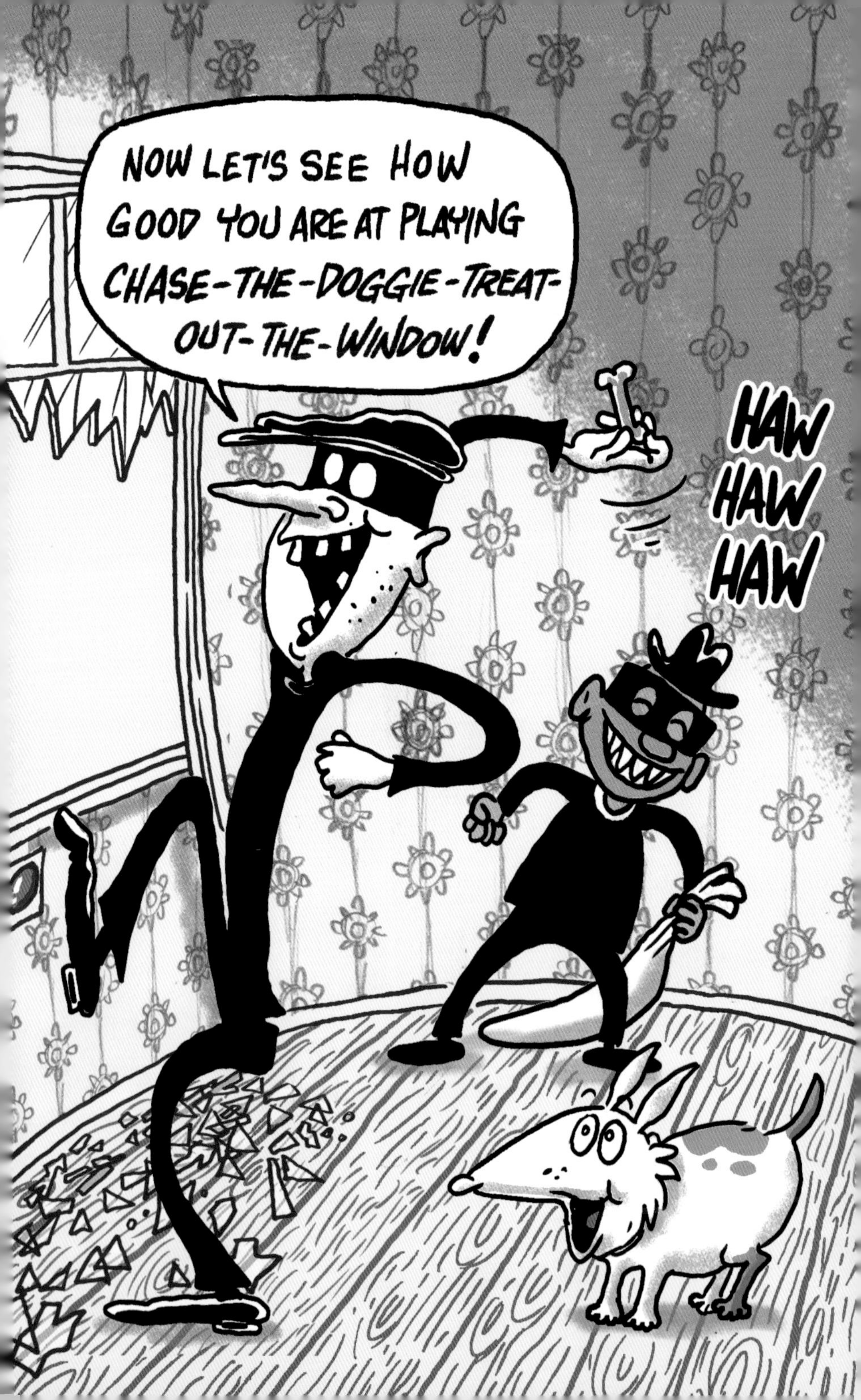
NOW LET'S SEE HOW GOOD YOU ARE AT PLAYING CHASE-THE-DOGGIE-TREAT-OUT-THE-WINDOW!
HAW HAW HAW

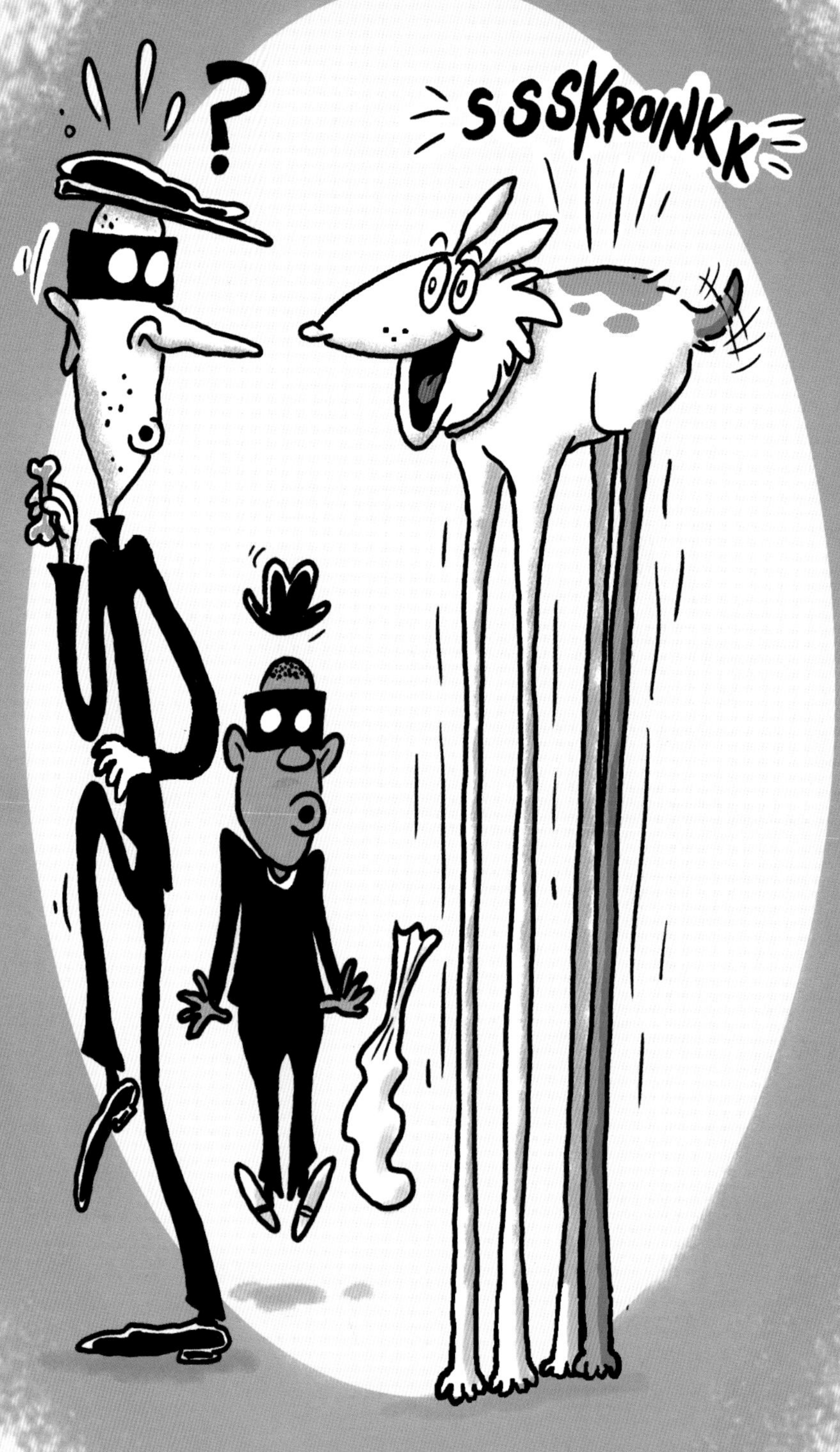
?
SSSKROINKK

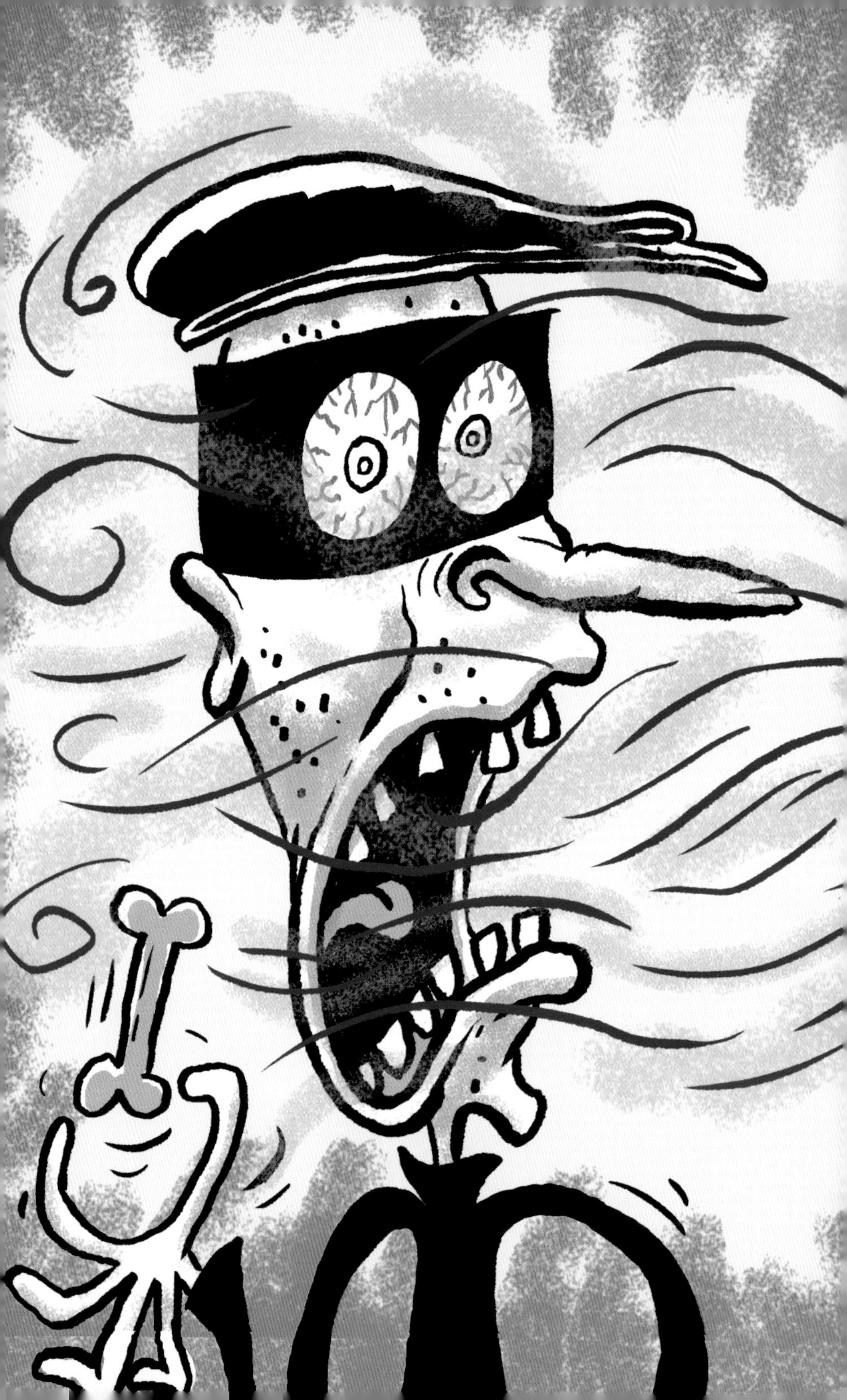

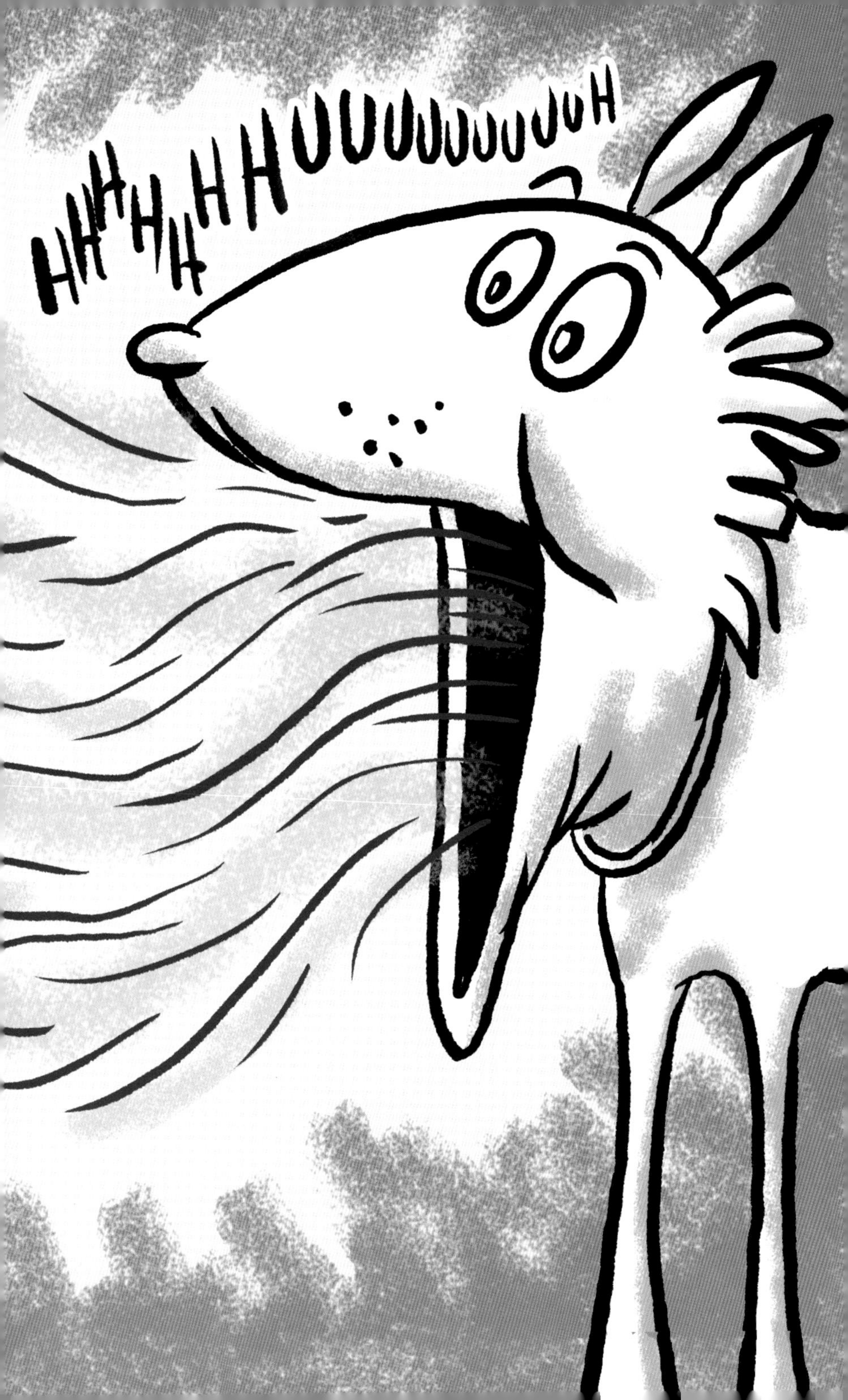
HHHHHHHUUUUUUUUUH

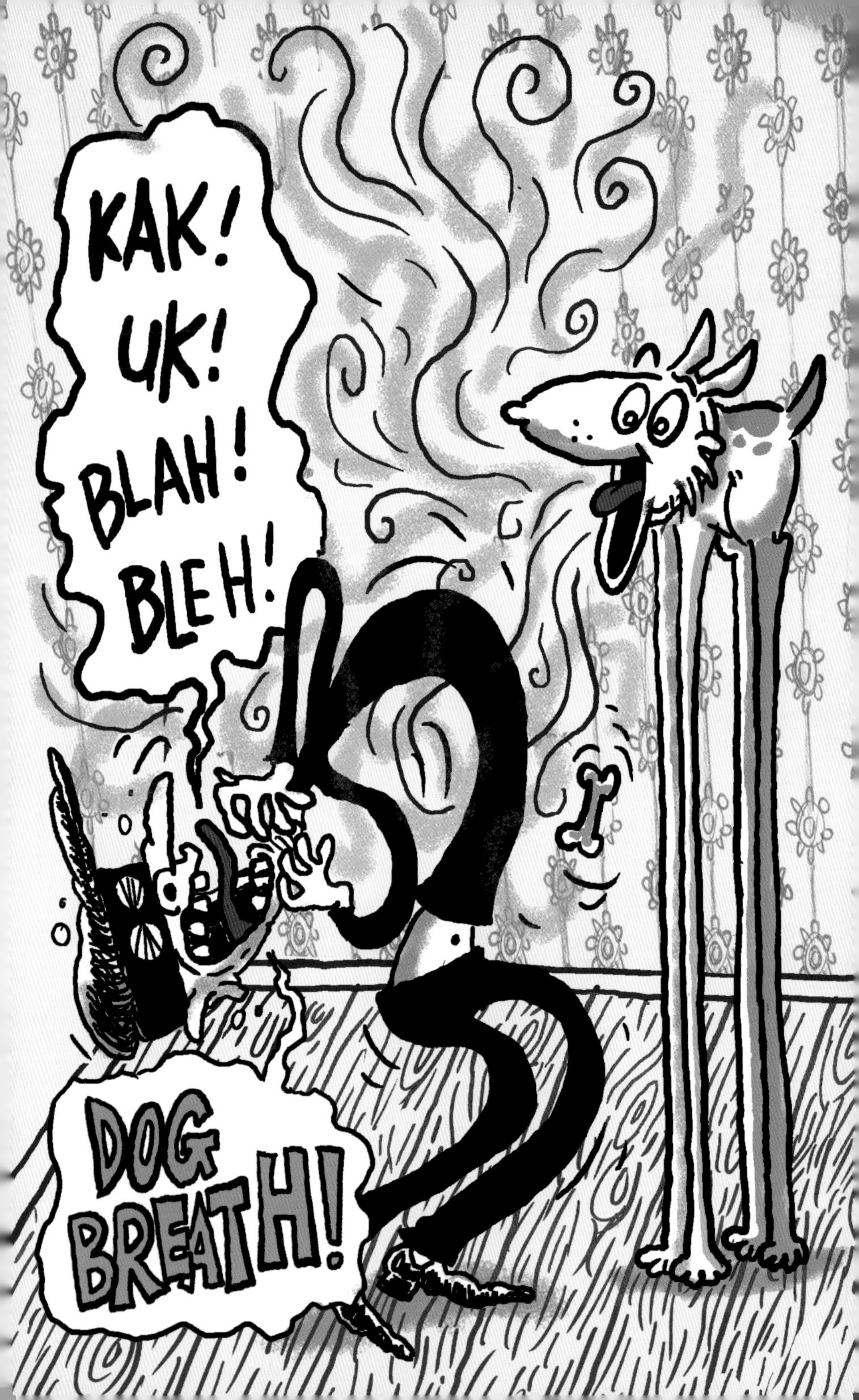
KAK! UK! BLAH! BLEH!
DOG BREATH!

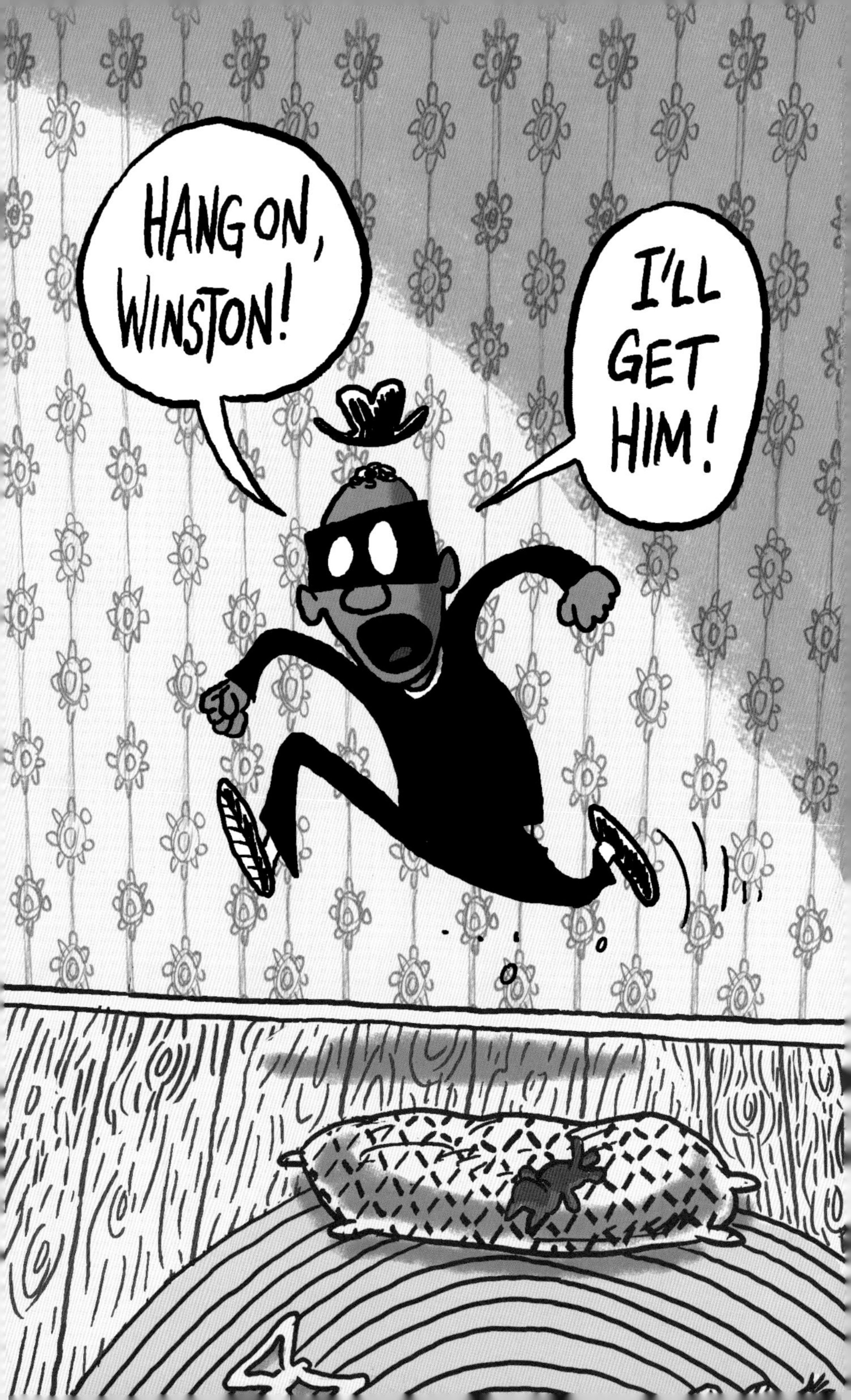
HANG ON, WINSTON!
I'LL GET HIM!

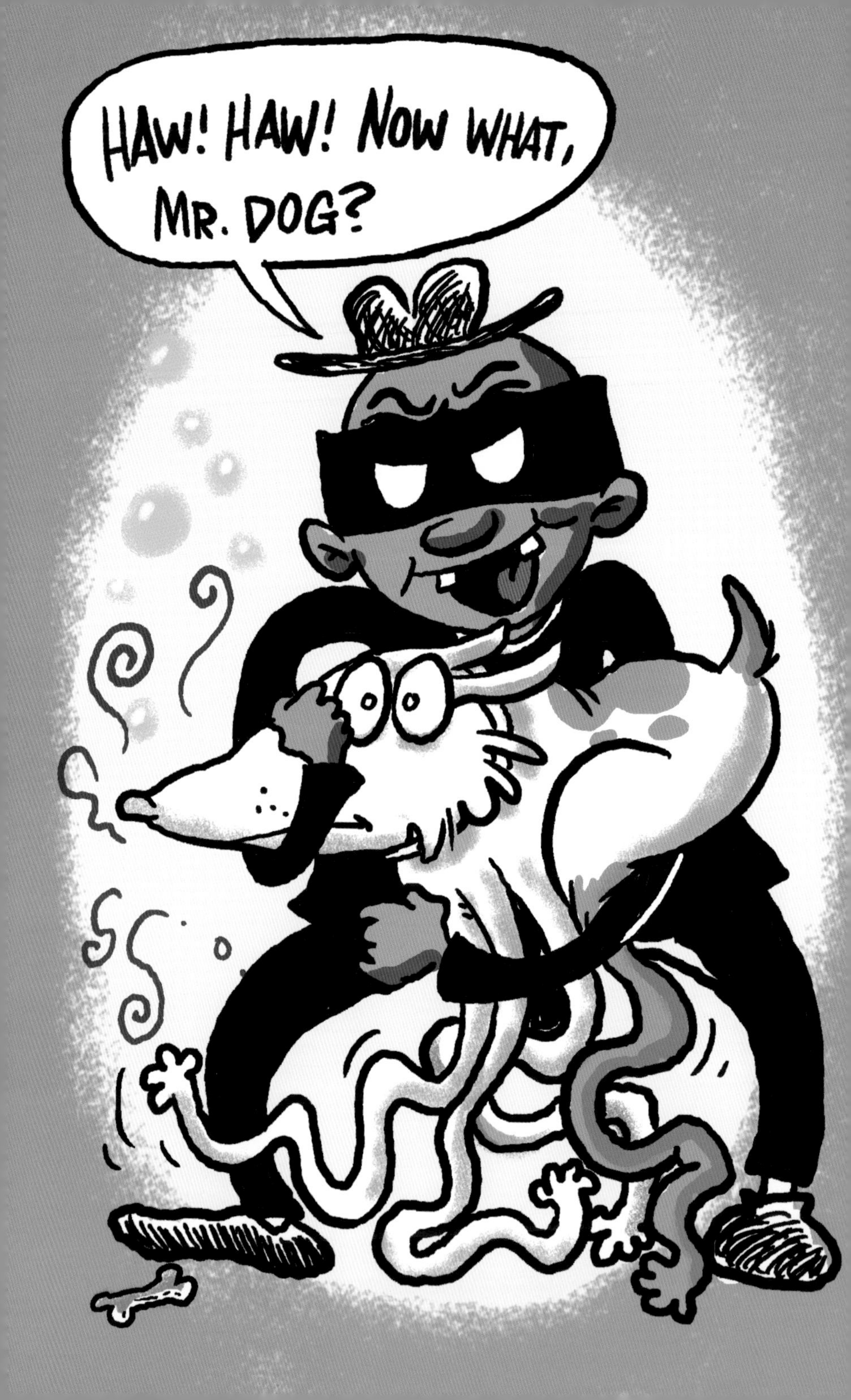
HAW! HAW! NOW WHAT, MR. DOG?

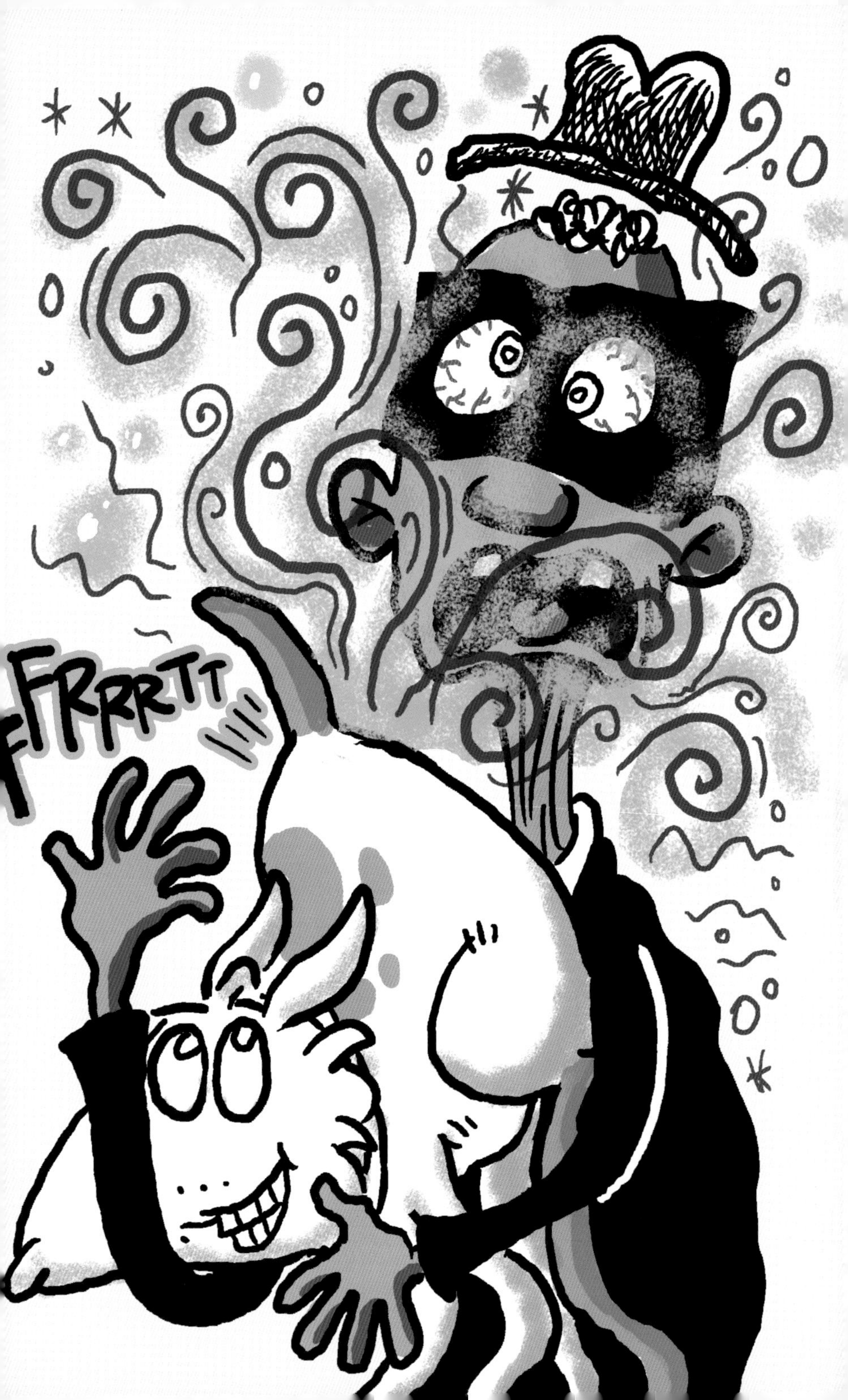
FRRRTT

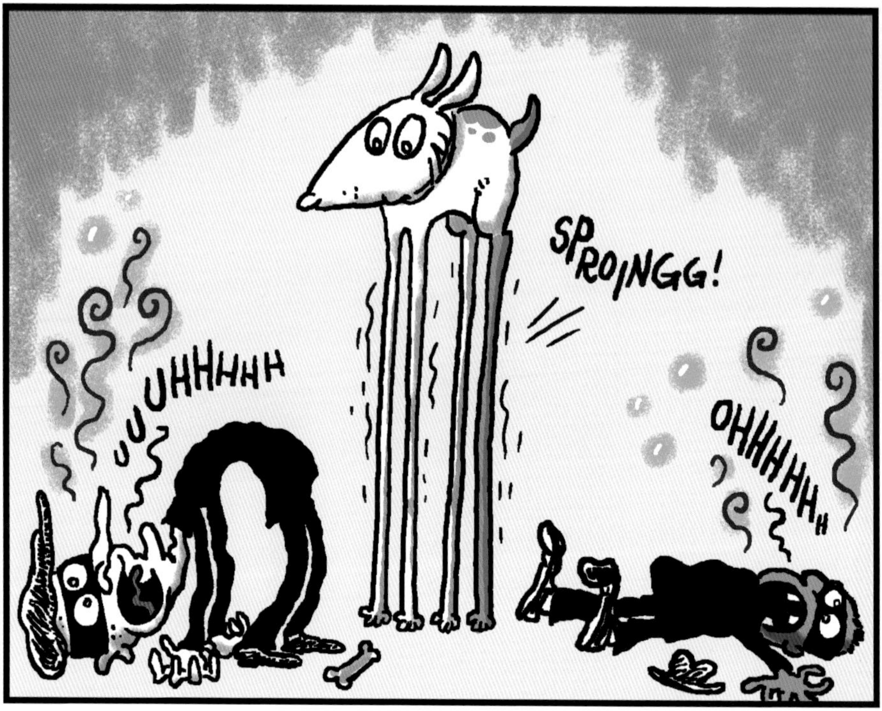
SPROINGG!
UUUHHHHHH
OHHHHHHH

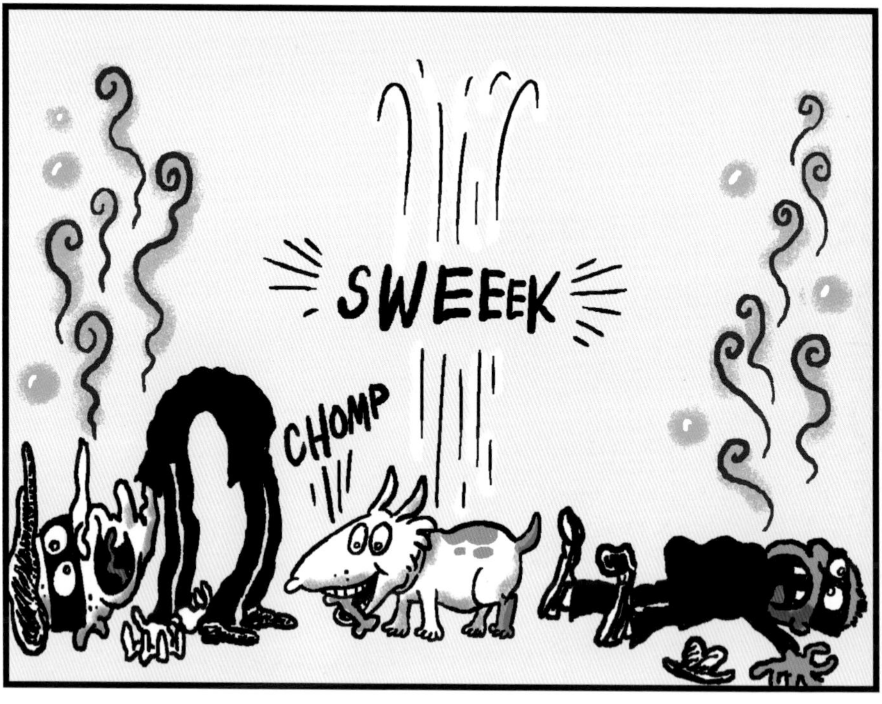
SWEEEK
CHOMP

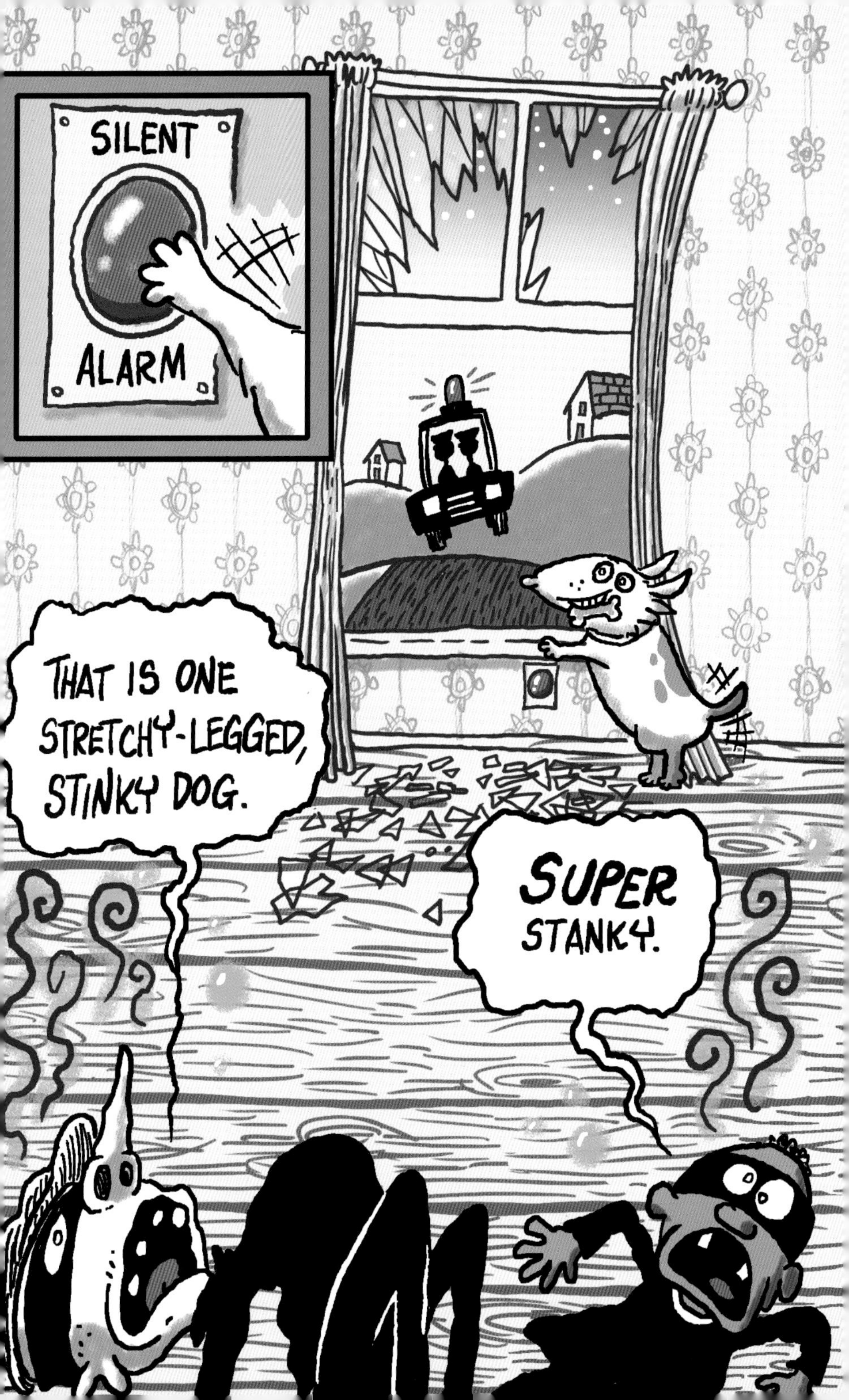
SILENT
ALARM
THAT IS ONE STRETCHY-LEGGED, STINKY DOG.
SUPER STANKY.

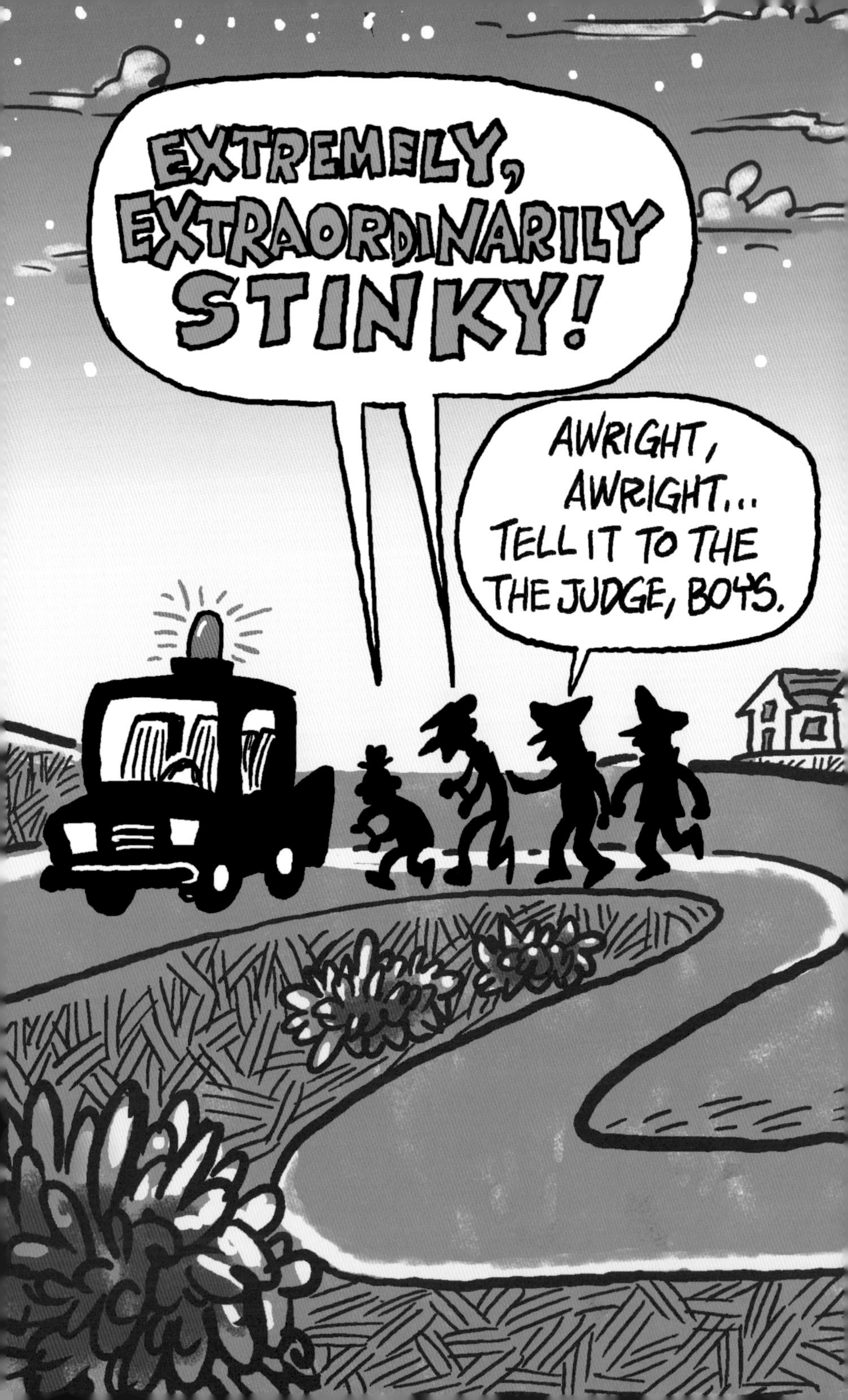
EXTREMELY, EXTRAORDINARILY STINKY!
AWRIGHT, AWRIGHT... TELL IT TO THE THE JUDGE, BOYS.

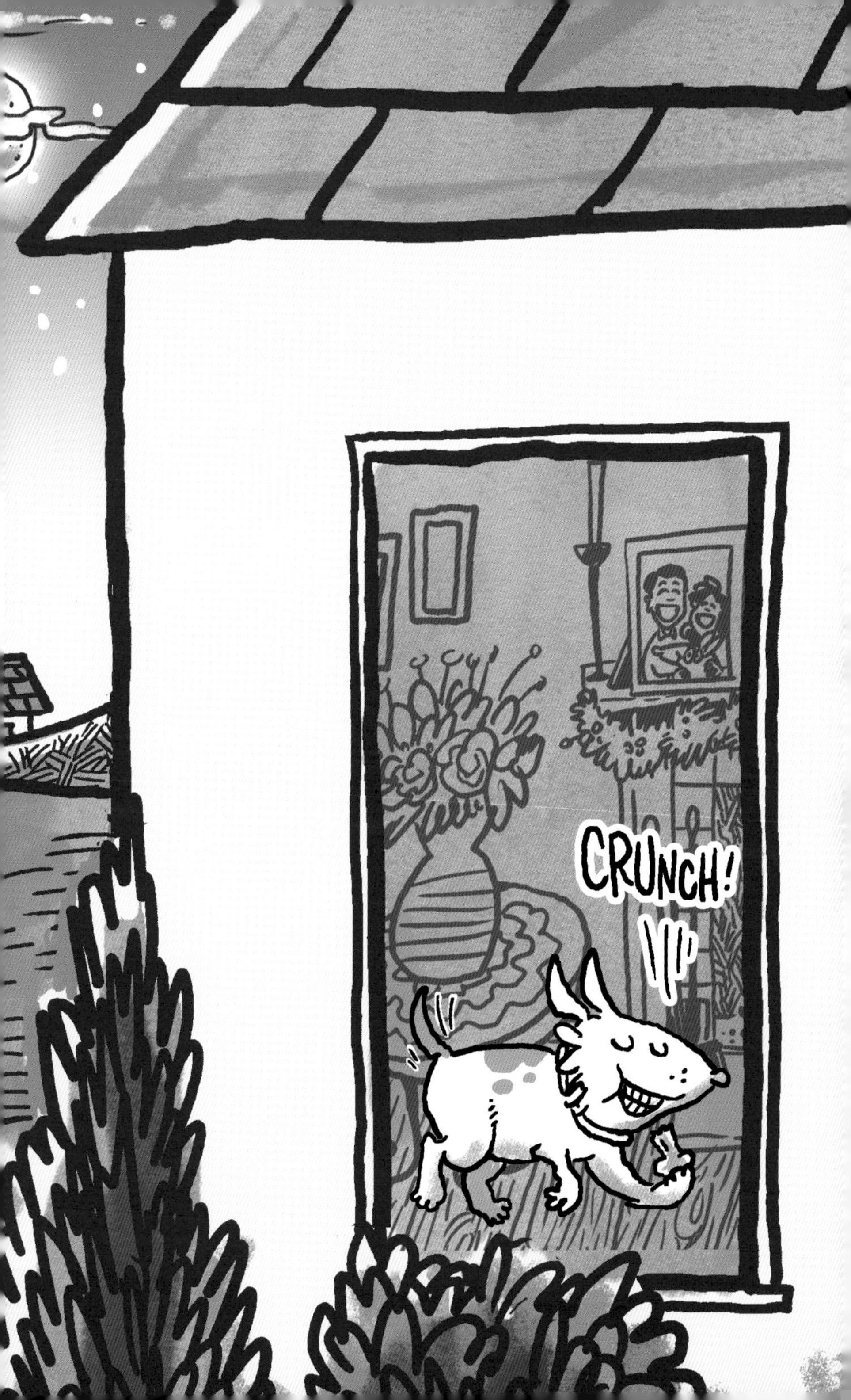
CRUNCH!

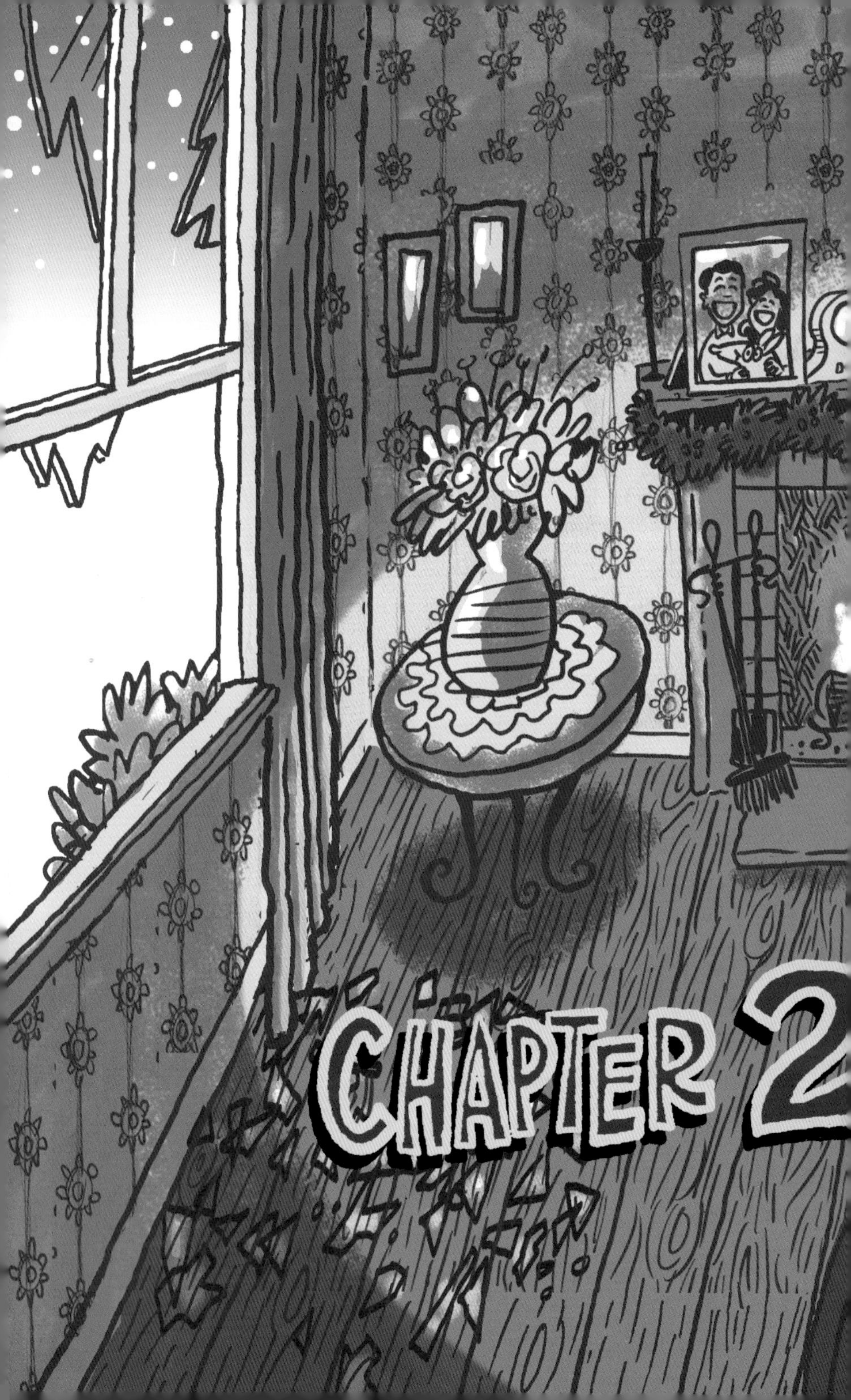
CHAPTER 2

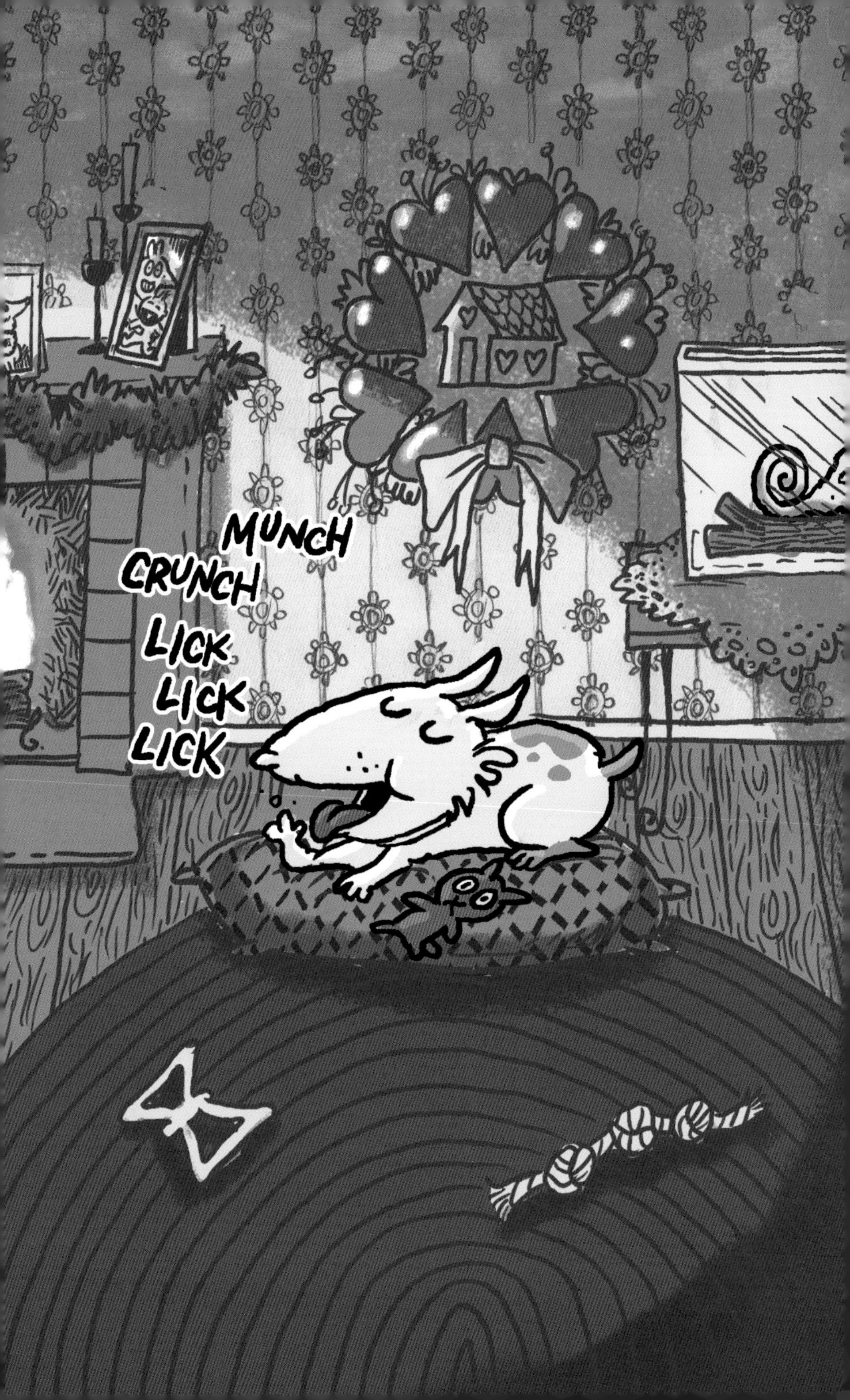
MUNCH
CRUNCH
LICK
LICK
LICK

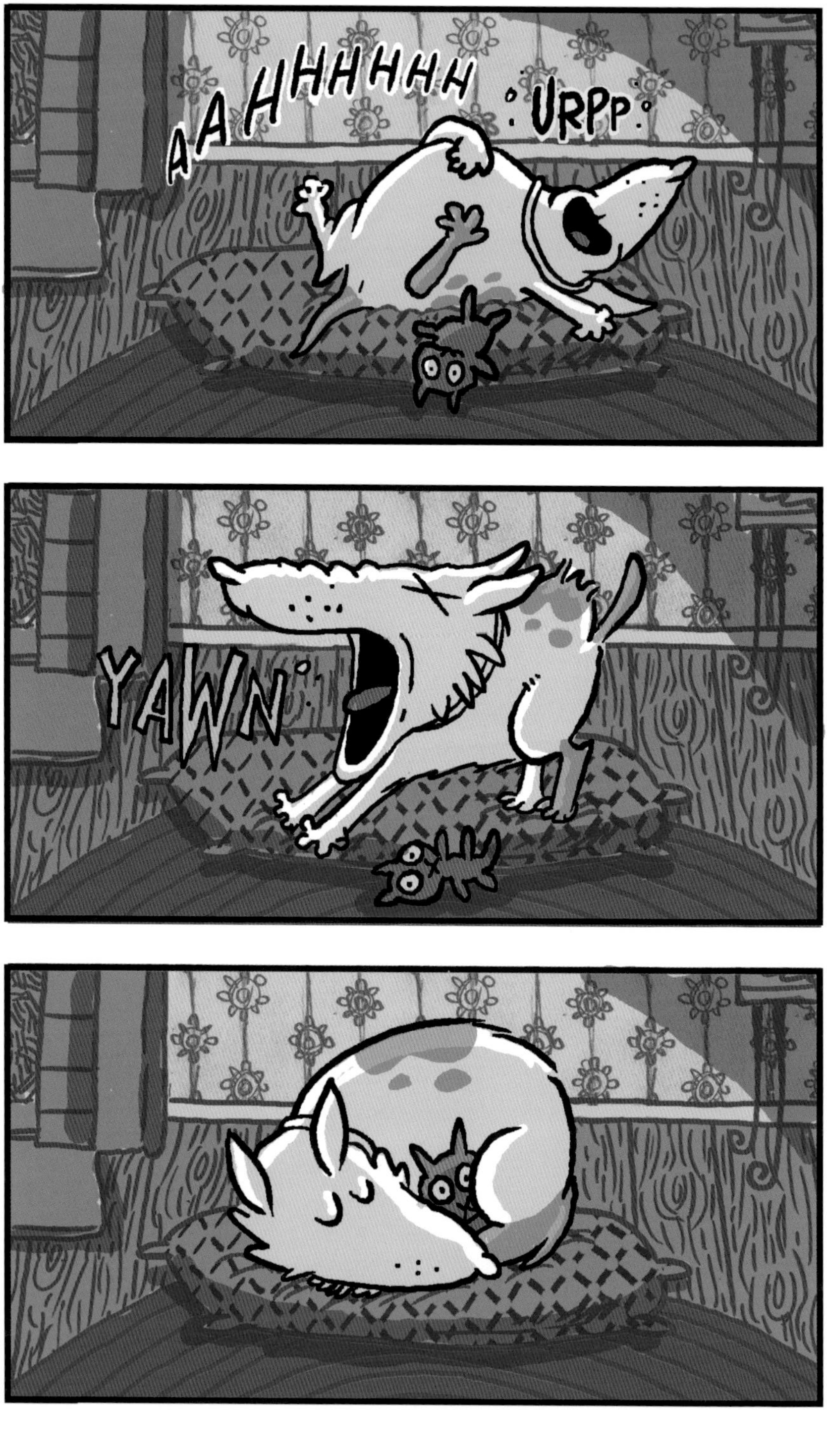
AAHHHHHHH
URPP
YAWN

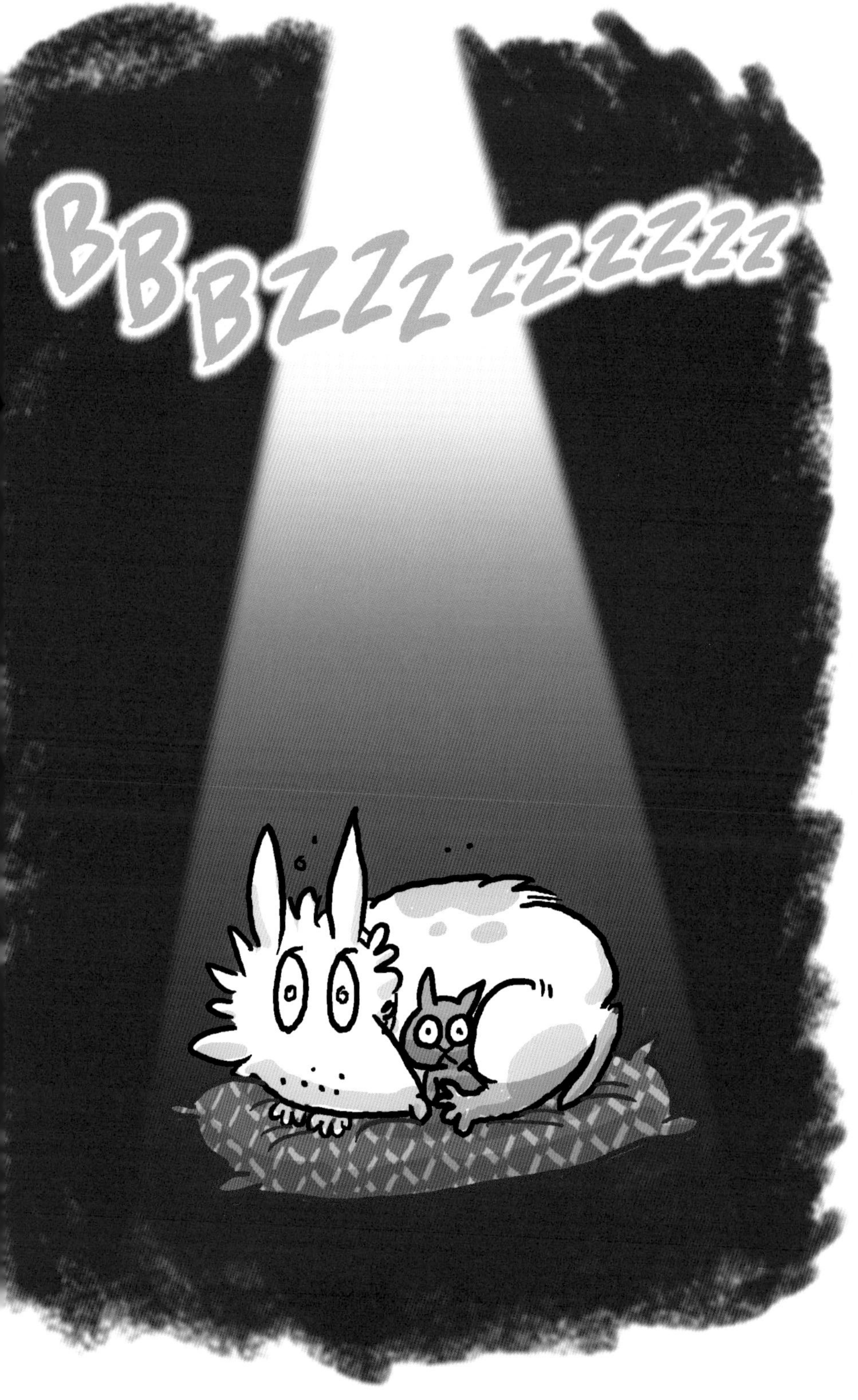
BBBZZZzzzzzzzz

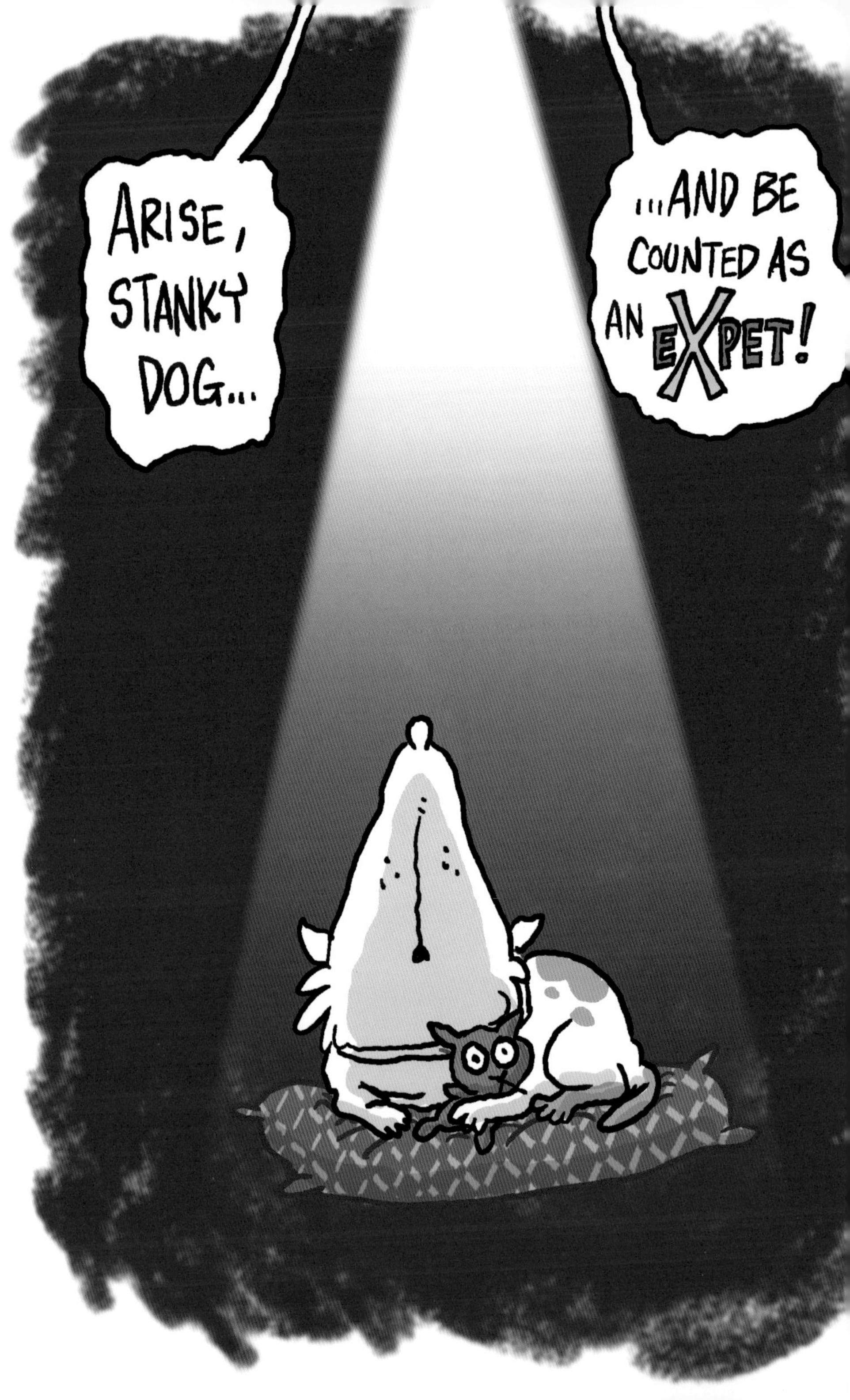
ARISE, STANKY DOG...
...AND BE COUNTED AS AN EXPET!

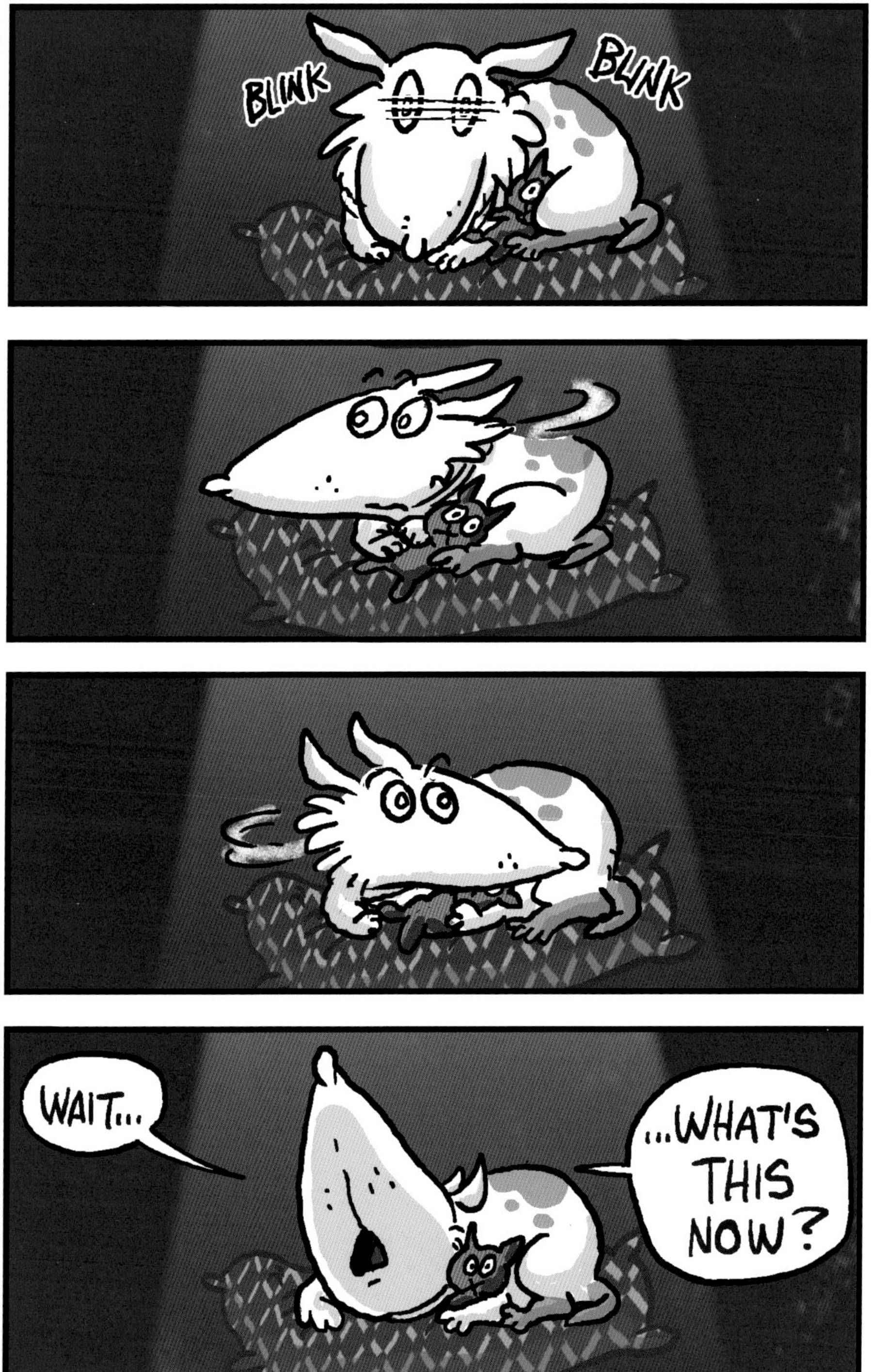
BLINK
BLINK
WAIT...
...WHAT'S THIS NOW?

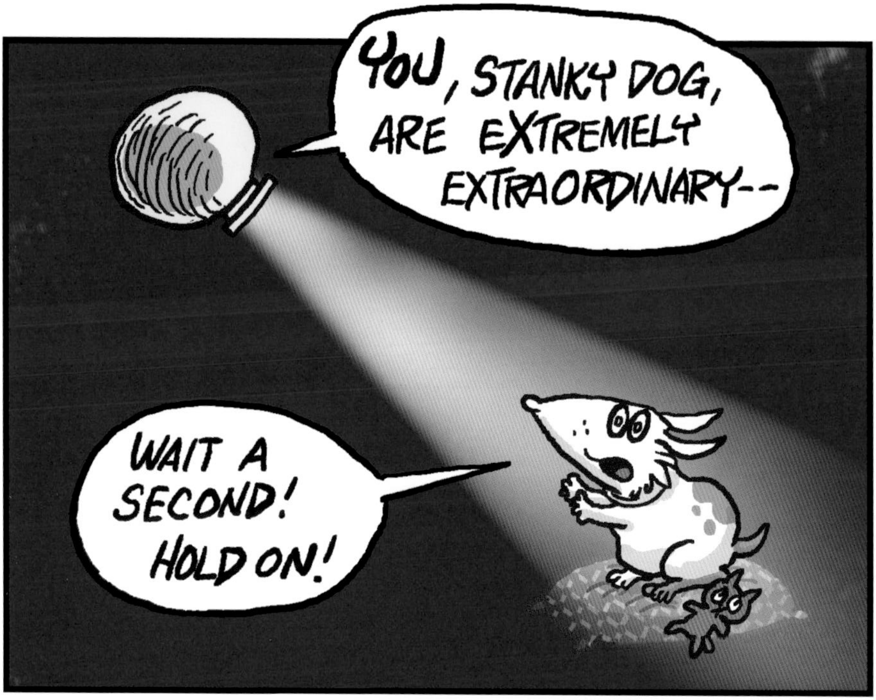
YOU, STANKY DOG, ARE EXTREMELY EXTRAORDINARY--
WAIT A SECOND! HOLD ON!

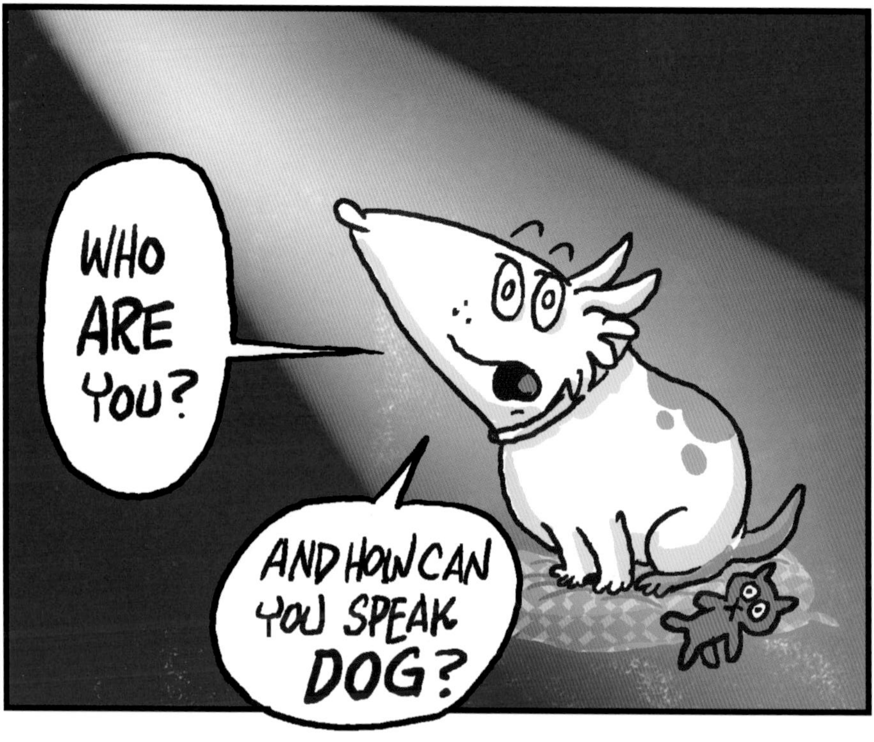
WHO ARE YOU?
AND HOW CAN YOU SPEAK DOG?

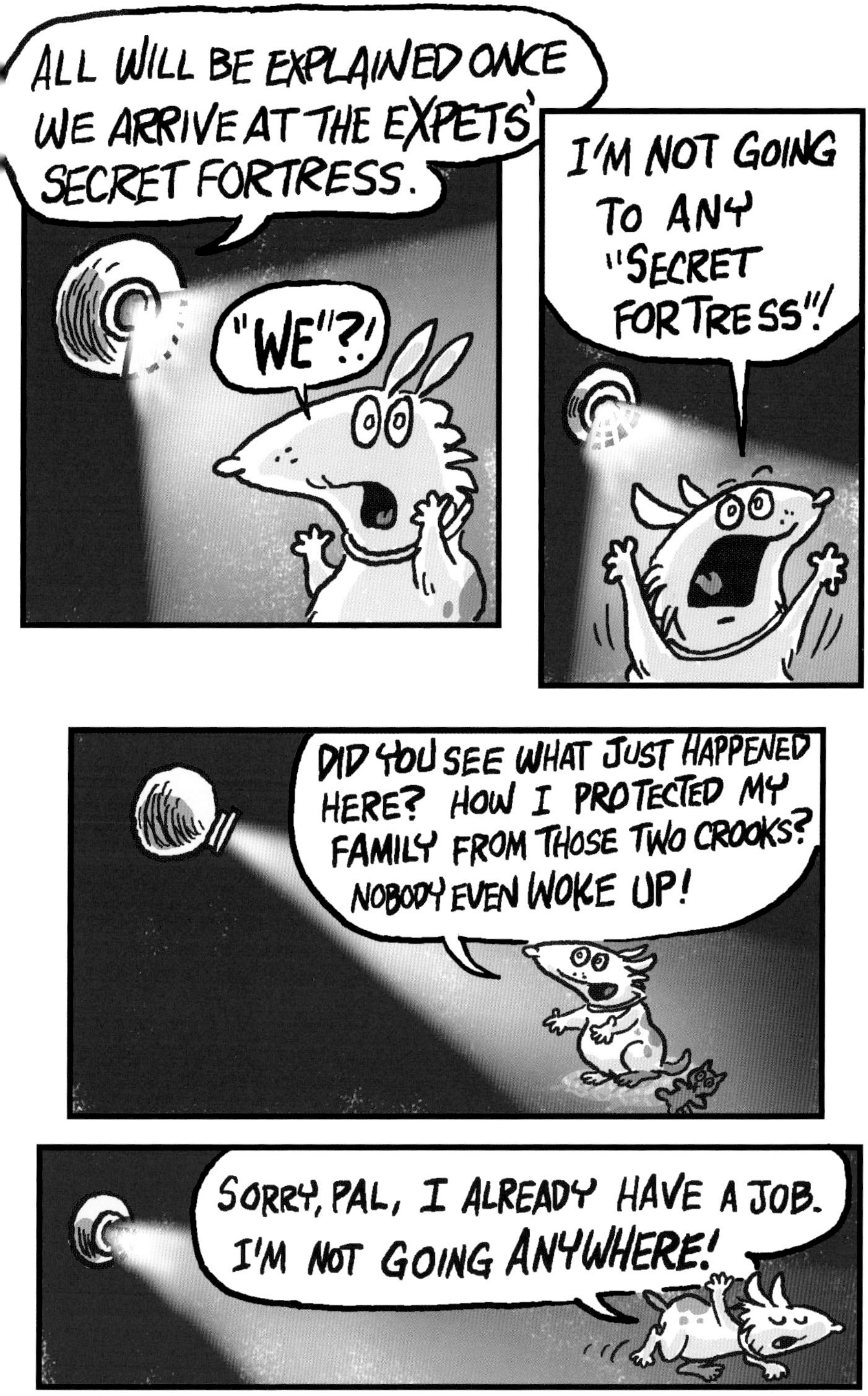
ALL WILL BE EXPLAINED ONCE WE ARRIVE AT THE EXPETS' SECRET FORTRESS.
"WE"?!
I'M NOT GOING TO ANY "SECRET FORTRESS"!
DID YOU SEE WHAT JUST HAPPENED HERE? HOW I PROTECTED MY FAMILY FROM THOSE TWO CROOKS? NOBODY EVEN WOKE UP!
SORRY, PAL, I ALREADY HAVE A JOB. I'M NOT GOING ANYWHERE!

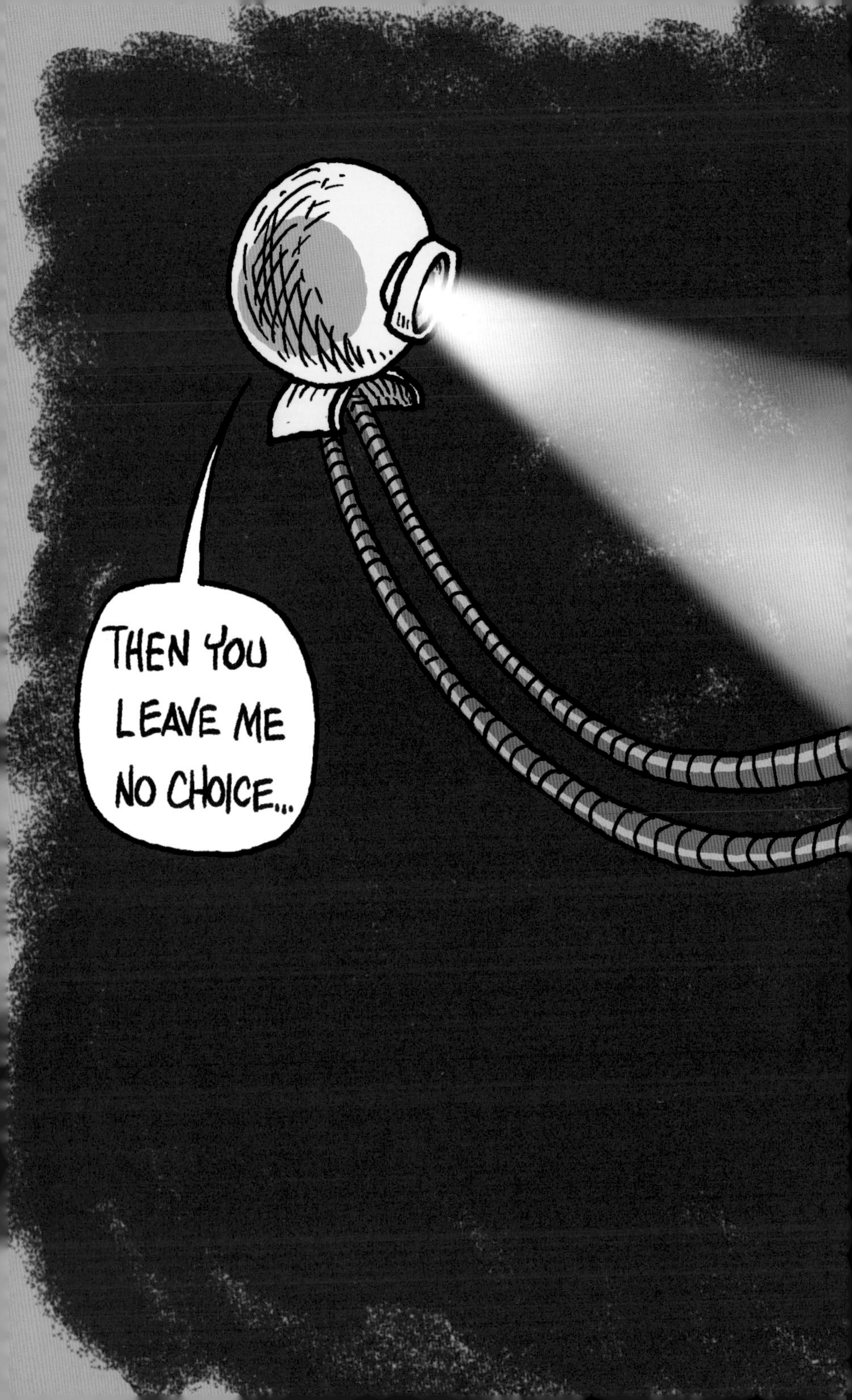
THEN YOU LEAVE ME NO CHOICE...

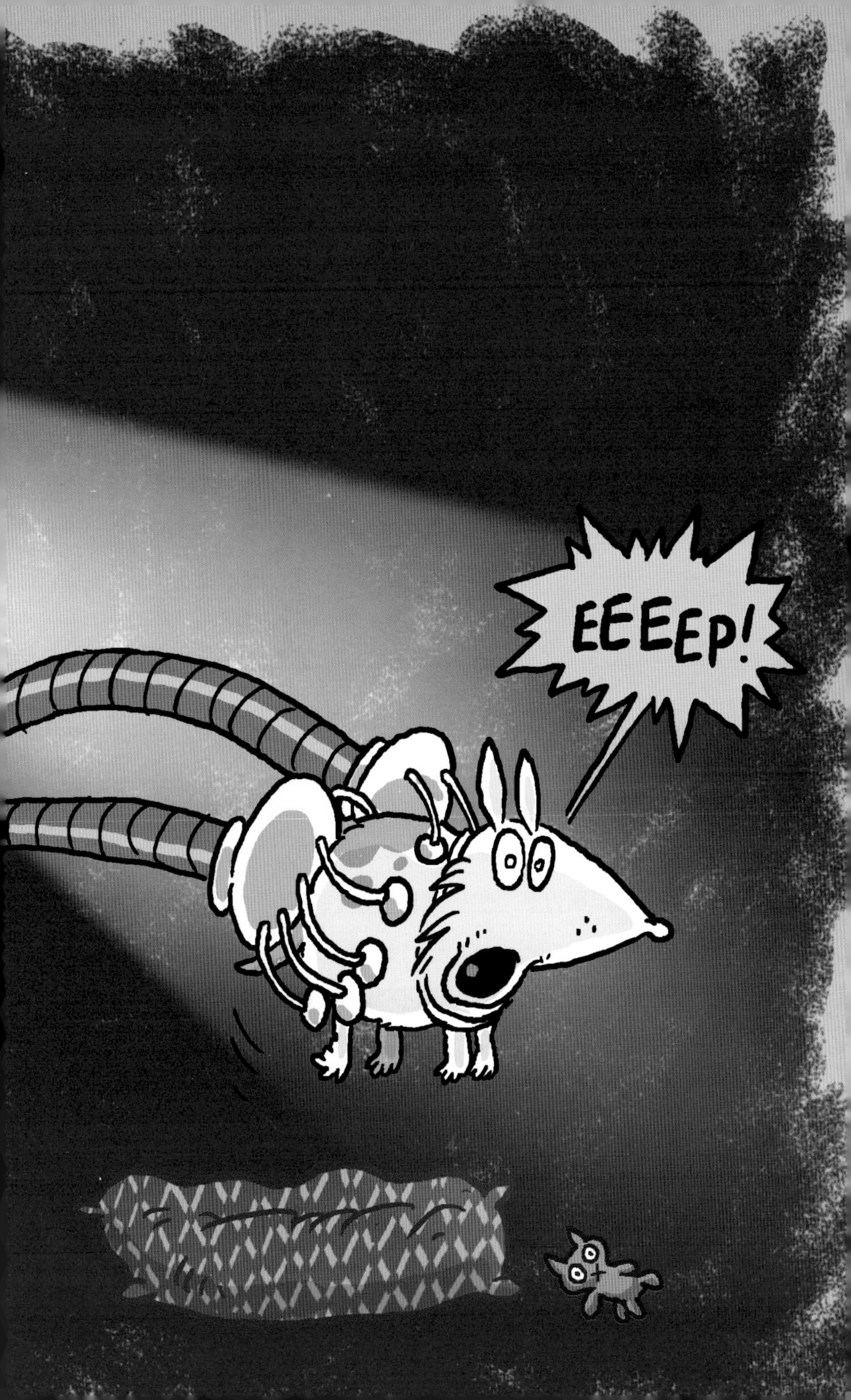
EEEEP!

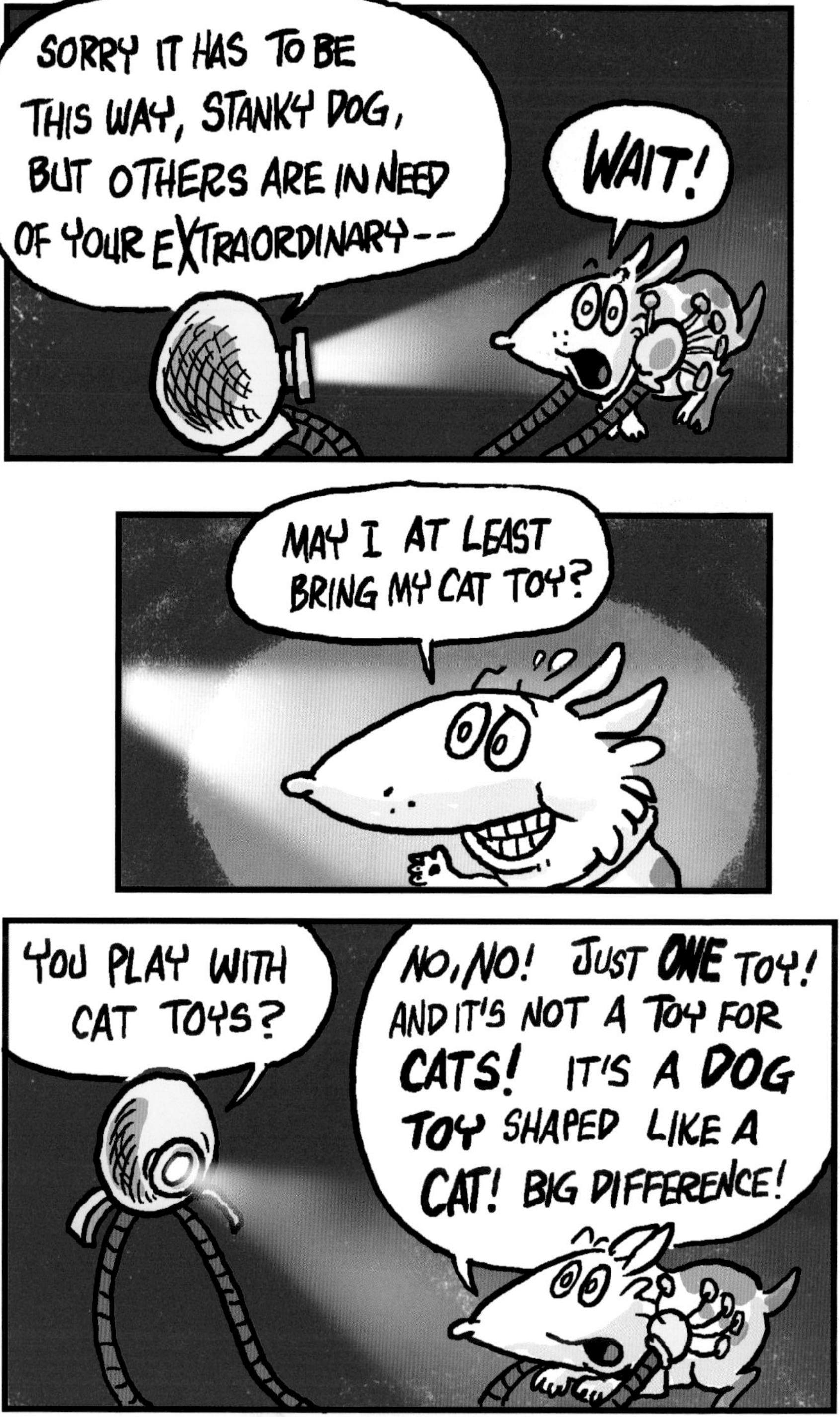
SORRY IT HAS TO BE THIS WAY, STANKY DOG, BUT OTHERS ARE IN NEED OF YOUR EXTRAORDINARY--
WAIT!
MAY I AT LEAST BRING MY CAT TOY?
YOU PLAY WITH CAT TOYS?
NO, NO! JUST ONE TOY! AND IT'S NOT A TOY FOR CATS! IT'S A DOG TOY SHAPED LIKE A CAT! BIG DIFFERENCE!

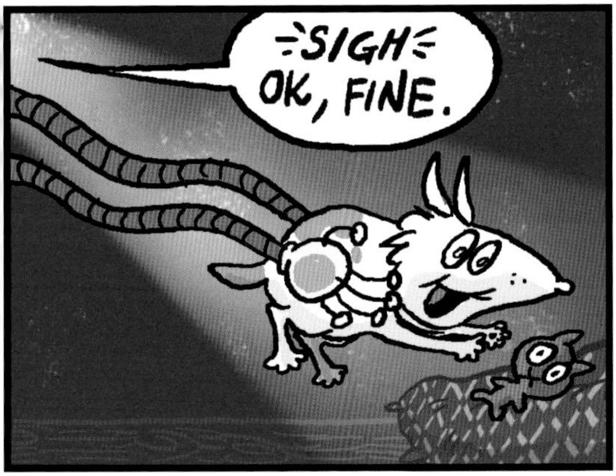
SIGH
OK, FINE.

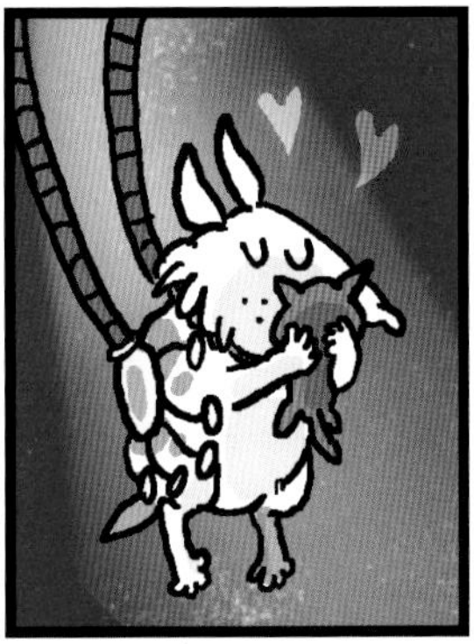

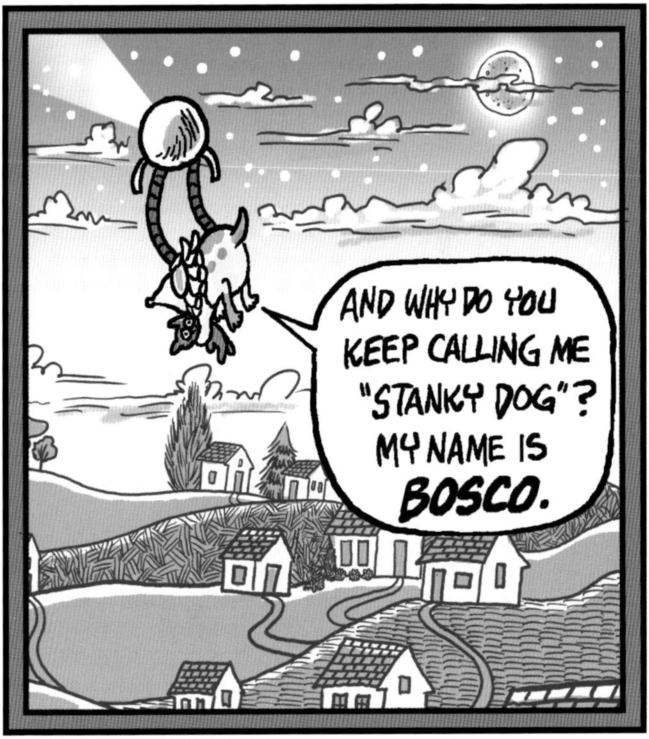
AND WHY DO YOU KEEP CALLING ME "STANKY DOG"? MY NAME IS BOSCO.

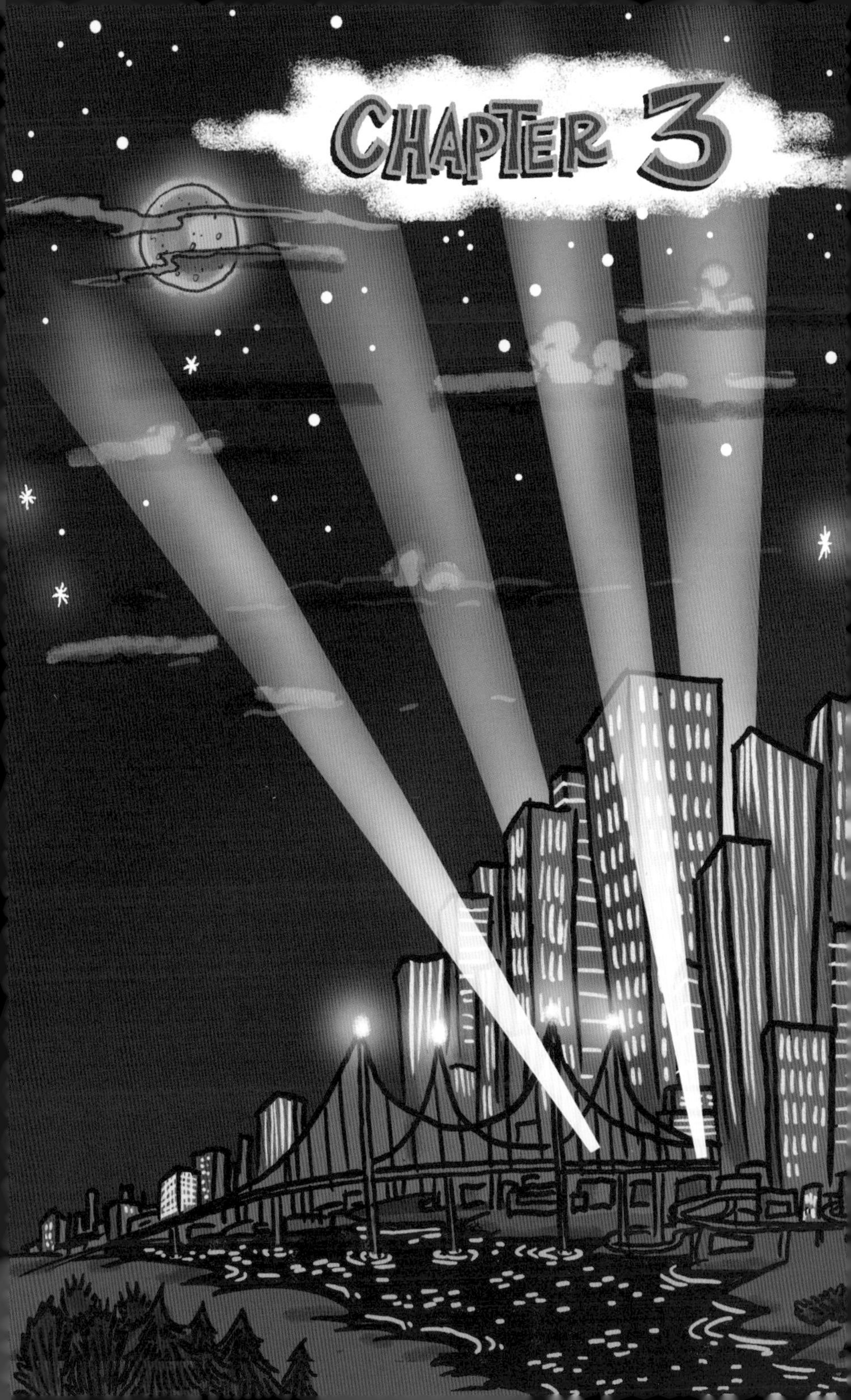
CHAPTER 3

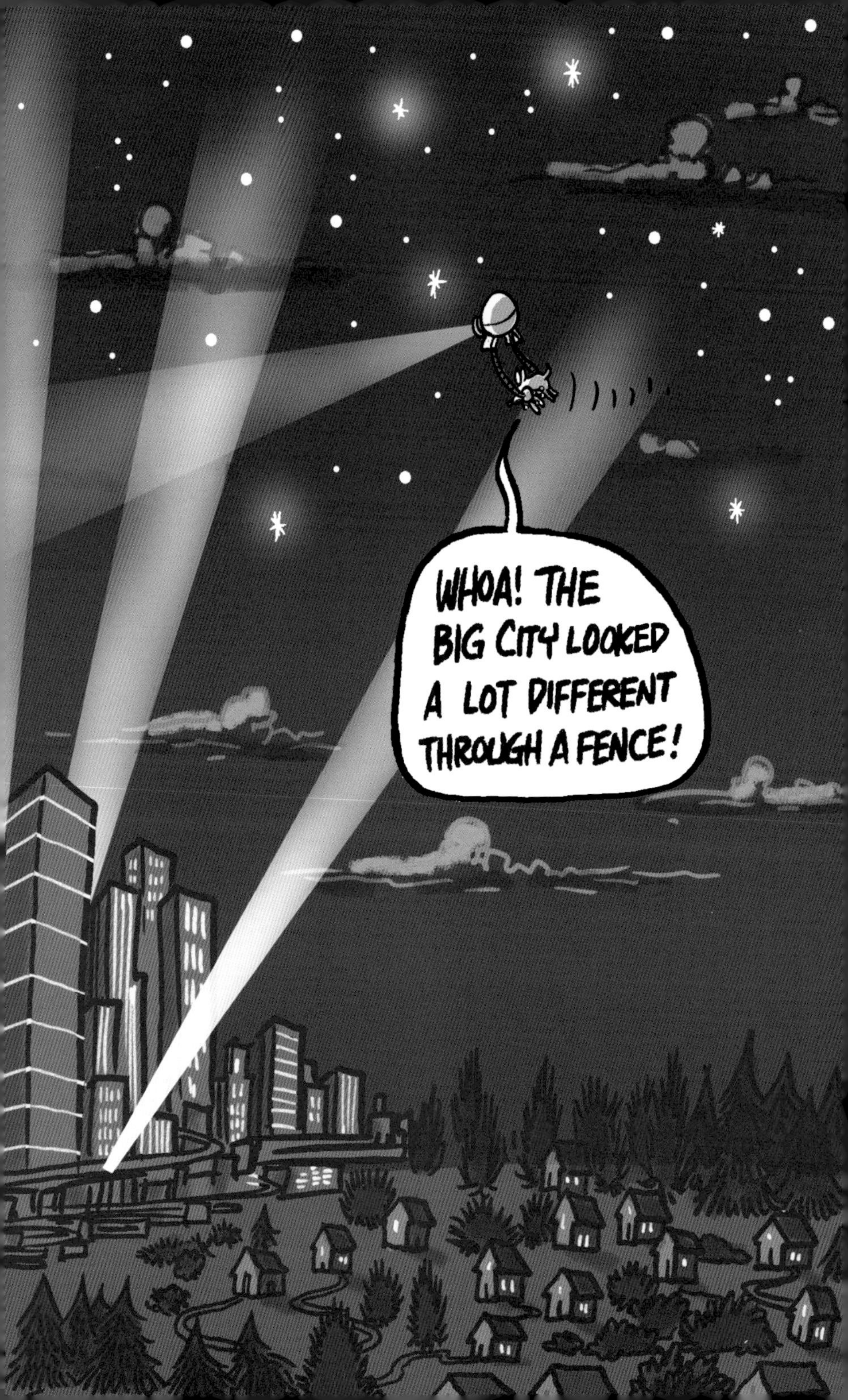
WHOA! THE BIG CITY LOOKED A LOT DIFFERENT THROUGH A FENCE!

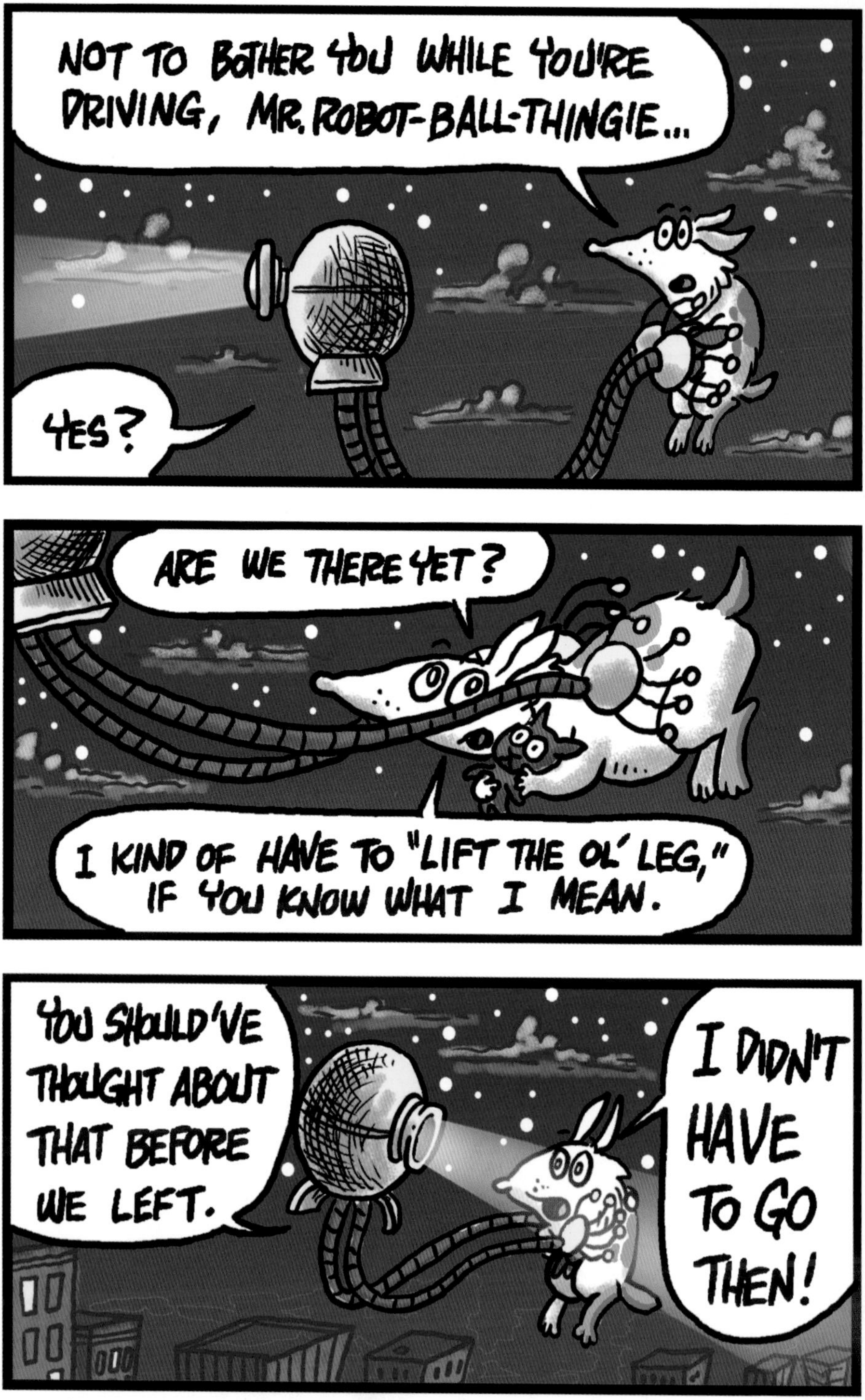
NOT TO BOTHER YOU WHILE YOU'RE DRIVING, MR. ROBOT-BALL-THINGIE...
YES?
ARE WE THERE YET?
I KIND OF HAVE TO "LIFT THE OL' LEG," IF YOU KNOW WHAT I MEAN.
YOU SHOULD'VE THOUGHT ABOUT THAT BEFORE WE LEFT.
I DIDN'T HAVE TO GO THEN!

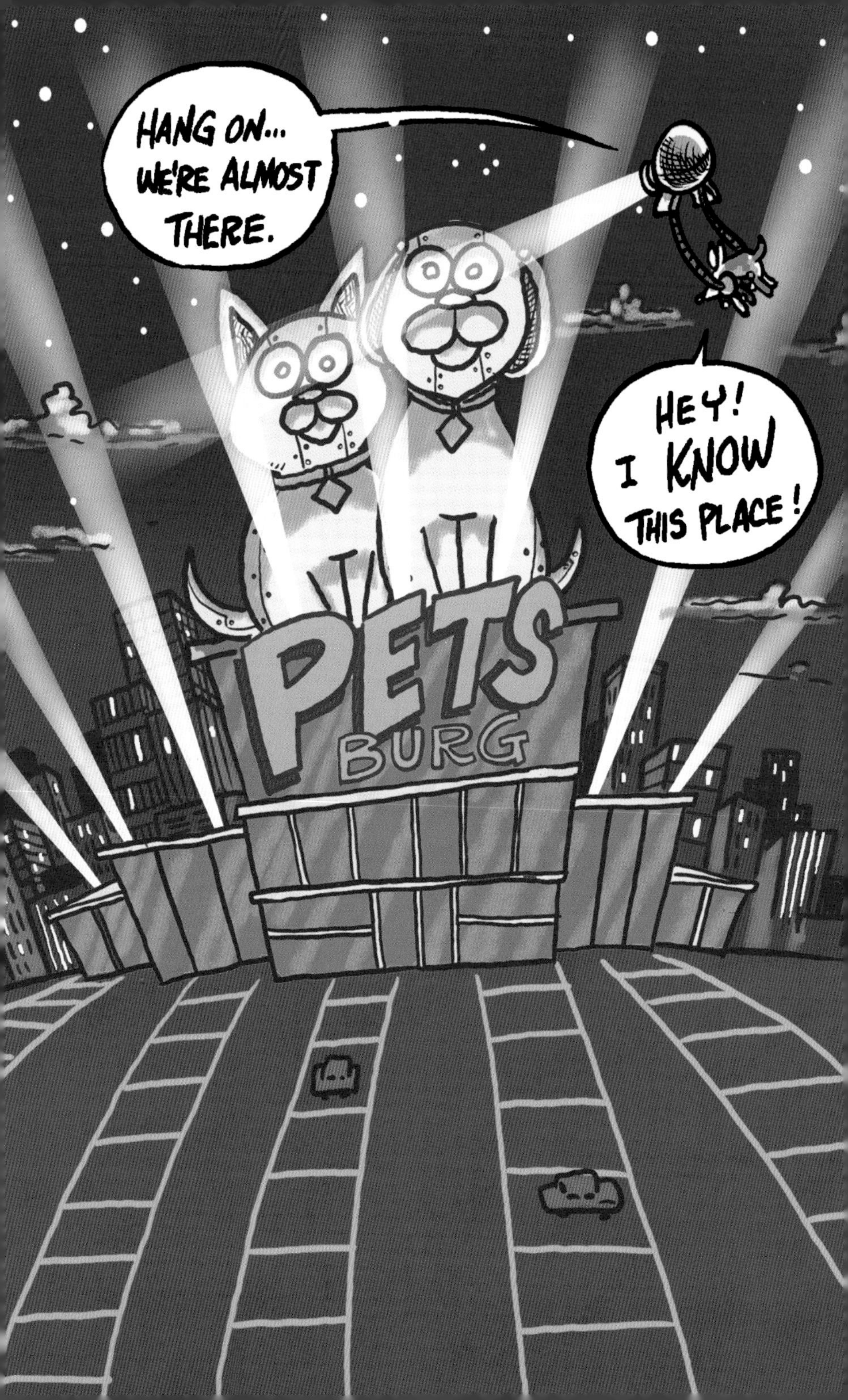
HANG ON... WE'RE ALMOST THERE.
HEY! I KNOW THIS PLACE!
PETS BURG

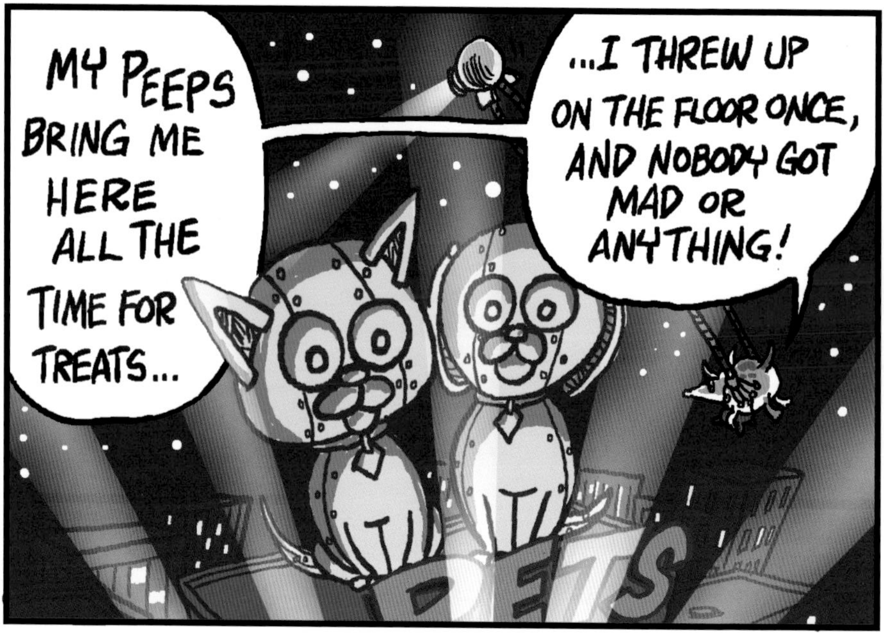
MY PEEPS BRING ME HERE ALL THE TIME FOR TREATS...
...I THREW UP ON THE FLOOR ONCE, AND NOBODY GOT MAD OR ANYTHING!
PETS

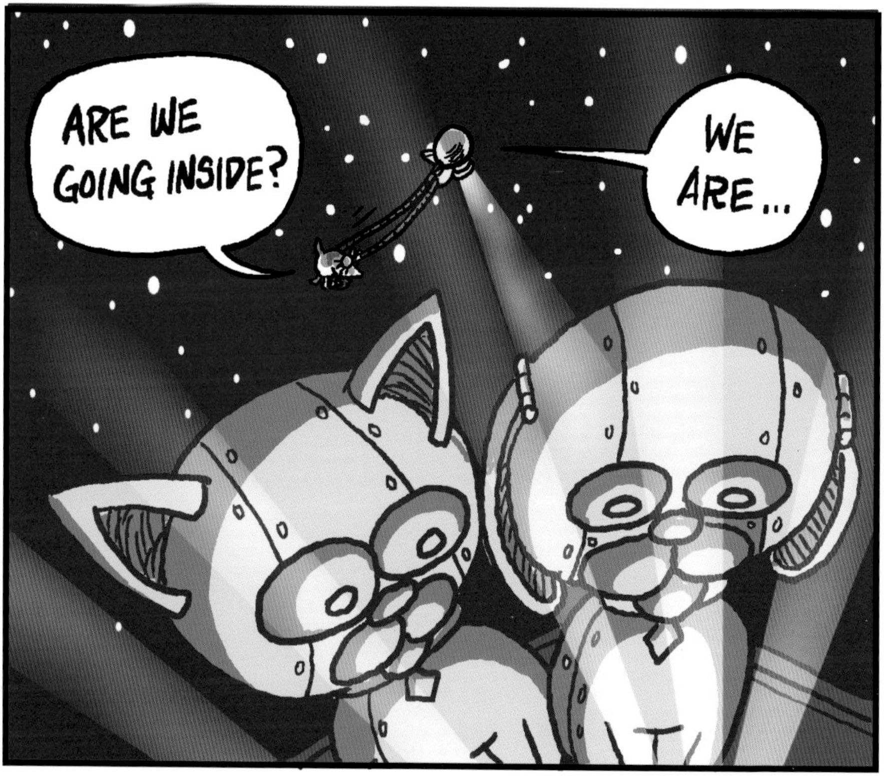
ARE WE GOING INSIDE?
WE ARE...

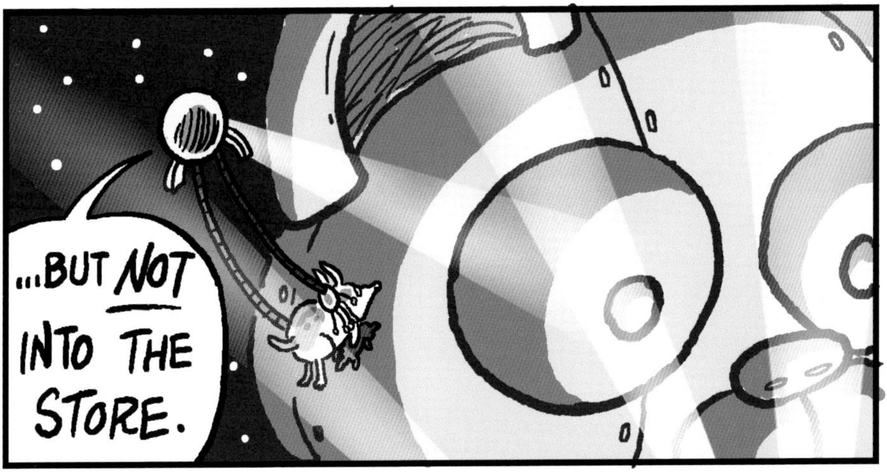
...BUT NOT INTO THE STORE.

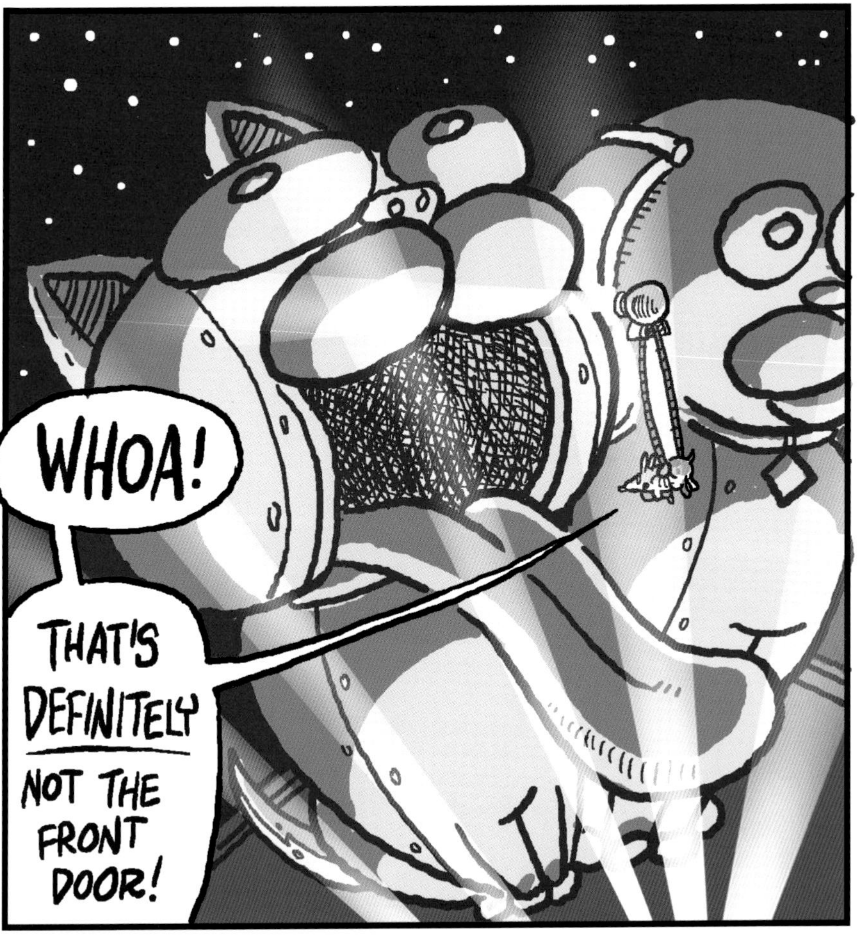
WHOA!
THAT'S DEFINITELY NOT THE FRONT DOOR!

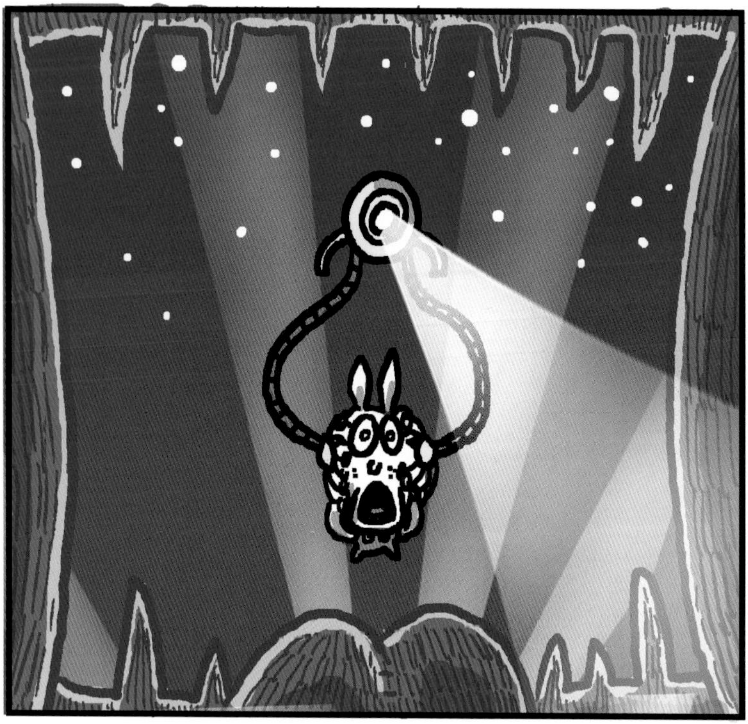

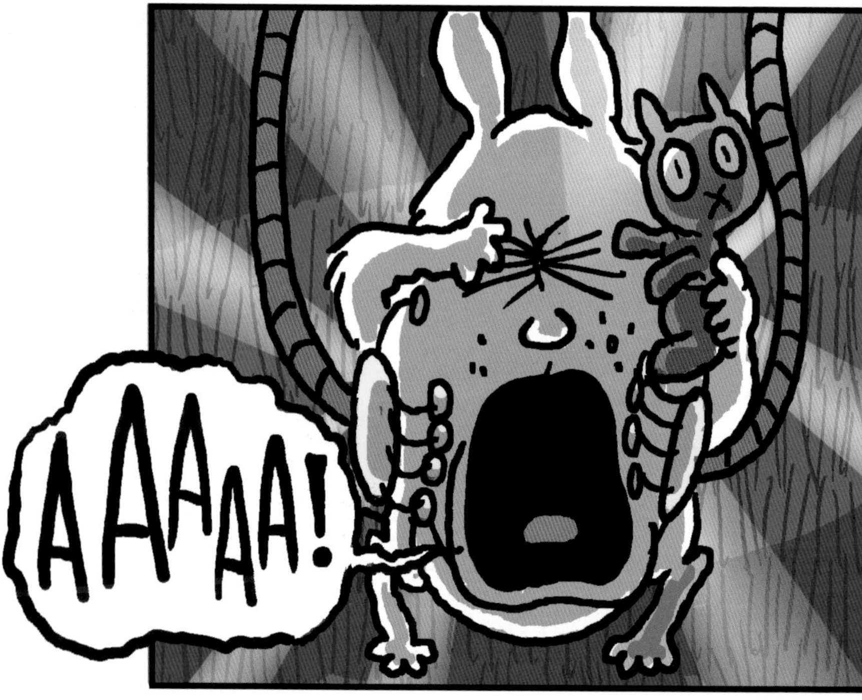
AAAAA!

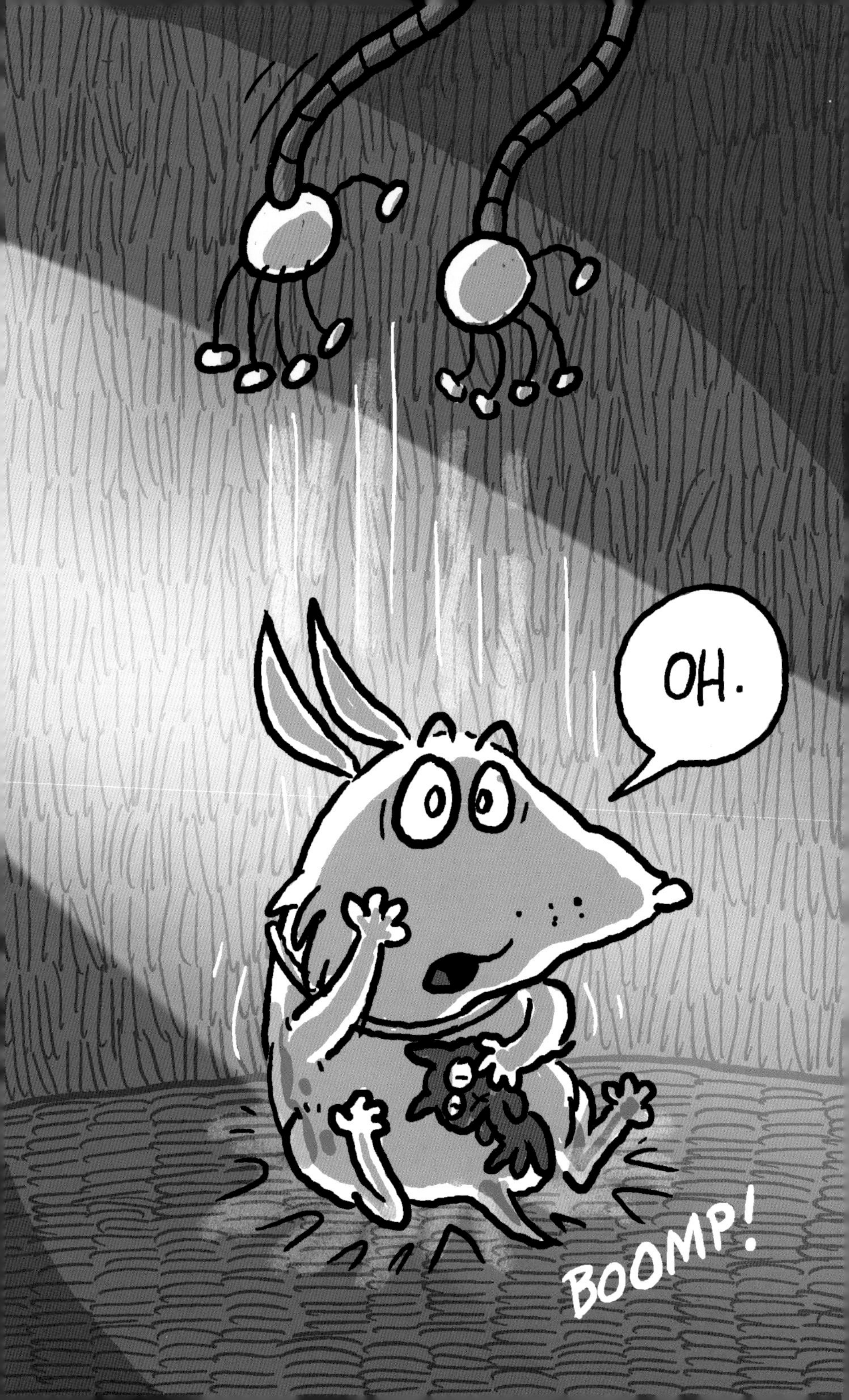
OH.
BOOMP!

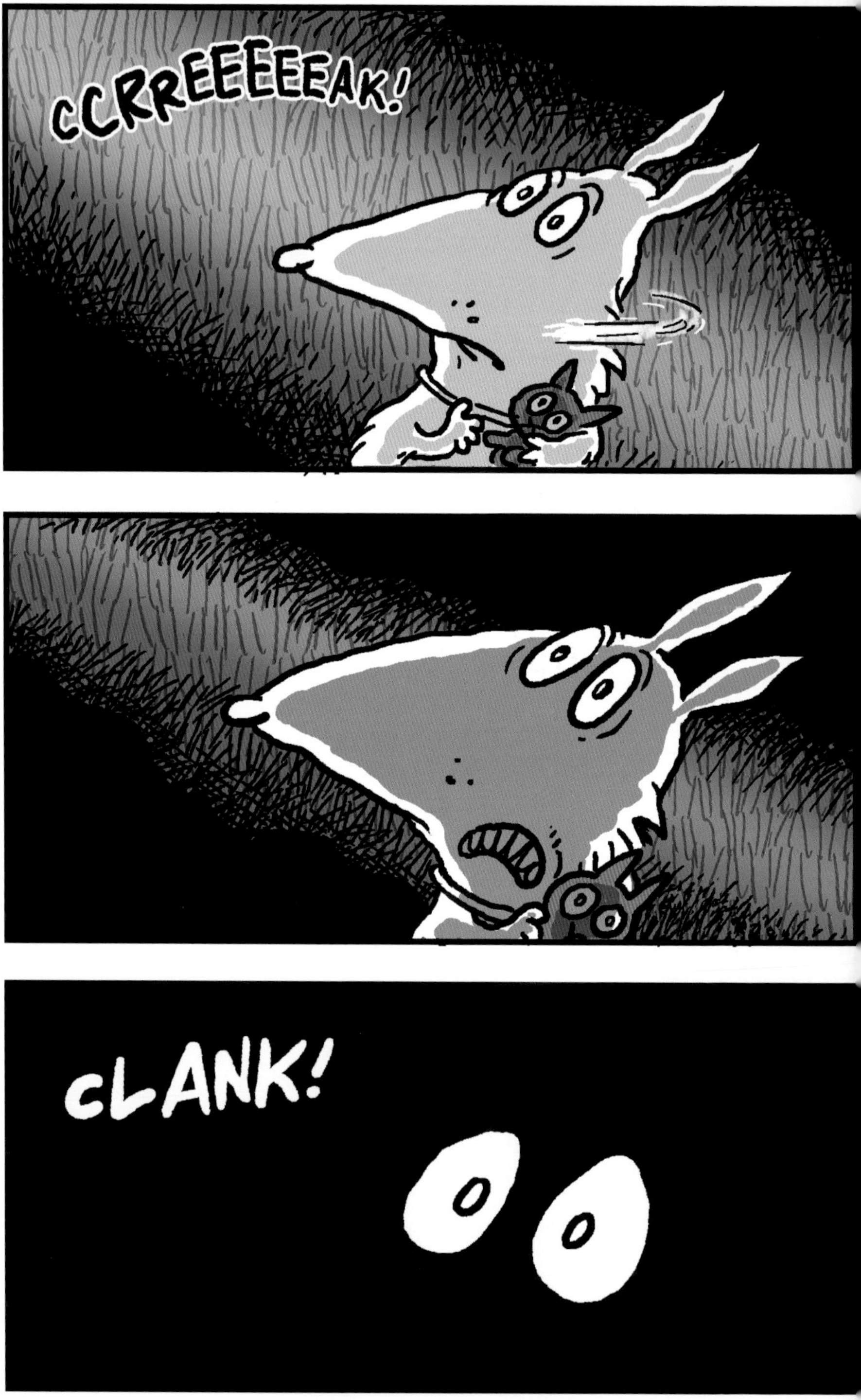
CCRREEEEEEAK!
CLANK!

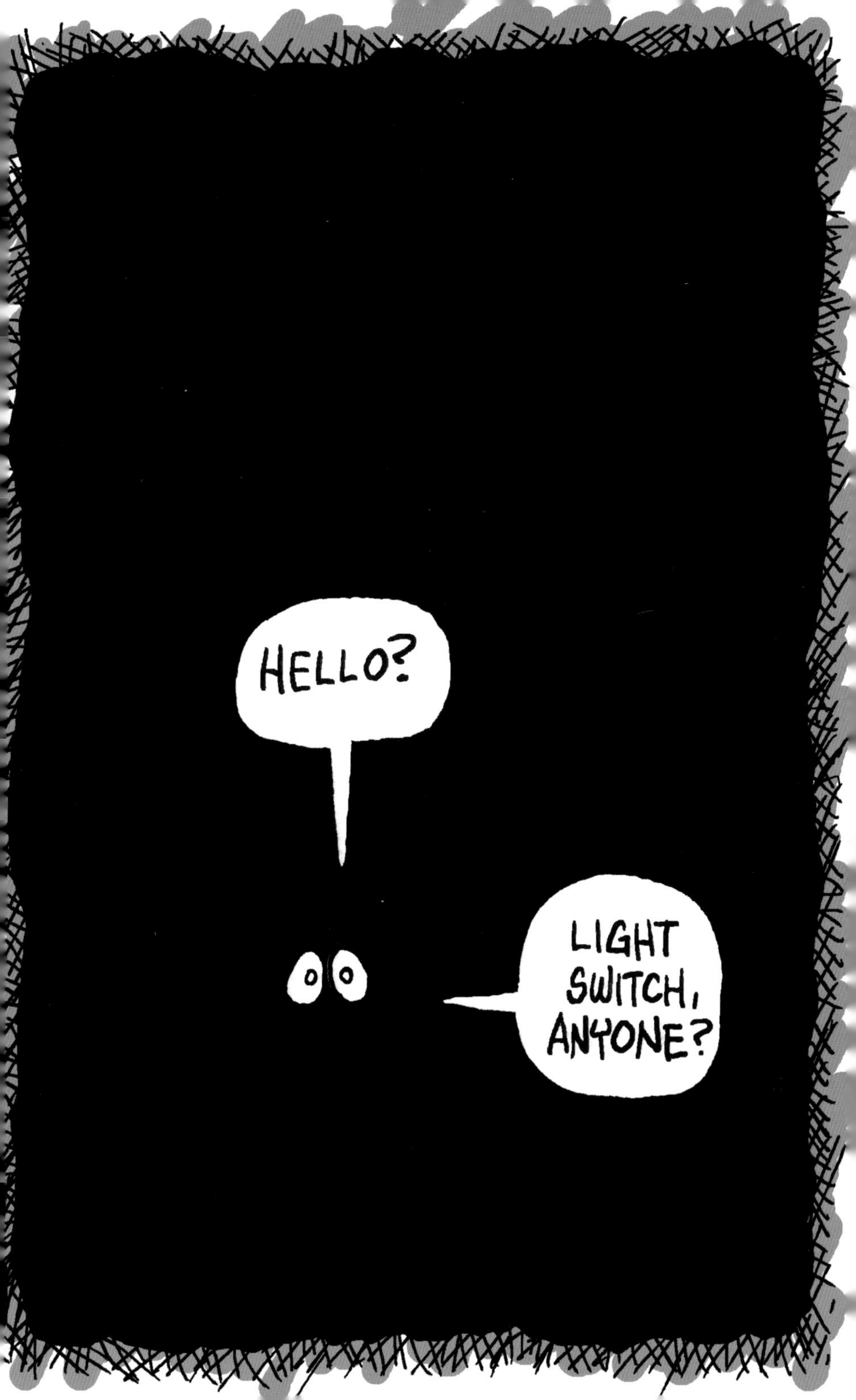
HELLO?
LIGHT SWITCH, ANYONE?

CHAPTER 4

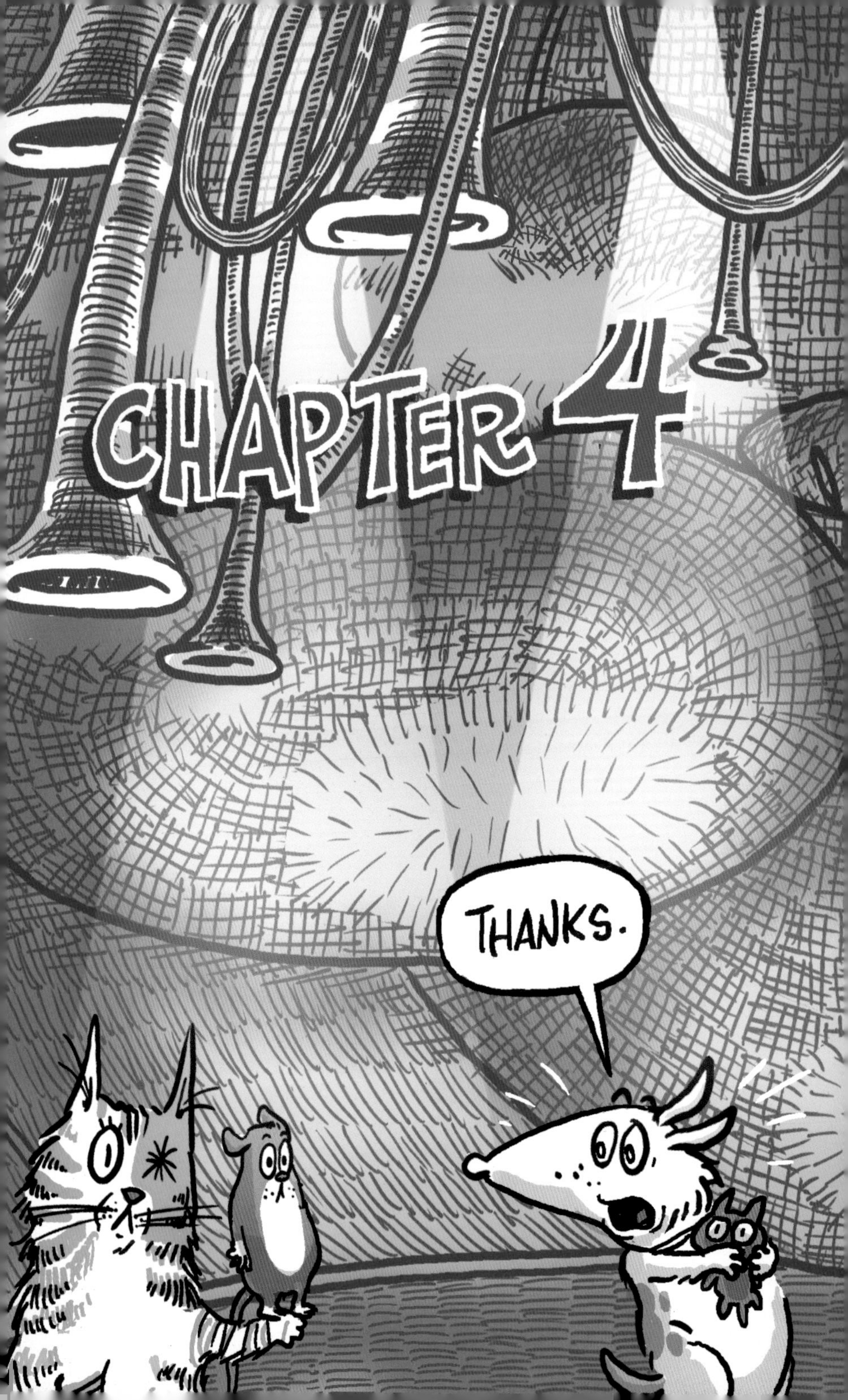
THANKS.

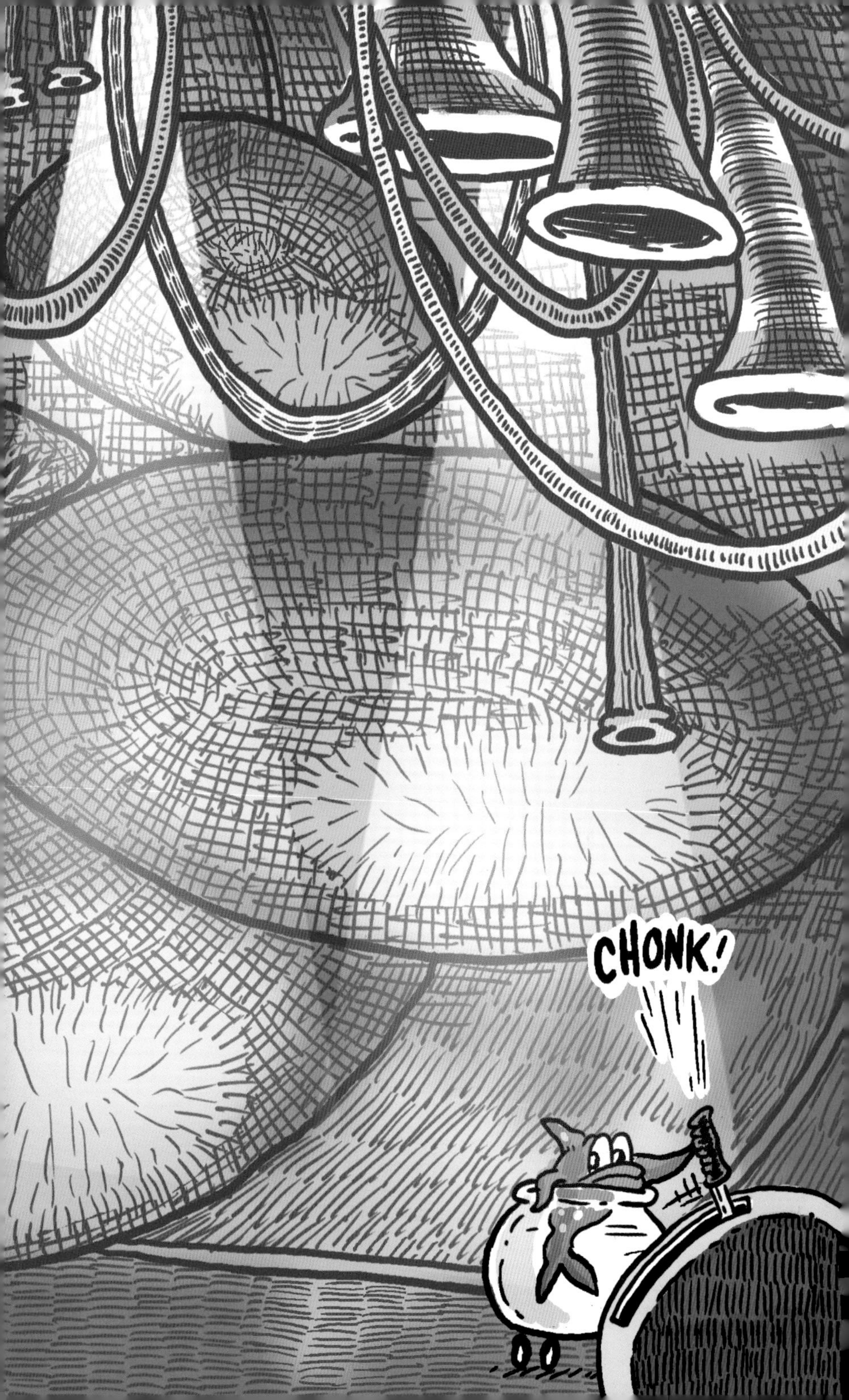
CHONK!

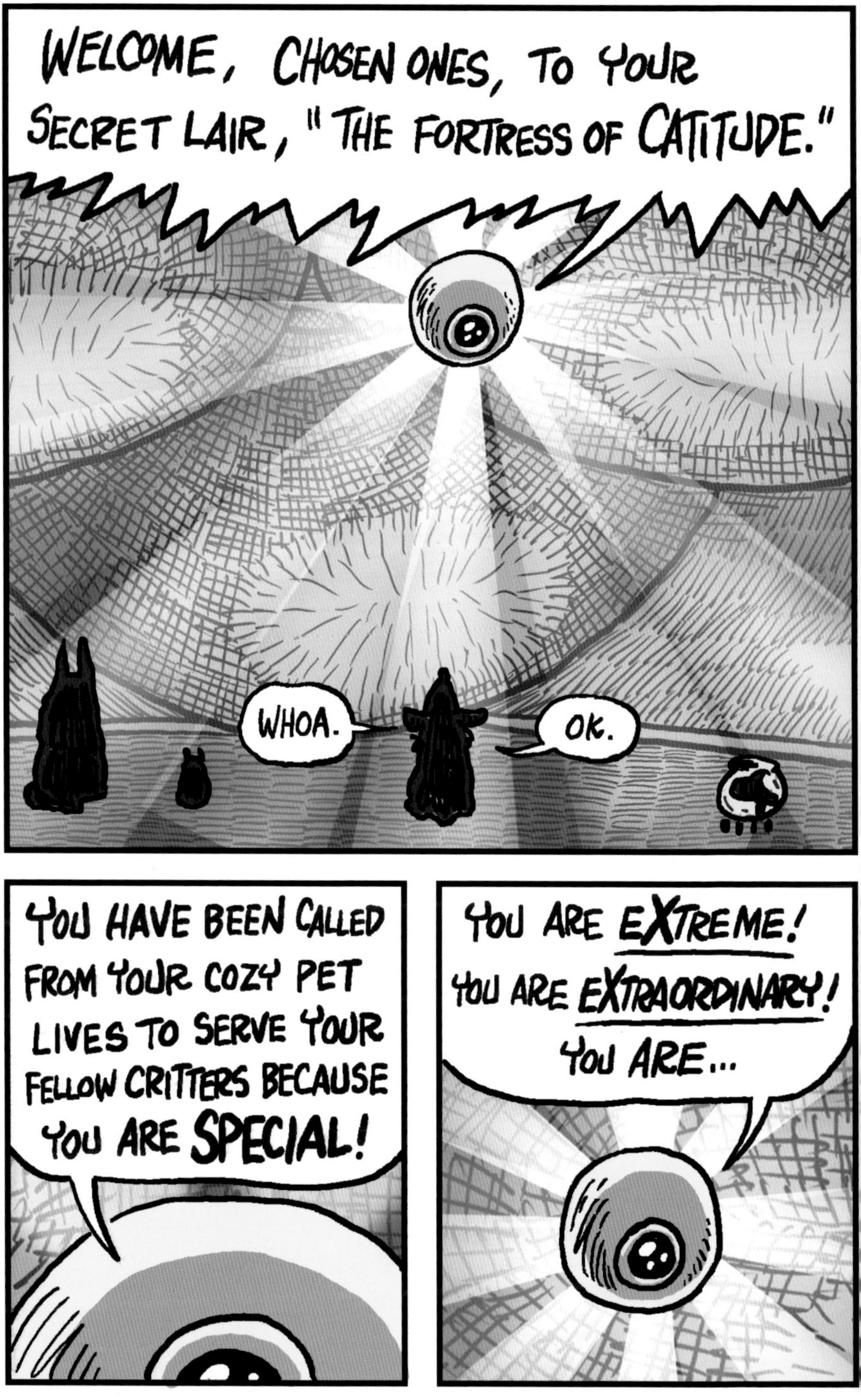
WELCOME, CHOSEN ONES, TO YOUR SECRET LAIR, "THE FORTRESS OF CATITUDE."
WHOA.
OK.
YOU HAVE BEEN CALLED FROM YOUR COZY PET LIVES TO SERVE YOUR FELLOW CRITTERS BECAUSE YOU ARE SPECIAL!
YOU ARE EXTREME! YOU ARE EXTRAORDINARY! YOU ARE...

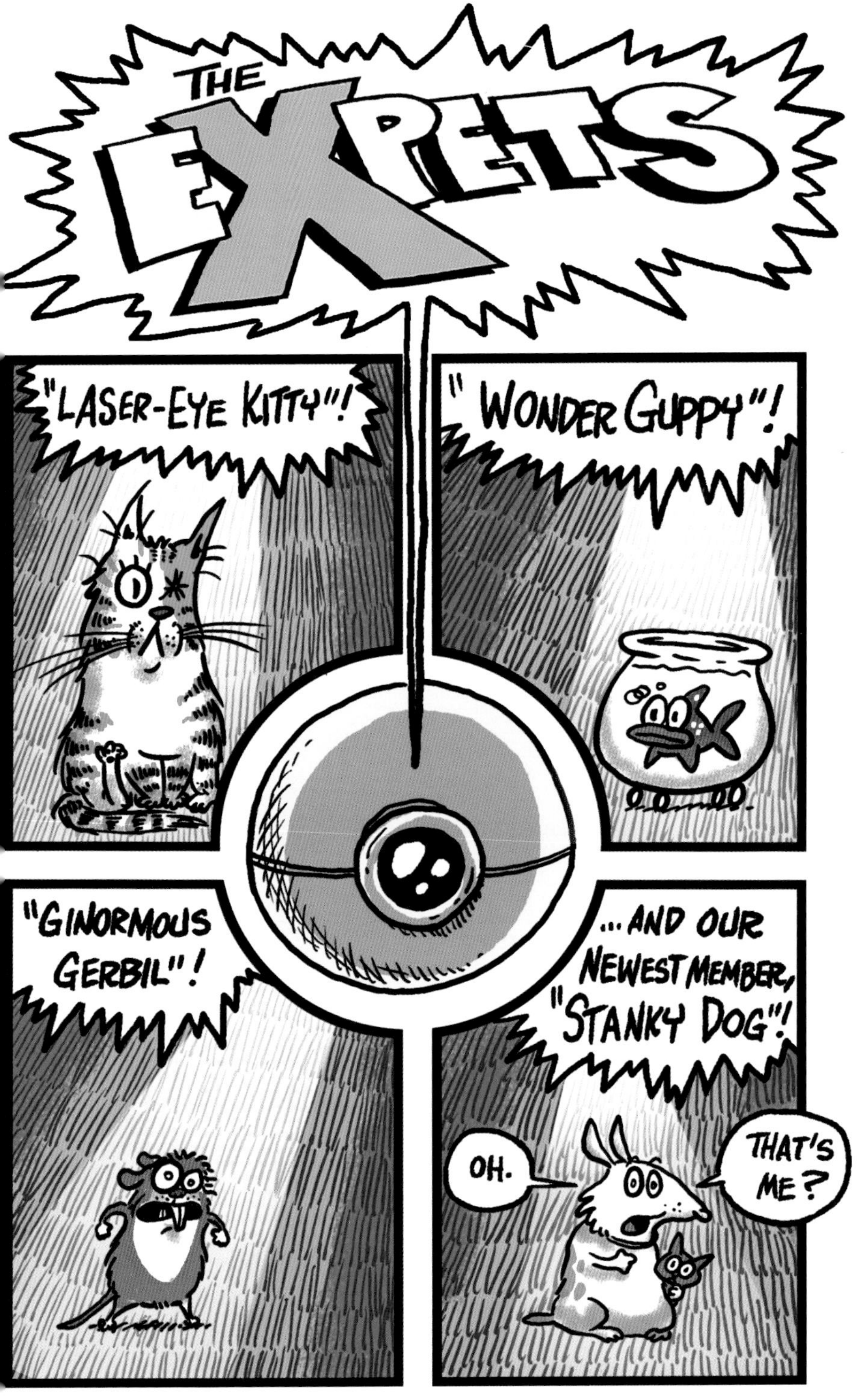
THE EXPETS
"LASER-EYE KITTY"!
"WONDER GUPPY"!
"GINORMOUS GERBIL"!
...AND OUR NEWEST MEMBER, "STANKY DOG"!
OH.
THAT'S ME?

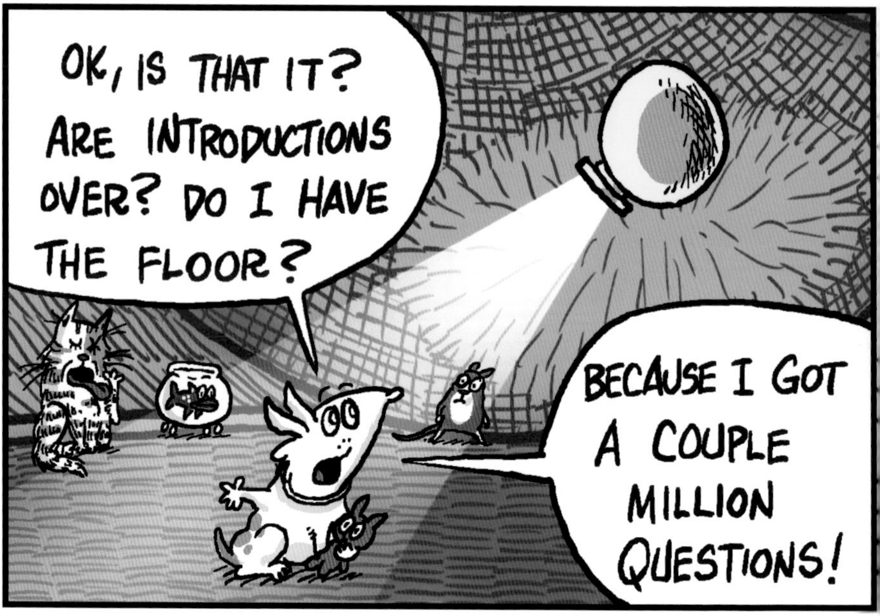
OK, IS THAT IT? ARE INTRODUCTIONS OVER? DO I HAVE THE FLOOR?
BECAUSE I GOT A COUPLE MILLION QUESTIONS!

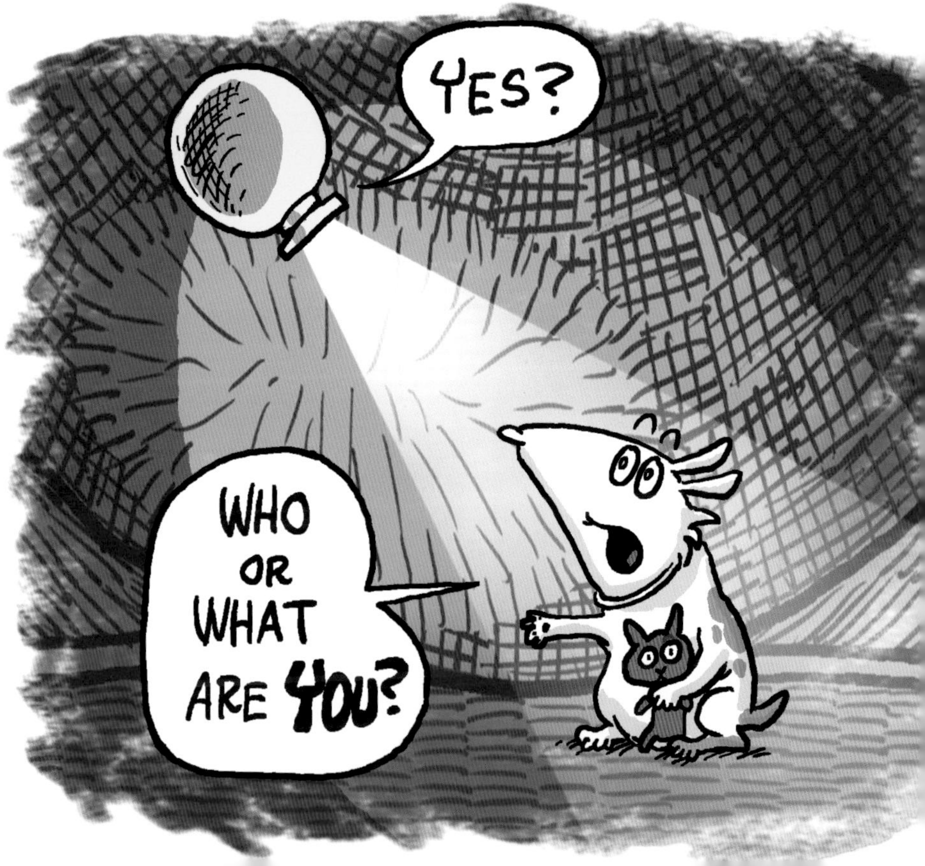
YES?
WHO OR WHAT ARE YOU?

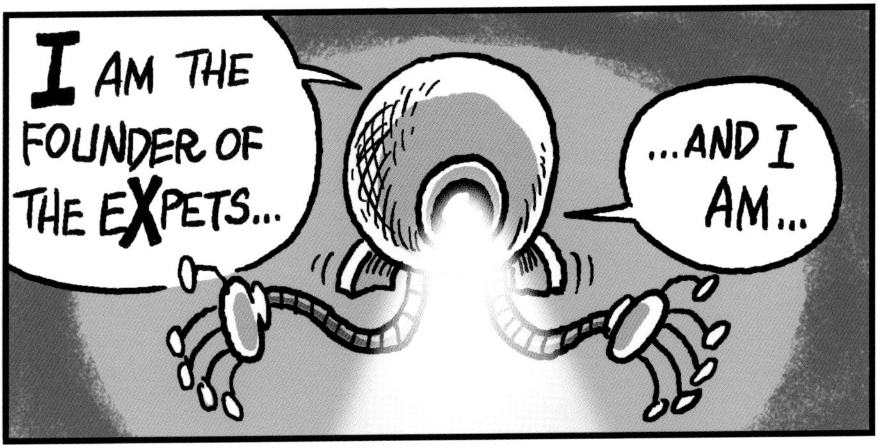
I AM THE FOUNDER OF THE EXPETS...
...AND I AM...

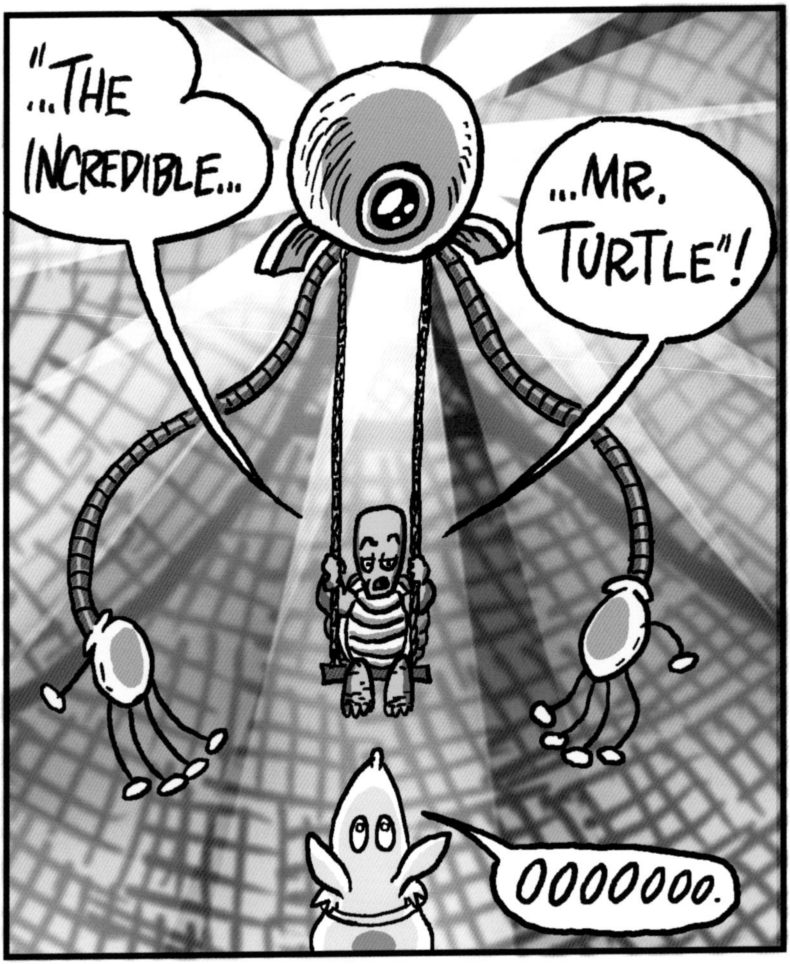
"...THE INCREDIBLE...
...MR. TURTLE"!
OOOOOOO.

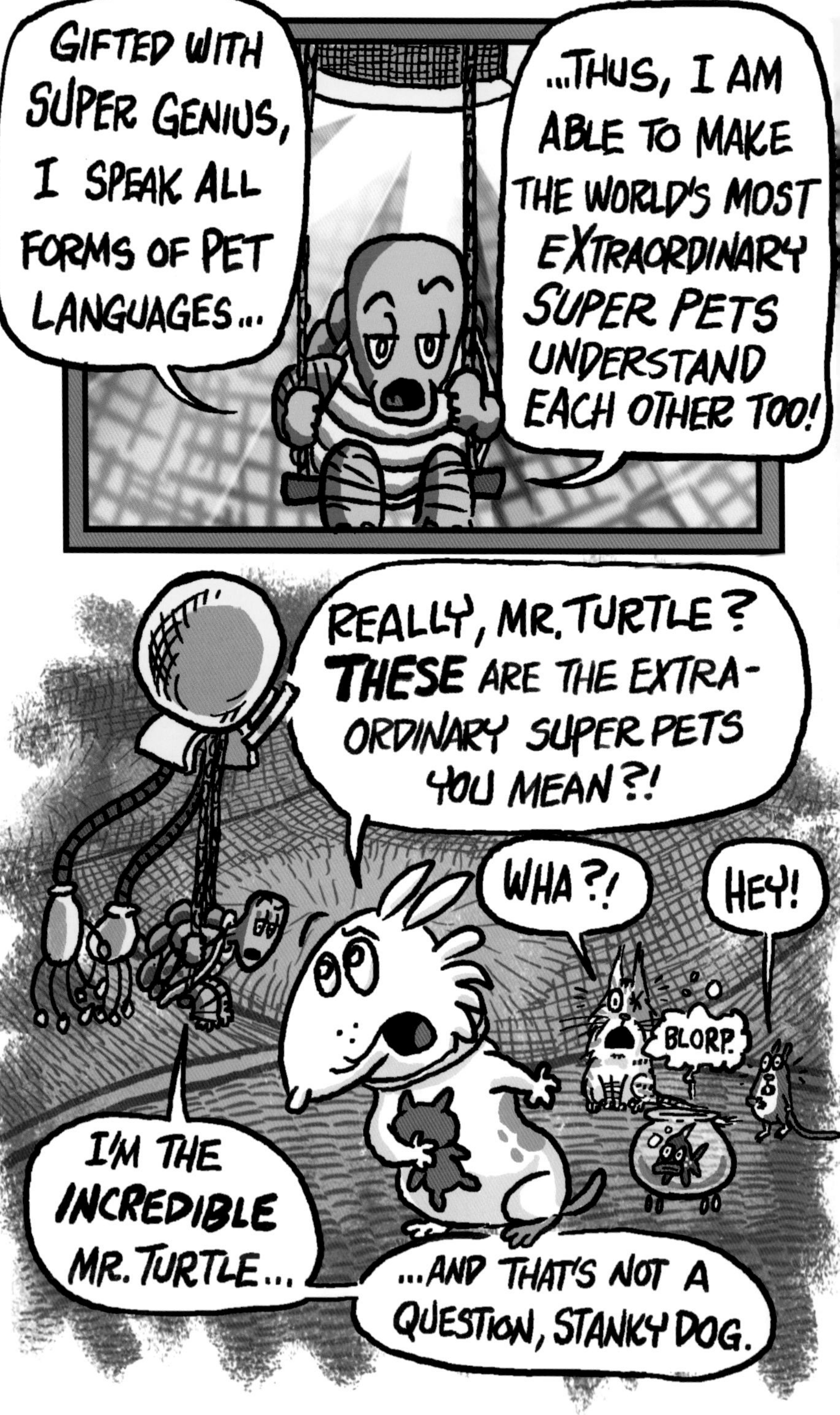
GIFTED WITH SUPER GENIUS, I SPEAK ALL FORMS OF PET LANGUAGES...
...THUS, I AM ABLE TO MAKE THE WORLD'S MOST EXTRAORDINARY SUPER PETS UNDERSTAND EACH OTHER TOO!
REALLY, MR. TURTLE? THESE ARE THE EXTRA-ORDINARY SUPER PETS YOU MEAN?!
WHA?!
BLORP.
HEY!
I'M THE INCREDIBLE MR. TURTLE...
...AND THAT'S NOT A QUESTION, STANKY DOG.

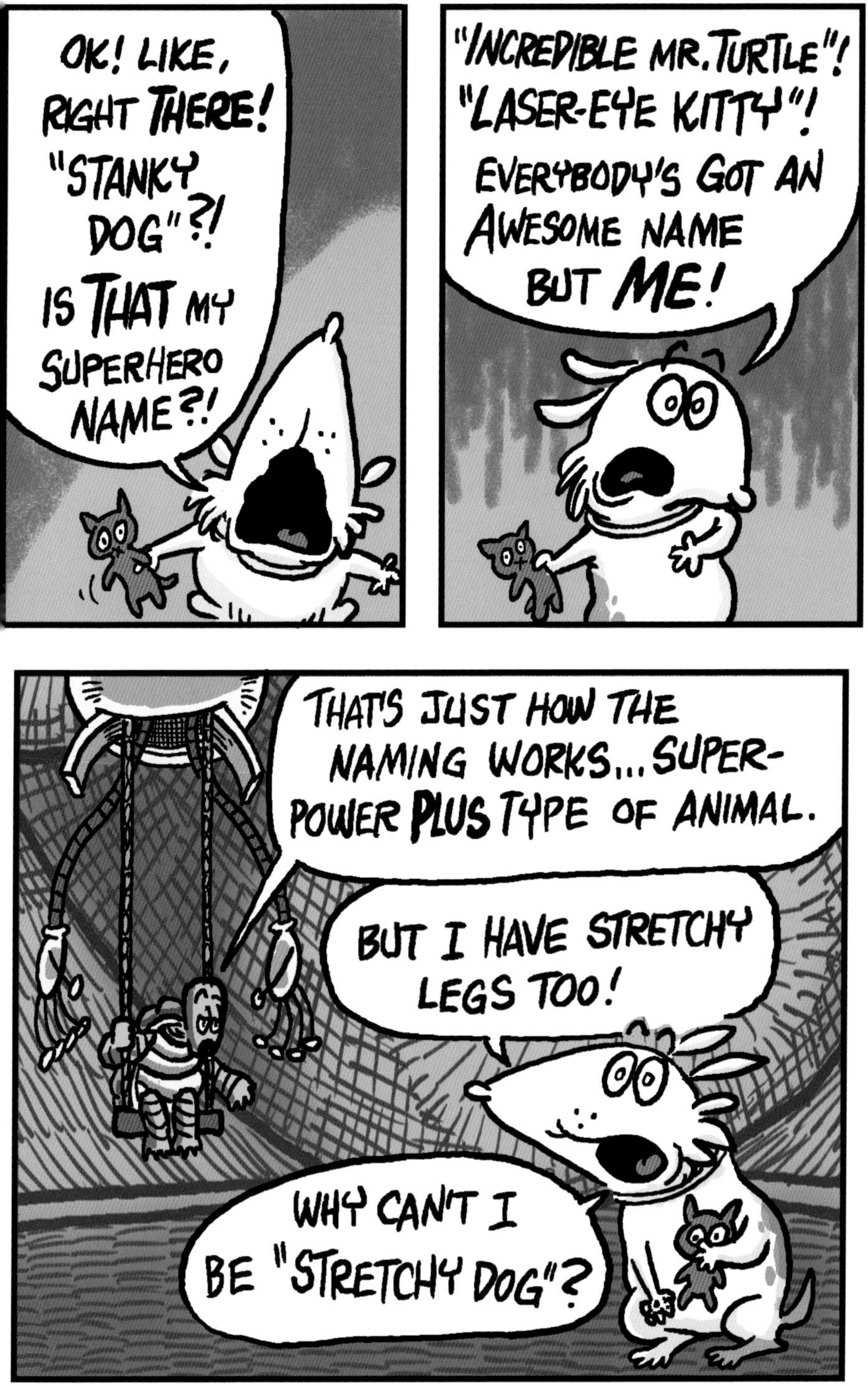
OK! LIKE, RIGHT THERE! "STANKY DOG"?! IS THAT MY SUPERHERO NAME?!
"INCREDIBLE MR. TURTLE"! "LASER-EYE KITTY"! EVERYBODY'S GOT AN AWESOME NAME BUT ME!
THAT'S JUST HOW THE NAMING WORKS... SUPER-POWER PLUS TYPE OF ANIMAL.
BUT I HAVE STRETCHY LEGS TOO!
WHY CAN'T I BE "STRETCHY DOG"?

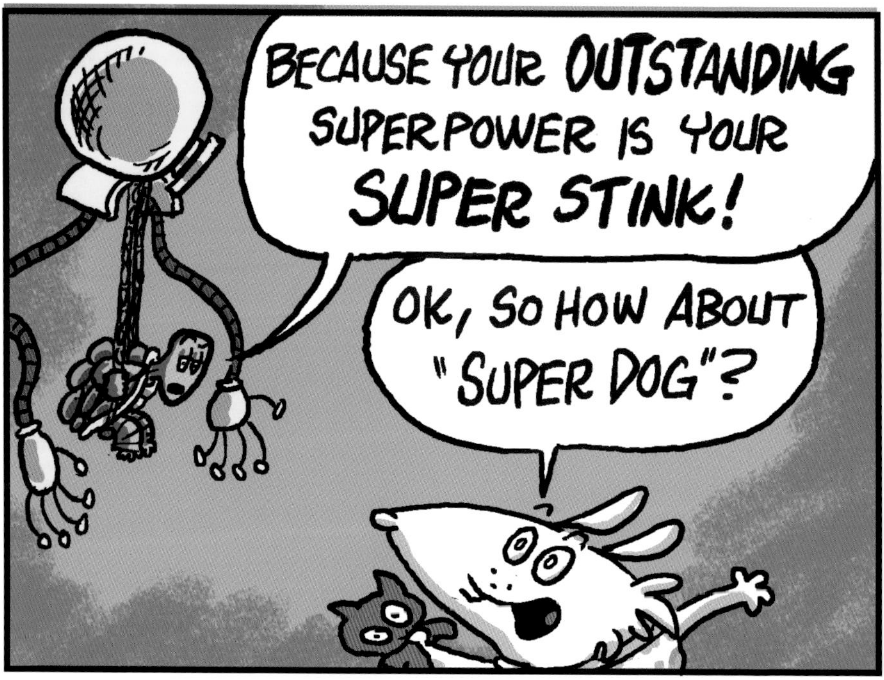
BECAUSE YOUR OUTSTANDING SUPERPOWER IS YOUR SUPER STINK!
OK, SO HOW ABOUT "SUPER DOG"?

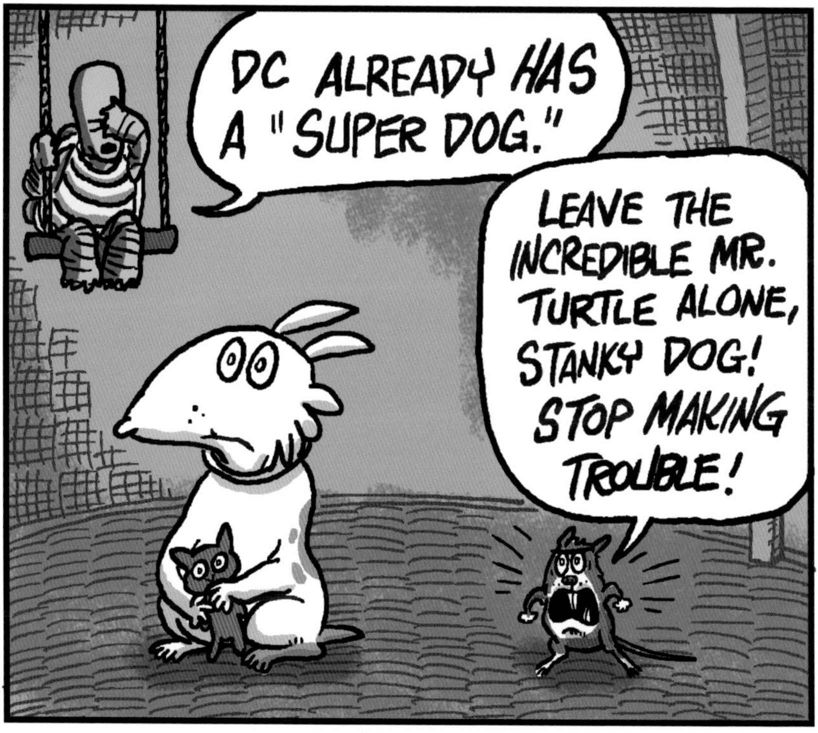
DC ALREADY HAS A "SUPER DOG."
LEAVE THE INCREDIBLE MR. TURTLE ALONE, STANKY DOG! STOP MAKING TROUBLE!

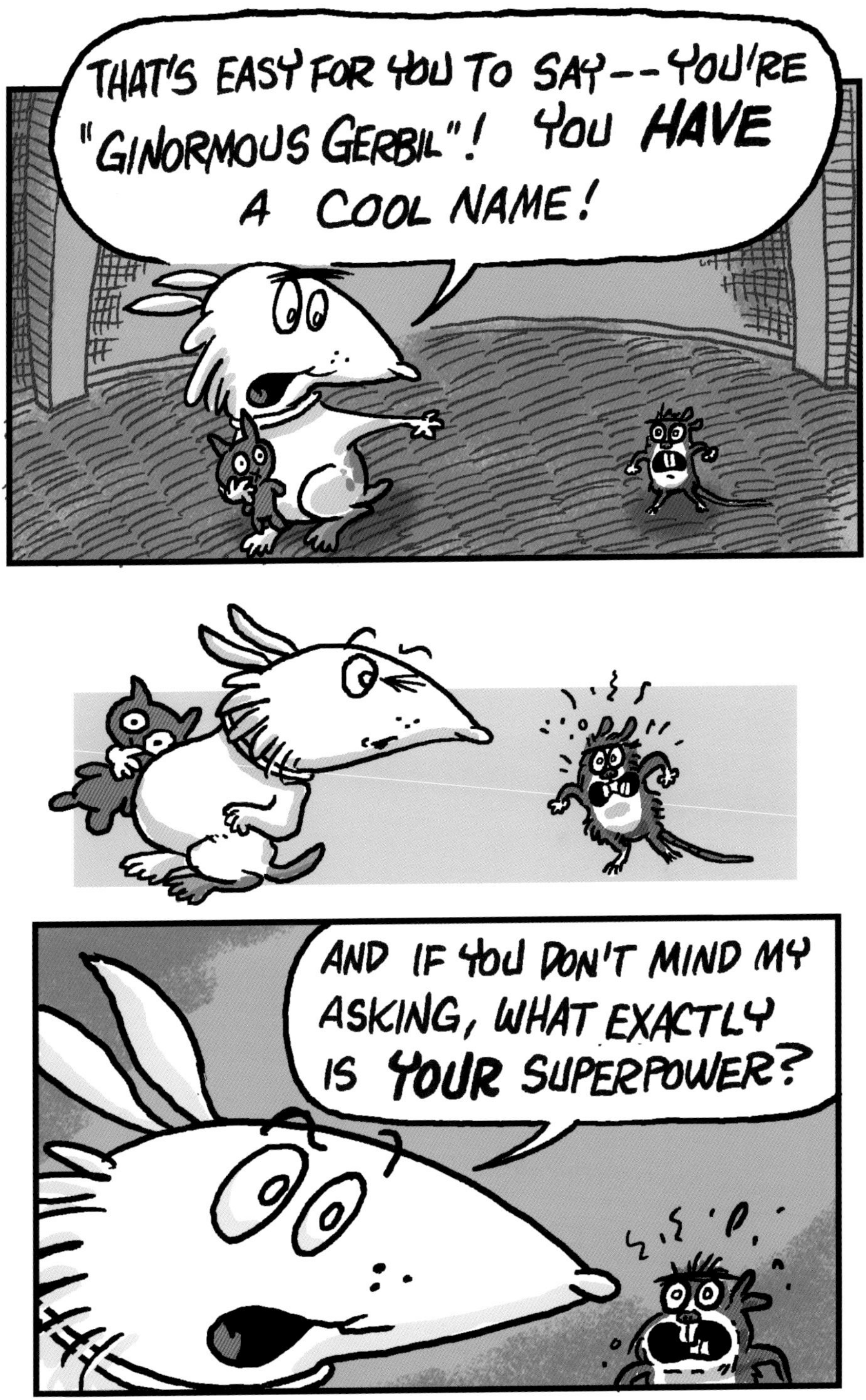
THAT'S EASY FOR YOU TO SAY--YOU'RE "GINORMOUS GERBIL"! YOU HAVE A COOL NAME!
AND IF YOU DON'T MIND MY ASKING, WHAT EXACTLY IS YOUR SUPERPOWER?

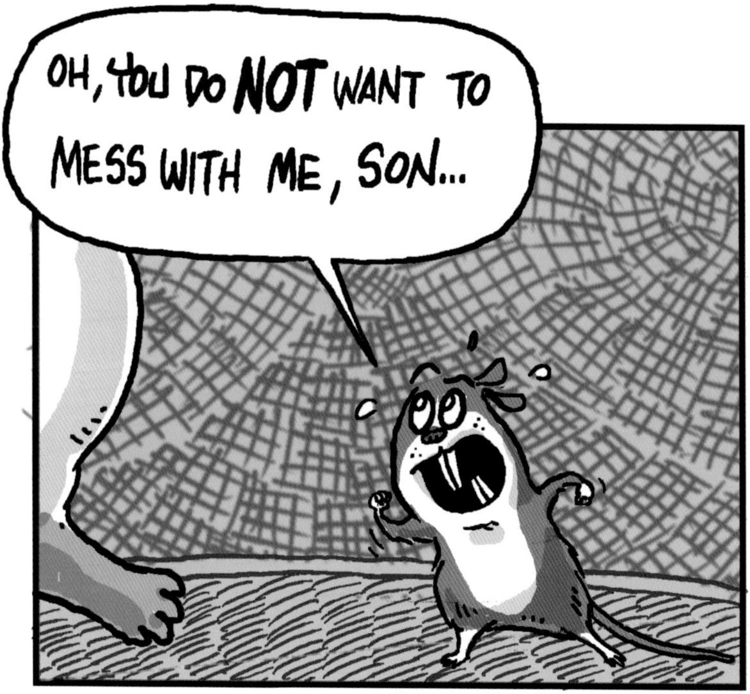
OH, YOU DO NOT WANT TO MESS WITH ME, SON...

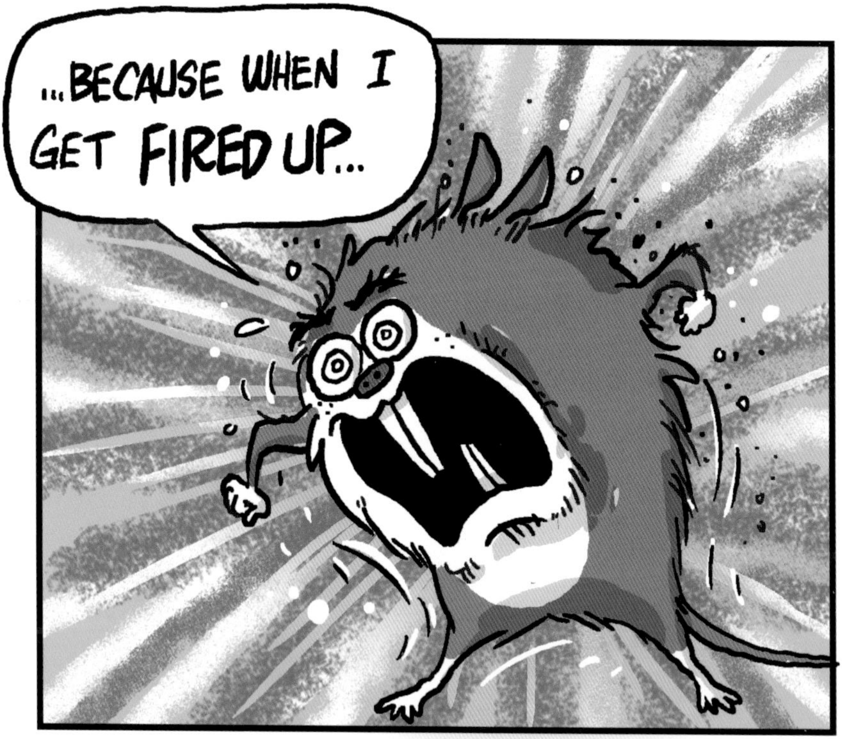
...BECAUSE WHEN I GET FIRED UP...

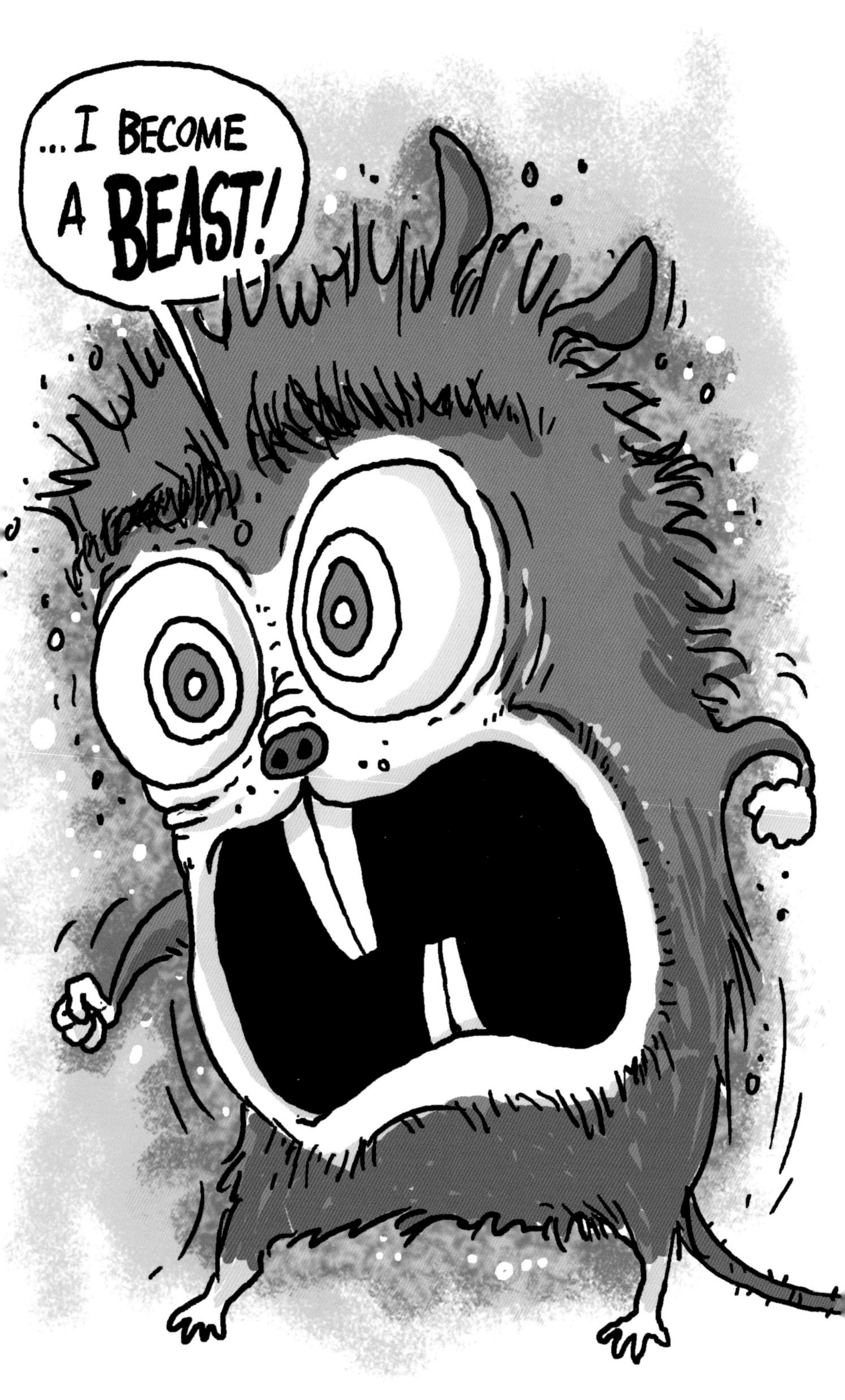
...I BECOME A BEAST!

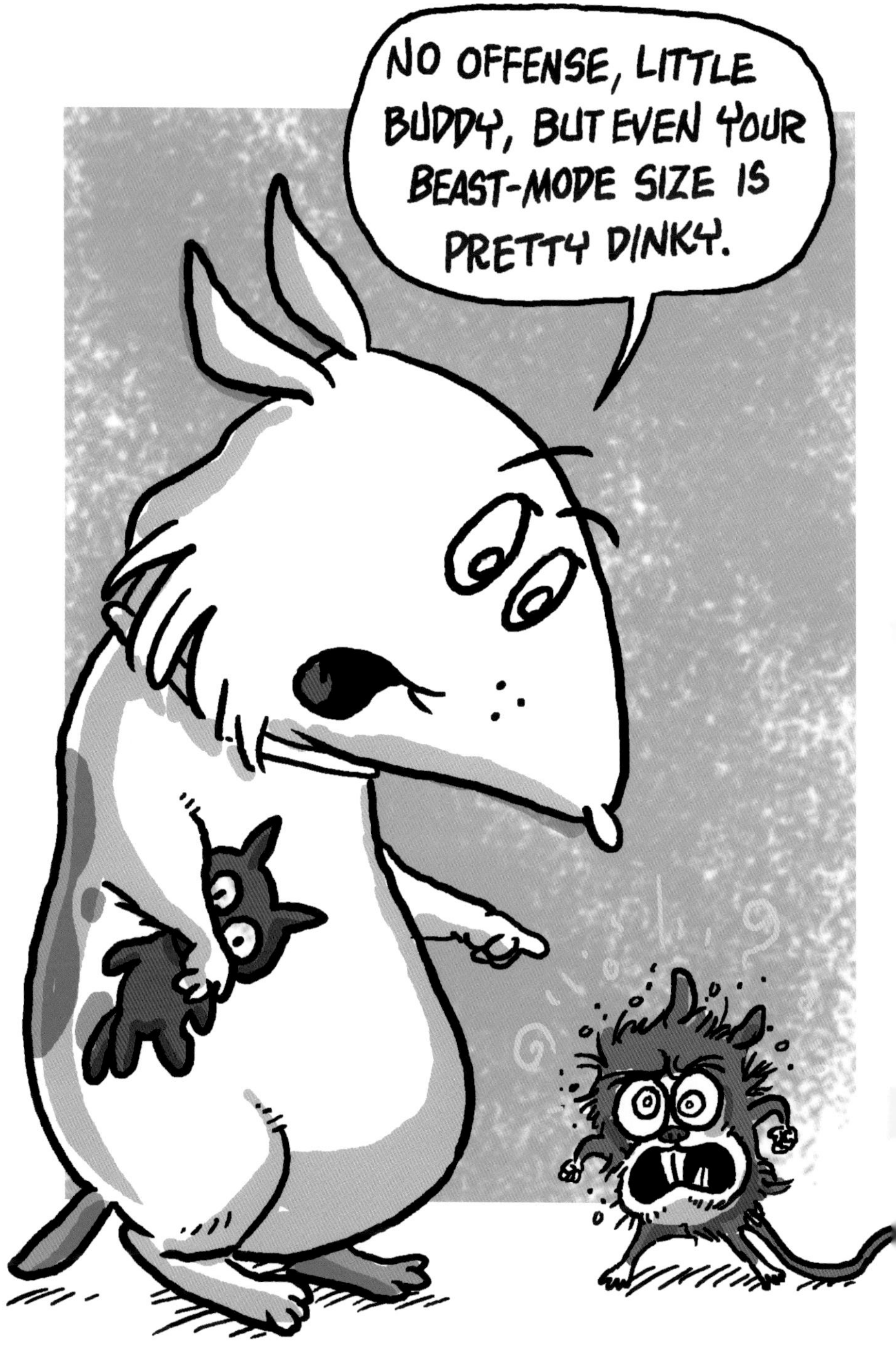
NO OFFENSE, LITTLE BUDDY, BUT EVEN YOUR BEAST-MODE SIZE IS PRETTY DINKY.

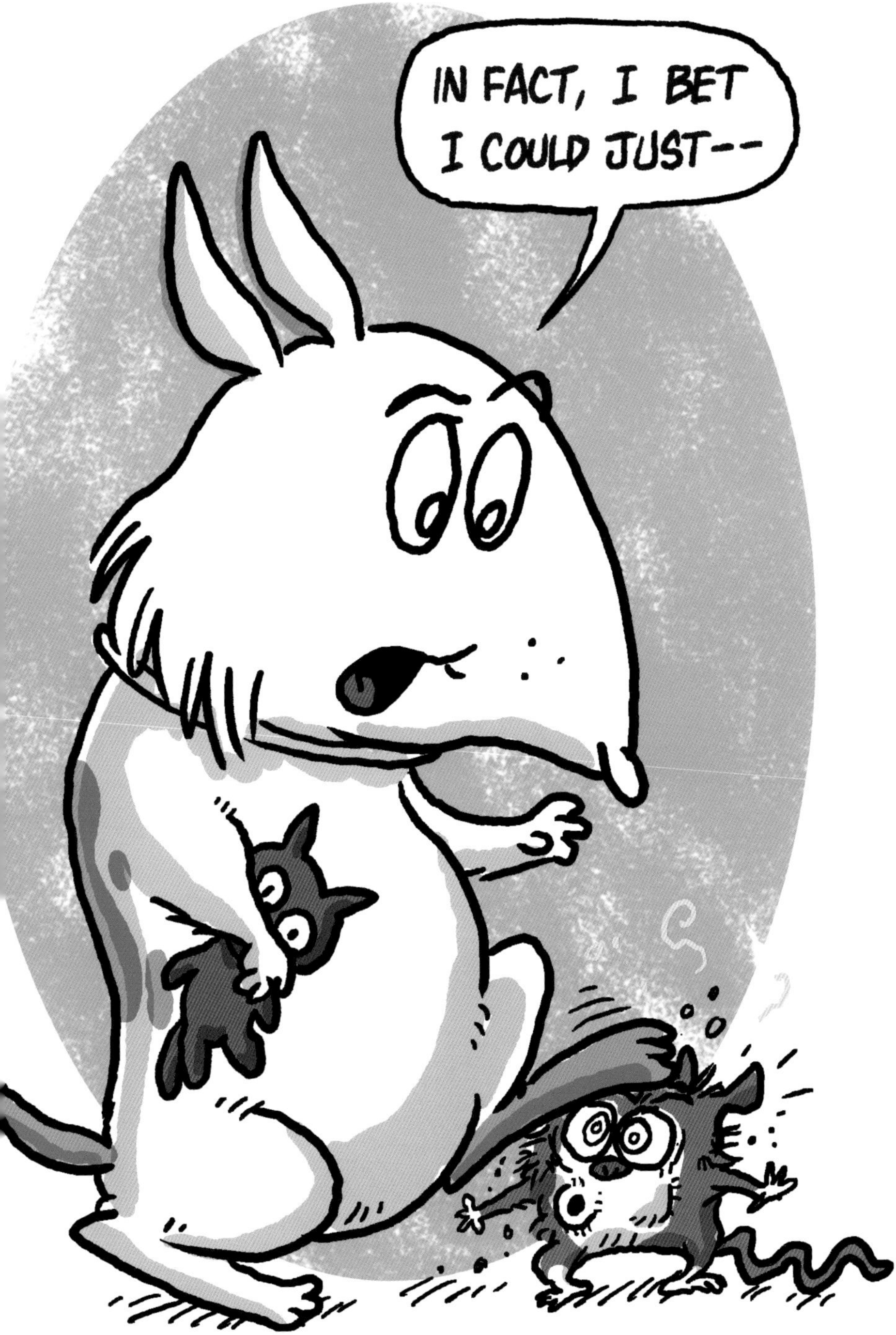
IN FACT, I BET I COULD JUST--

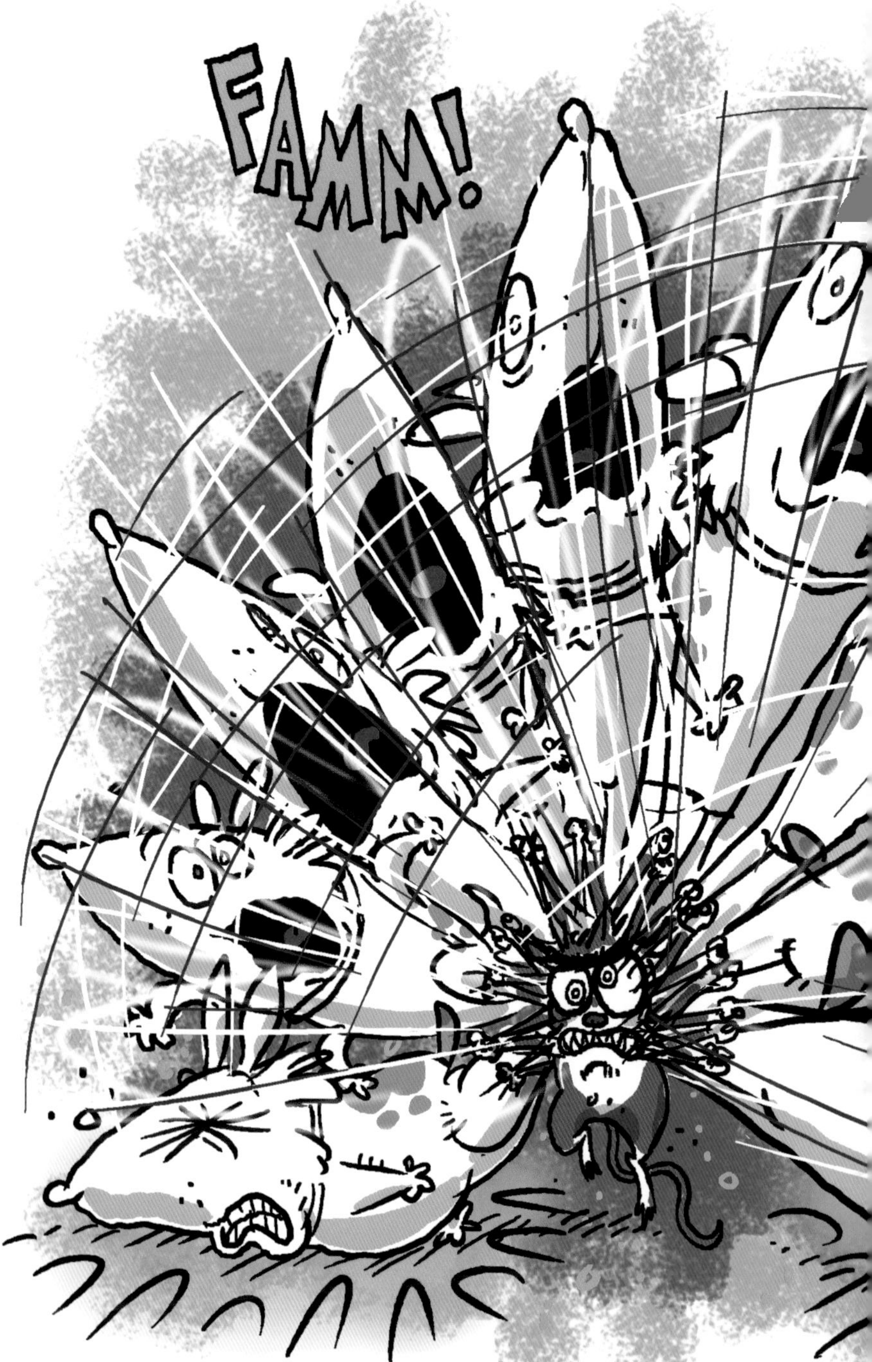
FAMM!

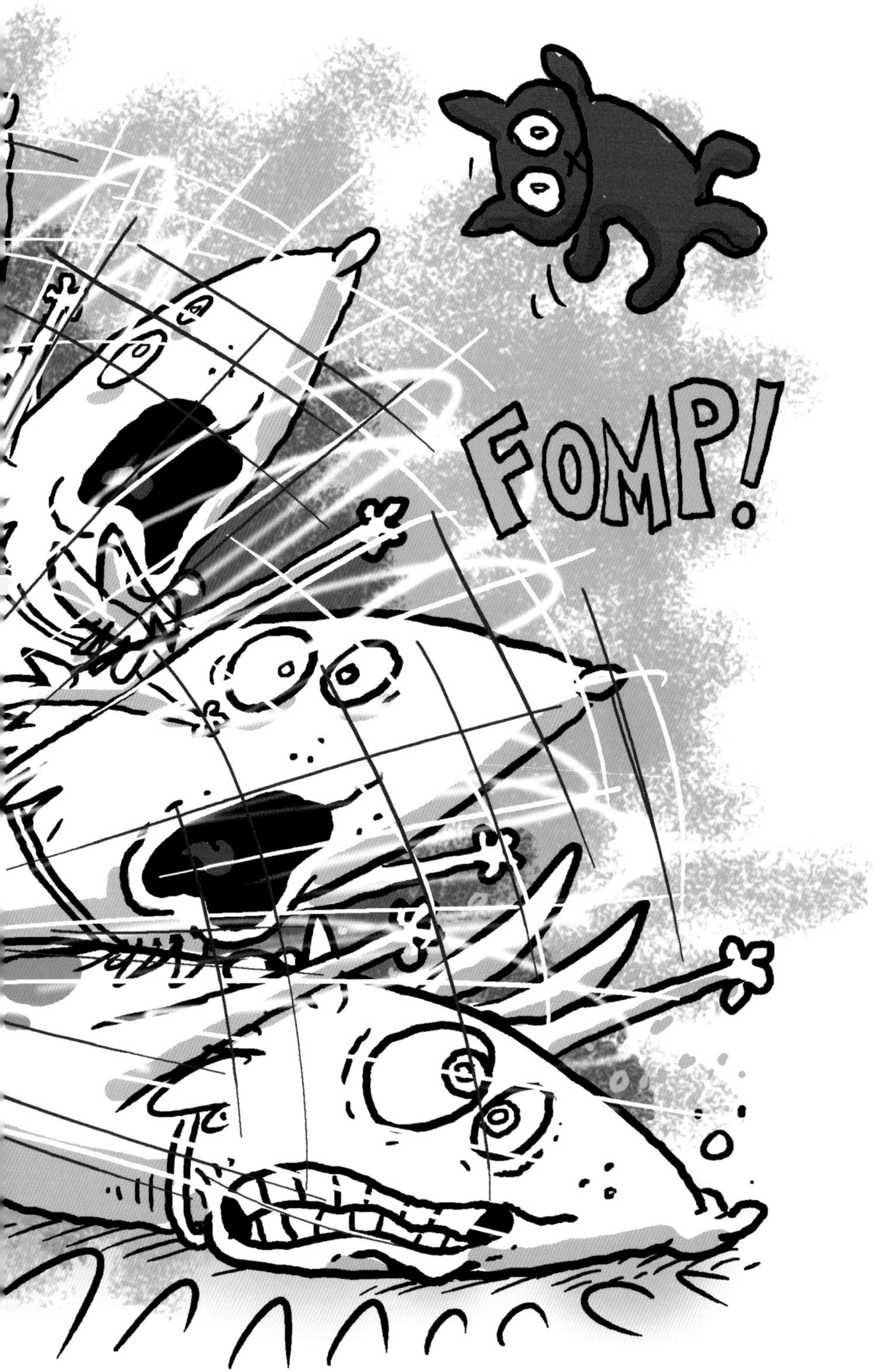
FOMP!

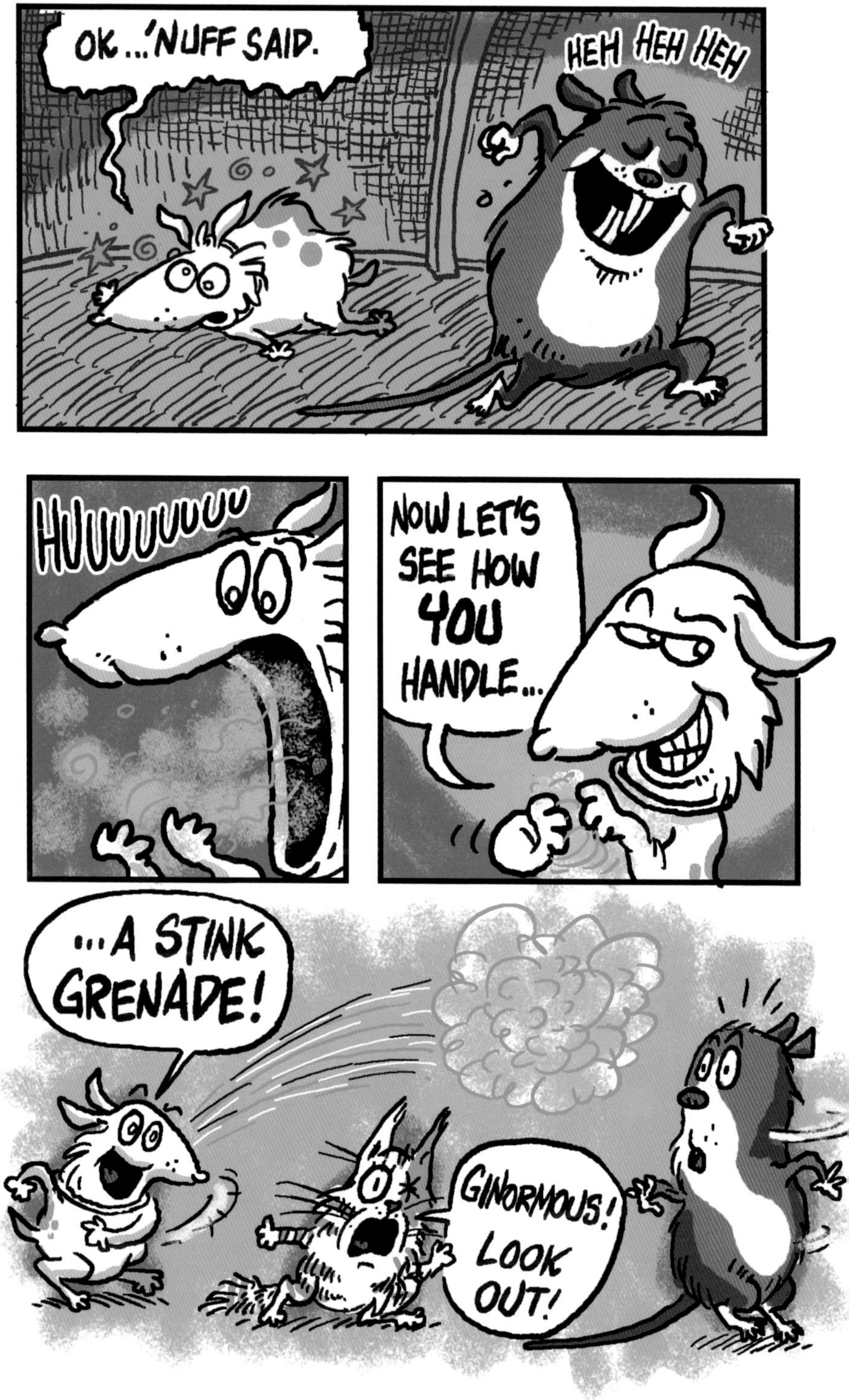
OK...'NUFF SAID.
HEH HEH HEH
HUUUUUUUU
NOW LET'S SEE HOW YOU HANDLE...
...A STINK GRENADE!
GINORMOUS! LOOK OUT!

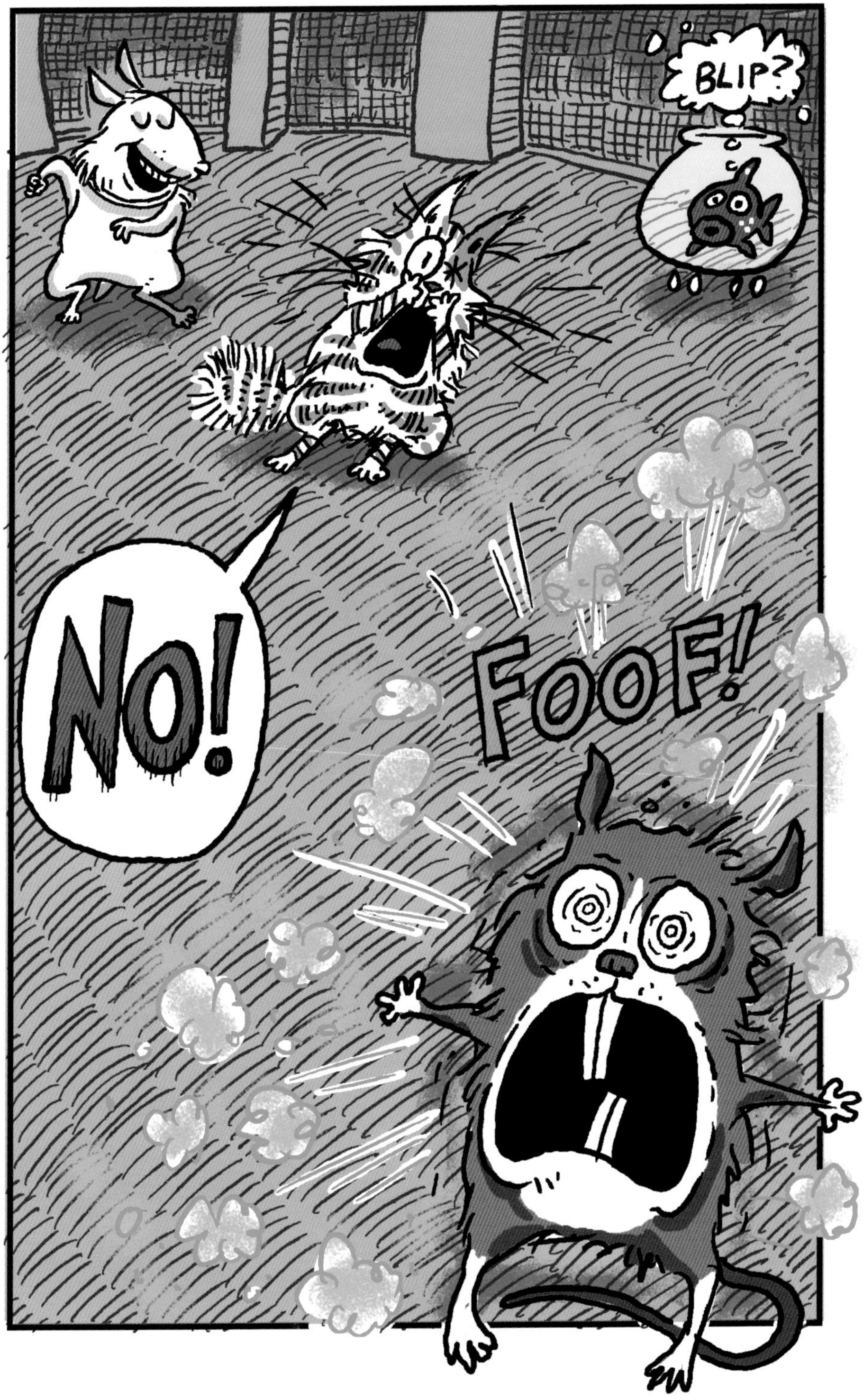
BLIP?
NO!
FOOF!

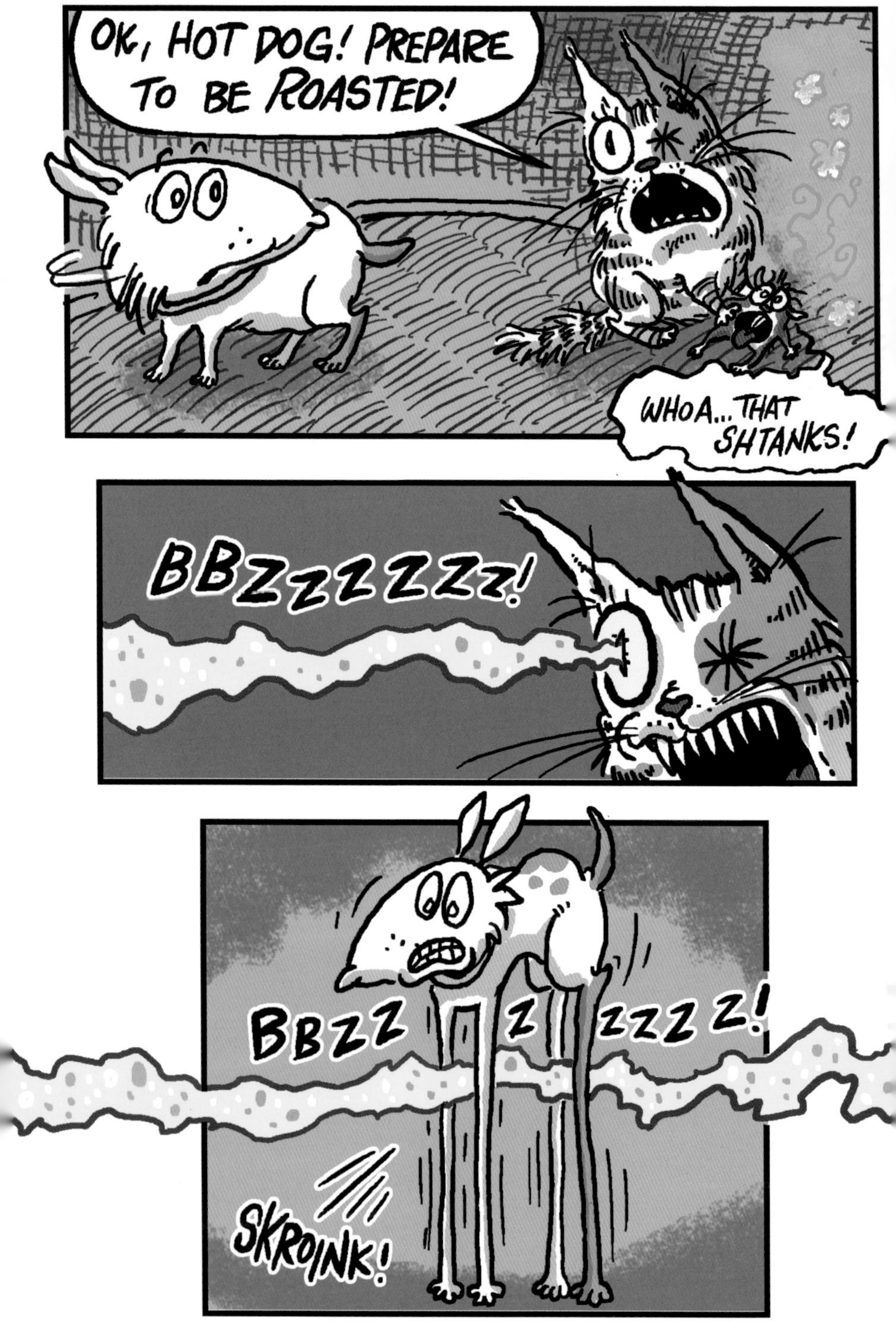
OK, HOT DOG! PREPARE TO BE ROASTED!
WHOA... THAT SHTANKS!
BBZZZZZZZ!
BBZZ Z ZZZ Z!
SKROINK!

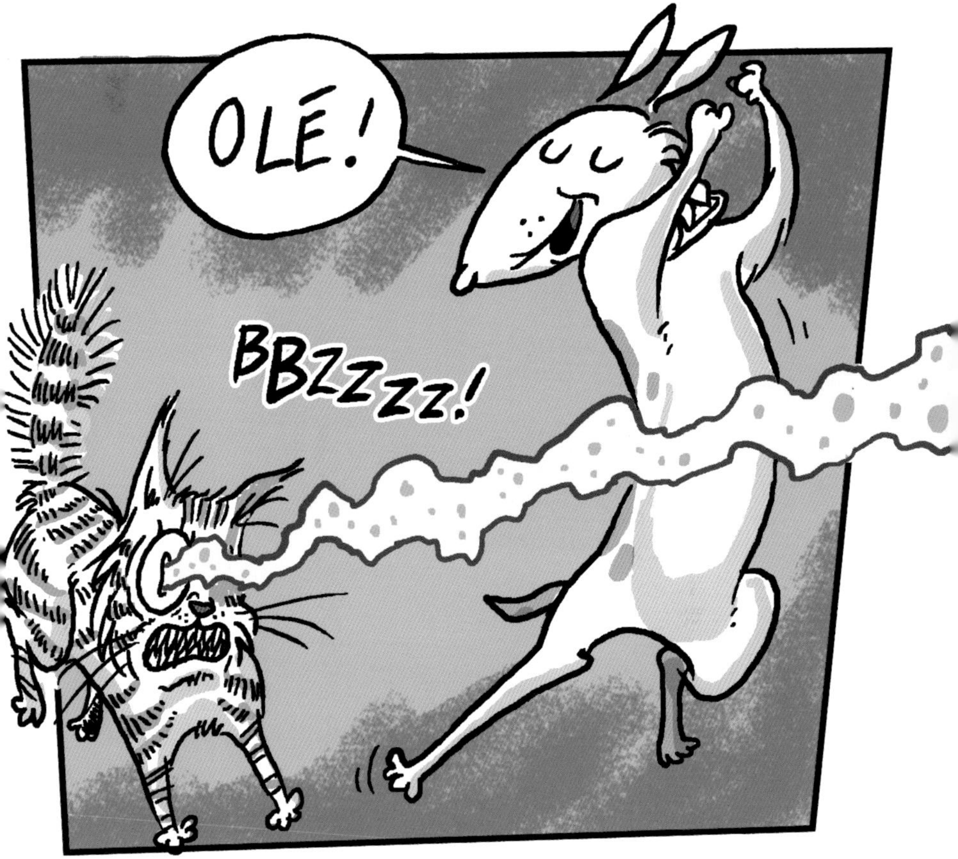
OLÉ!
BBZZZZZ!

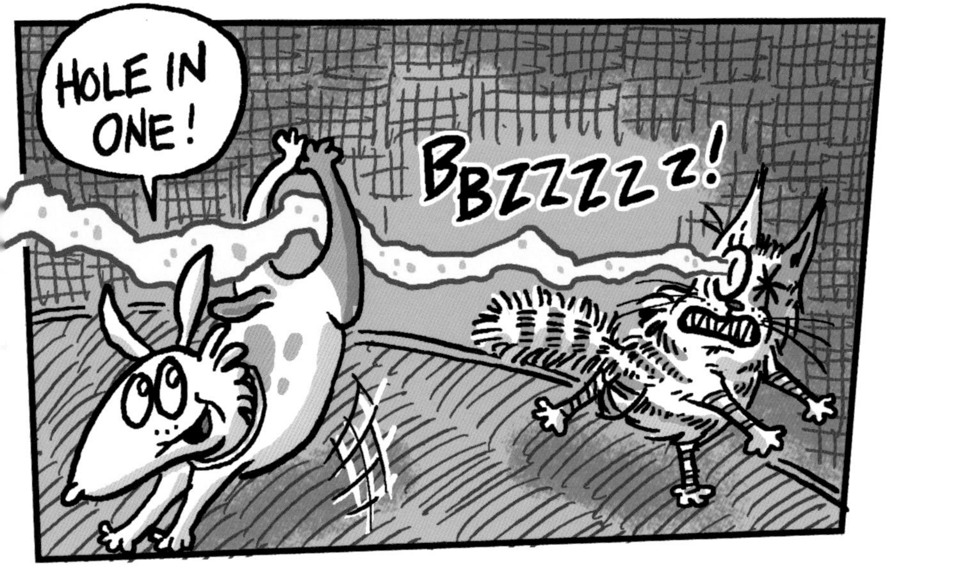
HOLE IN ONE!
BBZZZZZZ!

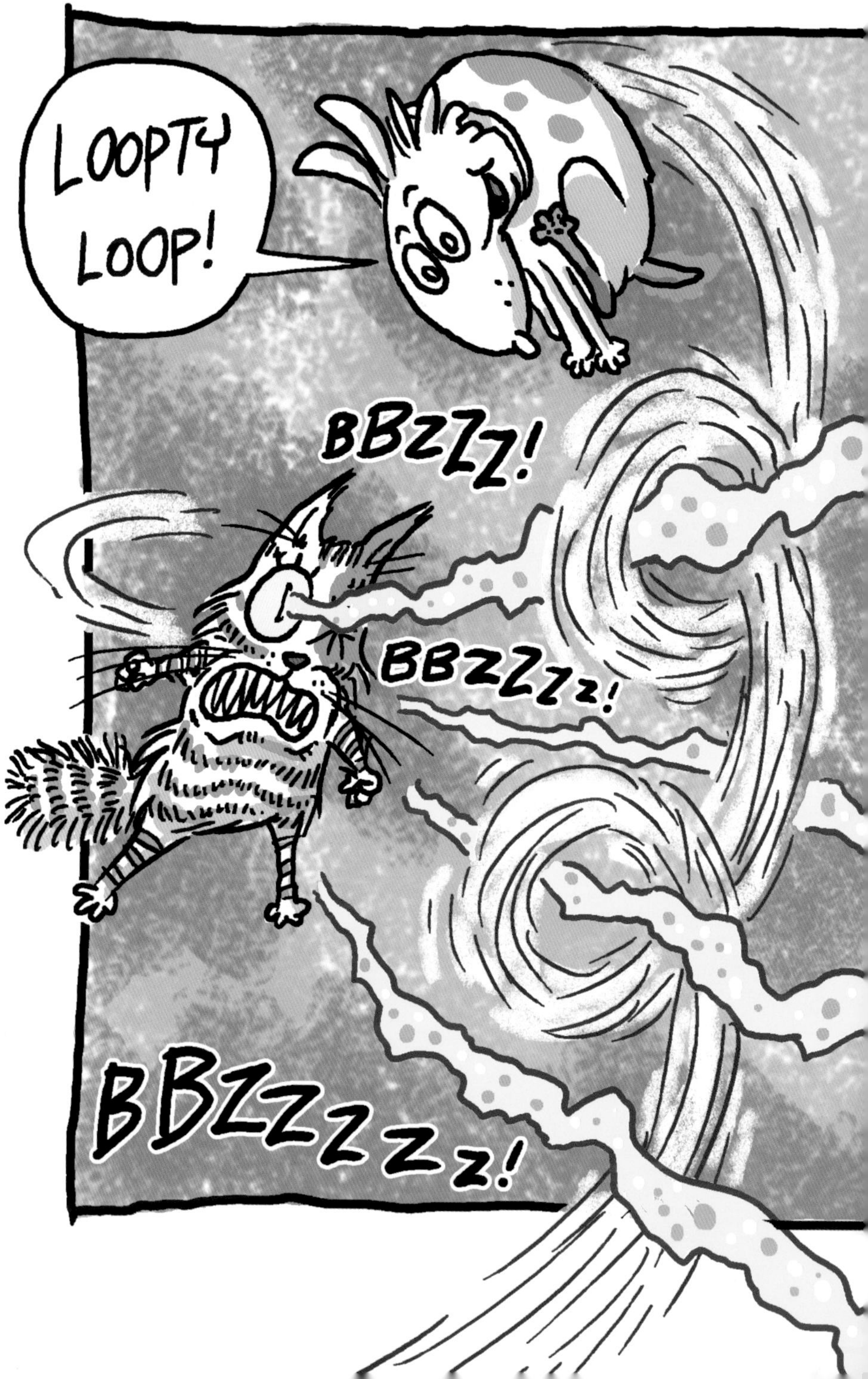
LOOPTY LOOP!
BBZZZ!
BBZZZzz!
BBZZZZZz!

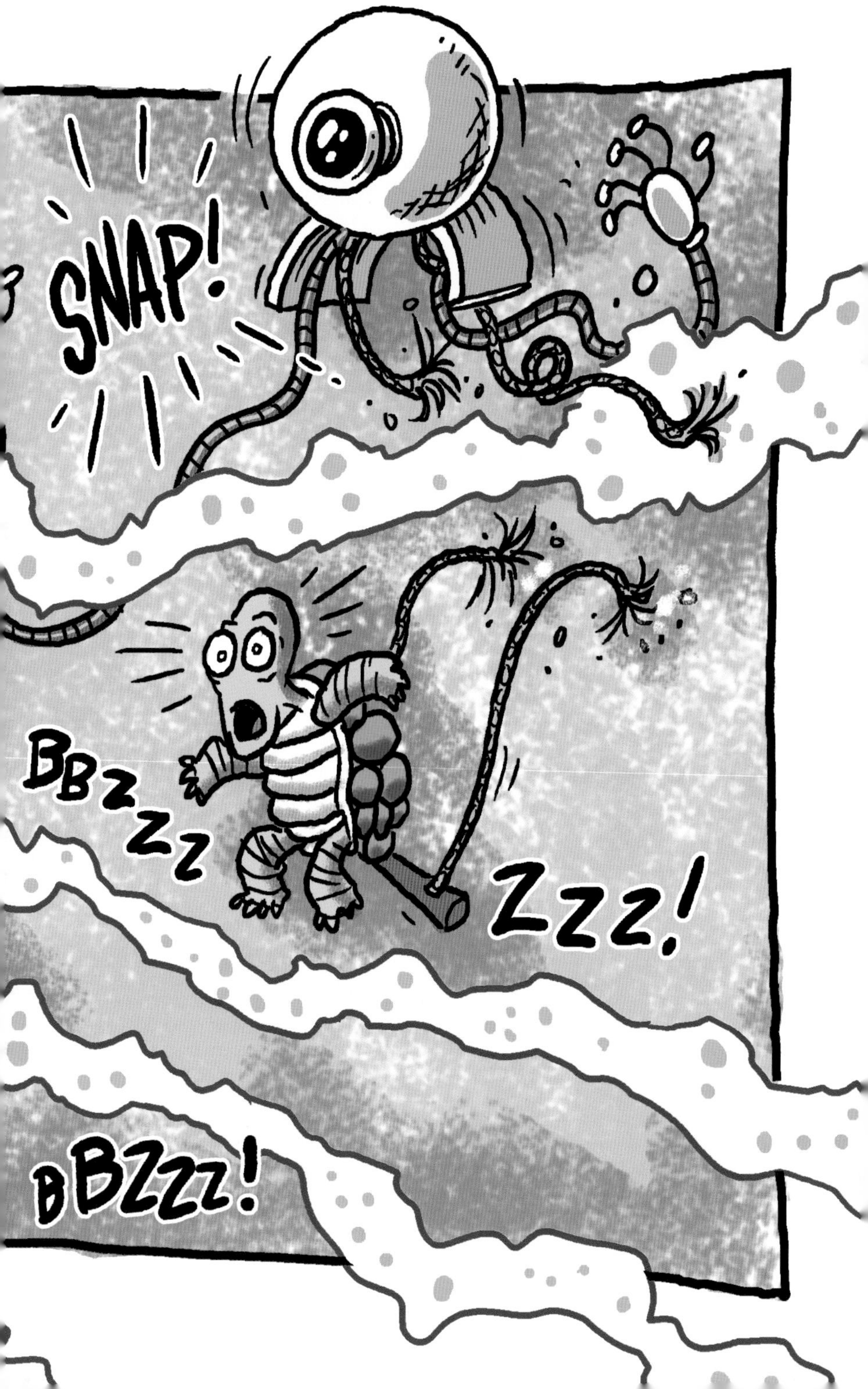
SNAP!
BBzzZz
Zzz!
BBZzz!

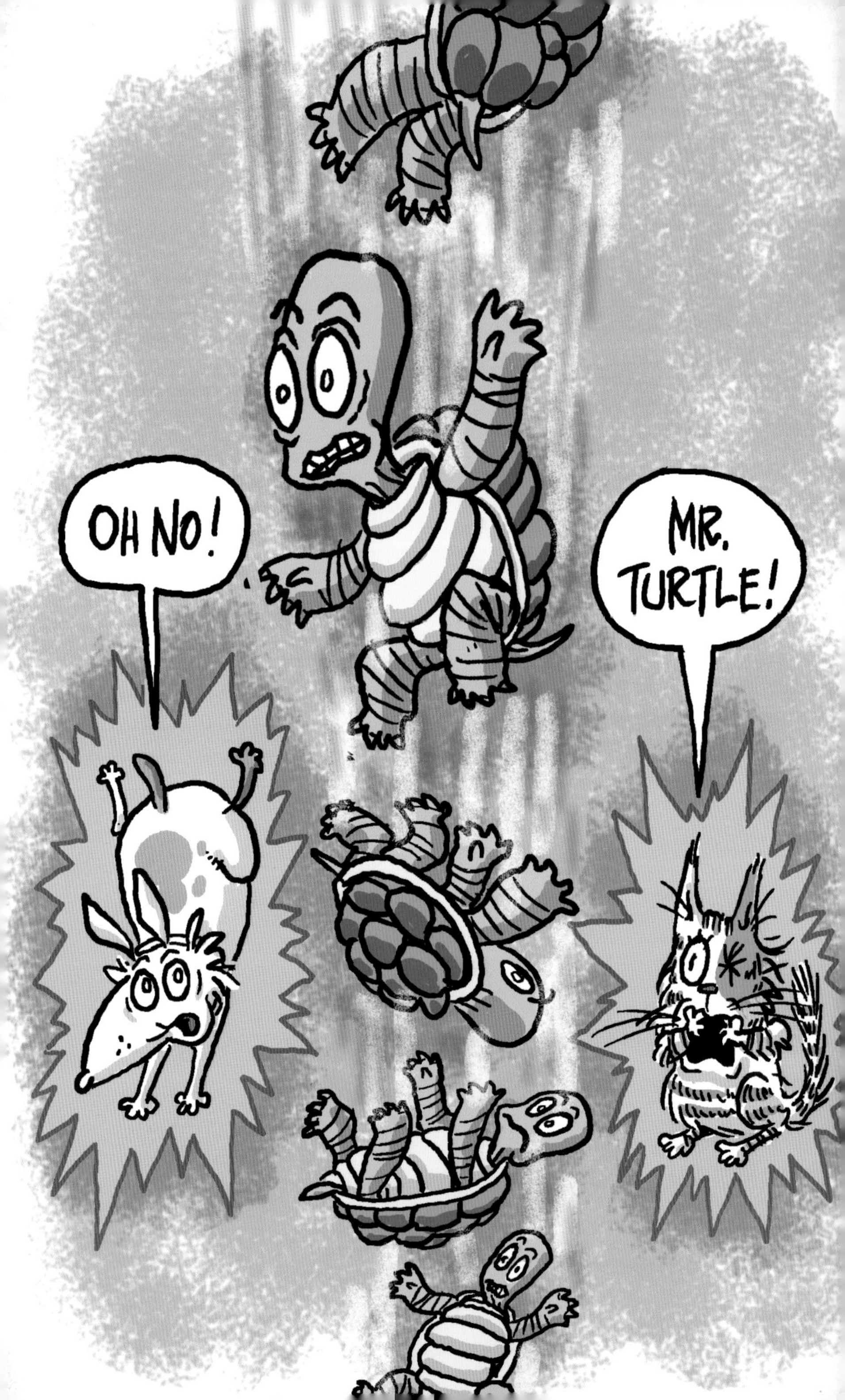
OH NO!
MR. TURTLE!

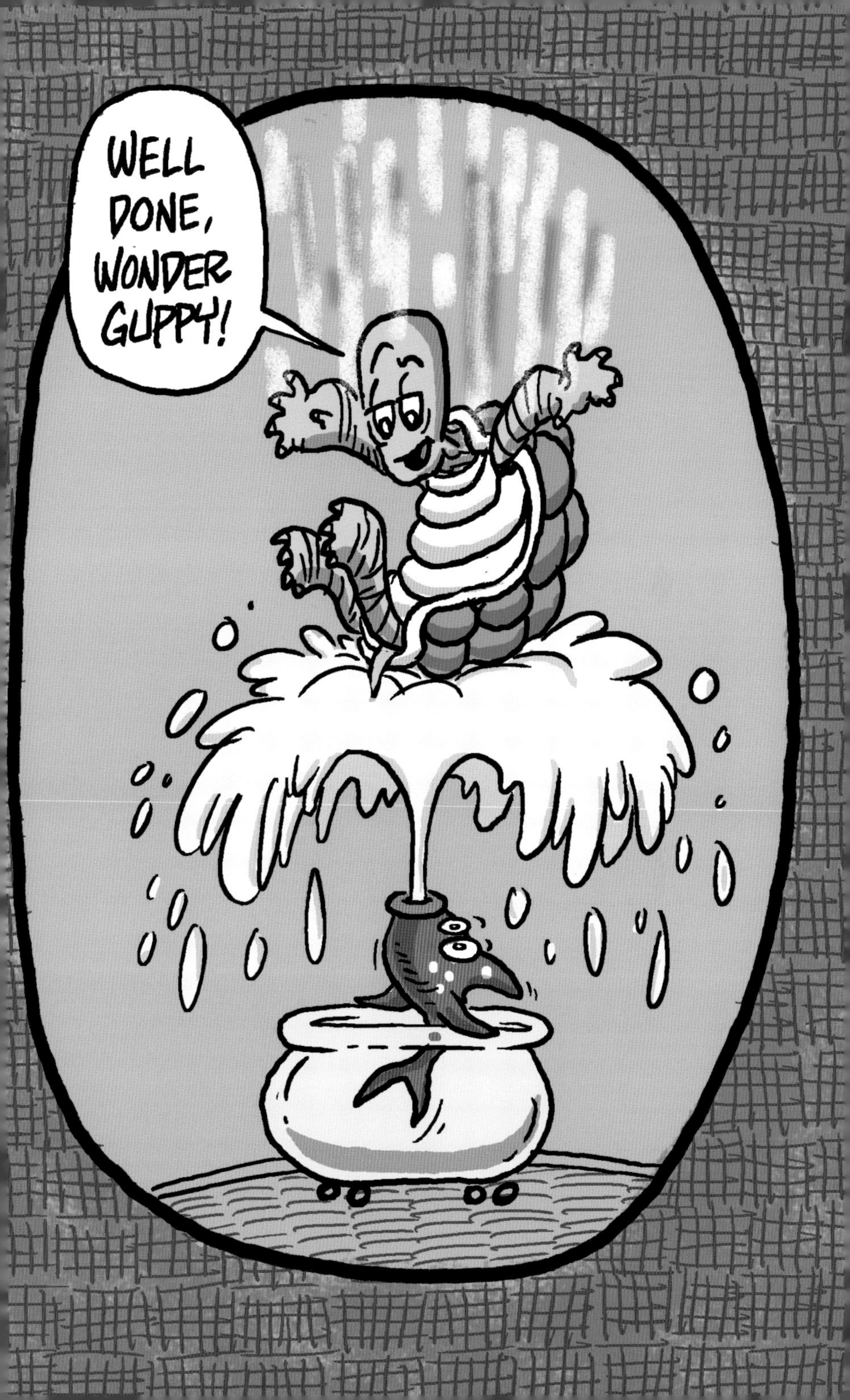
WELL DONE, WONDER GUPPY!

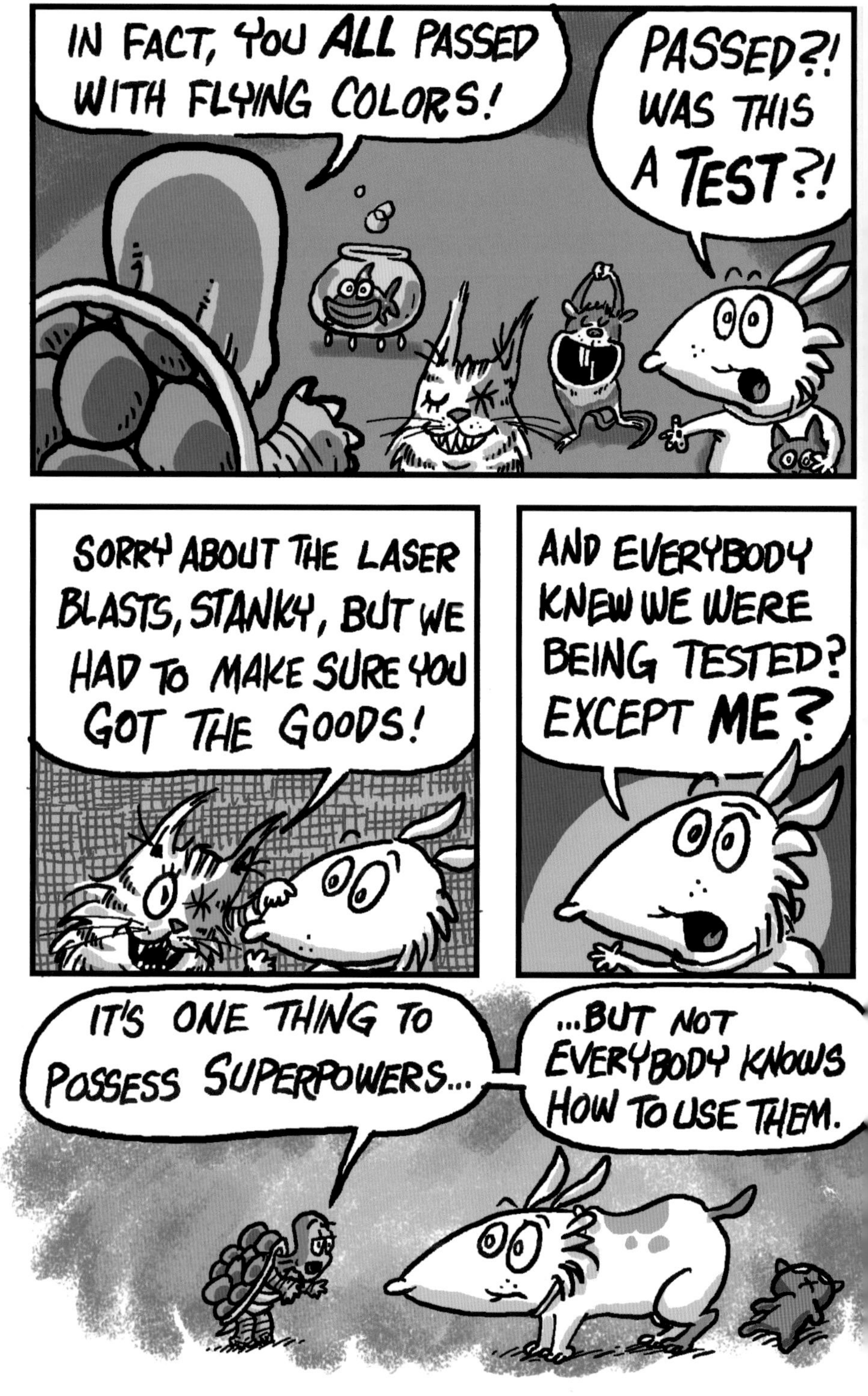
IN FACT, YOU ALL PASSED WITH FLYING COLORS!
PASSED?! WAS THIS A TEST?!
SORRY ABOUT THE LASER BLASTS, STANKY, BUT WE HAD TO MAKE SURE YOU GOT THE GOODS!
AND EVERYBODY KNEW WE WERE BEING TESTED? EXCEPT ME?
IT'S ONE THING TO POSSESS SUPERPOWERS...
...BUT NOT EVERYBODY KNOWS HOW TO USE THEM.

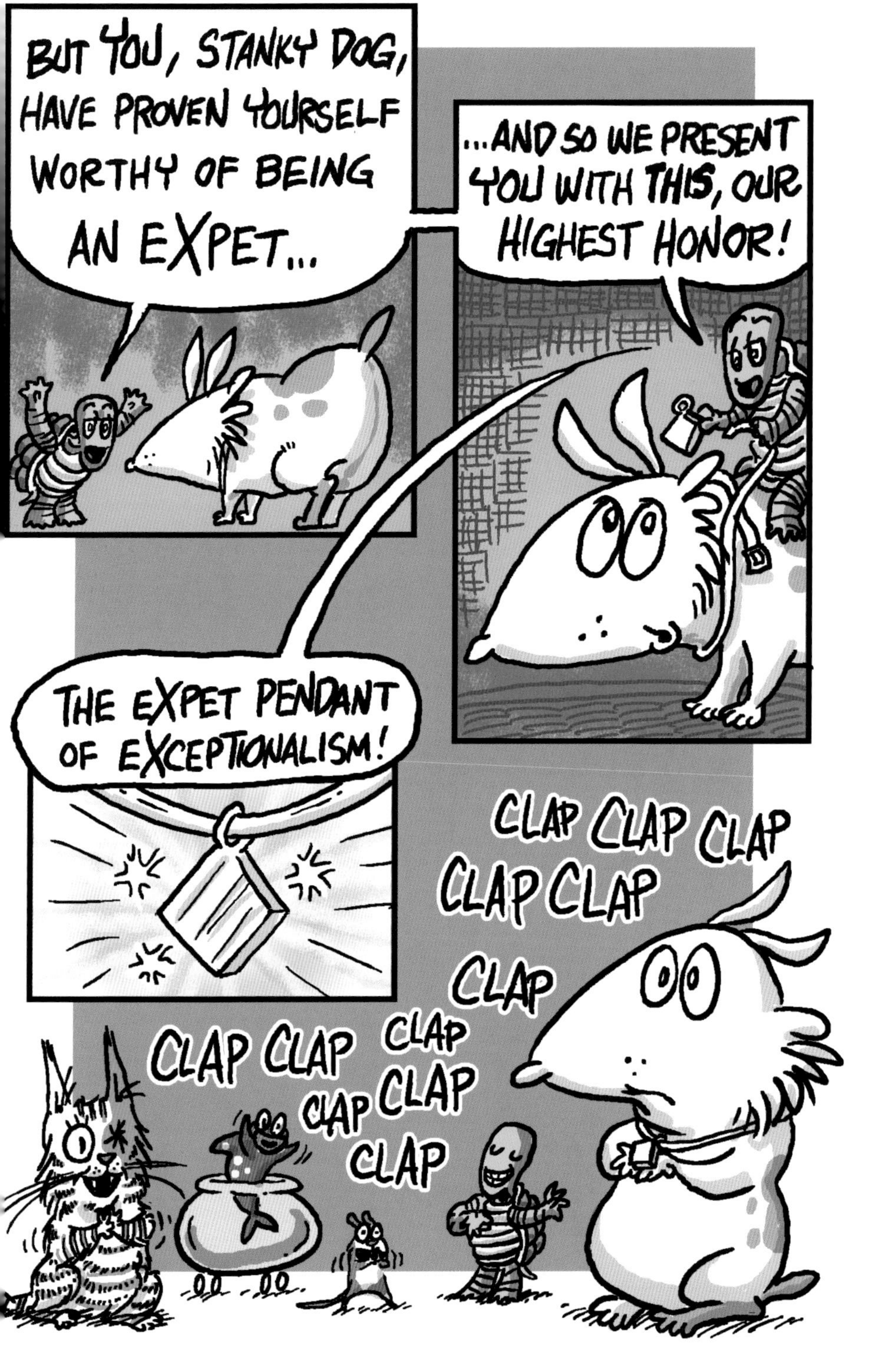
BUT YOU, STANKY DOG, HAVE PROVEN YOURSELF WORTHY OF BEING AN EXPET...
...AND SO WE PRESENT YOU WITH THIS, OUR HIGHEST HONOR!
THE EXPET PENDANT OF EXCEPTIONALISM!
CLAP CLAP CLAP
CLAP CLAP
CLAP
CLAP CLAP
CLAP
CLAP
CLAP CLAP
CLAP

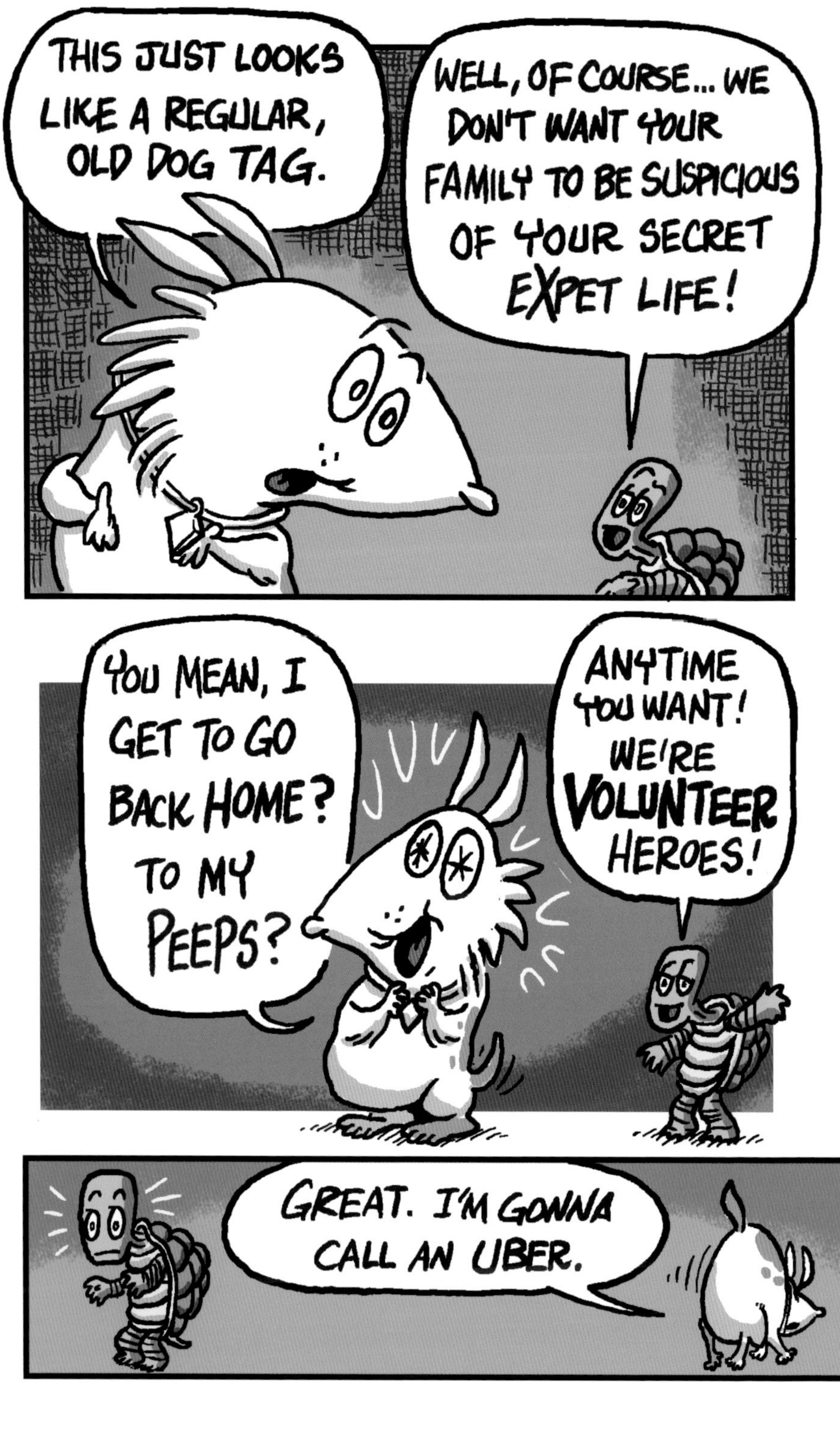
THIS JUST LOOKS LIKE A REGULAR, OLD DOG TAG.
WELL, OF COURSE... WE DON'T WANT YOUR FAMILY TO BE SUSPICIOUS OF YOUR SECRET EXPET LIFE!
YOU MEAN, I GET TO GO BACK HOME? TO MY PEEPS?
ANYTIME YOU WANT! WE'RE VOLUNTEER HEROES!
GREAT. I'M GONNA CALL AN UBER.

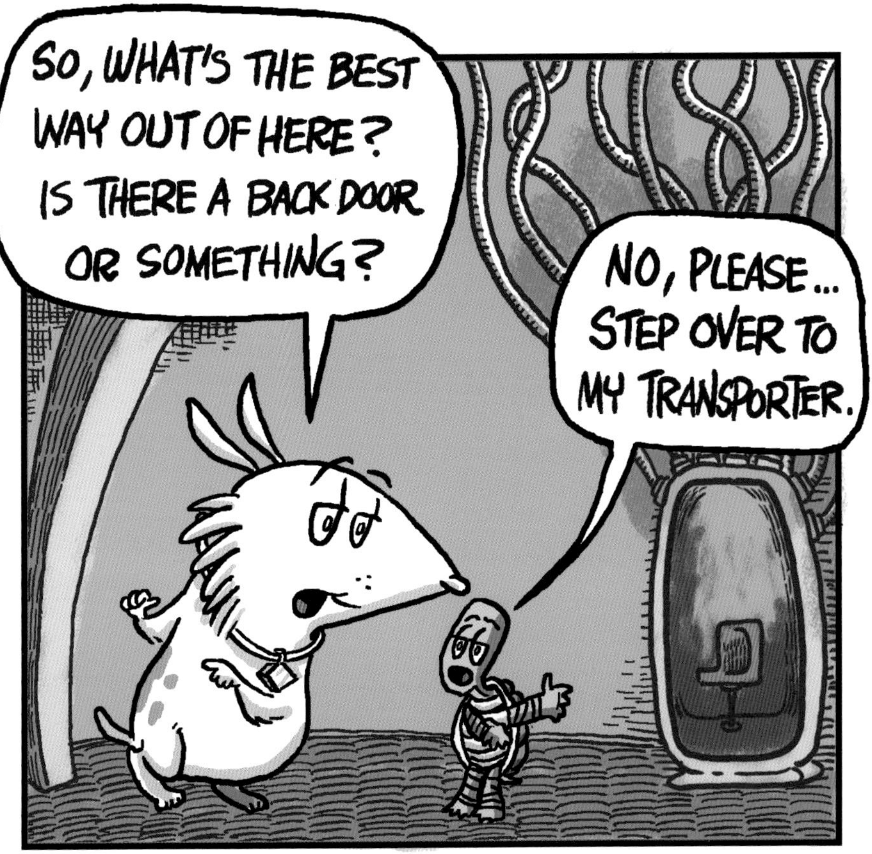
SO, WHAT'S THE BEST WAY OUT OF HERE? IS THERE A BACK DOOR OR SOMETHING?
NO, PLEASE... STEP OVER TO MY TRANSPORTER.

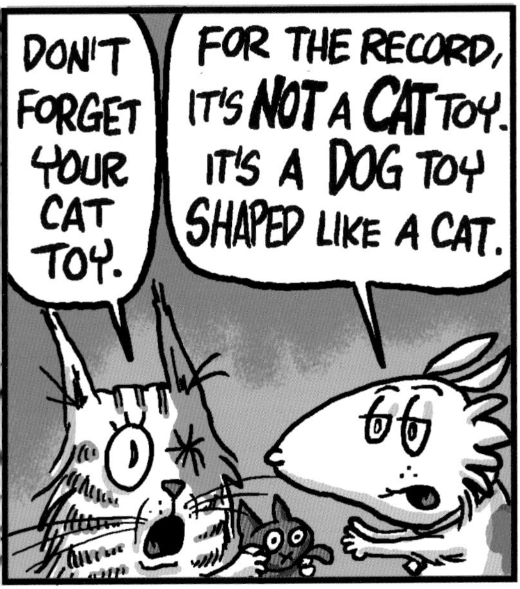
DON'T FORGET YOUR CAT TOY.
FOR THE RECORD, IT'S **NOT** A **CAT** TOY. IT'S A DOG TOY SHAPED LIKE A CAT.

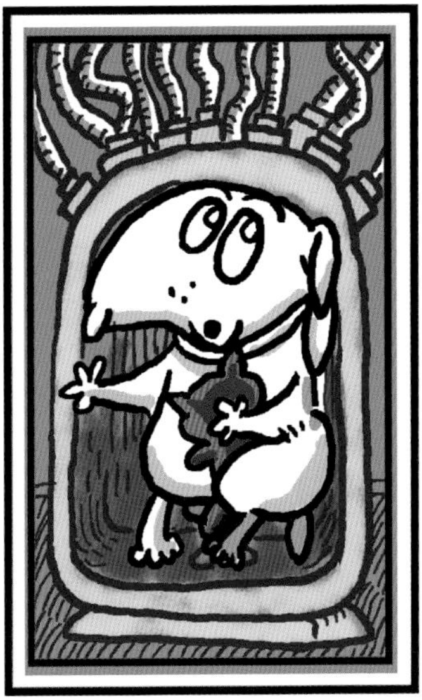

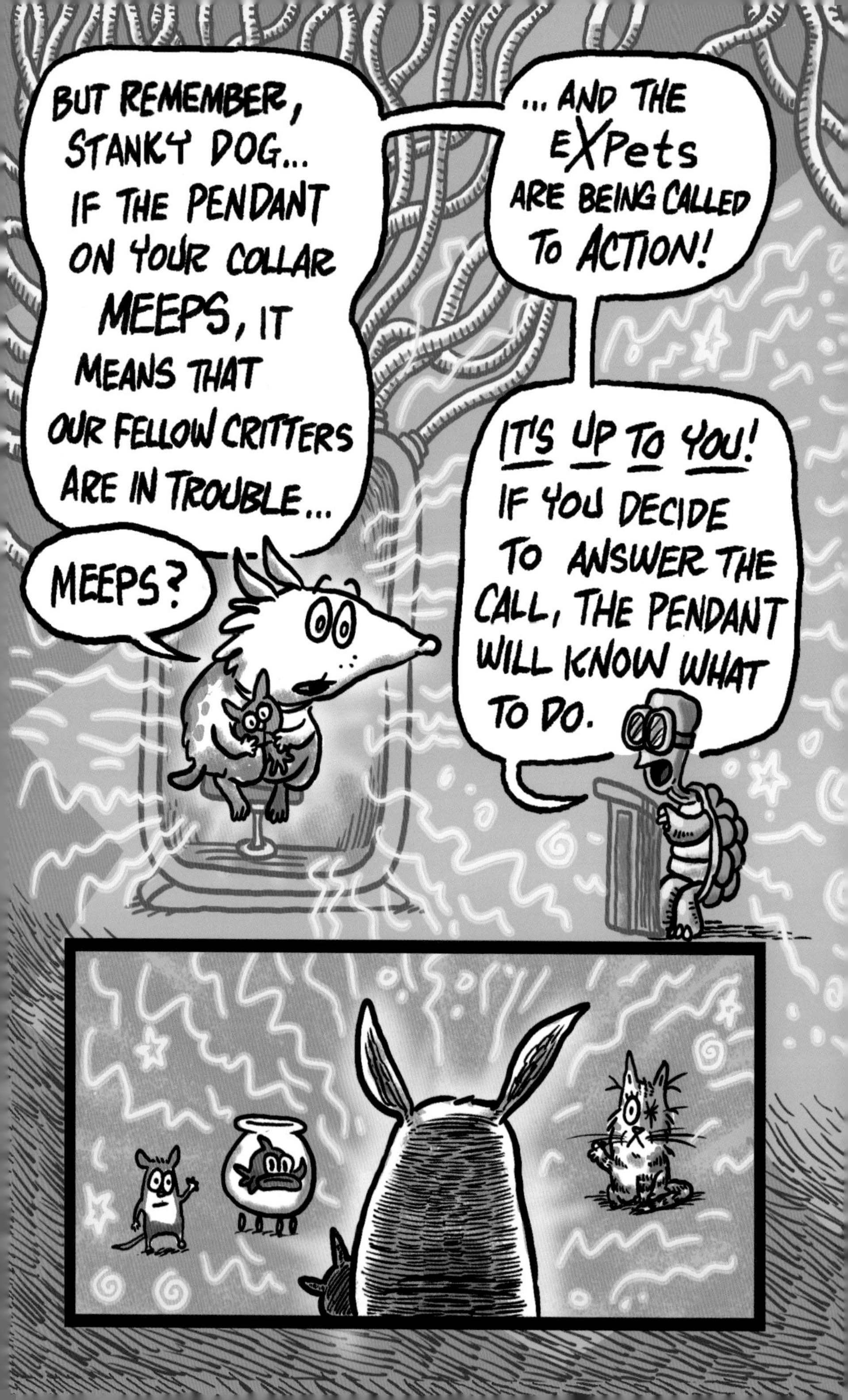
BUT REMEMBER, STANKY DOG... IF THE PENDANT ON YOUR COLLAR MEEPS, IT MEANS THAT OUR FELLOW CRITTERS ARE IN TROUBLE...
... AND THE EXPets ARE BEING CALLED TO ACTION!
MEEPS?
IT'S UP TO YOU! IF YOU DECIDE TO ANSWER THE CALL, THE PENDANT WILL KNOW WHAT TO DO.

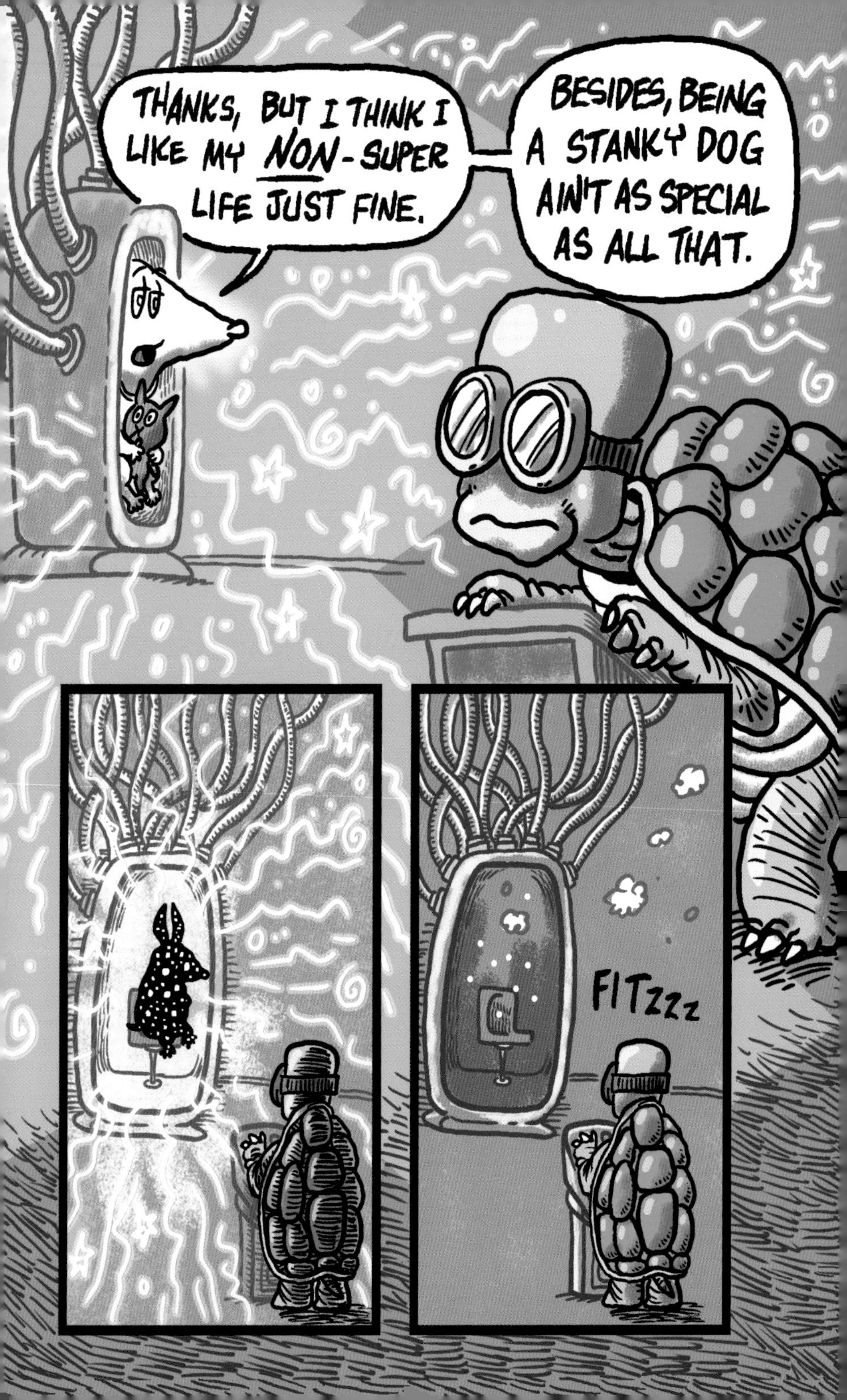
THANKS, BUT I THINK I LIKE MY NON-SUPER LIFE JUST FINE.
BESIDES, BEING A STANKY DOG AIN'T AS SPECIAL AS ALL THAT.
FITzzz

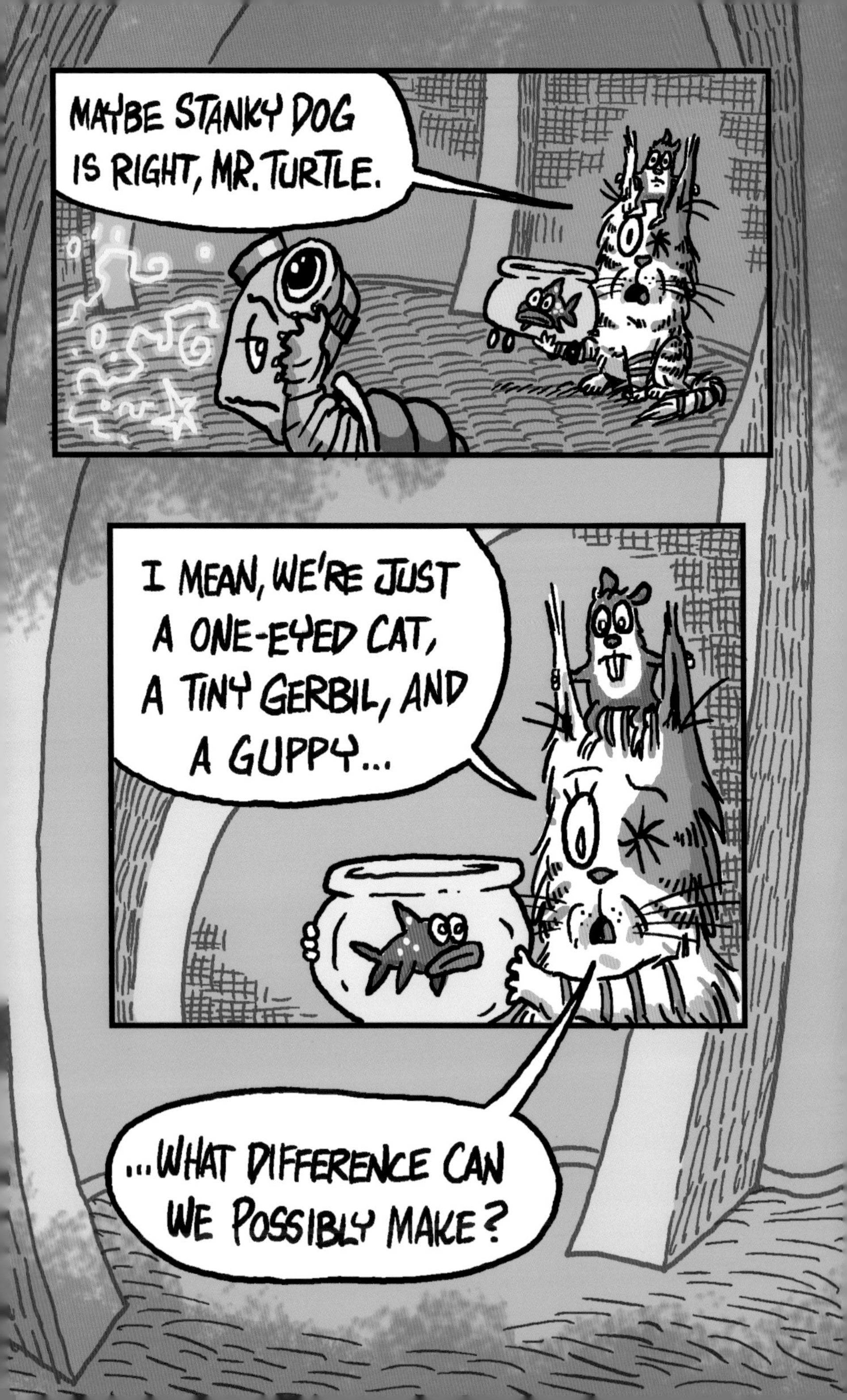
MAYBE STANKY DOG IS RIGHT, MR. TURTLE.
I MEAN, WE'RE JUST A ONE-EYED CAT, A TINY GERBIL, AND A GUPPY...
...WHAT DIFFERENCE CAN WE POSSIBLY MAKE?

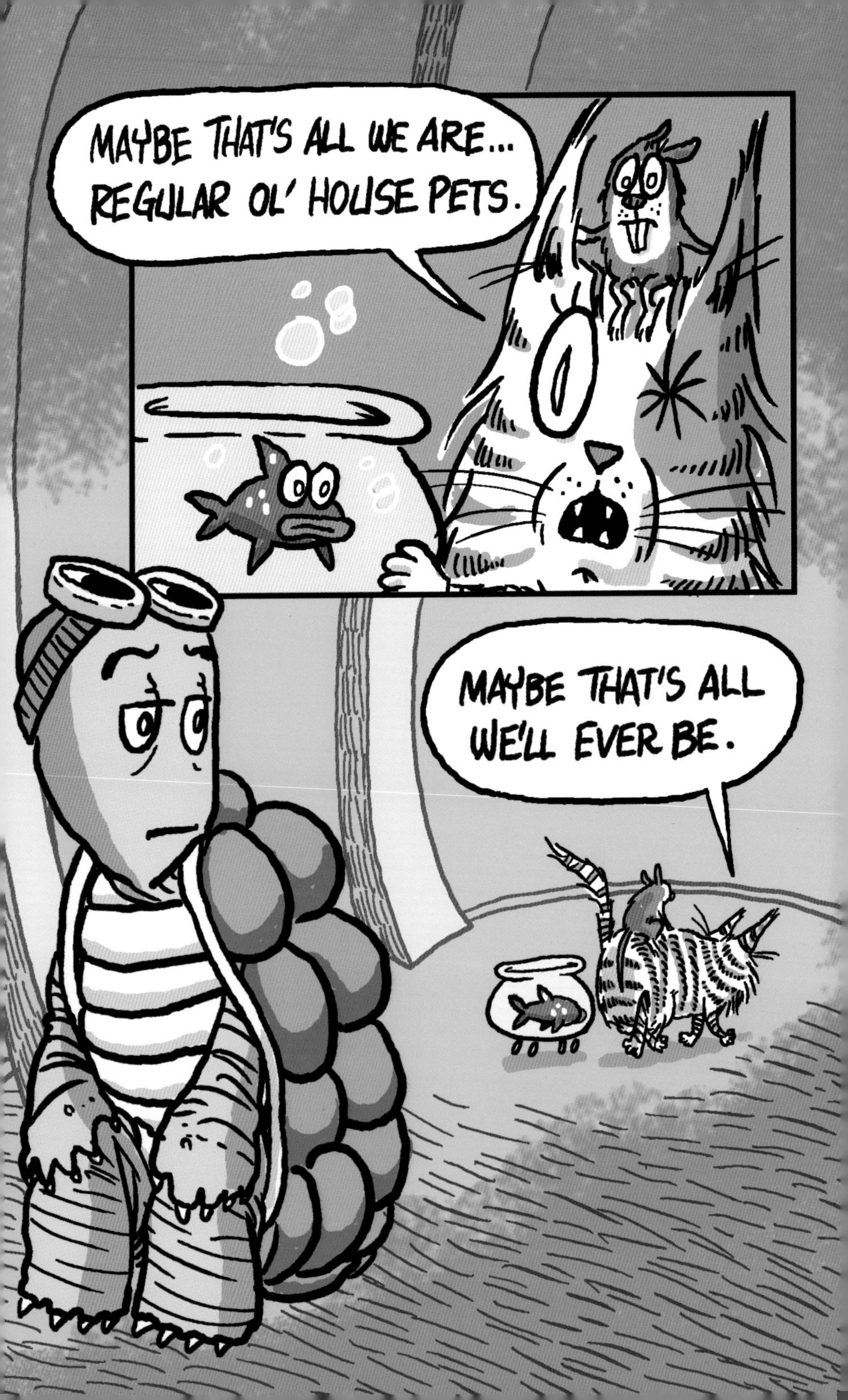
MAYBE THAT'S ALL WE ARE... REGULAR OL' HOUSE PETS.
MAYBE THAT'S ALL WE'LL EVER BE.

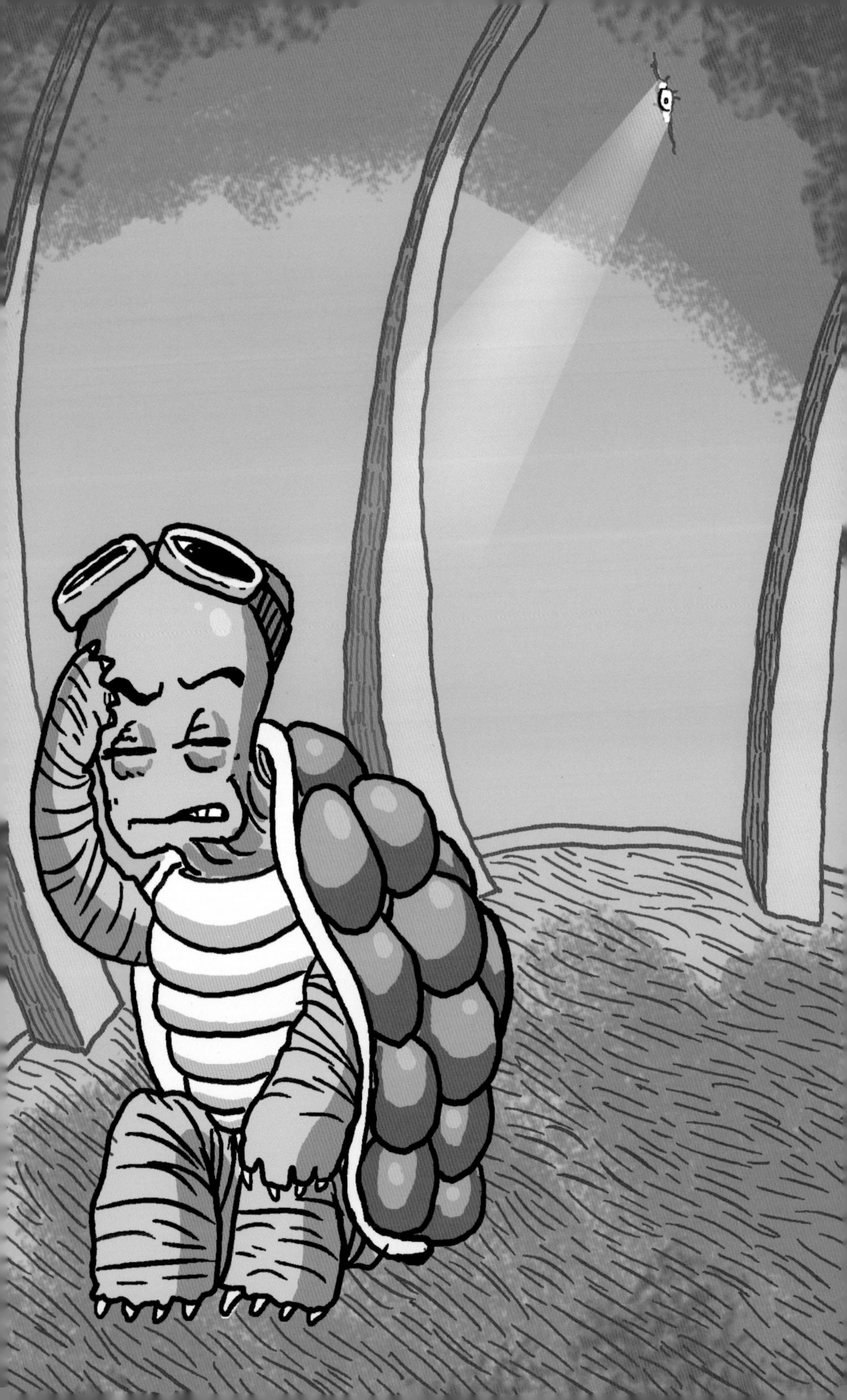

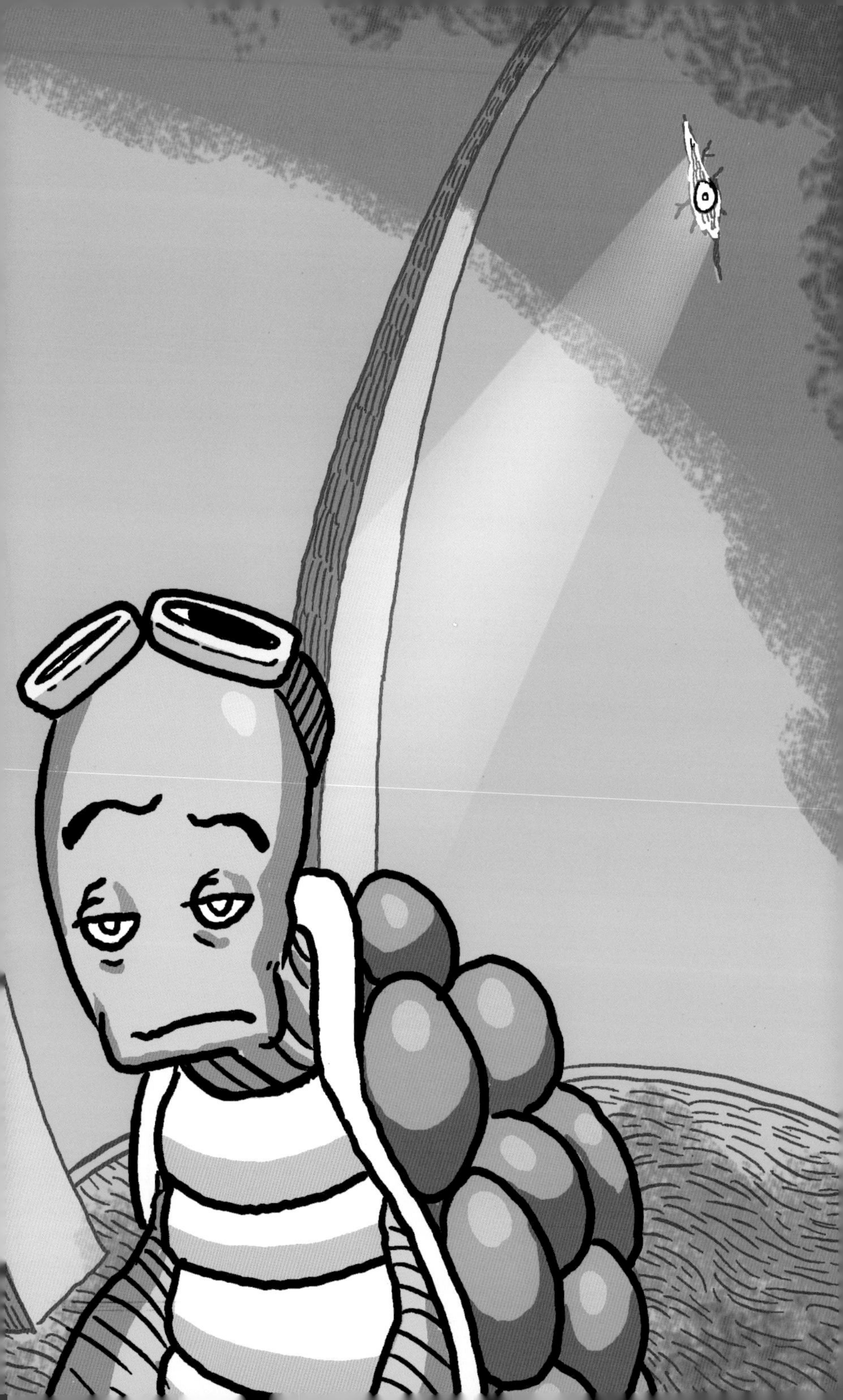

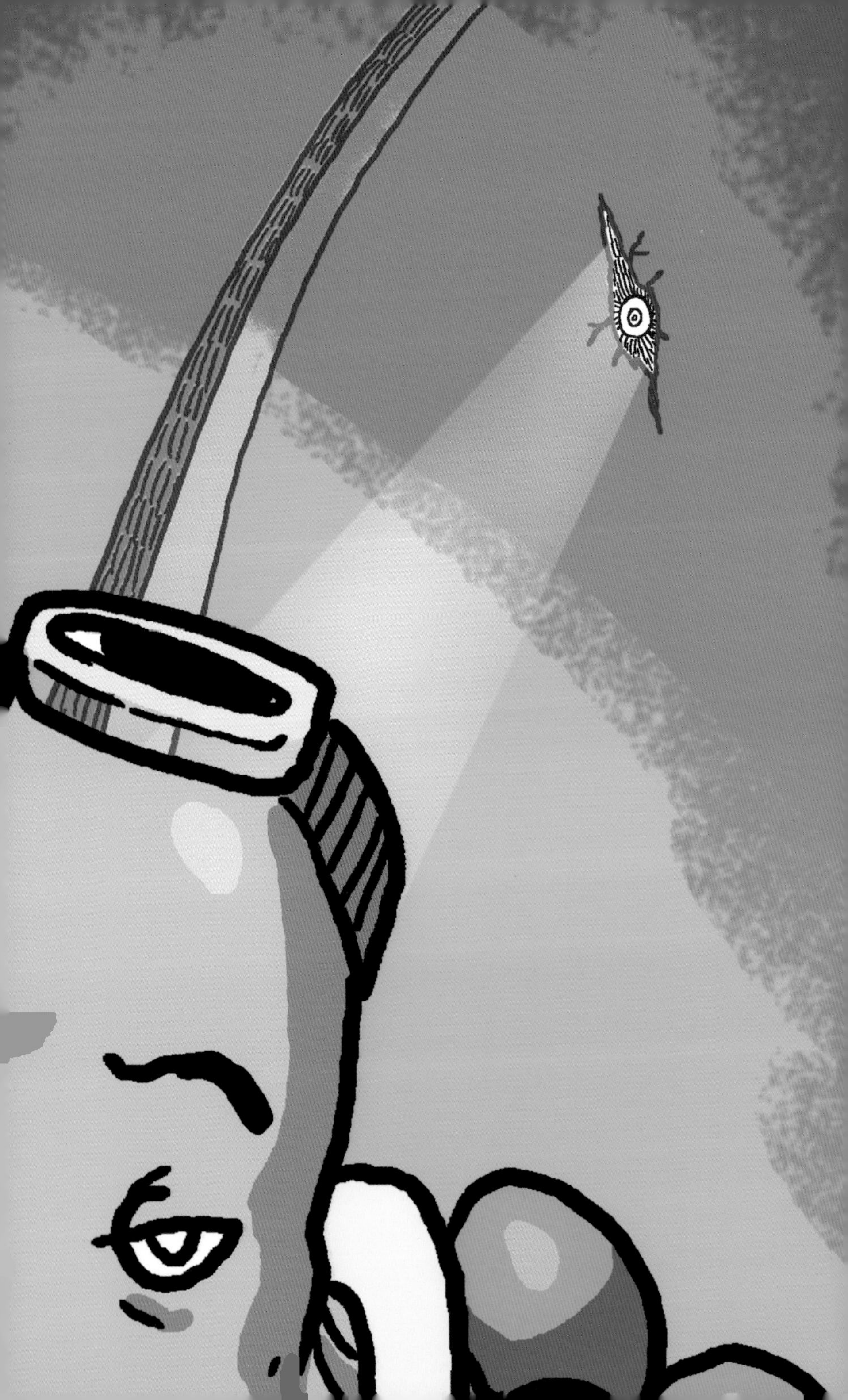

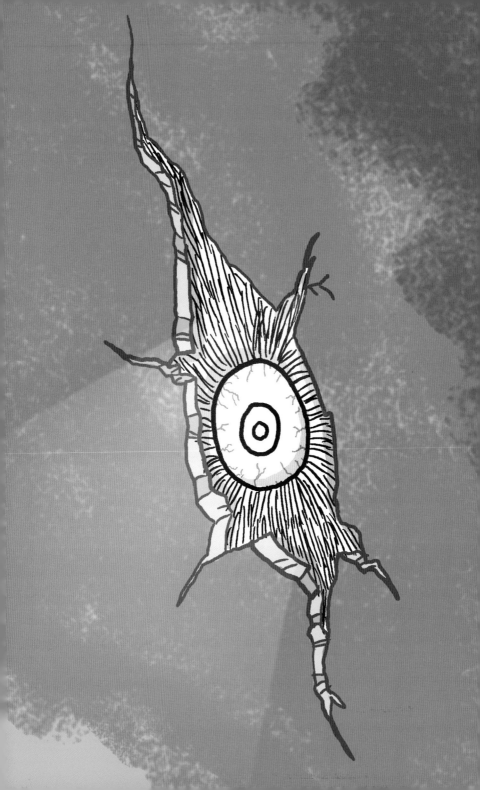

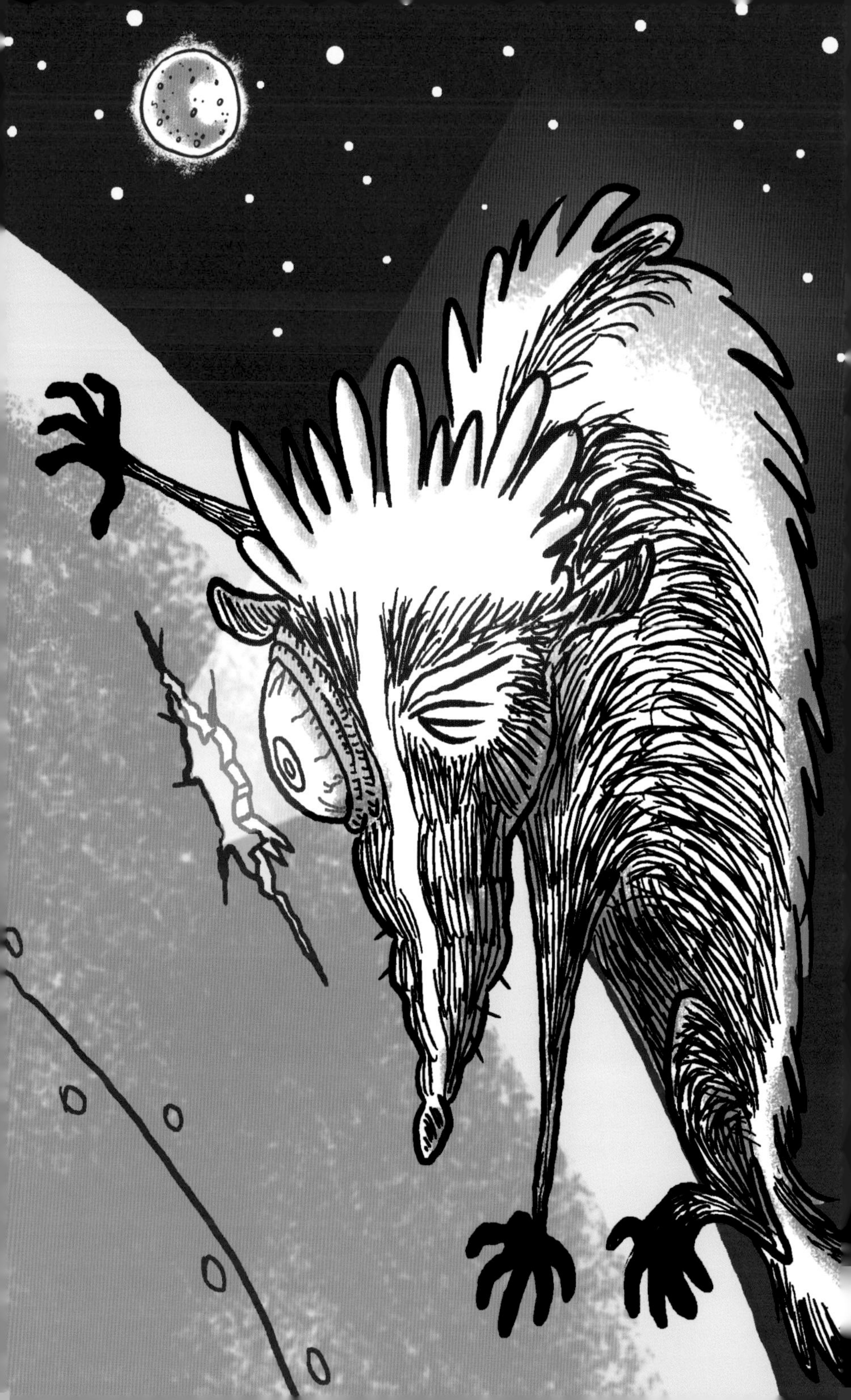

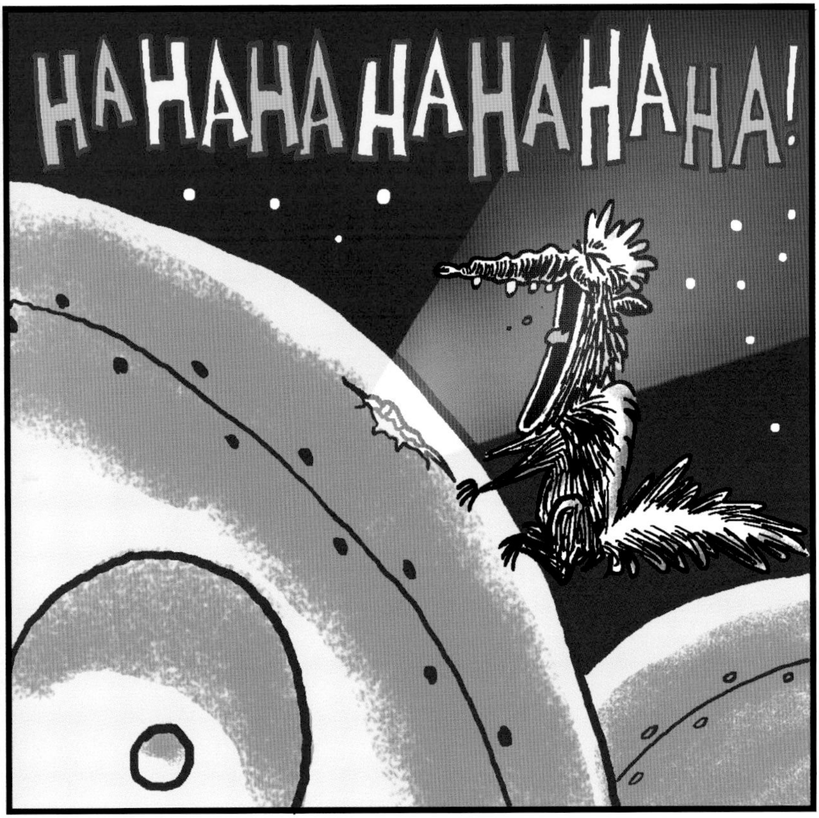
HAHAHAHAHAHAHAHAHA!

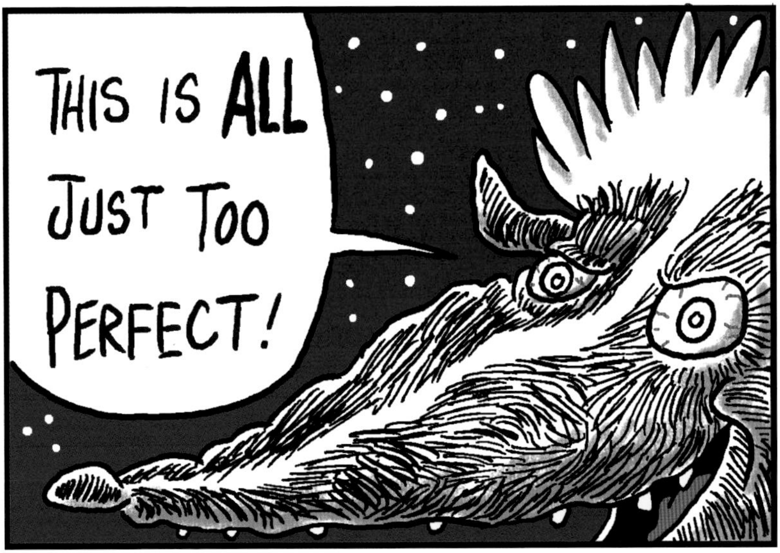
THIS IS ALL JUST TOO PERFECT!

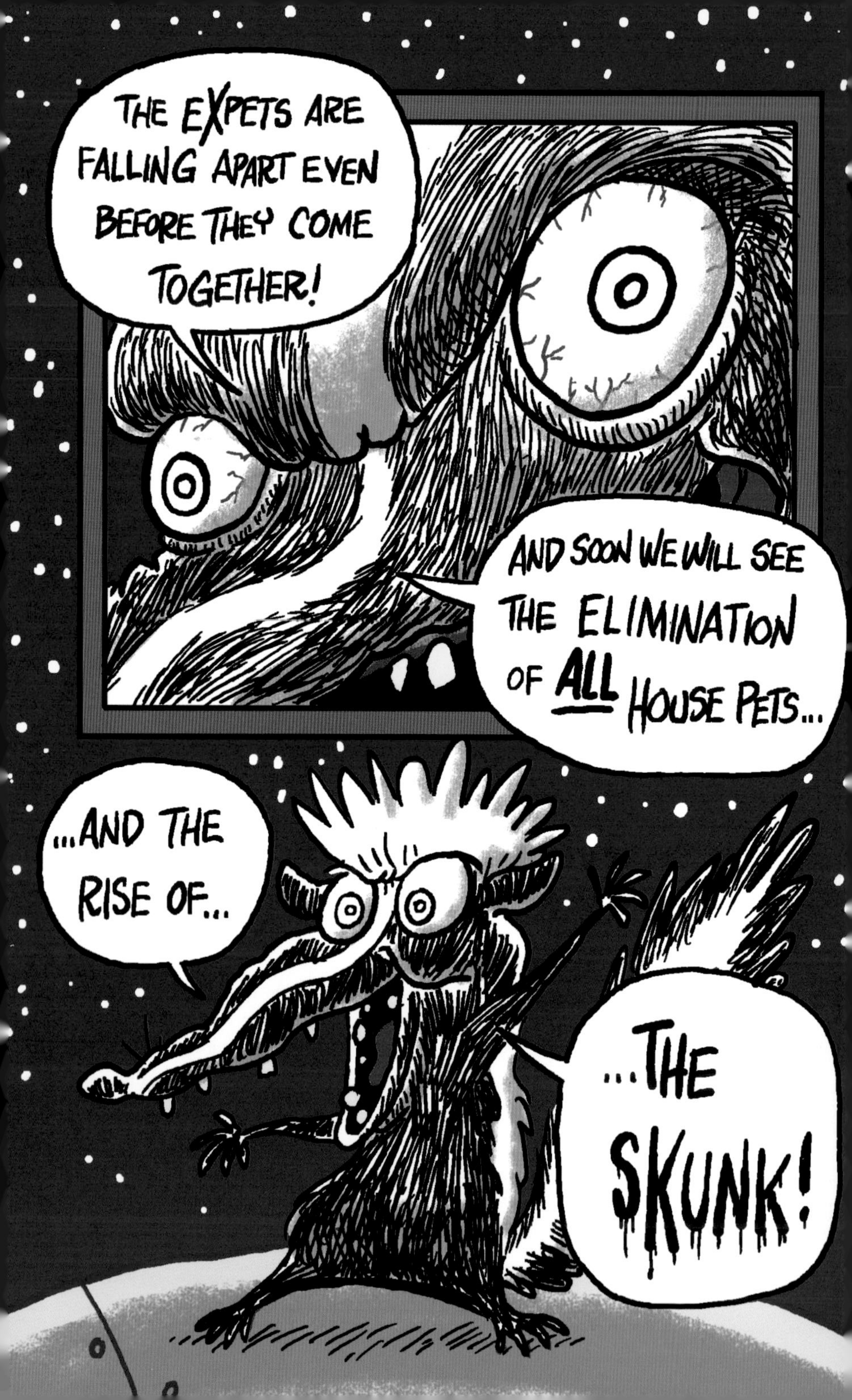
THE EXPETS ARE FALLING APART EVEN BEFORE THEY COME TOGETHER!
AND SOON WE WILL SEE THE ELIMINATION OF ALL HOUSE PETS...
...AND THE RISE OF...
...THE SKUNK!

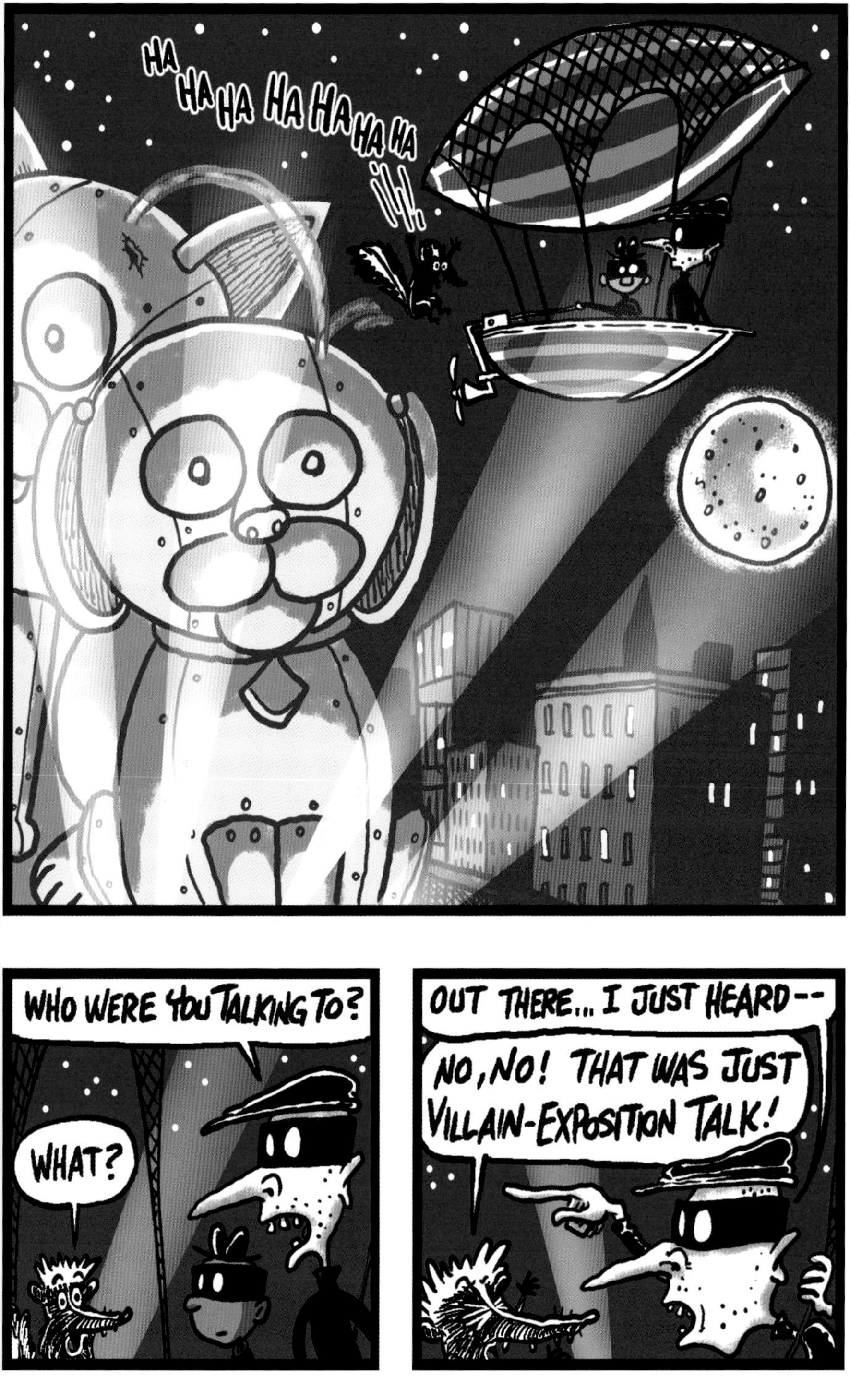
HA HA HA HA HA HA HA HA !!!
WHO WERE YOU TALKING TO?
WHAT?
OUT THERE... I JUST HEARD--
NO, NO! THAT WAS JUST VILLAIN-EXPOSITION TALK!

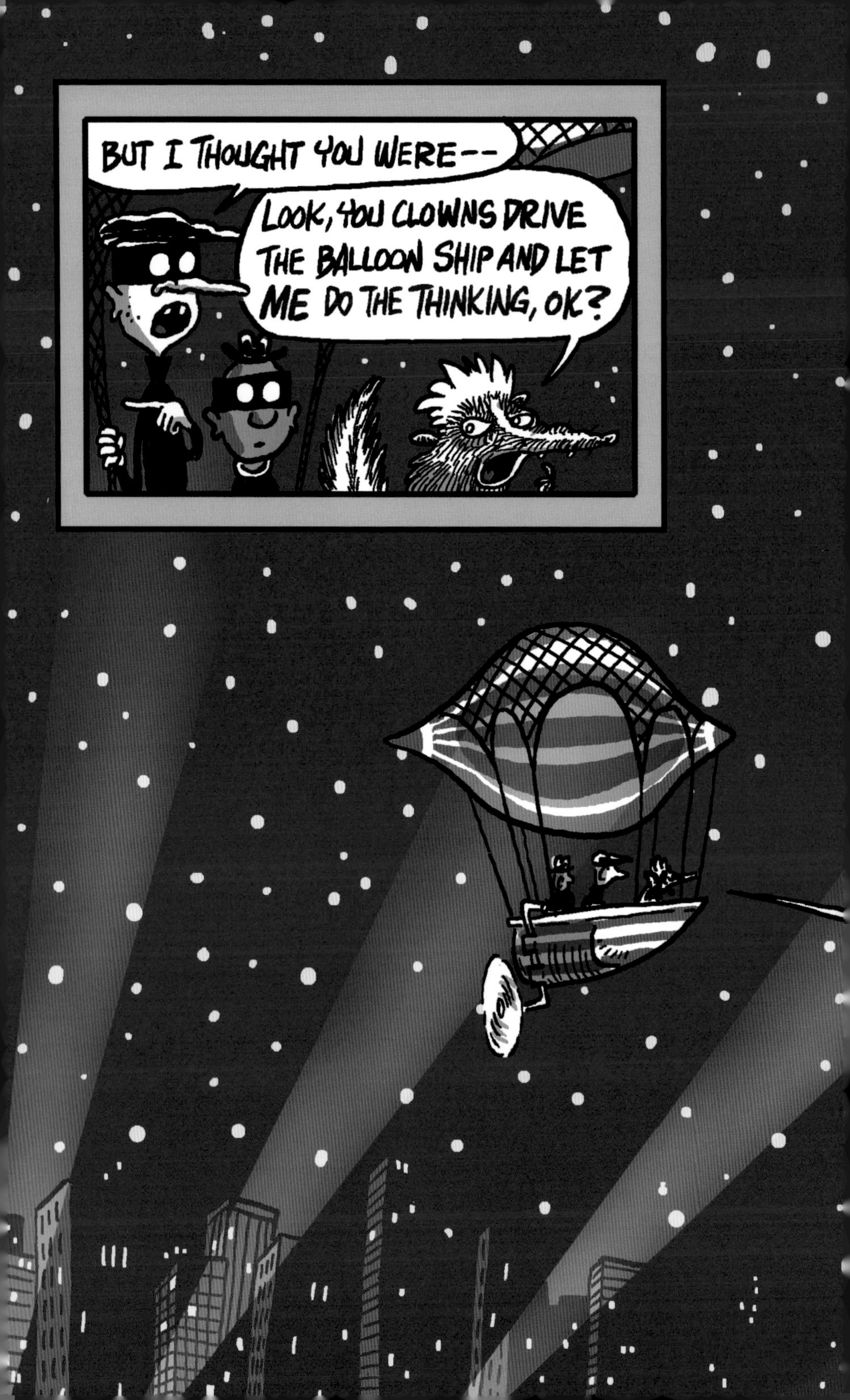
BUT I THOUGHT YOU WERE--
LOOK, YOU CLOWNS DRIVE THE BALLOON SHIP AND LET ME DO THE THINKING, OK?

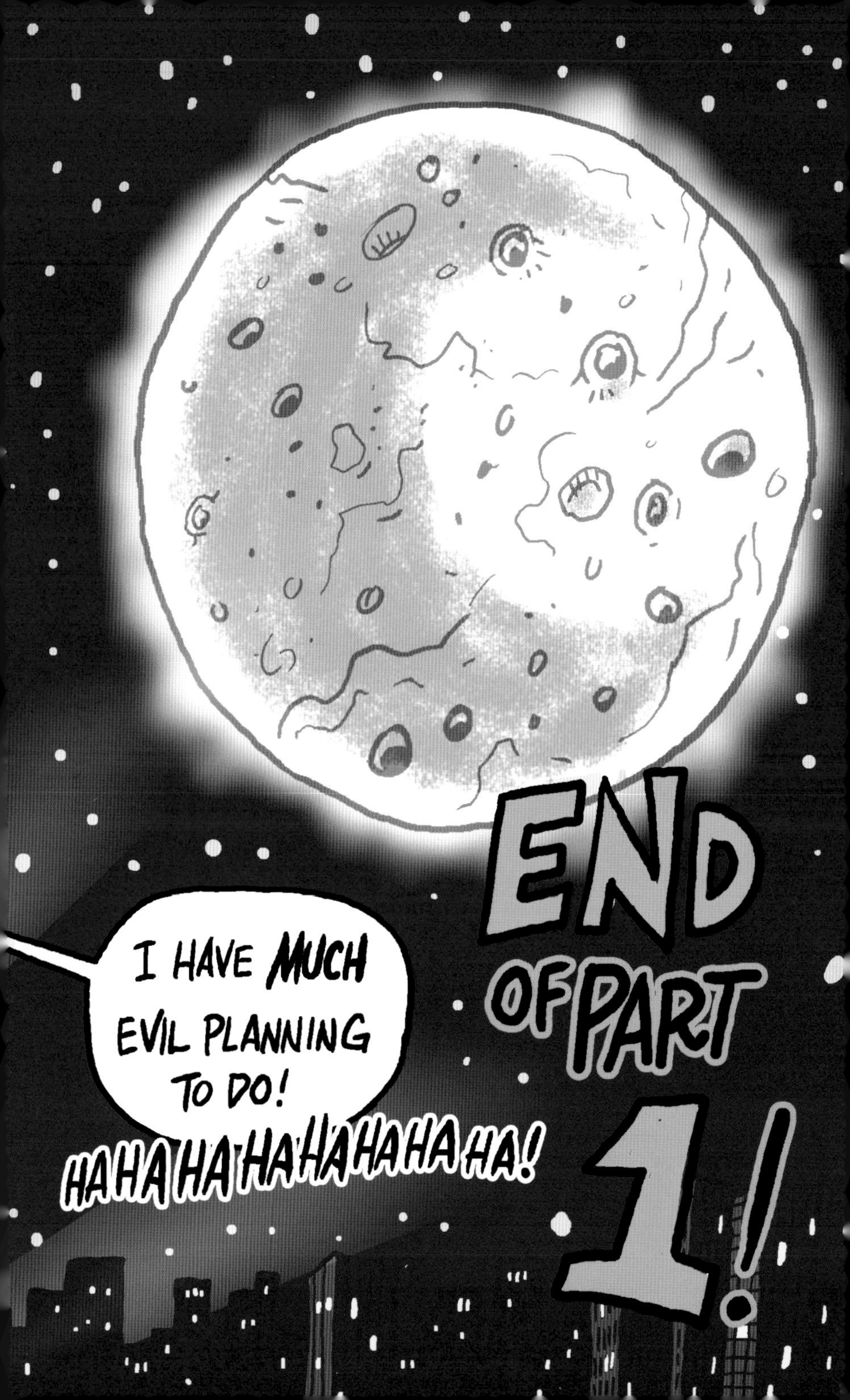
I HAVE MUCH EVIL PLANNING TO DO!
HAHAHAHAHAHAHAHAHAHA!
END OF PART 1!

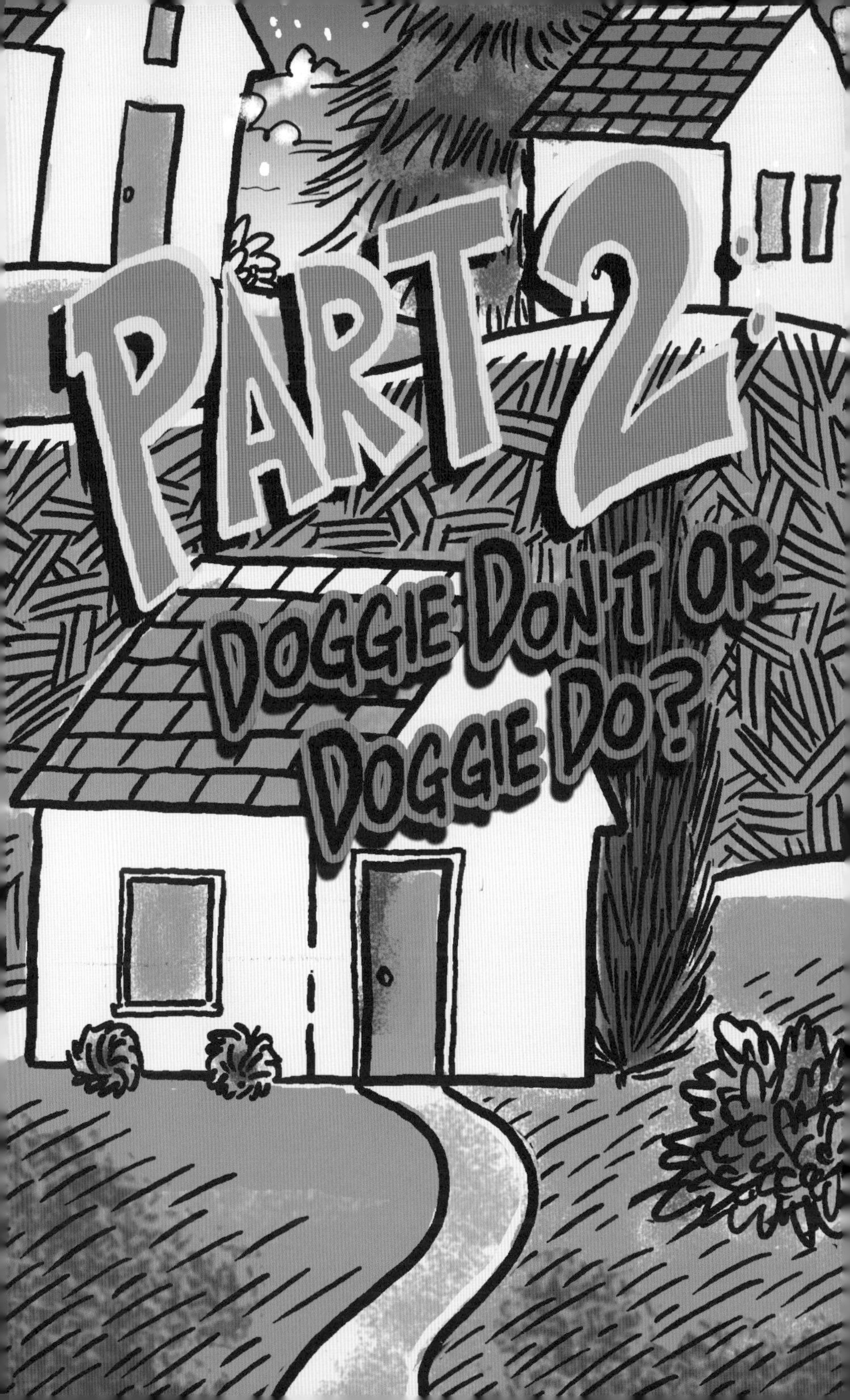
PART 2:
DOGGIE DON'T OR DOGGIE DO?

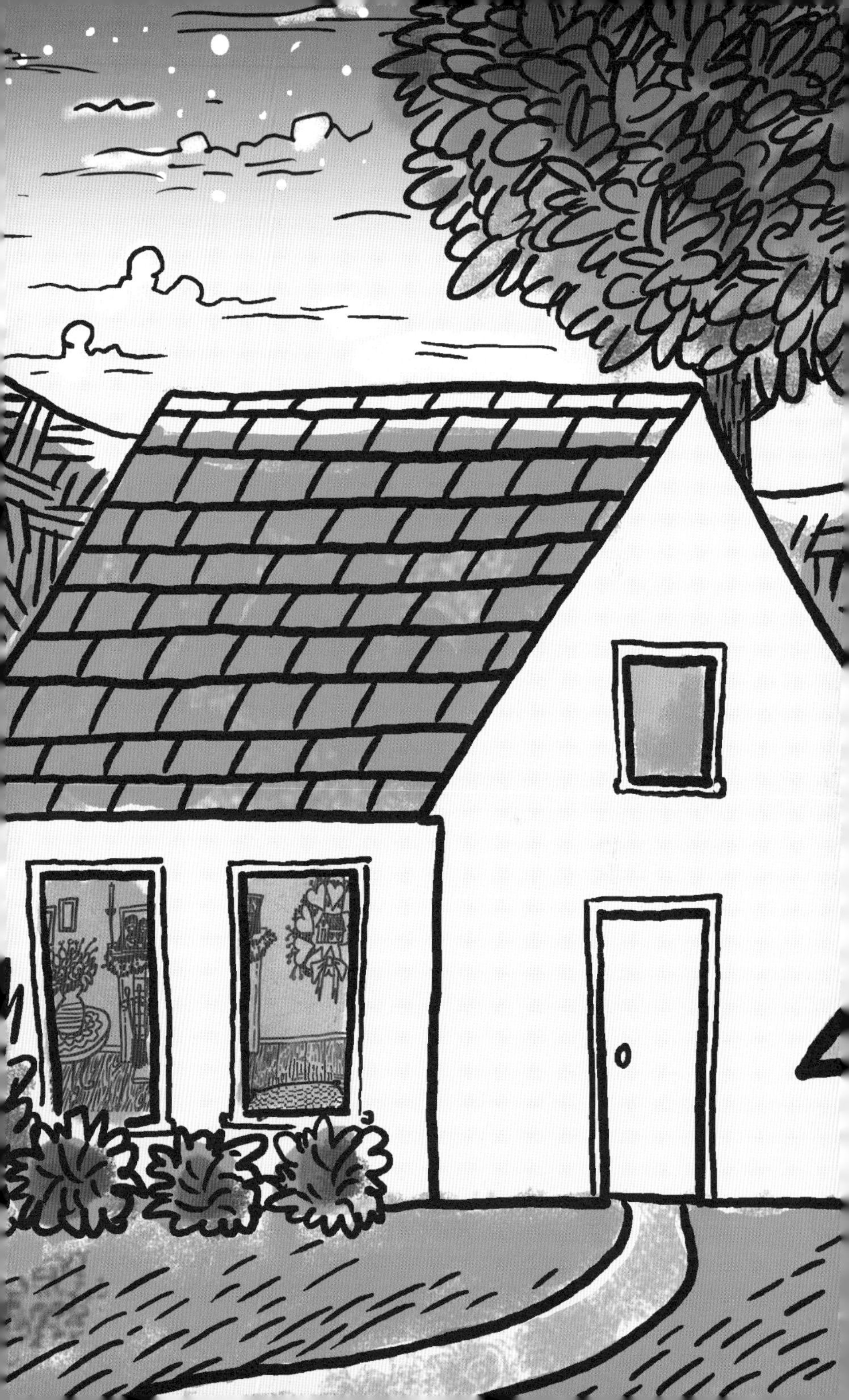

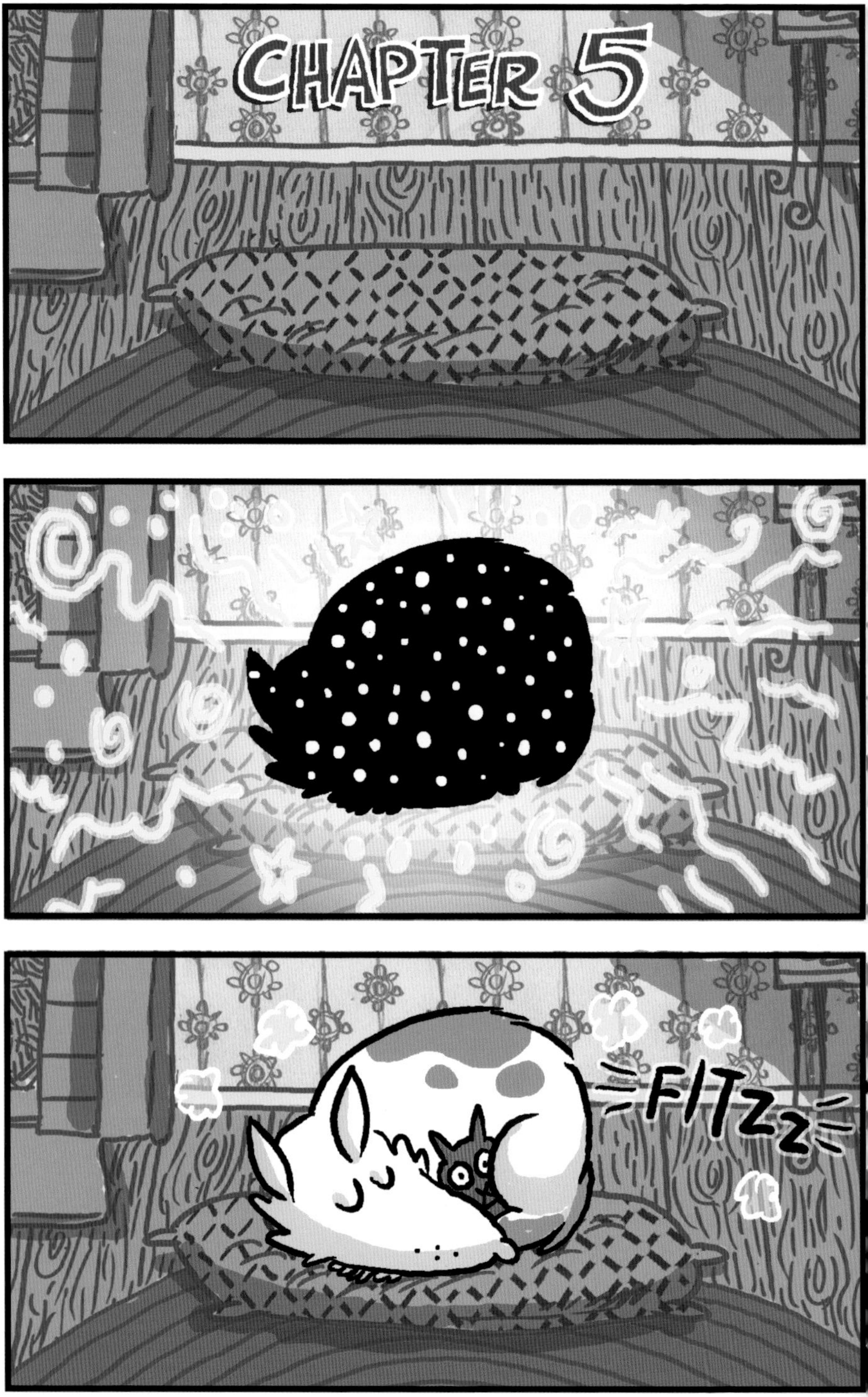
CHAPTER 5
FITZz

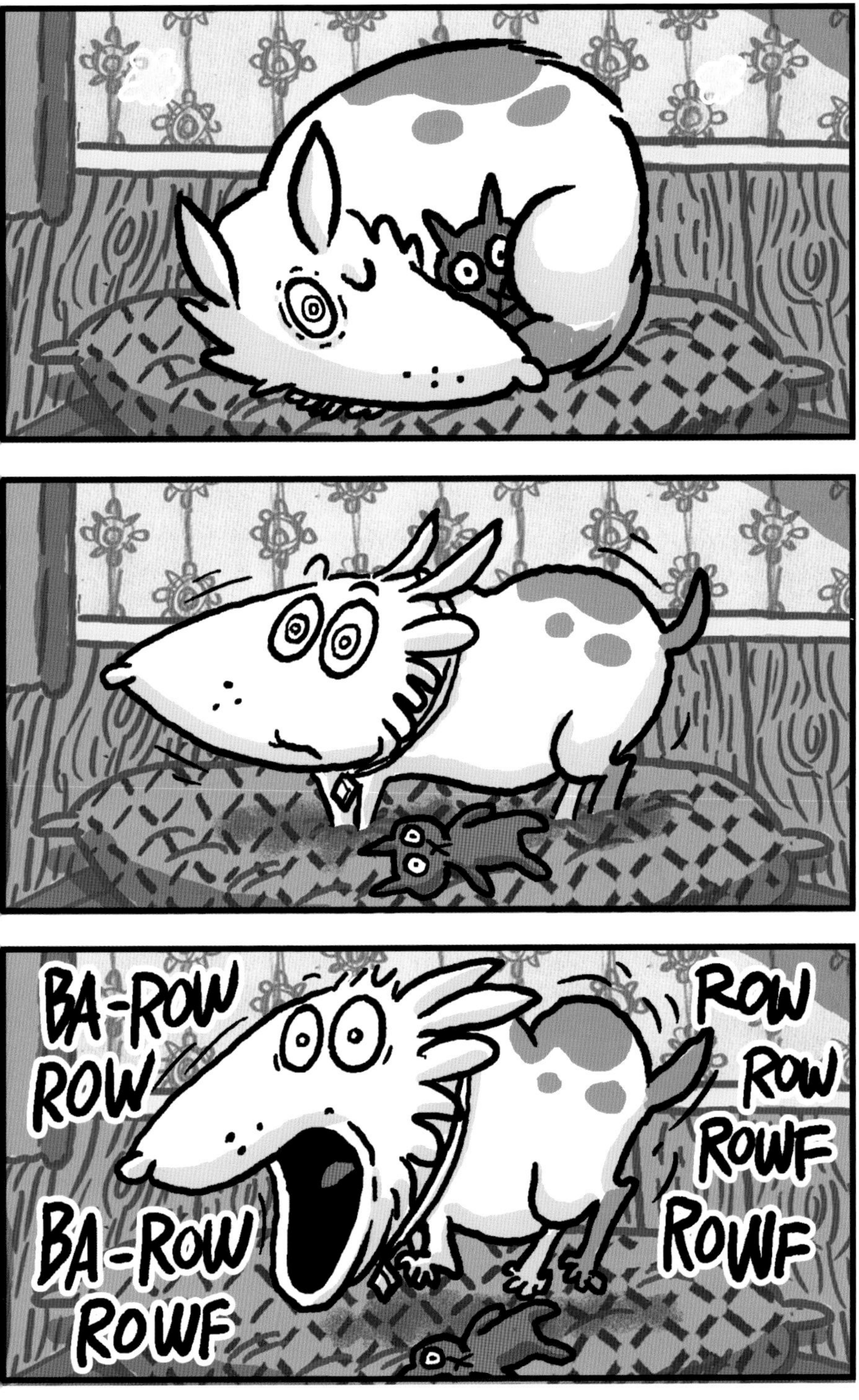
BA-ROW
ROW
ROW
ROW
ROWF
ROWF
BA-ROW
ROWF

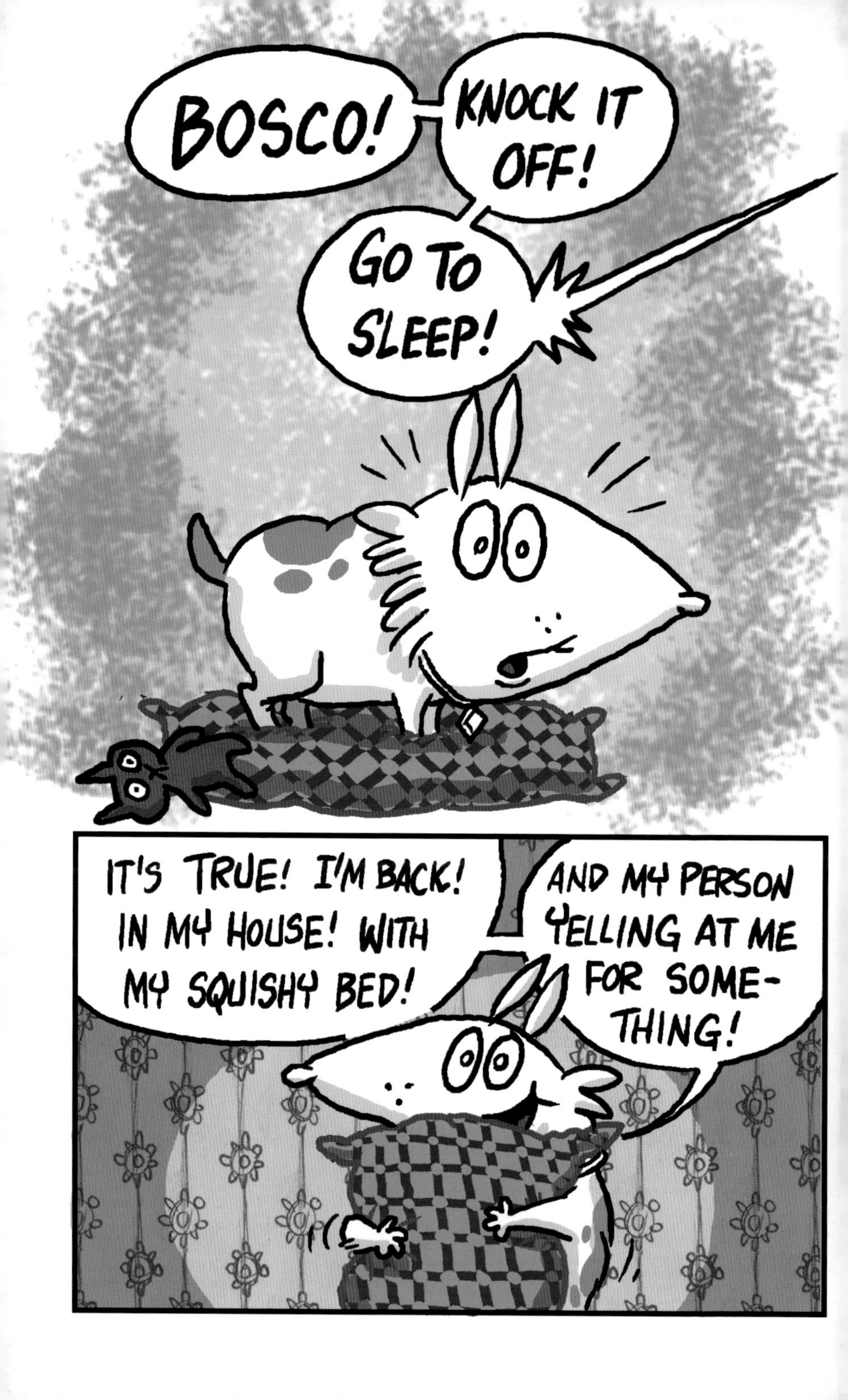
BOSCO!
KNOCK IT OFF!
GO TO SLEEP!
IT'S TRUE! I'M BACK! IN MY HOUSE! WITH MY SQUISHY BED!
AND MY PERSON YELLING AT ME FOR SOME-THING!

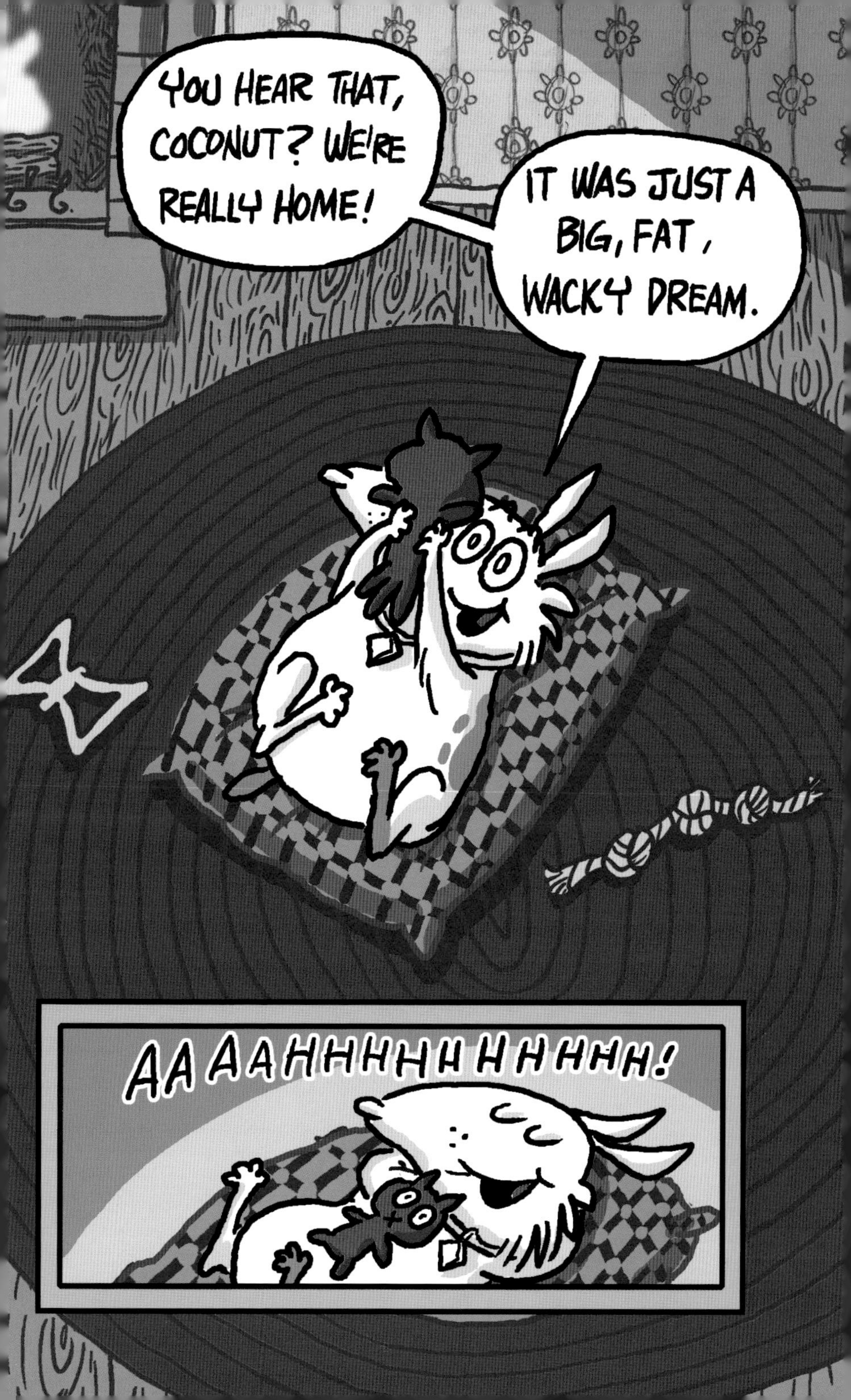
YOU HEAR THAT, COCONUT? WE'RE REALLY HOME!
IT WAS JUST A BIG, FAT, WACKY DREAM.
AAAAHHHHHHHHHHH!

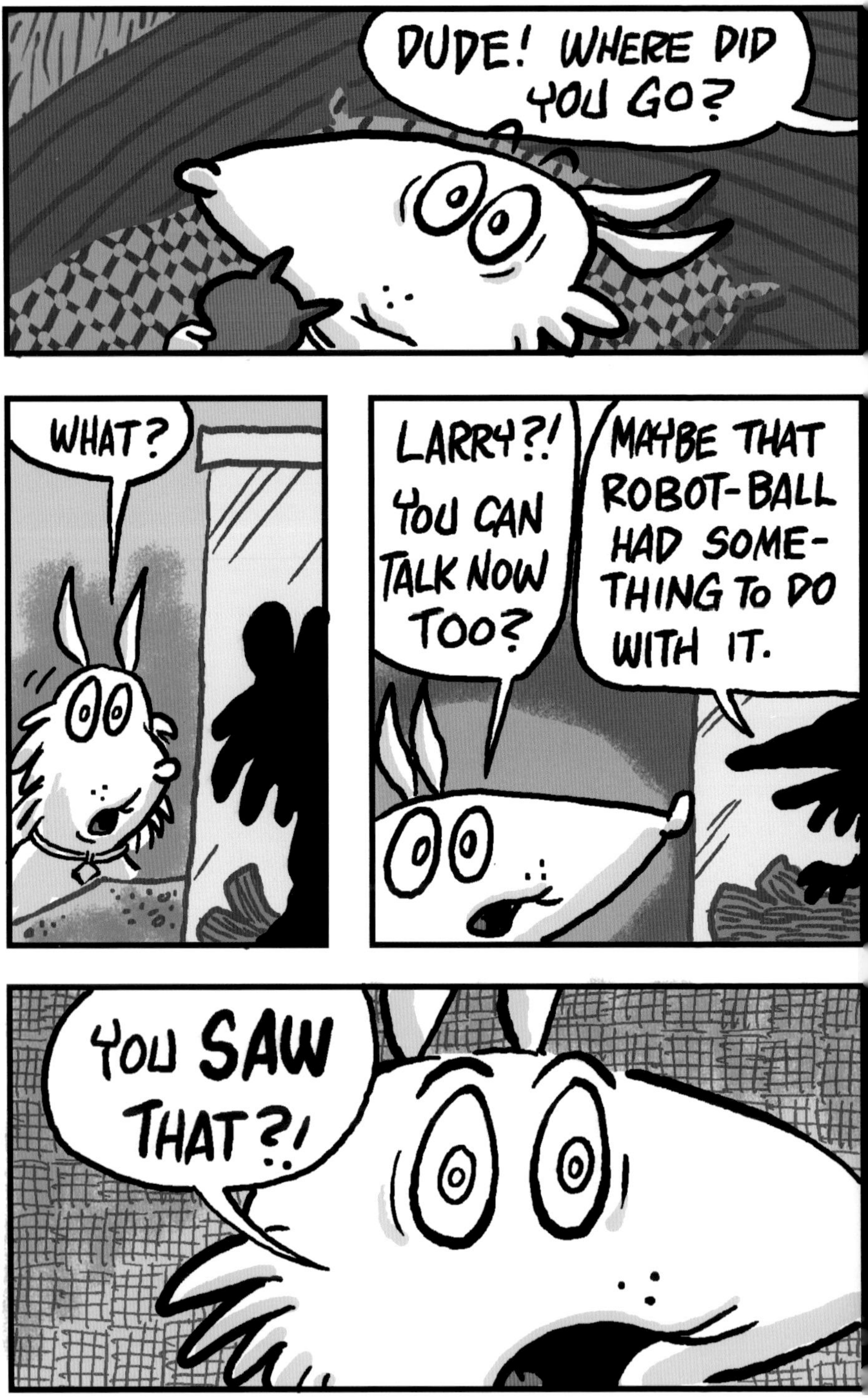
DUDE! WHERE DID YOU GO?
WHAT?
LARRY?! YOU CAN TALK NOW TOO?
MAYBE THAT ROBOT-BALL HAD SOME-THING TO DO WITH IT.
YOU SAW THAT?!

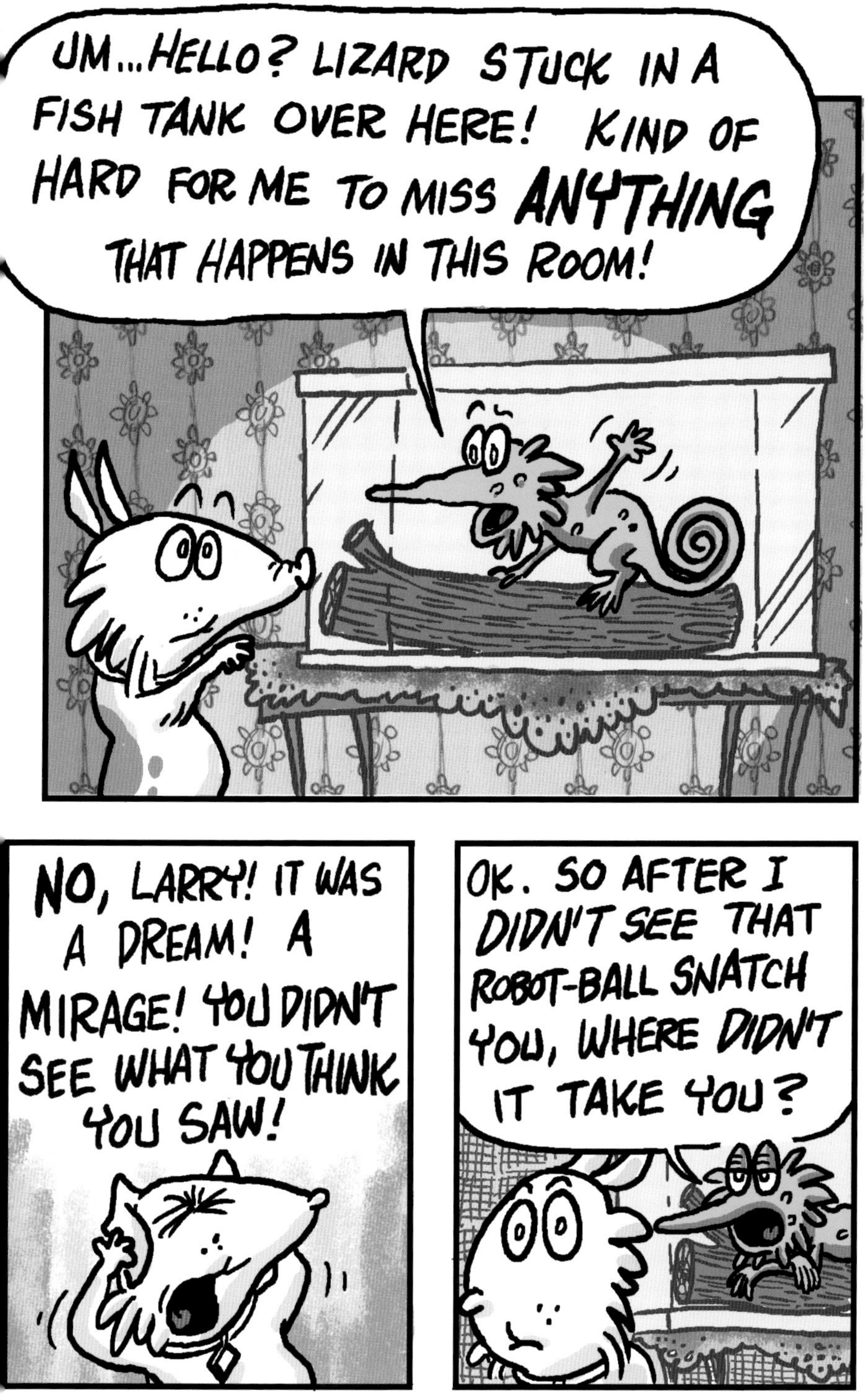
UM...HELLO? LIZARD STUCK IN A FISH TANK OVER HERE! KIND OF HARD FOR ME TO MISS ANYTHING THAT HAPPENS IN THIS ROOM!
NO, LARRY! IT WAS A DREAM! A MIRAGE! YOU DIDN'T SEE WHAT YOU THINK YOU SAW!
OK. SO AFTER I DIDN'T SEE THAT ROBOT-BALL SNATCH YOU, WHERE DIDN'T IT TAKE YOU?

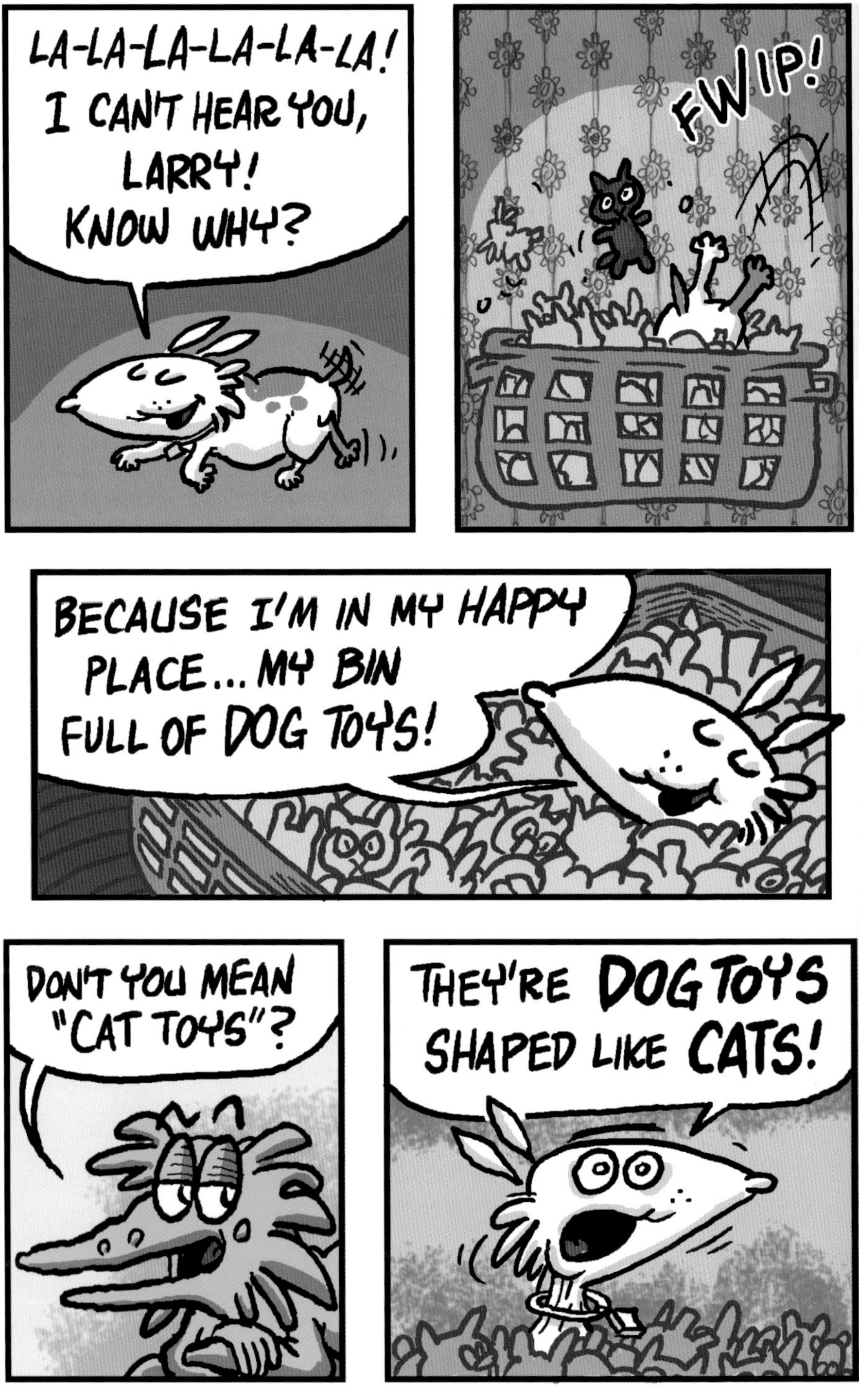
LA-LA-LA-LA-LA-LA! I CAN'T HEAR YOU, LARRY! KNOW WHY?
FWIP!
BECAUSE I'M IN MY HAPPY PLACE... MY BIN FULL OF DOG TOYS!
DON'T YOU MEAN "CAT TOYS"?
THEY'RE DOG TOYS SHAPED LIKE CATS!

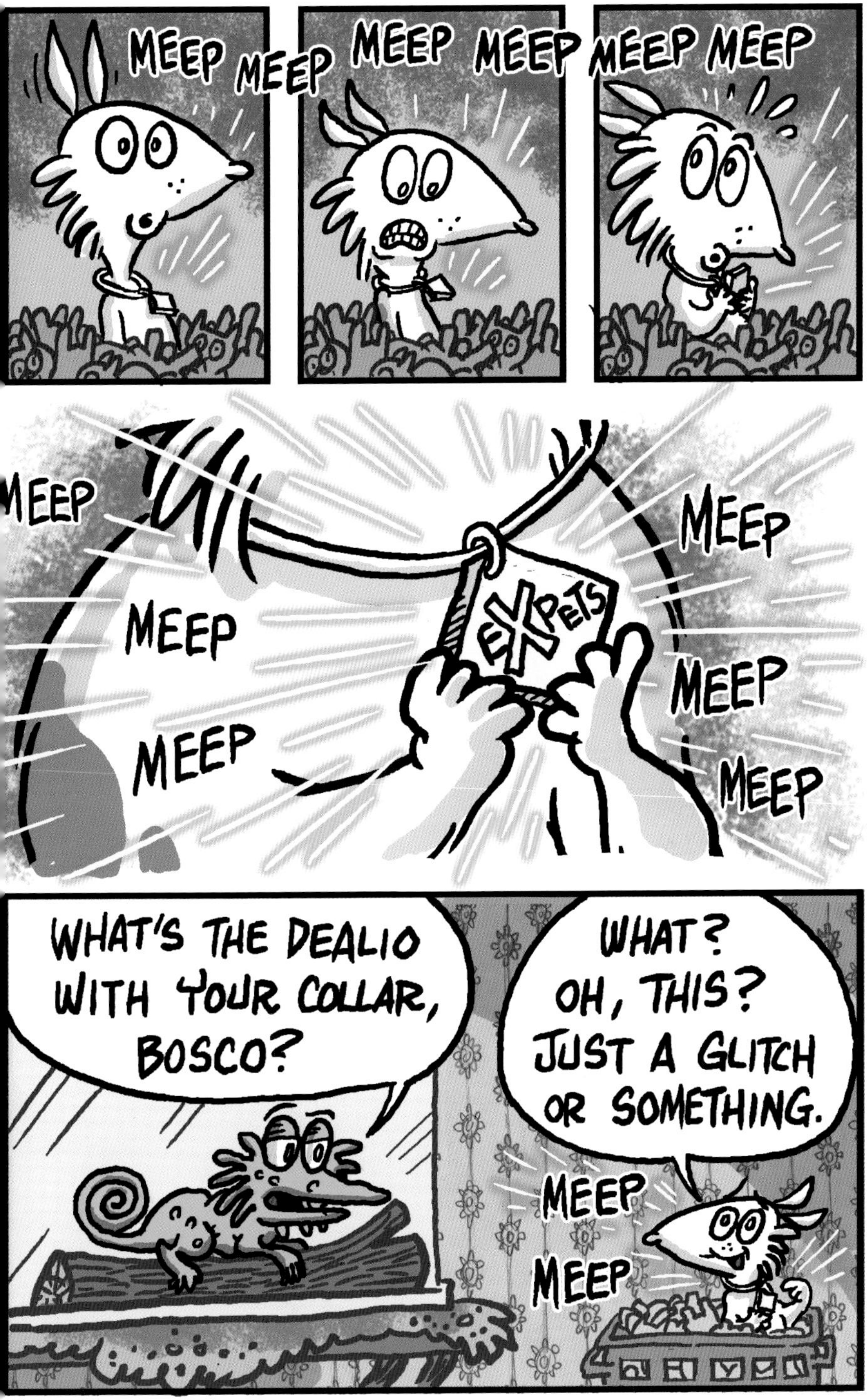
MEEP MEEP MEEP MEEP MEEP MEEP
MEEP
MEEP
MEEP
MEEP
MEEP
MEEP
EXPETS
WHAT'S THE DEALIO WITH YOUR COLLAR, BOSCO?
WHAT? OH, THIS? JUST A GLITCH OR SOMETHING.
MEEP
MEEP

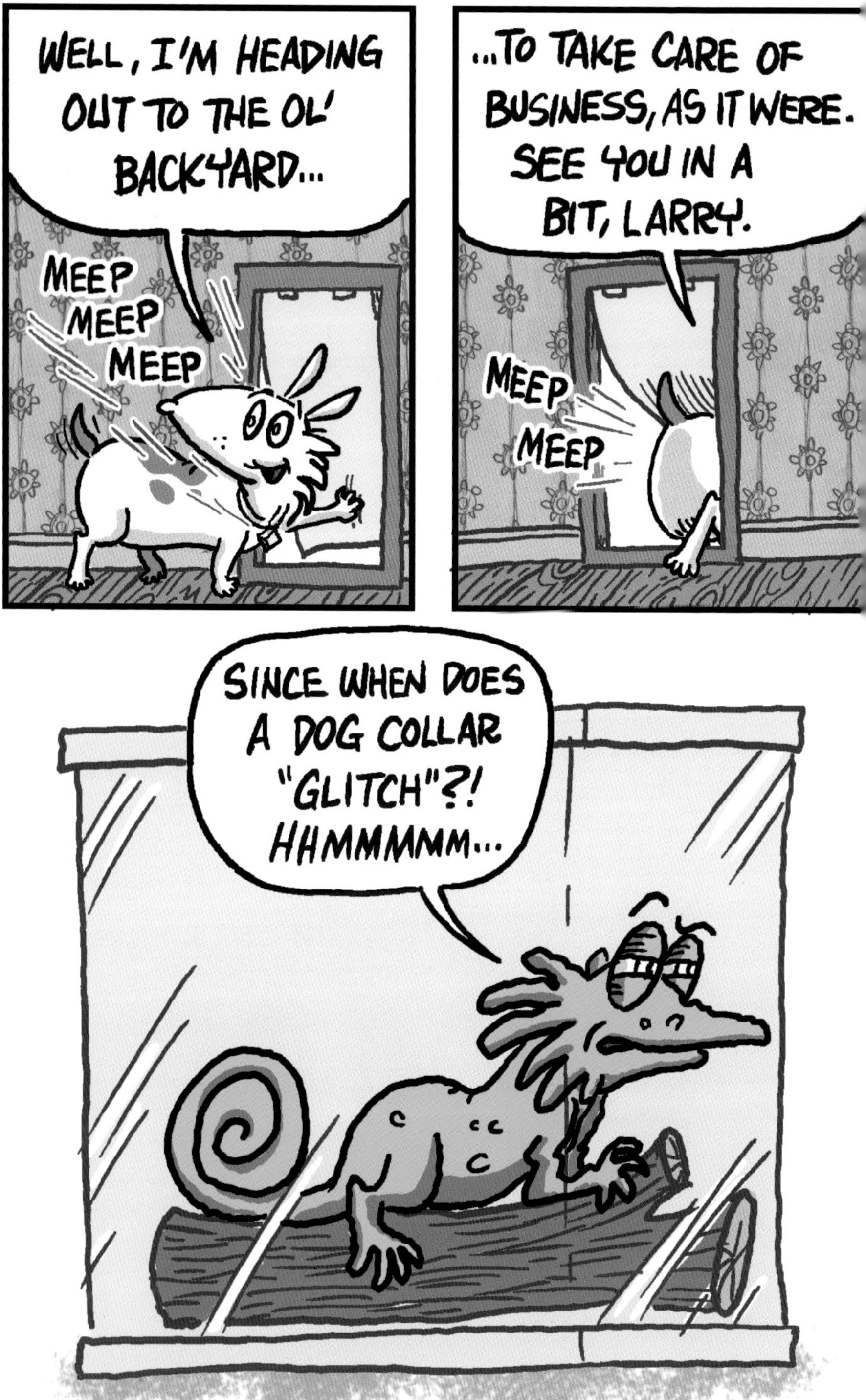
WELL, I'M HEADING OUT TO THE OL' BACKYARD...
MEEP MEEP MEEP
...TO TAKE CARE OF BUSINESS, AS IT WERE. SEE YOU IN A BIT, LARRY.
MEEP MEEP
SINCE WHEN DOES A DOG COLLAR "GLITCH"?! HHMMMMM...

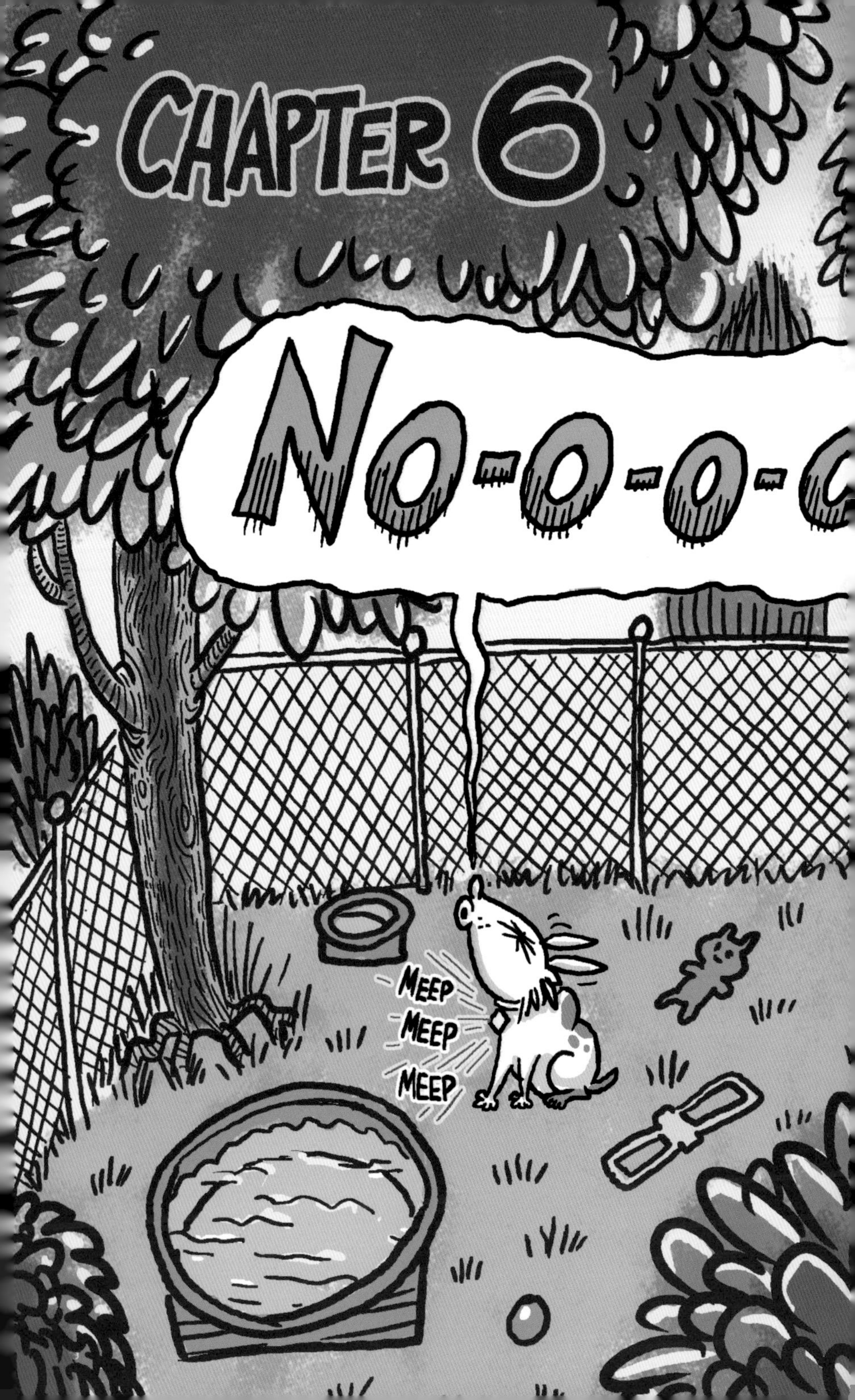
CHAPTER 6
NO-O-O-O
MEEP
MEEP
MEEP

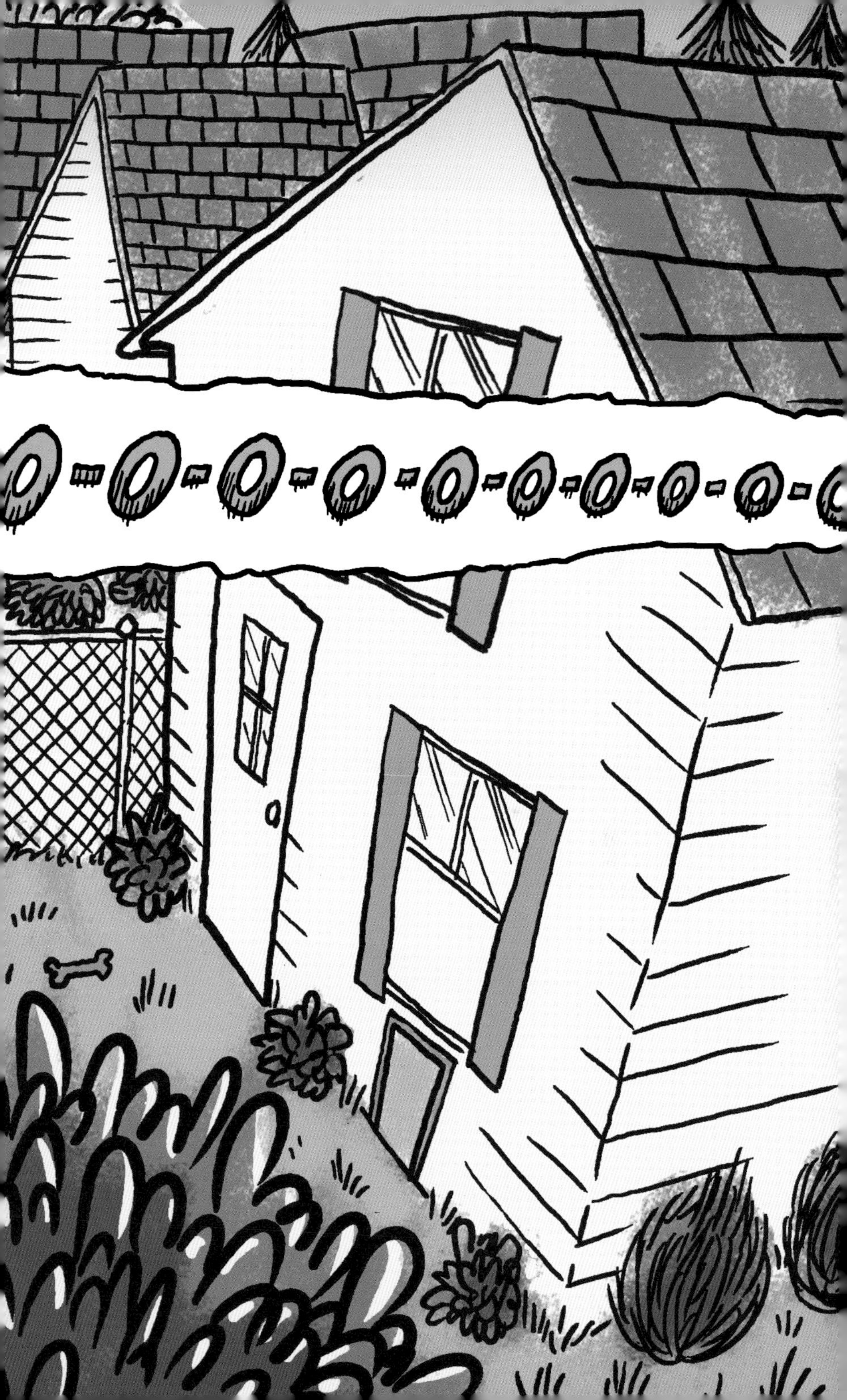
O-O-O-O-O-O-O-O-O-O

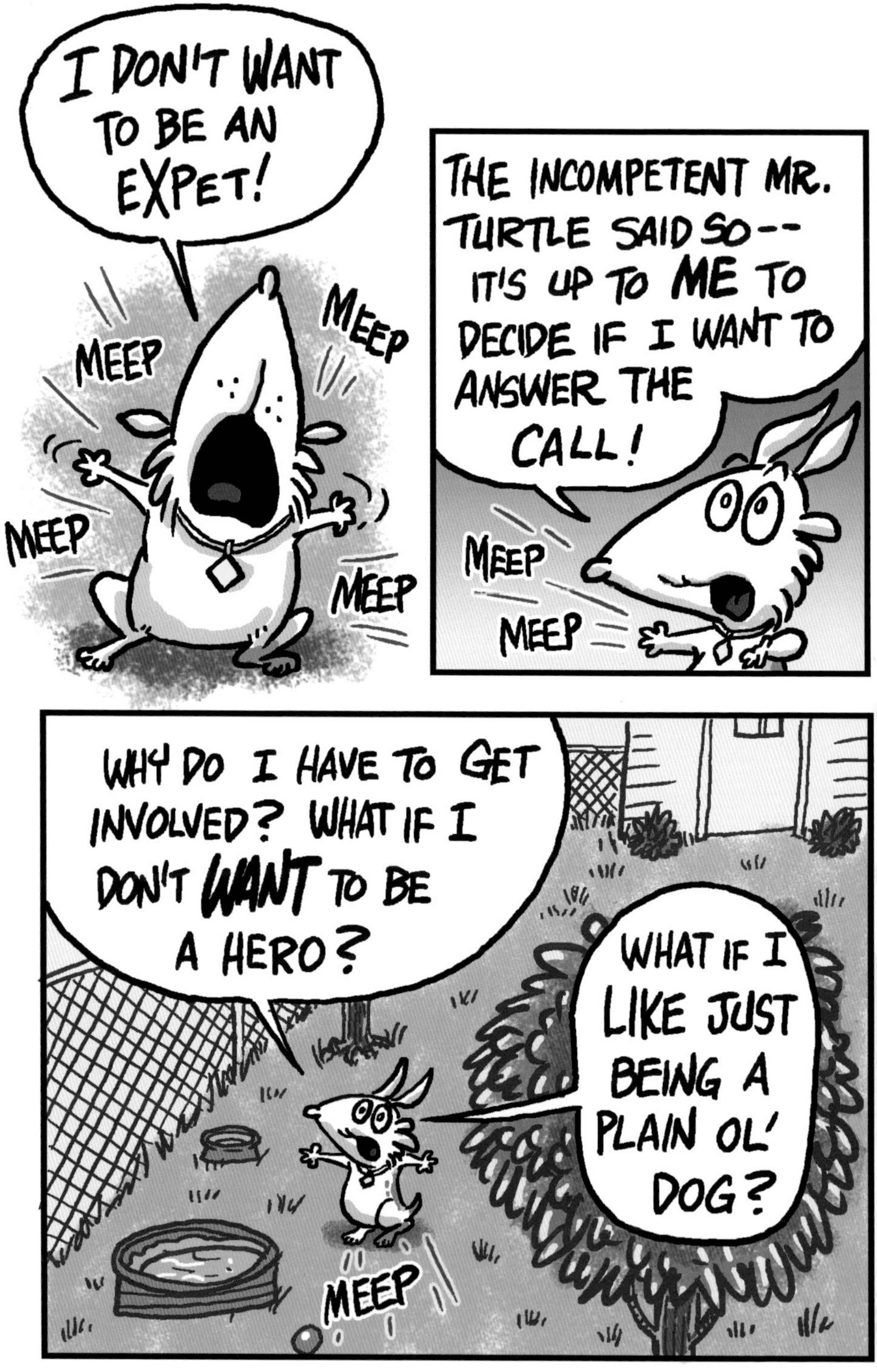
I DON'T WANT TO BE AN EXPET!
MEEP
MEEP
MEEP
MEEP
THE INCOMPETENT MR. TURTLE SAID SO-- IT'S UP TO ME TO DECIDE IF I WANT TO ANSWER THE CALL!
MEEP
MEEP
WHY DO I HAVE TO GET INVOLVED? WHAT IF I DON'T WANT TO BE A HERO?
WHAT IF I LIKE JUST BEING A PLAIN OL' DOG?
MEEP

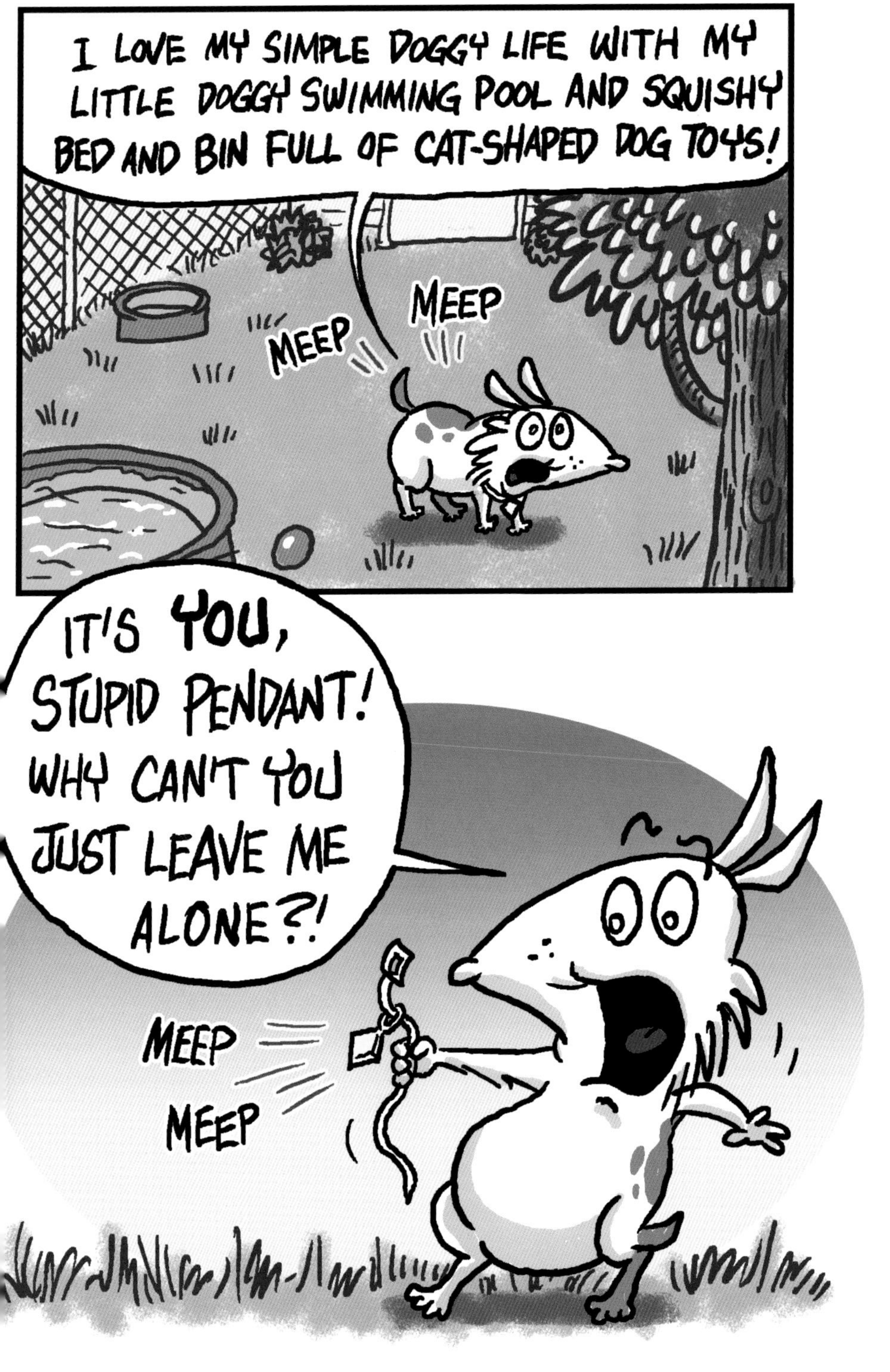
I LOVE MY SIMPLE DOGGY LIFE WITH MY LITTLE DOGGY SWIMMING POOL AND SQUISHY BED AND BIN FULL OF CAT-SHAPED DOG TOYS!
MEEP
MEEP
IT'S YOU, STUPID PENDANT! WHY CAN'T YOU JUST LEAVE ME ALONE?!
MEEP
MEEP

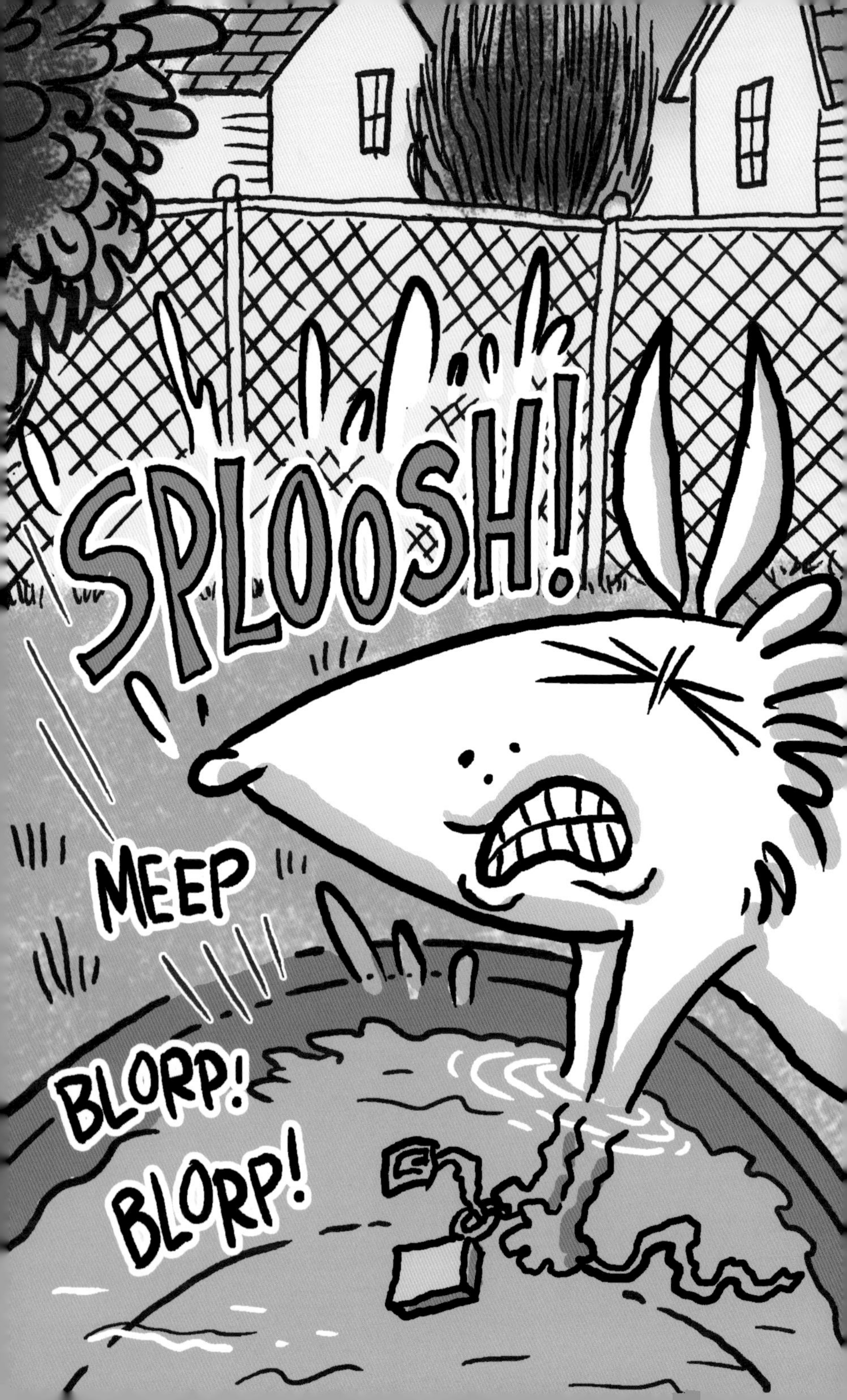
SPLOOSH!
MEEP
BLORP!
BLORP!

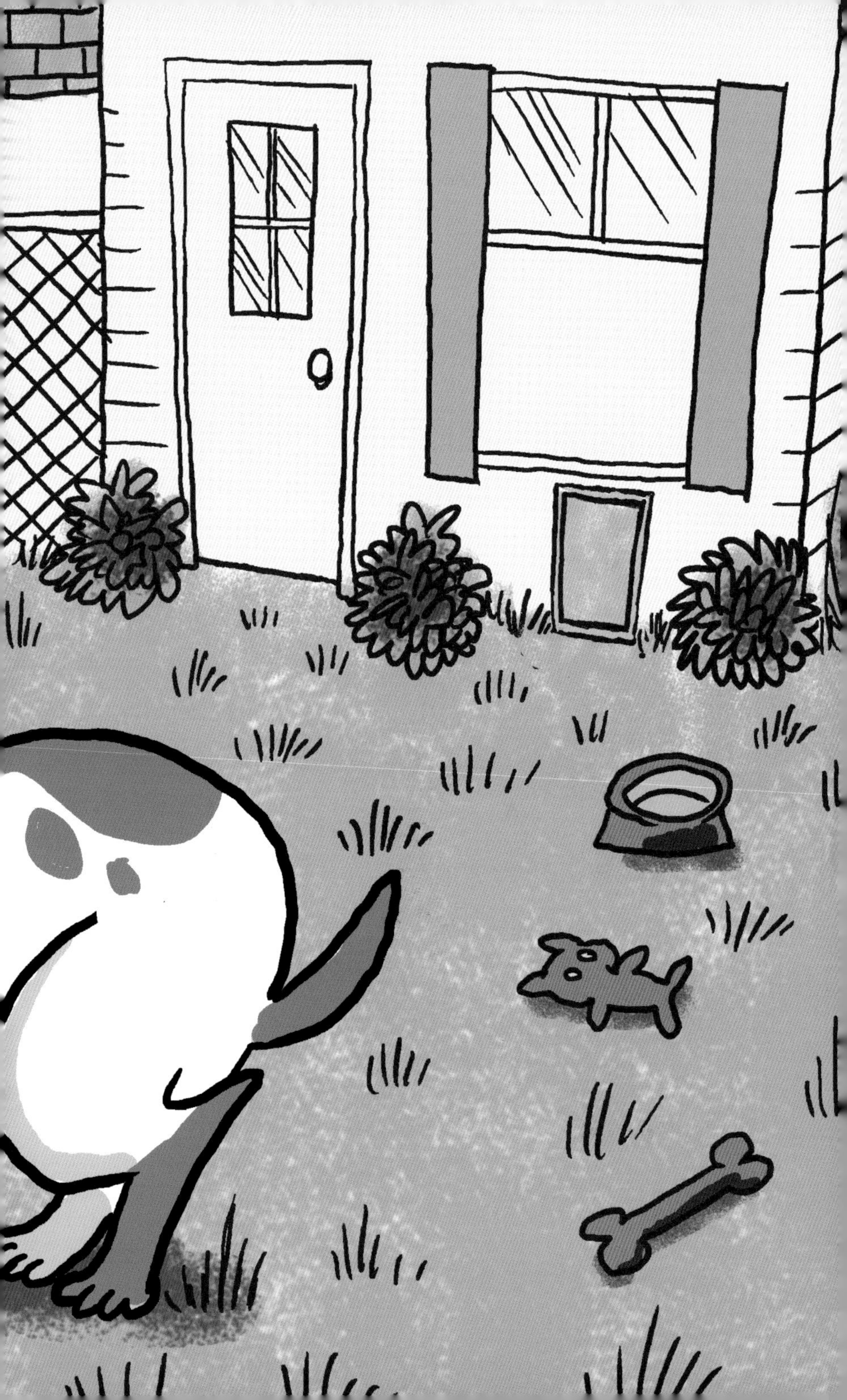

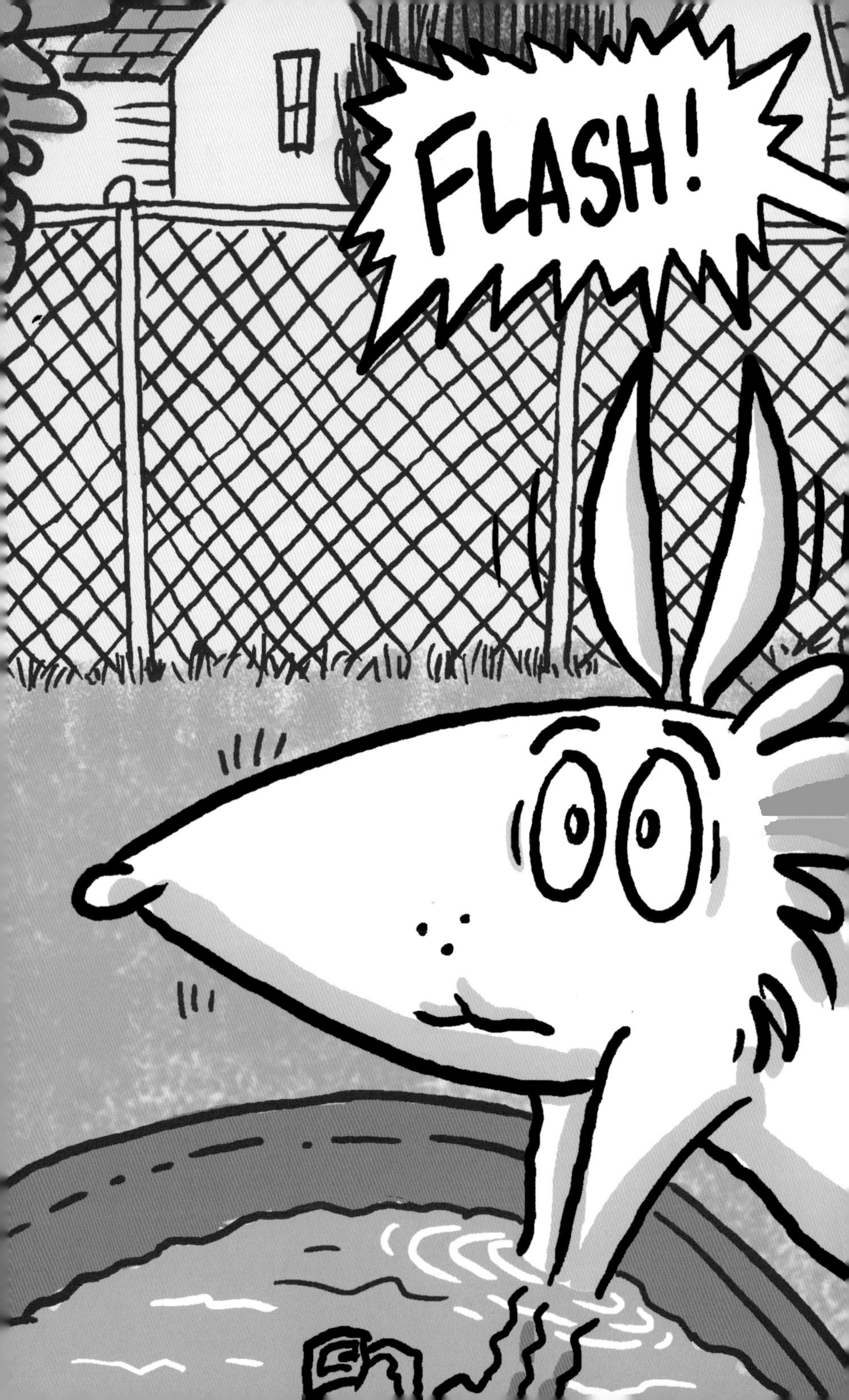
FLASH!

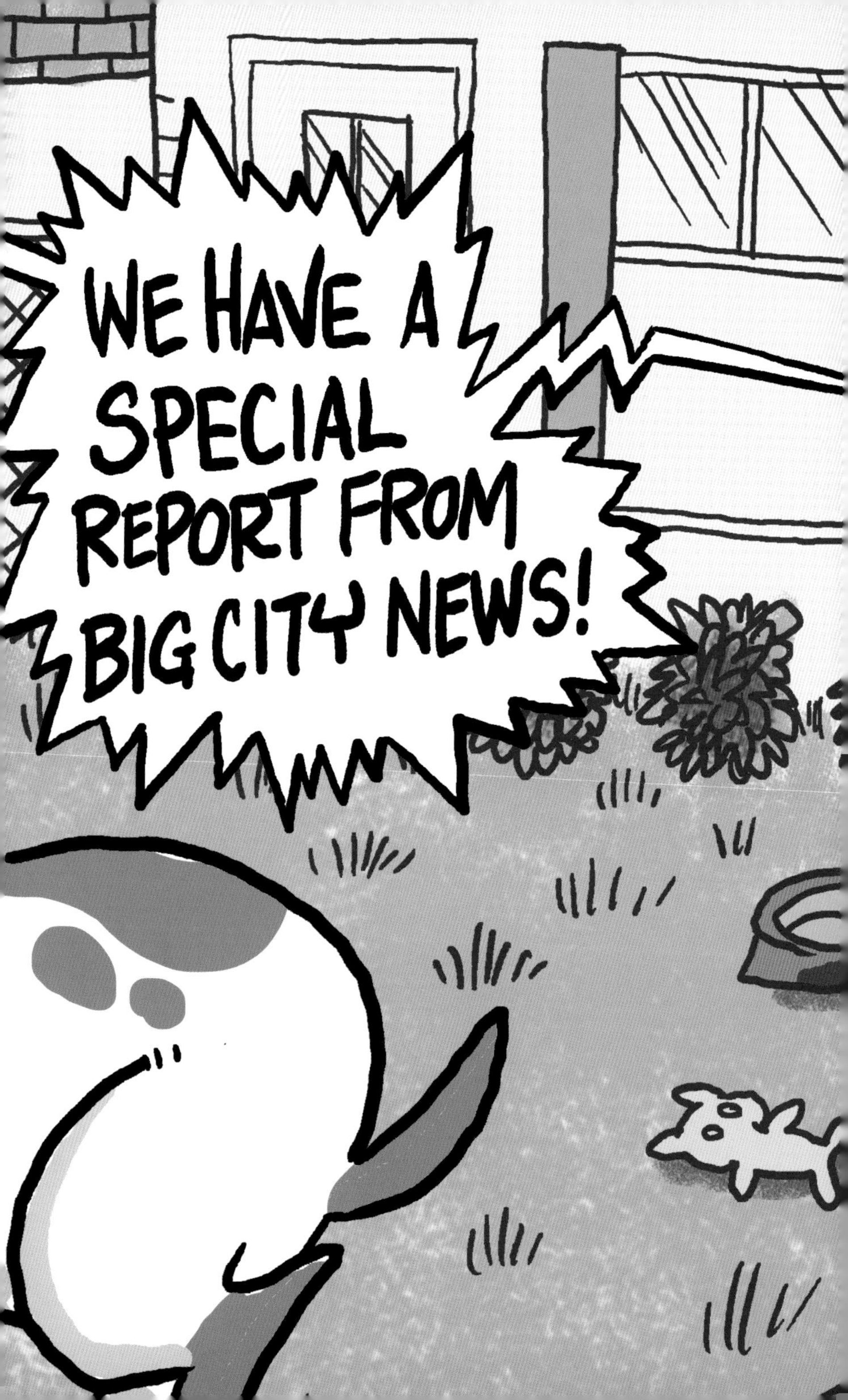
WE HAVE A SPECIAL REPORT FROM BIG CITY NEWS!

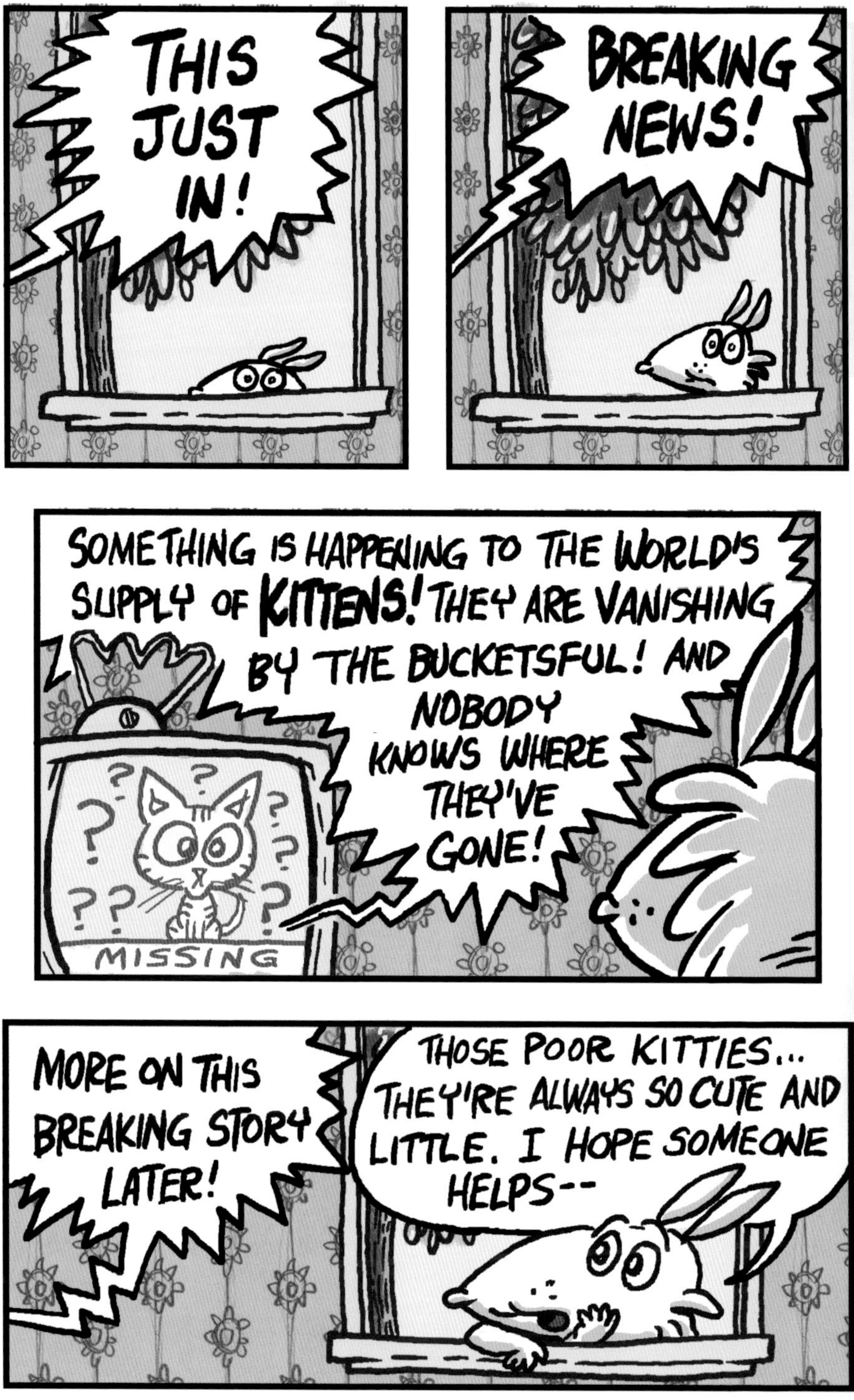
THIS JUST IN!
BREAKING NEWS!
SOMETHING IS HAPPENING TO THE WORLD'S SUPPLY OF KITTENS! THEY ARE VANISHING BY THE BUCKETSFUL! AND NOBODY KNOWS WHERE THEY'VE GONE!
MISSING
MORE ON THIS BREAKING STORY LATER!
THOSE POOR KITTIES... THEY'RE ALWAYS SO CUTE AND LITTLE. I HOPE SOMEONE HELPS--

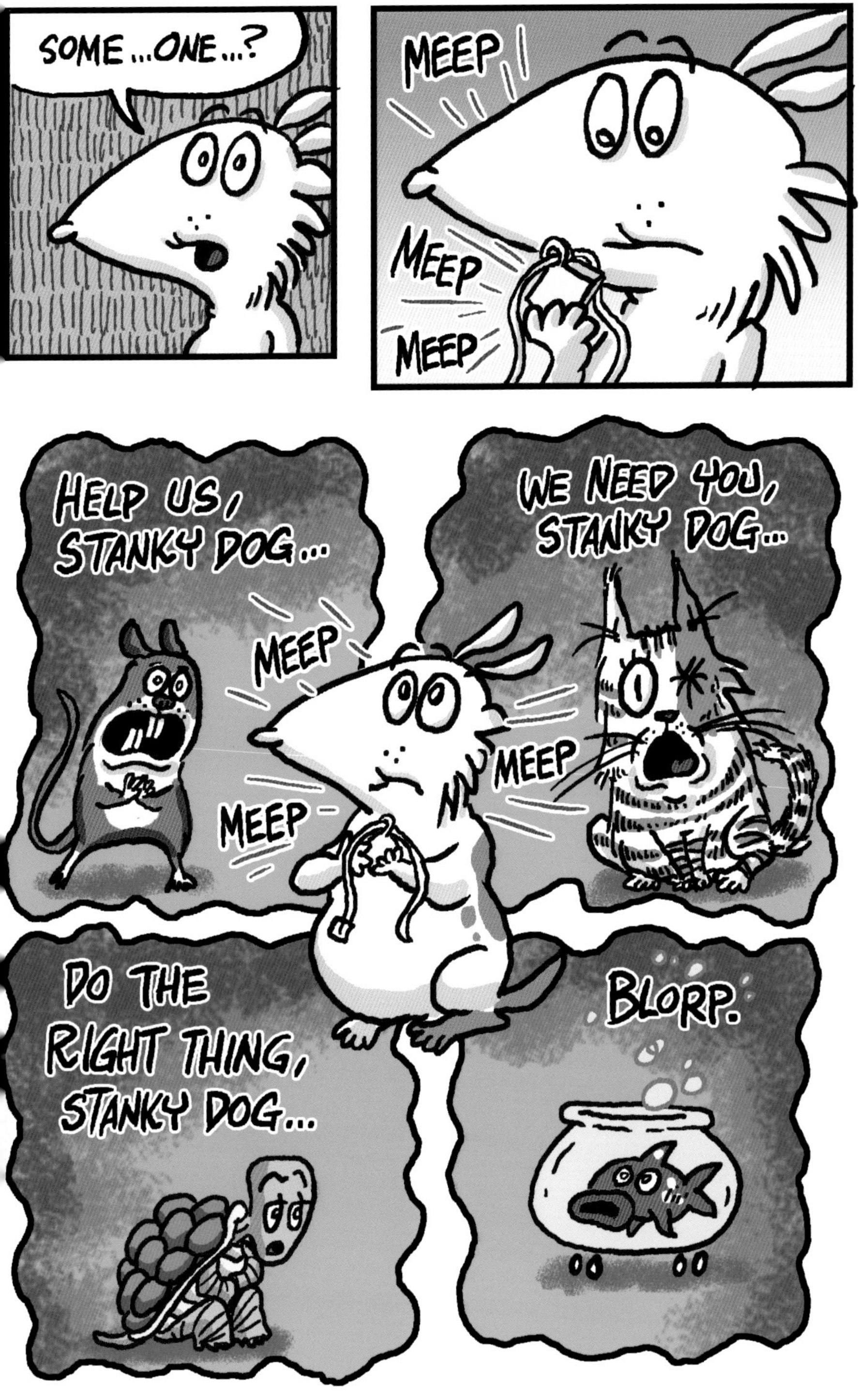
SOME...ONE...?
MEEP
MEEP
MEEP
HELP US, STANKY DOG...
WE NEED YOU, STANKY DOG...
MEEP
MEEP
MEEP
DO THE RIGHT THING, STANKY DOG...
BLORP.

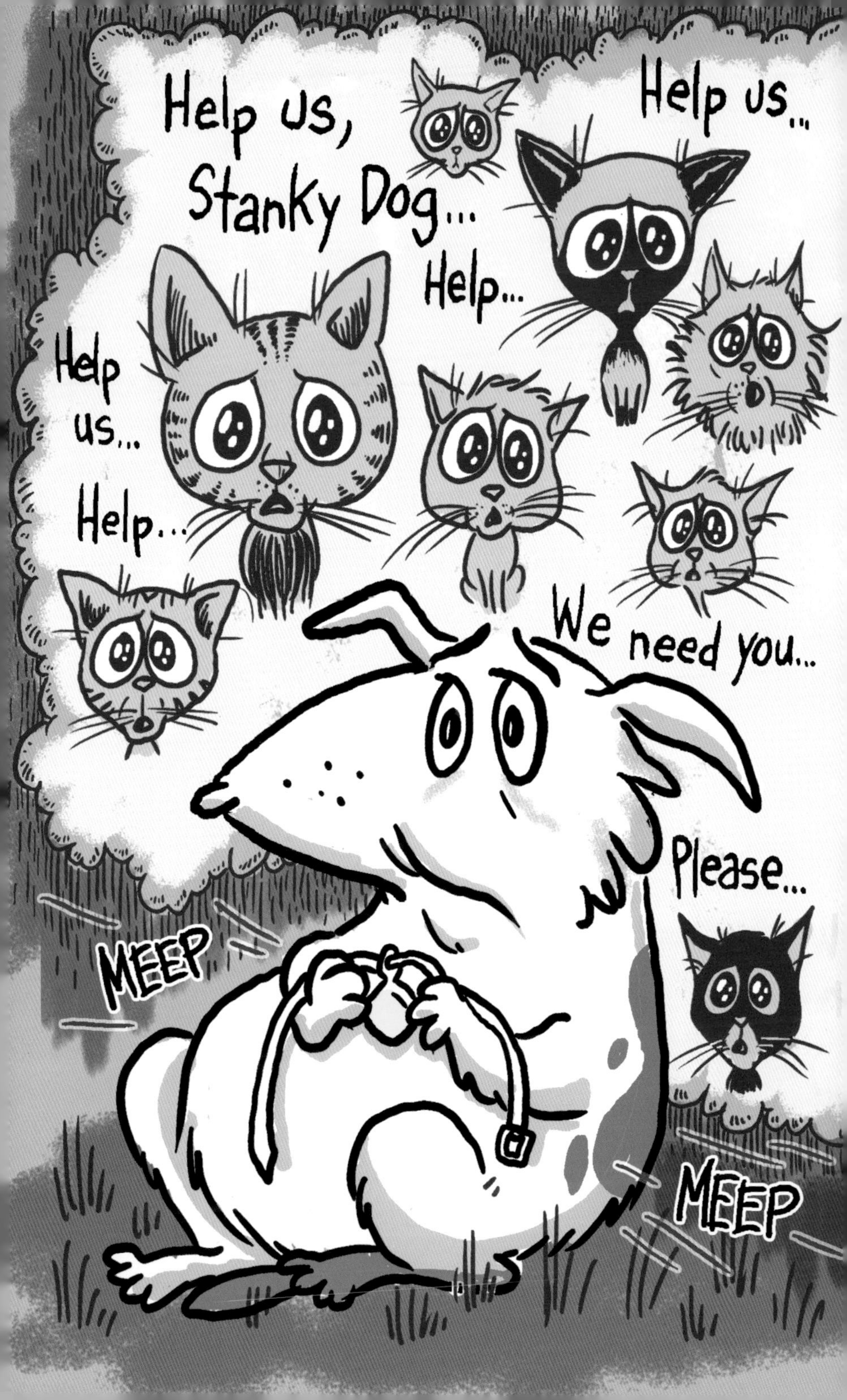
Help us, Stanky Dog...
Help us...
Help...
Help us...
Help...
We need you...
Please...
MEEP
MEEP

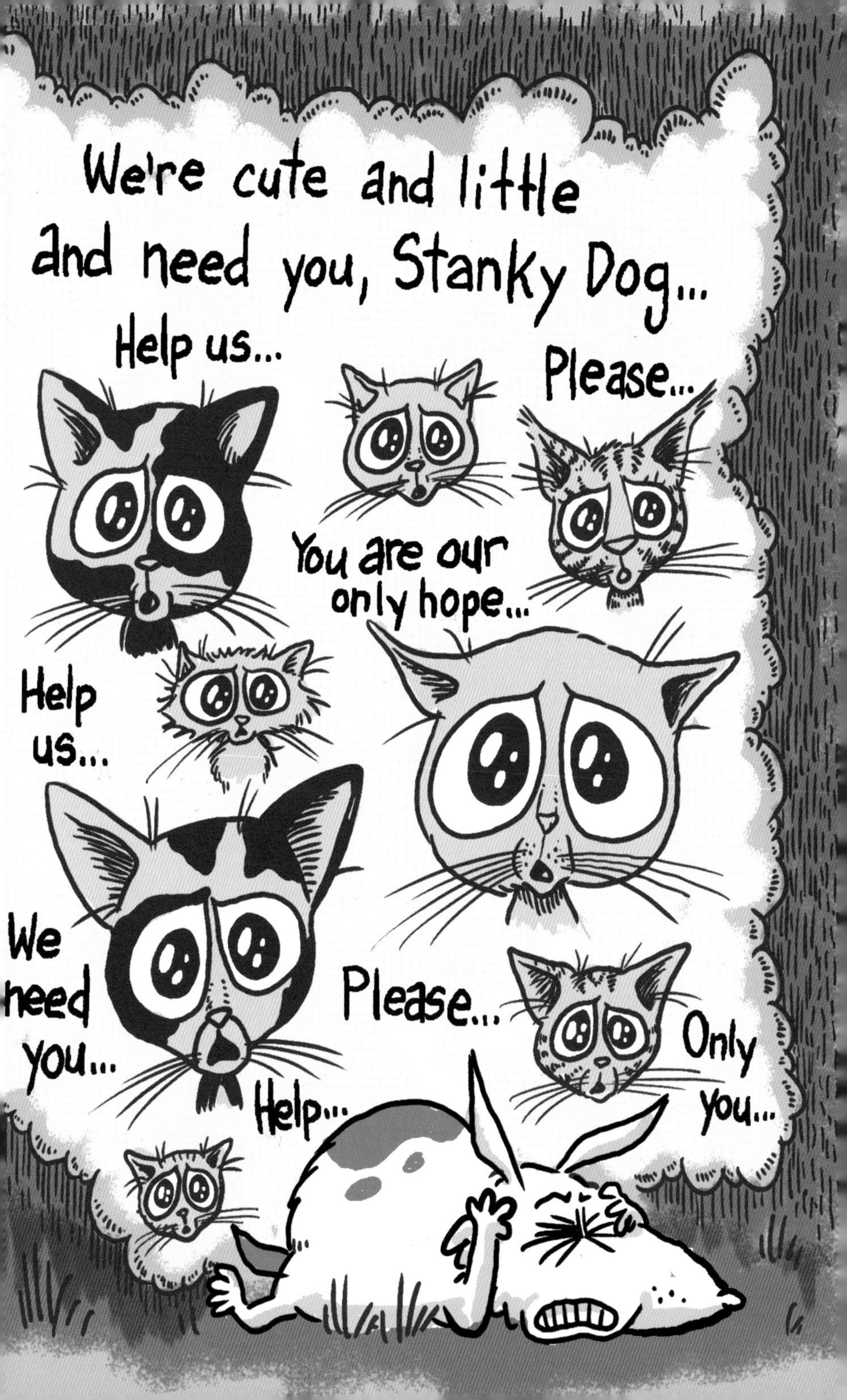
We're cute and little
and need you, Stanky Dog...
Help us...
Please...
You are our
only hope...
Help
us...
We
need
you...
Please...
Only
you...
Help...

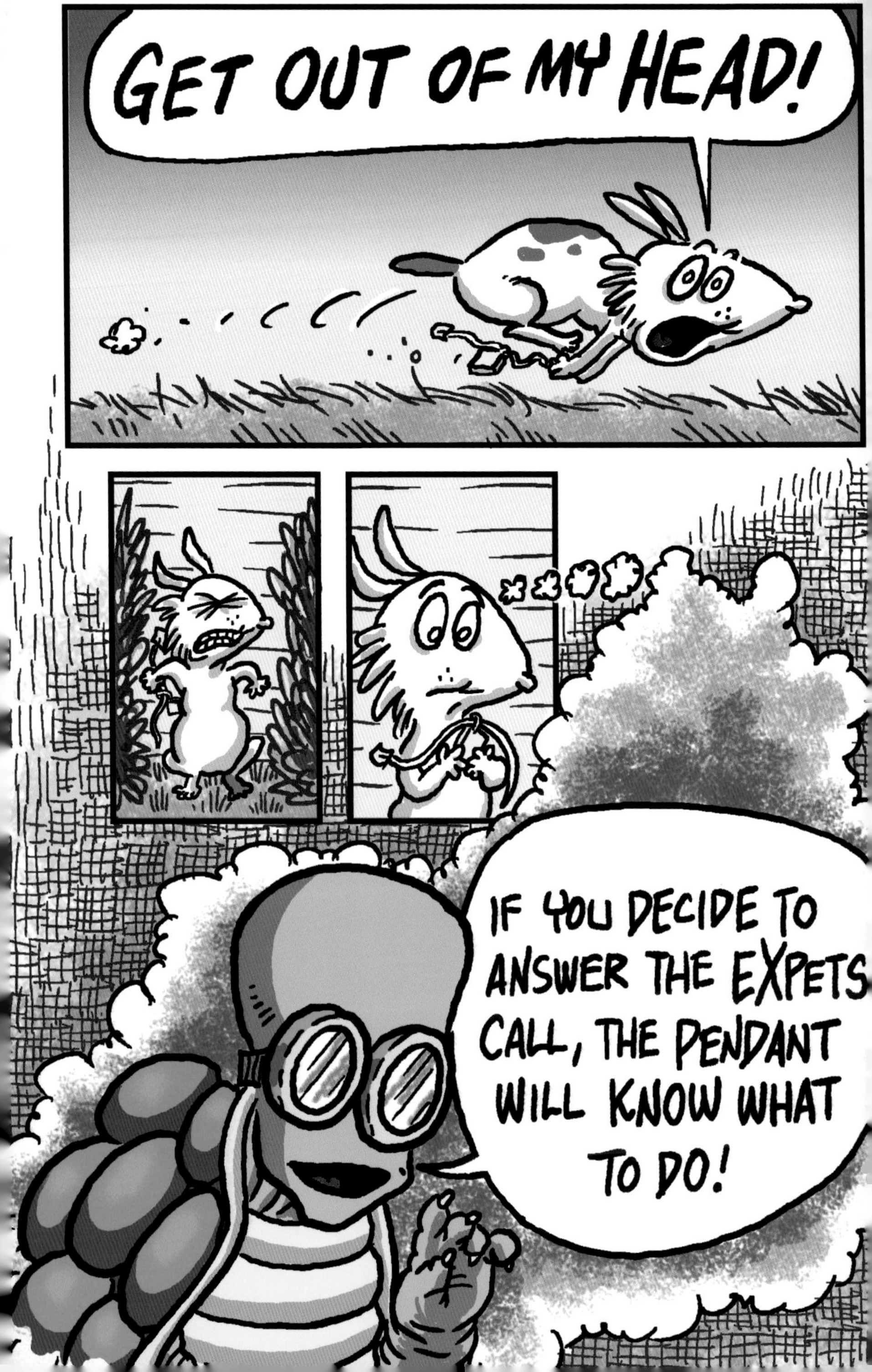
GET OUT OF MY HEAD!
IF YOU DECIDE TO ANSWER THE EXPETS CALL, THE PENDANT WILL KNOW WHAT TO DO!

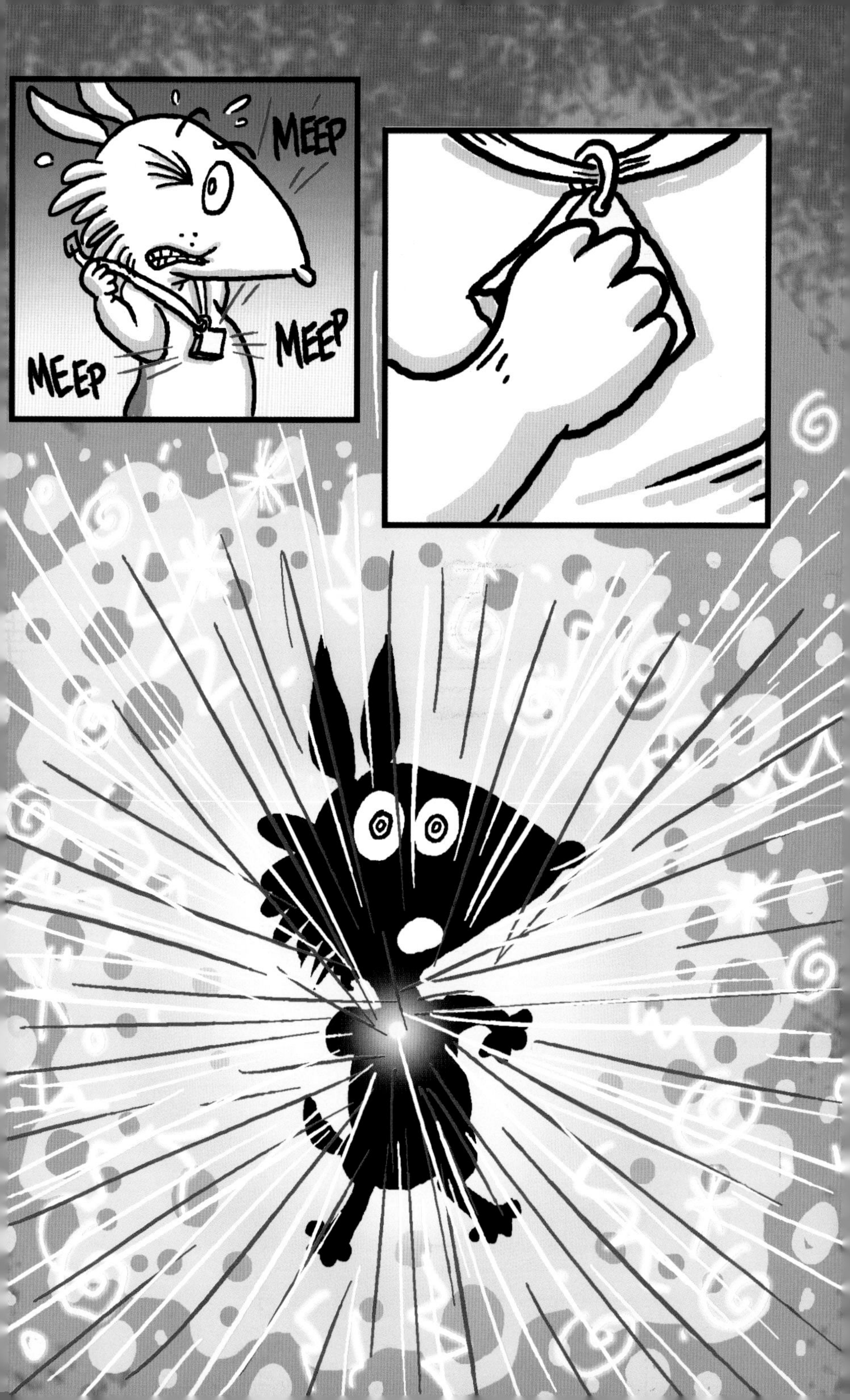
MEEP
MEEP
MEEP

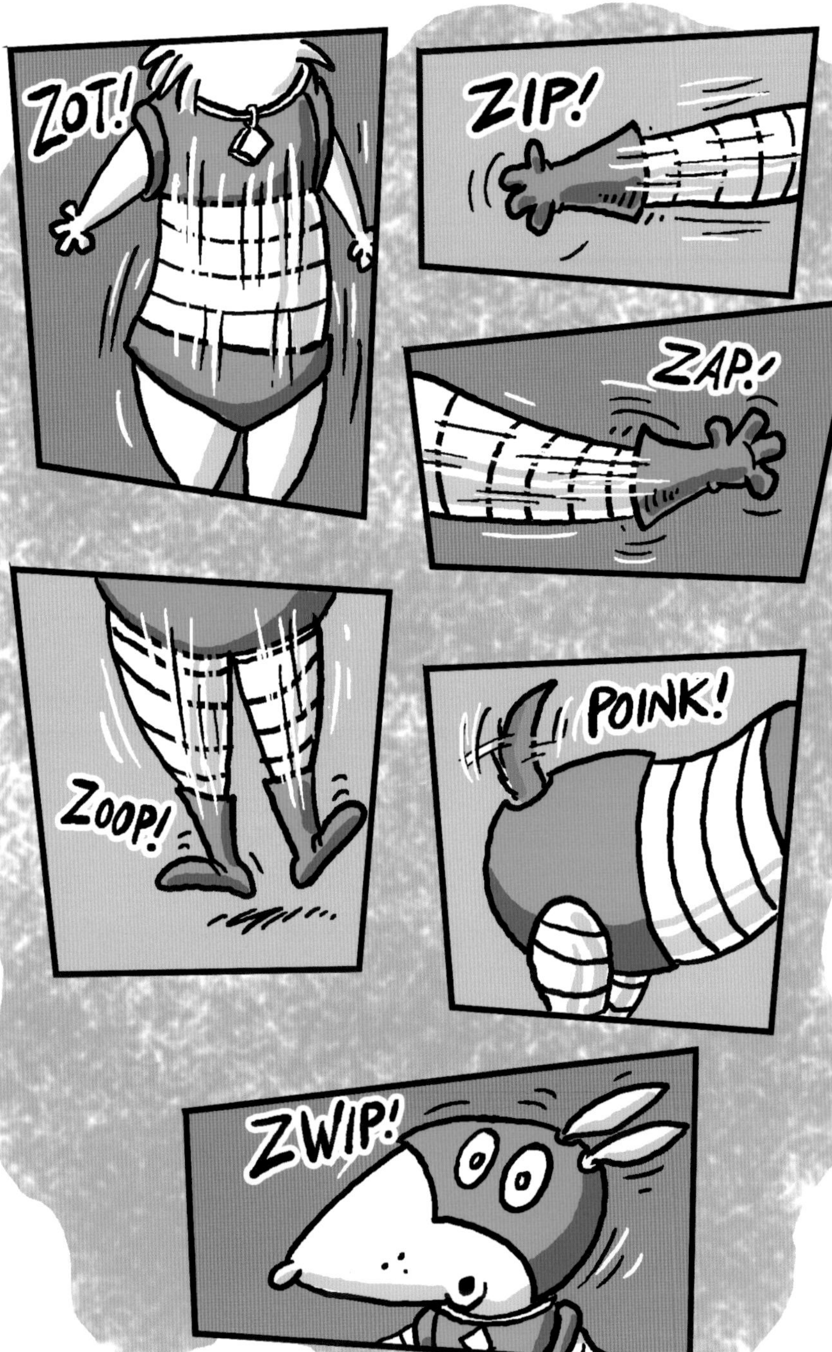
ZOT!
ZIP!
ZAP!
ZOOP!
POINK!
ZWIP!

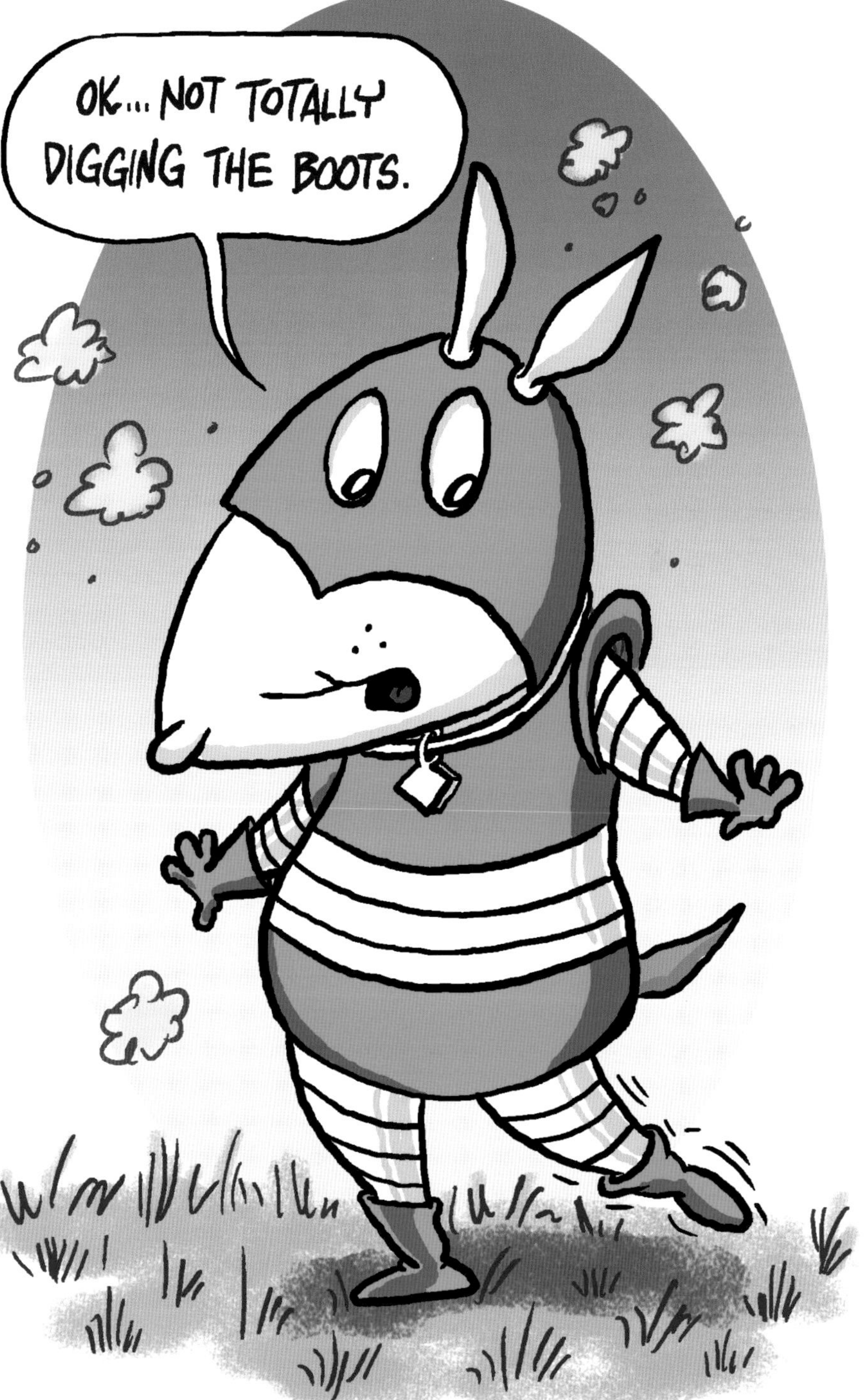
OK... NOT TOTALLY DIGGING THE BOOTS.

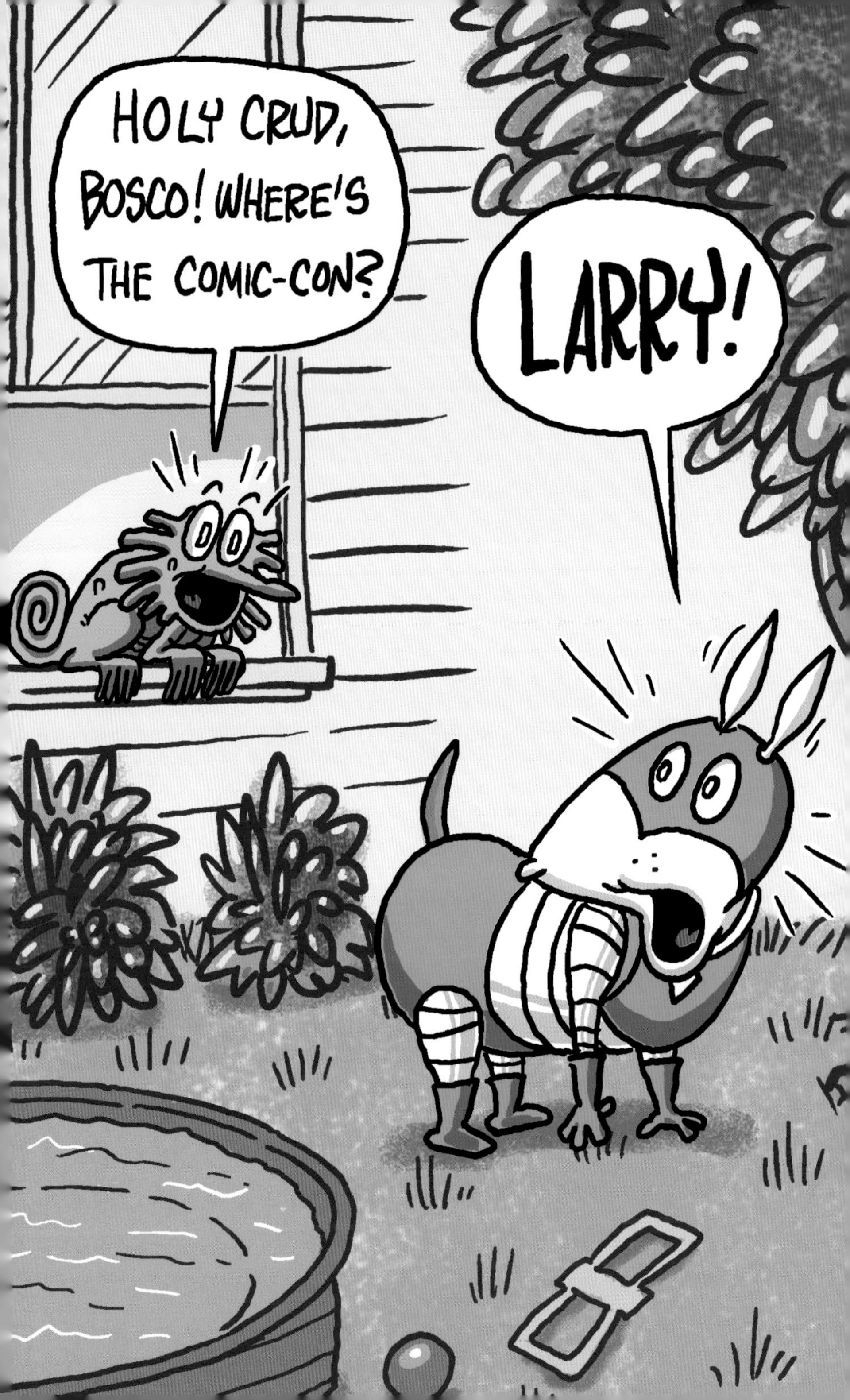
HOLY CRUD, BOSCO! WHERE'S THE COMIC-CON?
LARRY!

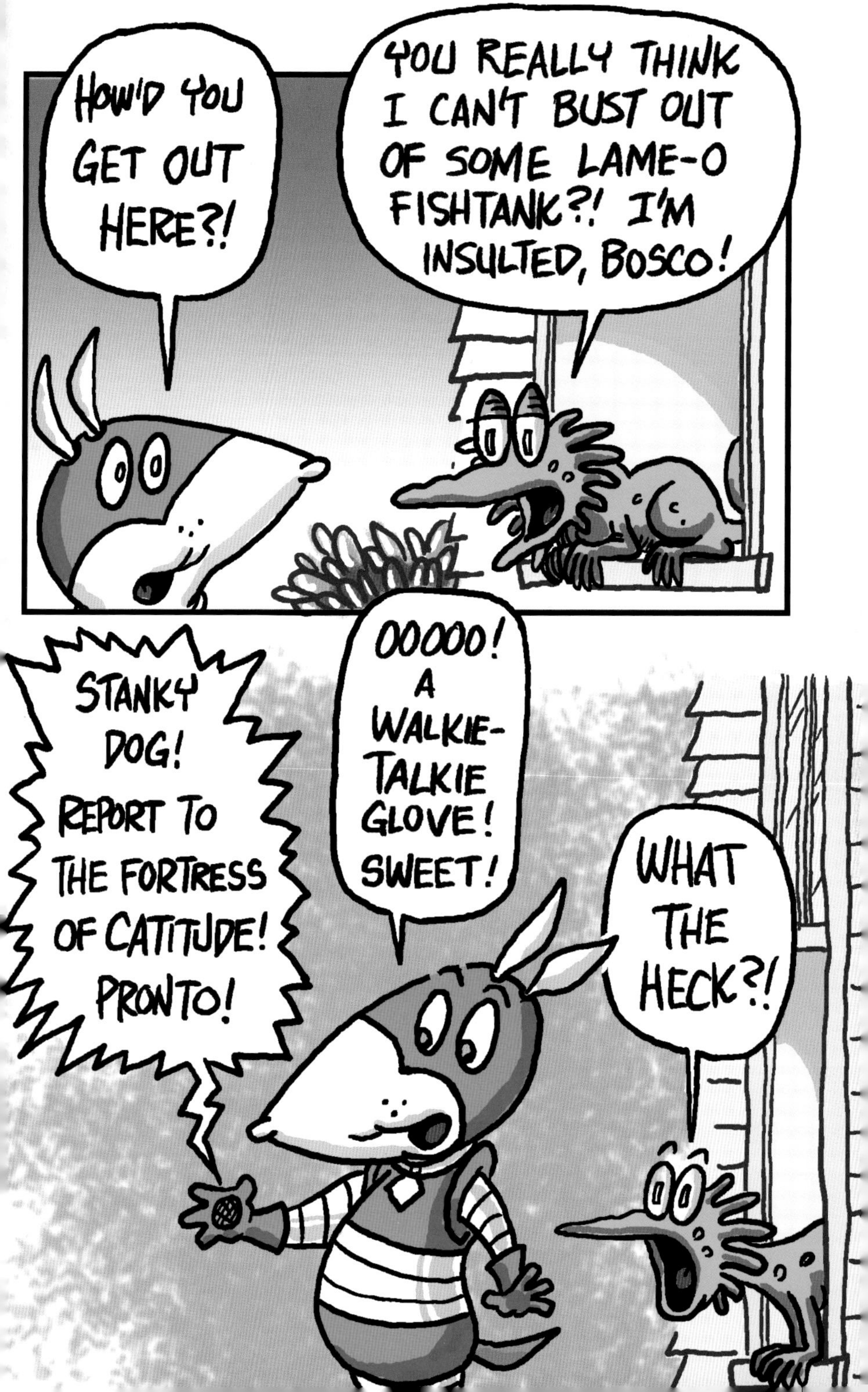
HOW'D YOU GET OUT HERE?!
YOU REALLY THINK I CAN'T BUST OUT OF SOME LAME-O FISHTANK?! I'M INSULTED, BOSCO!
STANKY DOG! REPORT TO THE FORTRESS OF CATITUDE! PRONTO!
OOOOO! A WALKIE-TALKIE GLOVE! SWEET!
WHAT THE HECK?!

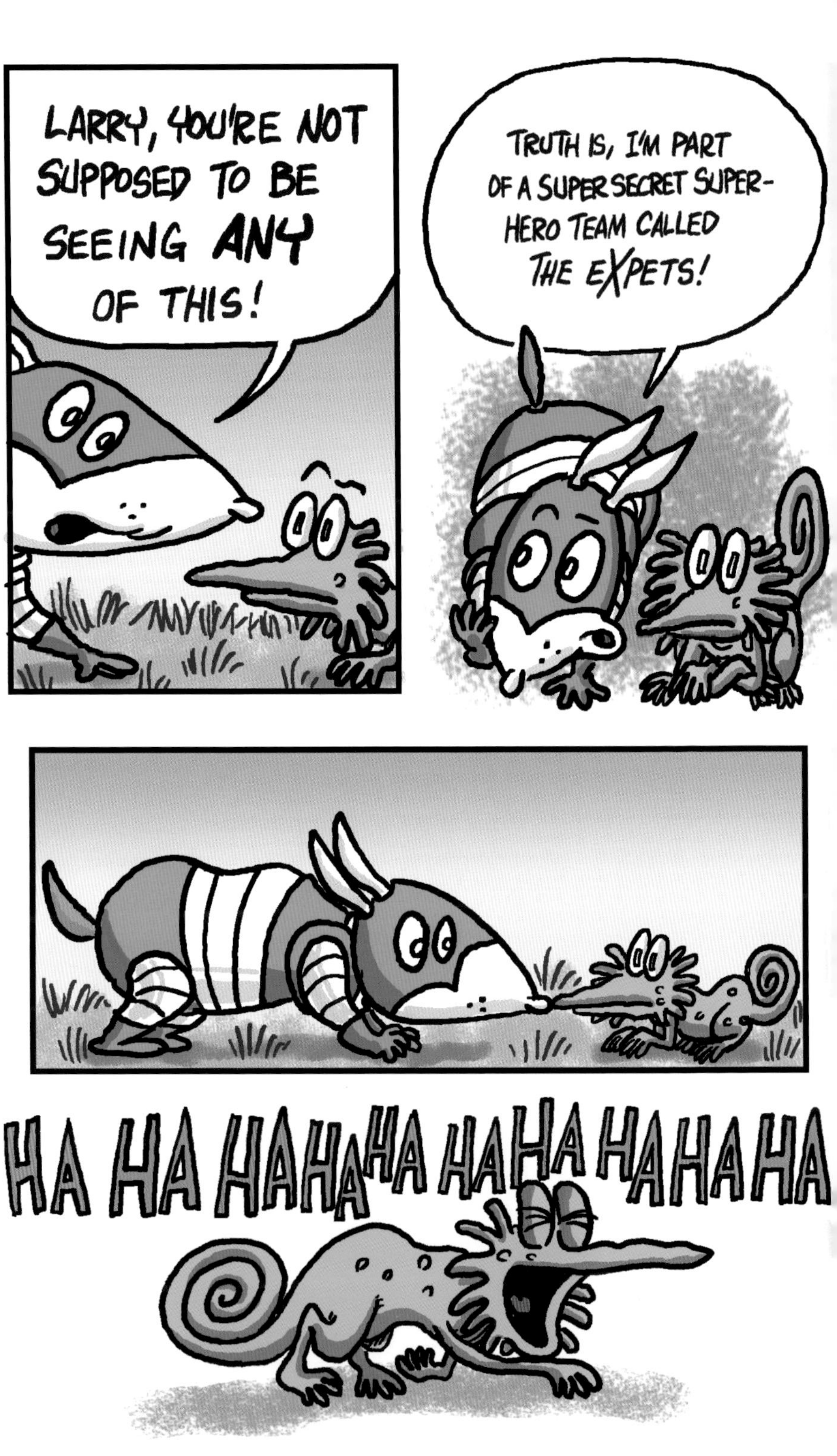
LARRY, YOU'RE NOT SUPPOSED TO BE SEEING ANY OF THIS!
TRUTH IS, I'M PART OF A SUPER SECRET SUPER-HERO TEAM CALLED THE EXPETS!
HA HA HAHAHA HAHAHA HAHAHAHA

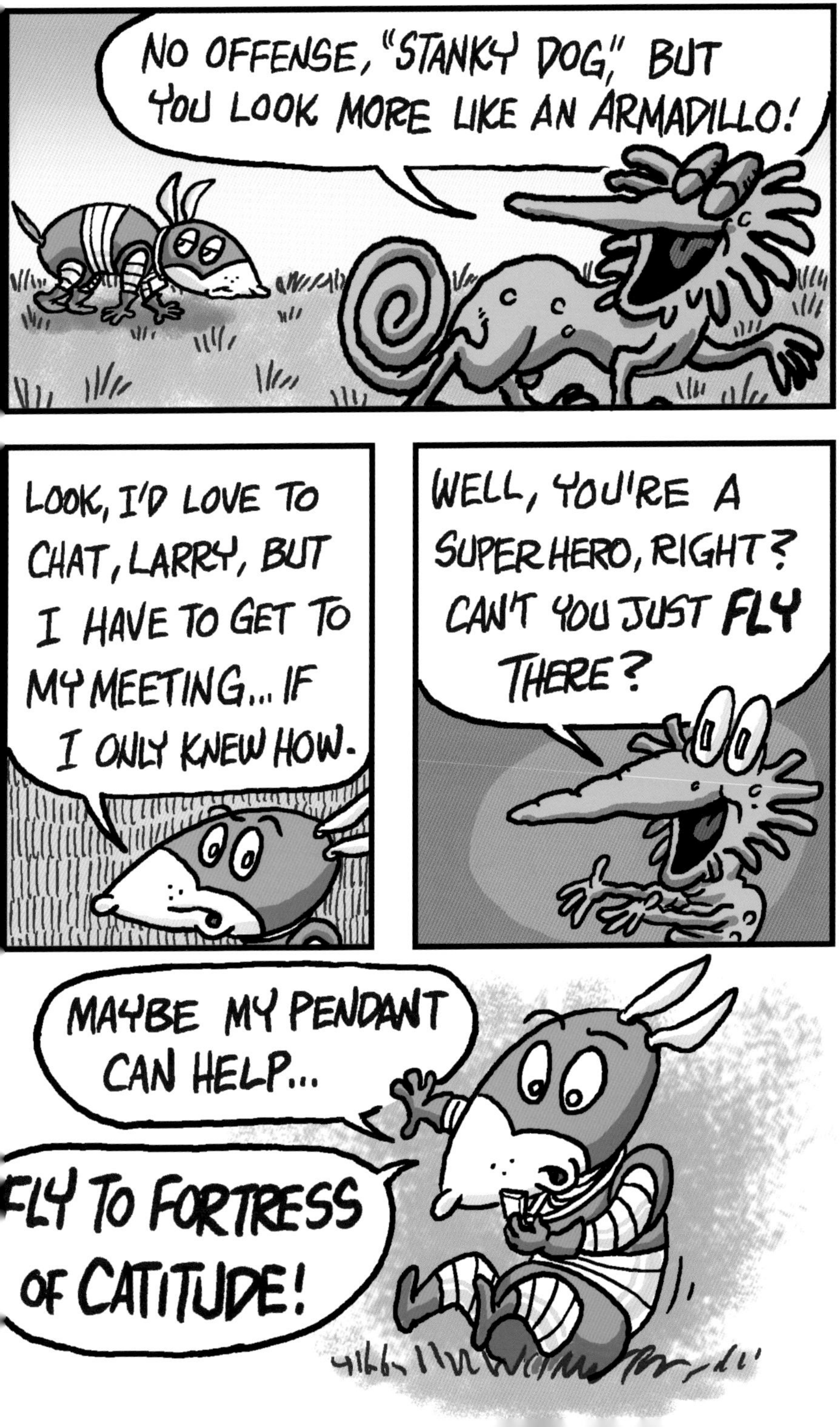
NO OFFENSE, "STANKY DOG," BUT YOU LOOK MORE LIKE AN ARMADILLO!
LOOK, I'D LOVE TO CHAT, LARRY, BUT I HAVE TO GET TO MY MEETING... IF I ONLY KNEW HOW.
WELL, YOU'RE A SUPERHERO, RIGHT? CAN'T YOU JUST **FLY** THERE?
MAYBE MY PENDANT CAN HELP...
FLY TO FORTRESS OF CATITUDE!

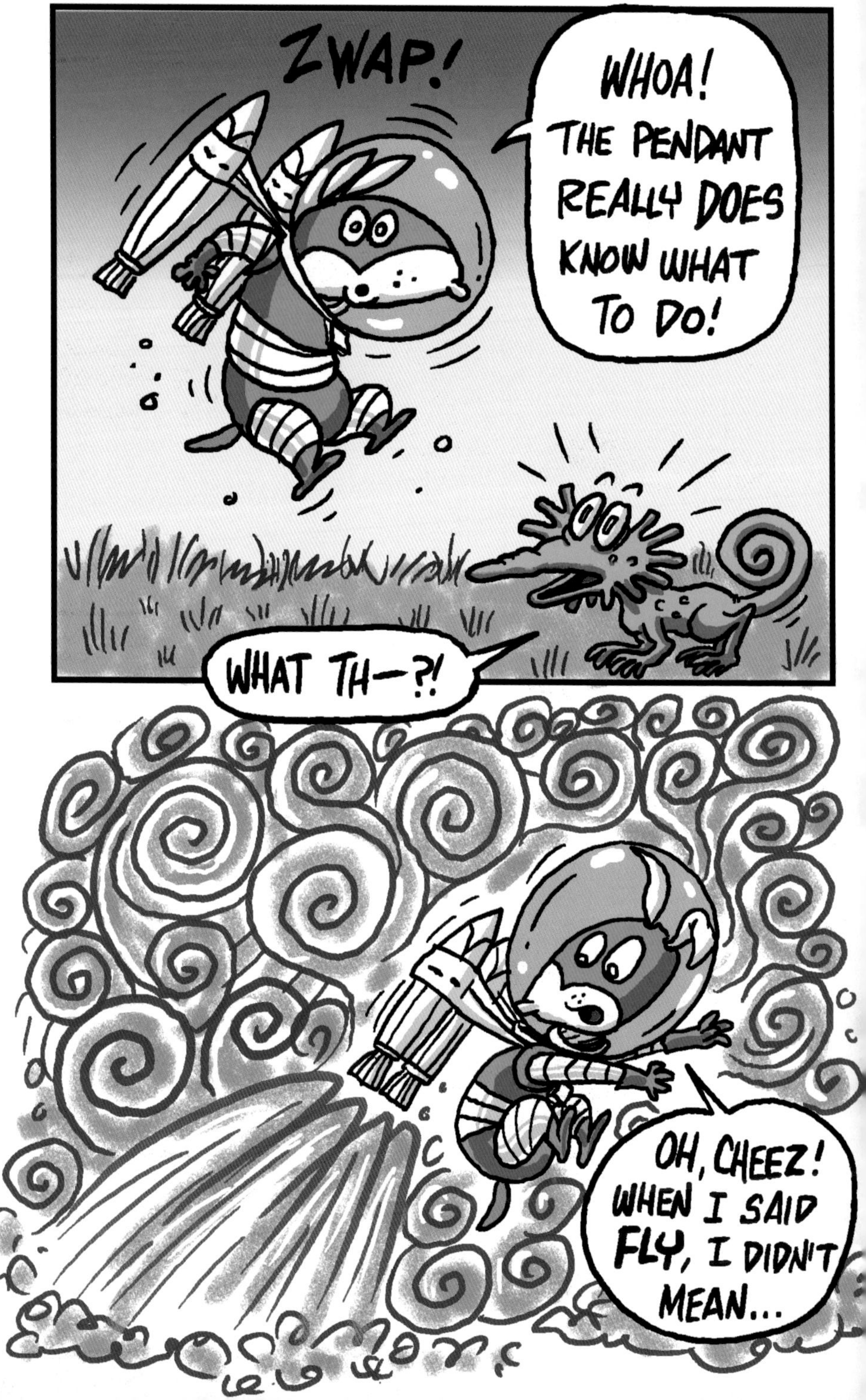
ZWAP!
WHOA! THE PENDANT REALLY DOES KNOW WHAT TO DO!
WHAT TH—?!
OH, CHEEZ! WHEN I SAID FLY, I DIDN'T MEAN...

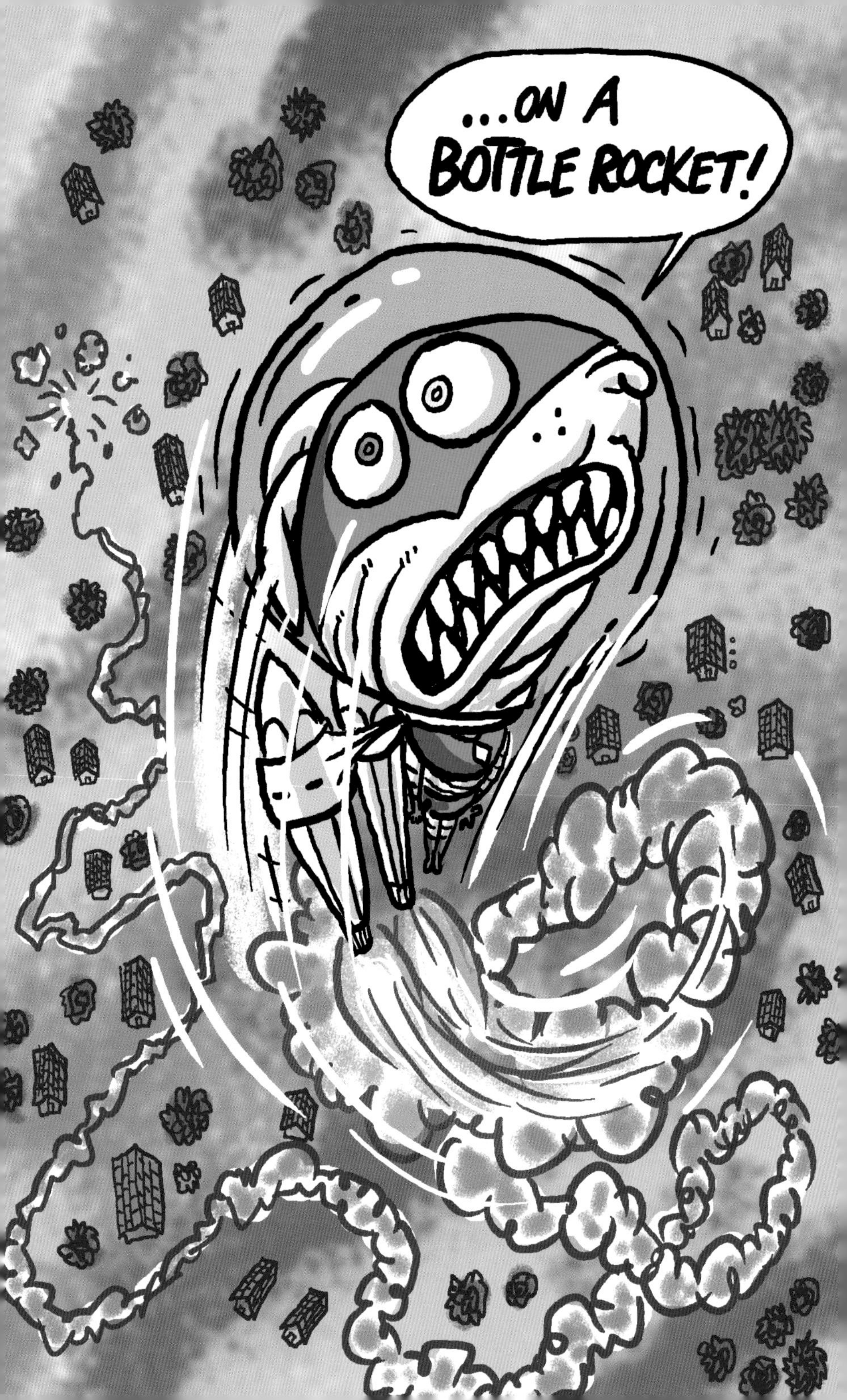
...ON A
BOTTLE ROCKET!

CHAPTER 7

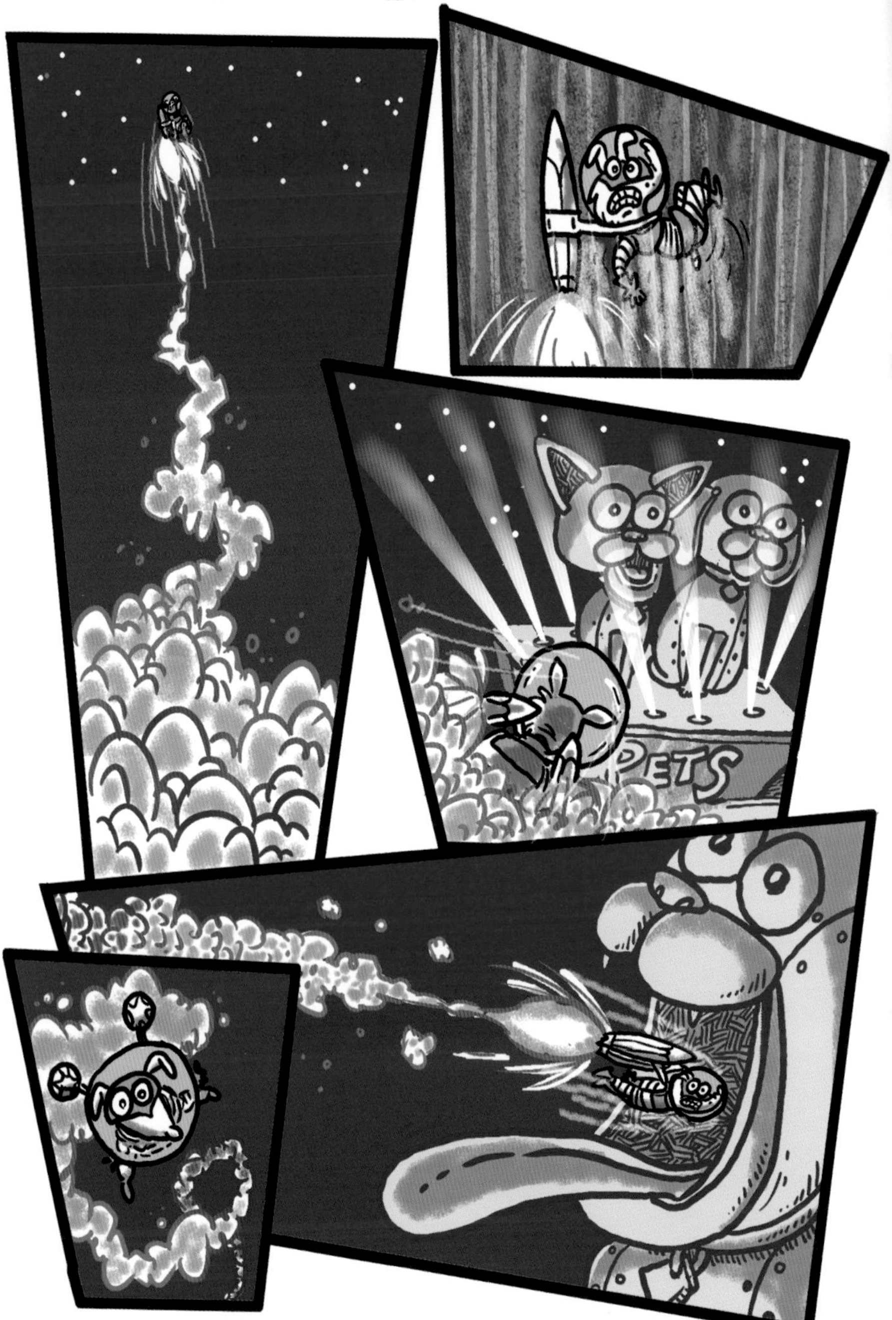

PETS

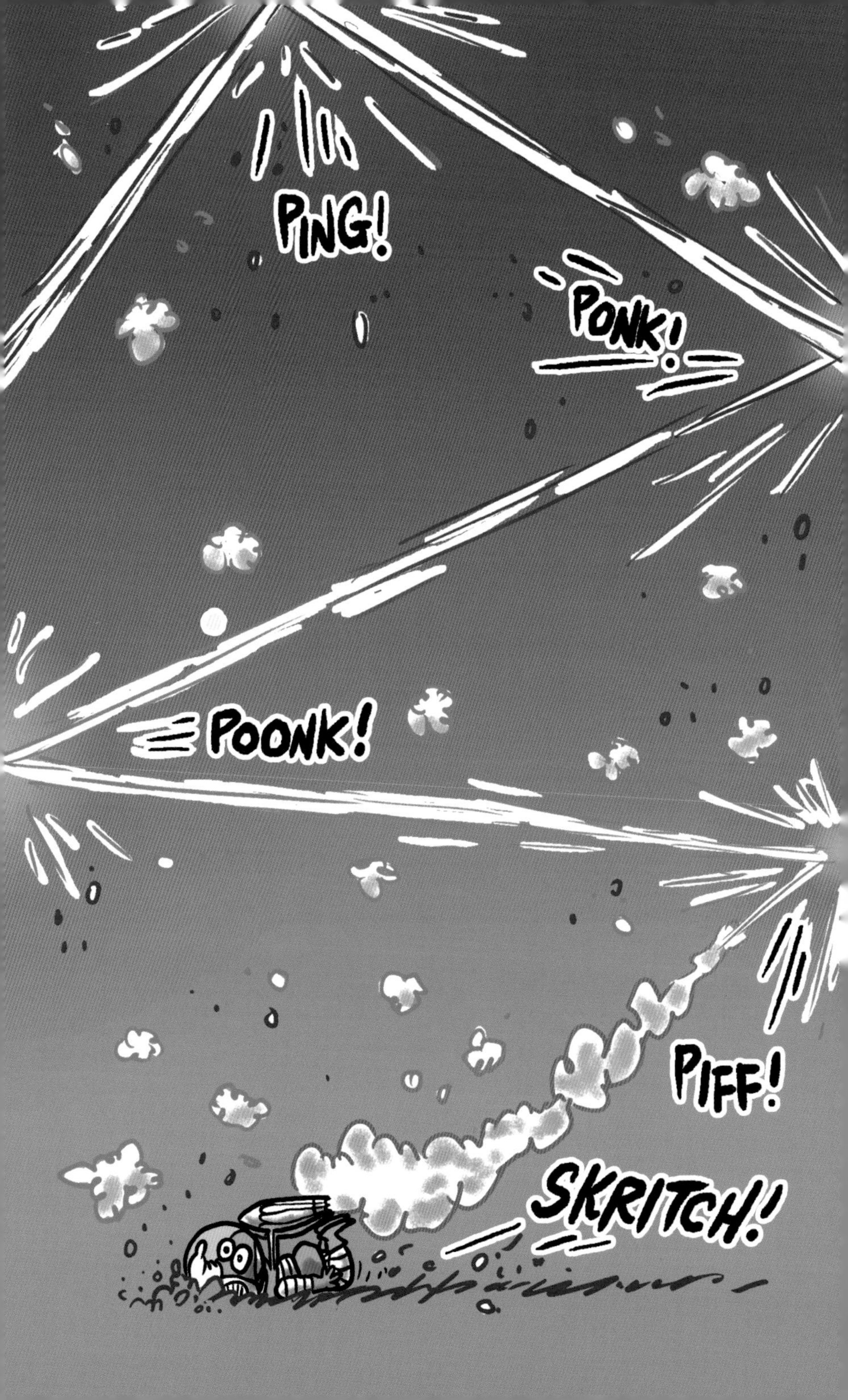
PING!
PONK!
POONK!
PIFF!
SKRITCH!

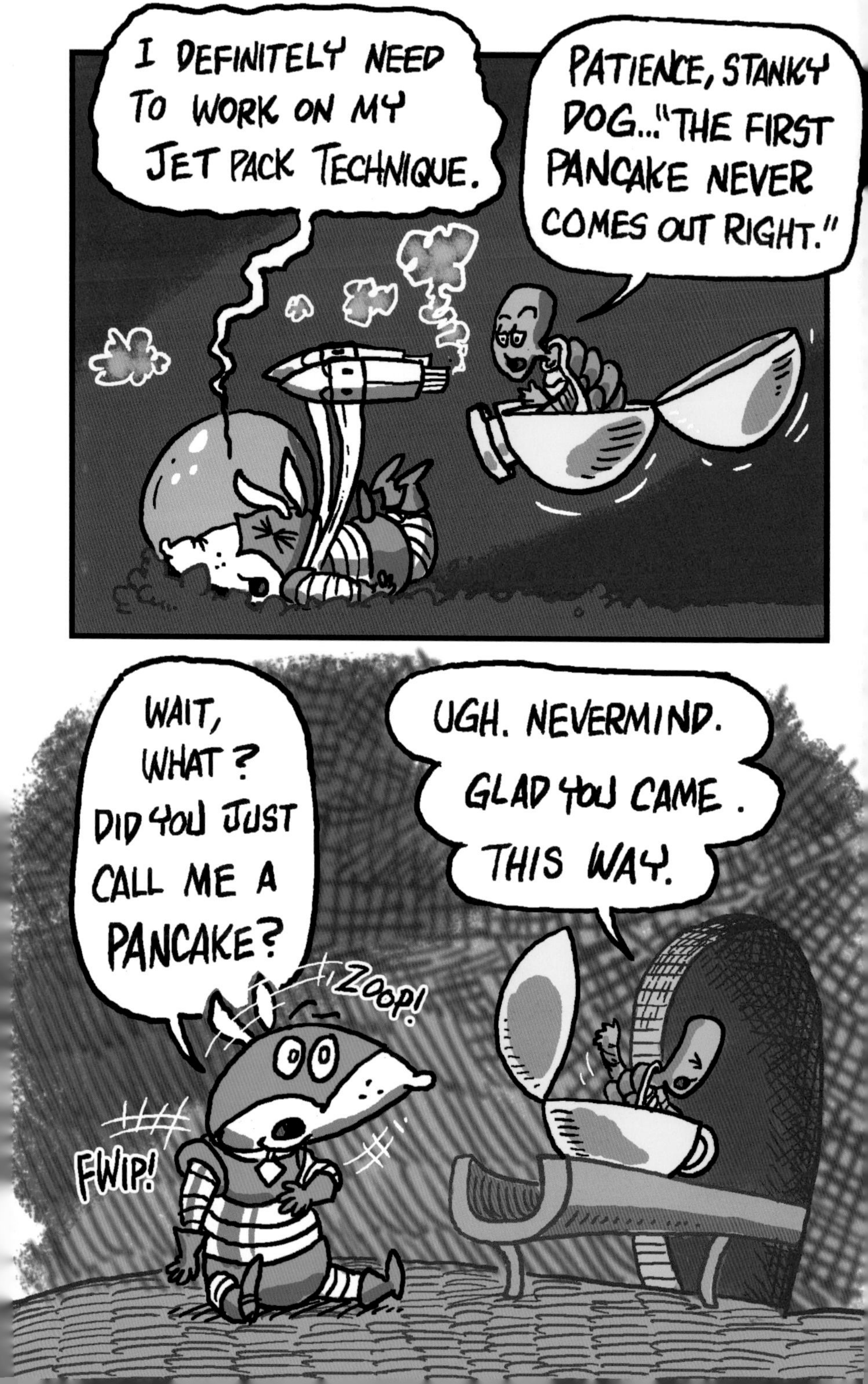
I DEFINITELY NEED TO WORK ON MY JET PACK TECHNIQUE.
PATIENCE, STANKY DOG..."THE FIRST PANCAKE NEVER COMES OUT RIGHT."
WAIT, WHAT? DID YOU JUST CALL ME A PANCAKE?
ZOOP!
FWIP!
UGH. NEVERMIND. GLAD YOU CAME. THIS WAY.

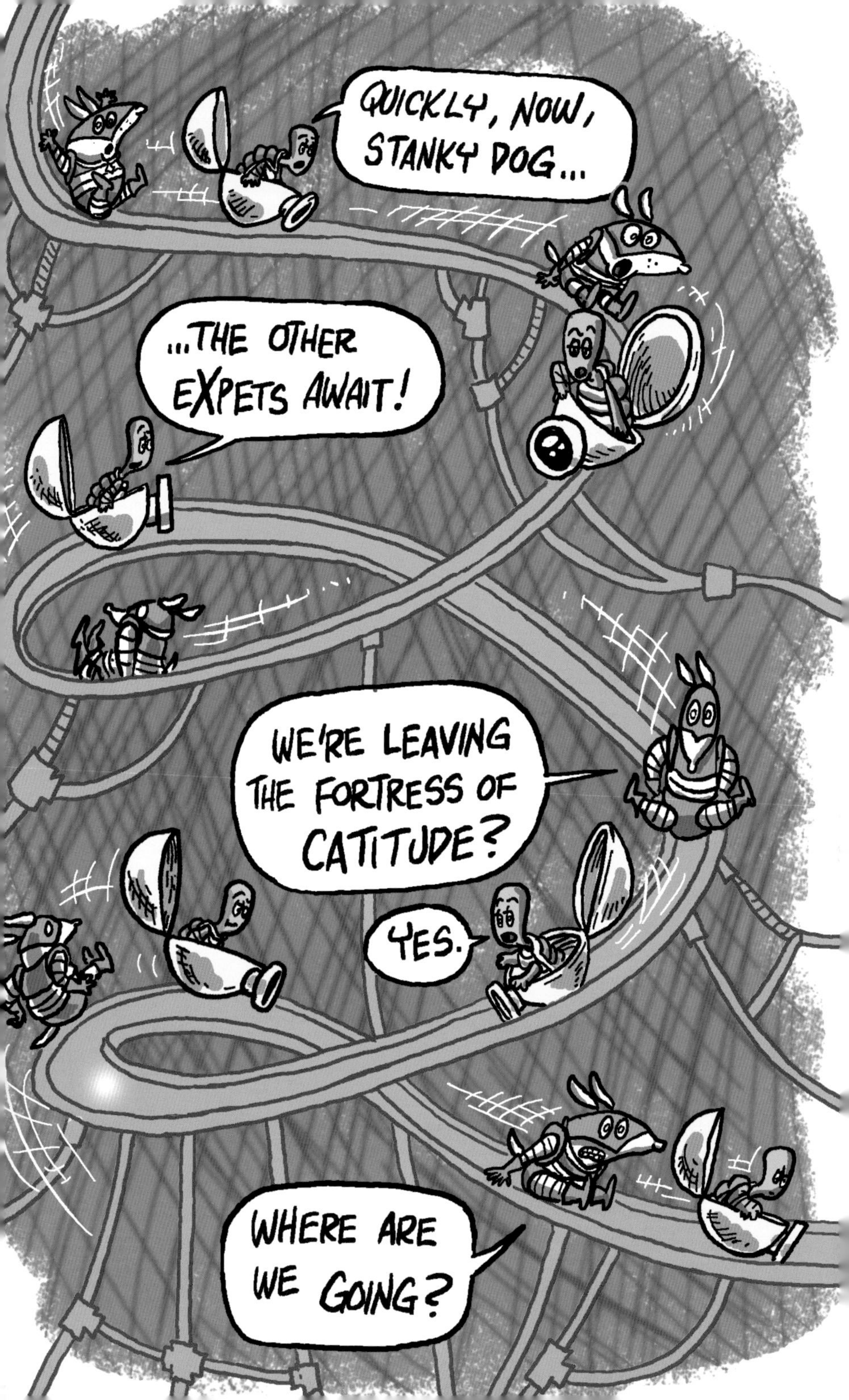
QUICKLY, NOW, STANKY DOG...
...THE OTHER EXPETS AWAIT!
WE'RE LEAVING THE FORTRESS OF CATITUDE?
YES.
WHERE ARE WE GOING?

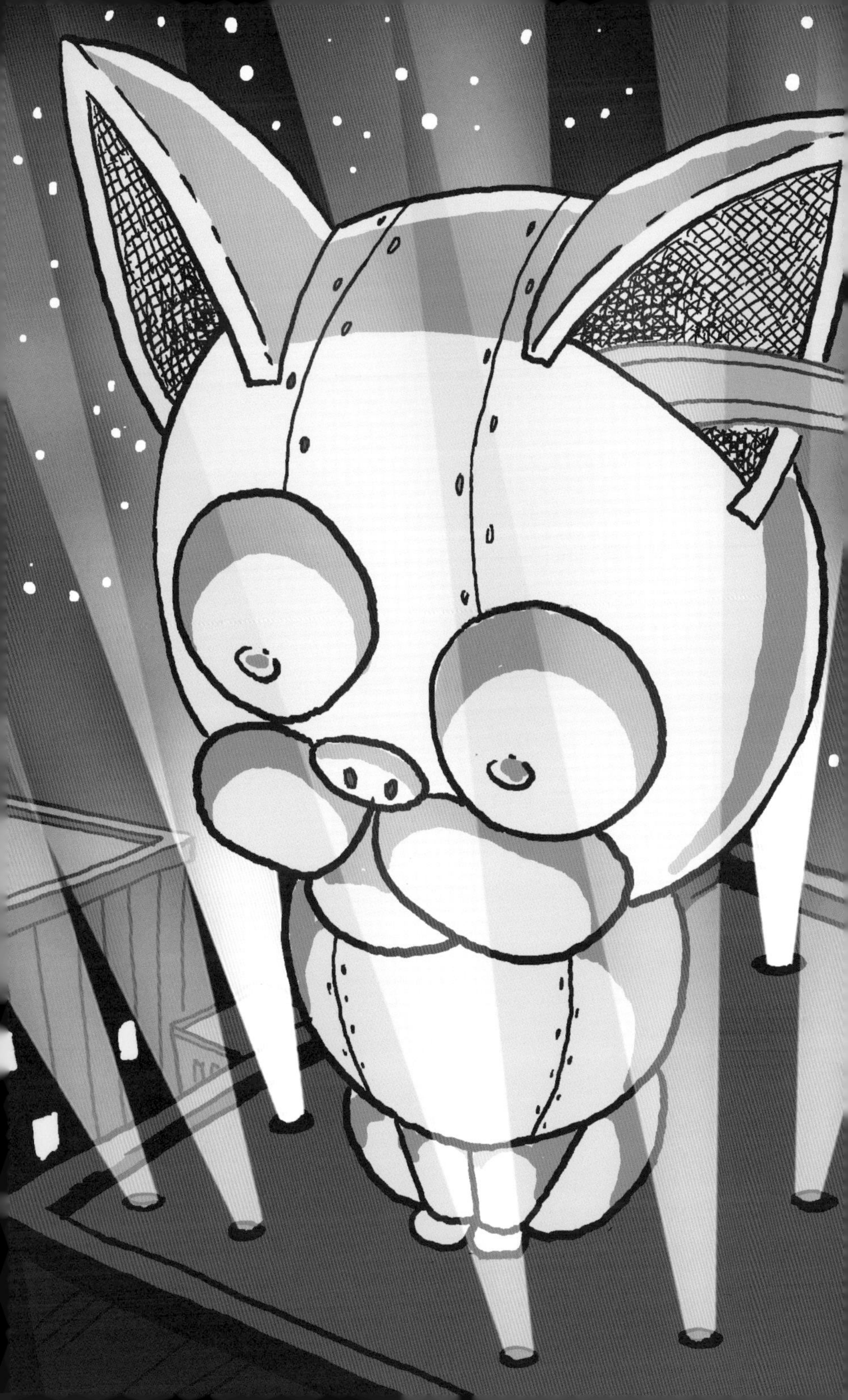

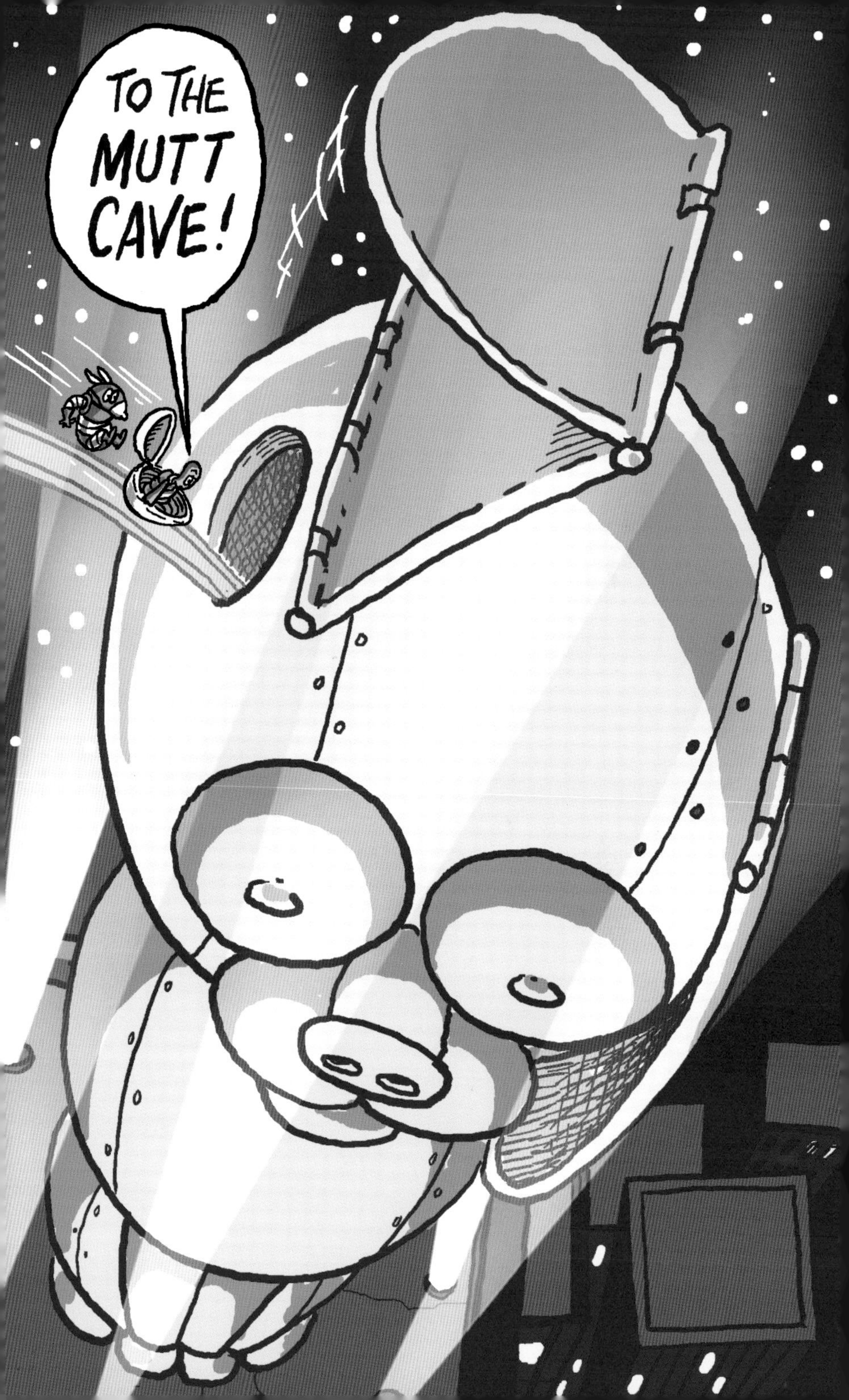
TO THE MUTT CAVE!

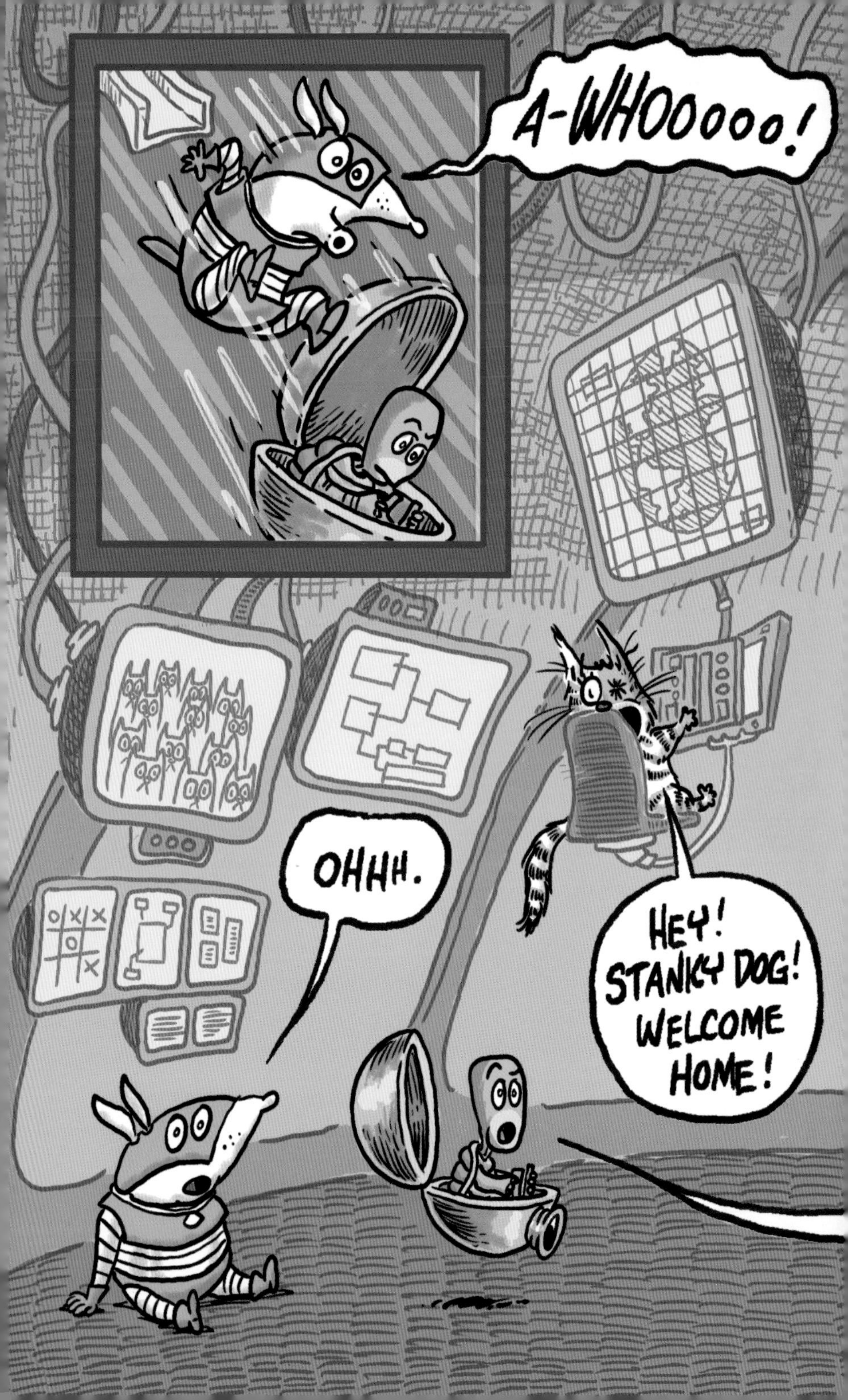
A-WHOOOOOO!
OHHH.
HEY! STANKY DOG! WELCOME HOME!

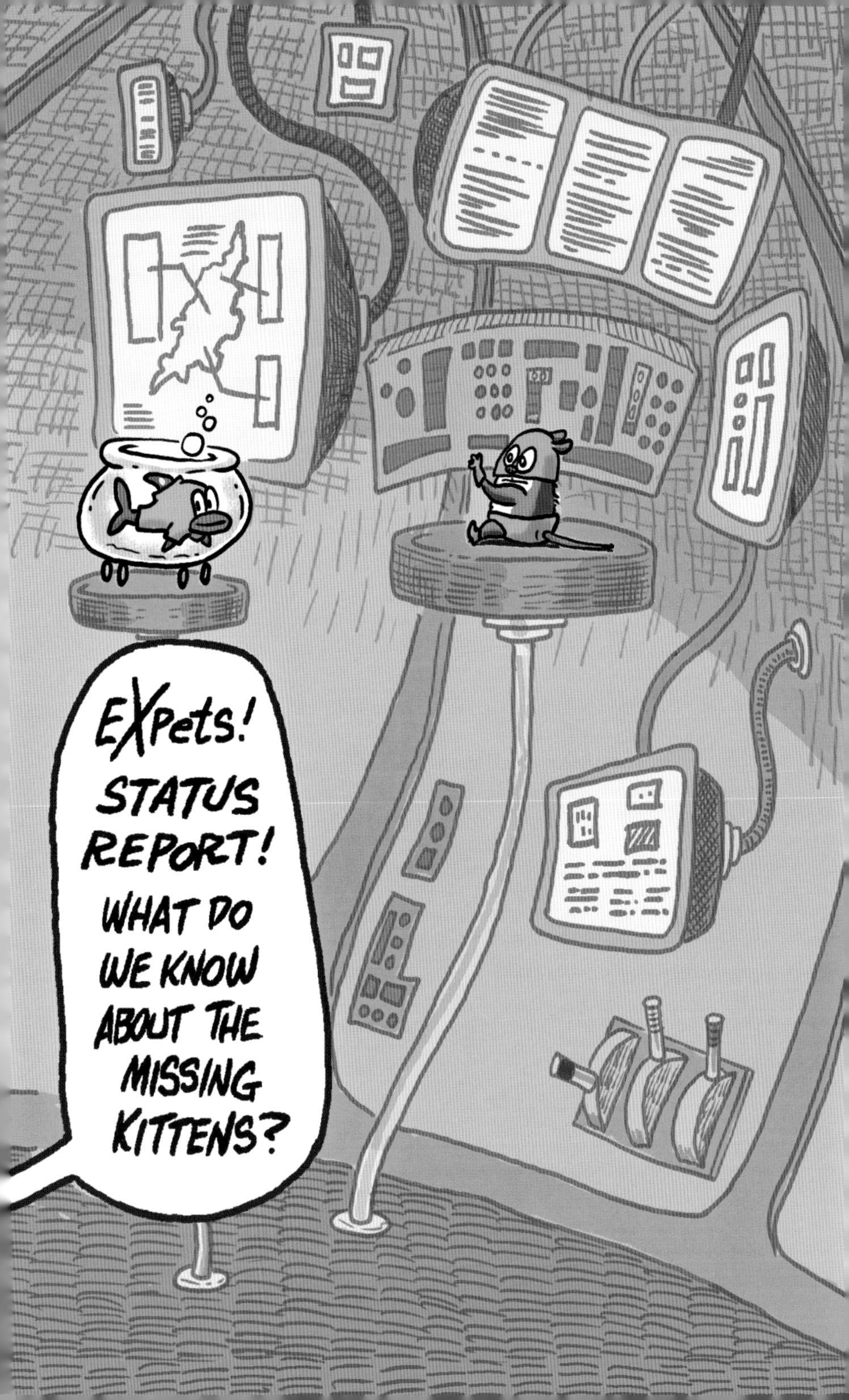
EXPets! STATUS REPORT! WHAT DO WE KNOW ABOUT THE MISSING KITTENS?

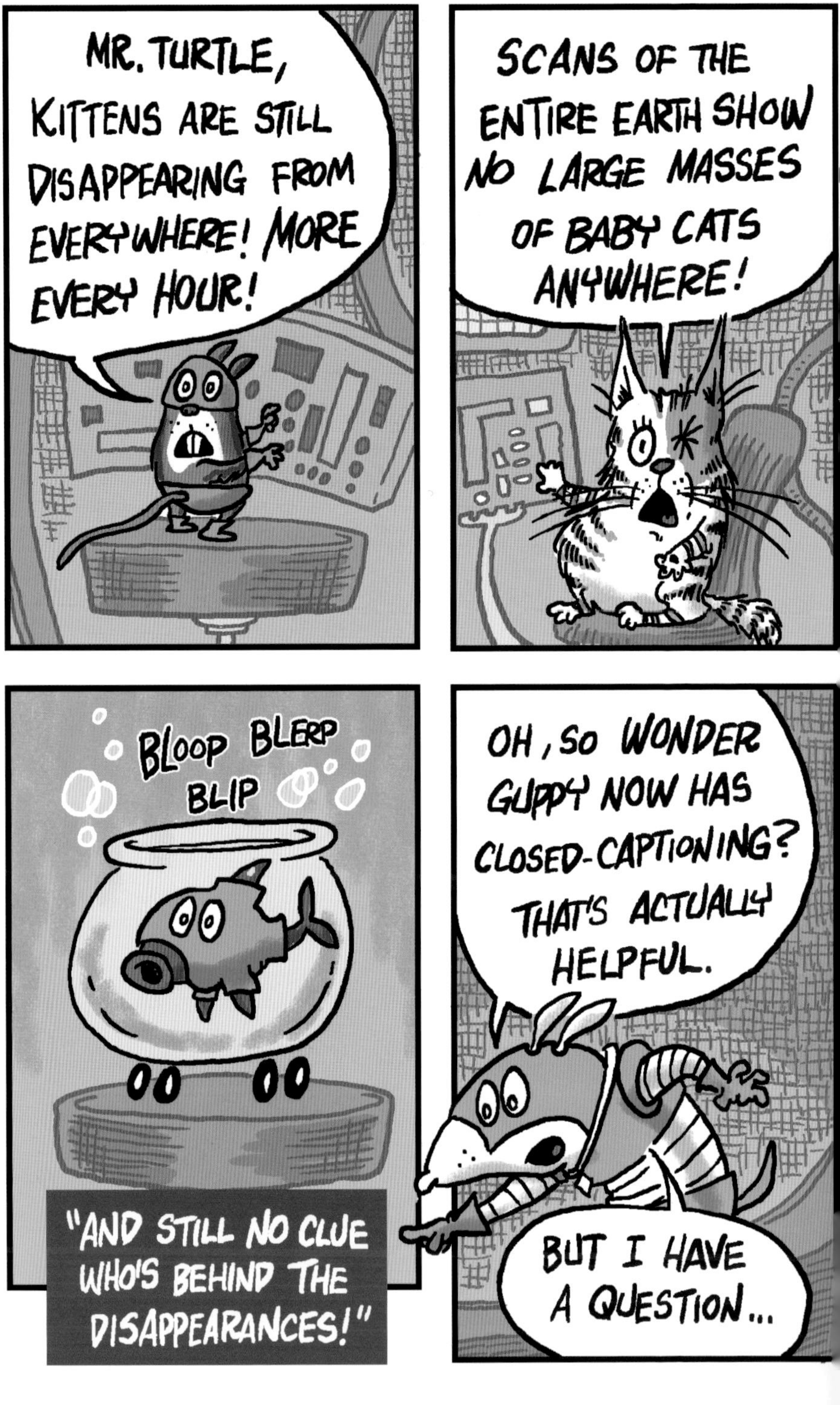
MR. TURTLE, KITTENS ARE STILL DISAPPEARING FROM EVERYWHERE! MORE EVERY HOUR!
SCANS OF THE ENTIRE EARTH SHOW NO LARGE MASSES OF BABY CATS ANYWHERE!
BLOOP BLERP BLIP
"AND STILL NO CLUE WHO'S BEHIND THE DISAPPEARANCES!"
OH, SO WONDER GUPPY NOW HAS CLOSED-CAPTIONING? THAT'S ACTUALLY HELPFUL.
BUT I HAVE A QUESTION...

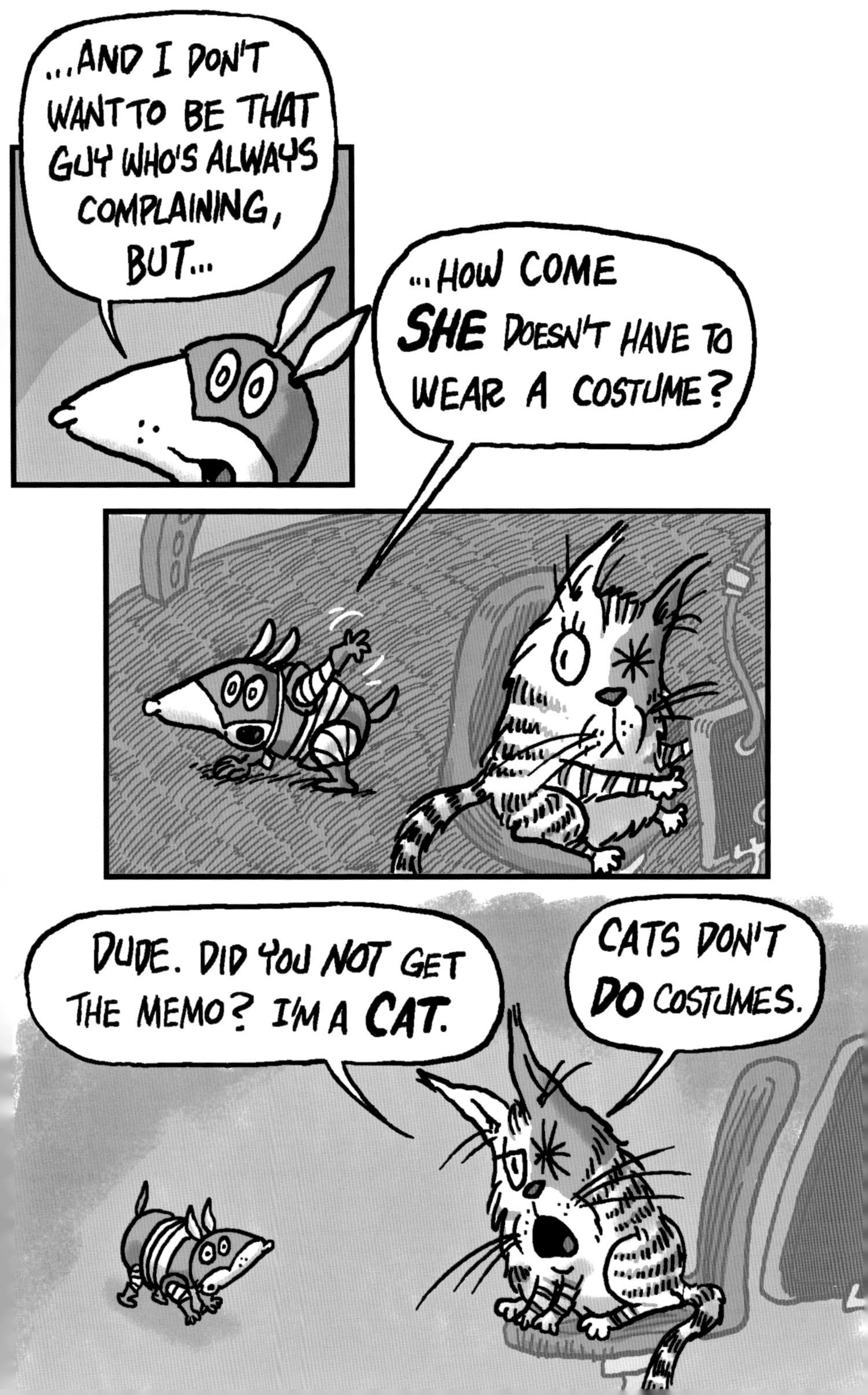
...AND I DON'T WANT TO BE THAT GUY WHO'S ALWAYS COMPLAINING, BUT...
...HOW COME SHE DOESN'T HAVE TO WEAR A COSTUME?
DUDE. DID YOU NOT GET THE MEMO? I'M A CAT.
CATS DON'T DO COSTUMES.

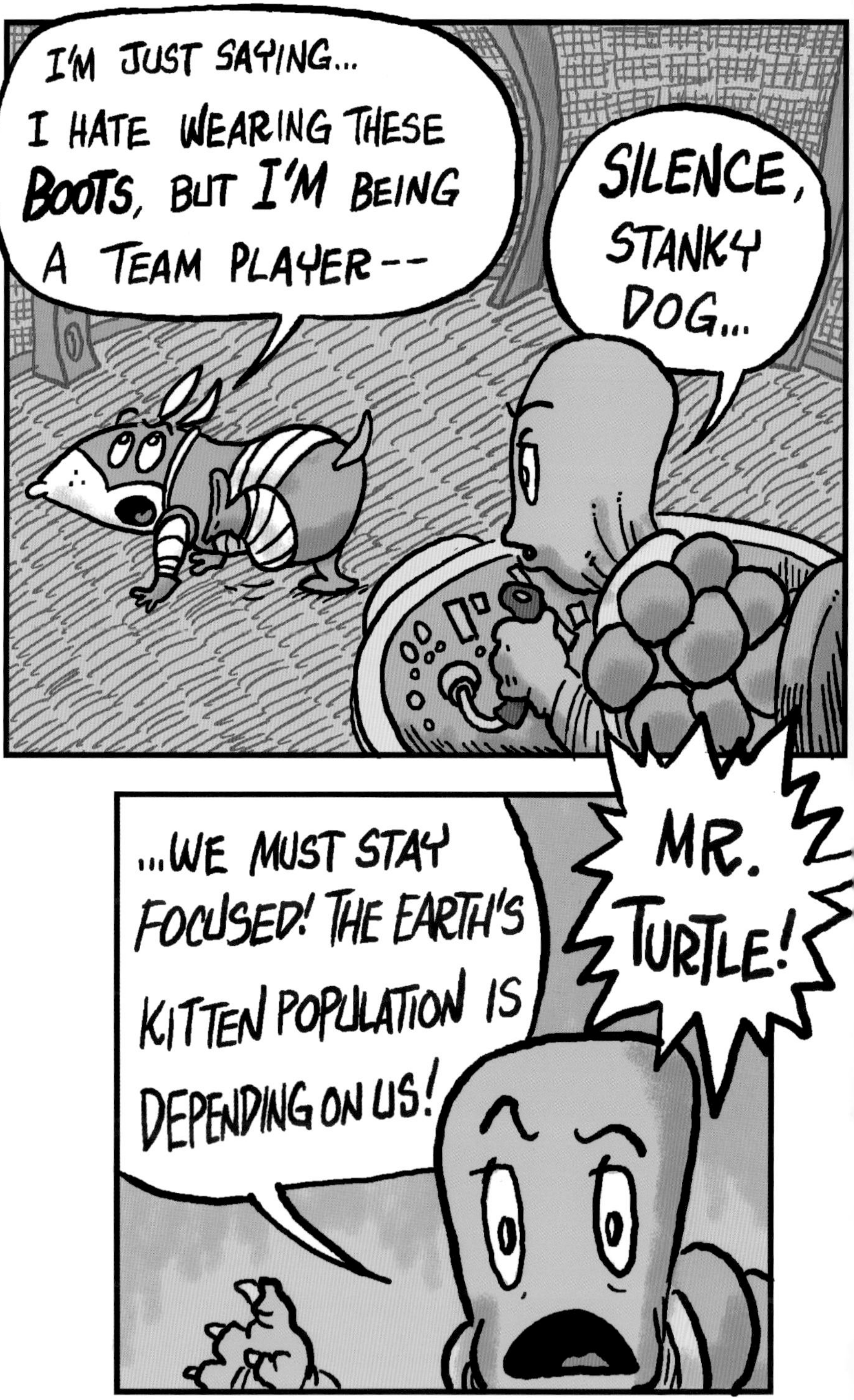
I'M JUST SAYING... I HATE WEARING THESE BOOTS, BUT I'M BEING A TEAM PLAYER--
SILENCE, STANKY DOG...
...WE MUST STAY FOCUSED! THE EARTH'S KITTEN POPULATION IS DEPENDING ON US!
MR. TURTLE!

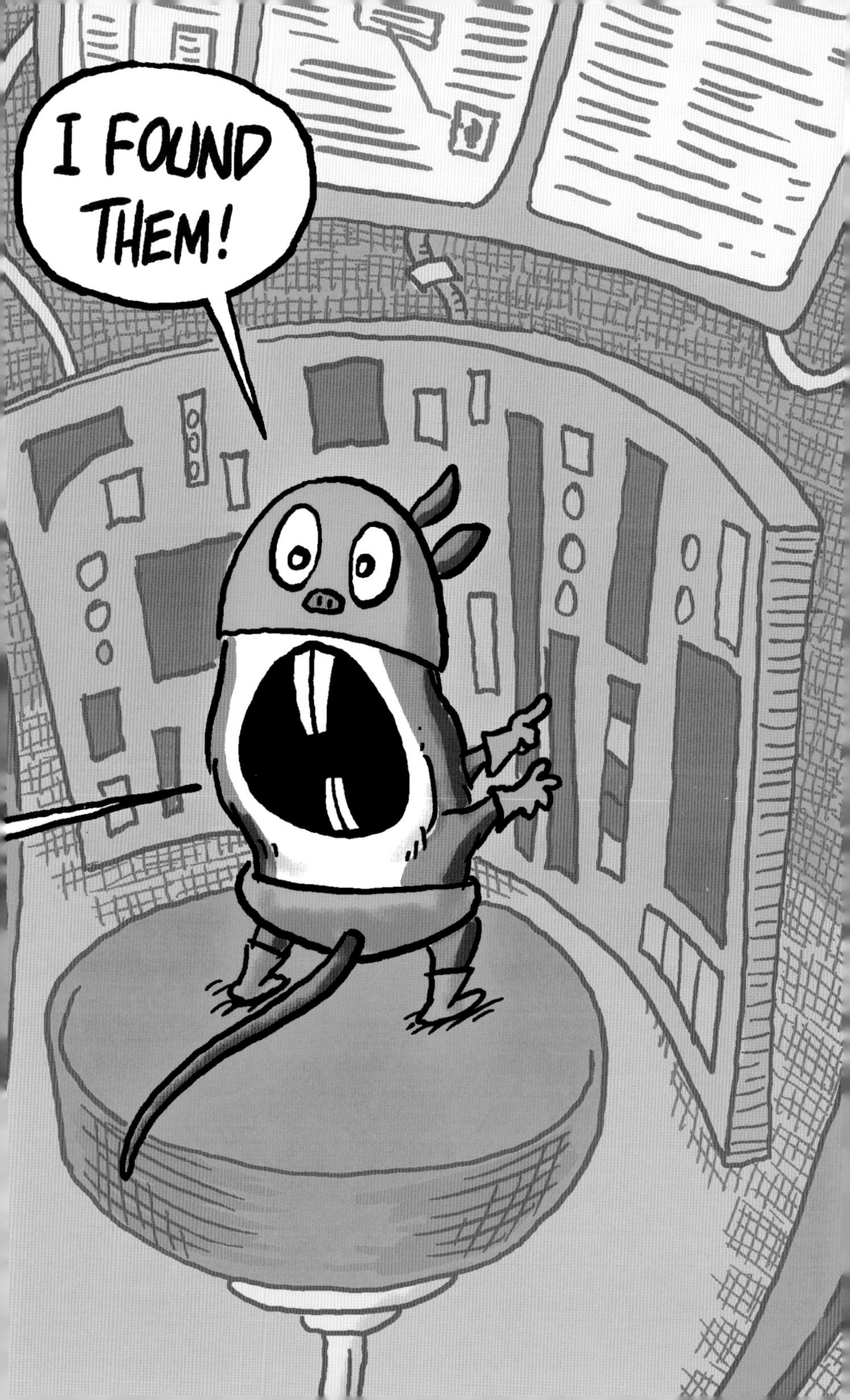
I FOUND THEM!

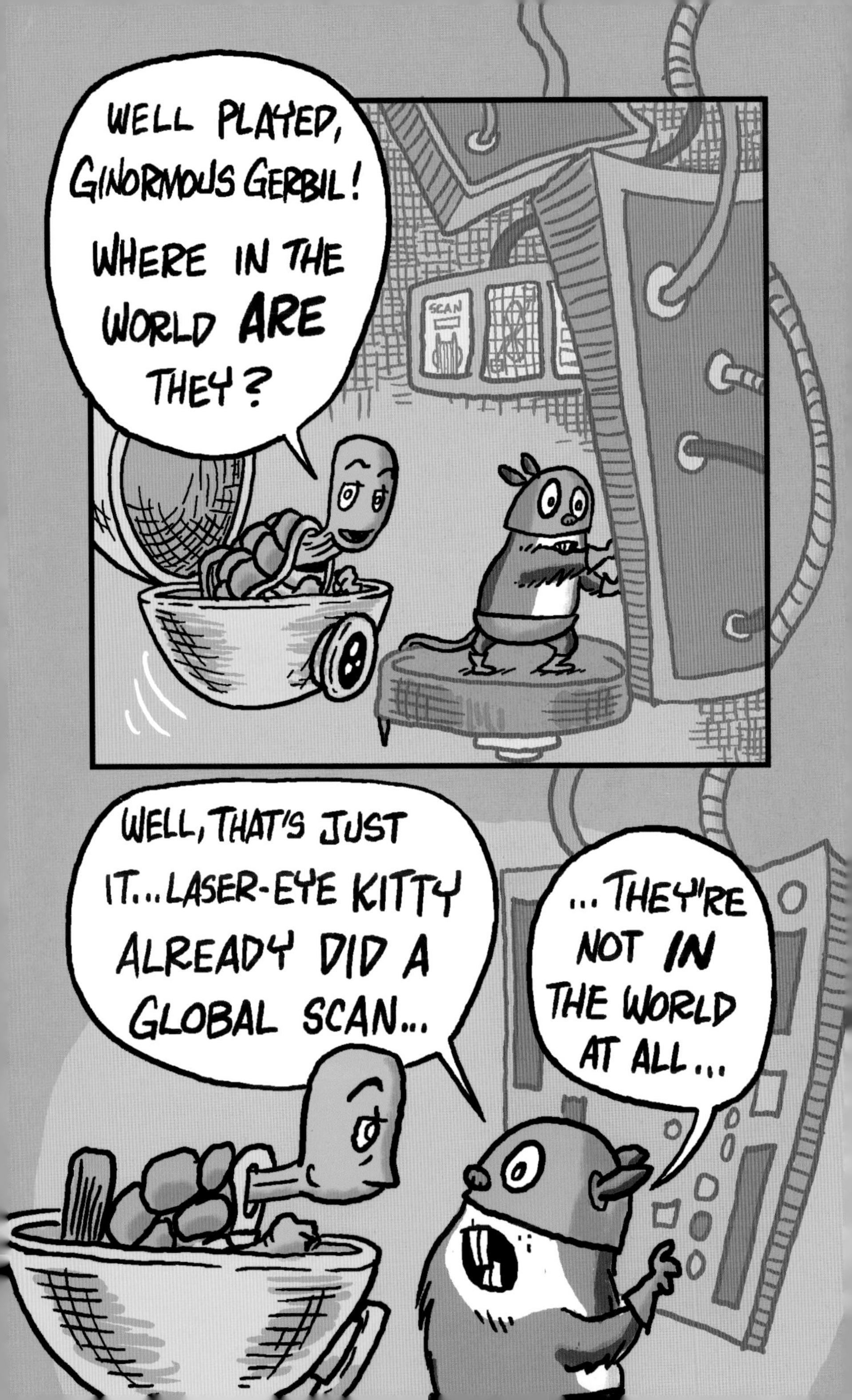
WELL PLAYED, GINORMOUS GERBIL! WHERE IN THE WORLD ARE THEY?
SCAN
WELL, THAT'S JUST IT...LASER-EYE KITTY ALREADY DID A GLOBAL SCAN...
...THEY'RE NOT IN THE WORLD AT ALL...

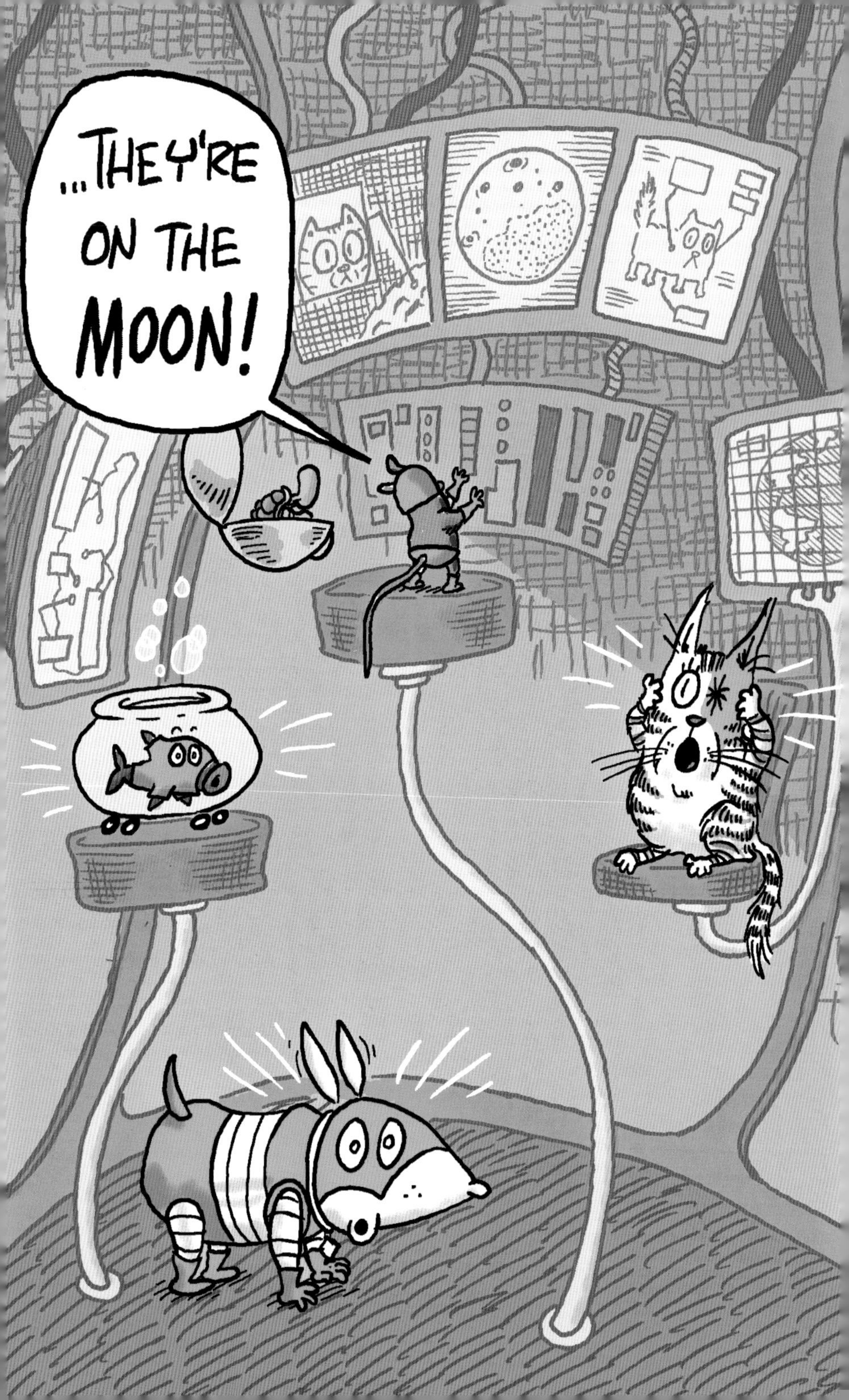
...THEY'RE ON THE MOON!

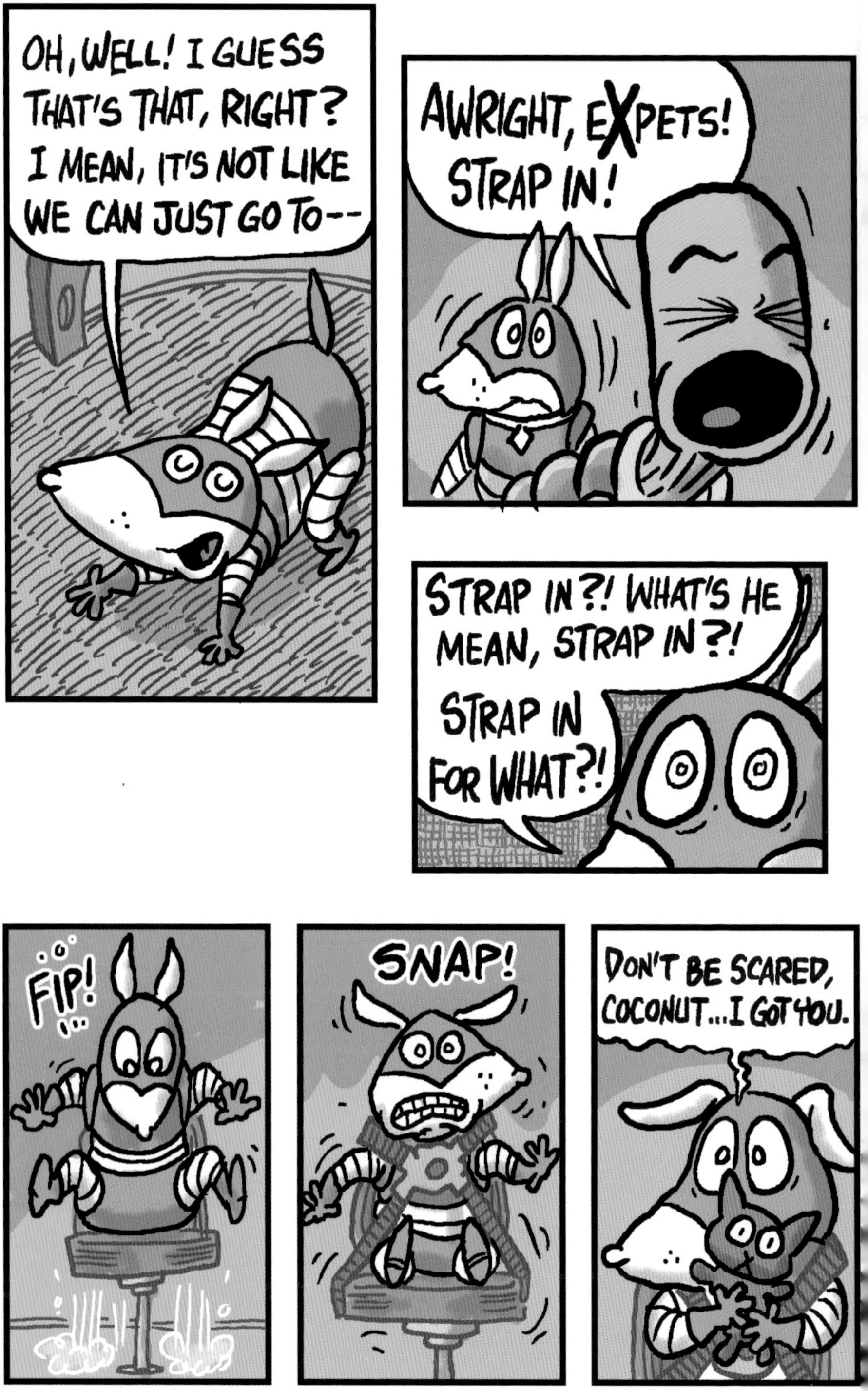
OH, WELL! I GUESS THAT'S THAT, RIGHT? I MEAN, IT'S NOT LIKE WE CAN JUST GO TO--
AWRIGHT, EXPETS! STRAP IN!
STRAP IN?! WHAT'S HE MEAN, STRAP IN?!
STRAP IN FOR WHAT?!
FIP!
SNAP!
DON'T BE SCARED, COCONUT...I GOT YOU.

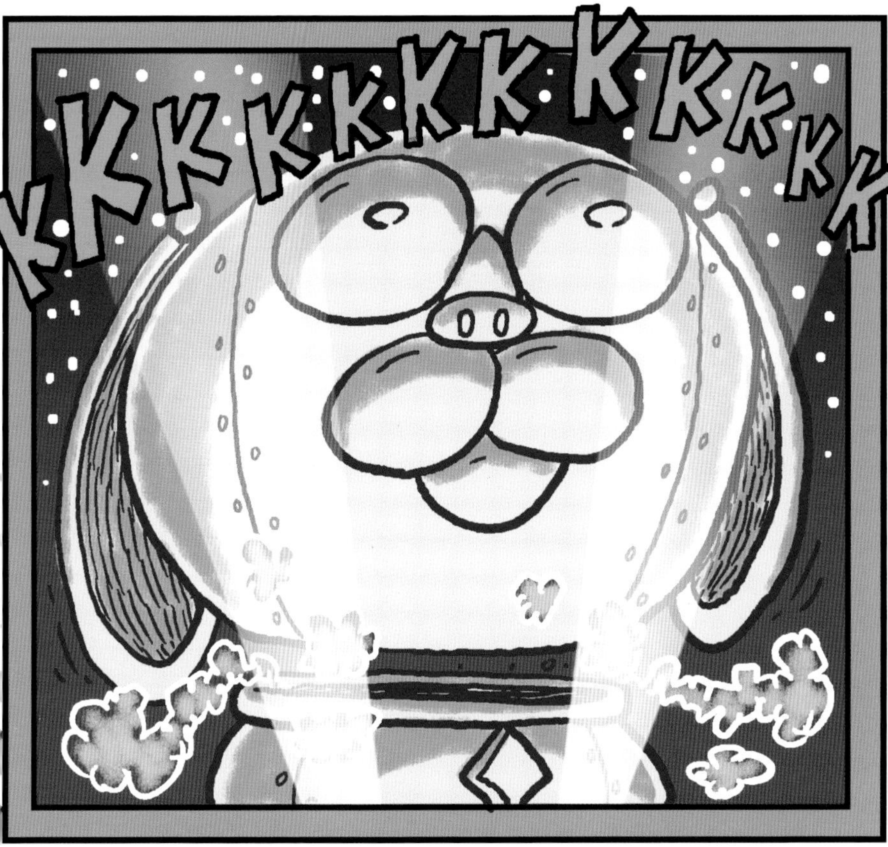
KKKKKKKKKKKKKK

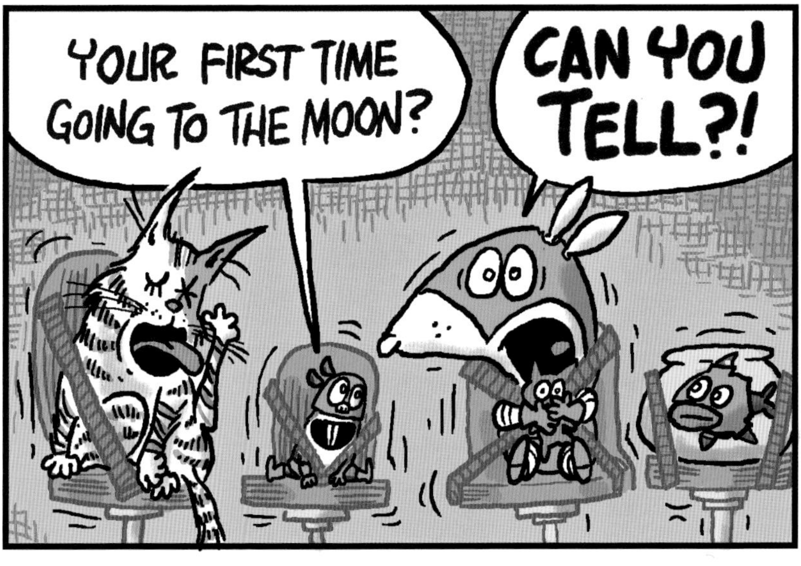
YOUR FIRST TIME GOING TO THE MOON?
CAN YOU TELL?!

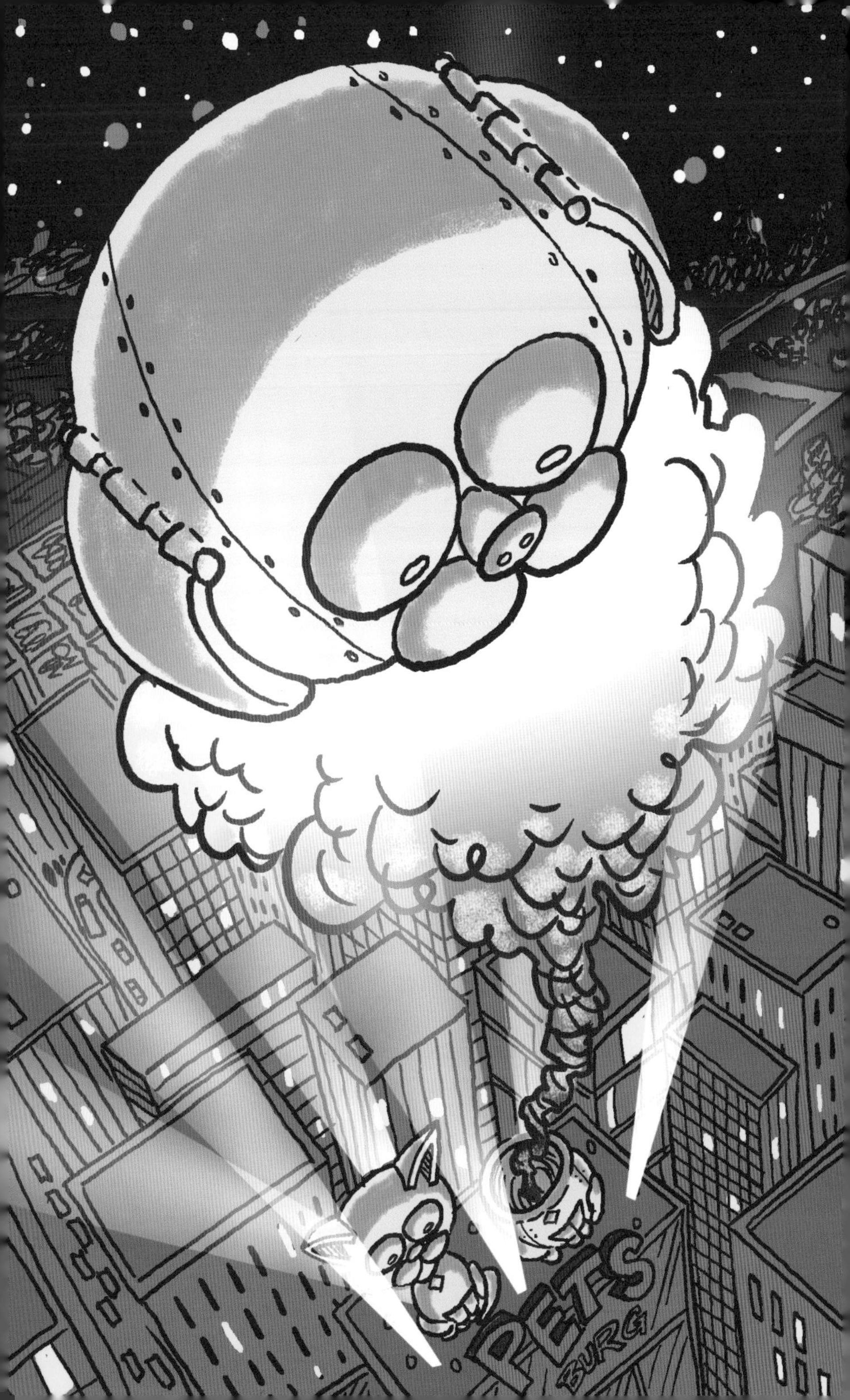
PETS
BURG

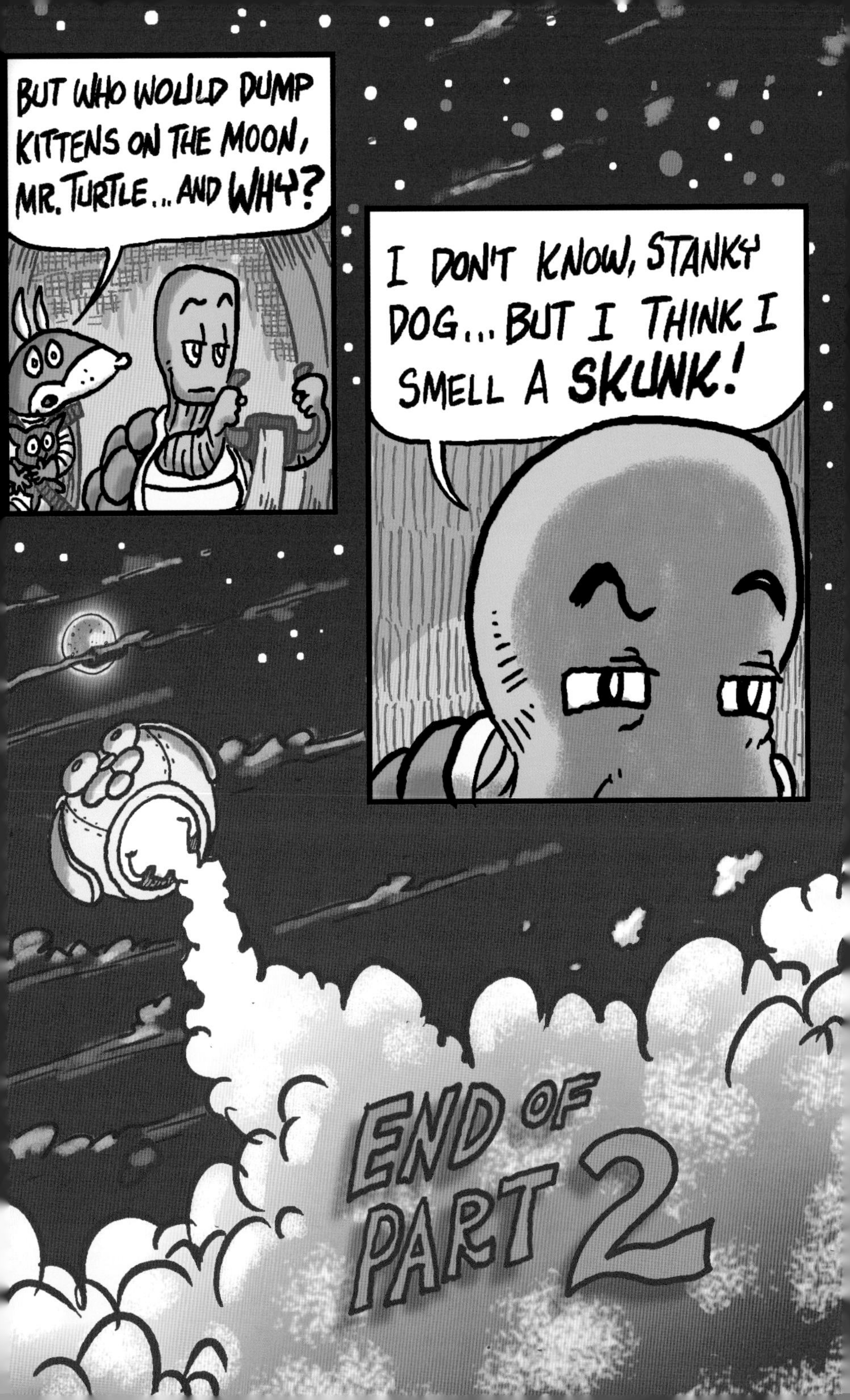
BUT WHO WOULD DUMP KITTENS ON THE MOON, MR. TURTLE... AND WHY?
I DON'T KNOW, STANKY DOG... BUT I THINK I SMELL A SKUNK!
END OF PART 2

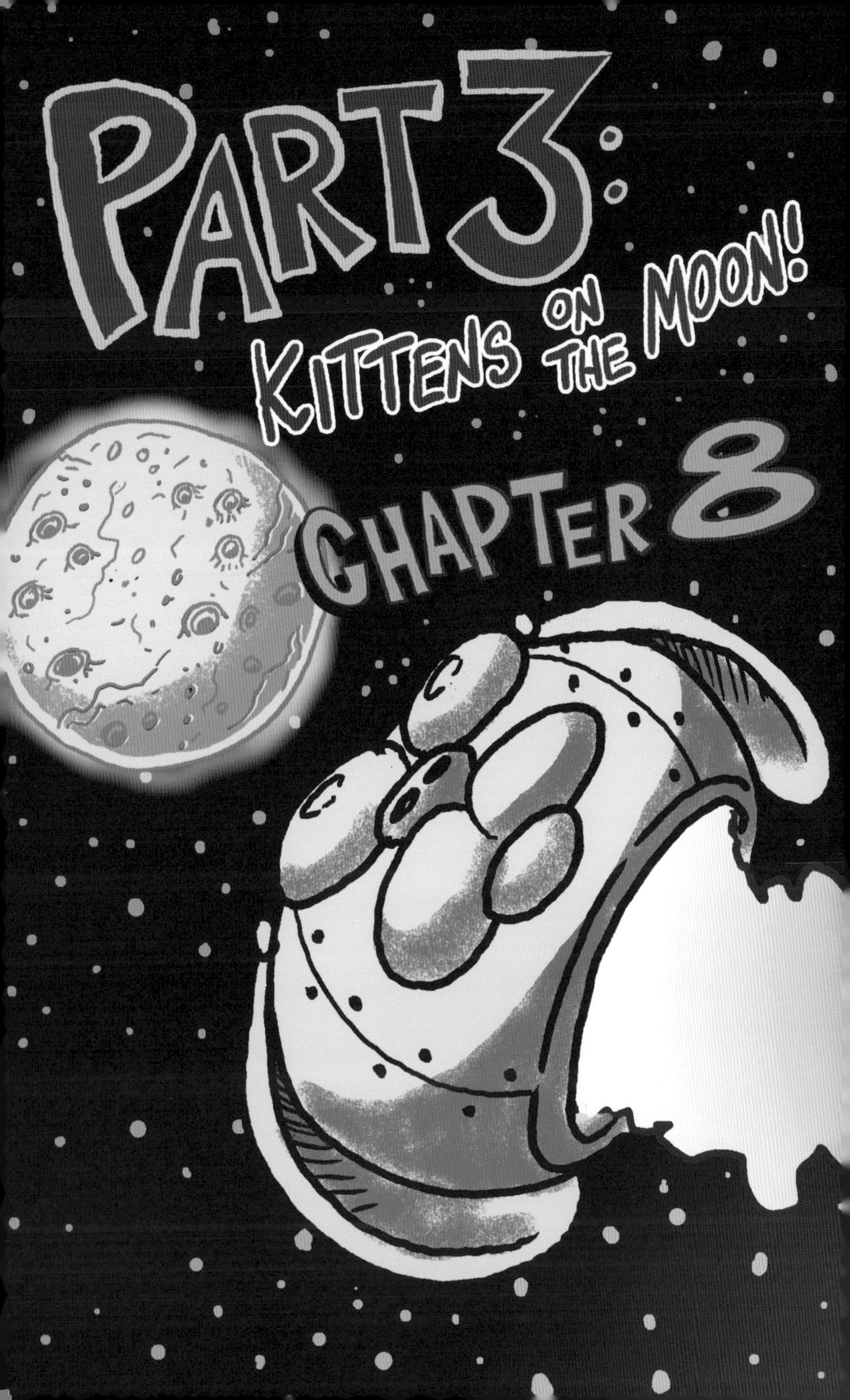
PART 3:
KITTENS ON THE MOON!
CHAPTER 8

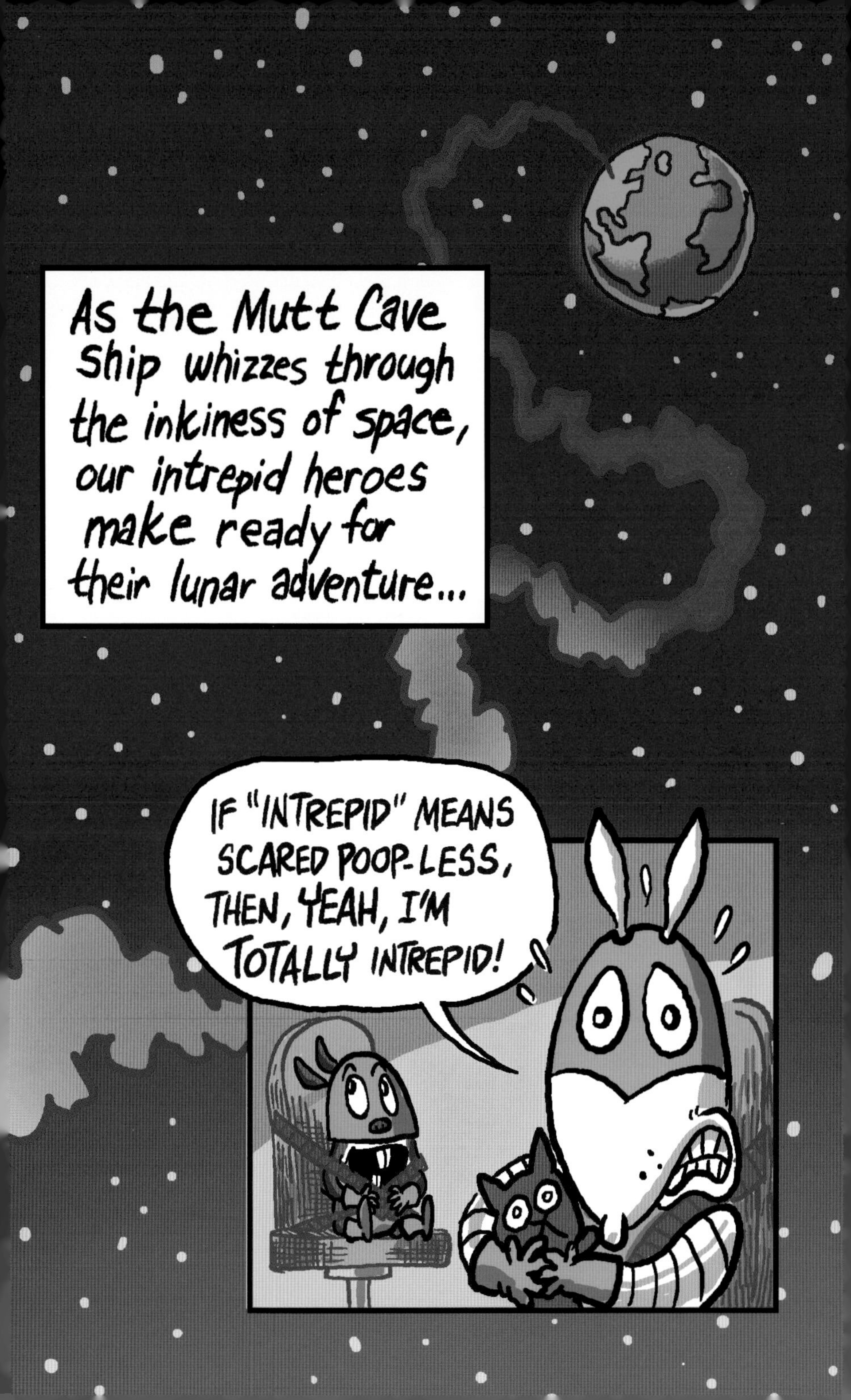
As the Mutt Cave Ship whizzes through the inkiness of space, our intrepid heroes make ready for their lunar adventure...
IF "INTREPID" MEANS SCARED POOP-LESS, THEN, YEAH, I'M TOTALLY INTREPID!

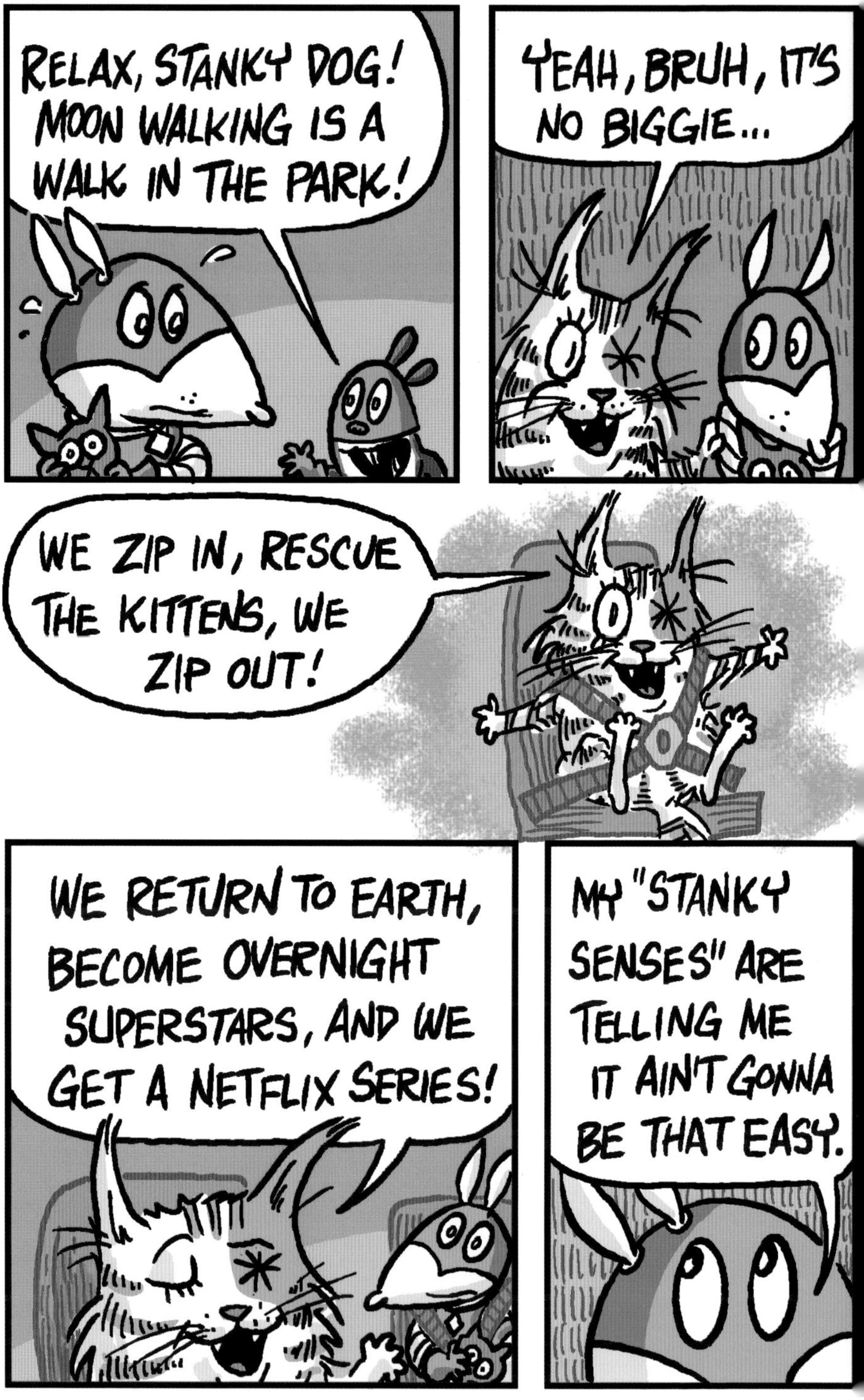
RELAX, STANKY DOG! MOON WALKING IS A WALK IN THE PARK!
YEAH, BRUH, IT'S NO BIGGIE...
WE ZIP IN, RESCUE THE KITTENS, WE ZIP OUT!
WE RETURN TO EARTH, BECOME OVERNIGHT SUPERSTARS, AND WE GET A NETFLIX SERIES!
MY "STANKY SENSES" ARE TELLING ME IT AIN'T GONNA BE THAT EASY.

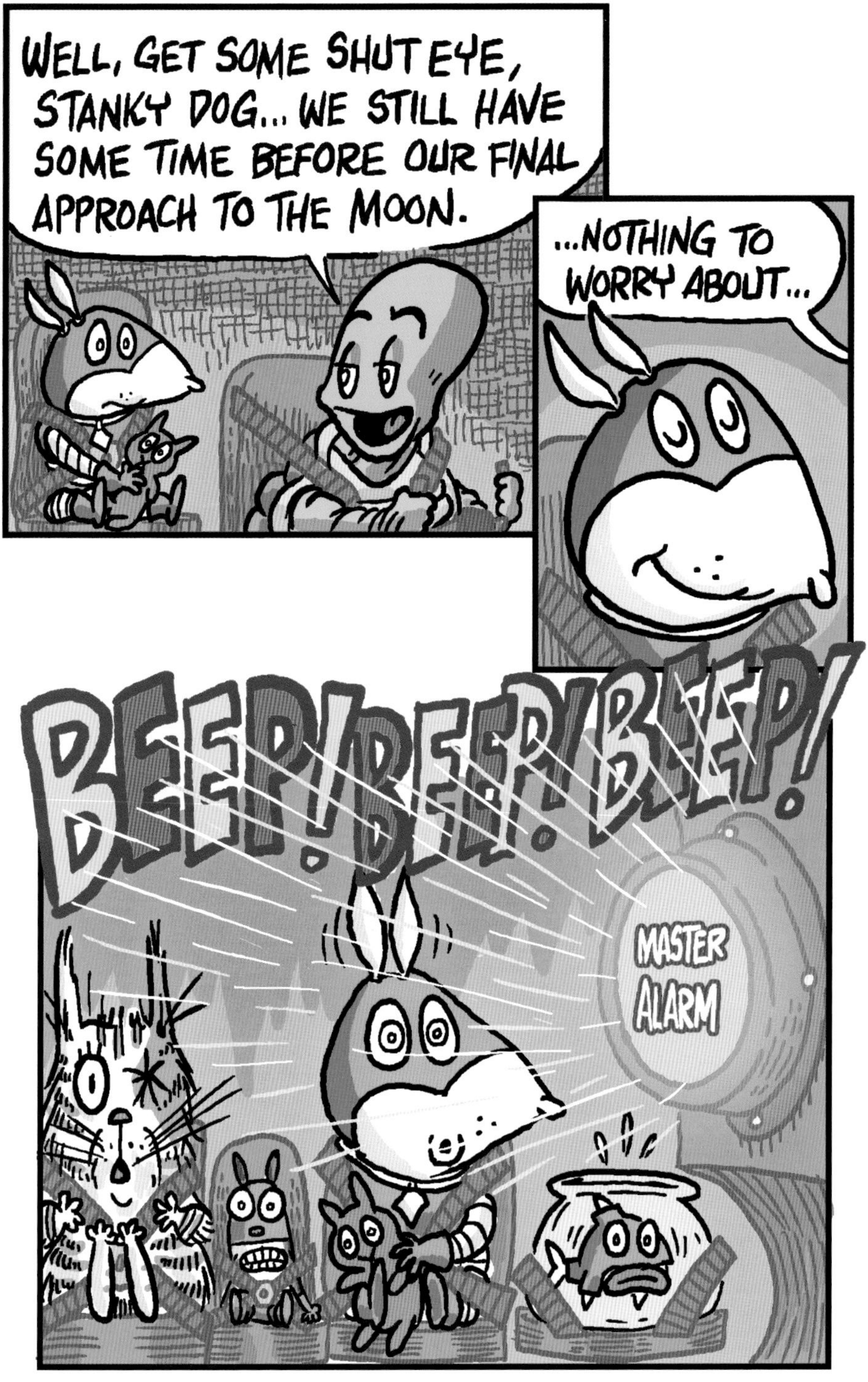
WELL, GET SOME SHUT EYE, STANKY DOG... WE STILL HAVE SOME TIME BEFORE OUR FINAL APPROACH TO THE MOON.
...NOTHING TO WORRY ABOUT...
BEEP! BEEP! BEEP!
MASTER ALARM

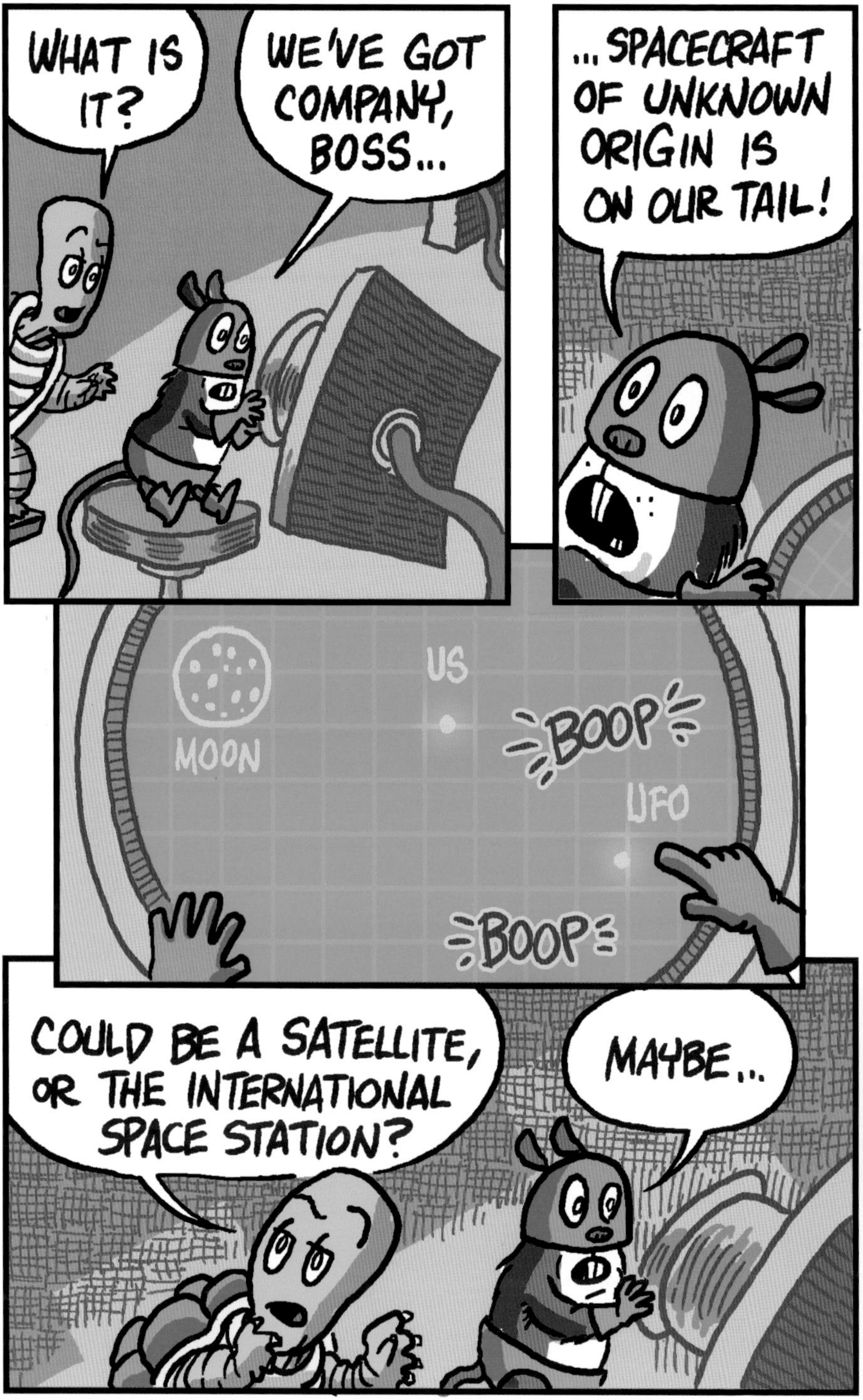
WHAT IS IT?
WE'VE GOT COMPANY, BOSS...
...SPACECRAFT OF UNKNOWN ORIGIN IS ON OUR TAIL!
MOON
US
BOOP
UFO
BOOP
COULD BE A SATELLITE, OR THE INTERNATIONAL SPACE STATION?
MAYBE...

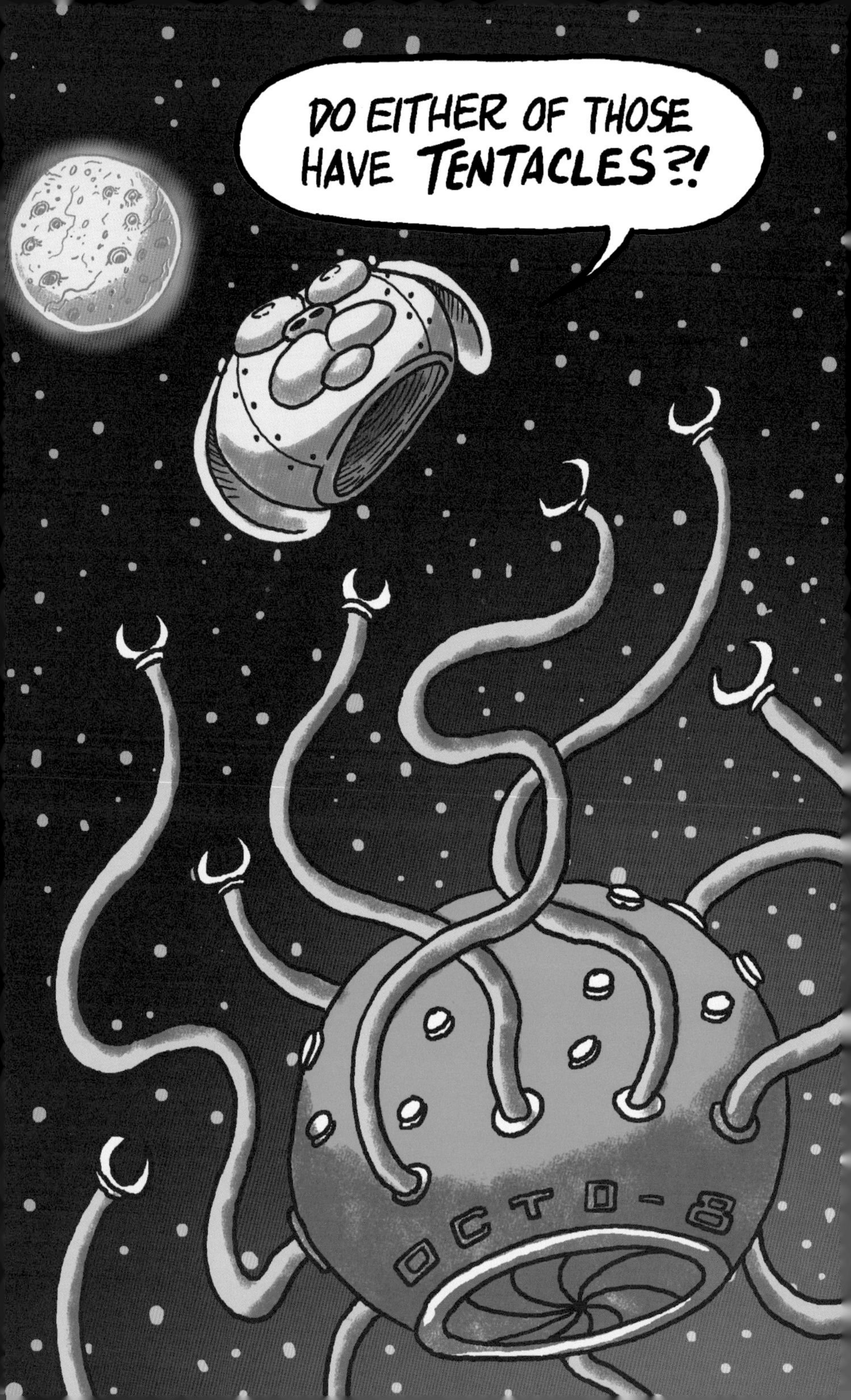
DO EITHER OF THOSE HAVE TENTACLES?!
OCTO-8

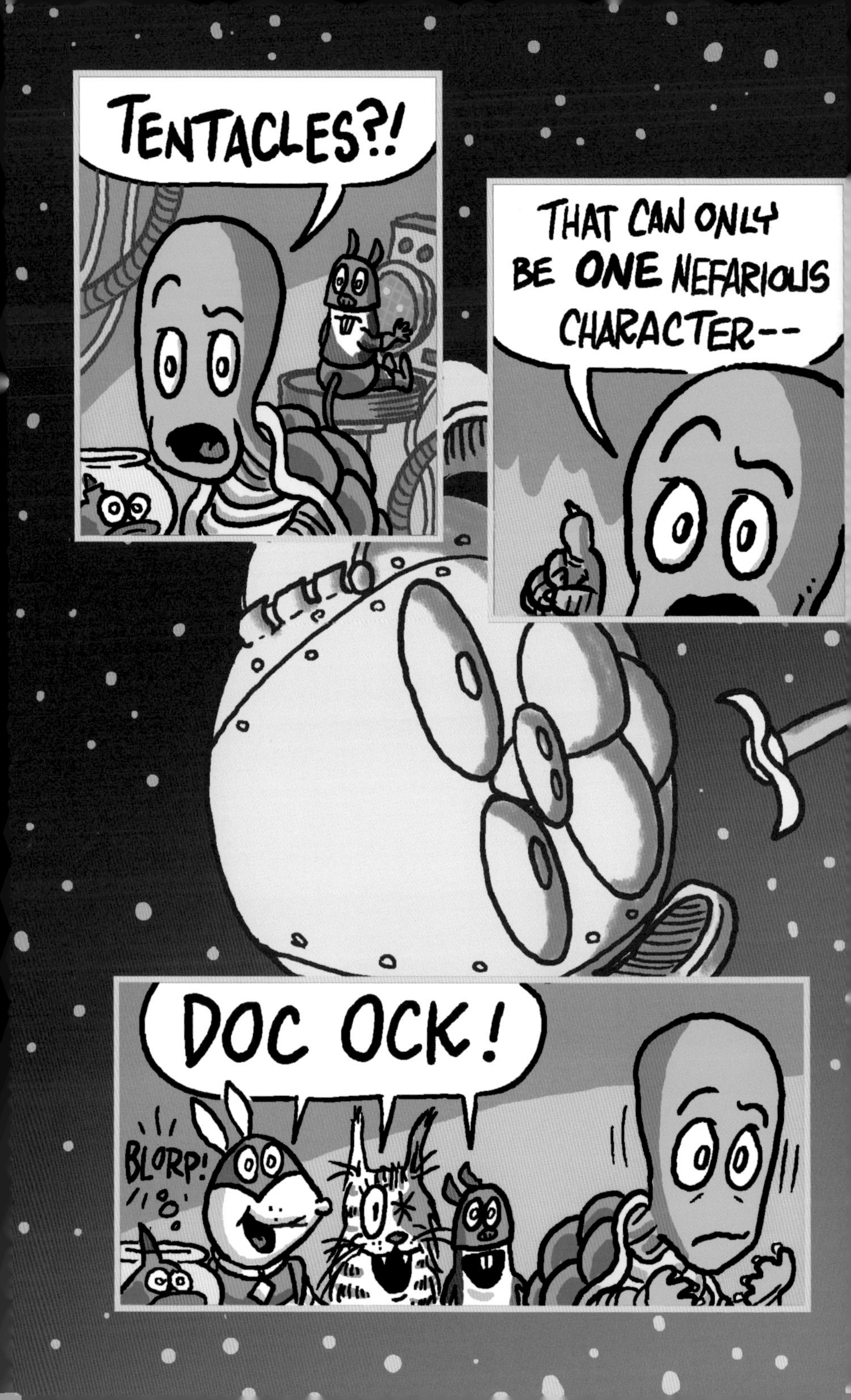
TENTACLES?!
THAT CAN ONLY BE ONE NEFARIOUS CHARACTER--
DOC OCK!
BLORP!

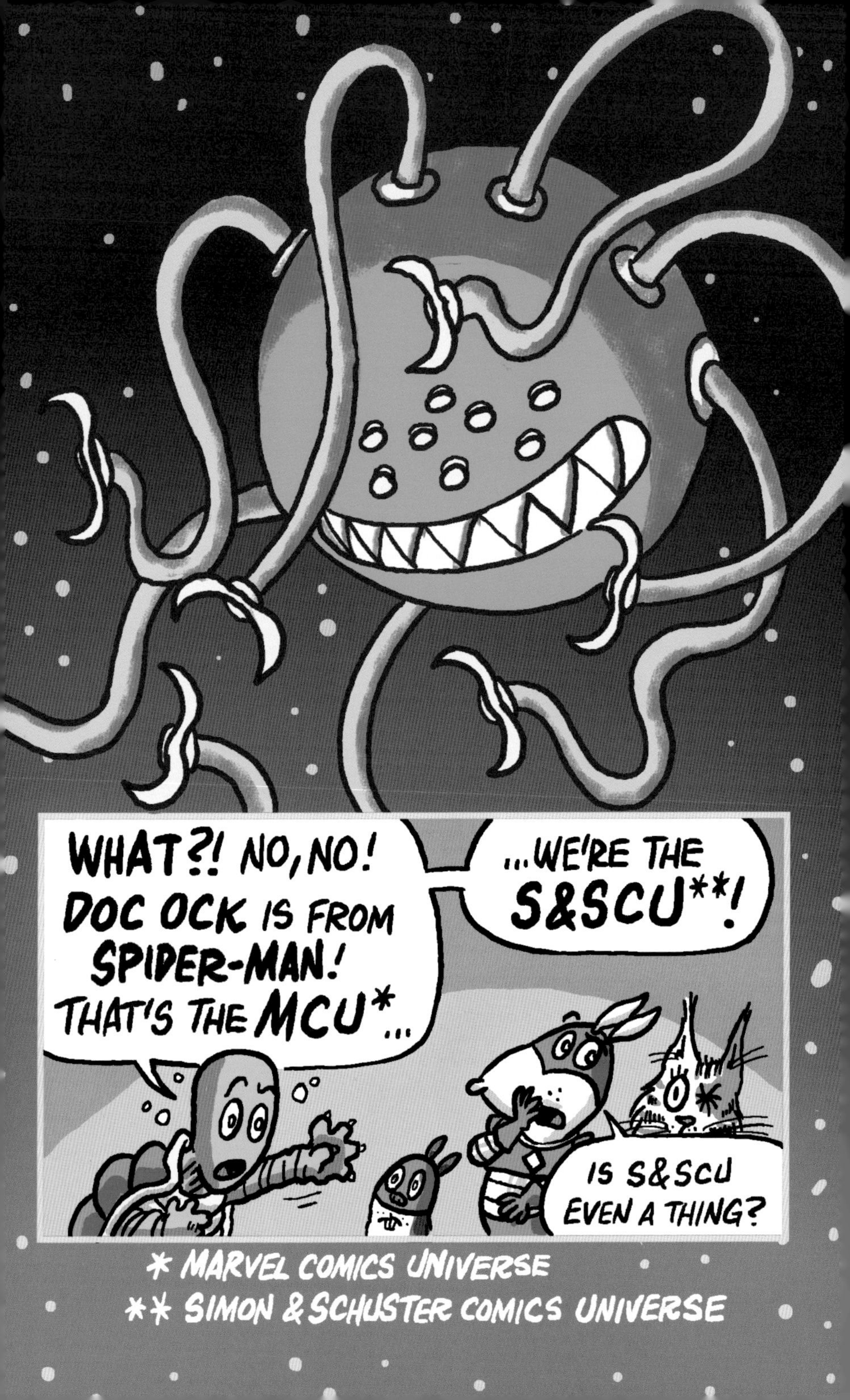
WHAT?! NO, NO! DOC OCK IS FROM SPIDER-MAN! THAT'S THE MCU*...
...WE'RE THE S&SCU**!
IS S&SCU EVEN A THING?

* MARVEL COMICS UNIVERSE

** SIMON & SCHUSTER COMICS UNIVERSE

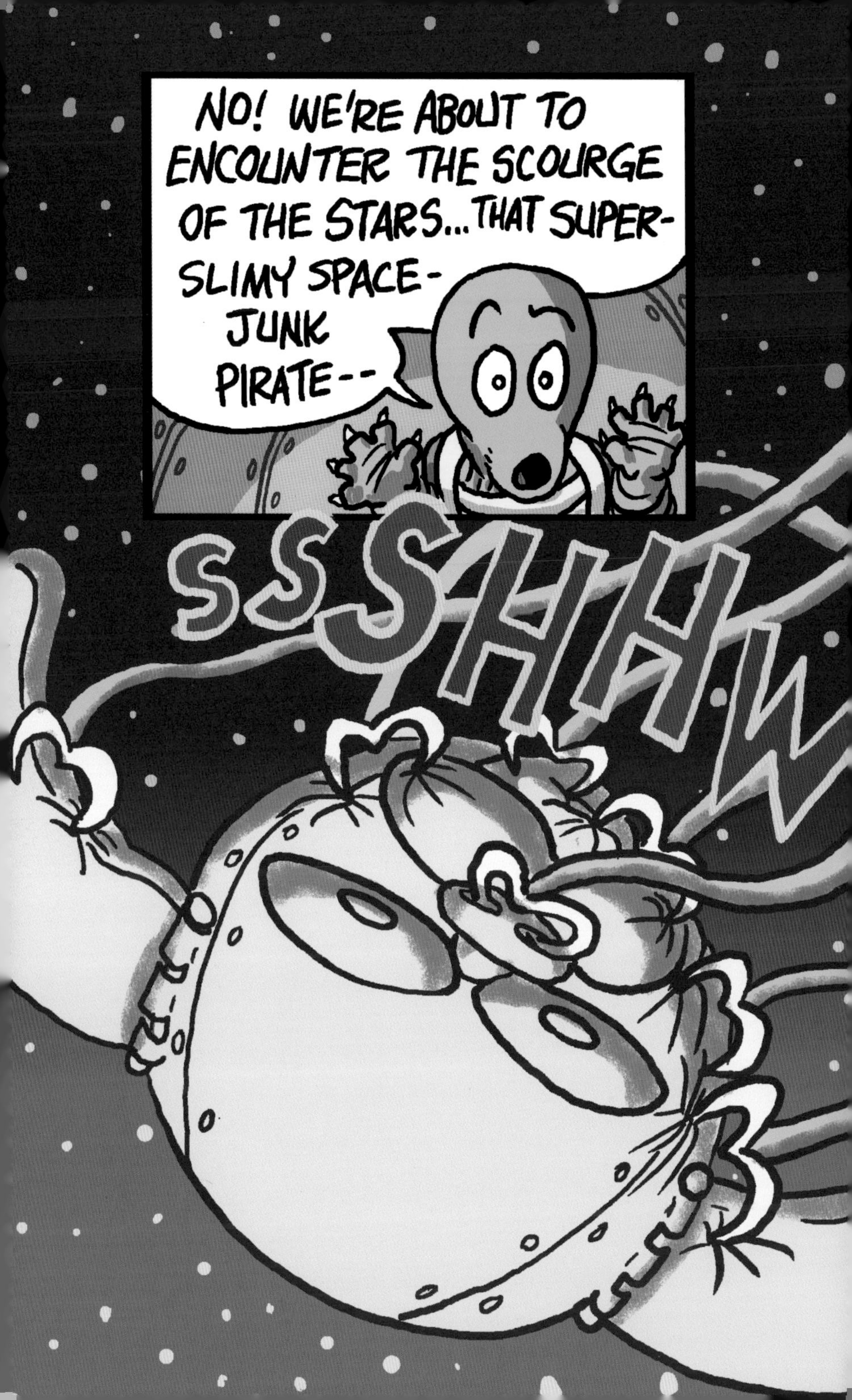
NO! WE'RE ABOUT TO ENCOUNTER THE SCOURGE OF THE STARS... THAT SUPER-SLIMY SPACE-JUNK PIRATE--
SSSHHHW

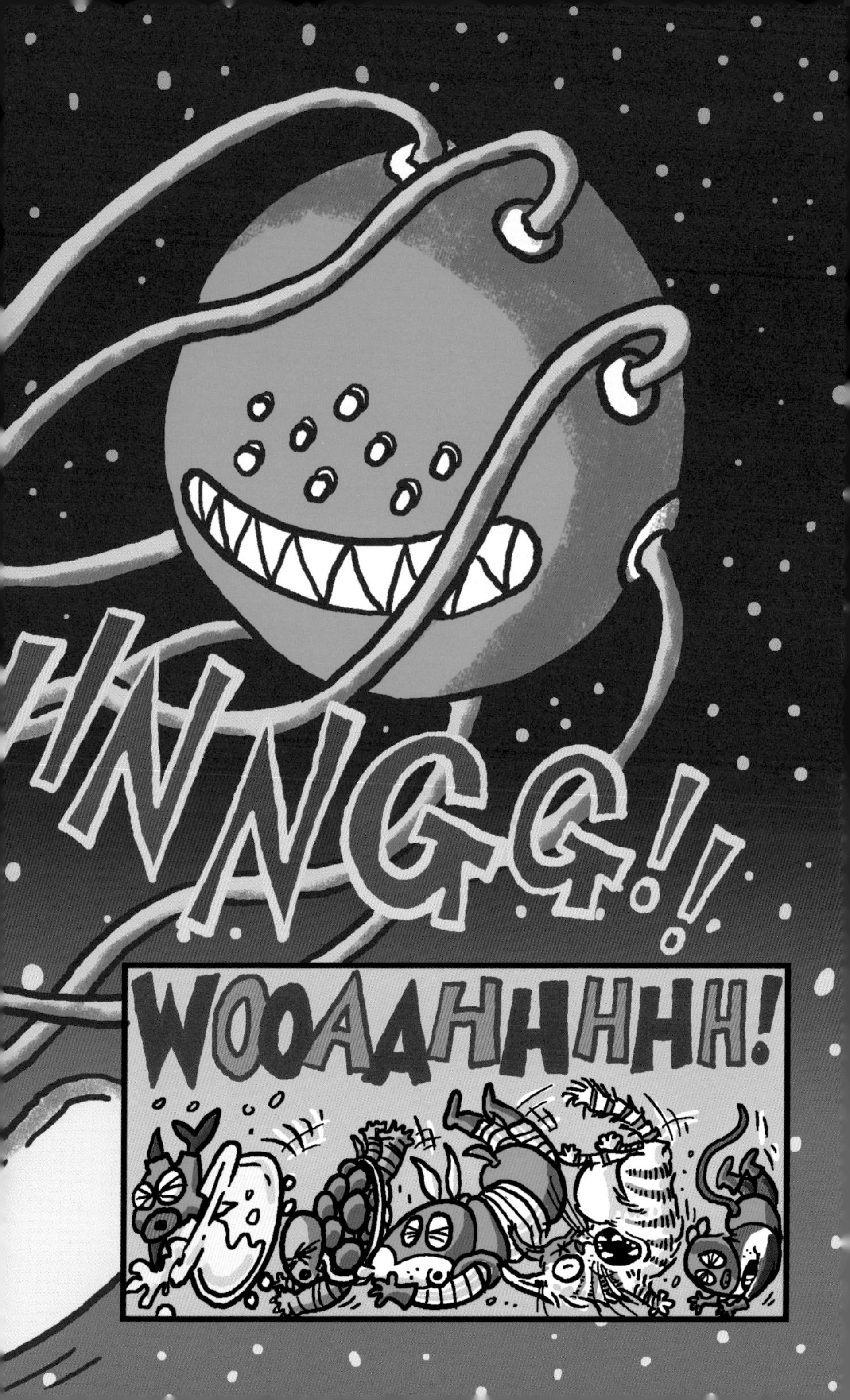
NANGG!!
WOOAAHHHHH!

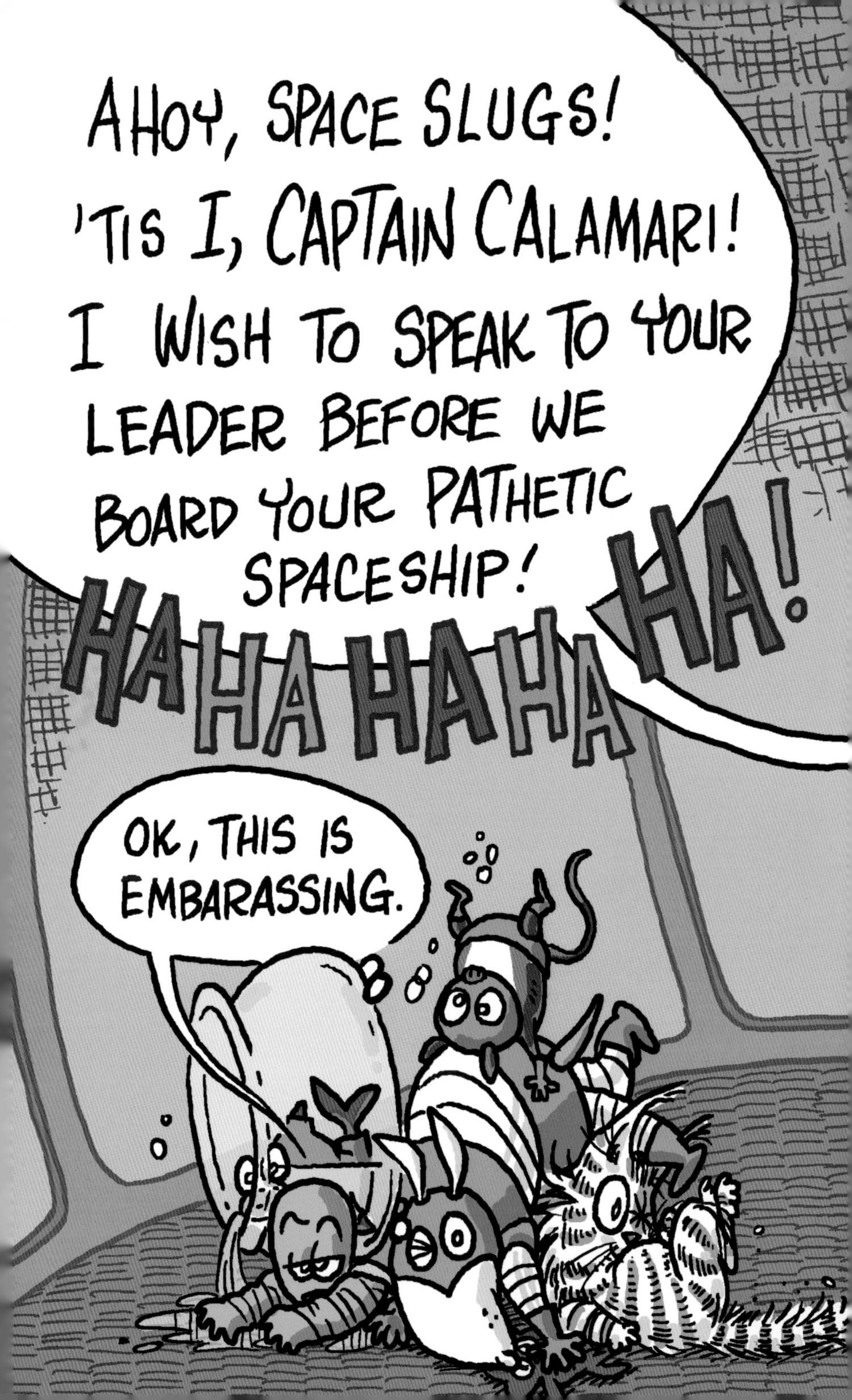
AHOY, SPACE SLUGS! 'TIS I, CAPTAIN CALAMARI! I WISH TO SPEAK TO YOUR LEADER BEFORE WE BOARD YOUR PATHETIC SPACESHIP!
HAHA HAHA HA!
OK, THIS IS EMBARASSING.

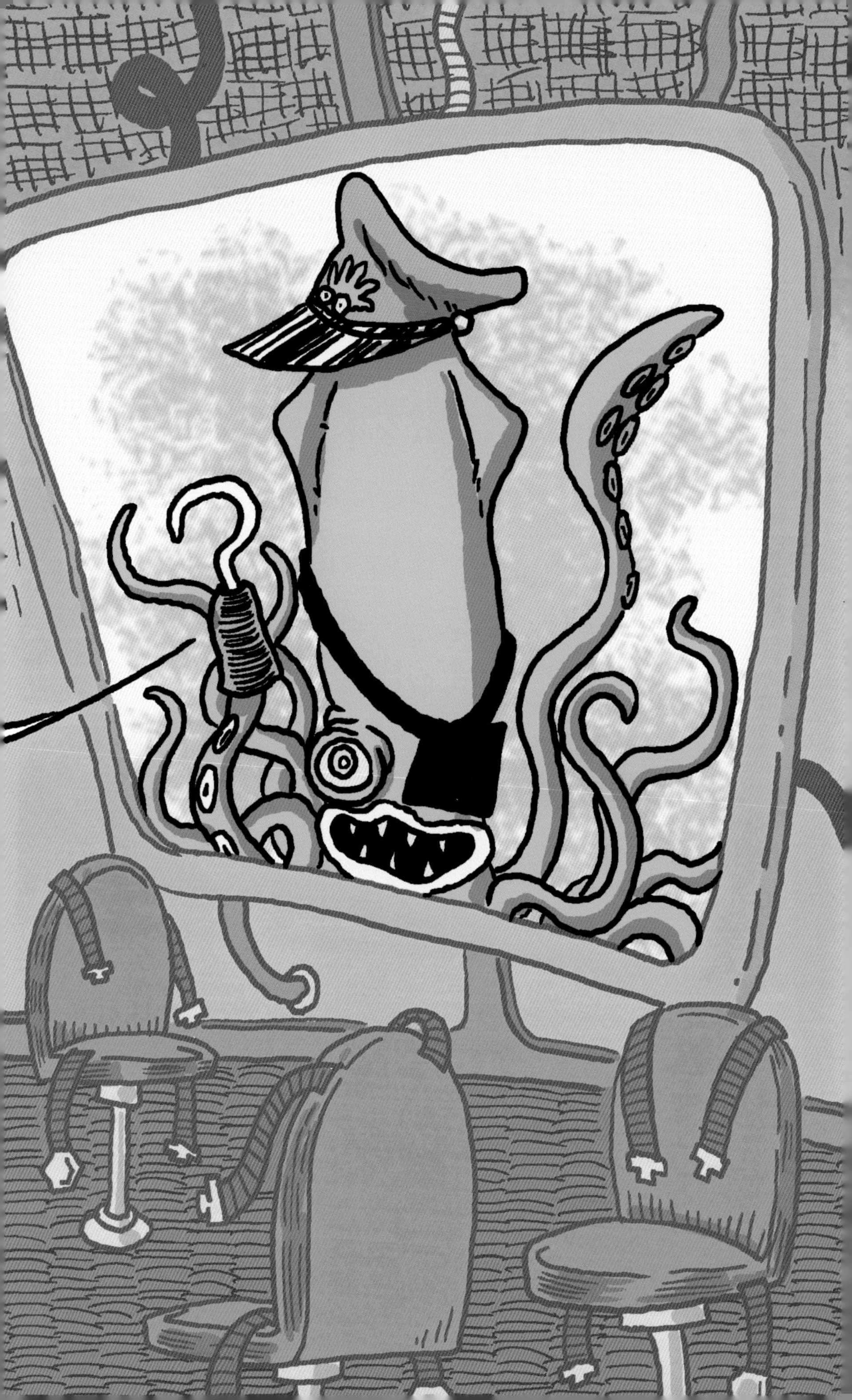

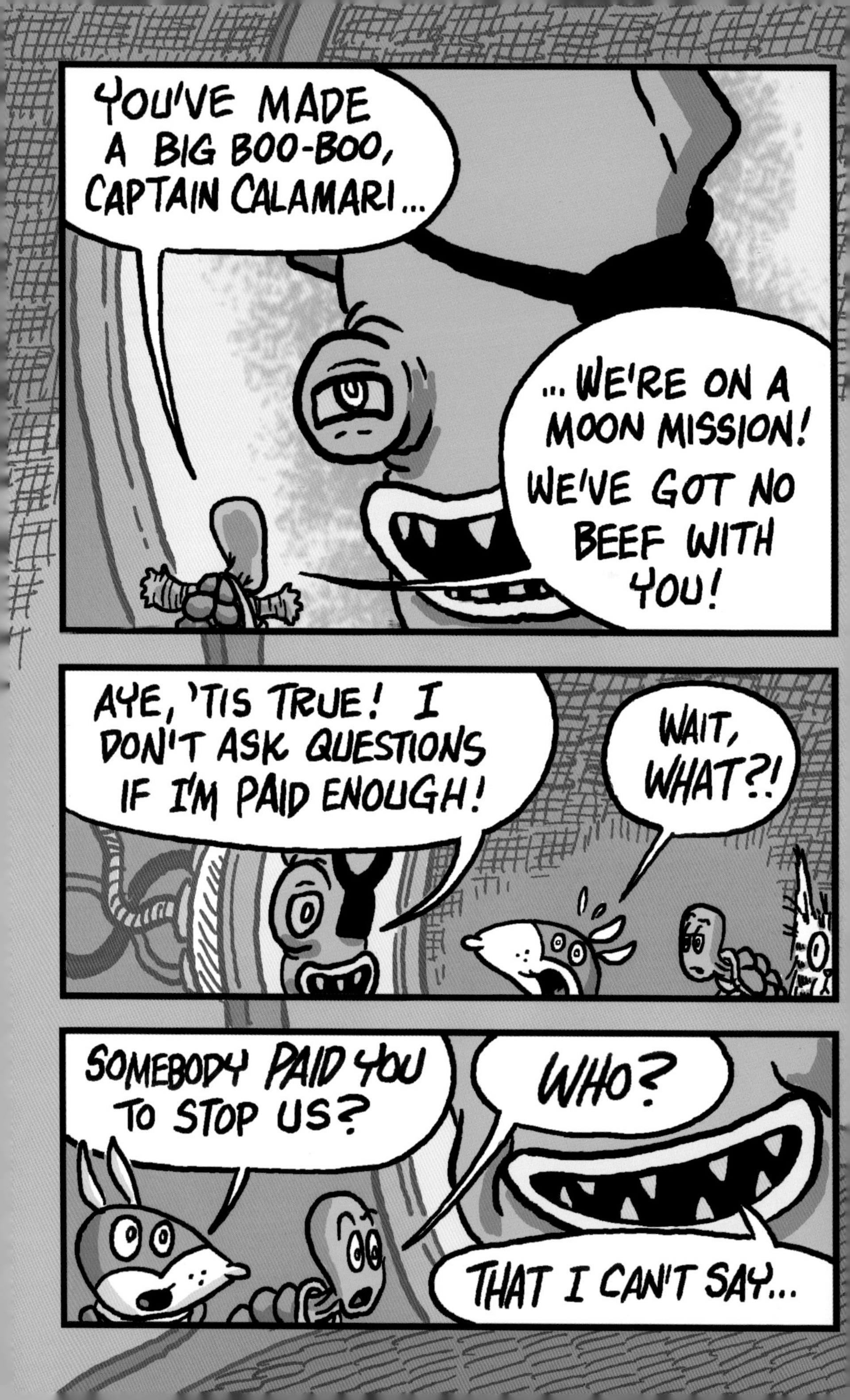
YOU'VE MADE A BIG BOO-BOO, CAPTAIN CALAMARI...
...WE'RE ON A MOON MISSION!
WE'VE GOT NO BEEF WITH YOU!
AYE, 'TIS TRUE! I DON'T ASK QUESTIONS IF I'M PAID ENOUGH!
WAIT, WHAT?!
SOMEBODY PAID YOU TO STOP US?
WHO?
THAT I CAN'T SAY...

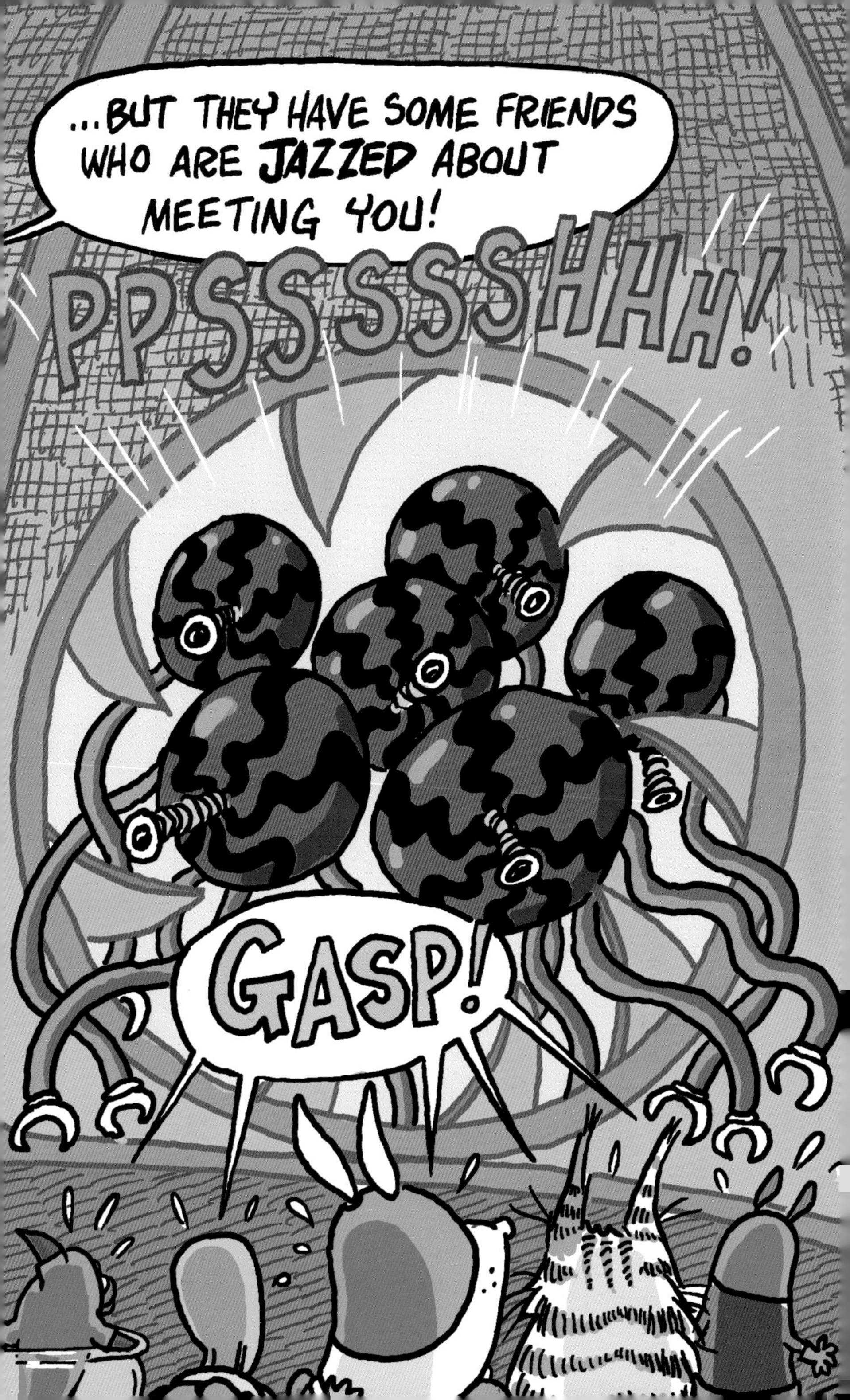
...BUT THEY HAVE SOME FRIENDS WHO ARE JAZZED ABOUT MEETING YOU!
PPSSSSSSHHH!
GASP!

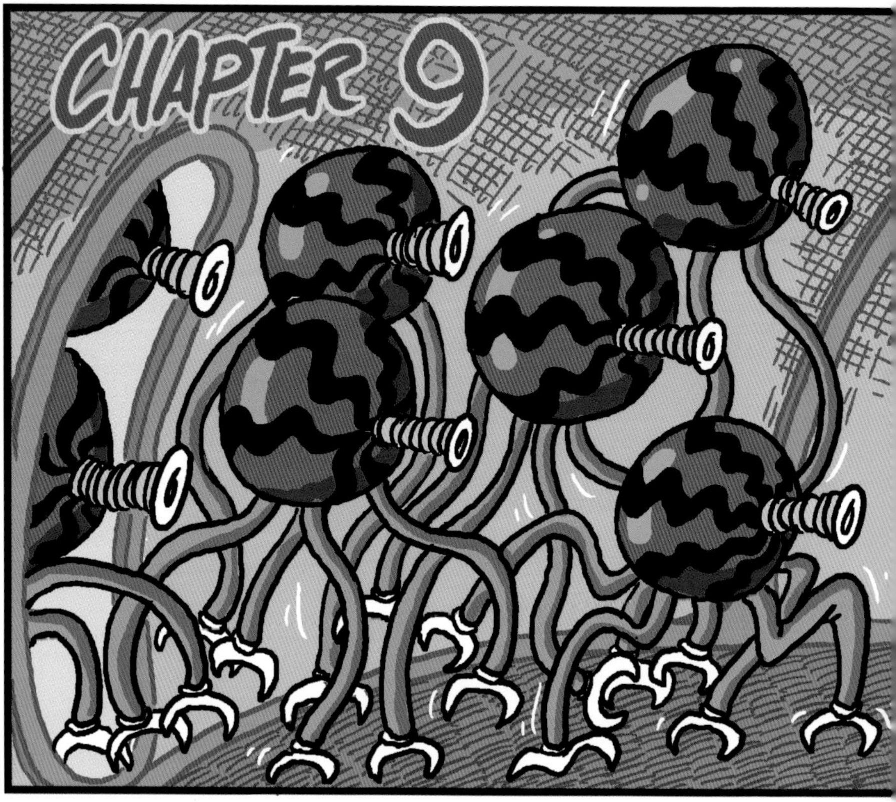
CHAPTER 9

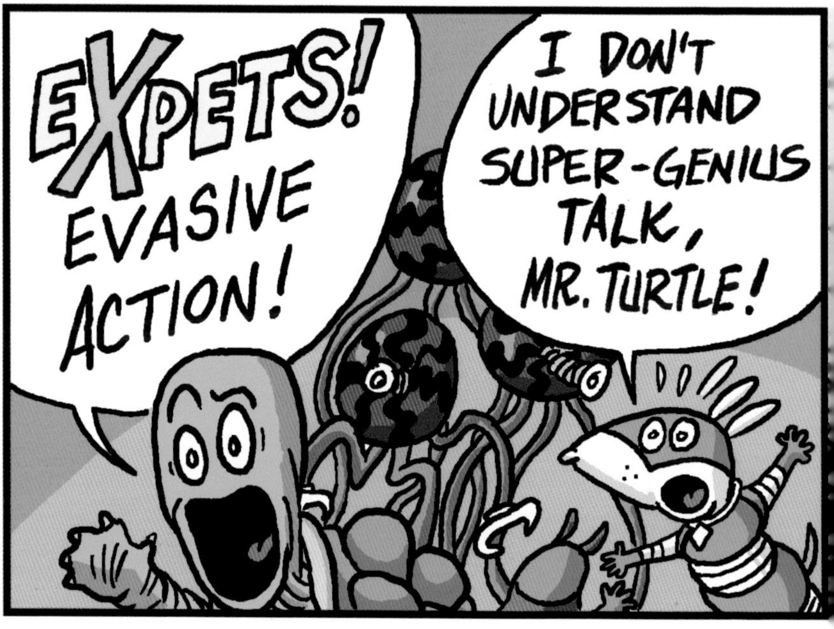
EXPETS! EVASIVE ACTION!
I DON'T UNDERSTAND SUPER-GENIUS TALK, MR. TURTLE!

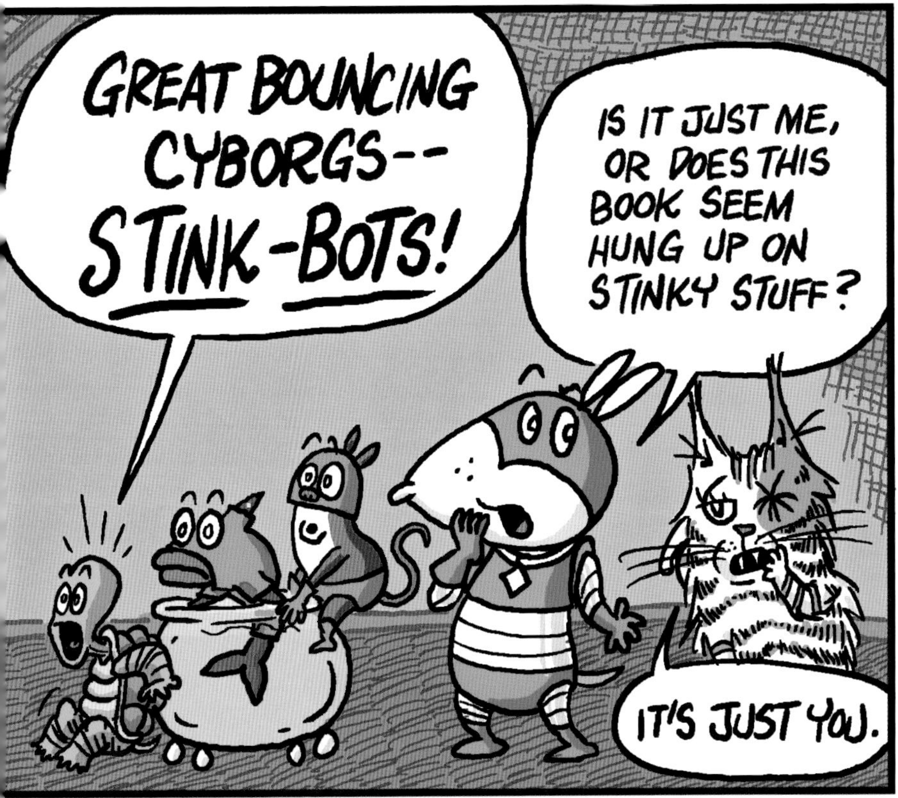
GREAT BOUNCING CYBORGS-- STINK-BOTS!
IS IT JUST ME, OR DOES THIS BOOK SEEM HUNG UP ON STINKY STUFF?
IT'S JUST YOU.

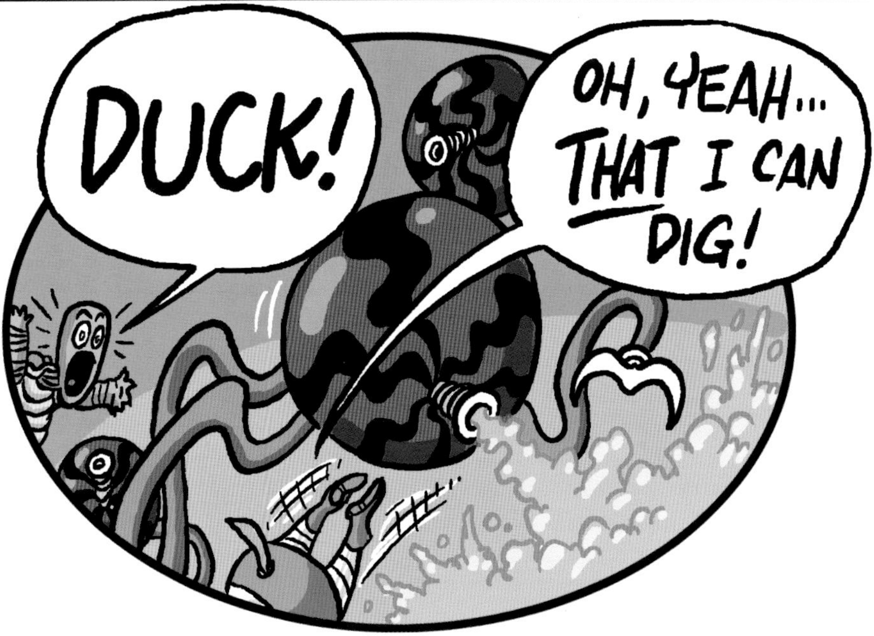
DUCK!
OH, YEAH... THAT I CAN DIG!

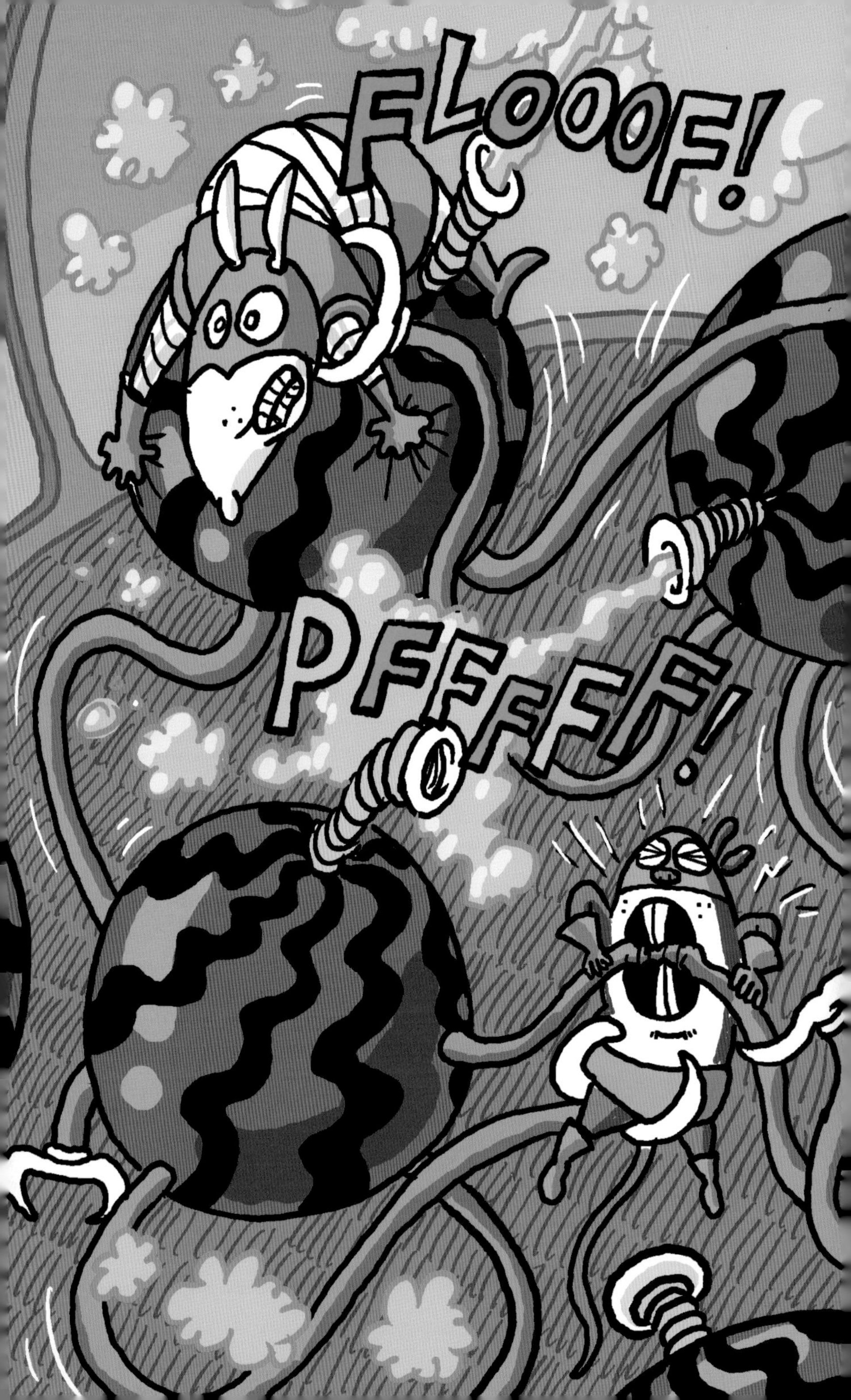
FLOOOF!
PFFFFF!

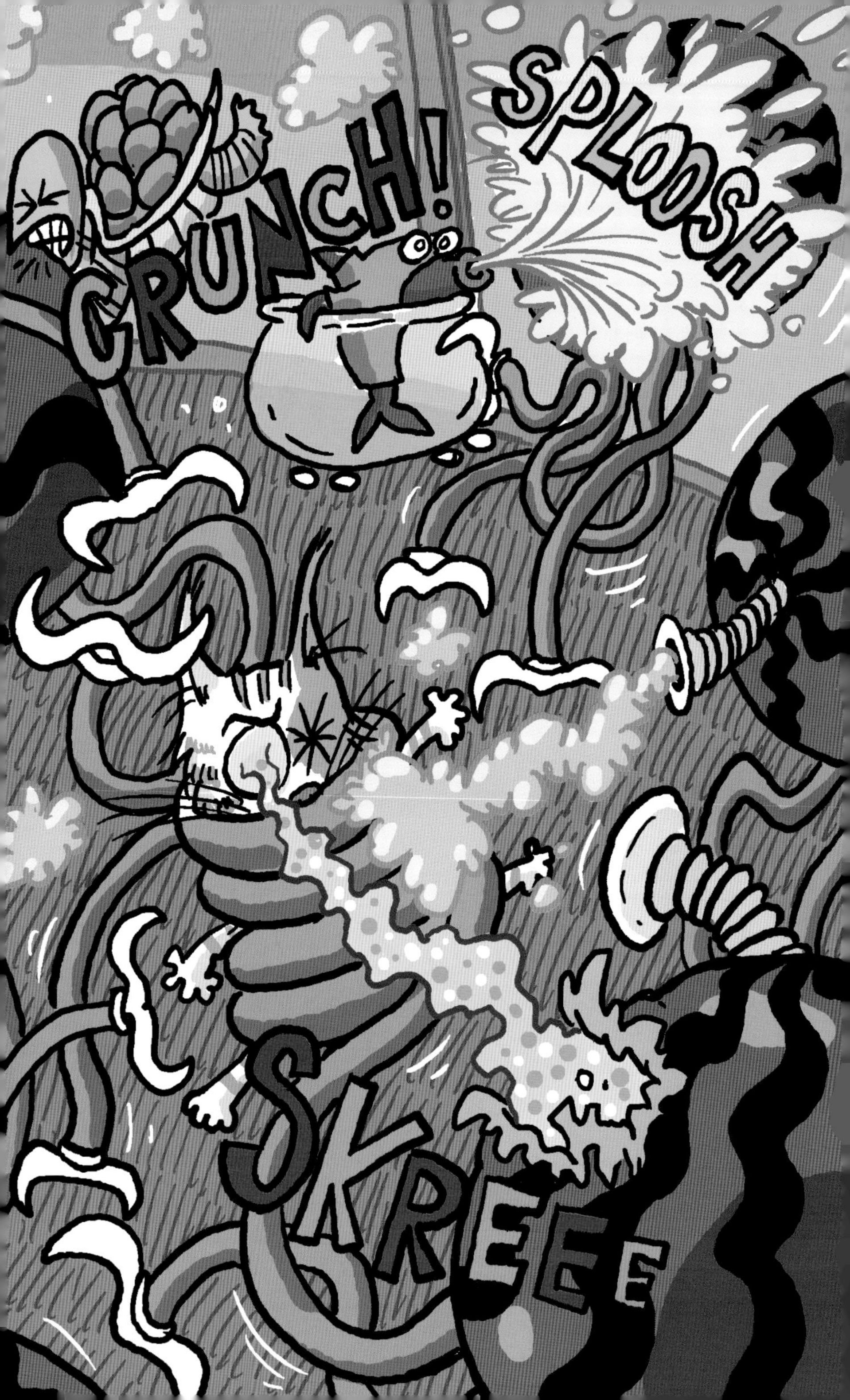
CRUNCH!
SPLOOSH
SKREEEE

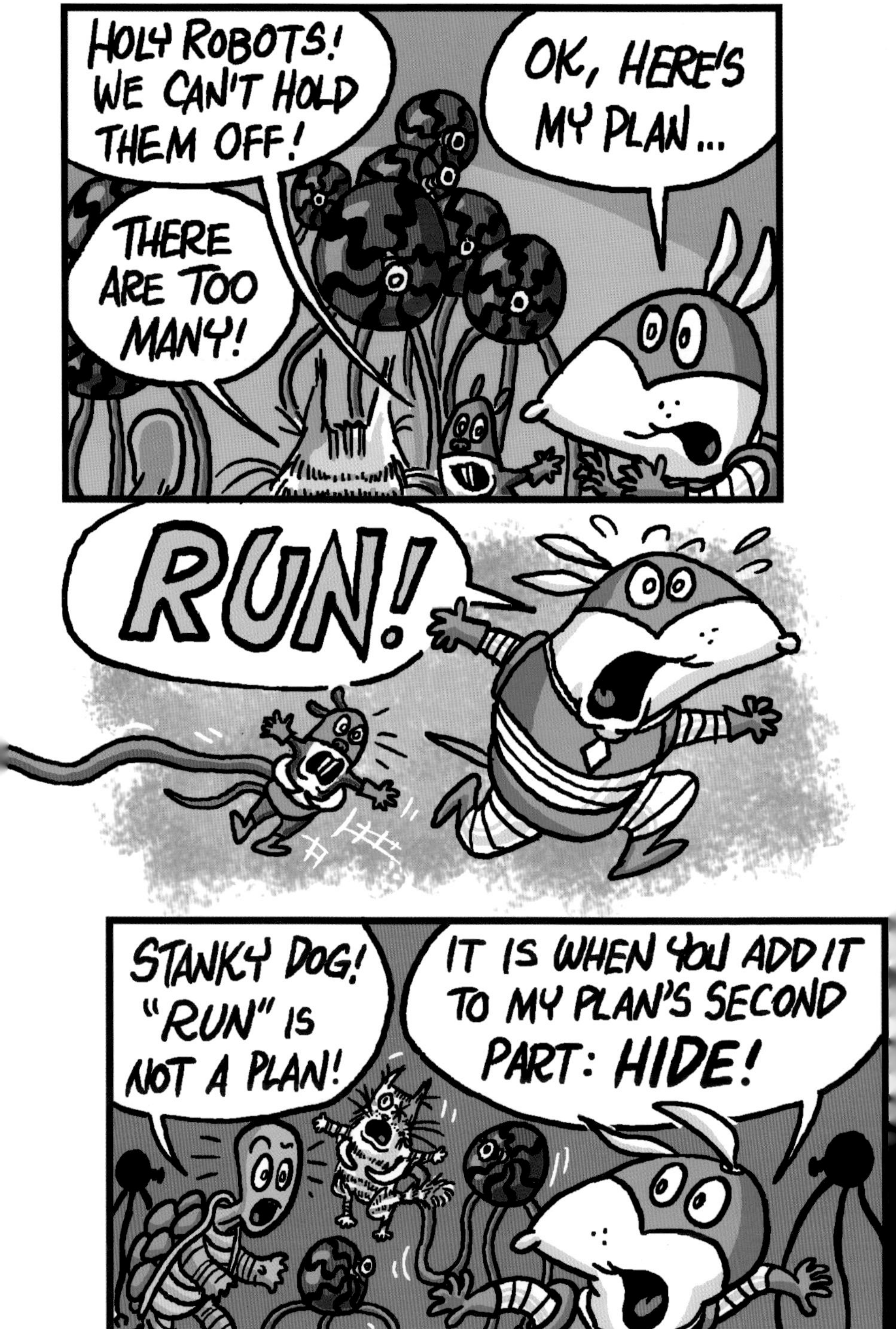
HOLY ROBOTS! WE CAN'T HOLD THEM OFF!
THERE ARE TOO MANY!
OK, HERE'S MY PLAN...
RUN!
STANKY DOG! "RUN" IS NOT A PLAN!
IT IS WHEN YOU ADD IT TO MY PLAN'S SECOND PART: HIDE!

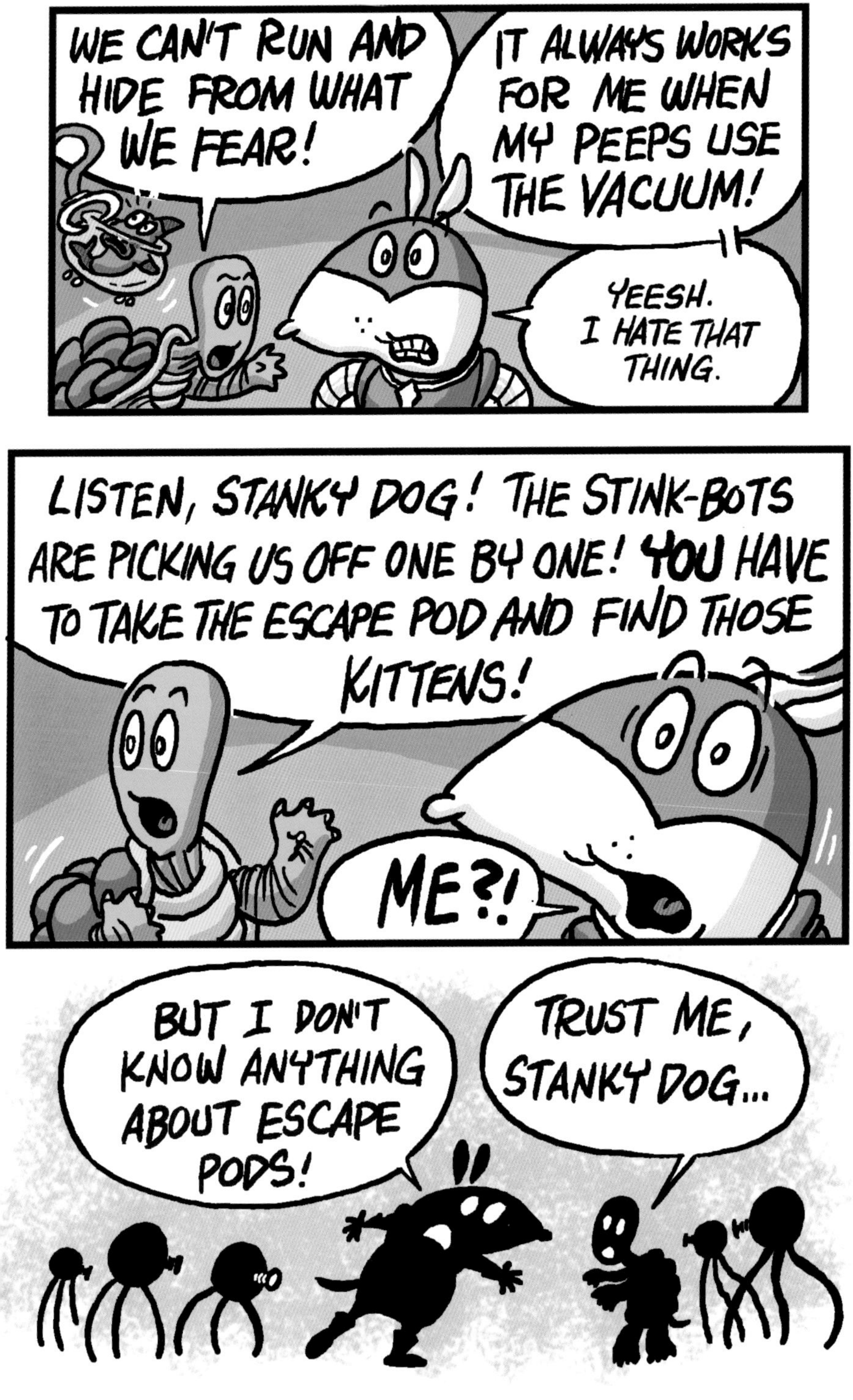

WE CAN'T RUN AND HIDE FROM WHAT WE FEAR!
IT ALWAYS WORKS FOR ME WHEN MY PEEPS USE THE VACUUM!
YEESH. I HATE THAT THING.
LISTEN, STANKY DOG! THE STINK-BOTS ARE PICKING US OFF ONE BY ONE! YOU HAVE TO TAKE THE ESCAPE POD AND FIND THOSE KITTENS!
ME?!
BUT I DON'T KNOW ANYTHING ABOUT ESCAPE PODS!
TRUST ME, STANKY DOG...

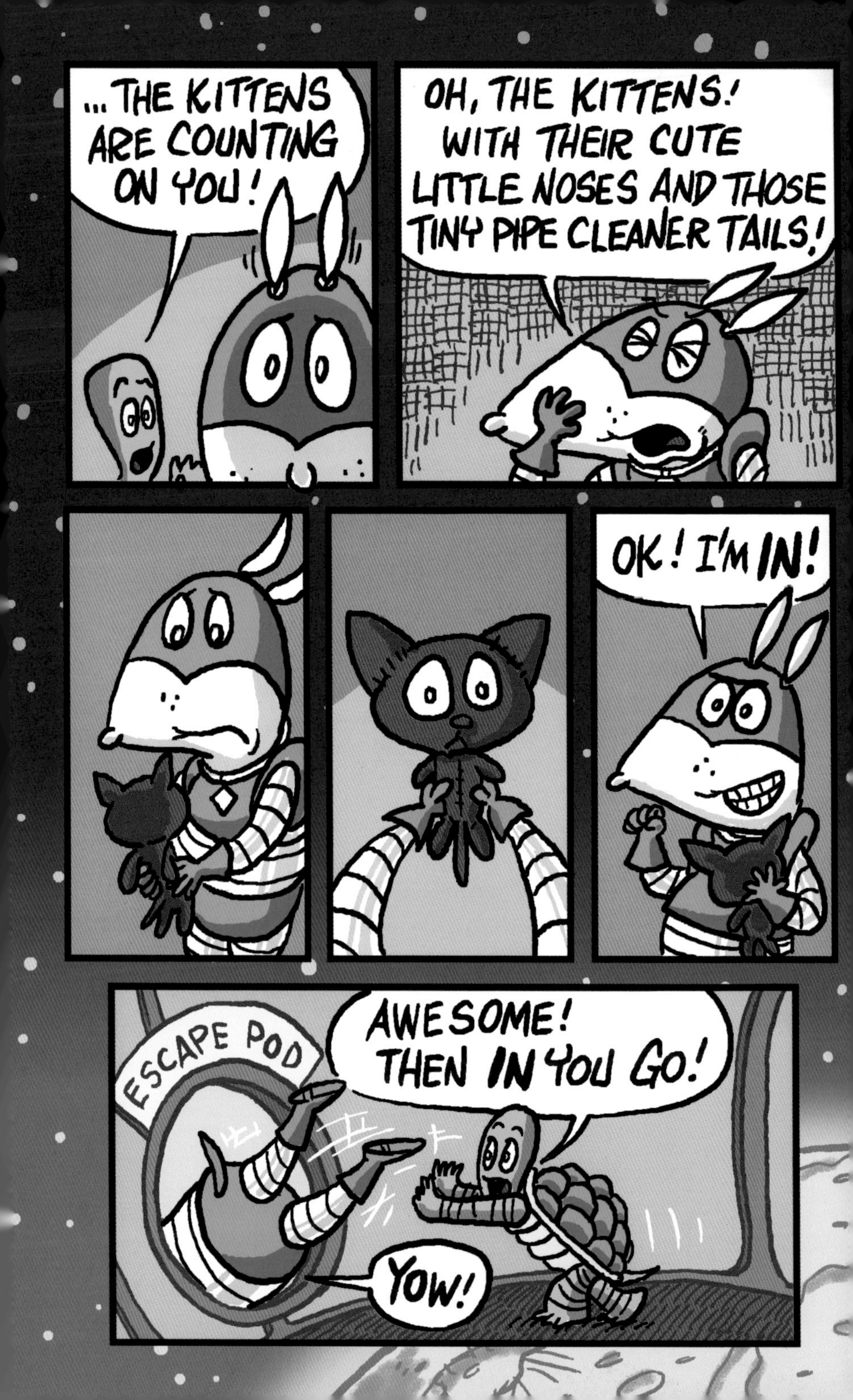
...THE KITTENS ARE COUNTING ON YOU!
OH, THE KITTENS! WITH THEIR CUTE LITTLE NOSES AND THOSE TINY PIPE CLEANER TAILS!
OK! I'M IN!
ESCAPE POD
AWESOME! THEN IN YOU GO!
YOW!

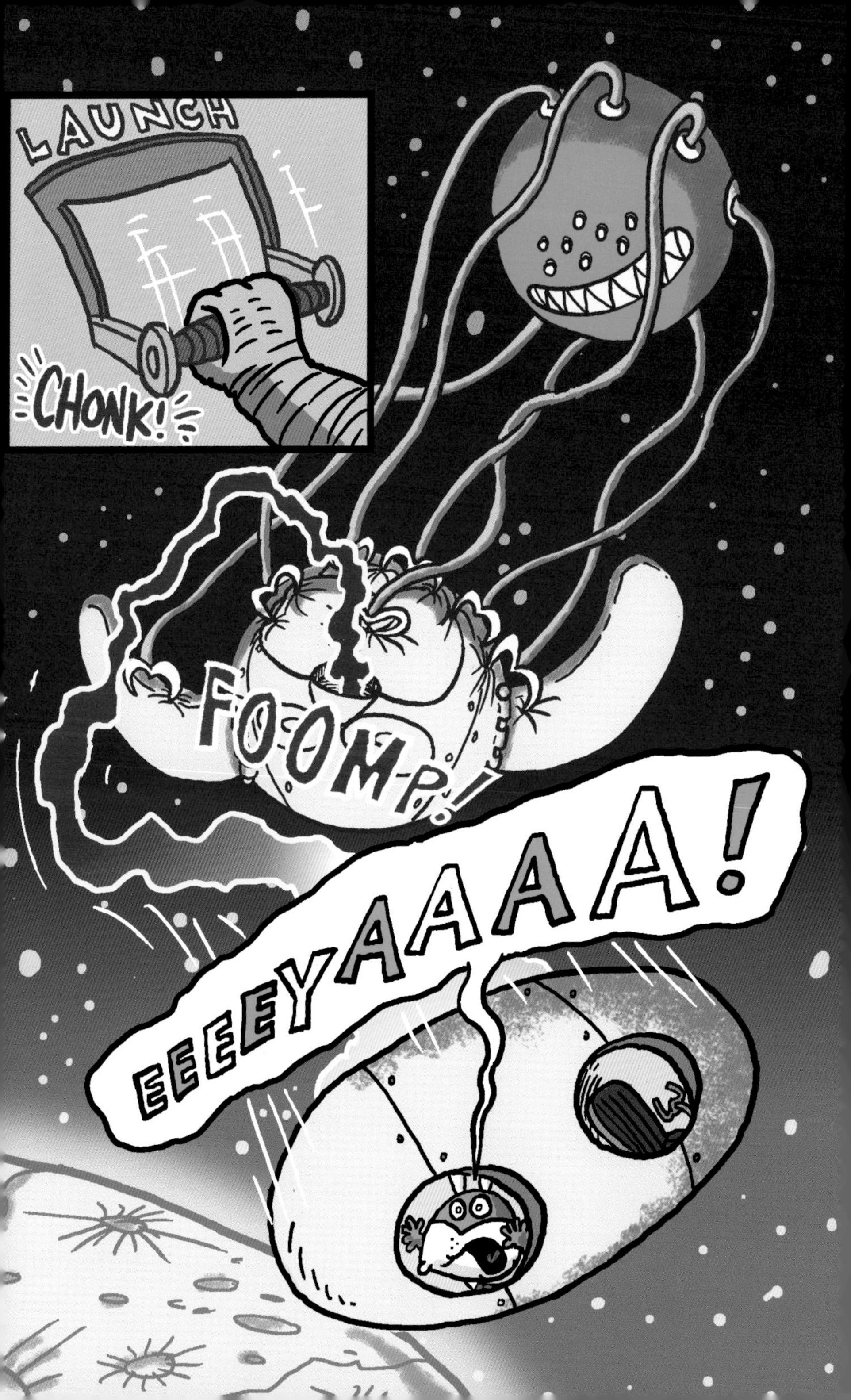
LAUNCH
CHONK!
FOOMP!
EEEEYAAAAA!

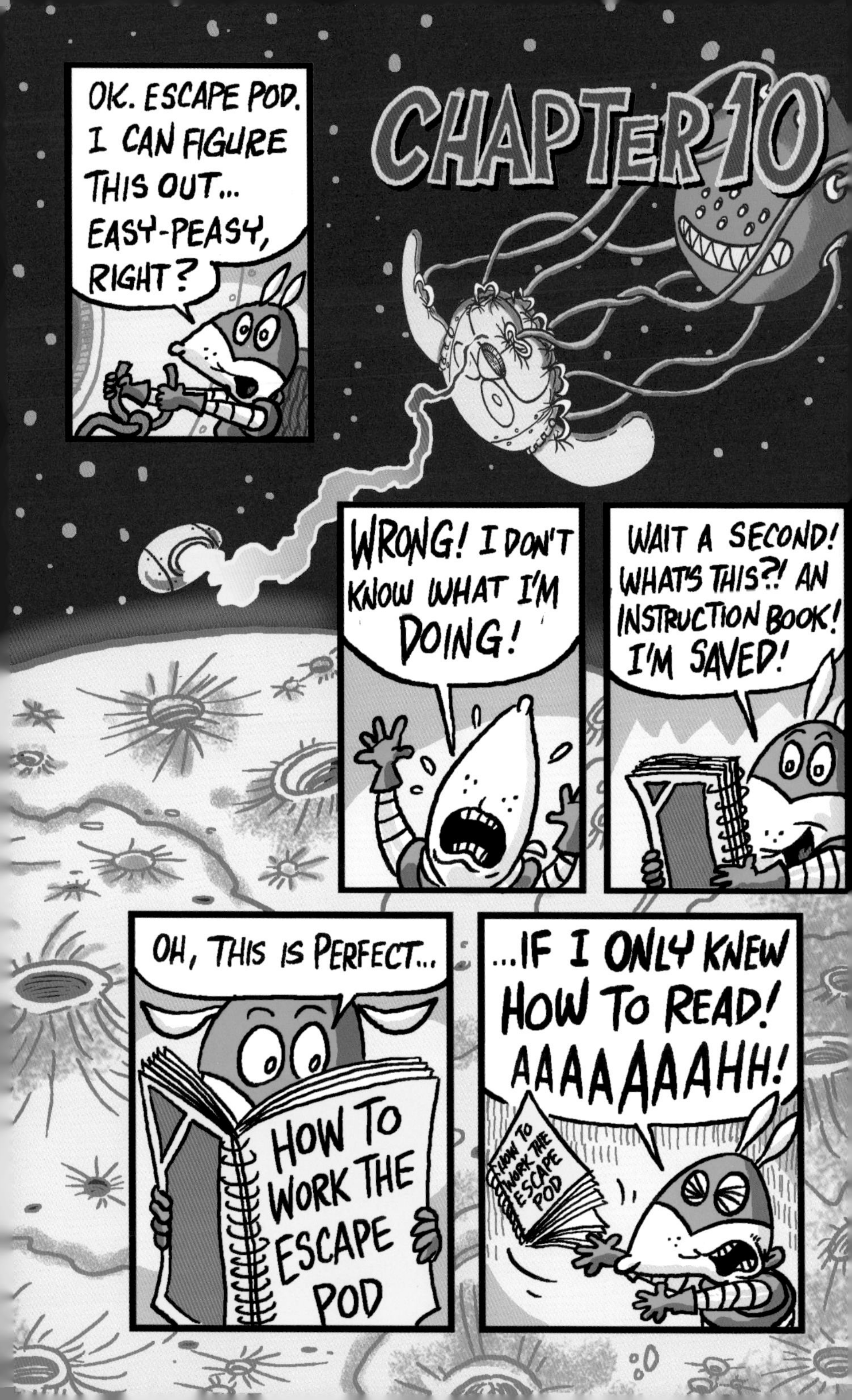
CHAPTER 10
OK. ESCAPE POD. I CAN FIGURE THIS OUT... EASY-PEASY, RIGHT?
WRONG! I DON'T KNOW WHAT I'M DOING!
WAIT A SECOND! WHAT'S THIS?! AN INSTRUCTION BOOK! I'M SAVED!
OH, THIS IS PERFECT...
HOW TO WORK THE ESCAPE POD
...IF I ONLY KNEW HOW TO READ! AAAAAAAHH!
HOW TO WORK THE ESCAPE POD

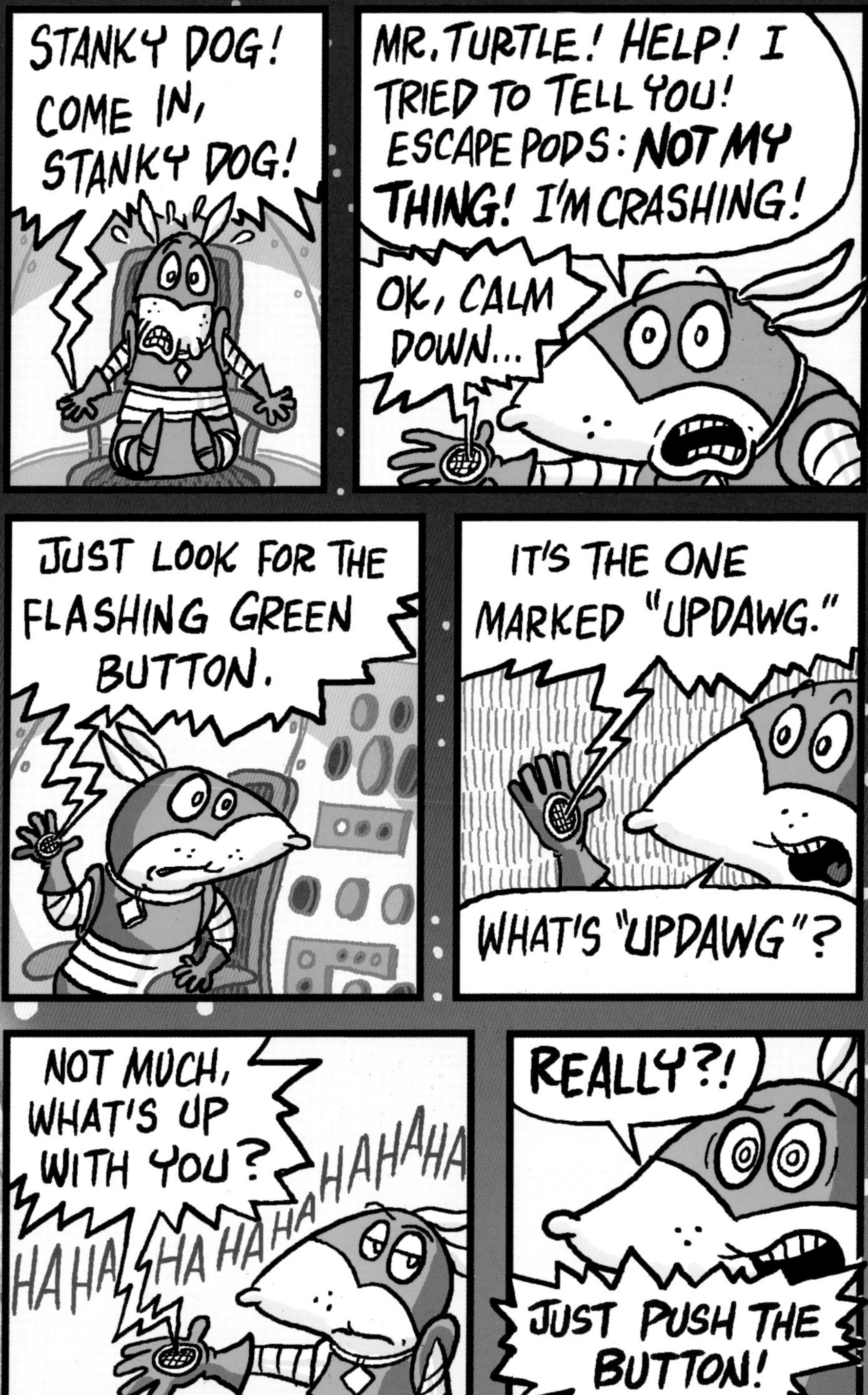
STANKY DOG! COME IN, STANKY DOG!
MR. TURTLE! HELP! I TRIED TO TELL YOU! ESCAPE PODS: NOT MY THING! I'M CRASHING!
OK, CALM DOWN...
JUST LOOK FOR THE FLASHING GREEN BUTTON.
IT'S THE ONE MARKED "UPDAWG."
WHAT'S "UPDAWG"?
NOT MUCH, WHAT'S UP WITH YOU?
HAHAHAHA
HAHA HA HA HA HA
REALLY?!
JUST PUSH THE BUTTON!

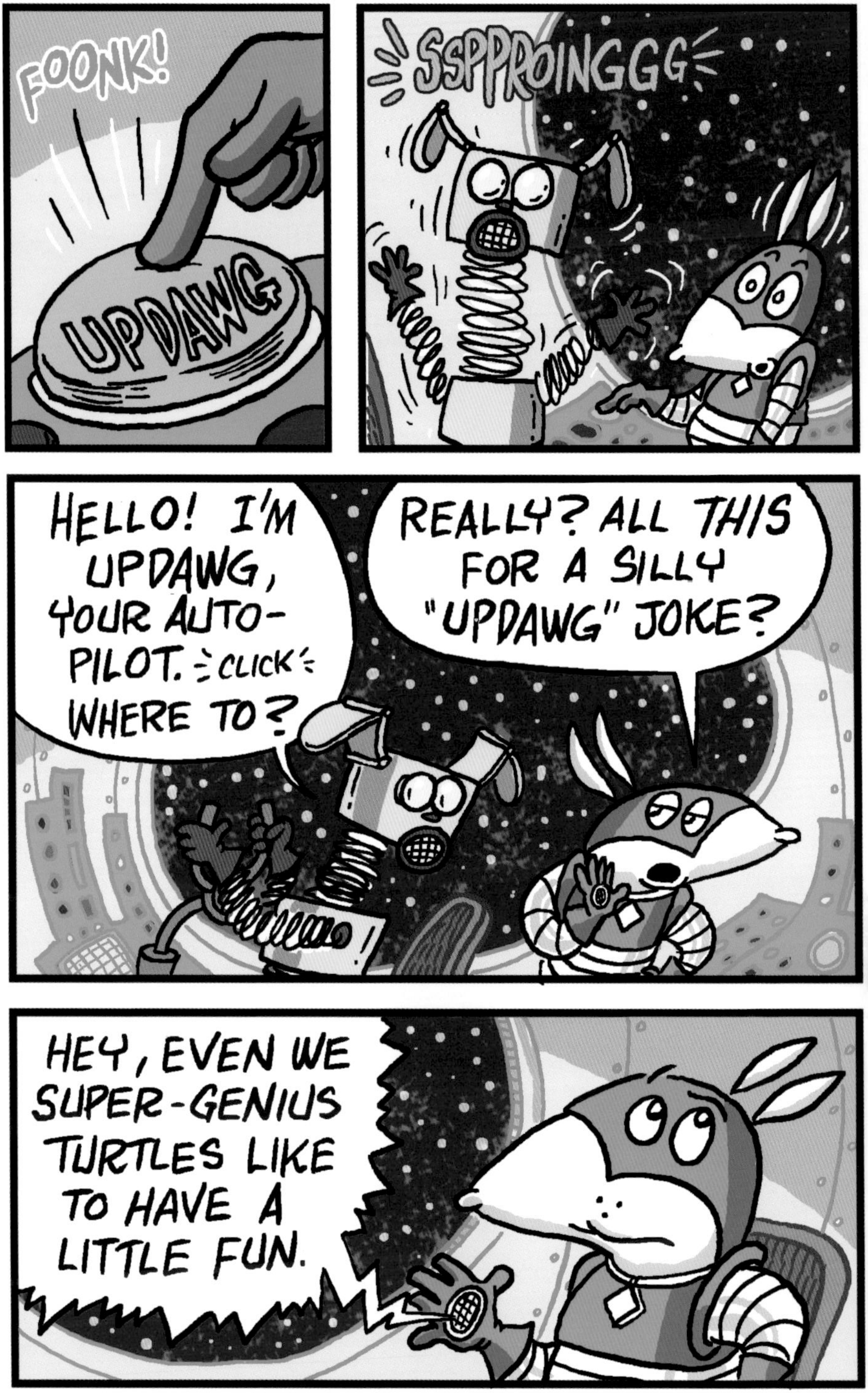
FOONK!
UPDAWG
SSPPROINGGG
HELLO! I'M UPDAWG, YOUR AUTO-PILOT. CLICK WHERE TO?
REALLY? ALL THIS FOR A SILLY "UPDAWG" JOKE?
HEY, EVEN WE SUPER-GENIUS TURTLES LIKE TO HAVE A LITTLE FUN.

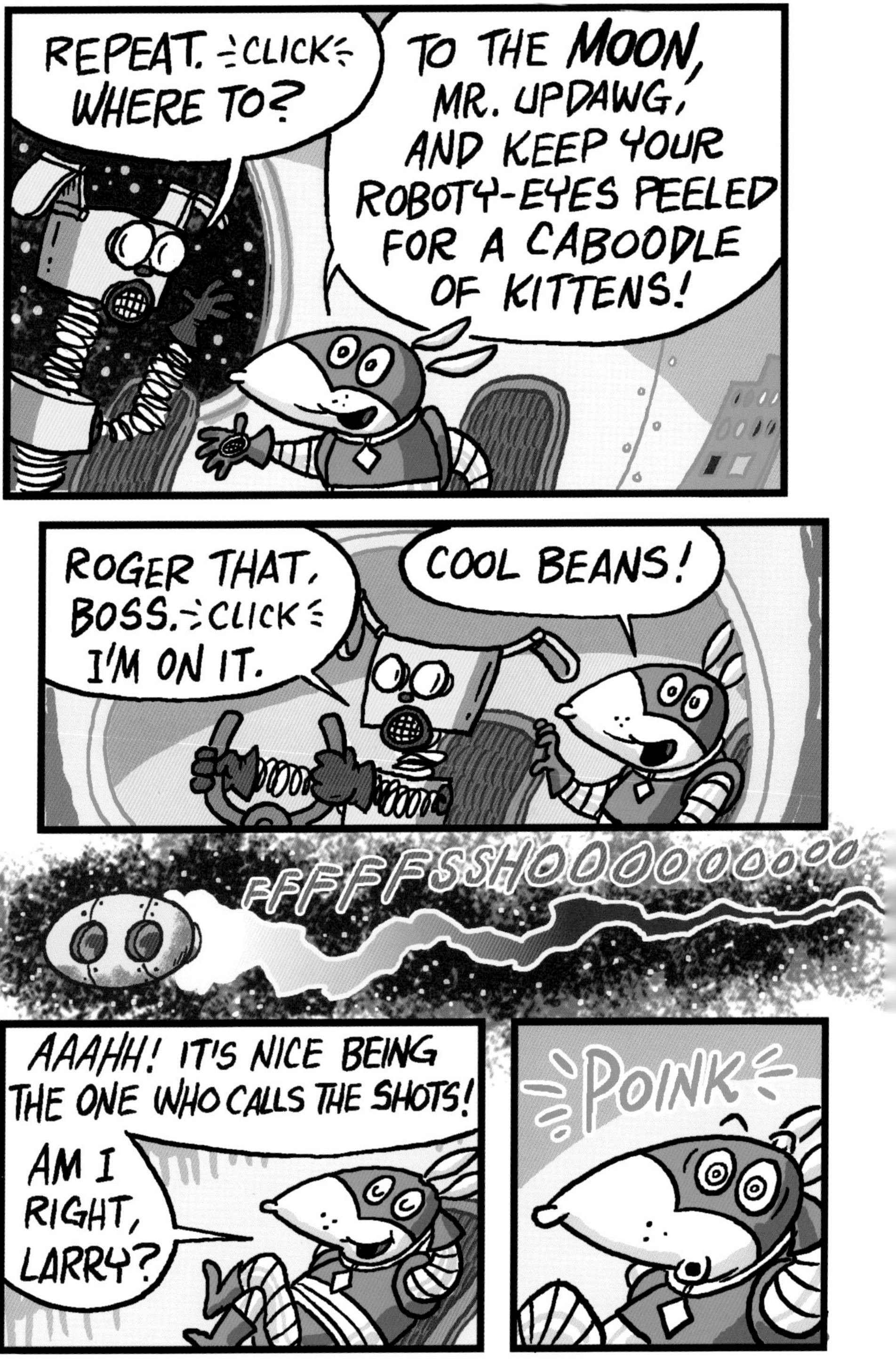

REPEAT. CLICK WHERE TO?
TO THE MOON, MR. UPDAWG, AND KEEP YOUR ROBOTY-EYES PEELED FOR A CABOODLE OF KITTENS!
ROGER THAT, BOSS. CLICK I'M ON IT.
COOL BEANS!
FFFFFFSSHOOOOOOOOOOO
AAAHH! IT'S NICE BEING THE ONE WHO CALLS THE SHOTS!
AM I RIGHT, LARRY?
POINK

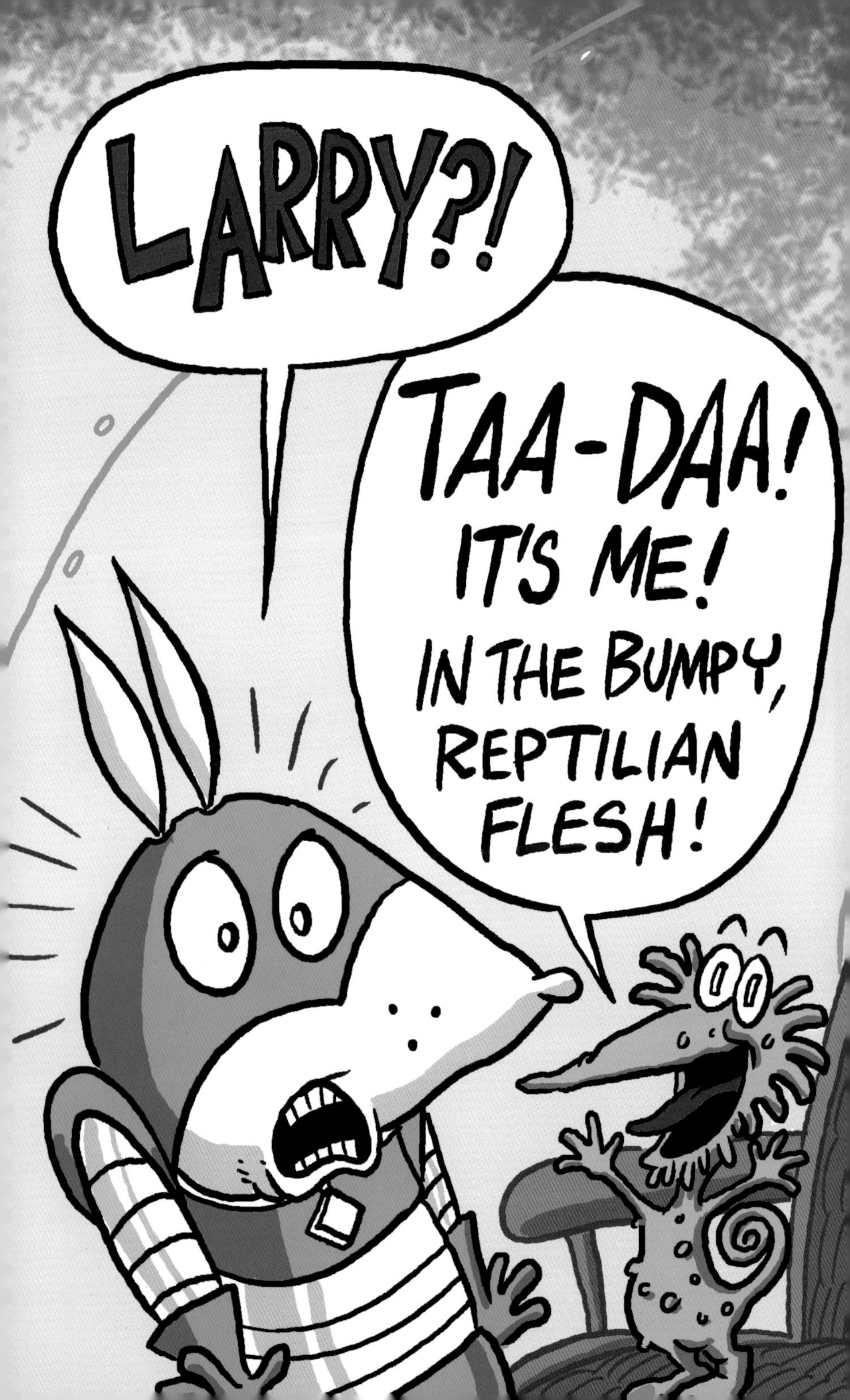
LARRY?!
TAA-DAA! IT'S ME! IN THE BUMPY, REPTILIAN FLESH!

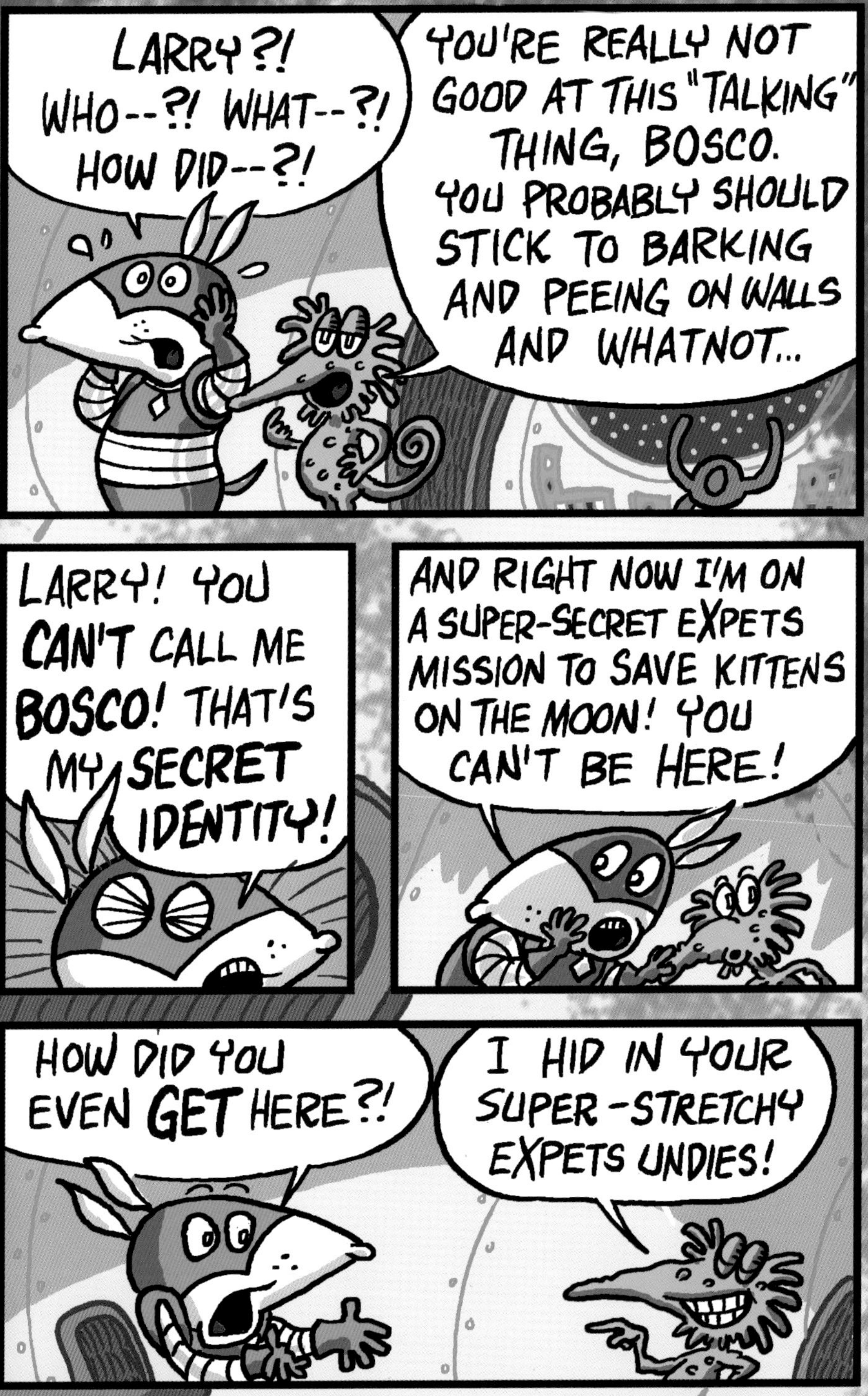
LARRY?! WHO--?! WHAT--?! HOW DID--?!
YOU'RE REALLY NOT GOOD AT THIS "TALKING" THING, BOSCO. YOU PROBABLY SHOULD STICK TO BARKING AND PEEING ON WALLS AND WHATNOT...
LARRY! YOU CAN'T CALL ME BOSCO! THAT'S MY SECRET IDENTITY!
AND RIGHT NOW I'M ON A SUPER-SECRET EXPETS MISSION TO SAVE KITTENS ON THE MOON! YOU CAN'T BE HERE!
HOW DID YOU EVEN GET HERE?!
I HID IN YOUR SUPER-STRETCHY EXPETS UNDIES!

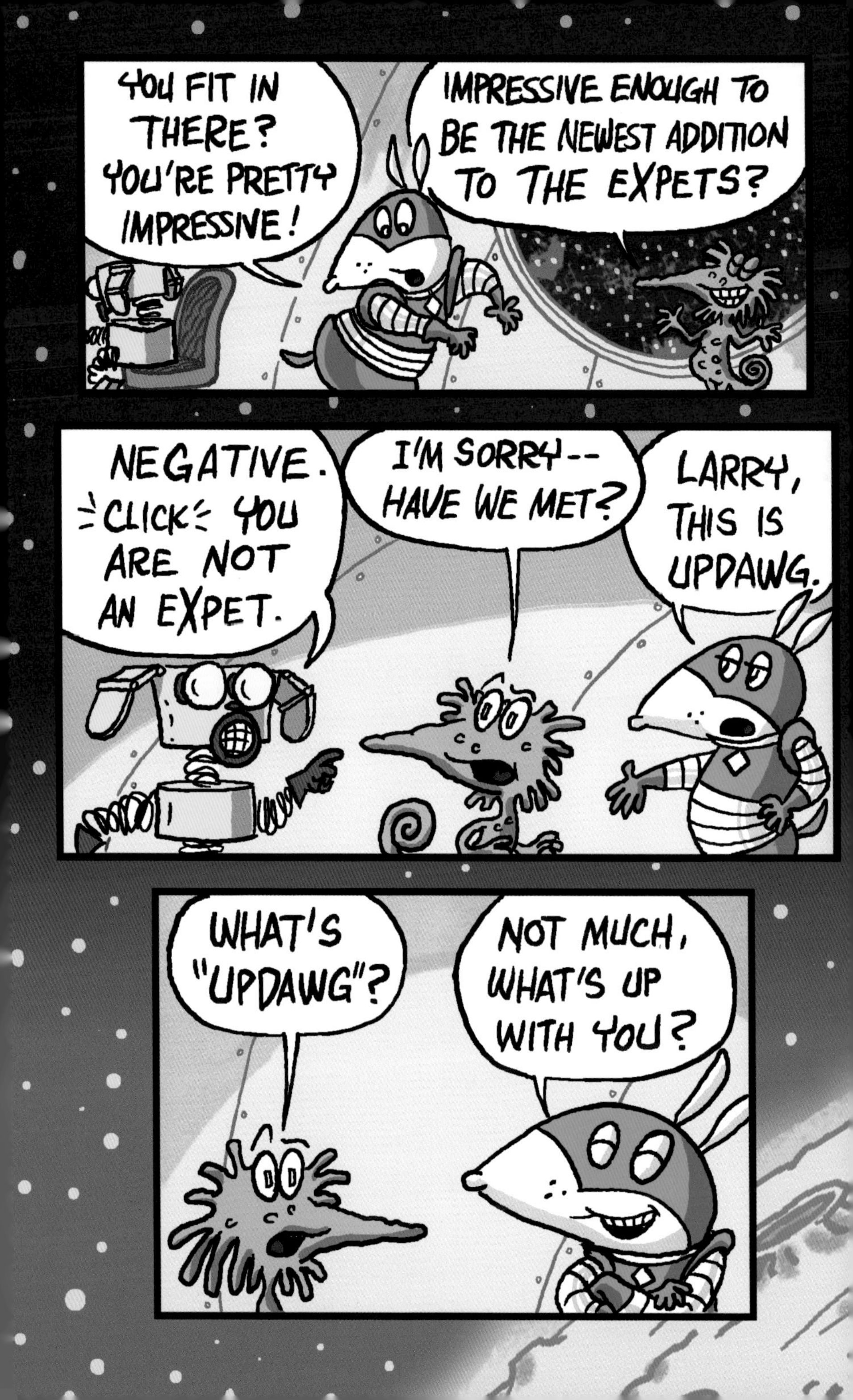
YOU FIT IN THERE? YOU'RE PRETTY IMPRESSIVE!
IMPRESSIVE ENOUGH TO BE THE NEWEST ADDITION TO THE EXPETS?
NEGATIVE. CLICK YOU ARE NOT AN EXPET.
I'M SORRY-- HAVE WE MET?
LARRY, THIS IS UPDAWG.
WHAT'S "UPDAWG"?
NOT MUCH, WHAT'S UP WITH YOU?

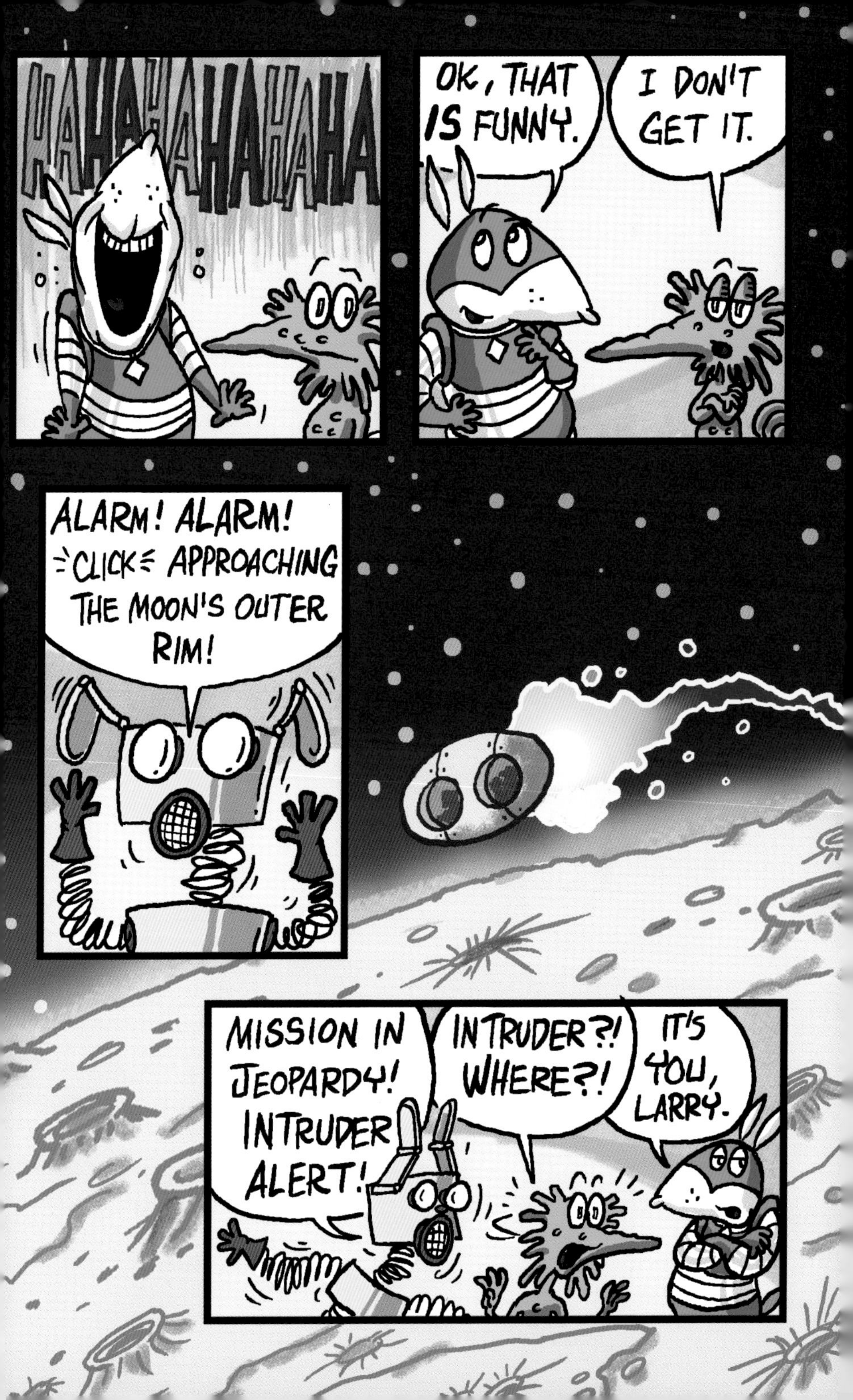
HAHAHAHAHAHAHA
OK, THAT IS FUNNY.
I DON'T GET IT.
ALARM! ALARM! CLICK APPROACHING THE MOON'S OUTER RIM!
MISSION IN JEOPARDY! INTRUDER ALERT!
INTRUDER?! WHERE?!
IT'S YOU, LARRY.

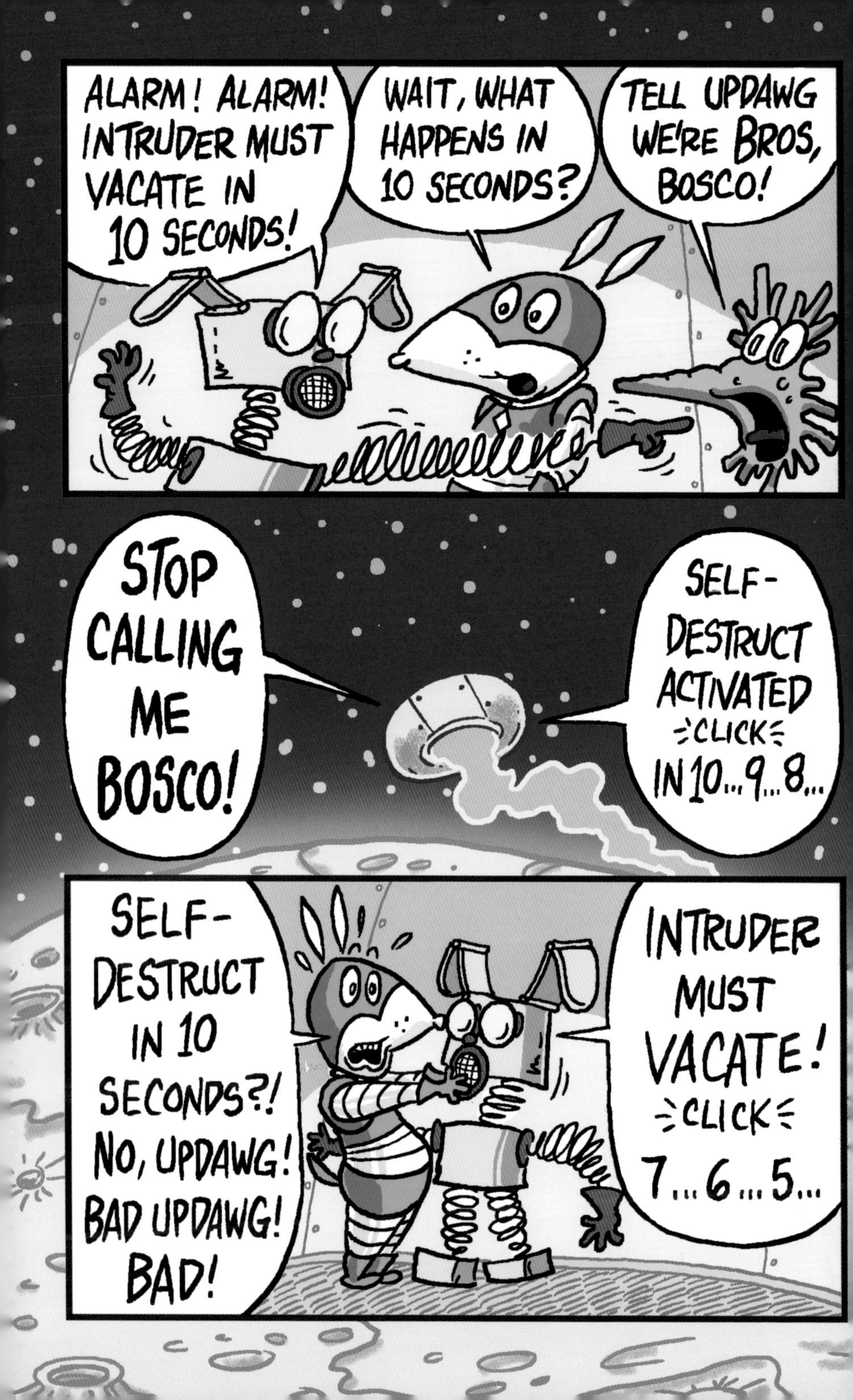
ALARM! ALARM! INTRUDER MUST VACATE IN 10 SECONDS!
WAIT, WHAT HAPPENS IN 10 SECONDS?
TELL UPDAWG WE'RE BROS, BOSCO!
STOP CALLING ME BOSCO!
SELF-DESTRUCT ACTIVATED
CLICK
IN 10...9...8...
SELF-DESTRUCT IN 10 SECONDS?! NO, UPDAWG! BAD UPDAWG! BAD!
INTRUDER MUST VACATE!
CLICK
7...6...5...

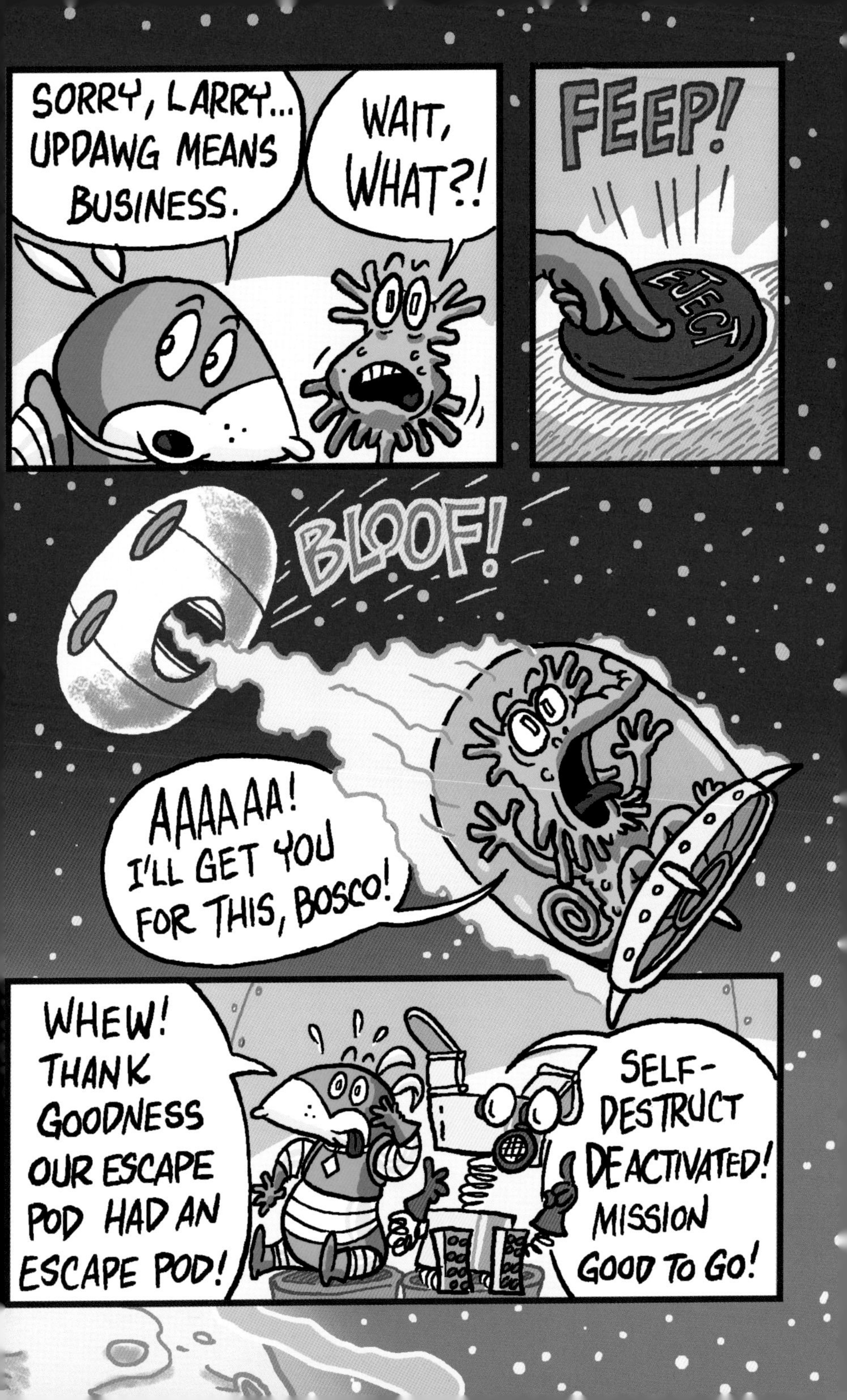

SORRY, LARRY... UPDAWG MEANS BUSINESS.
WAIT, WHAT?!
FEEP!
EJECT
BLOOF!
AAAAAA! I'LL GET YOU FOR THIS, BOSCO!
WHEW! THANK GOODNESS OUR ESCAPE POD HAD AN ESCAPE POD!
SELF-DESTRUCT DEACTIVATED! MISSION GOOD TO GO!

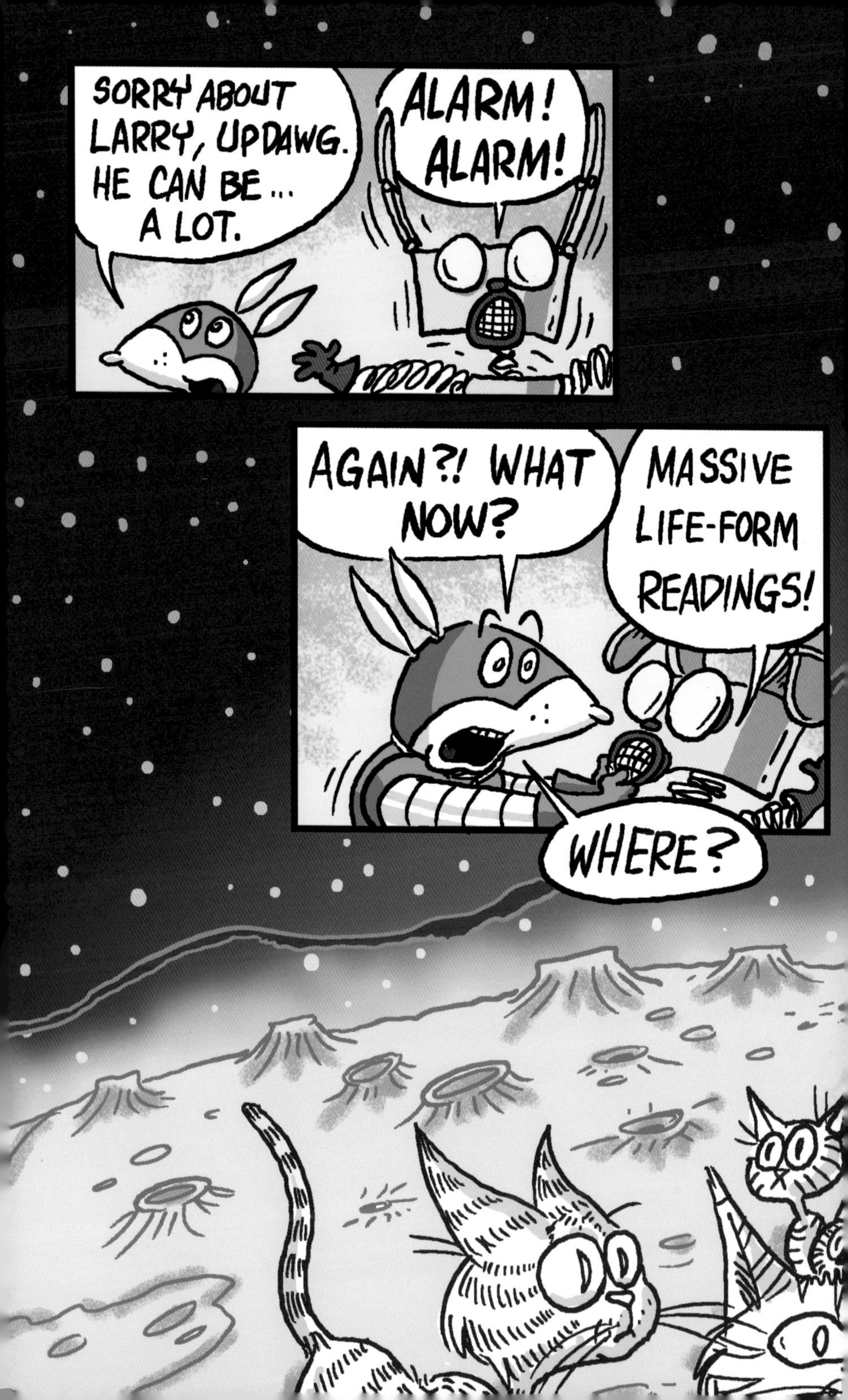
SORRY ABOUT LARRY, UPDAWG. HE CAN BE... A LOT.
ALARM! ALARM!
AGAIN?! WHAT NOW?
MASSIVE LIFE-FORM READINGS!
WHERE?

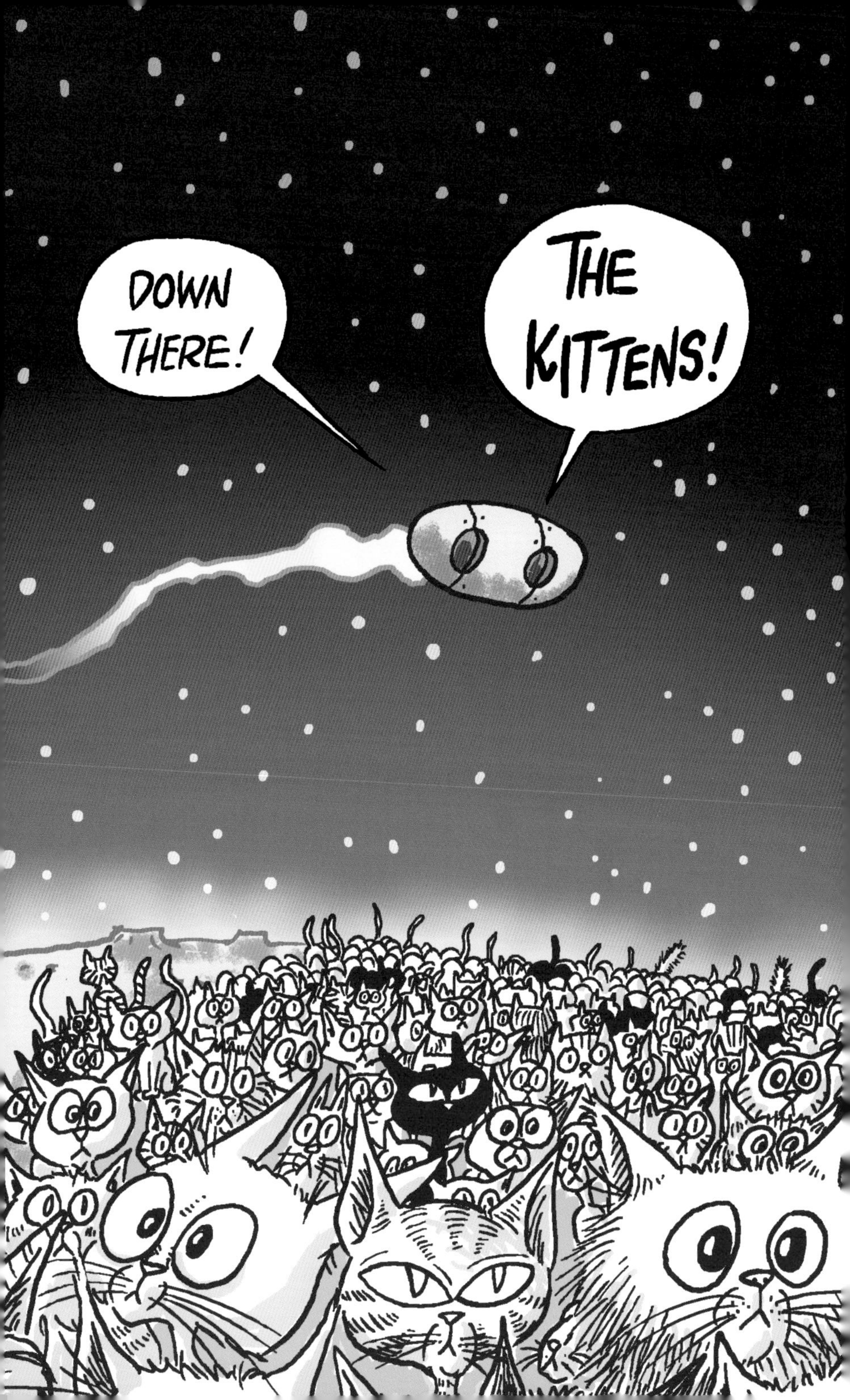
DOWN THERE!
THE KITTENS!

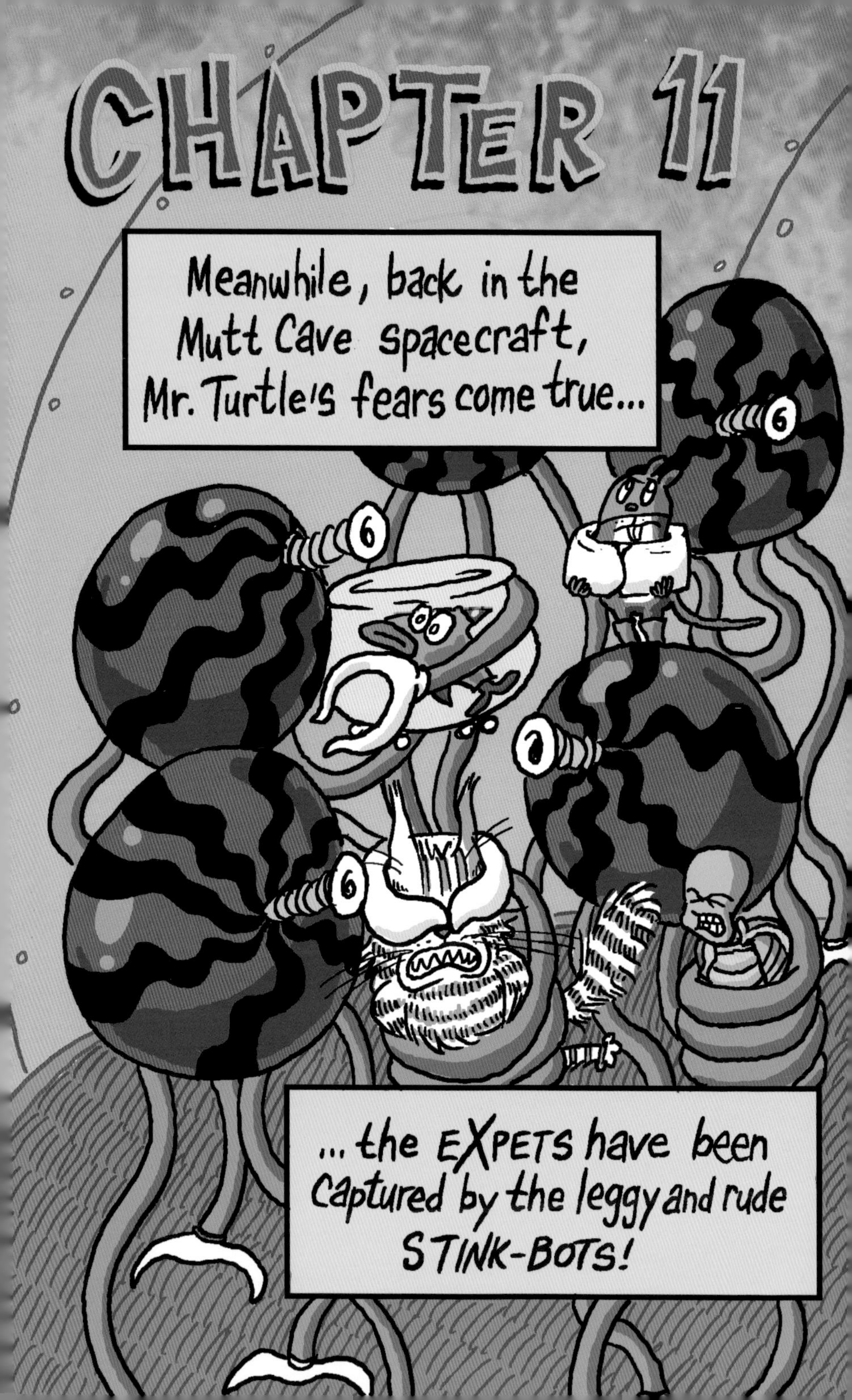
CHAPTER 11
Meanwhile, back in the Mutt Cave spacecraft, Mr. Turtle's fears come true...
6
6
6
2
... the EXPETS have been captured by the leggy and rude STINK-BOTS!

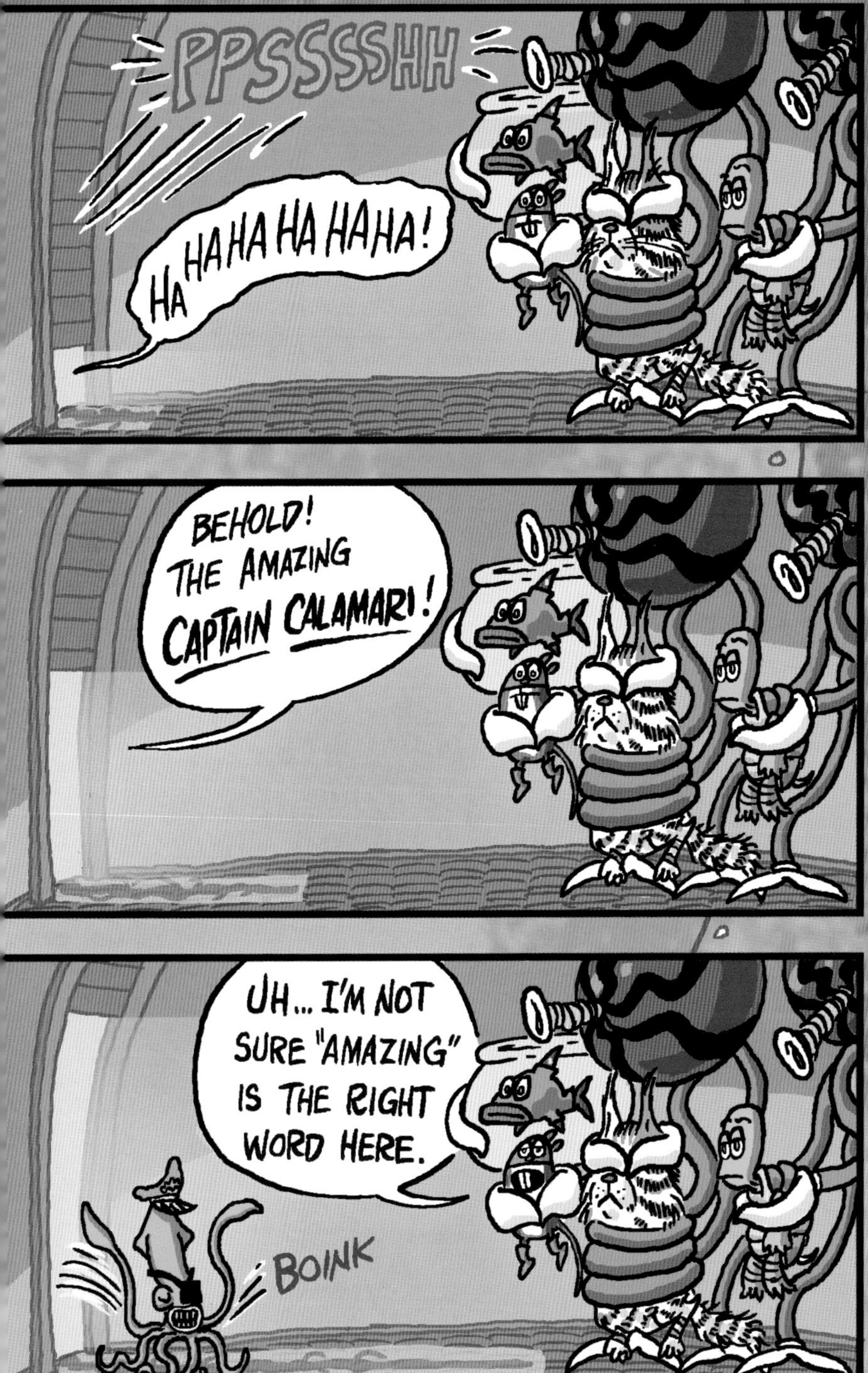
PPSSSSHH
HA HA HA HA HA HA HA!
BEHOLD! THE AMAZING CAPTAIN CALAMARI!
UH... I'M NOT SURE "AMAZING" IS THE RIGHT WORD HERE.
BOINK

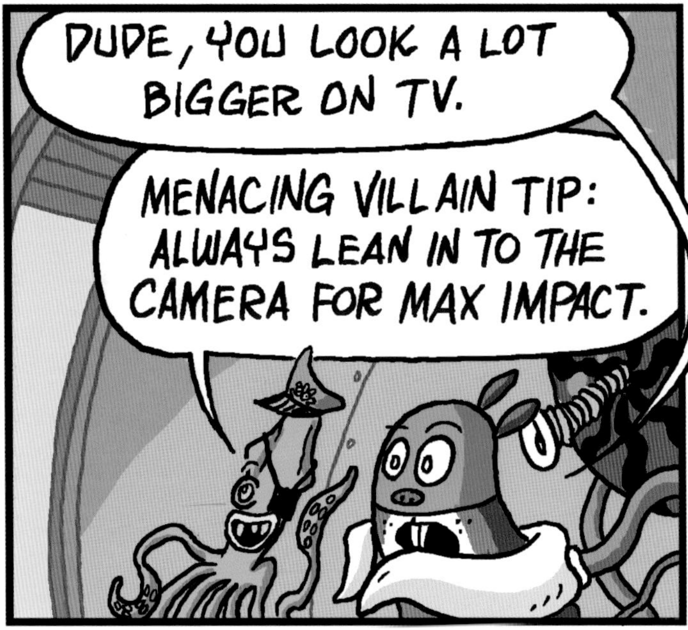
DUDE, YOU LOOK A LOT BIGGER ON TV.
MENACING VILLAIN TIP: ALWAYS LEAN IN TO THE CAMERA FOR MAX IMPACT.

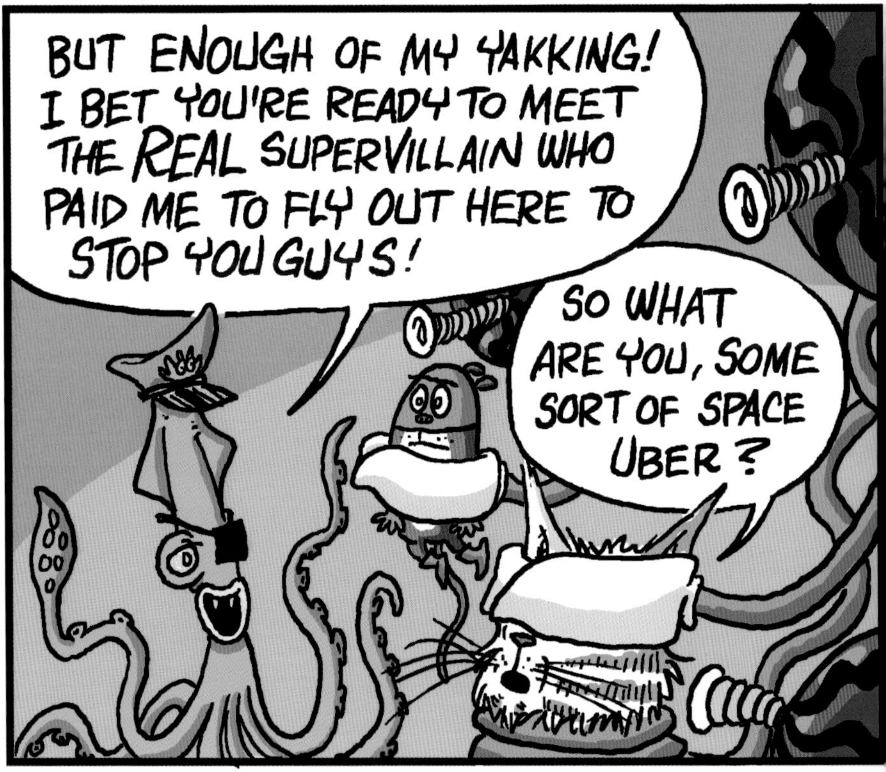
BUT ENOUGH OF MY YAKKING! I BET YOU'RE READY TO MEET THE *REAL* SUPERVILLAIN WHO PAID ME TO FLY OUT HERE TO STOP YOU GUYS!
SO WHAT ARE YOU, SOME SORT OF SPACE UBER?

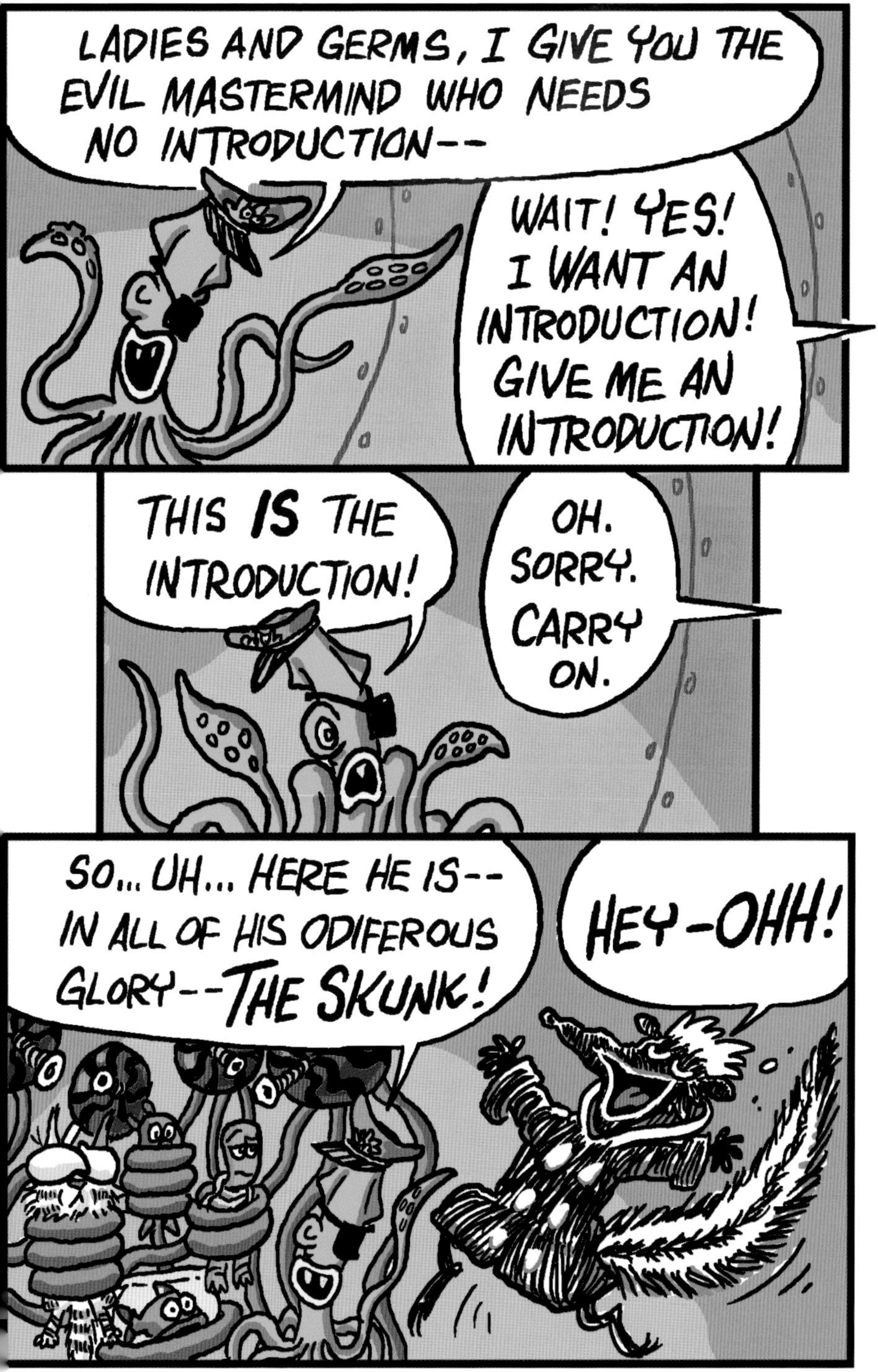
LADIES AND GERMS, I GIVE YOU THE EVIL MASTERMIND WHO NEEDS NO INTRODUCTION--
WAIT! YES! I WANT AN INTRODUCTION! GIVE ME AN INTRODUCTION!
THIS IS THE INTRODUCTION!
OH. SORRY. CARRY ON.
SO... UH... HERE HE IS-- IN ALL OF HIS ODIFEROUS GLORY--THE SKUNK!
HEY-OHH!

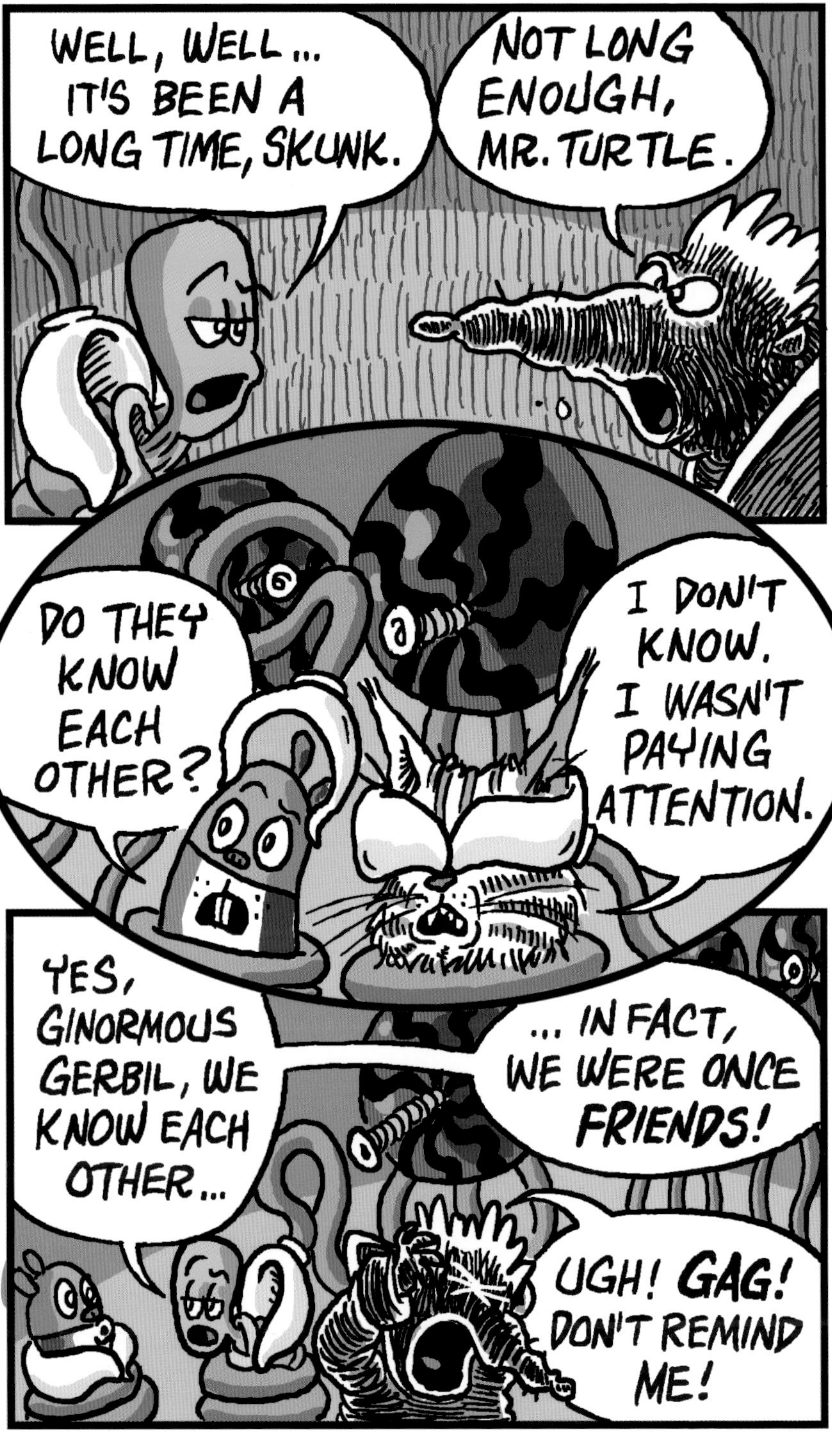
WELL, WELL... IT'S BEEN A LONG TIME, SKUNK.
NOT LONG ENOUGH, MR. TURTLE.
DO THEY KNOW EACH OTHER?
I DON'T KNOW. I WASN'T PAYING ATTENTION.
YES, GINORMOUS GERBIL, WE KNOW EACH OTHER...
... IN FACT, WE WERE ONCE FRIENDS!
UGH! GAG! DON'T REMIND ME!

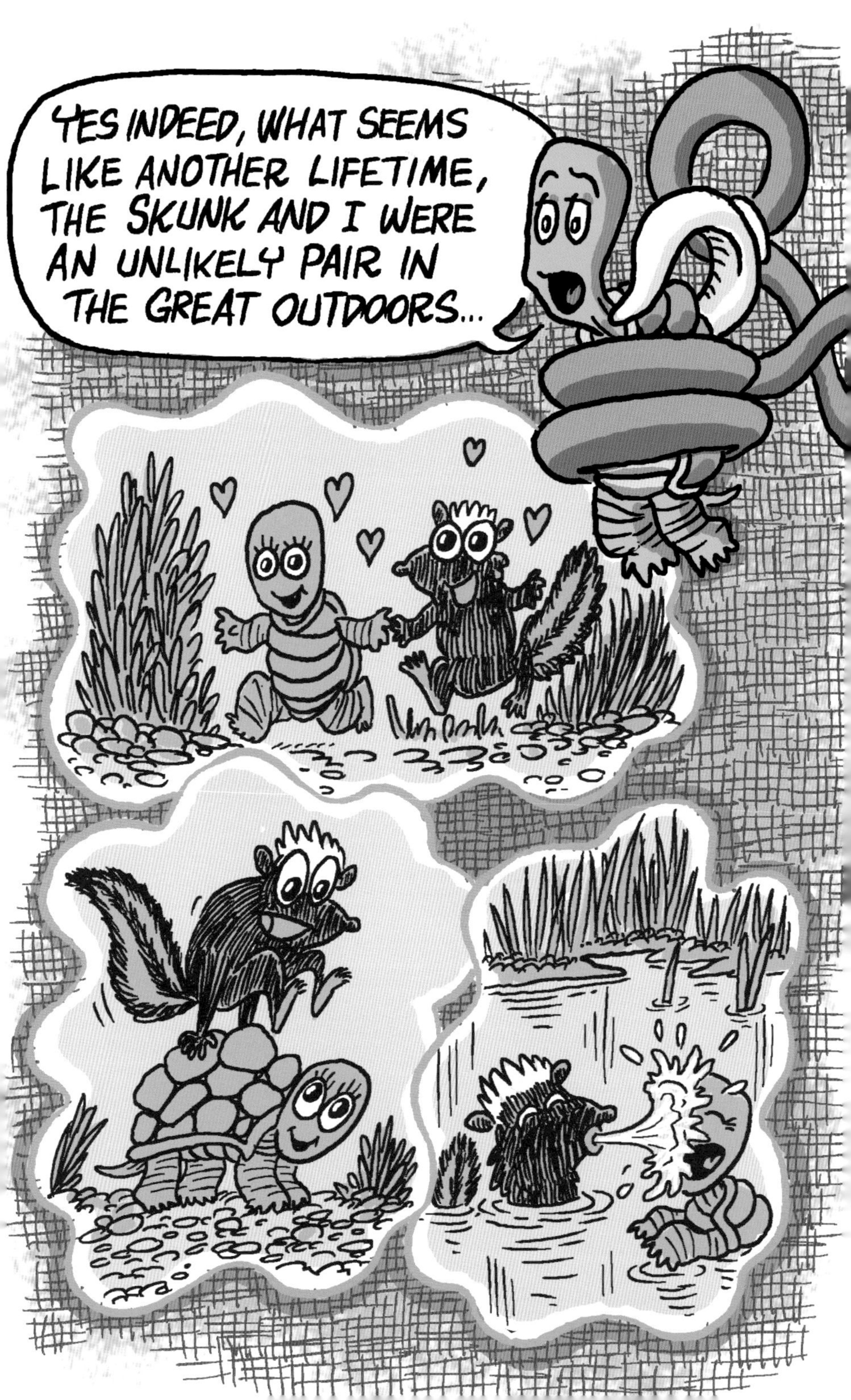
YES INDEED, WHAT SEEMS LIKE ANOTHER LIFETIME, THE SKUNK AND I WERE AN UNLIKELY PAIR IN THE GREAT OUTDOORS...

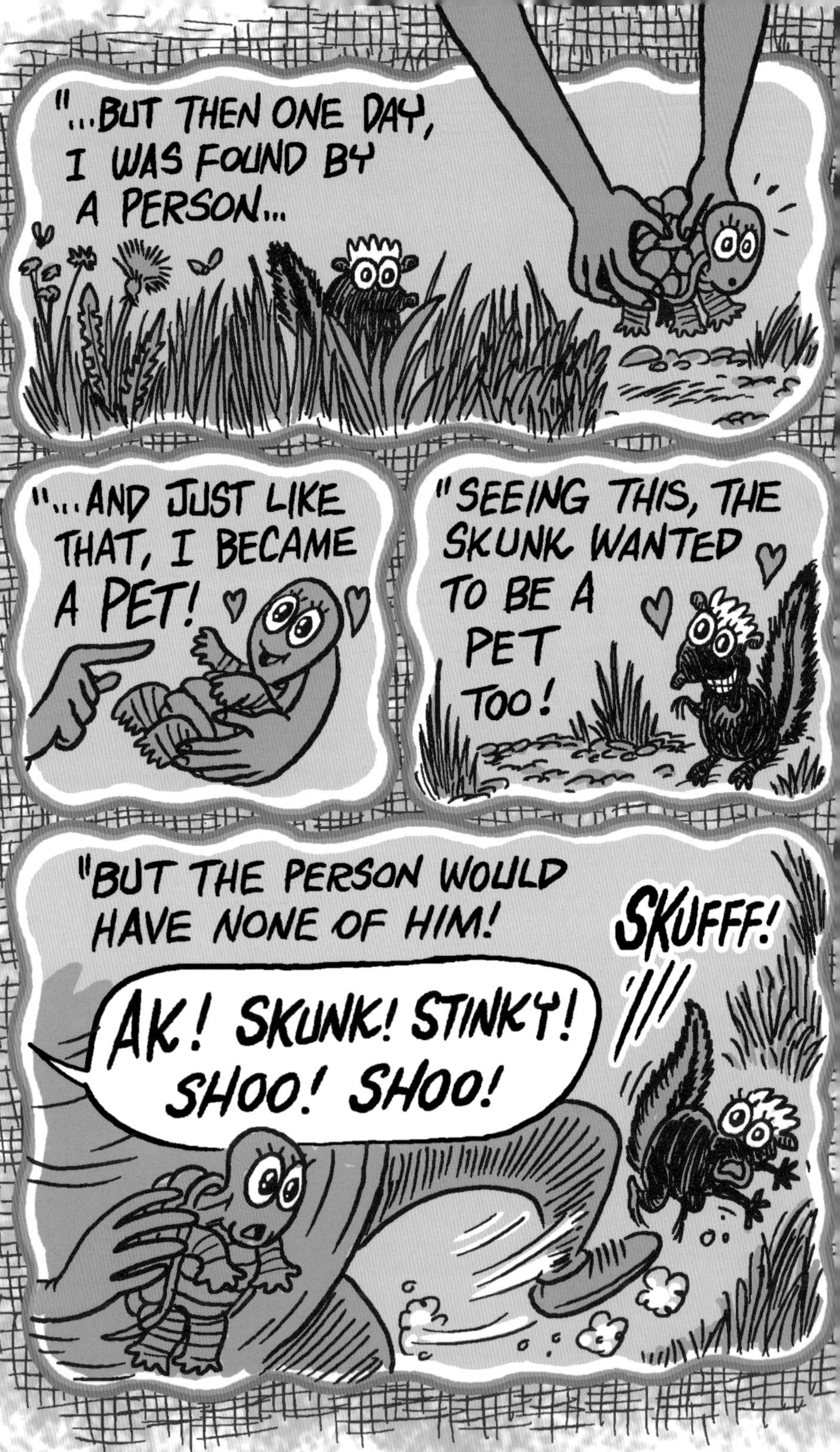
"...BUT THEN ONE DAY, I WAS FOUND BY A PERSON...
"...AND JUST LIKE THAT, I BECAME A PET!
"SEEING THIS, THE SKUNK WANTED TO BE A PET TOO!
"BUT THE PERSON WOULD HAVE NONE OF HIM!
SKUFFF!
AK! SKUNK! STINKY! SHOO! SHOO!

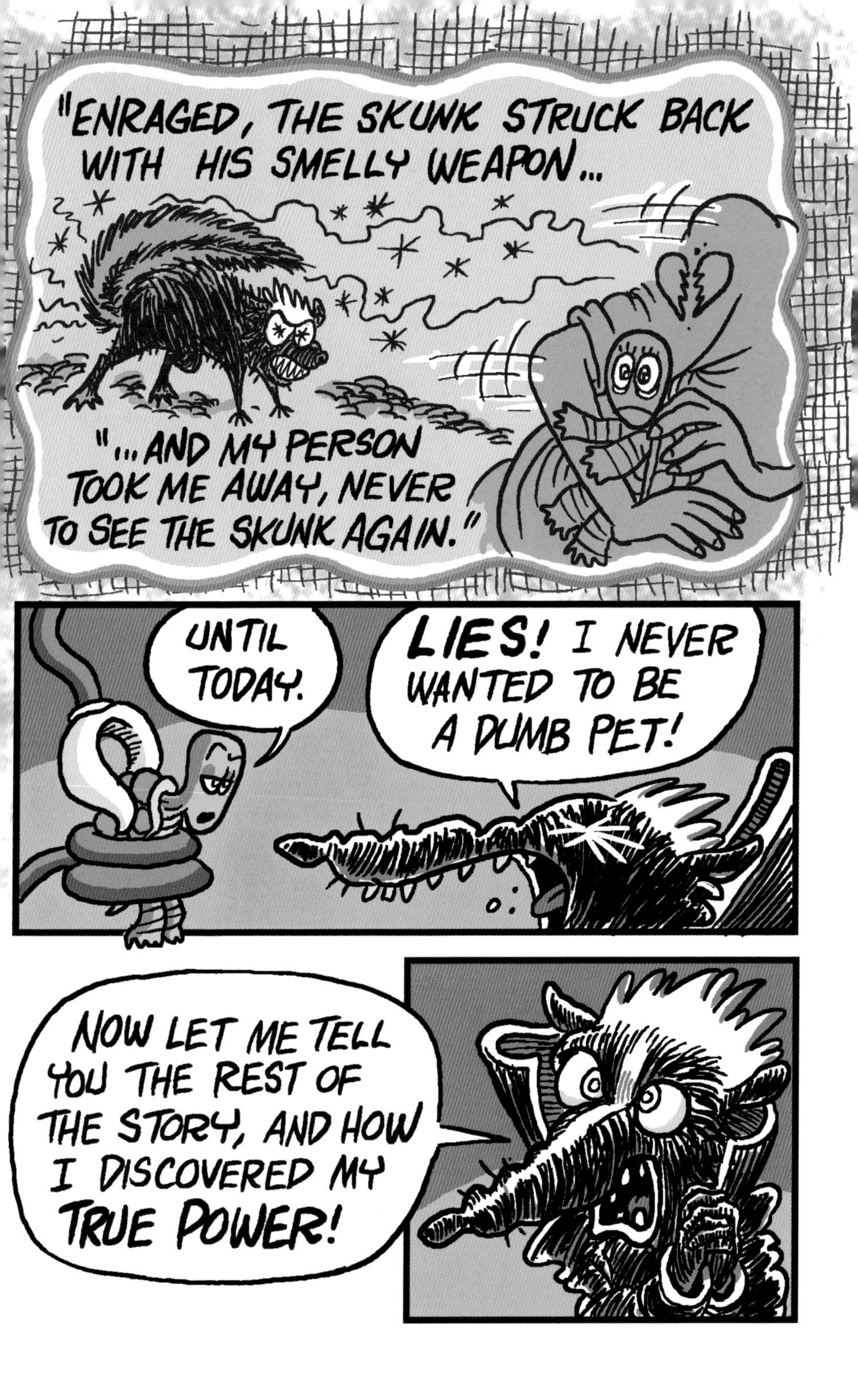
"ENRAGED, THE SKUNK STRUCK BACK WITH HIS SMELLY WEAPON...
"...AND MY PERSON TOOK ME AWAY, NEVER TO SEE THE SKUNK AGAIN."
UNTIL TODAY.
LIES! I NEVER WANTED TO BE A DUMB PET!
NOW LET ME TELL YOU THE REST OF THE STORY, AND HOW I DISCOVERED MY TRUE POWER!

CHAPTER 12

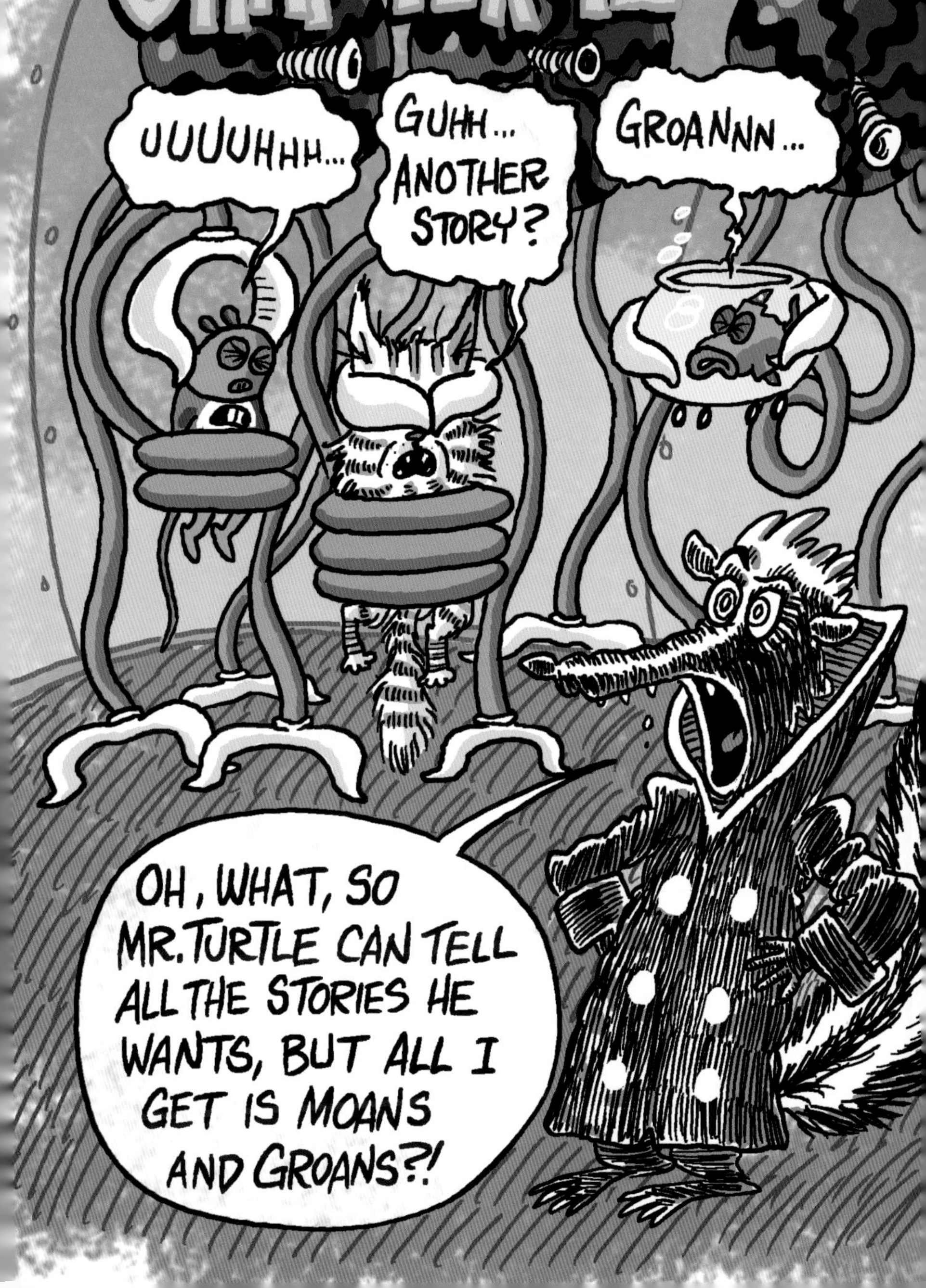
UUUUHHH...
GUHH... ANOTHER STORY?
GROANNN...
OH, WHAT, SO MR. TURTLE CAN TELL ALL THE STORIES HE WANTS, BUT ALL I GET IS MOANS AND GROANS?!

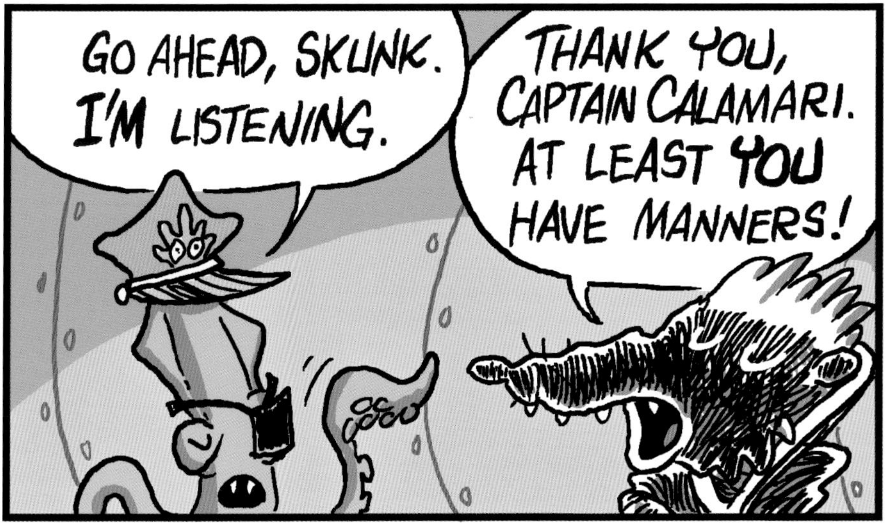
GO AHEAD, SKUNK. I'M LISTENING.
THANK YOU, CAPTAIN CALAMARI. AT LEAST YOU HAVE MANNERS!

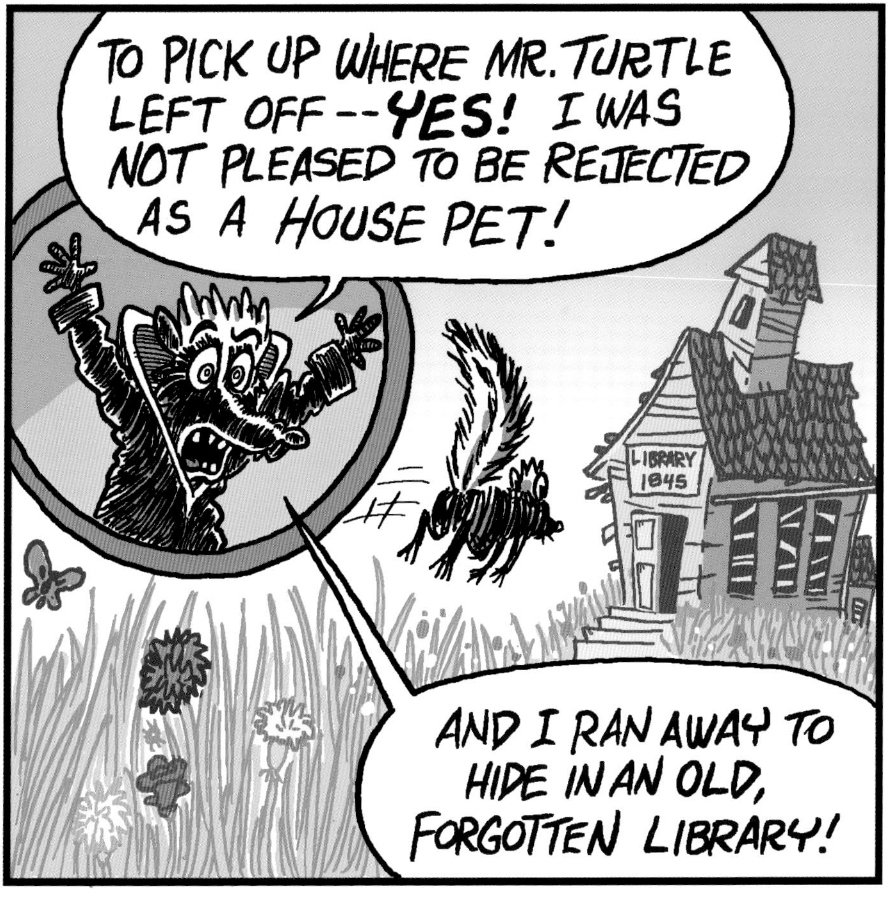
TO PICK UP WHERE MR. TURTLE LEFT OFF--YES! I WAS NOT PLEASED TO BE REJECTED AS A HOUSE PET!
LIBRARY 1845
AND I RAN AWAY TO HIDE IN AN OLD, FORGOTTEN LIBRARY!

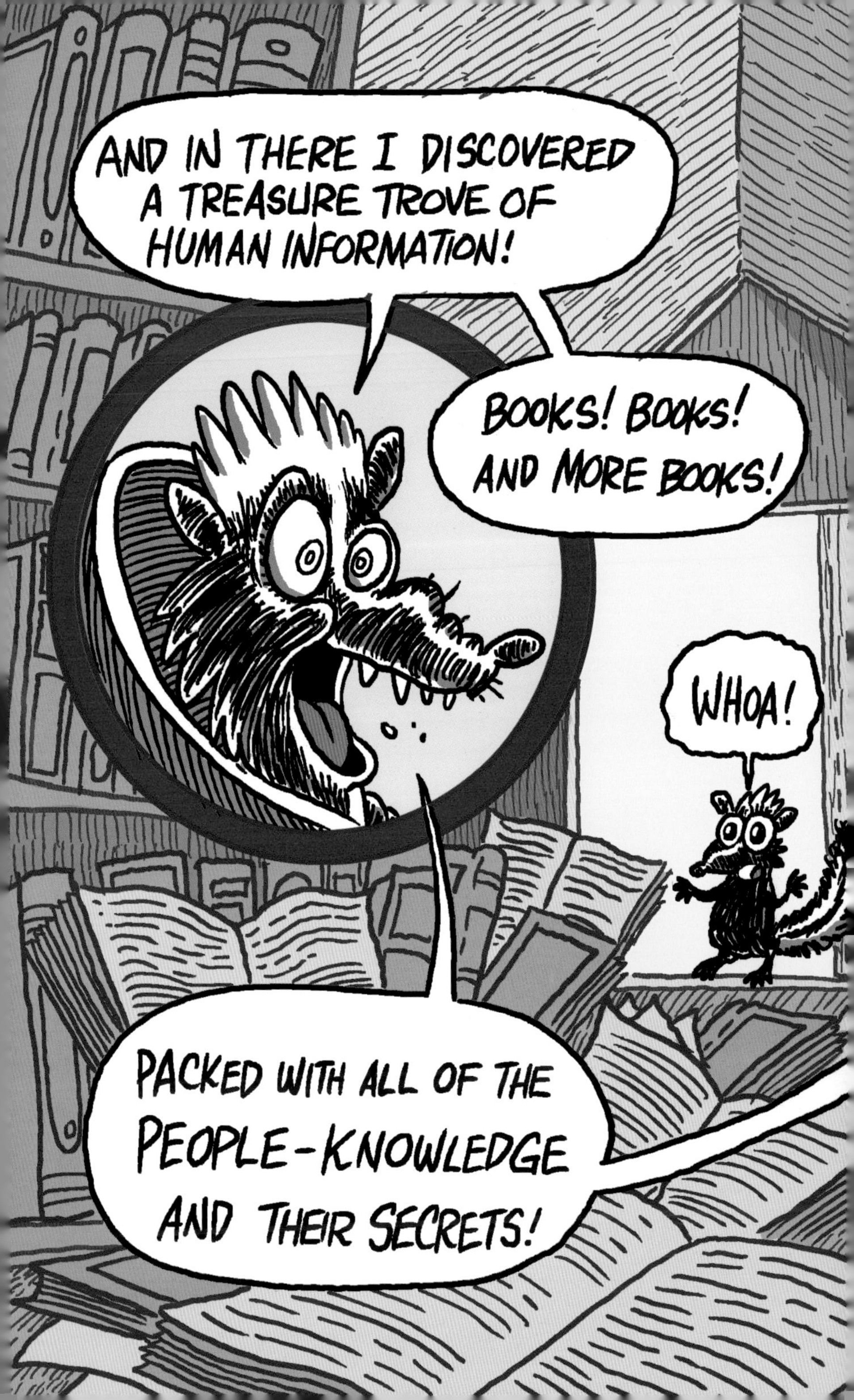
AND IN THERE I DISCOVERED A TREASURE TROVE OF HUMAN INFORMATION!
BOOKS! BOOKS! AND MORE BOOKS!
WHOA!
PACKED WITH ALL OF THE PEOPLE-KNOWLEDGE AND THEIR SECRETS!

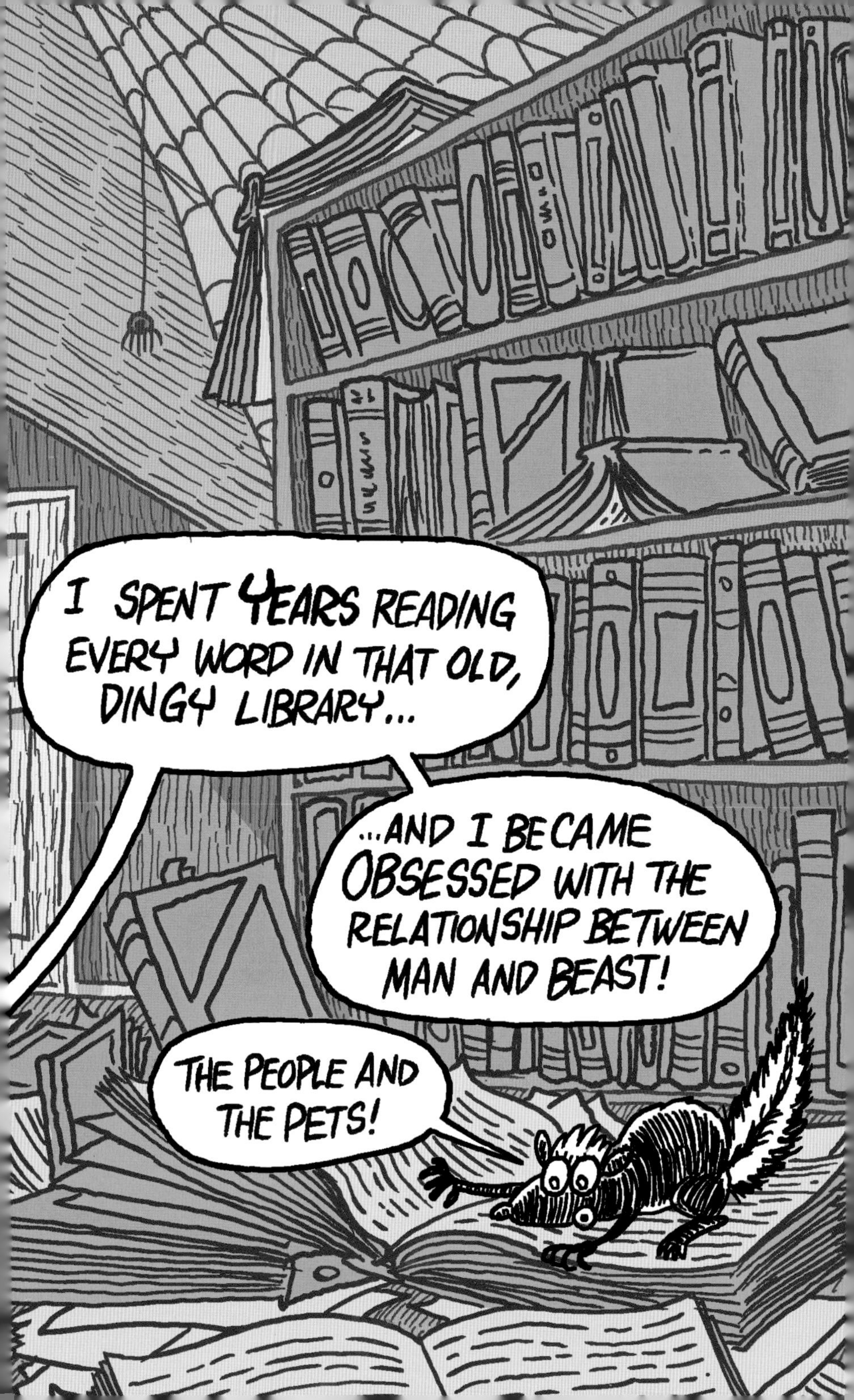

I SPENT YEARS READING EVERY WORD IN THAT OLD, DINGY LIBRARY...
...AND I BECAME OBSESSED WITH THE RELATIONSHIP BETWEEN MAN AND BEAST!
THE PEOPLE AND THE PETS!

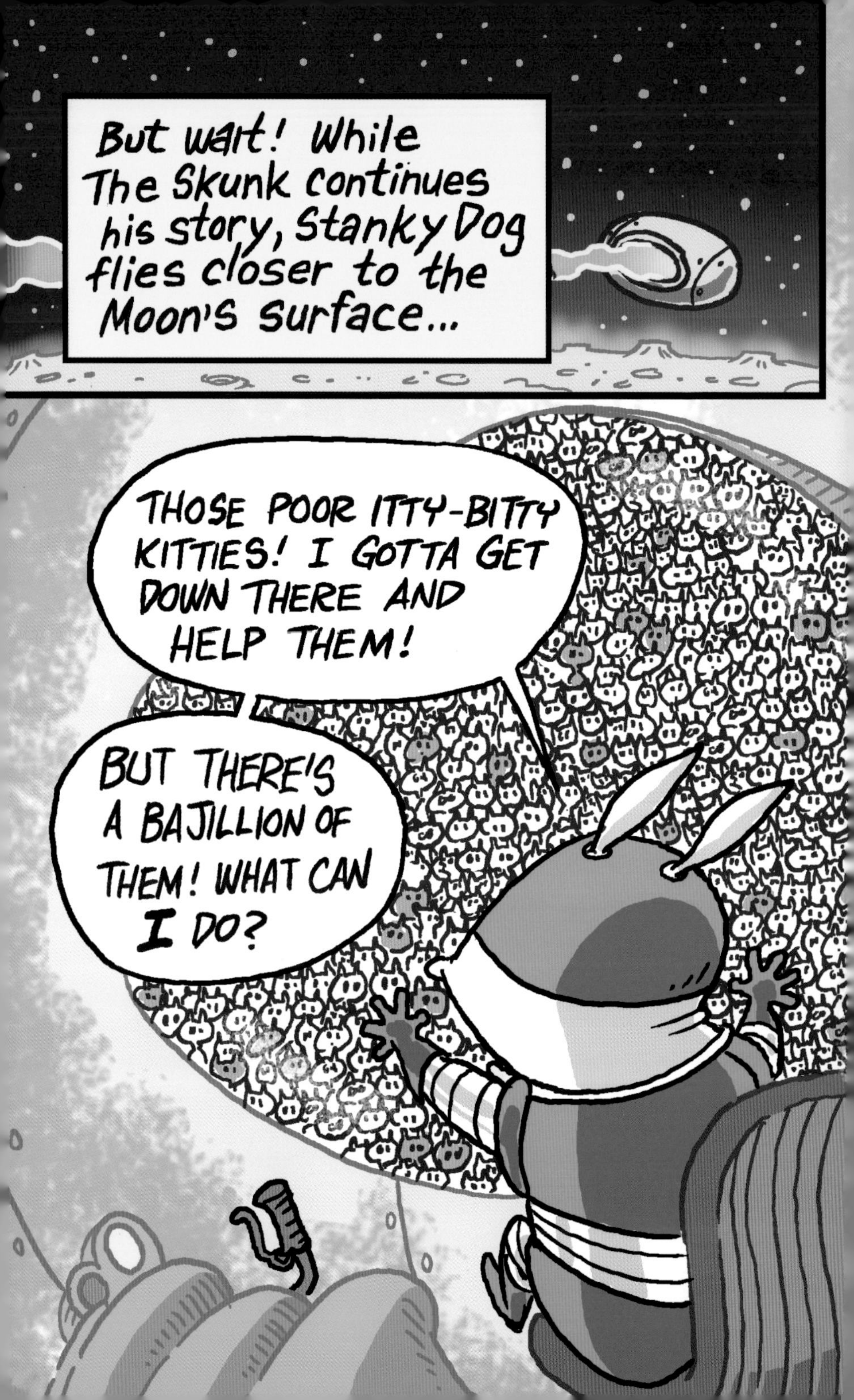

But wait! While The Skunk continues his story, Stanky Dog flies closer to the Moon's surface...
THOSE POOR ITTY-BITTY KITTIES! I GOTTA GET DOWN THERE AND HELP THEM!
BUT THERE'S A BAJILLION OF THEM! WHAT CAN I DO?

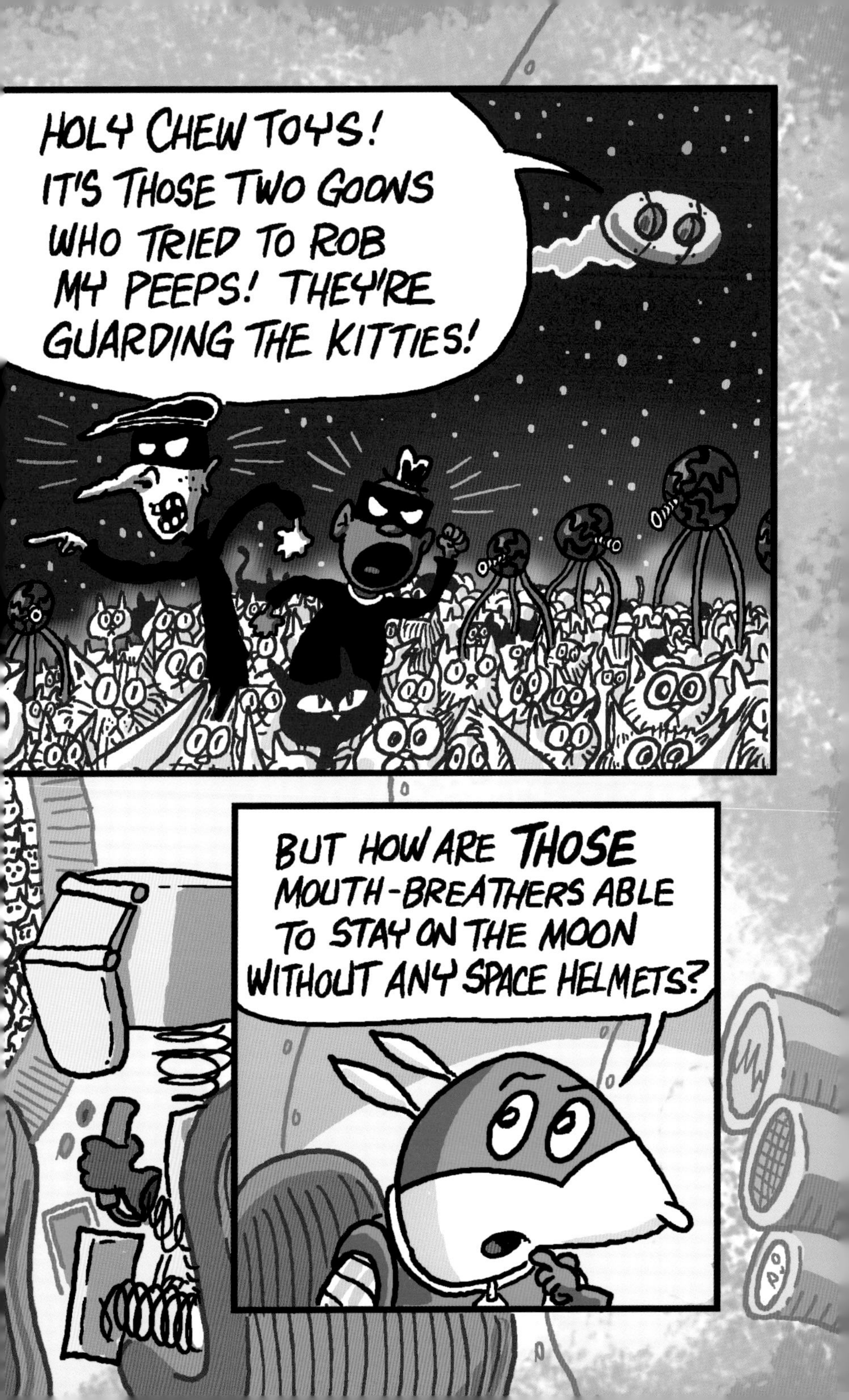
HOLY CHEW TOYS! IT'S THOSE TWO GOONS WHO TRIED TO ROB MY PEEPS! THEY'RE GUARDING THE KITTIES!
BUT HOW ARE THOSE MOUTH-BREATHERS ABLE TO STAY ON THE MOON WITHOUT ANY SPACE HELMETS?

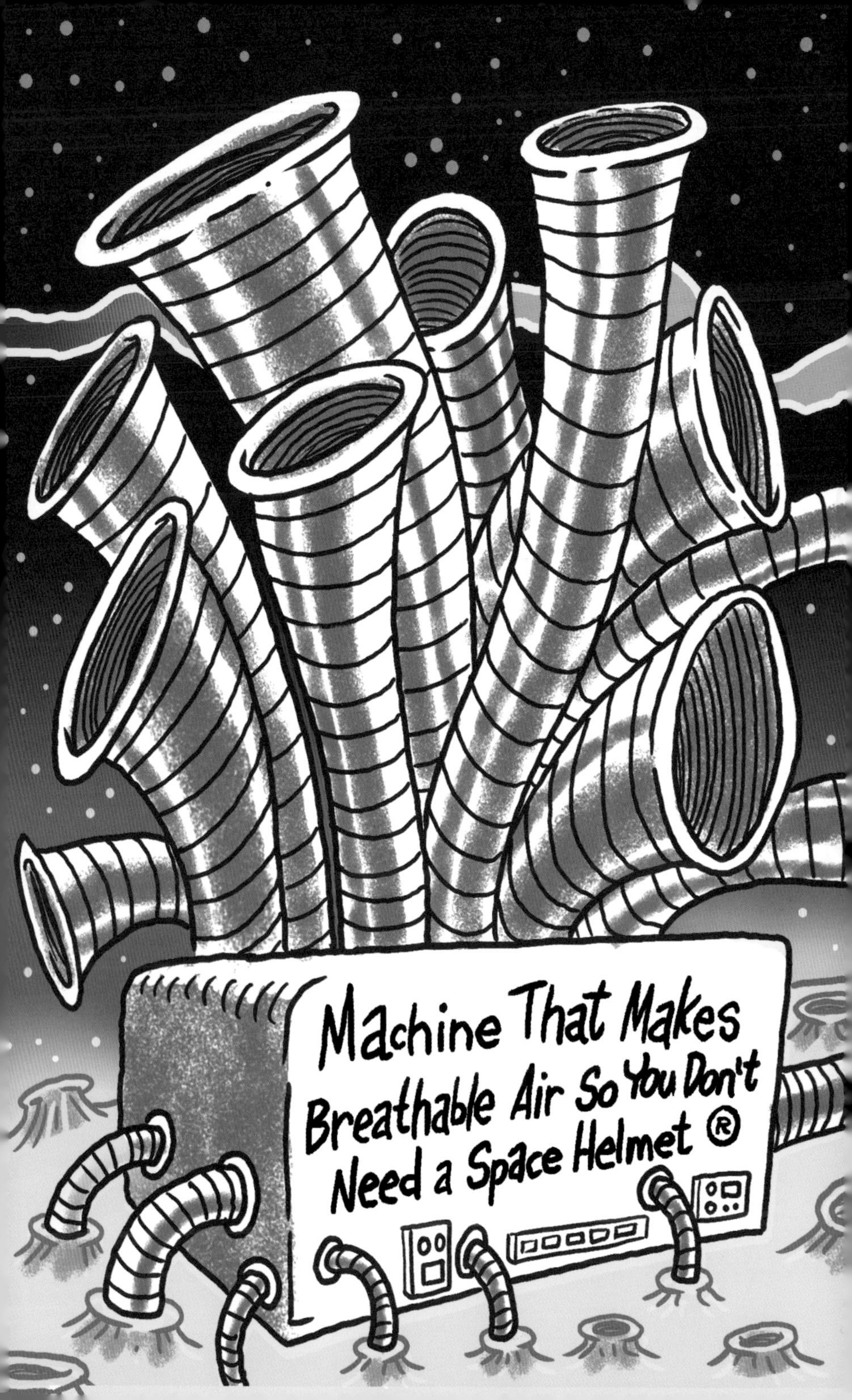
Machine That Makes Breathable Air So You Don't Need a Space Helmet ®

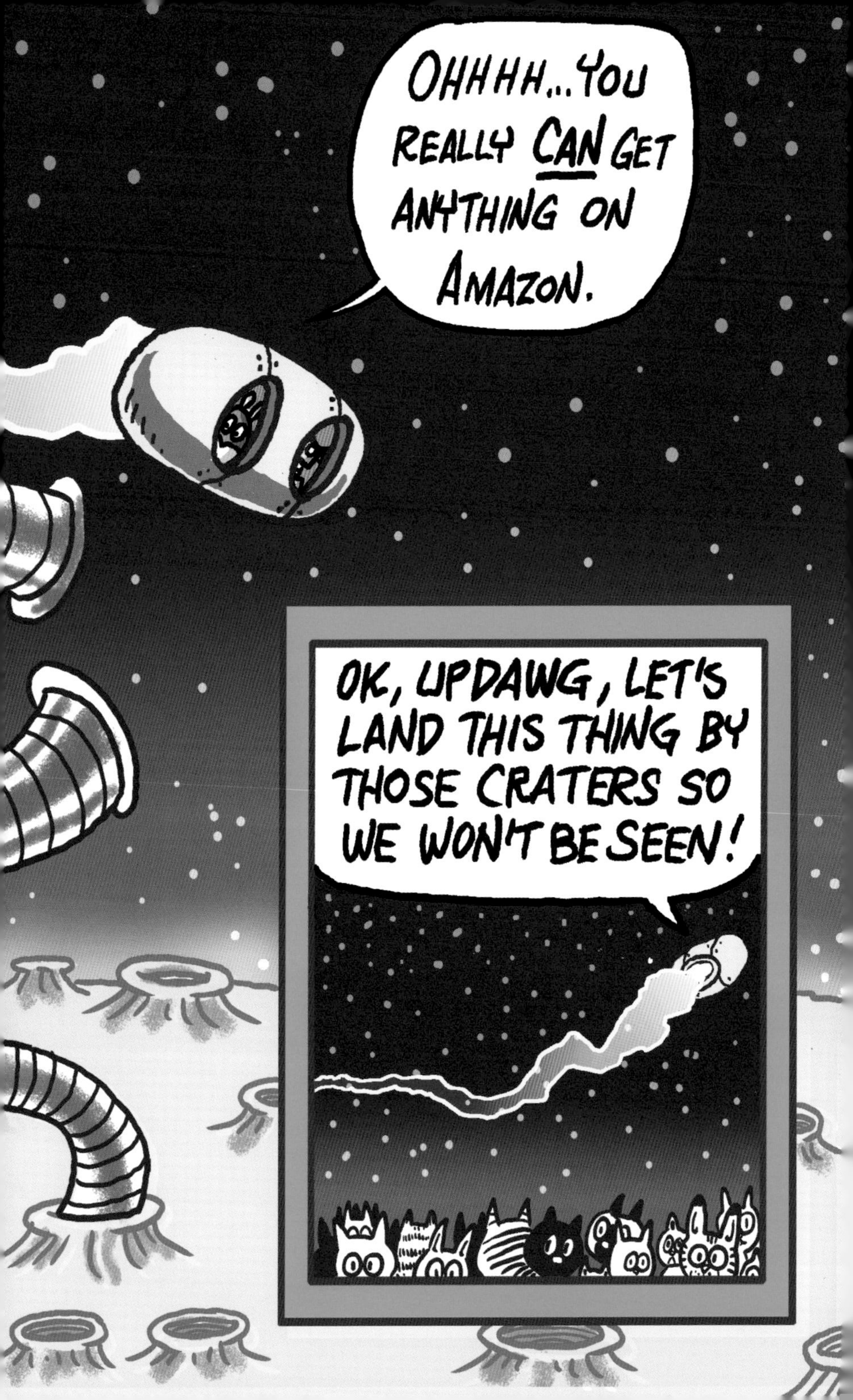
OHHHH... YOU REALLY CAN GET ANYTHING ON AMAZON.
OK, UPDAWG, LET'S LAND THIS THING BY THOSE CRATERS SO WE WON'T BE SEEN!

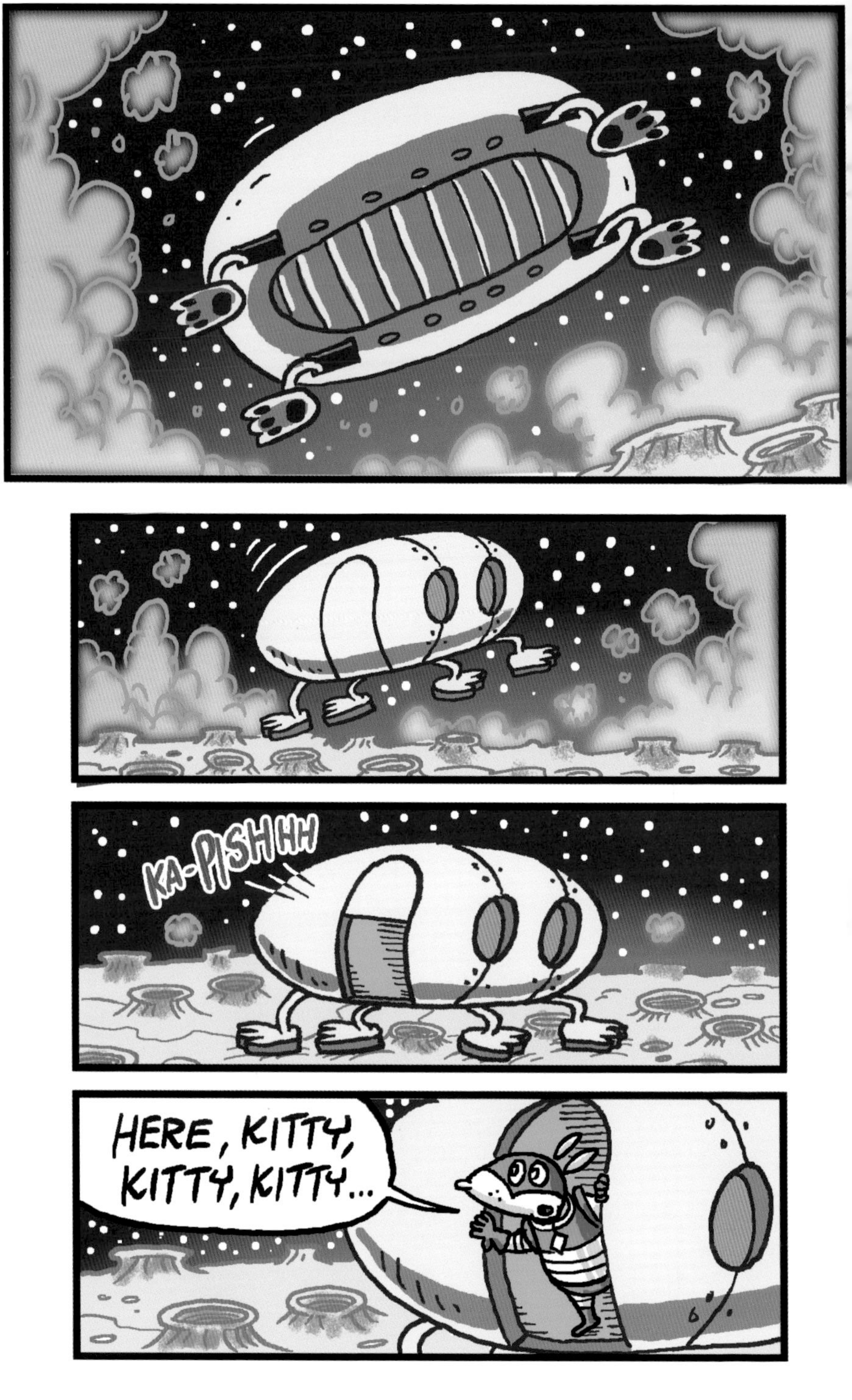
KA-PISHHH
HERE, KITTY, KITTY, KITTY, KITTY...

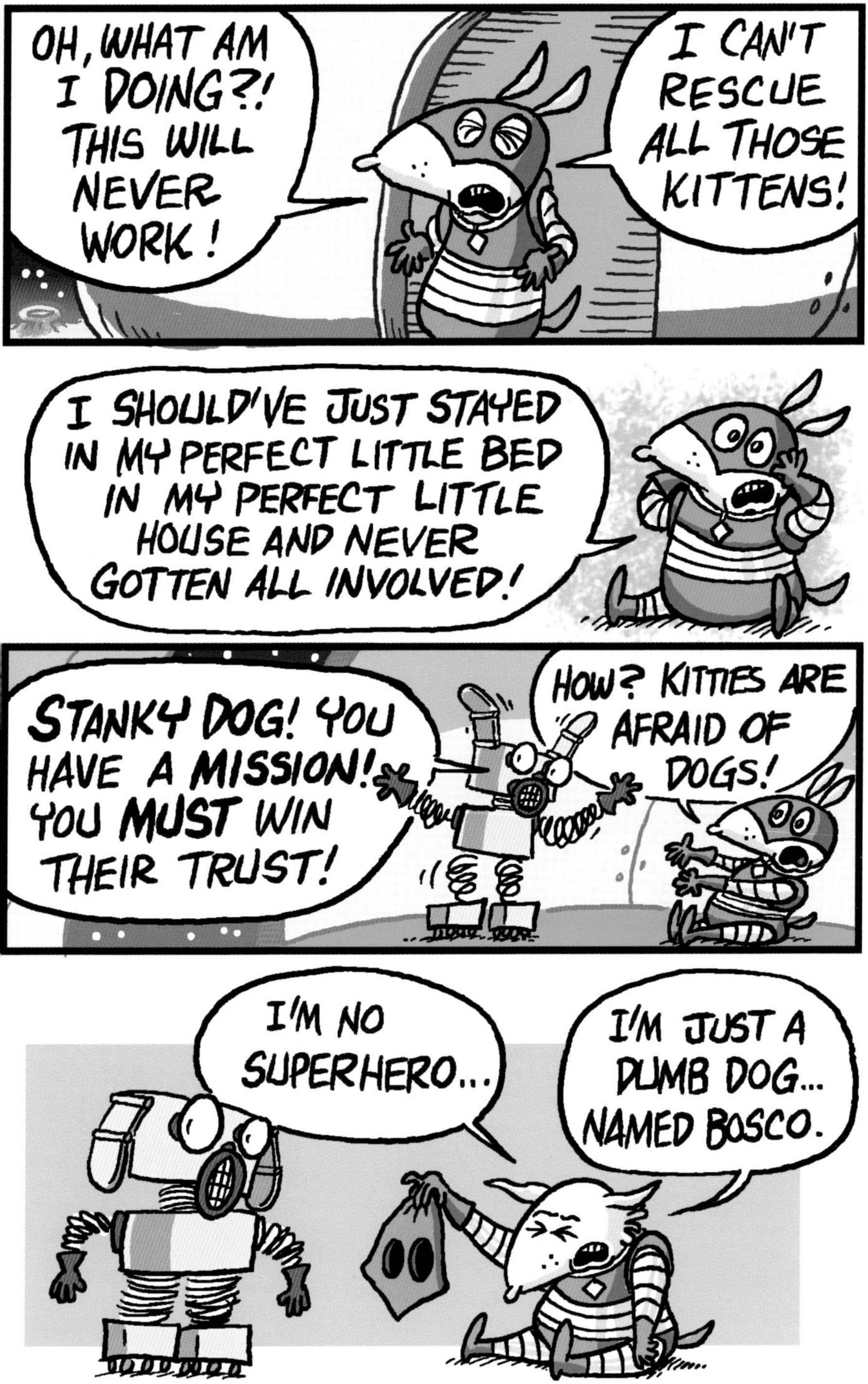
OH, WHAT AM I DOING?! THIS WILL NEVER WORK!
I CAN'T RESCUE ALL THOSE KITTENS!
I SHOULD'VE JUST STAYED IN MY PERFECT LITTLE BED IN MY PERFECT LITTLE HOUSE AND NEVER GOTTEN ALL INVOLVED!
STANKY DOG! YOU HAVE A **MISSION**! YOU **MUST** WIN THEIR TRUST!
HOW? KITTIES ARE AFRAID OF DOGS!
I'M NO SUPERHERO...
I'M JUST A DUMB DOG... NAMED BOSCO.

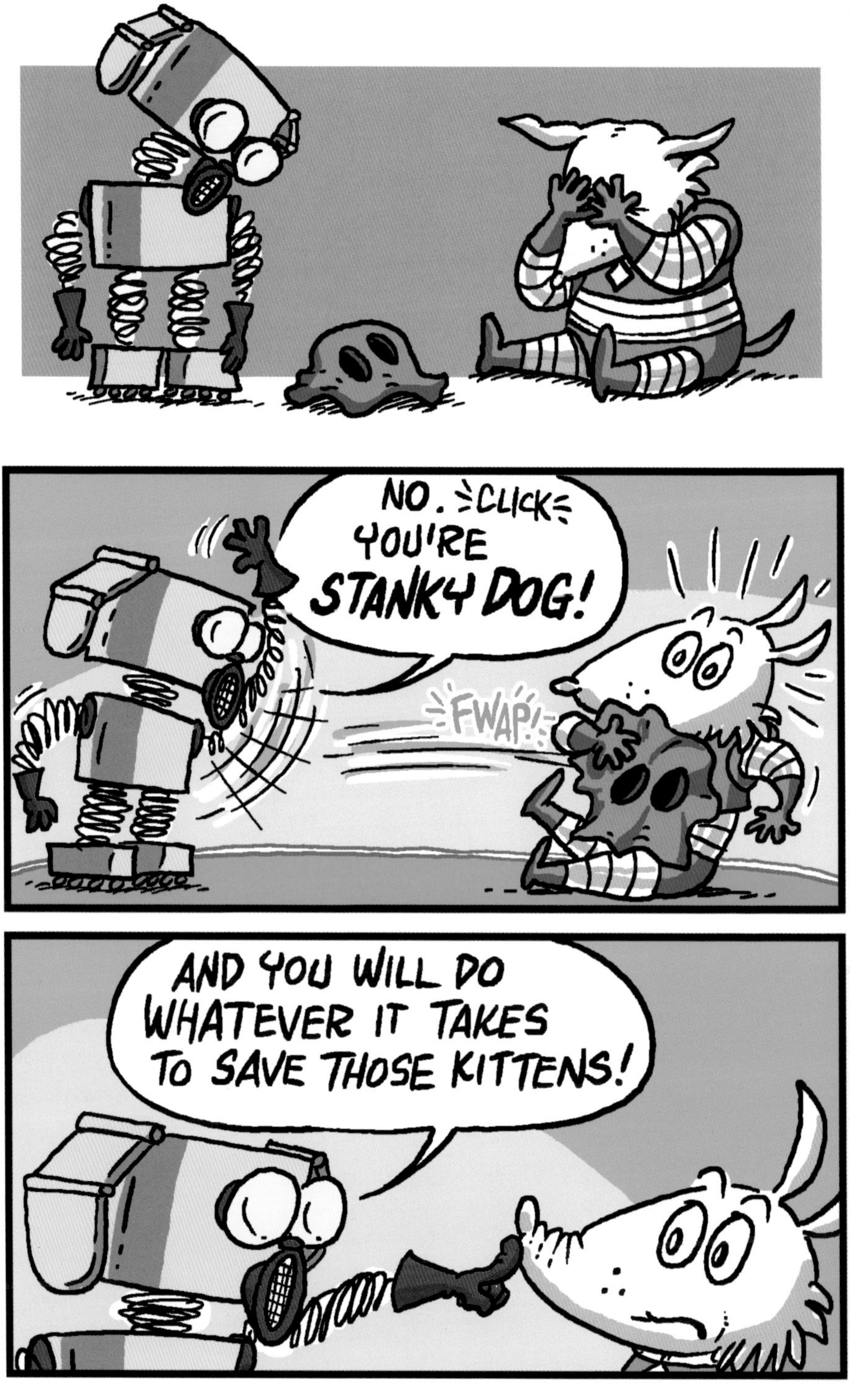
NO. CLICK YOU'RE STANKY DOG!
FWAP!
AND YOU WILL DO WHATEVER IT TAKES TO SAVE THOSE KITTENS!

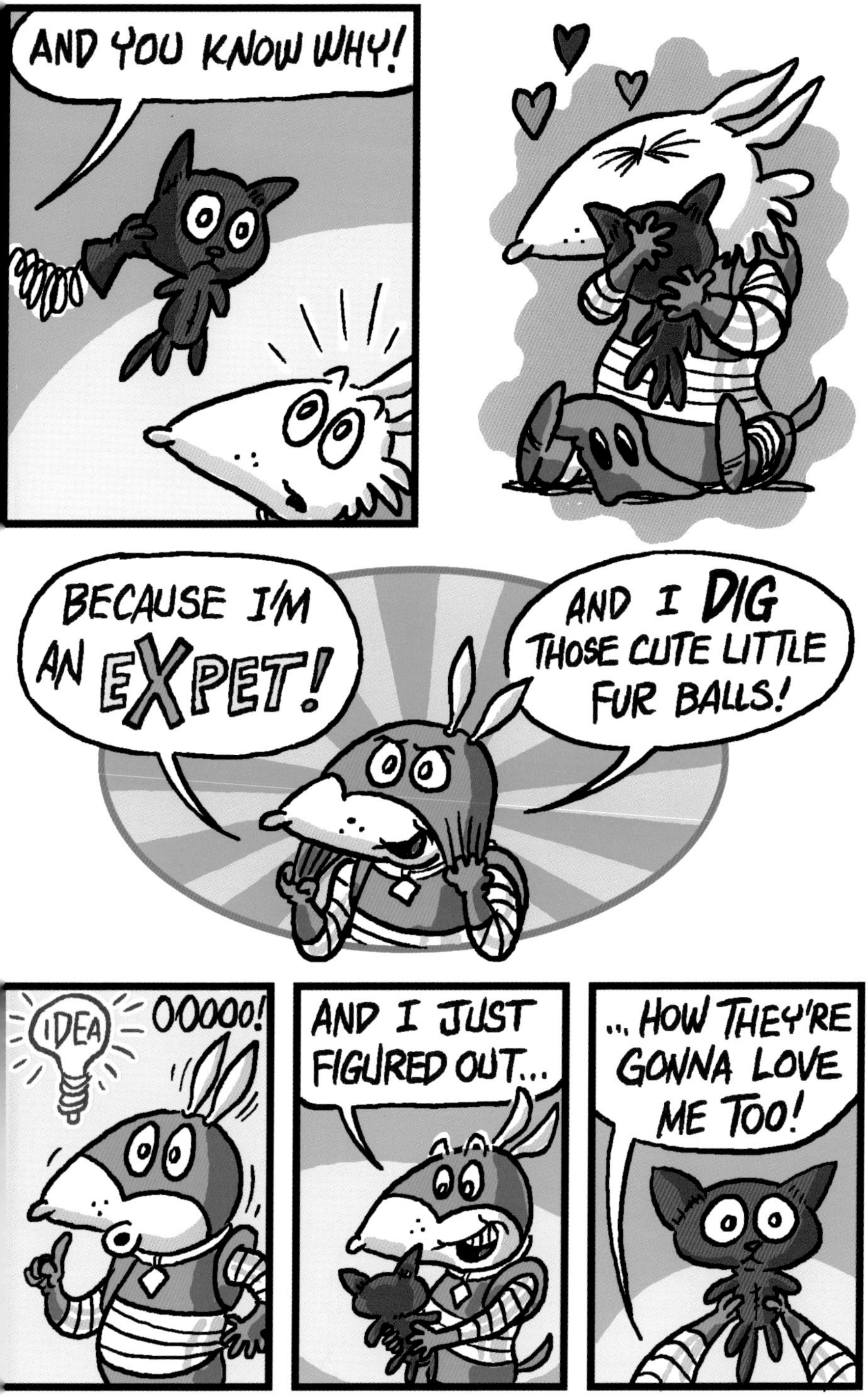
AND YOU KNOW WHY!
BECAUSE I'M AN EXPET!
AND I DIG THOSE CUTE LITTLE FUR BALLS!
IDEA
OOOOO!
AND I JUST FIGURED OUT...
... HOW THEY'RE GONNA LOVE ME TOO!

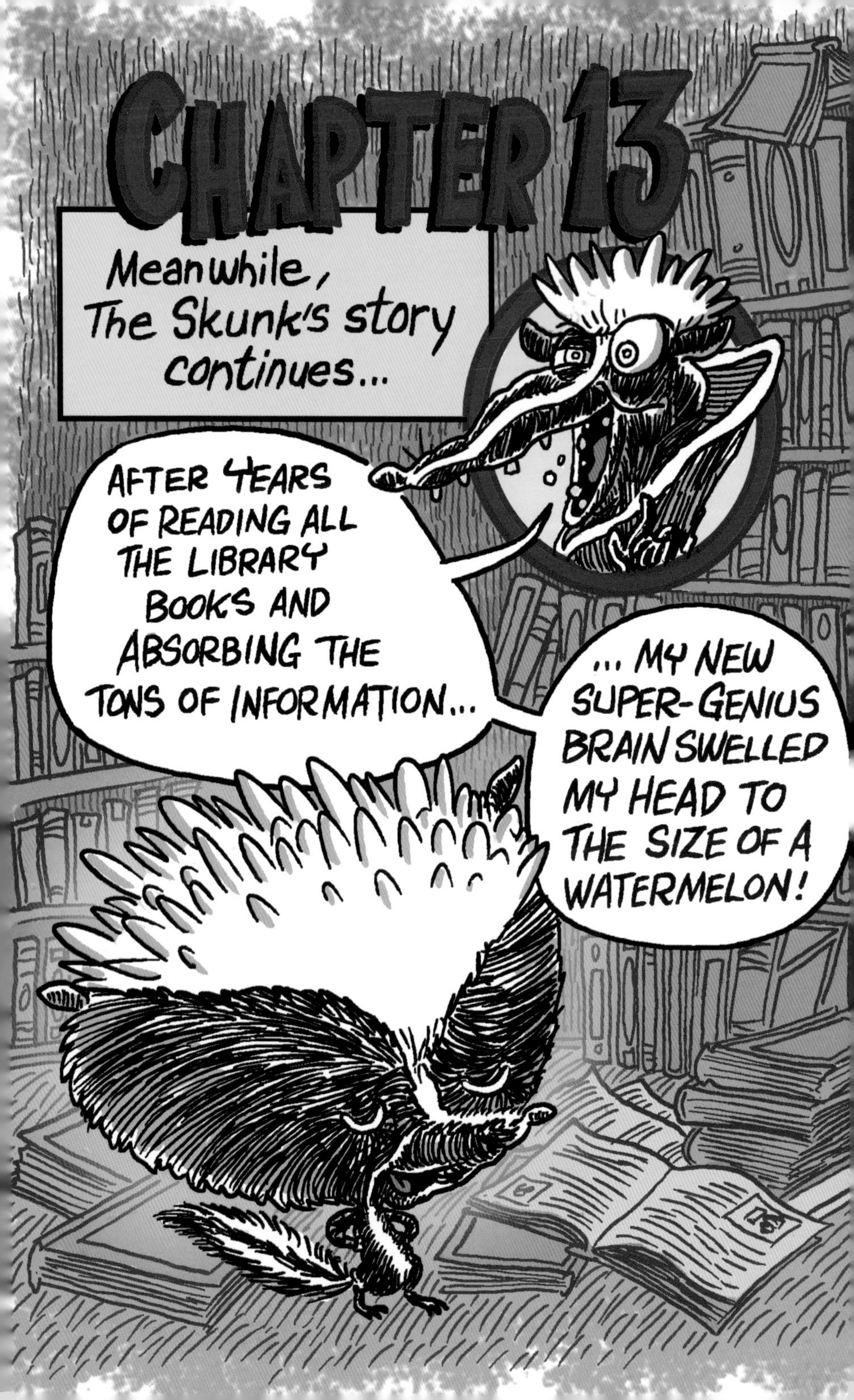
CHAPTER 13
Meanwhile, The Skunk's story continues...
AFTER YEARS OF READING ALL THE LIBRARY BOOKS AND ABSORBING THE TONS OF INFORMATION...
... MY NEW SUPER-GENIUS BRAIN SWELLED MY HEAD TO THE SIZE OF A WATERMELON!

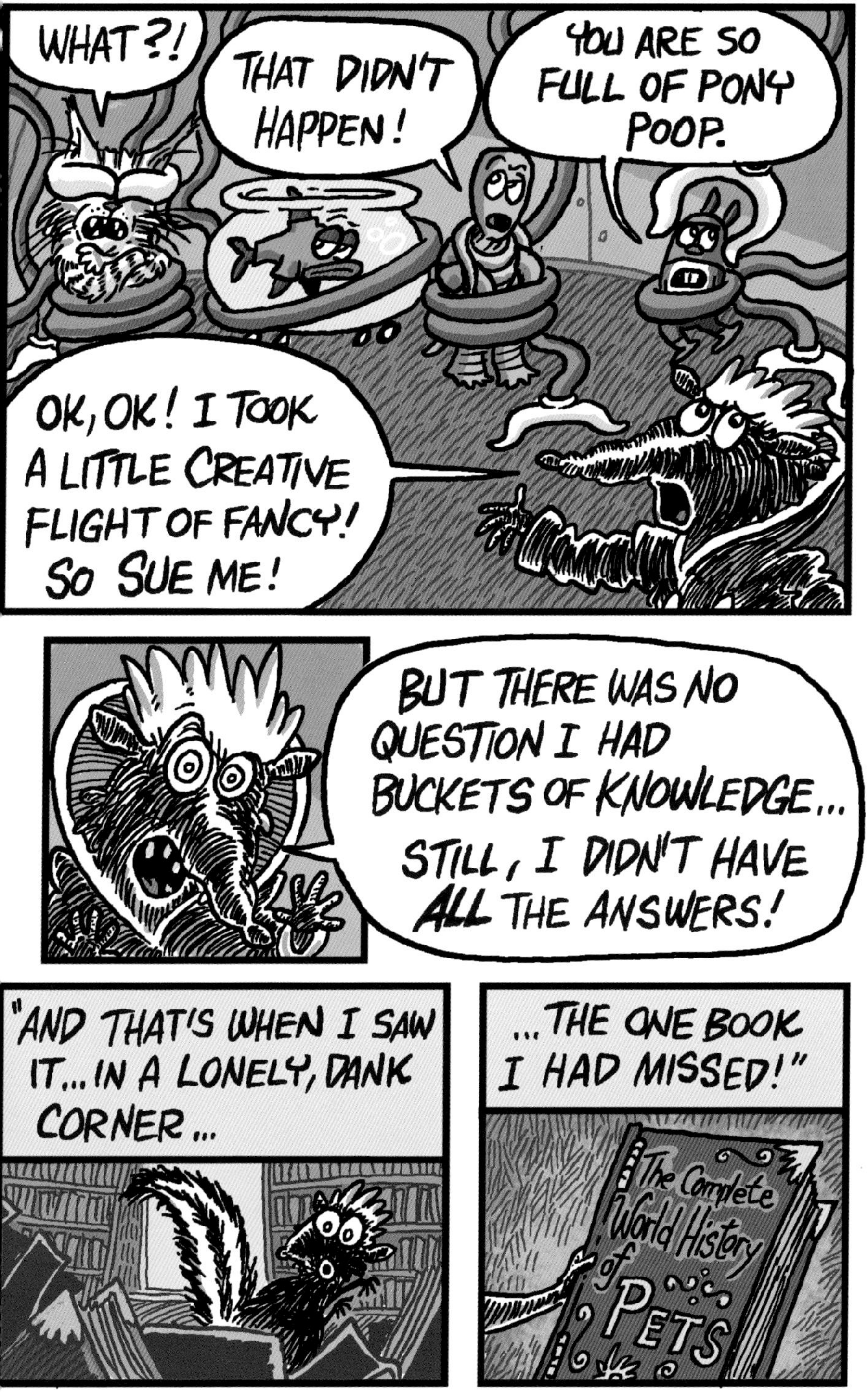
WHAT?!
THAT DIDN'T HAPPEN!
YOU ARE SO FULL OF PONY POOP.
OK, OK! I TOOK A LITTLE CREATIVE FLIGHT OF FANCY! SO SUE ME!
BUT THERE WAS NO QUESTION I HAD BUCKETS OF KNOWLEDGE... STILL, I DIDN'T HAVE ALL THE ANSWERS!
"AND THAT'S WHEN I SAW IT... IN A LONELY, DANK CORNER...
...THE ONE BOOK I HAD MISSED!"
The Complete World History of PETS

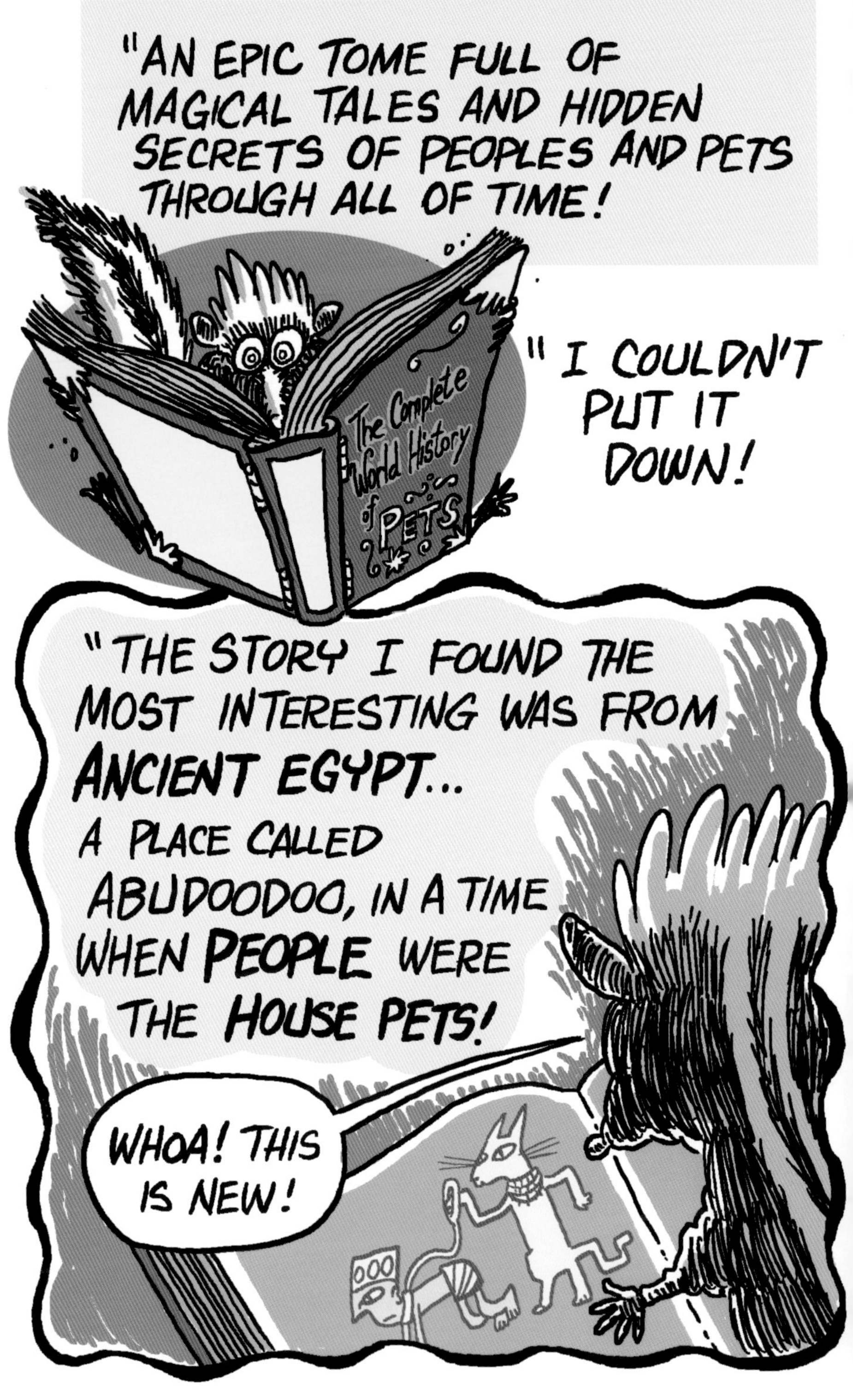

"AN EPIC TOME FULL OF MAGICAL TALES AND HIDDEN SECRETS OF PEOPLES AND PETS THROUGH ALL OF TIME!
The Complete World History of PETS
" I COULDN'T PUT IT DOWN!
"THE STORY I FOUND THE MOST INTERESTING WAS FROM ANCIENT EGYPT... A PLACE CALLED ABUDOODOO, IN A TIME WHEN PEOPLE WERE THE HOUSE PETS!
WHOA! THIS IS NEW!

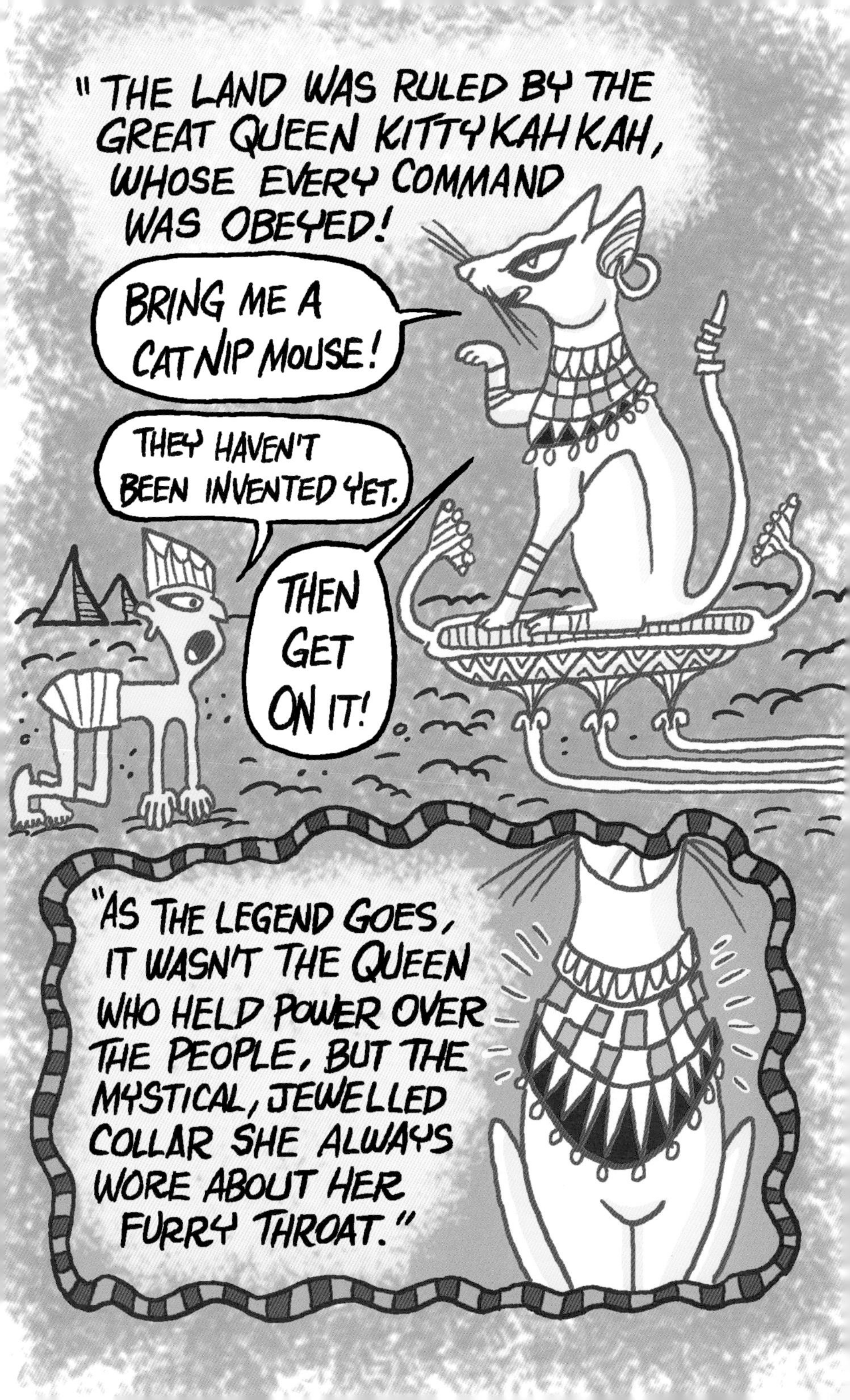
"THE LAND WAS RULED BY THE GREAT QUEEN KITTYKAHKAH, WHOSE EVERY COMMAND WAS OBEYED!
BRING ME A CATNIP MOUSE!
THEY HAVEN'T BEEN INVENTED YET.
THEN GET ON IT!
"AS THE LEGEND GOES, IT WASN'T THE QUEEN WHO HELD POWER OVER THE PEOPLE, BUT THE MYSTICAL, JEWELLED COLLAR SHE ALWAYS WORE ABOUT HER FURRY THROAT."

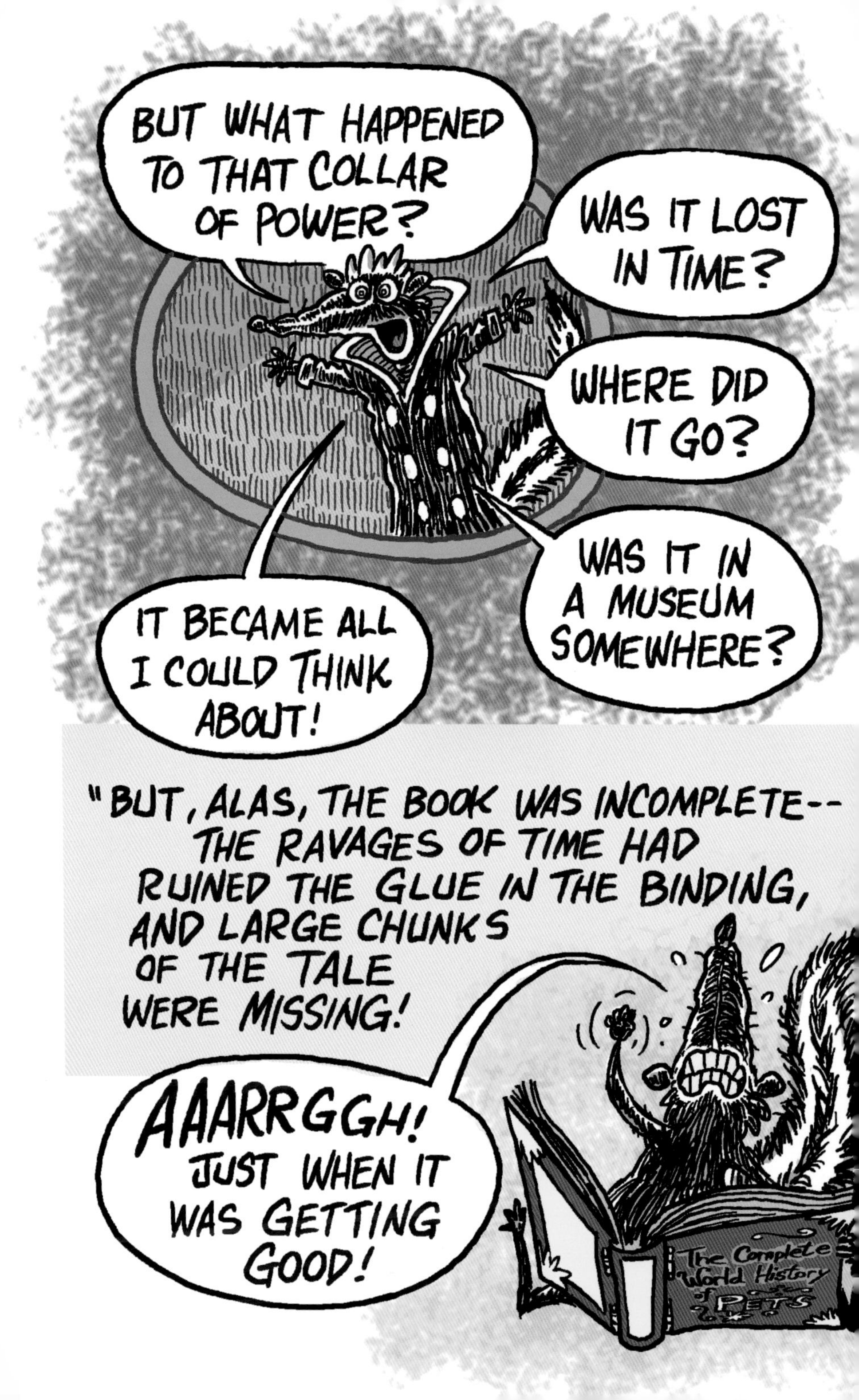
BUT WHAT HAPPENED TO THAT COLLAR OF POWER?
WAS IT LOST IN TIME?
WHERE DID IT GO?
WAS IT IN A MUSEUM SOMEWHERE?
IT BECAME ALL I COULD THINK ABOUT!
"BUT, ALAS, THE BOOK WAS INCOMPLETE-- THE RAVAGES OF TIME HAD RUINED THE GLUE IN THE BINDING, AND LARGE CHUNKS OF THE TALE WERE MISSING!
AAARRGGH! JUST WHEN IT WAS GETTING GOOD!
The Complete World History of PETS

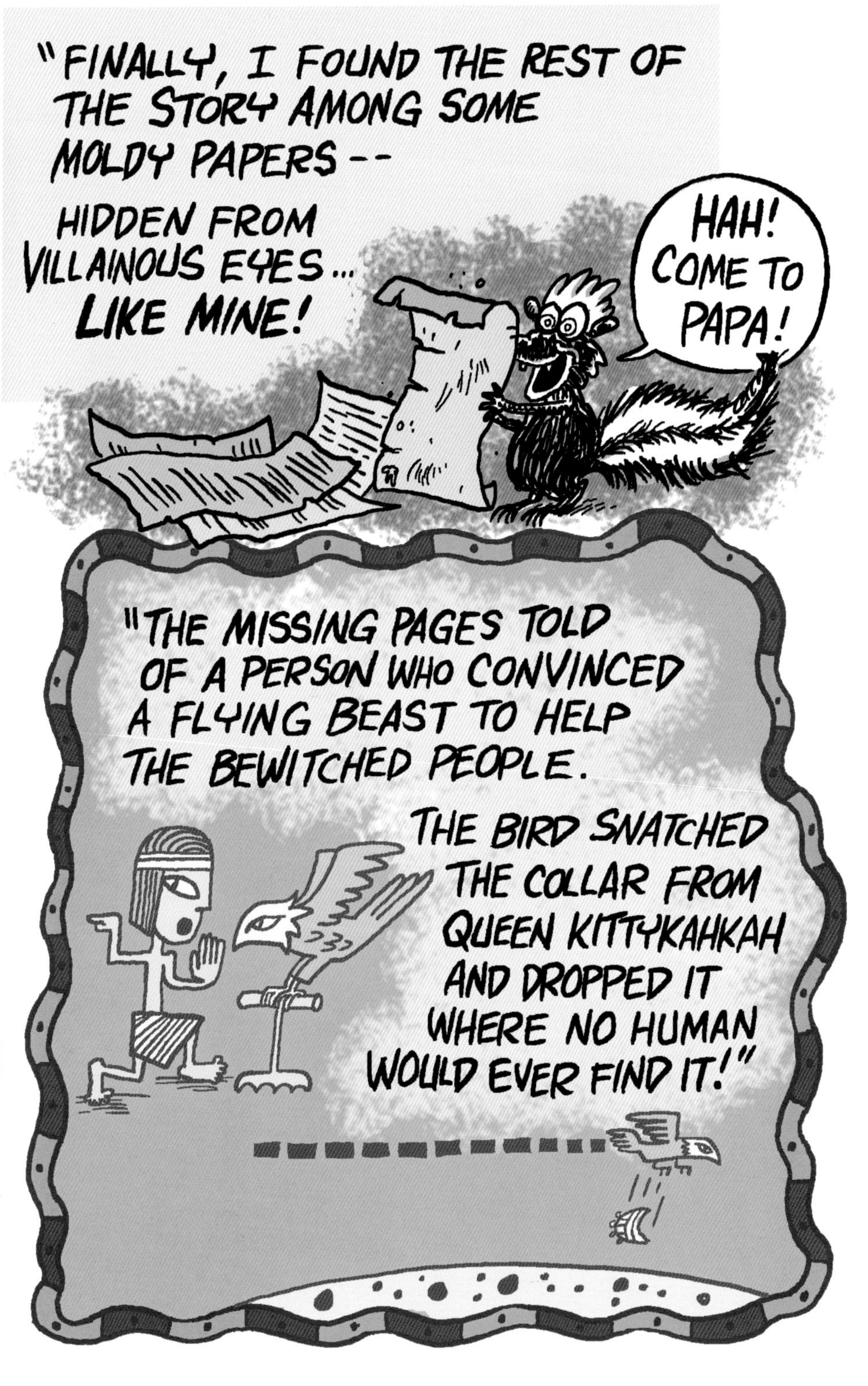
"FINALLY, I FOUND THE REST OF THE STORY AMONG SOME MOLDY PAPERS--
HIDDEN FROM VILLAINOUS EYES... LIKE MINE!
HAH! COME TO PAPA!
"THE MISSING PAGES TOLD OF A PERSON WHO CONVINCED A FLYING BEAST TO HELP THE BEWITCHED PEOPLE.
THE BIRD SNATCHED THE COLLAR FROM QUEEN KITTYKAHKAH AND DROPPED IT WHERE NO HUMAN WOULD EVER FIND IT!"

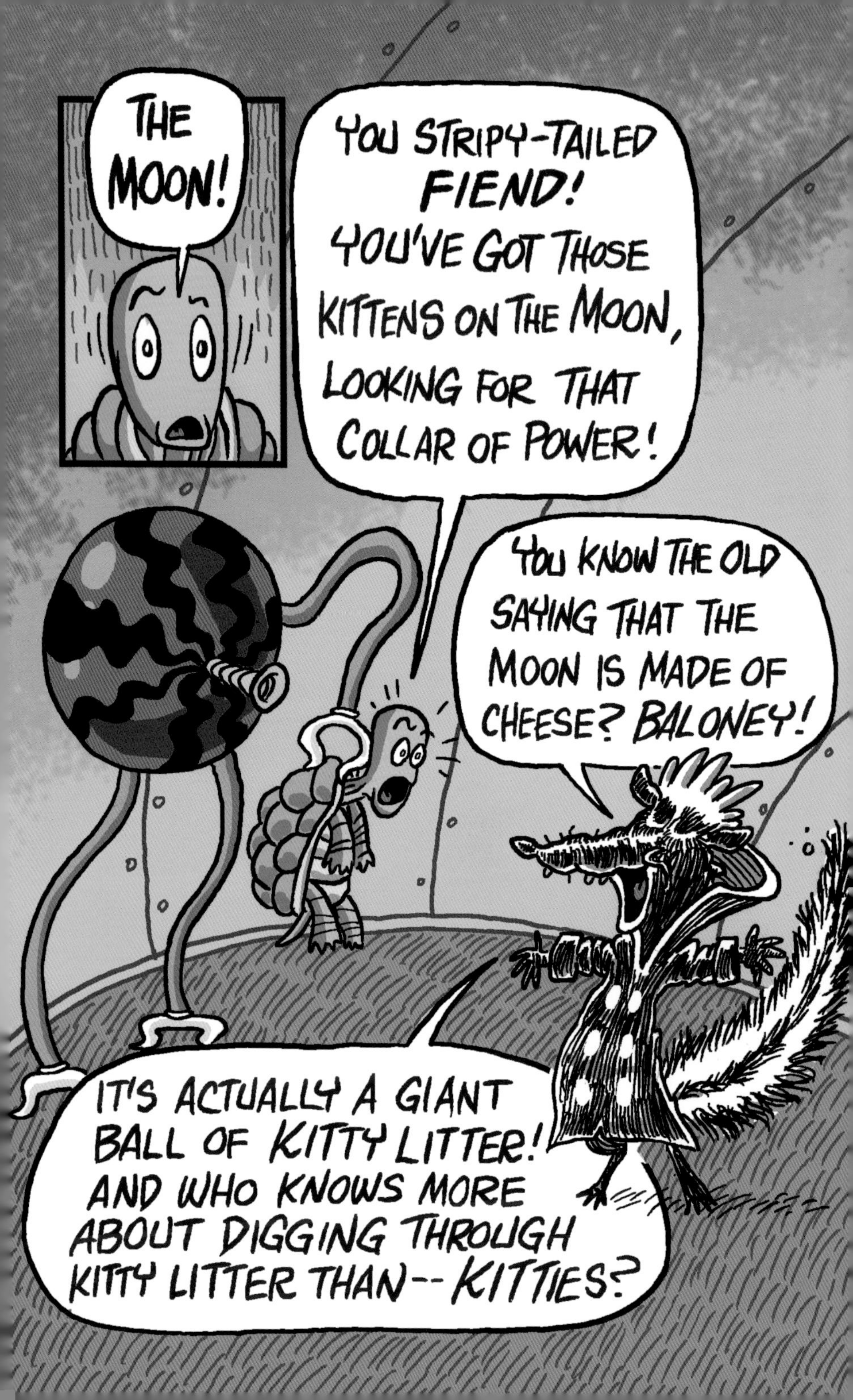
THE MOON!
YOU STRIPY-TAILED FIEND! YOU'VE GOT THOSE KITTENS ON THE MOON, LOOKING FOR THAT COLLAR OF POWER!
YOU KNOW THE OLD SAYING THAT THE MOON IS MADE OF CHEESE? BALONEY!
IT'S ACTUALLY A GIANT BALL OF KITTY LITTER! AND WHO KNOWS MORE ABOUT DIGGING THROUGH KITTY LITTER THAN-- KITTIES?

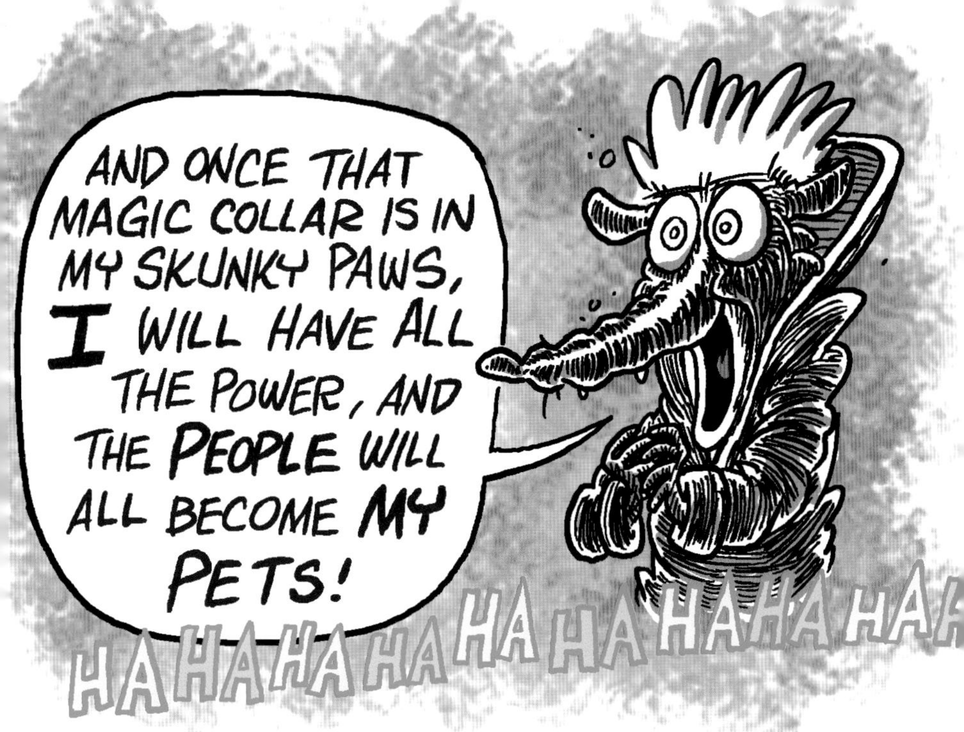
AND ONCE THAT MAGIC COLLAR IS IN MY SKUNKY PAWS, I WILL HAVE ALL THE POWER, AND THE PEOPLE WILL ALL BECOME MY PETS!
HAHAHAHAHAHAHAHAHAHAHA

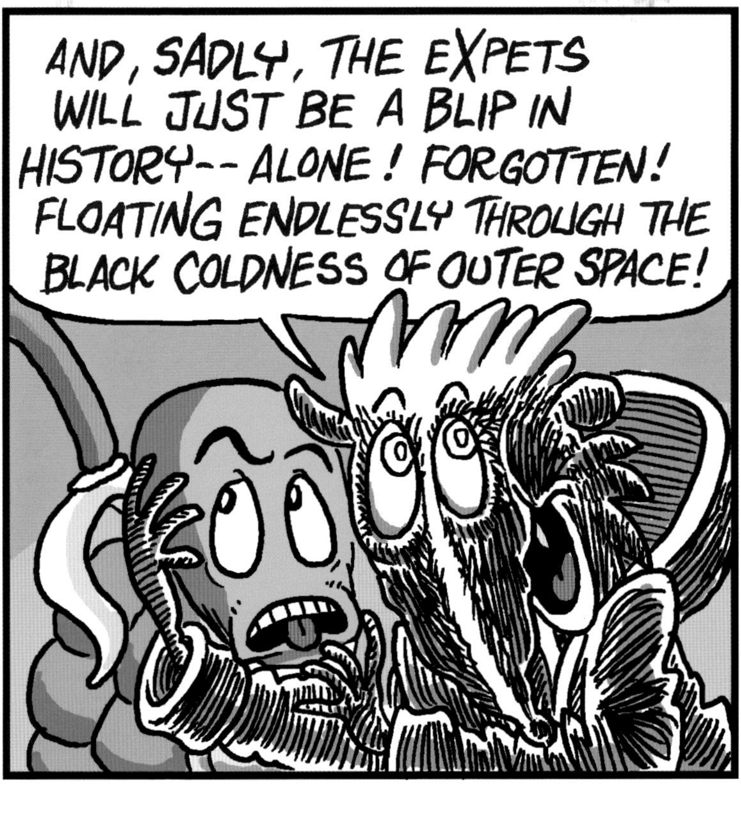
AND, SADLY, THE EXPETS WILL JUST BE A BLIP IN HISTORY-- ALONE! FORGOTTEN! FLOATING ENDLESSLY THROUGH THE BLACK COLDNESS OF OUTER SPACE!

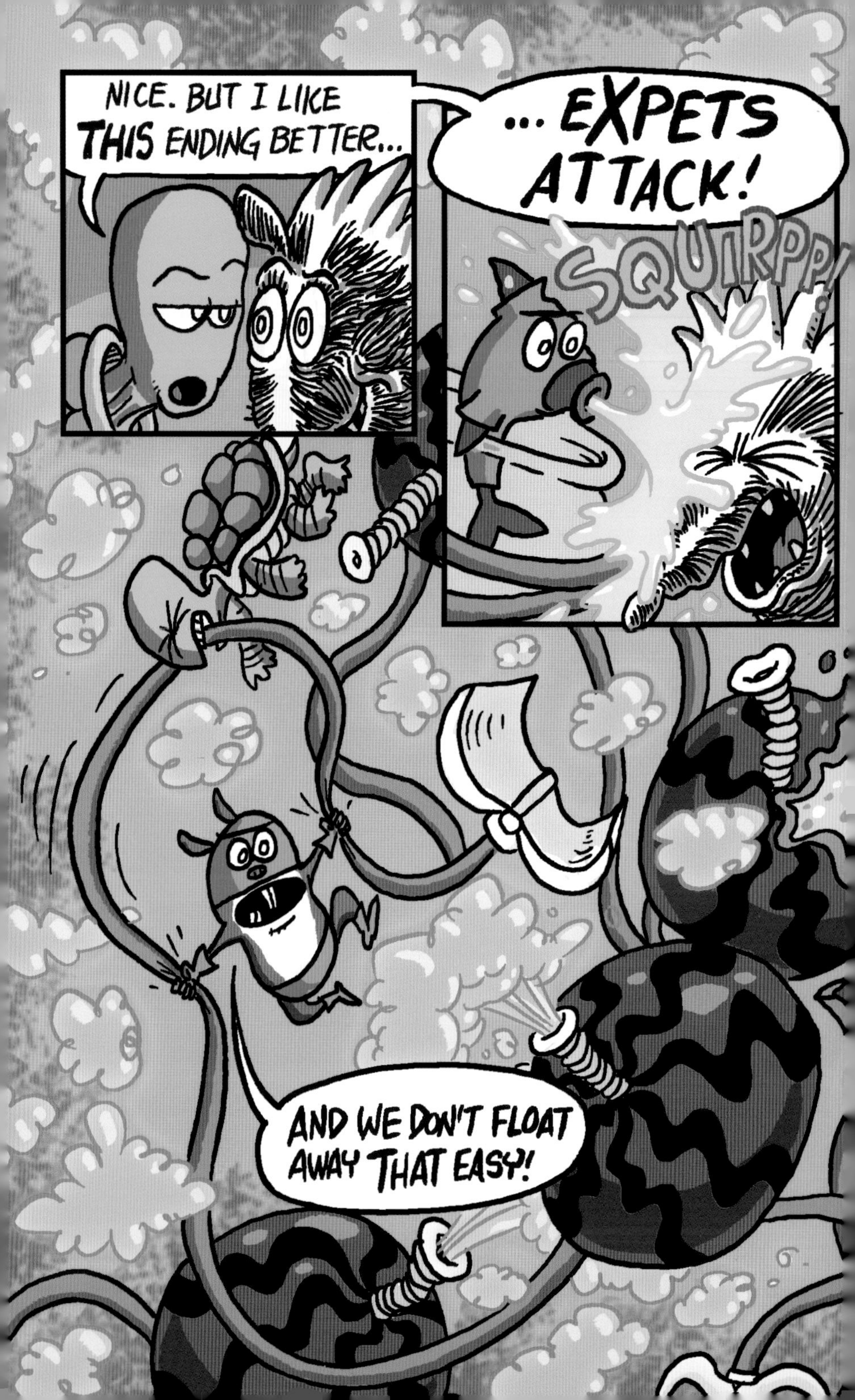
NICE. BUT I LIKE THIS ENDING BETTER...
...EXPETS ATTACK!
SQUIRPP!
AND WE DON'T FLOAT AWAY THAT EASY!

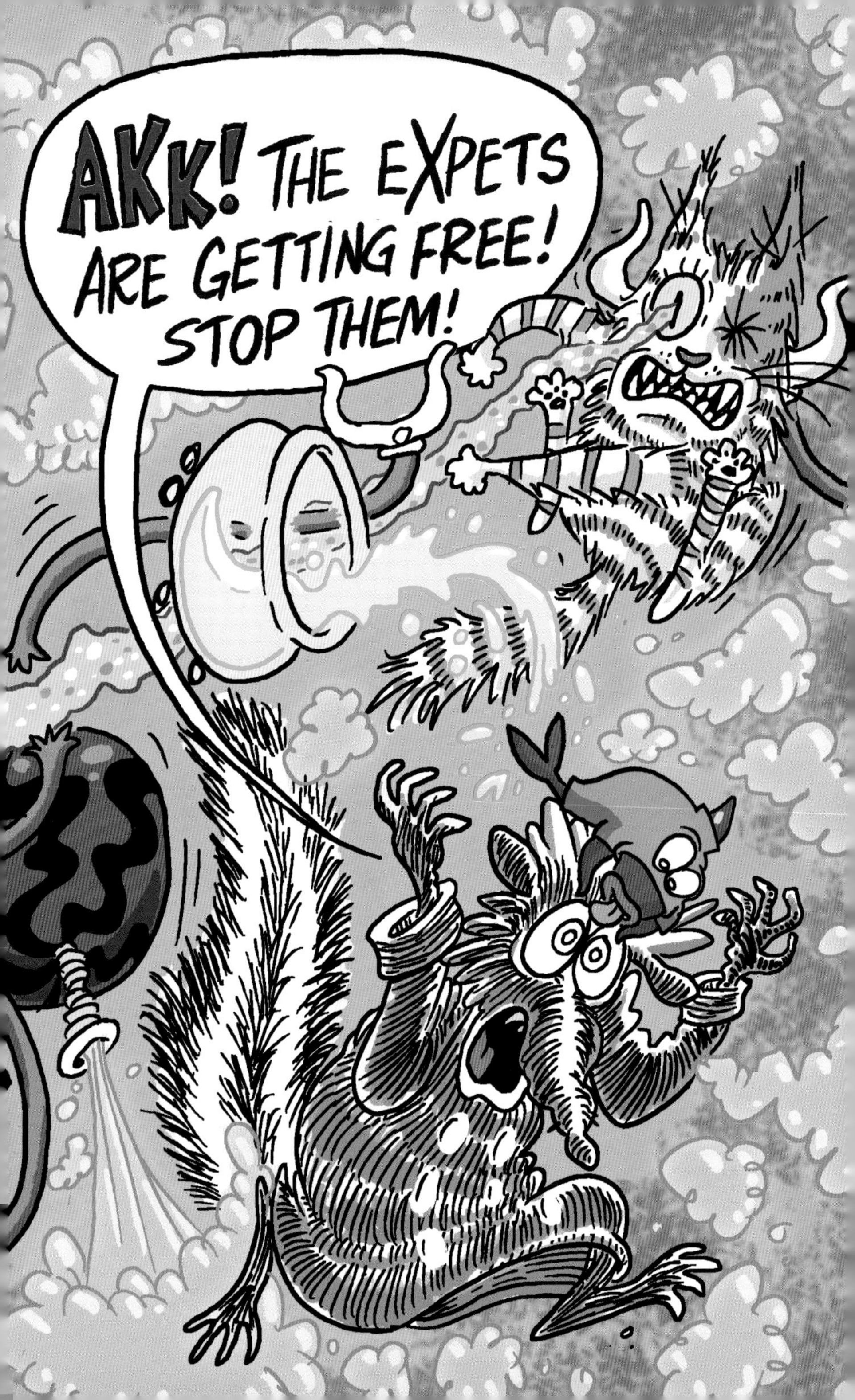
AKK! THE EXPETS ARE GETTING FREE! STOP THEM!

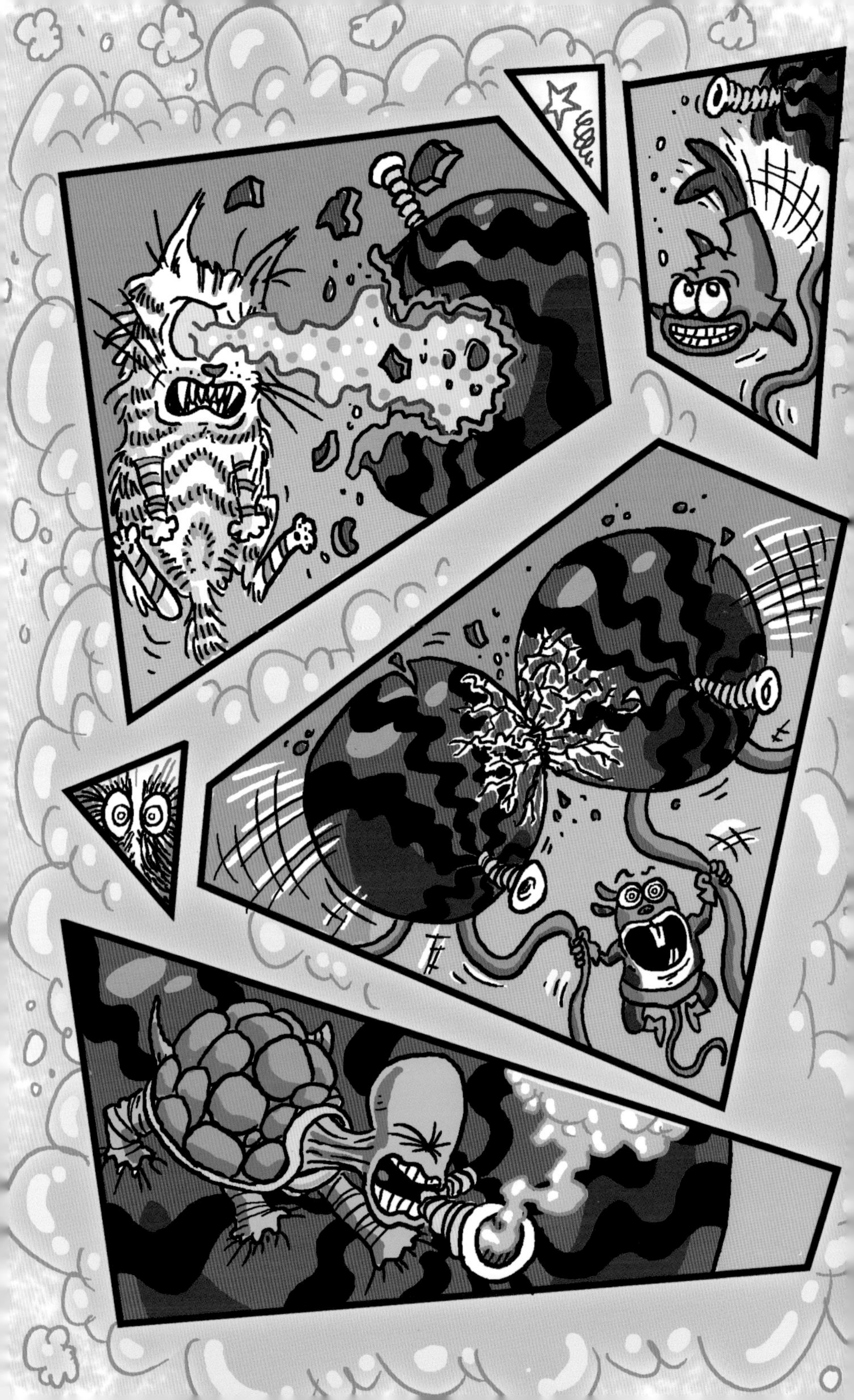

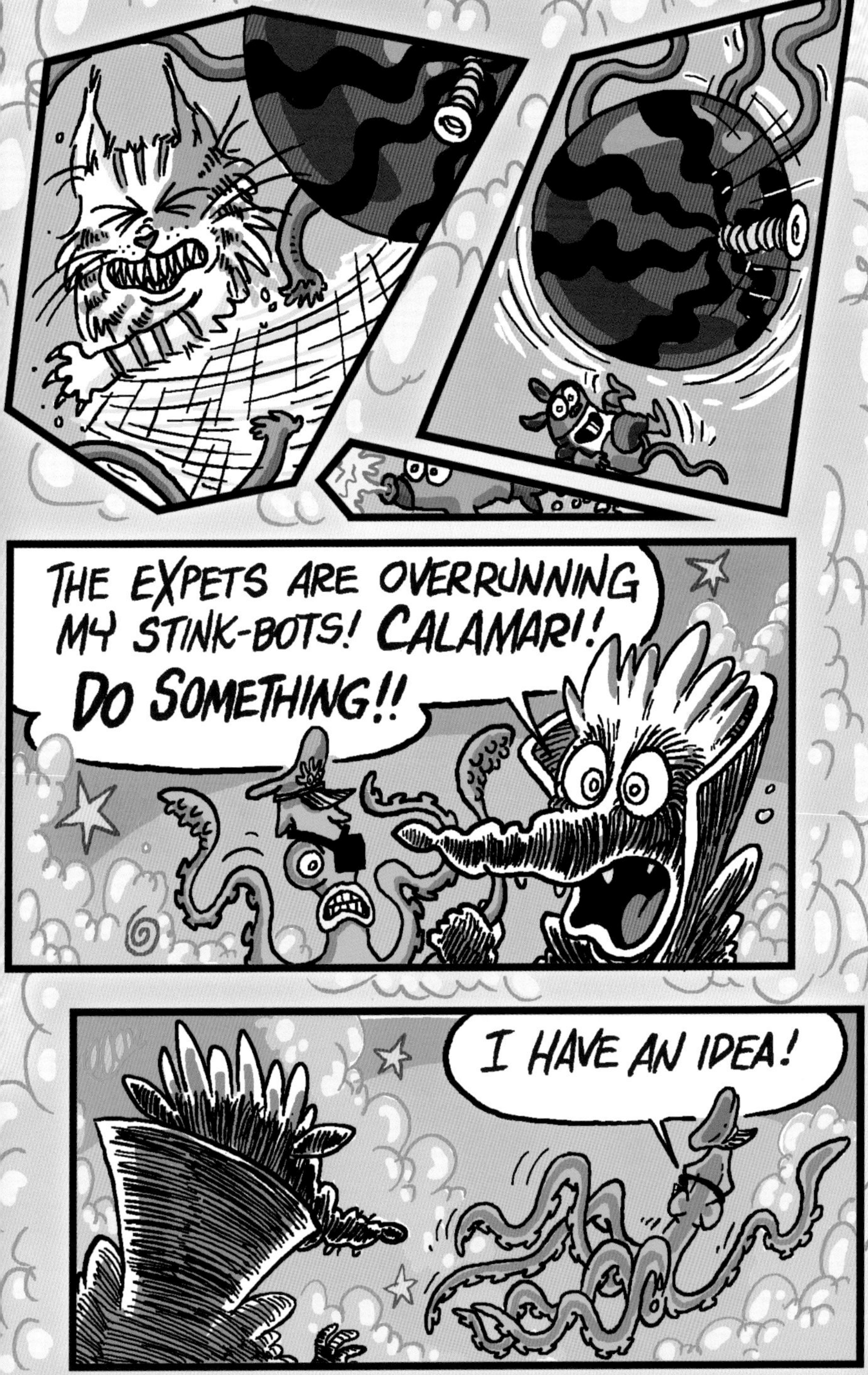
THE EXPETS ARE OVERRUNNING MY STINK-BOTS! CALAMARI! DO SOMETHING!!
I HAVE AN IDEA!

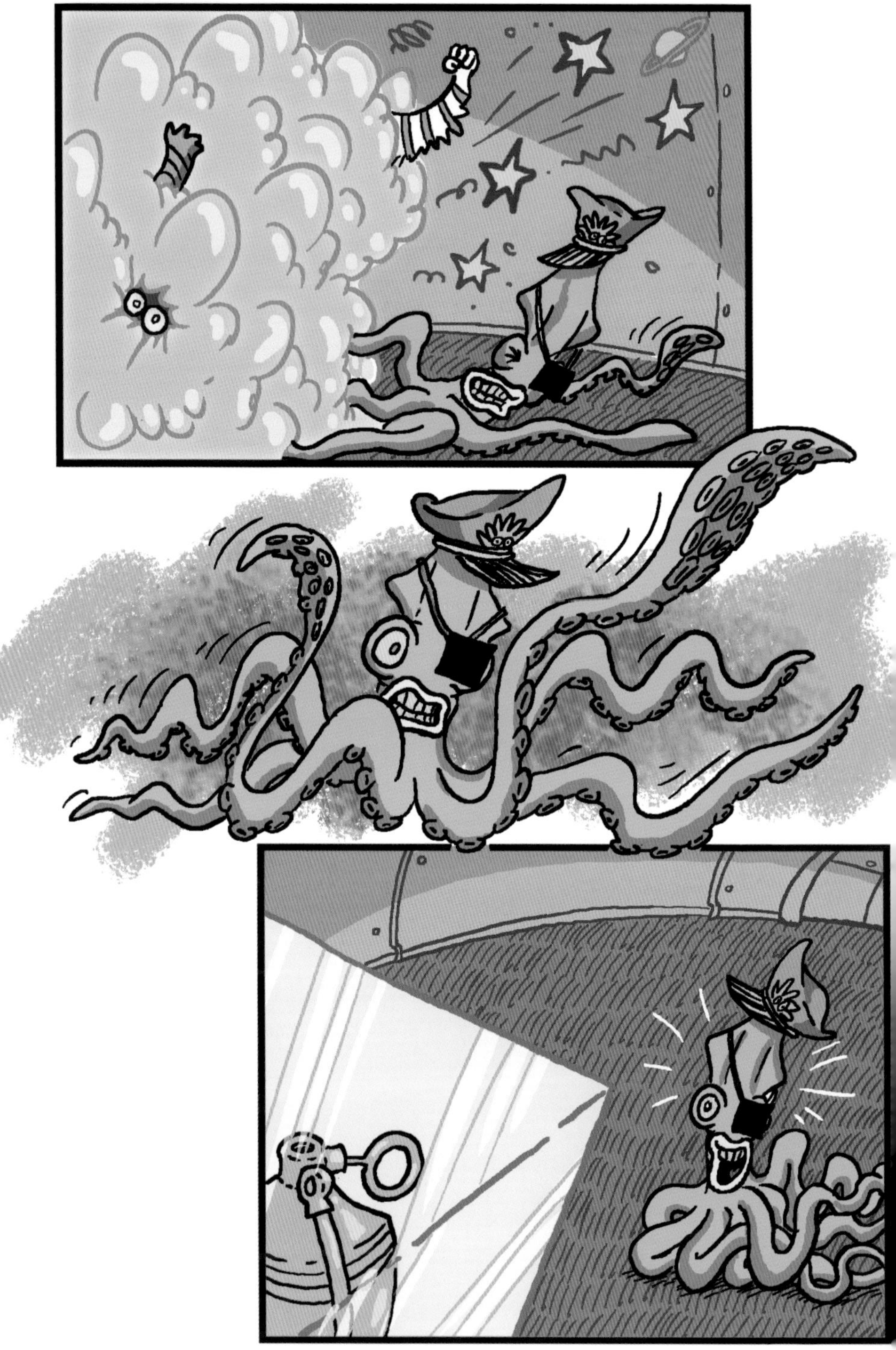

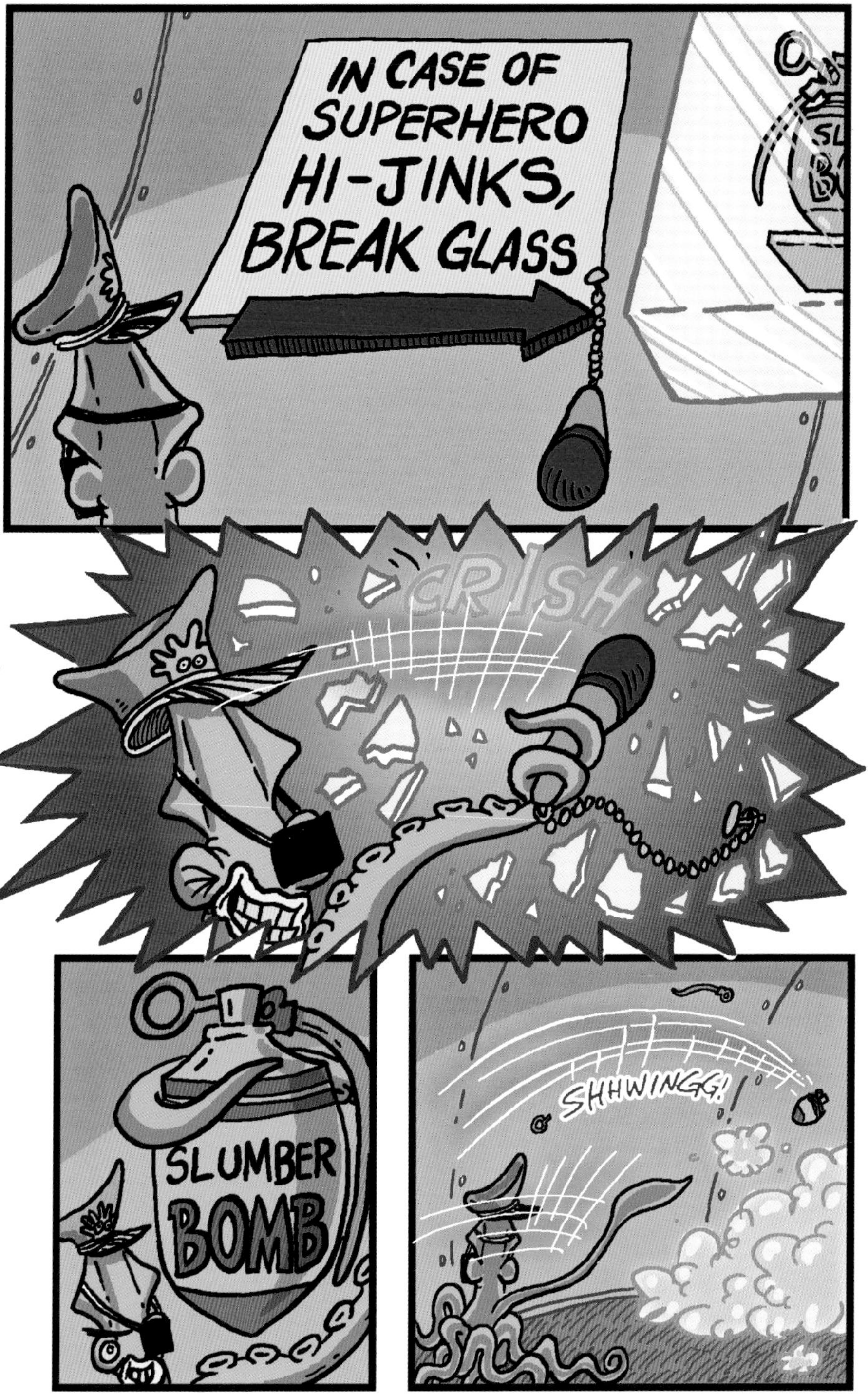
IN CASE OF SUPERHERO HI-JINKS, BREAK GLASS
CRISH
SLUMBER BOMB
SHHWINGG!

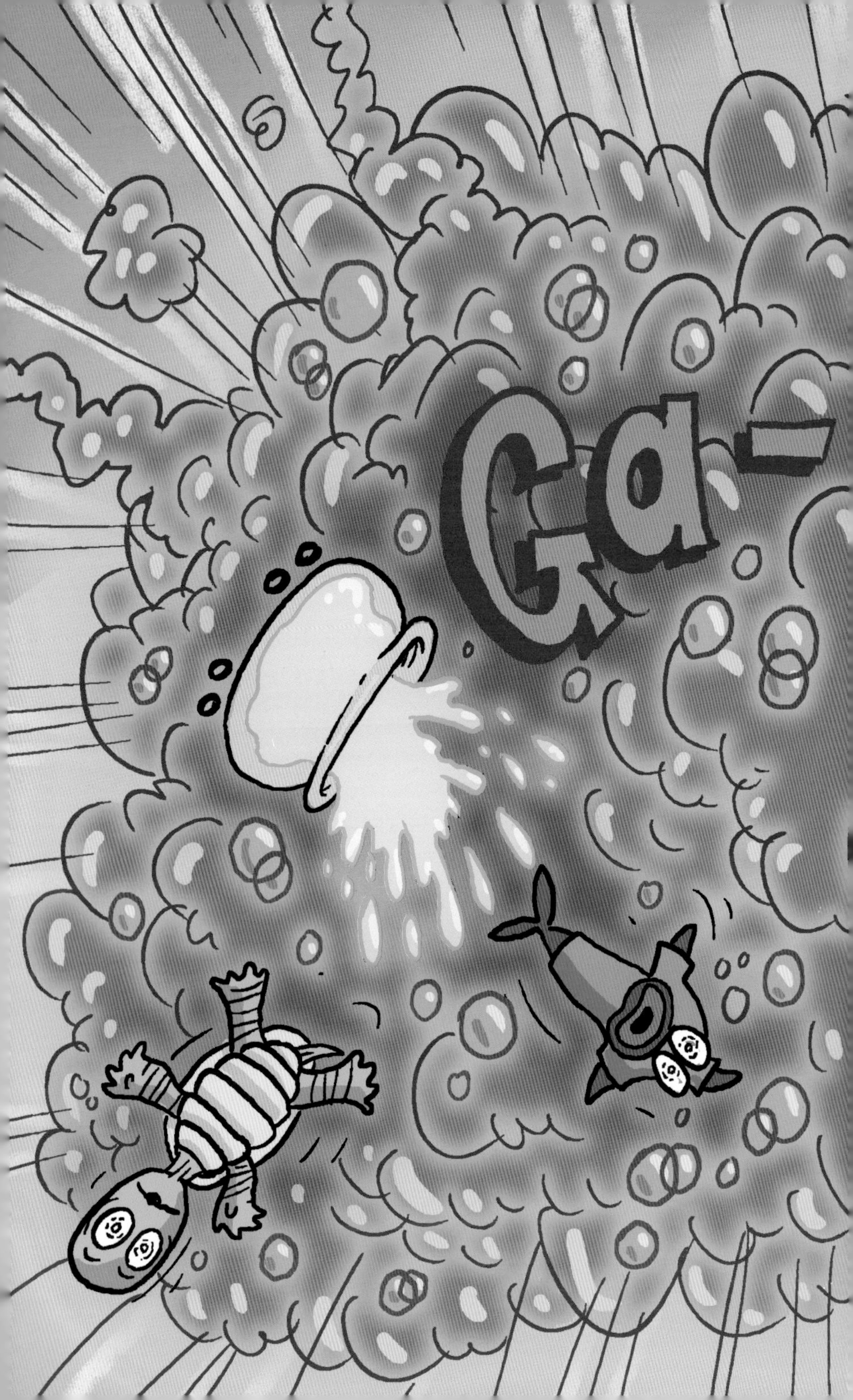
Ga-

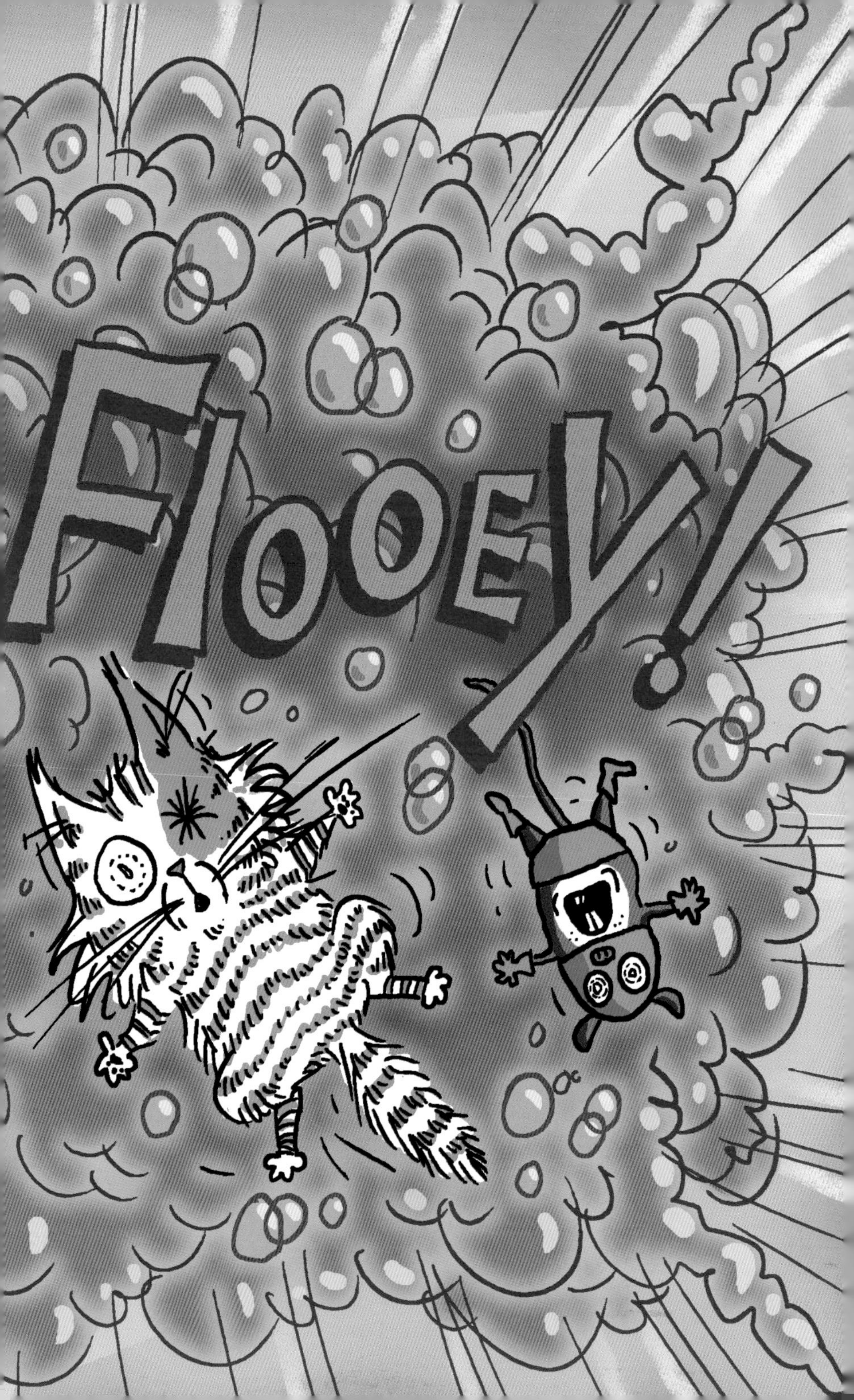
FLOOEY!

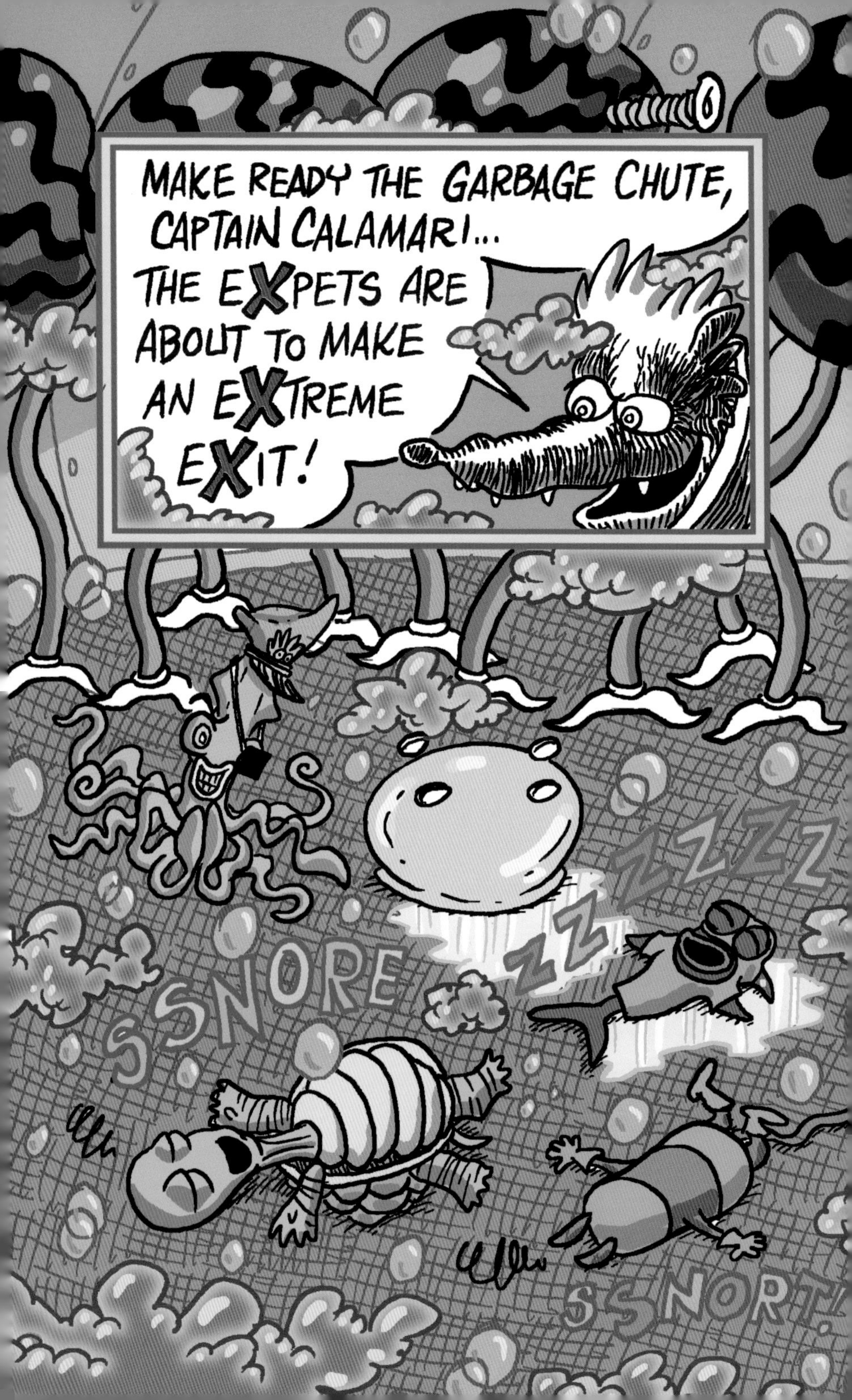
MAKE READY THE GARBAGE CHUTE, CAPTAIN CALAMARI... THE EXPETS ARE ABOUT TO MAKE AN EXTREME EXIT!
ZZZZ
ZZZ
SSNORE
SSNORT!

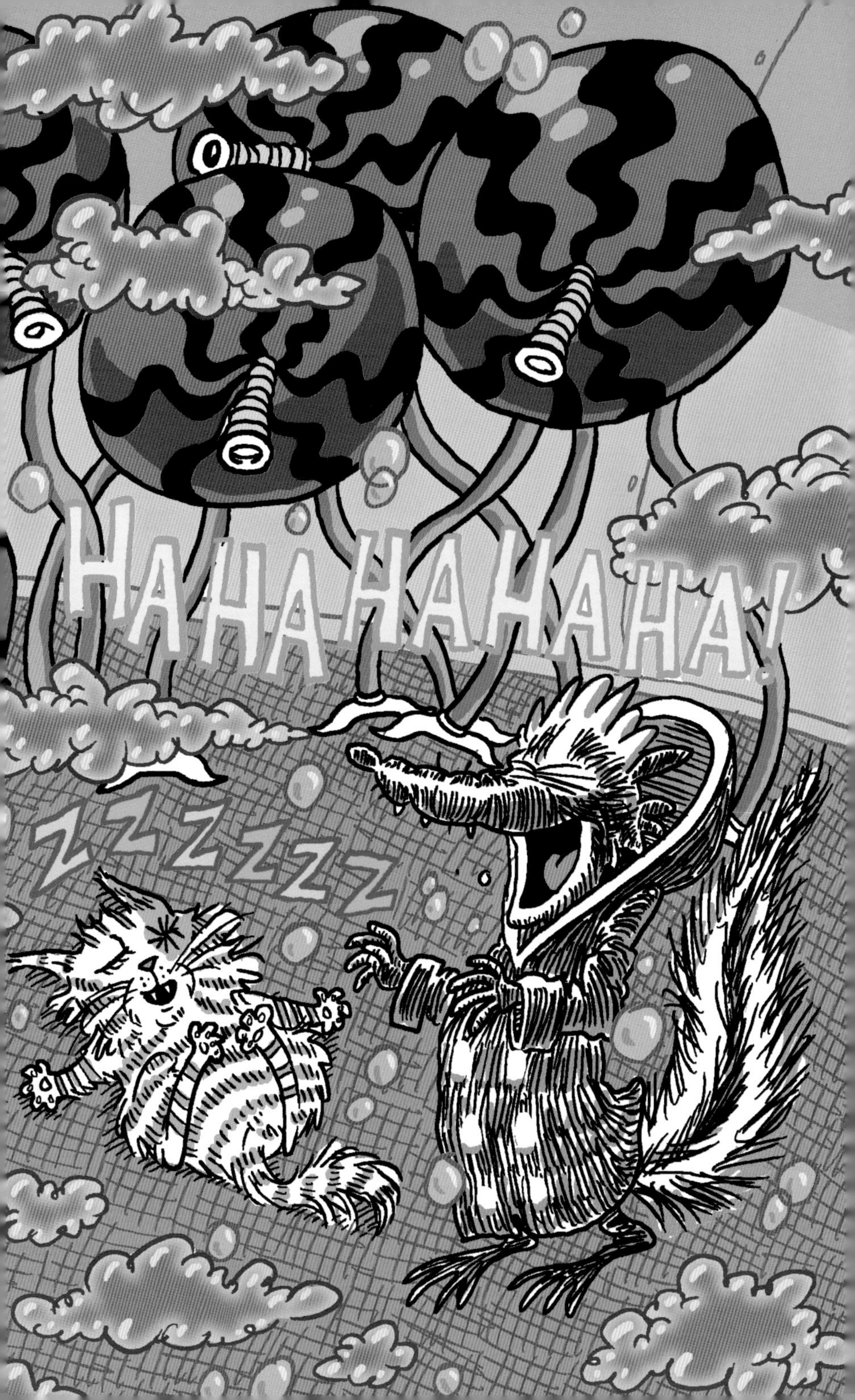
HAHAHAHAHAHA!
ZZZZZZZ

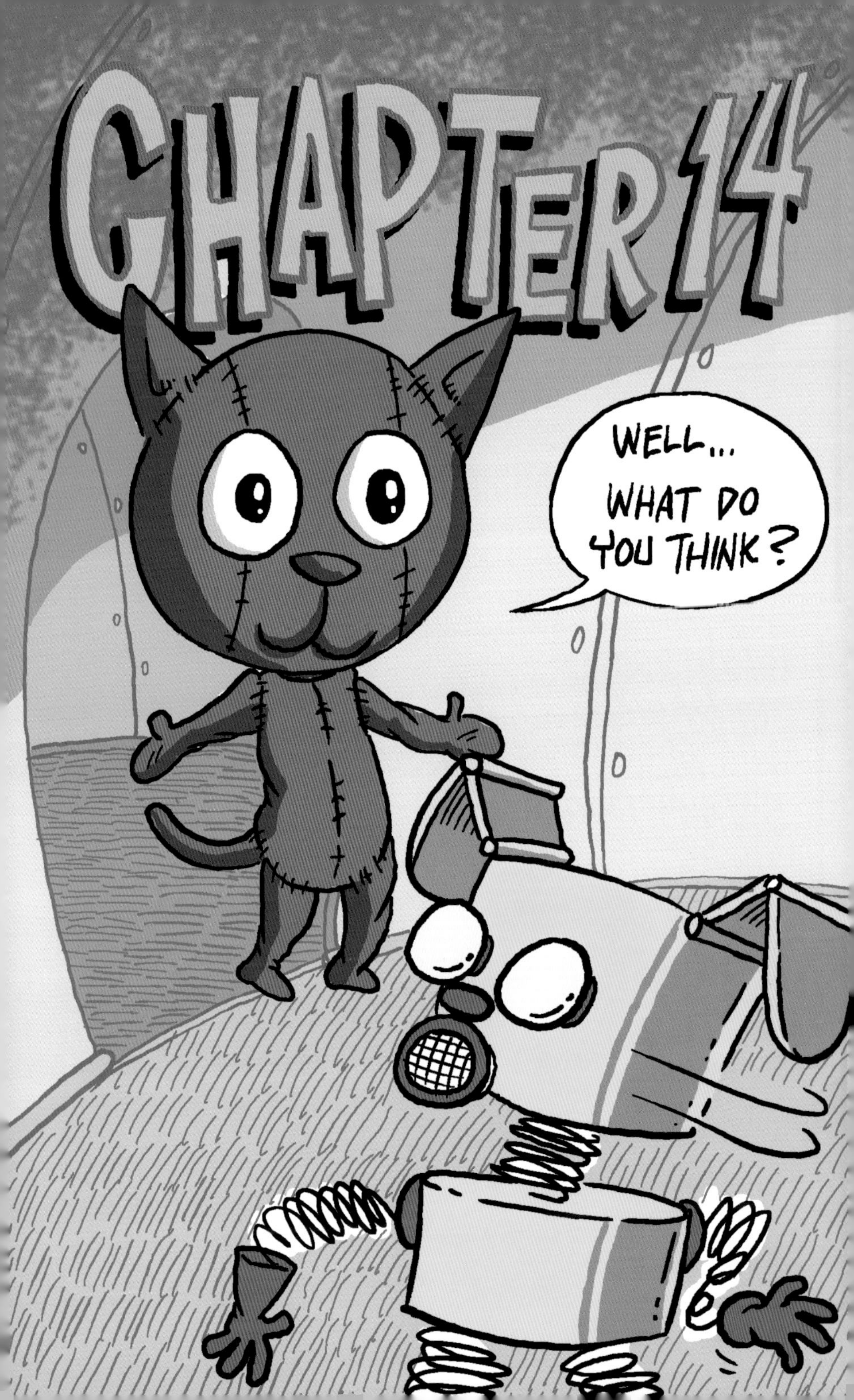
CHAPTER 14
WELL...
WHAT DO
YOU THINK?

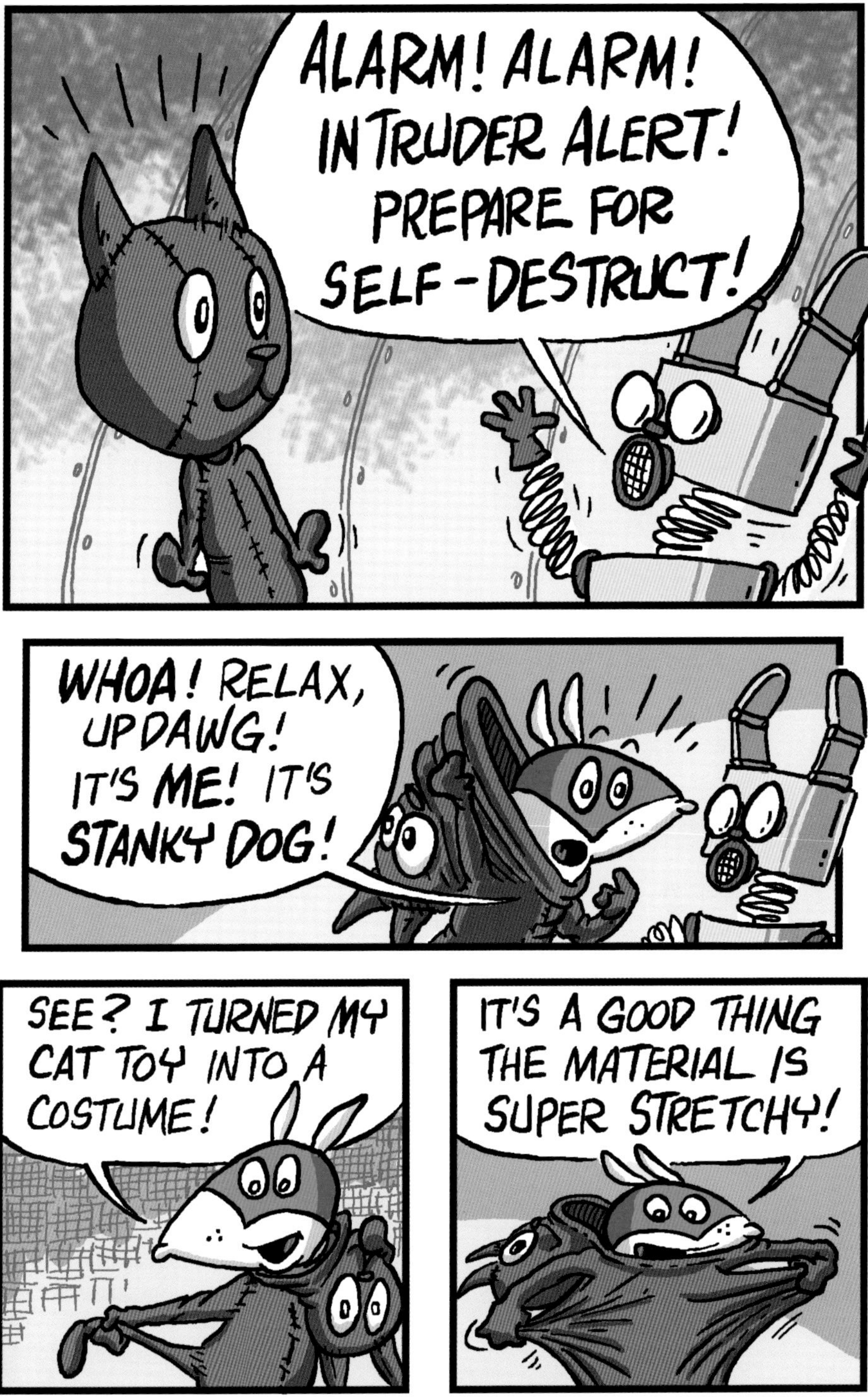
ALARM! ALARM! INTRUDER ALERT! PREPARE FOR SELF-DESTRUCT!
WHOA! RELAX, UPDAWG! IT'S ME! IT'S STANKY DOG!
SEE? I TURNED MY CAT TOY INTO A COSTUME!
IT'S A GOOD THING THE MATERIAL IS SUPER STRETCHY!

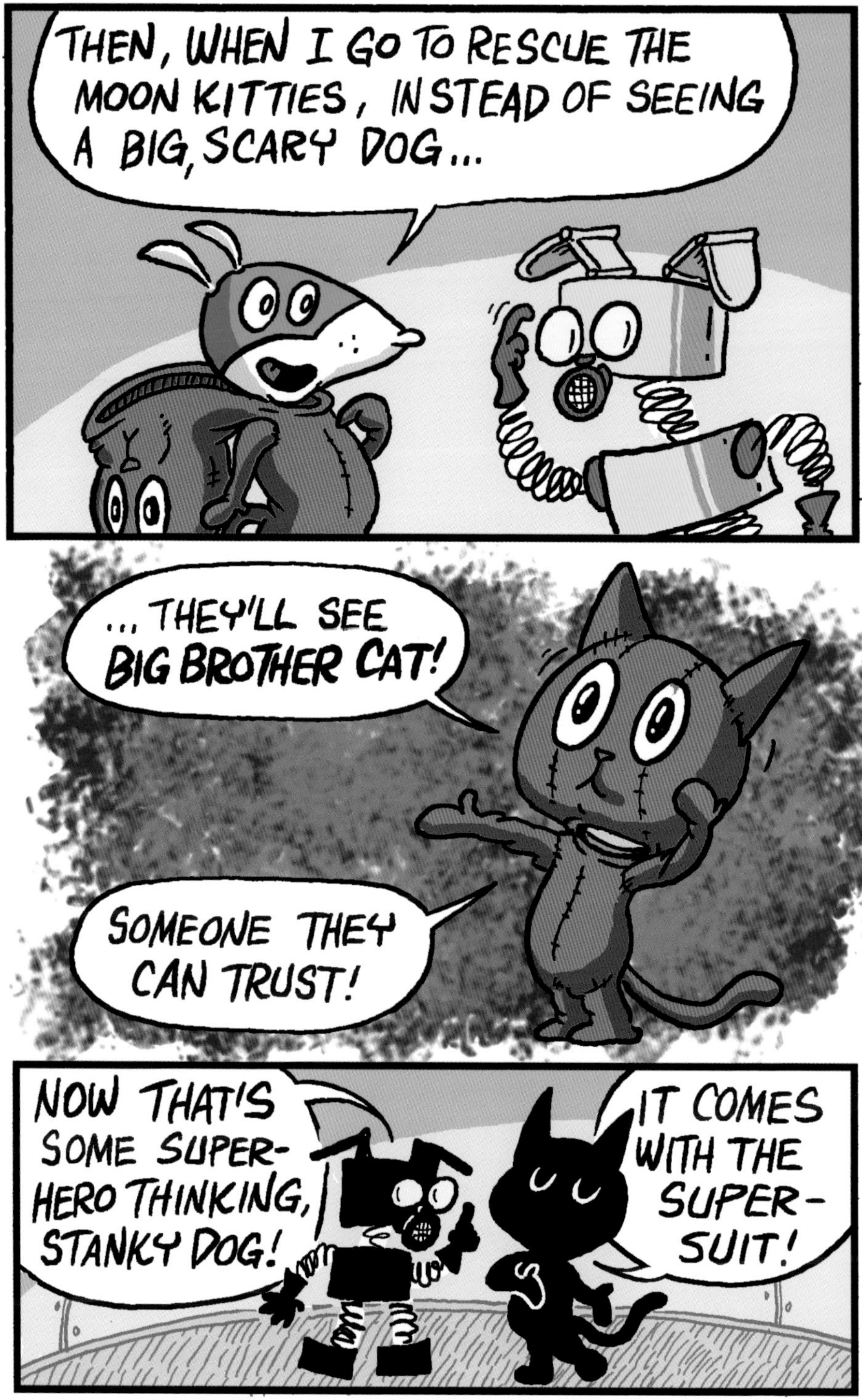
THEN, WHEN I GO TO RESCUE THE MOON KITTIES, INSTEAD OF SEEING A BIG, SCARY DOG...
...THEY'LL SEE BIG BROTHER CAT!
SOMEONE THEY CAN TRUST!
NOW THAT'S SOME SUPER-HERO THINKING, STANKY DOG!
IT COMES WITH THE SUPER-SUIT!

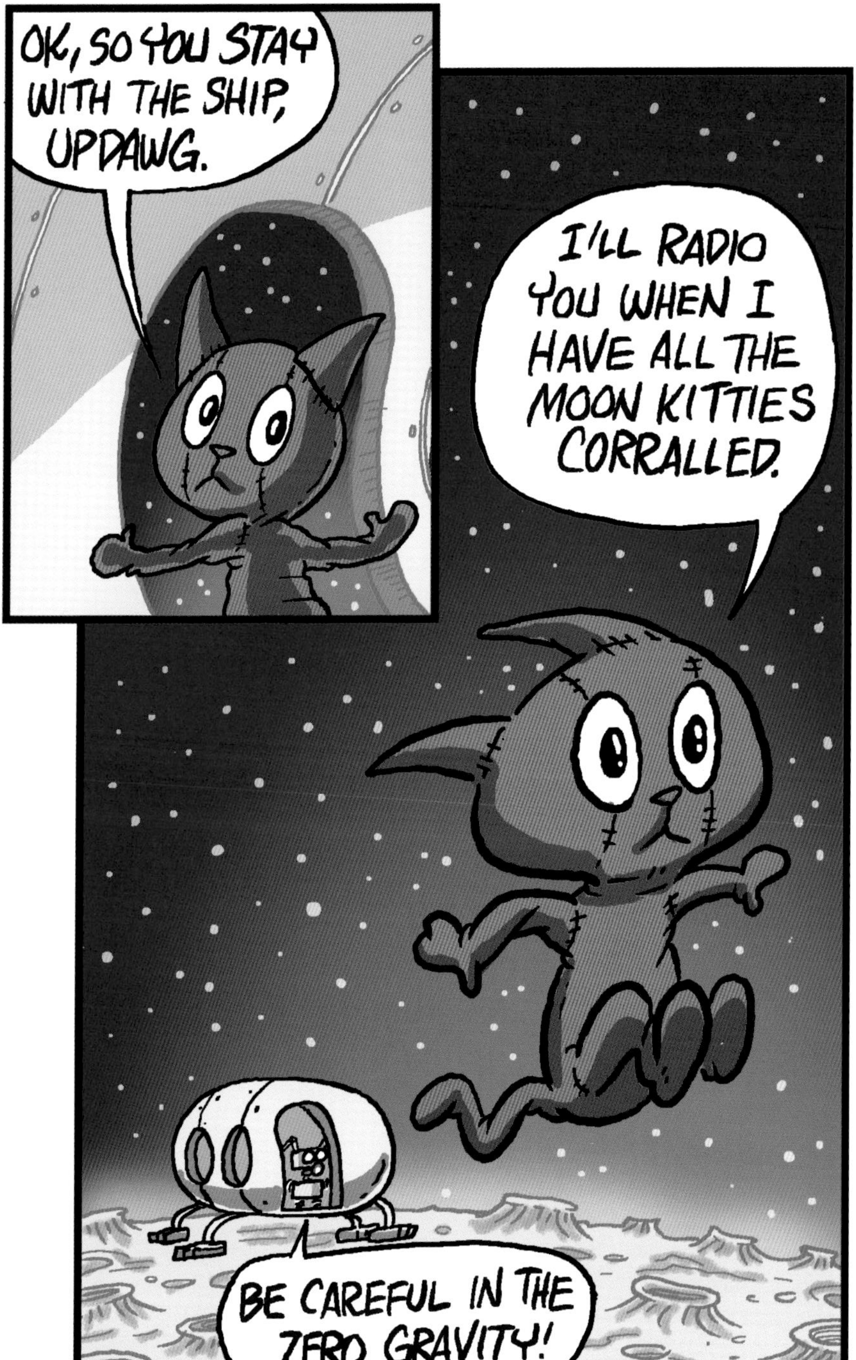
OK, SO YOU STAY WITH THE SHIP, UPDAWG.
I'LL RADIO YOU WHEN I HAVE ALL THE MOON KITTIES CORRALLED.
BE CAREFUL IN THE ZERO GRAVITY!

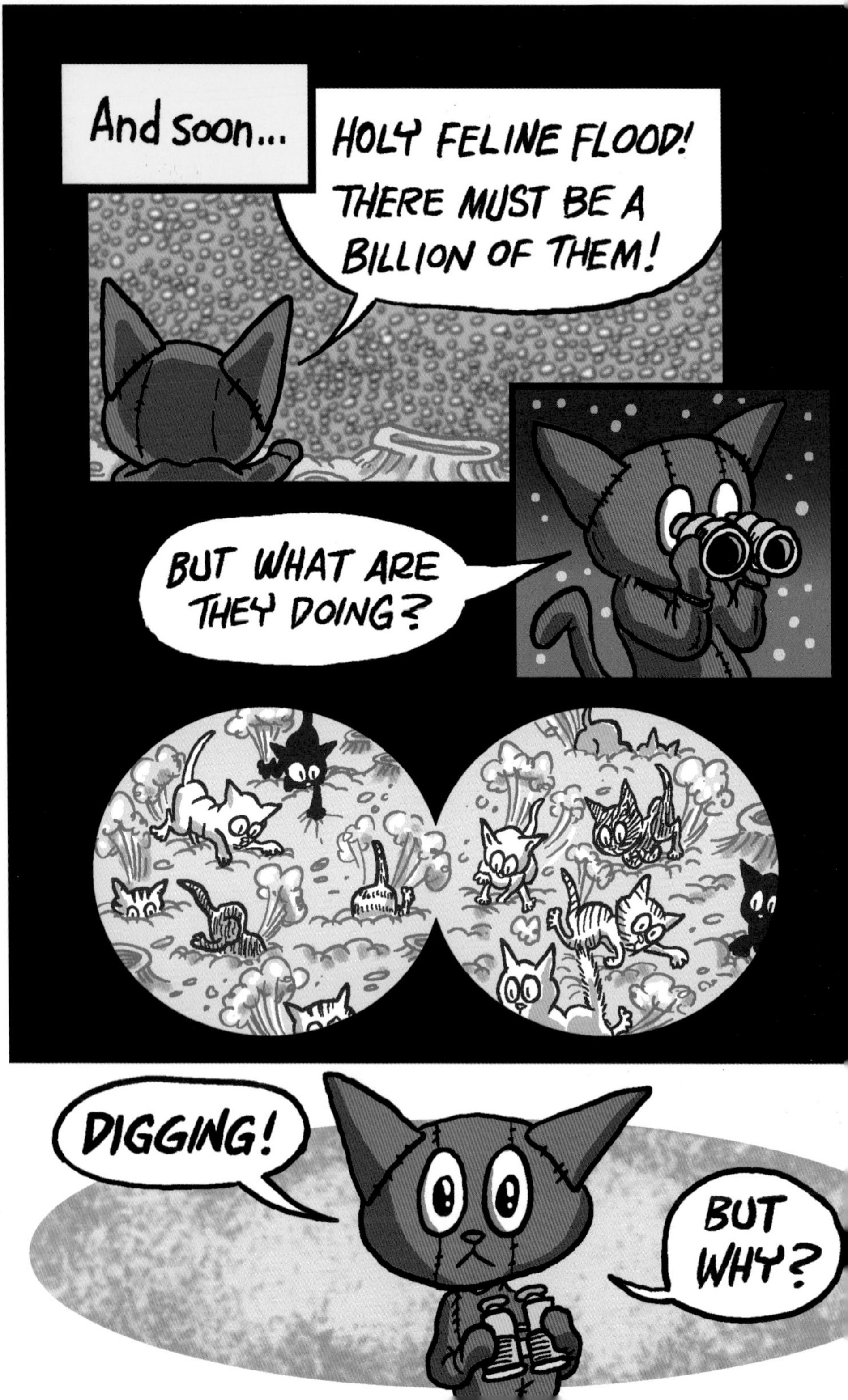
And soon...
HOLY FELINE FLOOD! THERE MUST BE A BILLION OF THEM!
BUT WHAT ARE THEY DOING?
DIGGING!
BUT WHY?

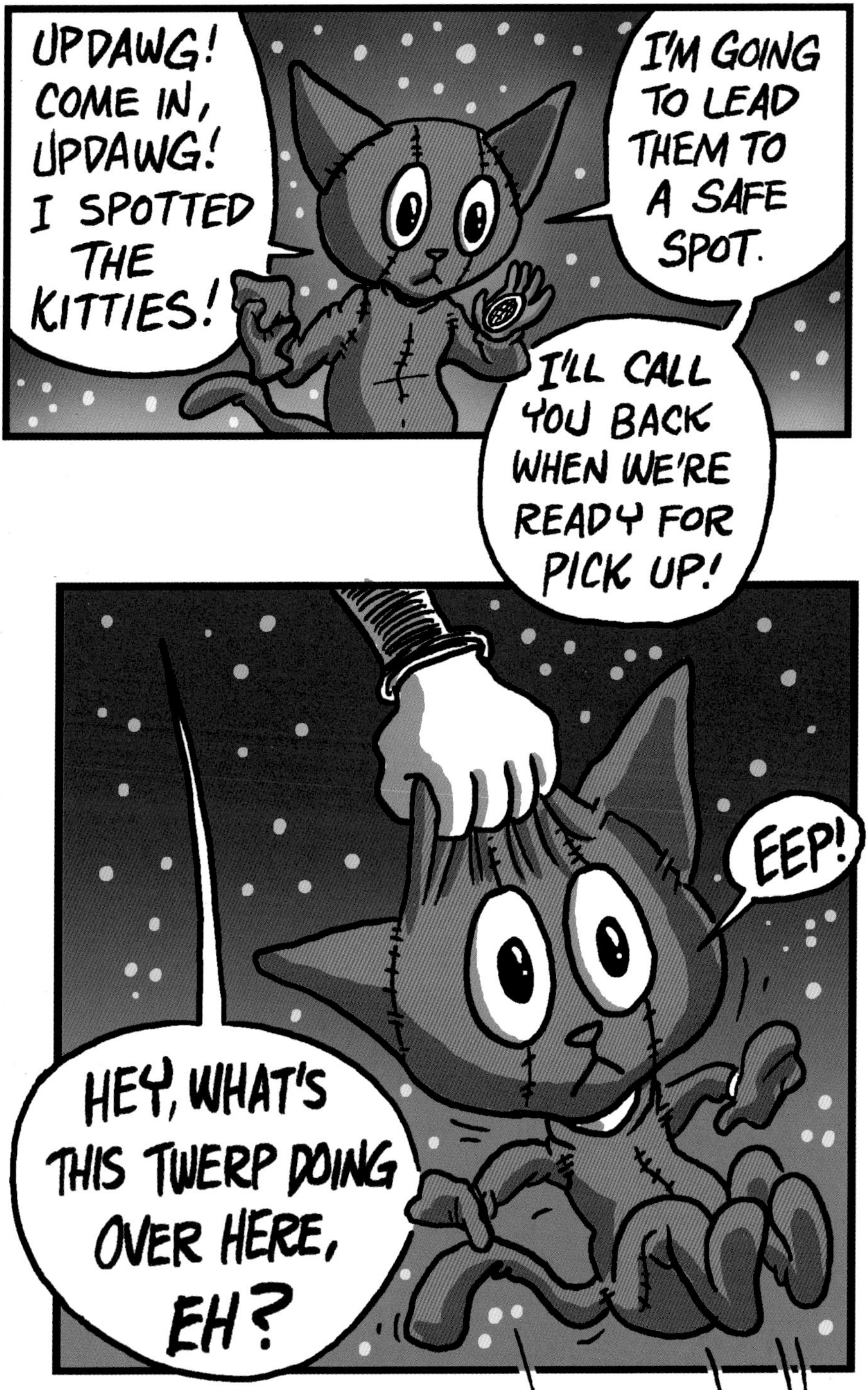
UPDAWG! COME IN, UPDAWG! I SPOTTED THE KITTIES!
I'M GOING TO LEAD THEM TO A SAFE SPOT.
I'LL CALL YOU BACK WHEN WE'RE READY FOR PICK UP!
EEP!
HEY, WHAT'S THIS TWERP DOING OVER HERE, EH?

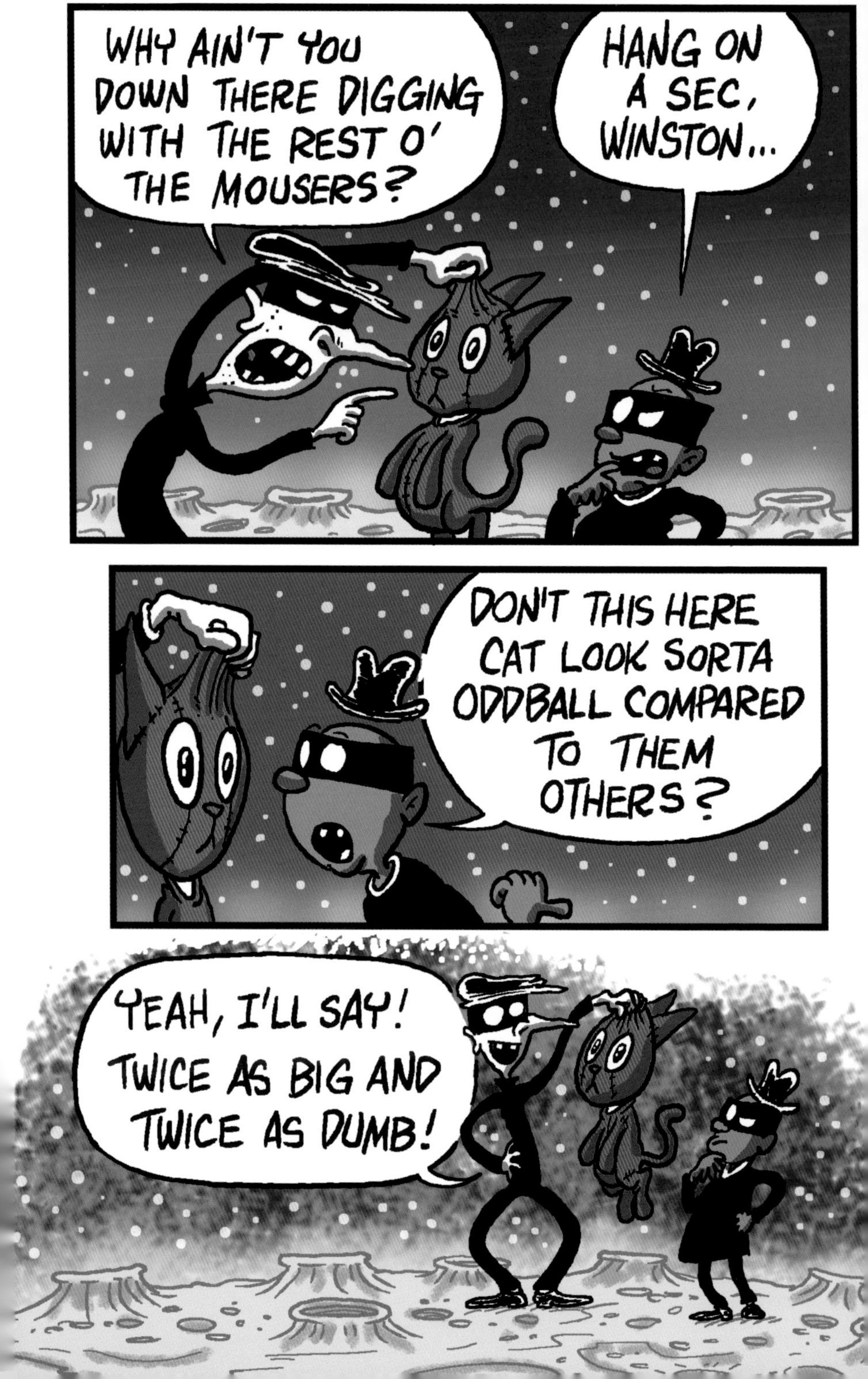
WHY AIN'T YOU DOWN THERE DIGGING WITH THE REST O' THE MOUSERS?
HANG ON A SEC, WINSTON...
DON'T THIS HERE CAT LOOK SORTA ODDBALL COMPARED TO THEM OTHERS?
YEAH, I'LL SAY! TWICE AS BIG AND TWICE AS DUMB!

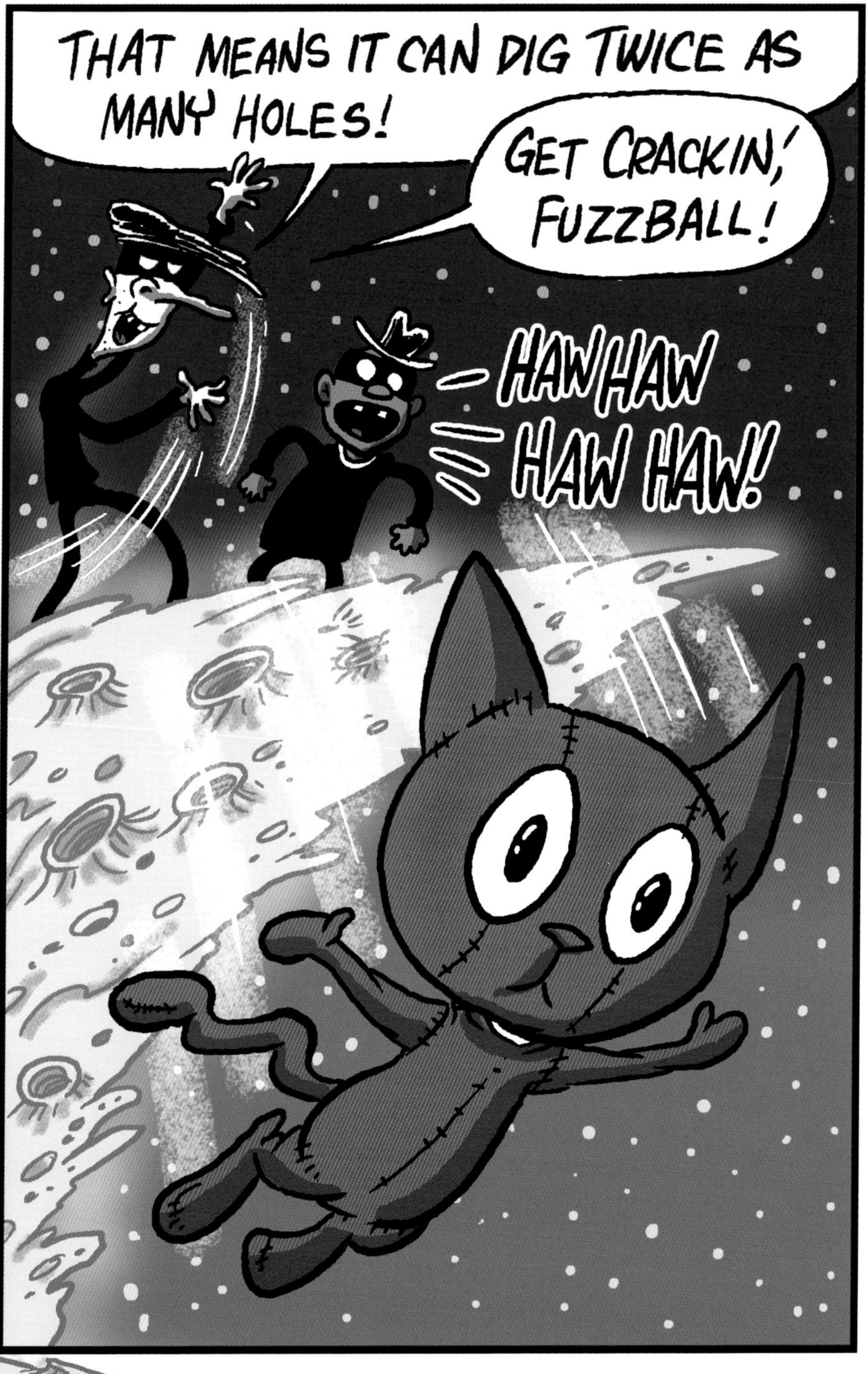
THAT MEANS IT CAN DIG TWICE AS MANY HOLES!
GET CRACKIN', FUZZBALL!
HAW HAW HAW HAW!

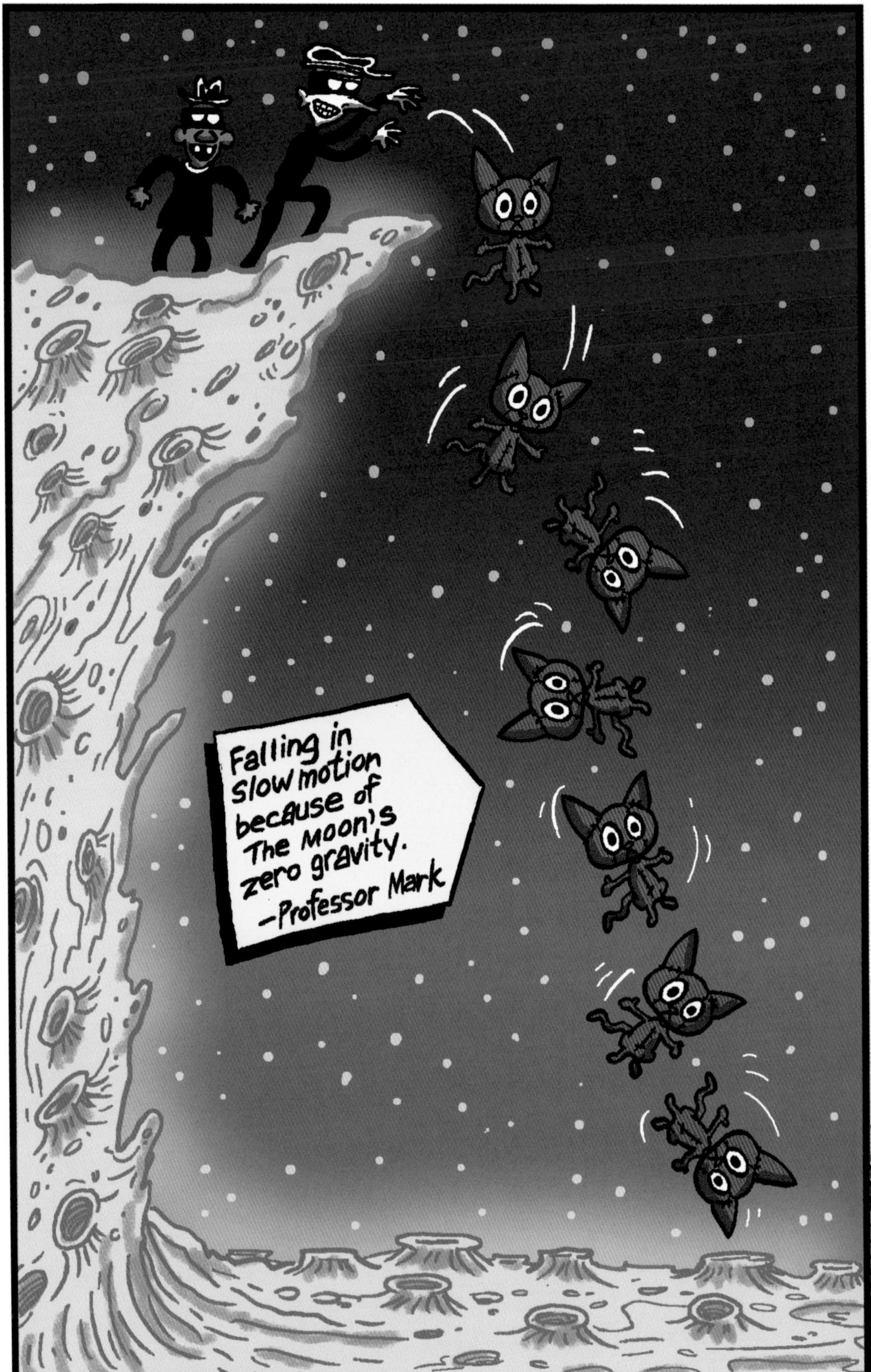
Falling in slow motion because of The Moon's zero gravity.
—Professor Mark

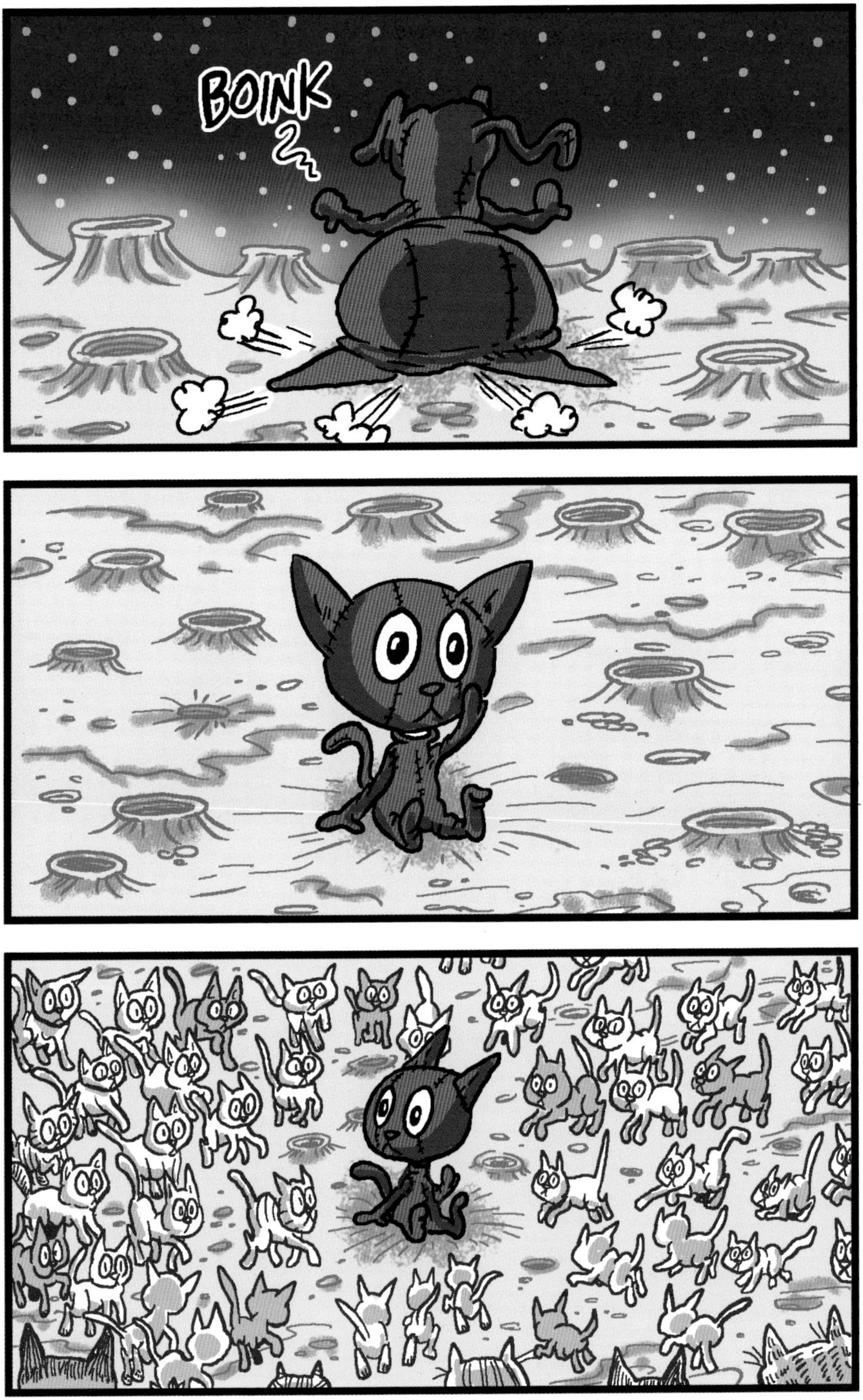
BOINK

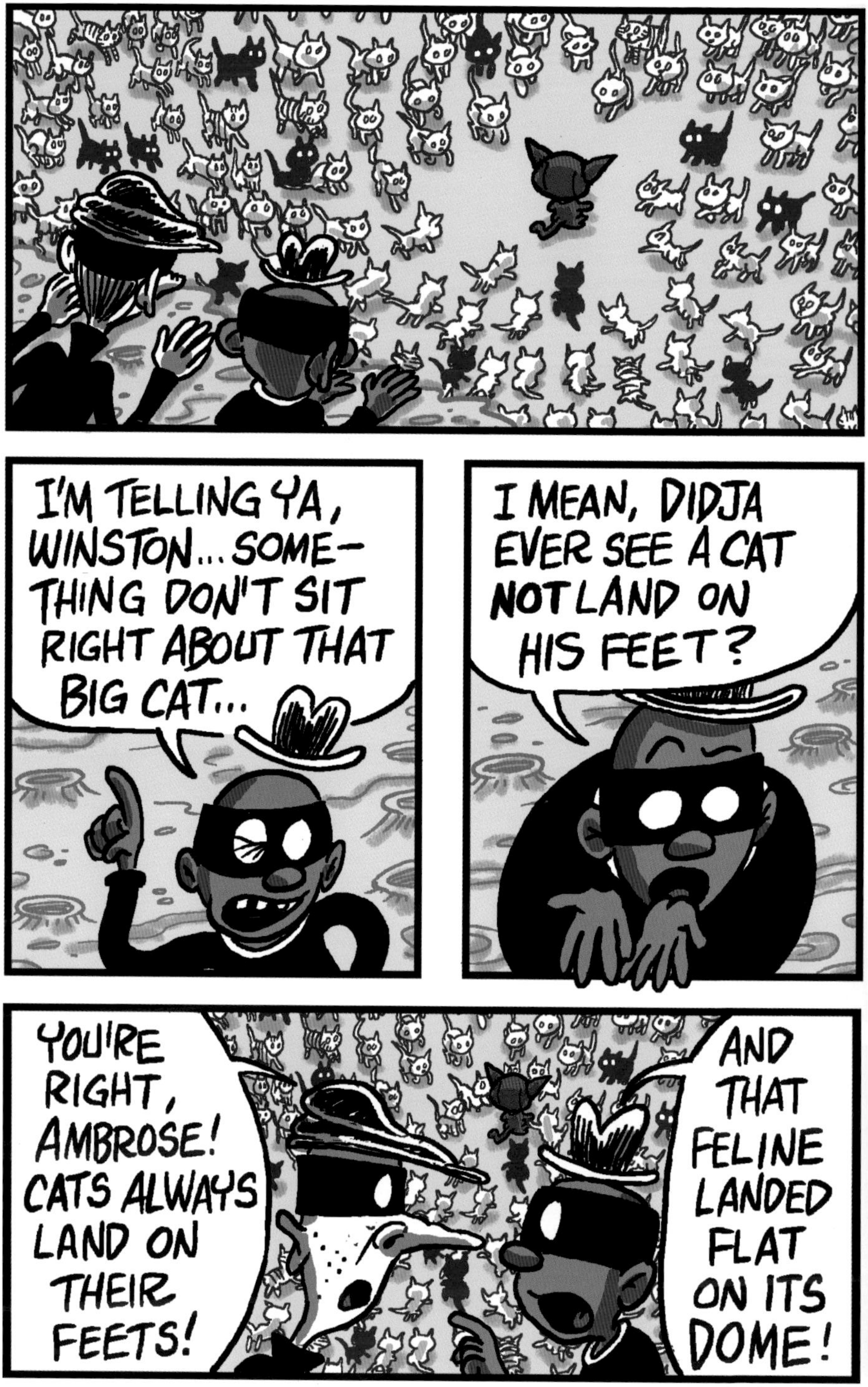
I'M TELLING YA, WINSTON... SOME-THING DON'T SIT RIGHT ABOUT THAT BIG CAT...
I MEAN, DIDJA EVER SEE A CAT NOT LAND ON HIS FEET?
YOU'RE RIGHT, AMBROSE! CATS ALWAYS LAND ON THEIR FEETS!
AND THAT FELINE LANDED FLAT ON ITS DOME!

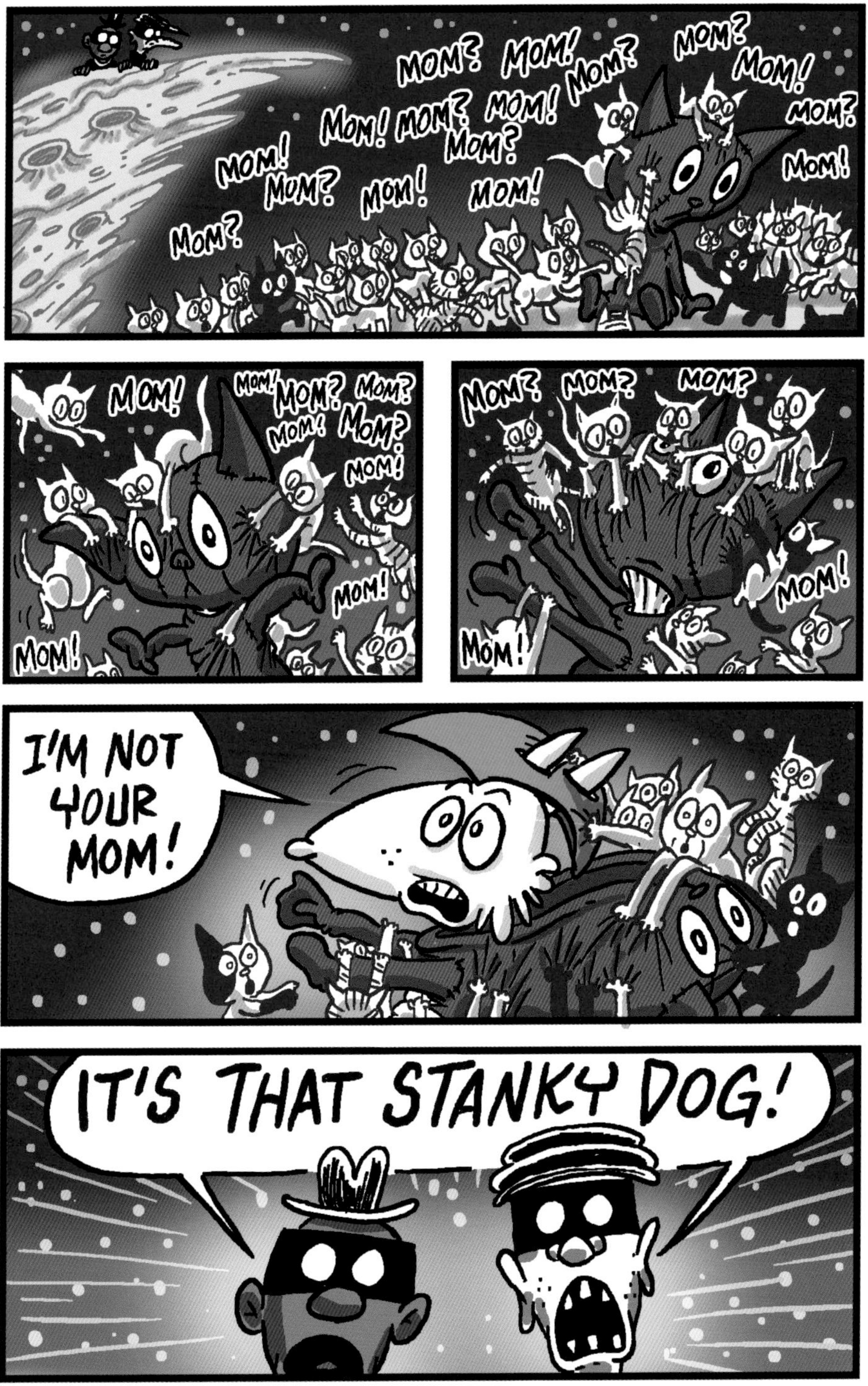
MOM? MOM! MOM? MOM? MOM!
MOM! MOM? MOM! MOM?
MOM! MOM? MOM! MOM!
MOM? MOM! MOM?
MOM! MOM? MOM! MOM? MOM!
MOM!
MOM!
MOM? MOM? MOM!
MOM!
I'M NOT YOUR MOM!
IT'S THAT STANKY DOG!

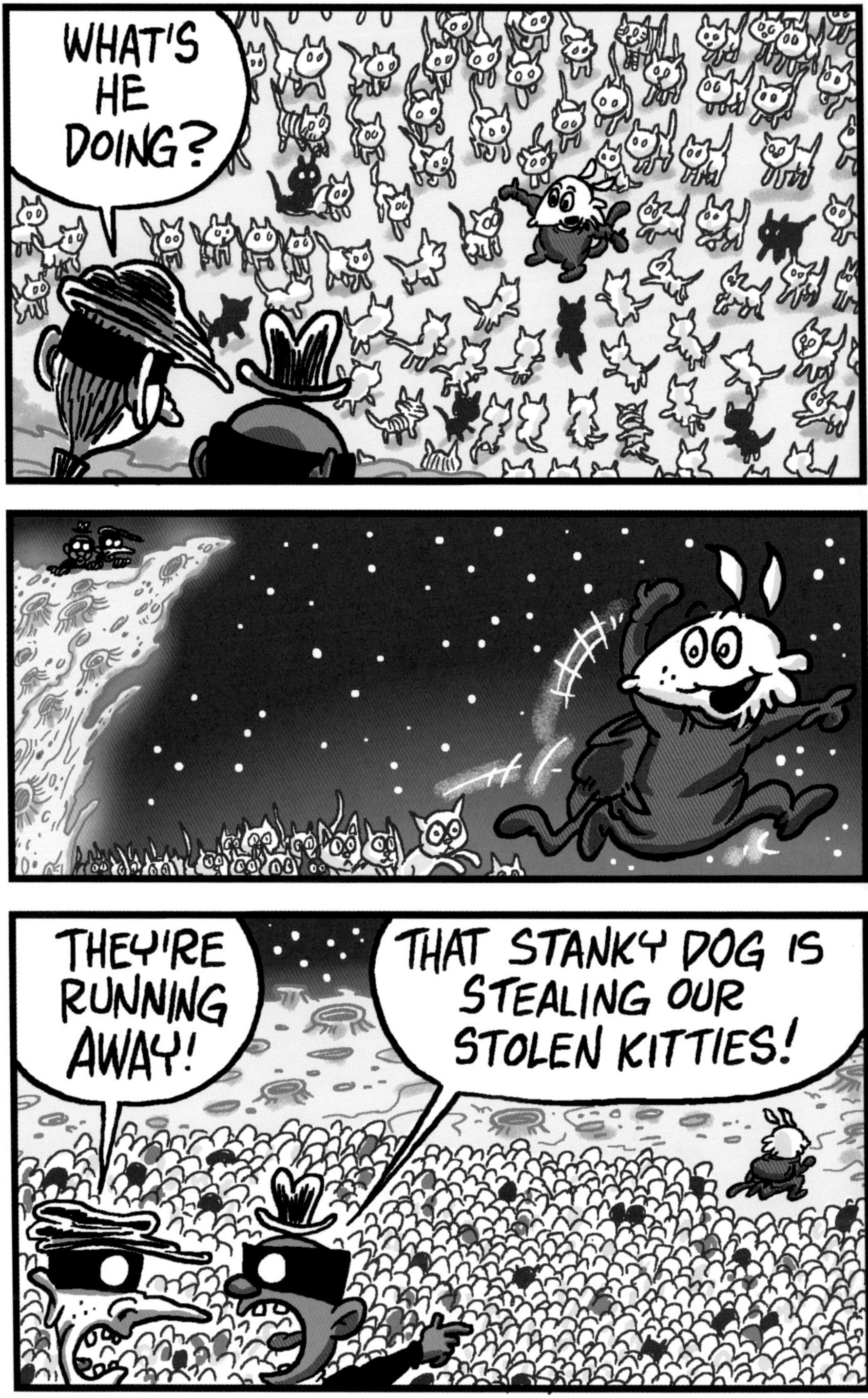
WHAT'S HE DOING?
THEY'RE RUNNING AWAY!
THAT STANKY DOG IS STEALING OUR STOLEN KITTIES!

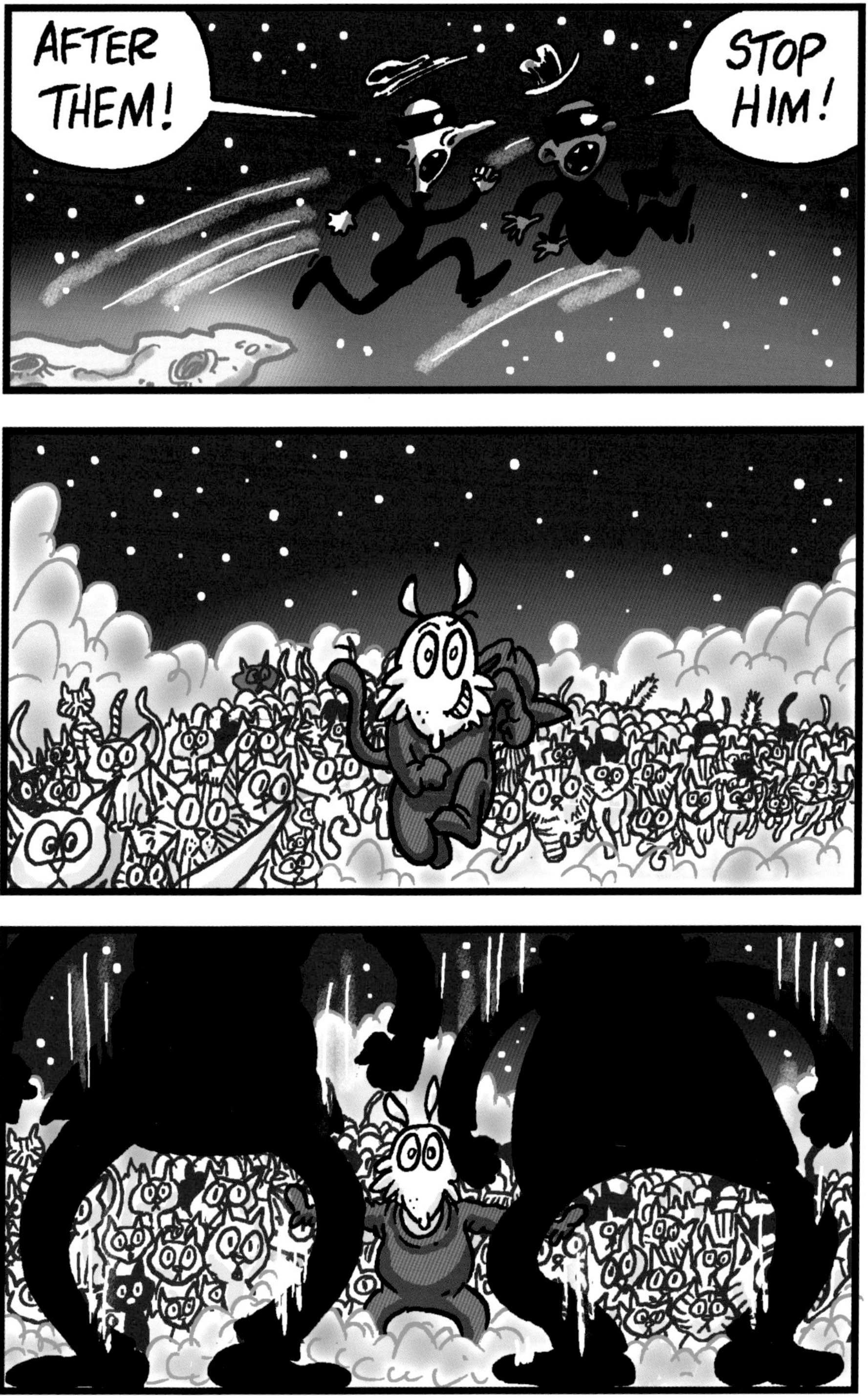
AFTER THEM!
STOP HIM!

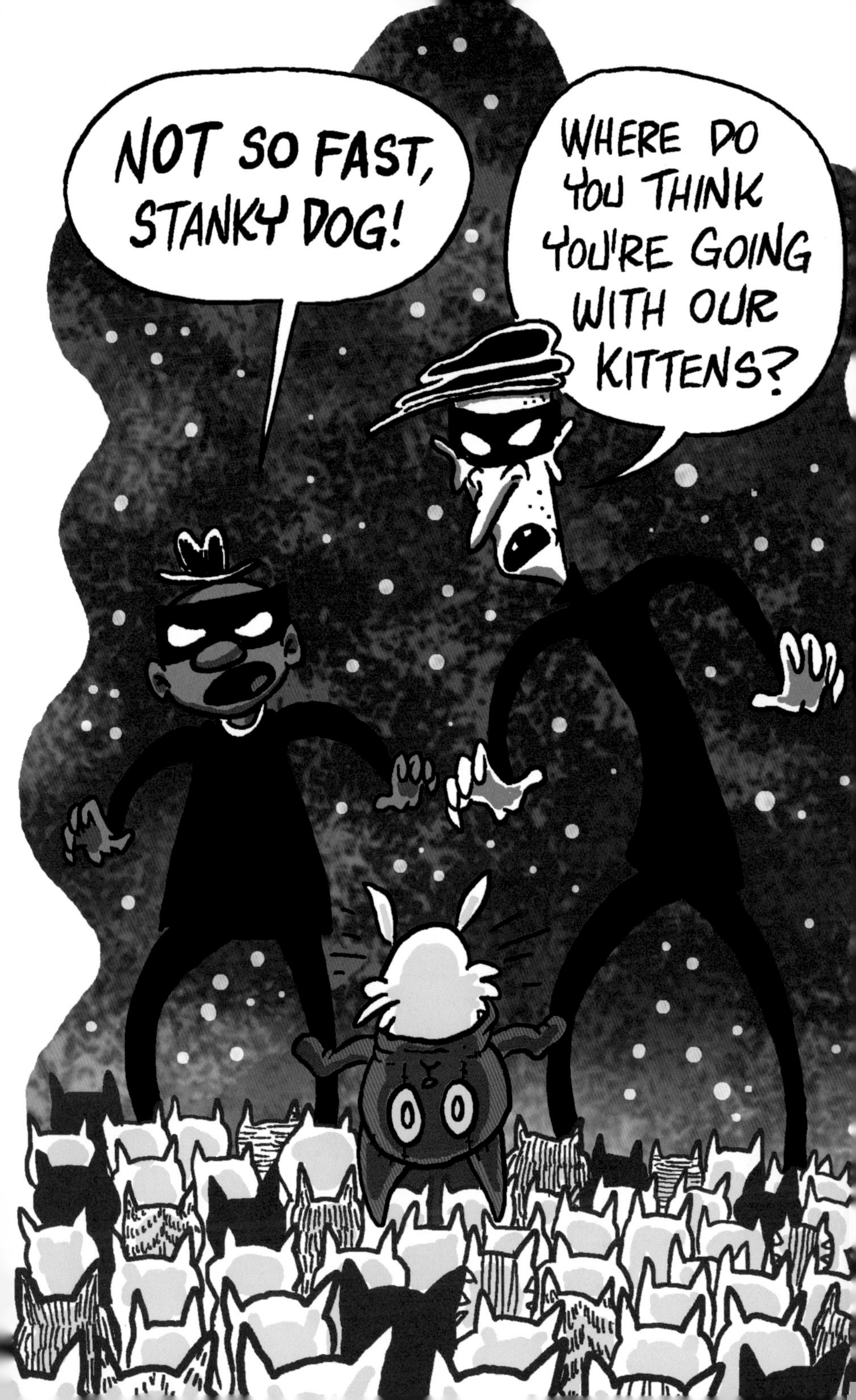
NOT SO FAST, STANKY DOG!
WHERE DO YOU THINK YOU'RE GOING WITH OUR KITTENS?

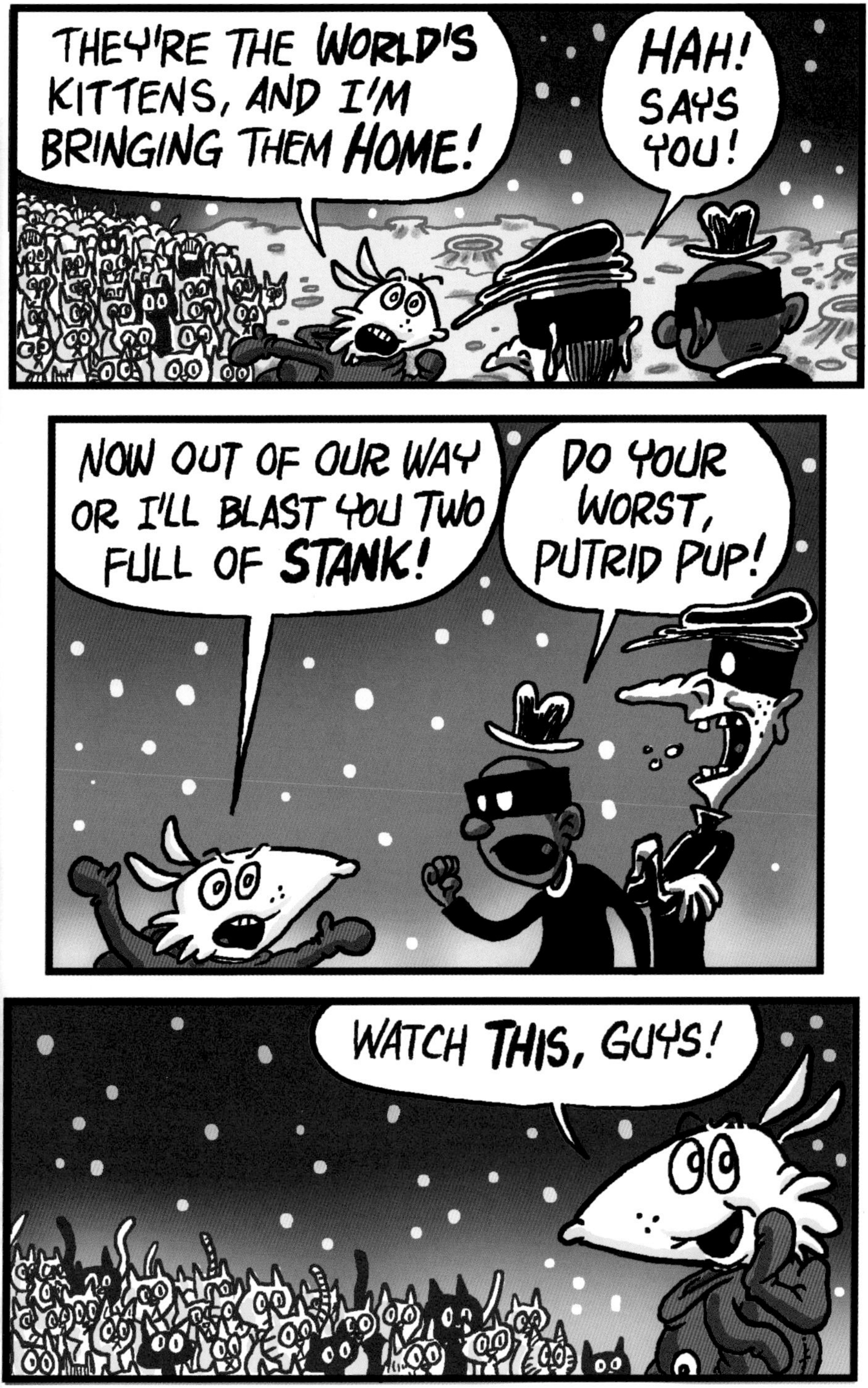
THEY'RE THE WORLD'S KITTENS, AND I'M BRINGING THEM HOME!
HAH! SAYS YOU!
NOW OUT OF OUR WAY OR I'LL BLAST YOU TWO FULL OF STANK!
DO YOUR WORST, PUTRID PUP!
WATCH THIS, GUYS!

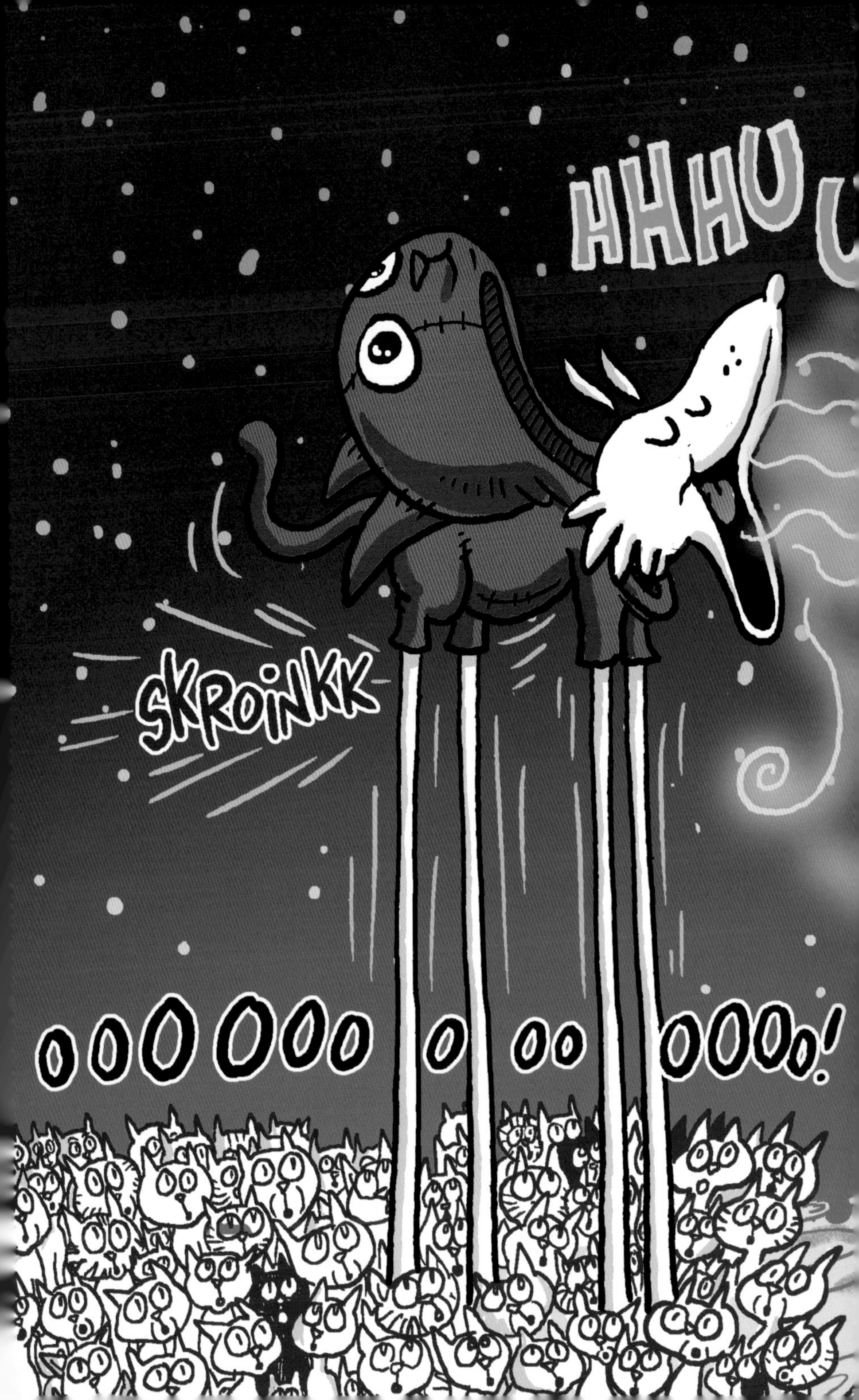
HHHUU
SKROINKK
OOOOOOO O OO OOOOO!

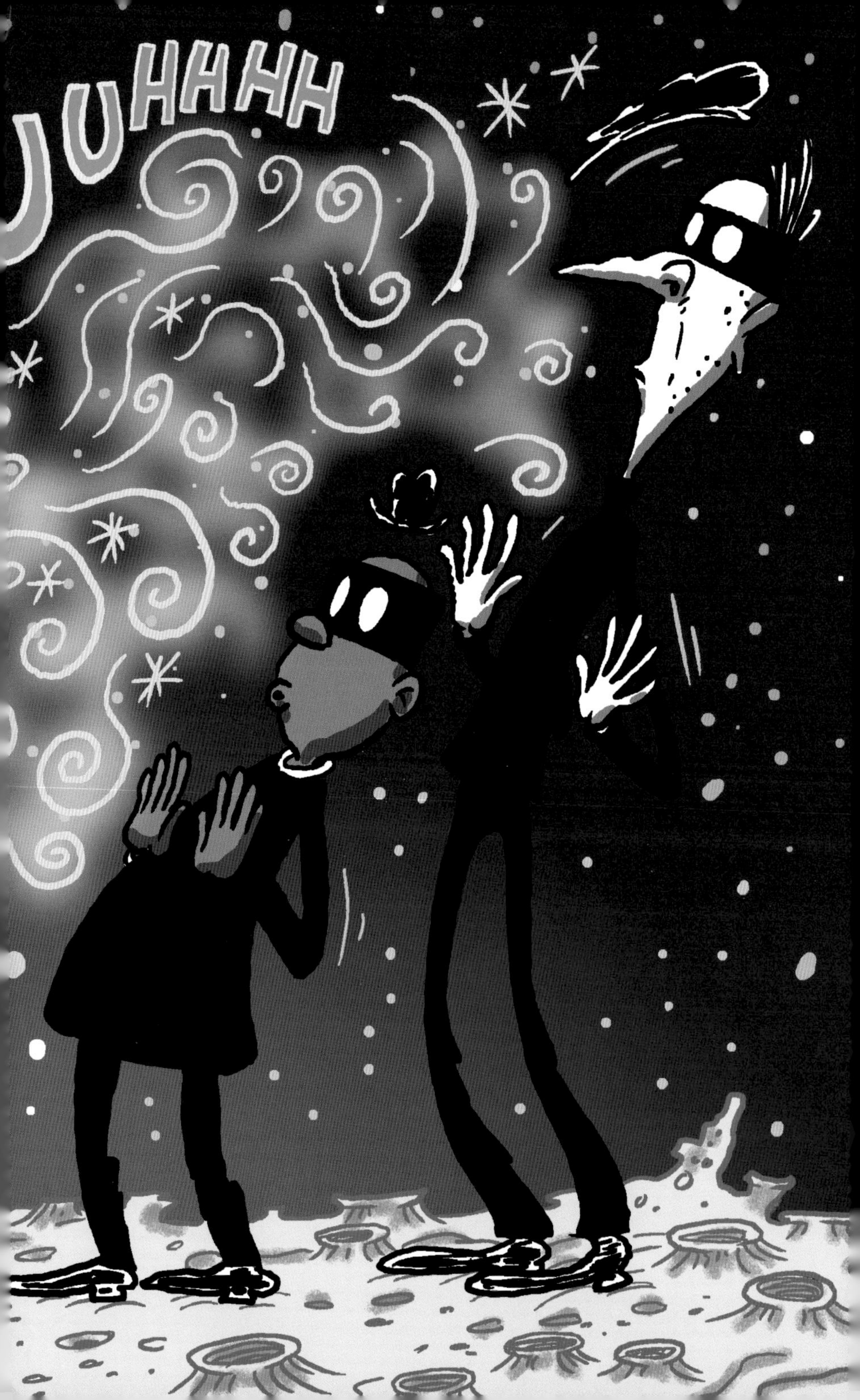
UHHHH

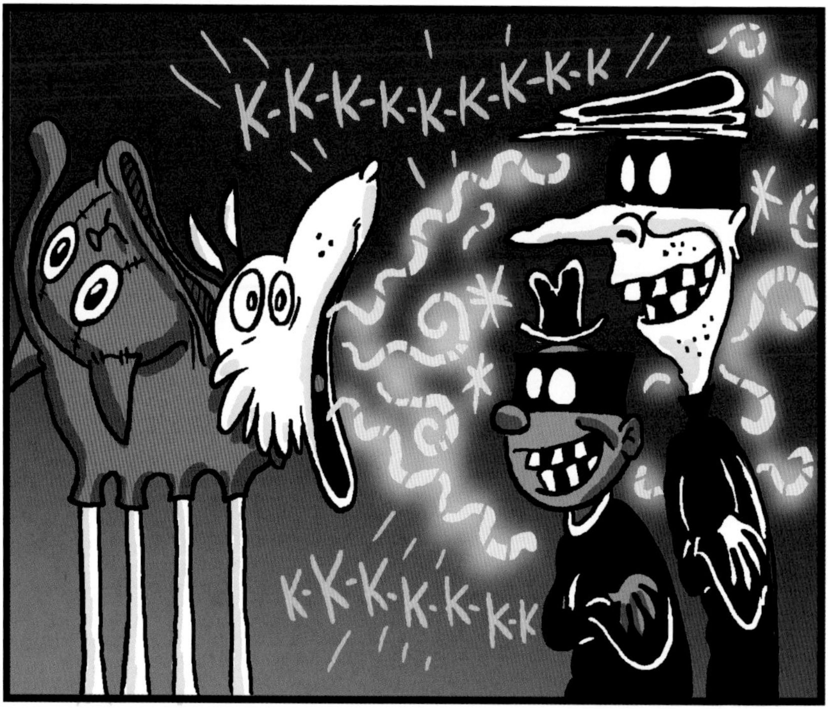
K-K-K-K-K-K-K-K-K-K
K-K-K-K-K-K-K

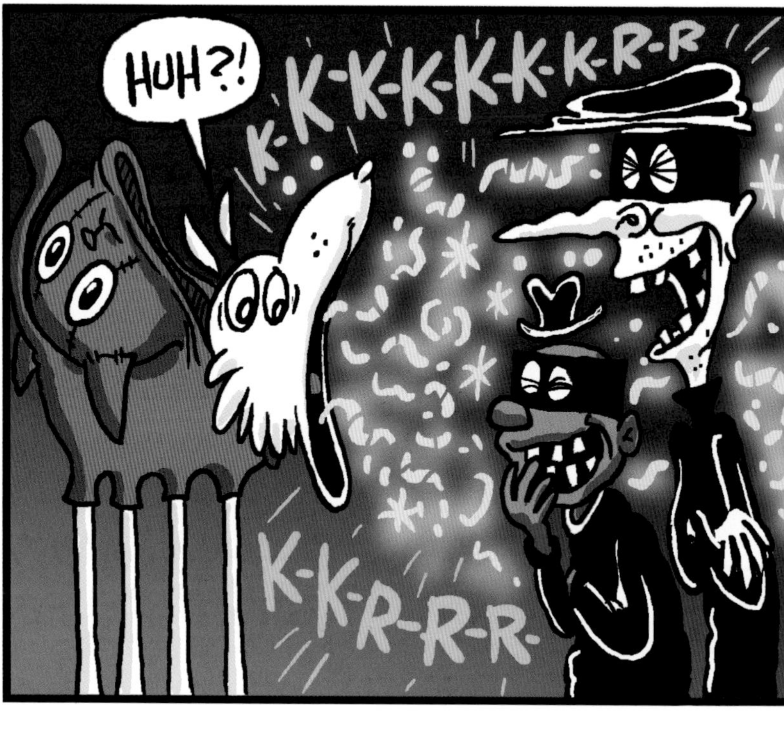
HUH?!
K-K-K-K-K-K-K-K-R-R
K-K-R-R-R-

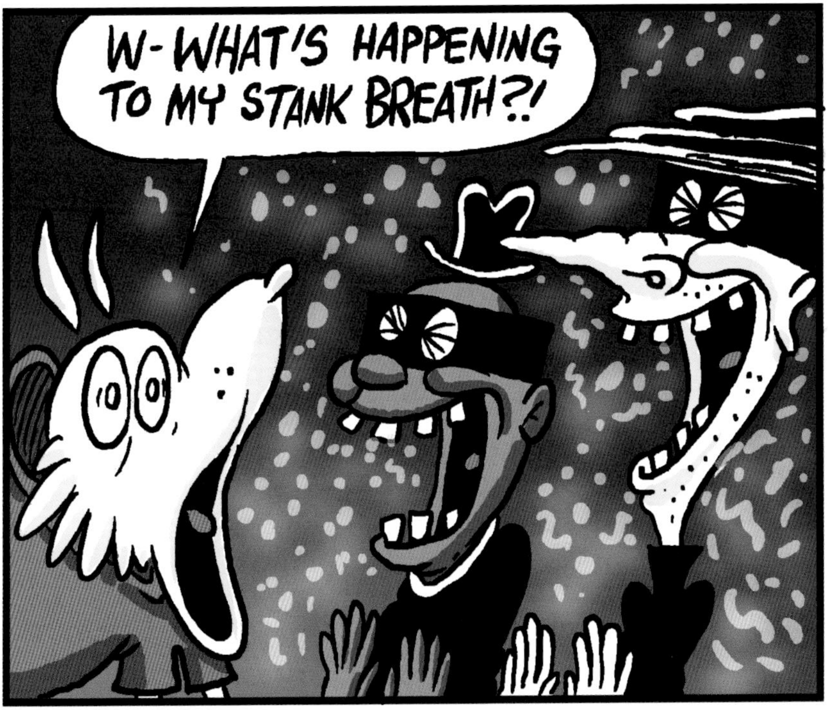
W-WHAT'S HAPPENING TO MY STANK BREATH?!

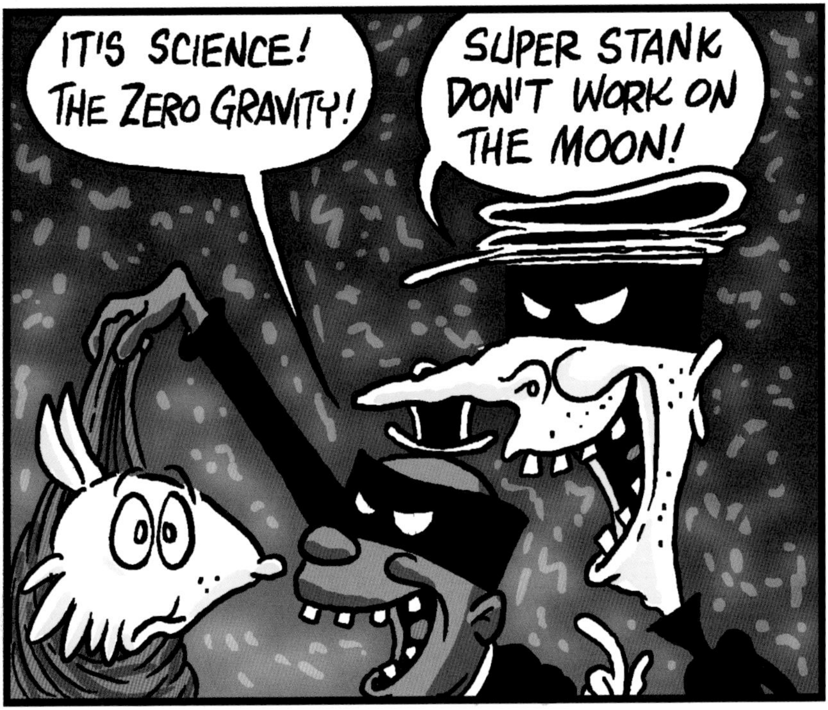
IT'S SCIENCE! THE ZERO GRAVITY!
SUPER STANK DON'T WORK ON THE MOON!

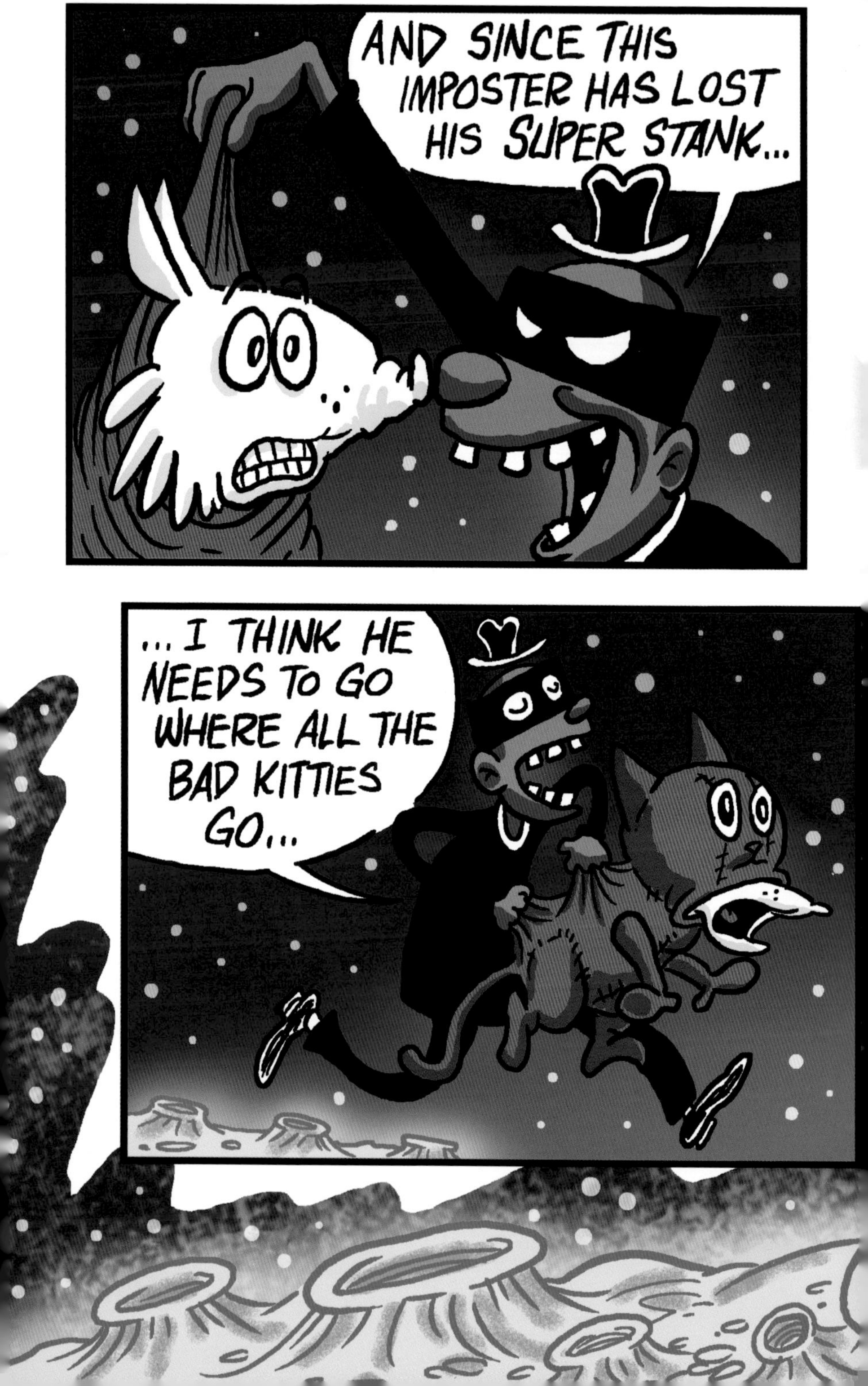
AND SINCE THIS IMPOSTER HAS LOST HIS SUPER STANK...
...I THINK HE NEEDS TO GO WHERE ALL THE BAD KITTIES GO...

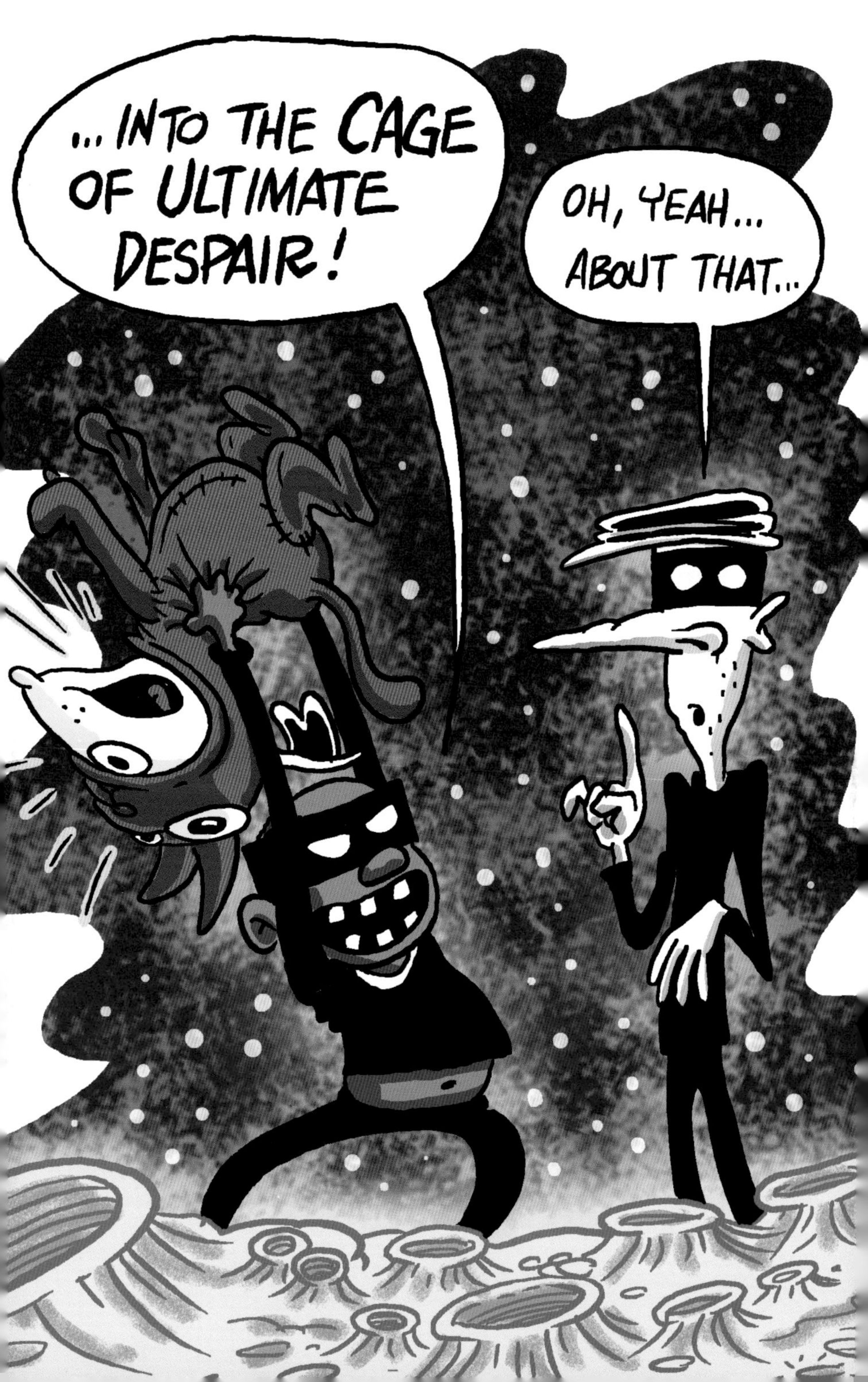
...INTO THE CAGE OF ULTIMATE DESPAIR!
OH, YEAH... ABOUT THAT...

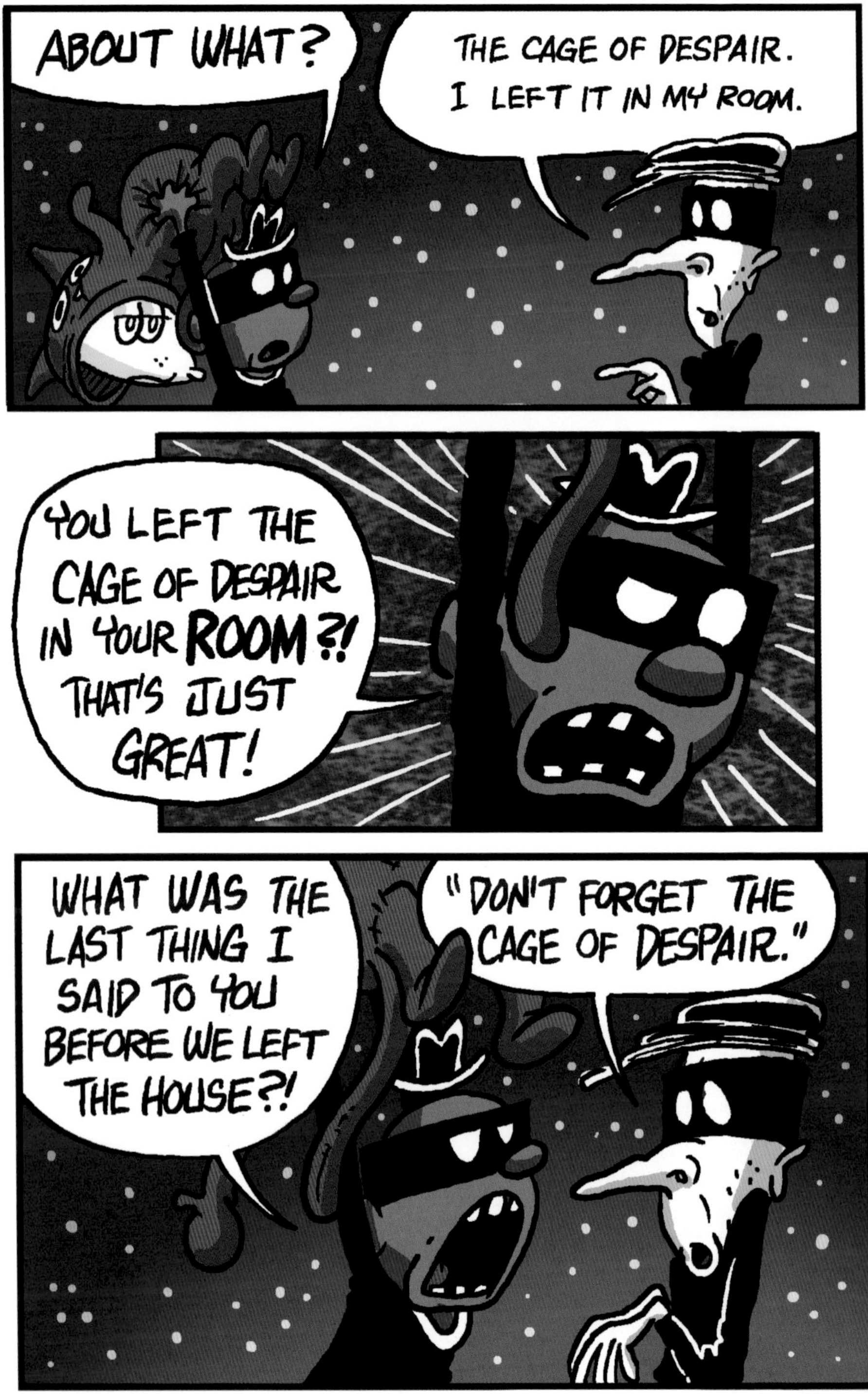
ABOUT WHAT?
THE CAGE OF DESPAIR. I LEFT IT IN MY ROOM.
YOU LEFT THE CAGE OF DESPAIR IN YOUR ROOM?! THAT'S JUST GREAT!
WHAT WAS THE LAST THING I SAID TO YOU BEFORE WE LEFT THE HOUSE?!
"DON'T FORGET THE CAGE OF DESPAIR."

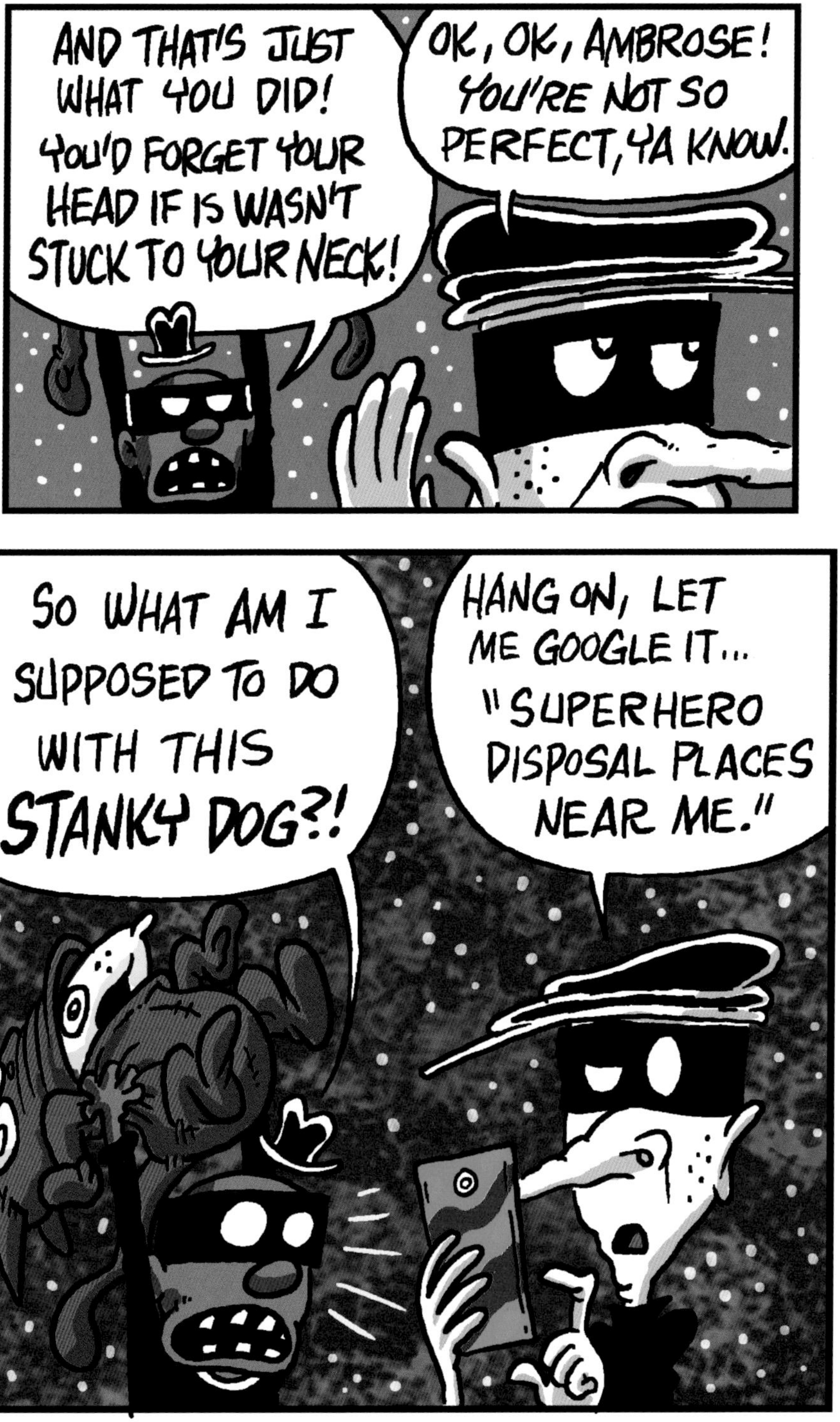
AND THAT'S JUST WHAT YOU DID! YOU'D FORGET YOUR HEAD IF IS WASN'T STUCK TO YOUR NECK!
OK, OK, AMBROSE! YOU'RE NOT SO PERFECT, YA KNOW.
SO WHAT AM I SUPPOSED TO DO WITH THIS STANKY DOG?!
HANG ON, LET ME GOOGLE IT... "SUPERHERO DISPOSAL PLACES NEAR ME."

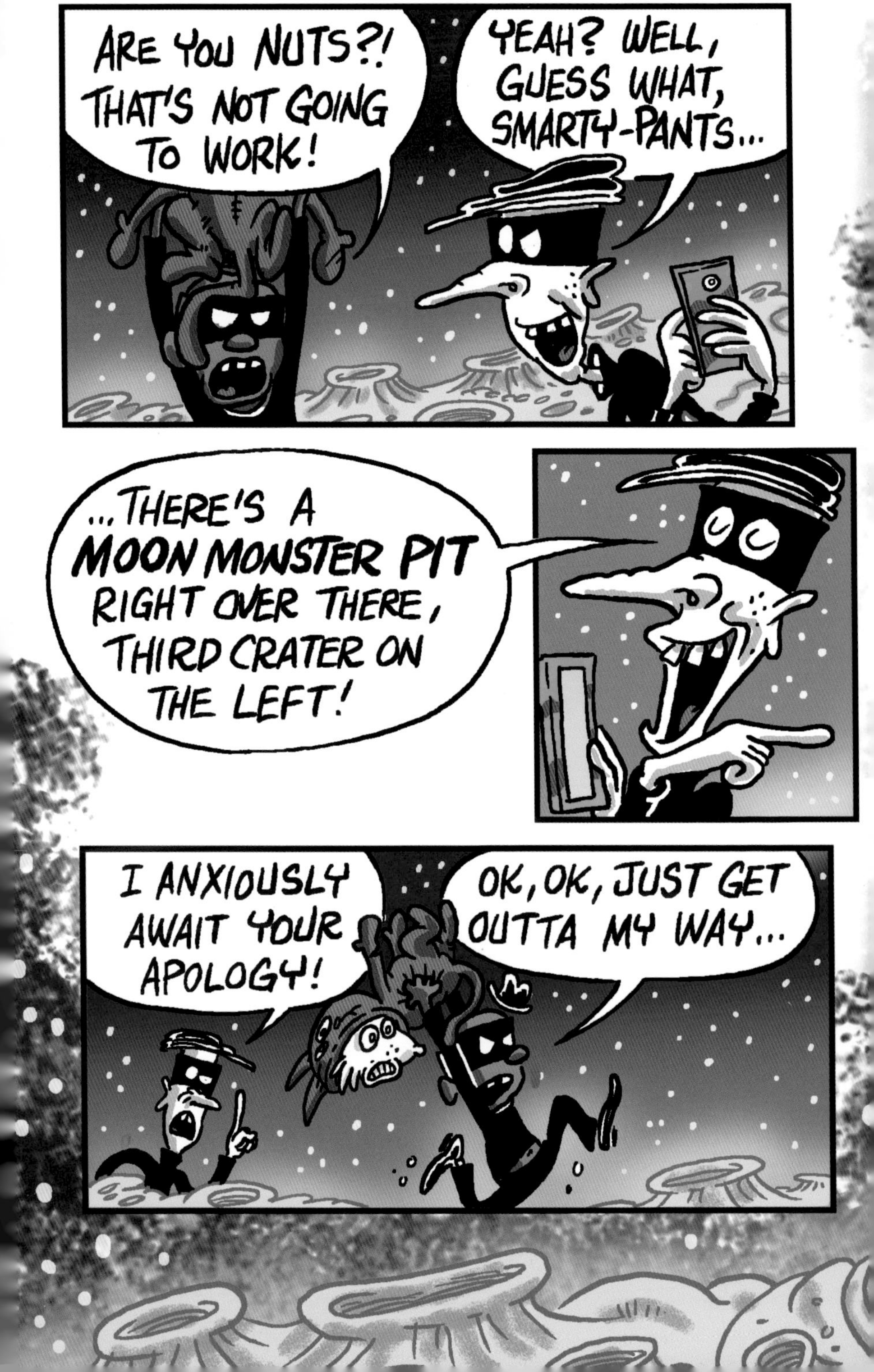
ARE YOU NUTS?! THAT'S NOT GOING TO WORK!
YEAH? WELL, GUESS WHAT, SMARTY-PANTS...
...THERE'S A MOON MONSTER PIT RIGHT OVER THERE, THIRD CRATER ON THE LEFT!
I ANXIOUSLY AWAIT YOUR APOLOGY!
OK, OK, JUST GET OUTTA MY WAY...

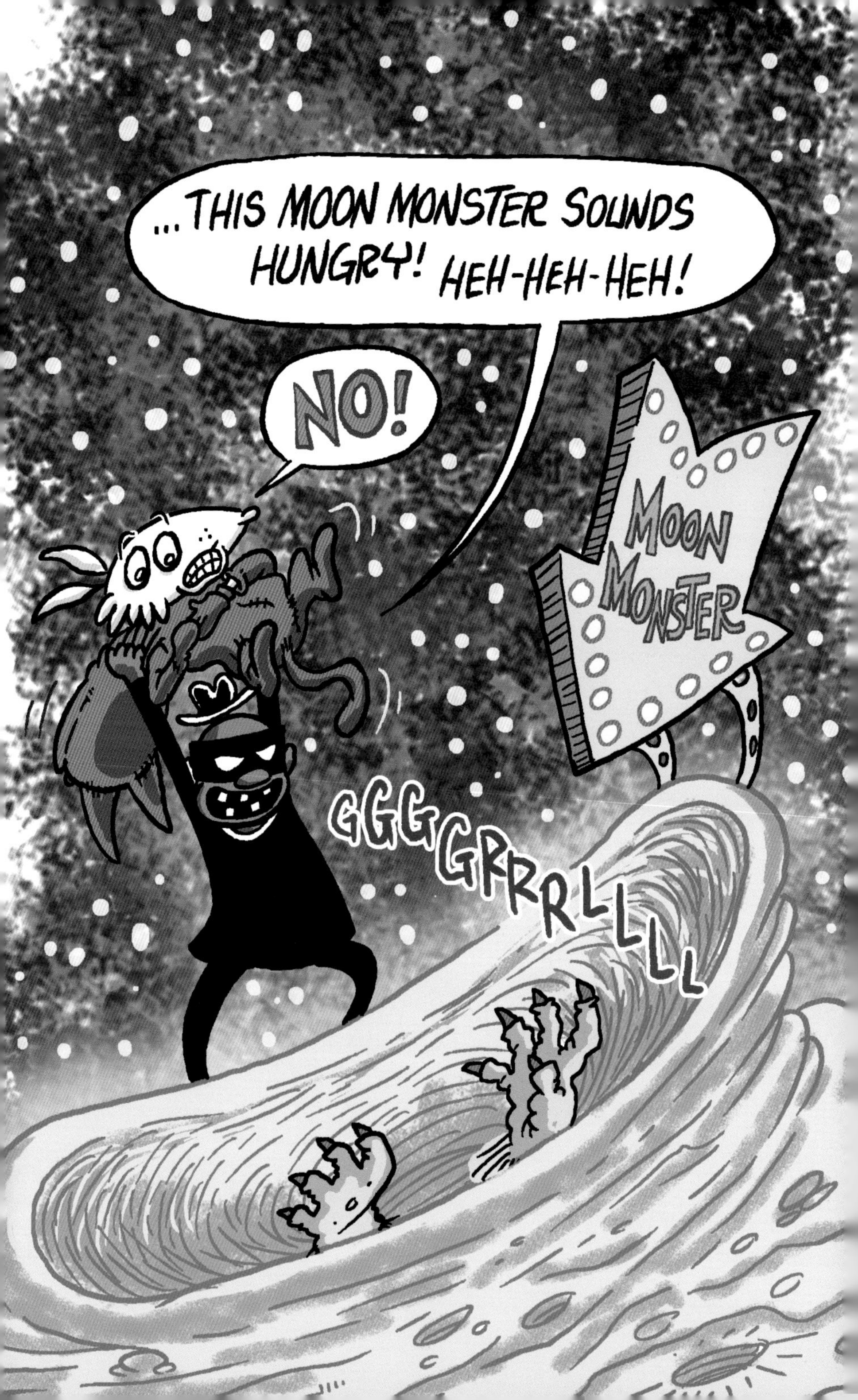
...THIS MOON MONSTER SOUNDS HUNGRY! HEH-HEH-HEH!
NO!
MOON MONSTER
GGGGRRRLLLLL

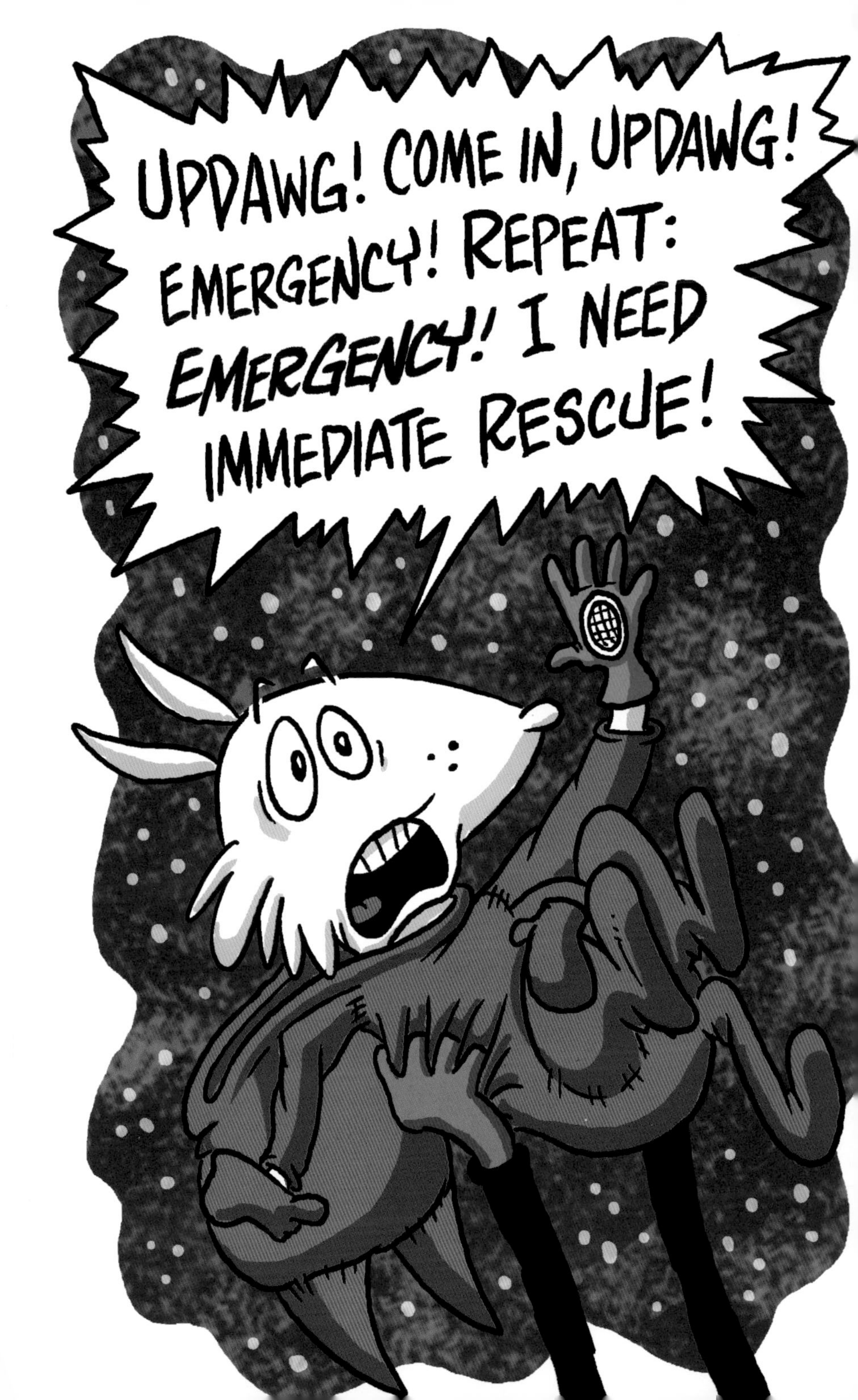
UPDAWG! COME IN, UPDAWG! EMERGENCY! REPEAT: EMERGENCY! I NEED IMMEDIATE RESCUE!

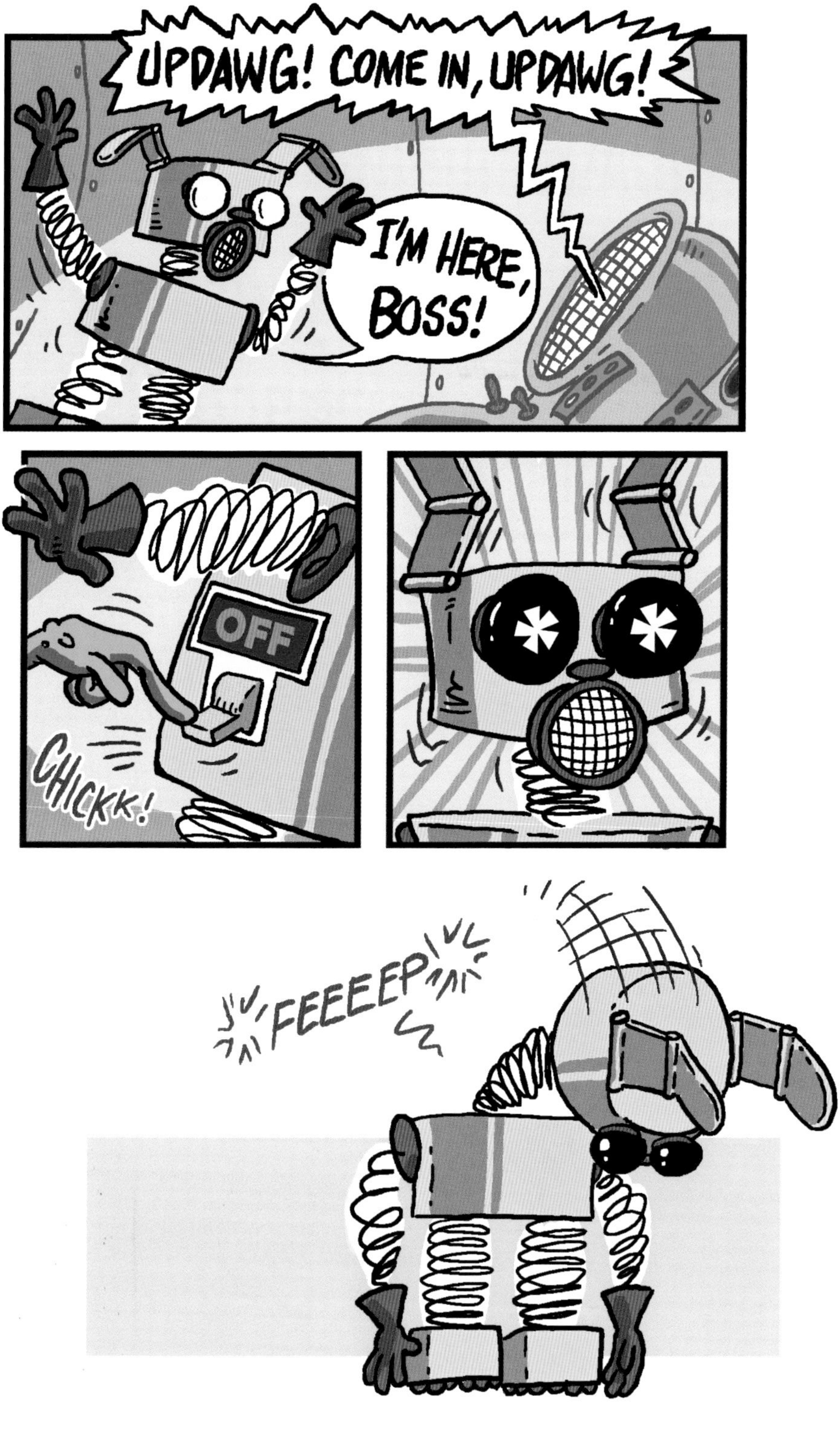

UPDAWG! COME IN, UPDAWG!
I'M HERE, BOSS!
OFF
CHICKK!
FEEEEP

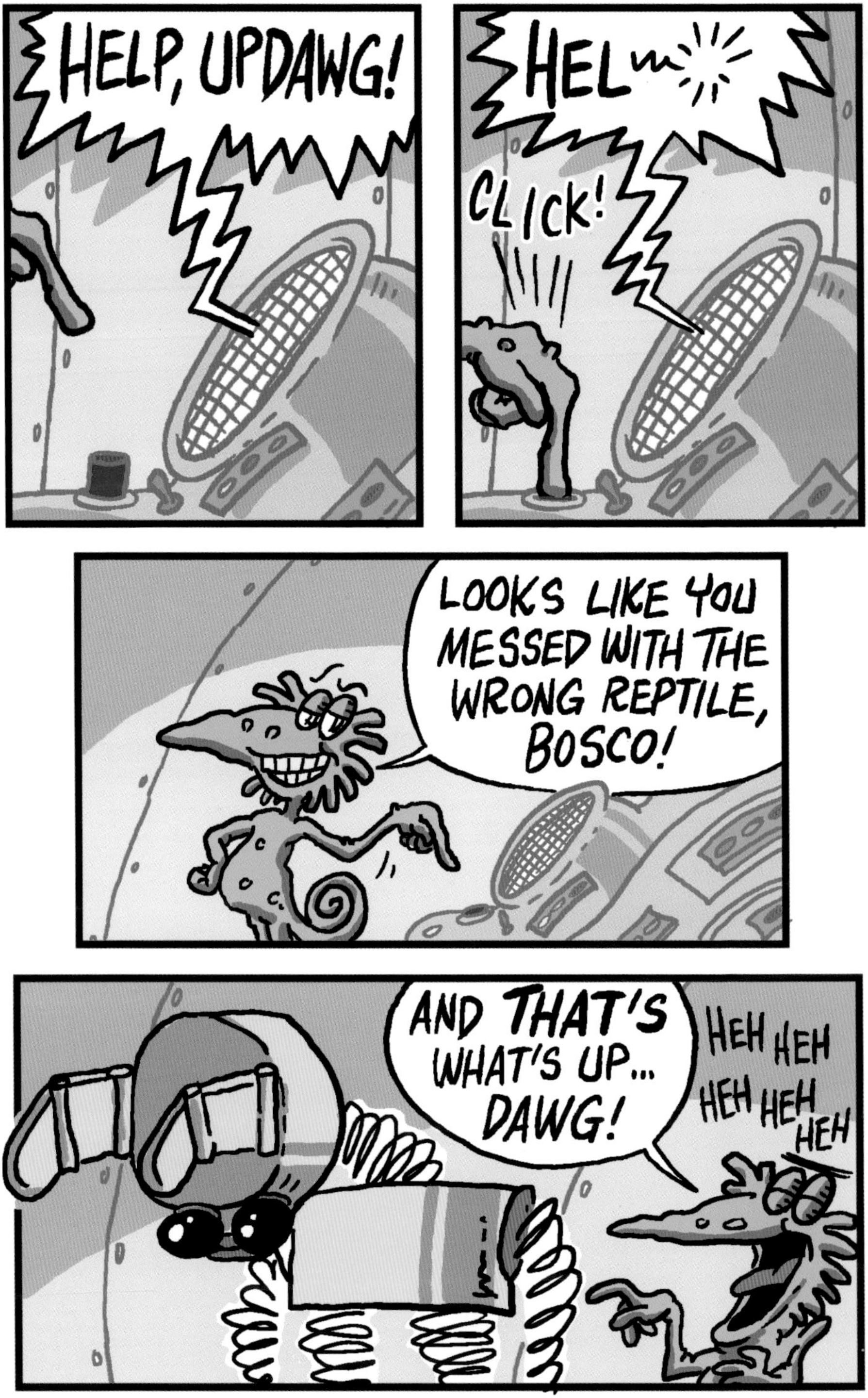
HELP, UPDAWG!
HEL
CLICK!
LOOKS LIKE YOU MESSED WITH THE WRONG REPTILE, BOSCO!
AND THAT'S WHAT'S UP... DAWG!
HEH HEH HEH HEH HEH

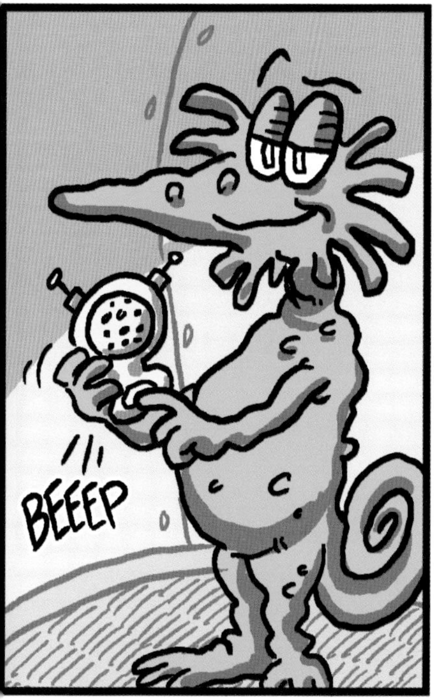
BEEEP

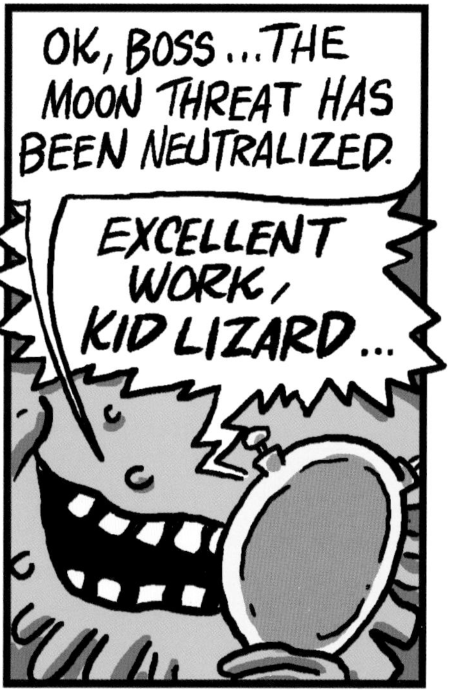
OK, BOSS...THE MOON THREAT HAS BEEN NEUTRALIZED.
EXCELLENT WORK, KID LIZARD...

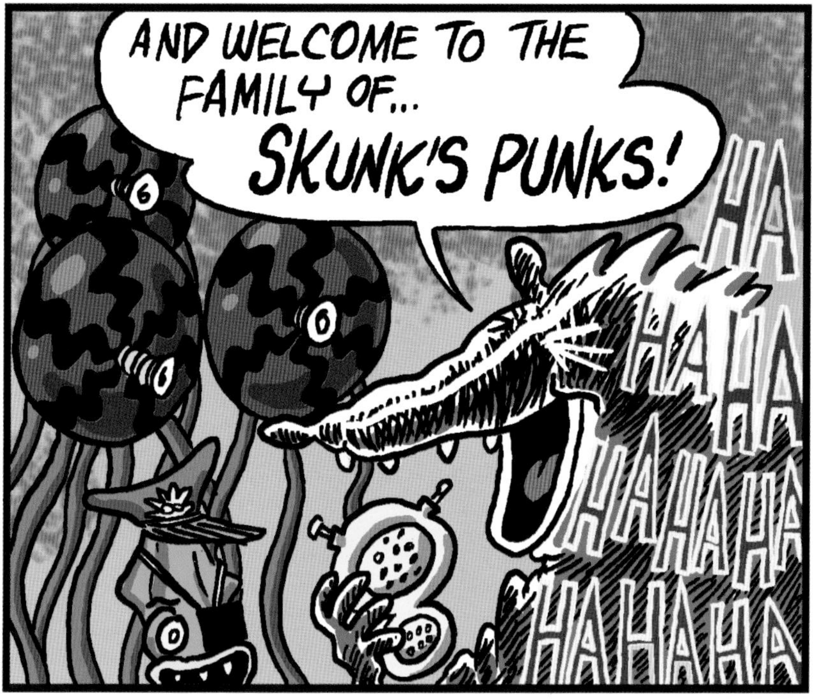
AND WELCOME TO THE FAMILY OF... SKUNK'S PUNKS!
HA HAHA HAHAHA HAHAHA

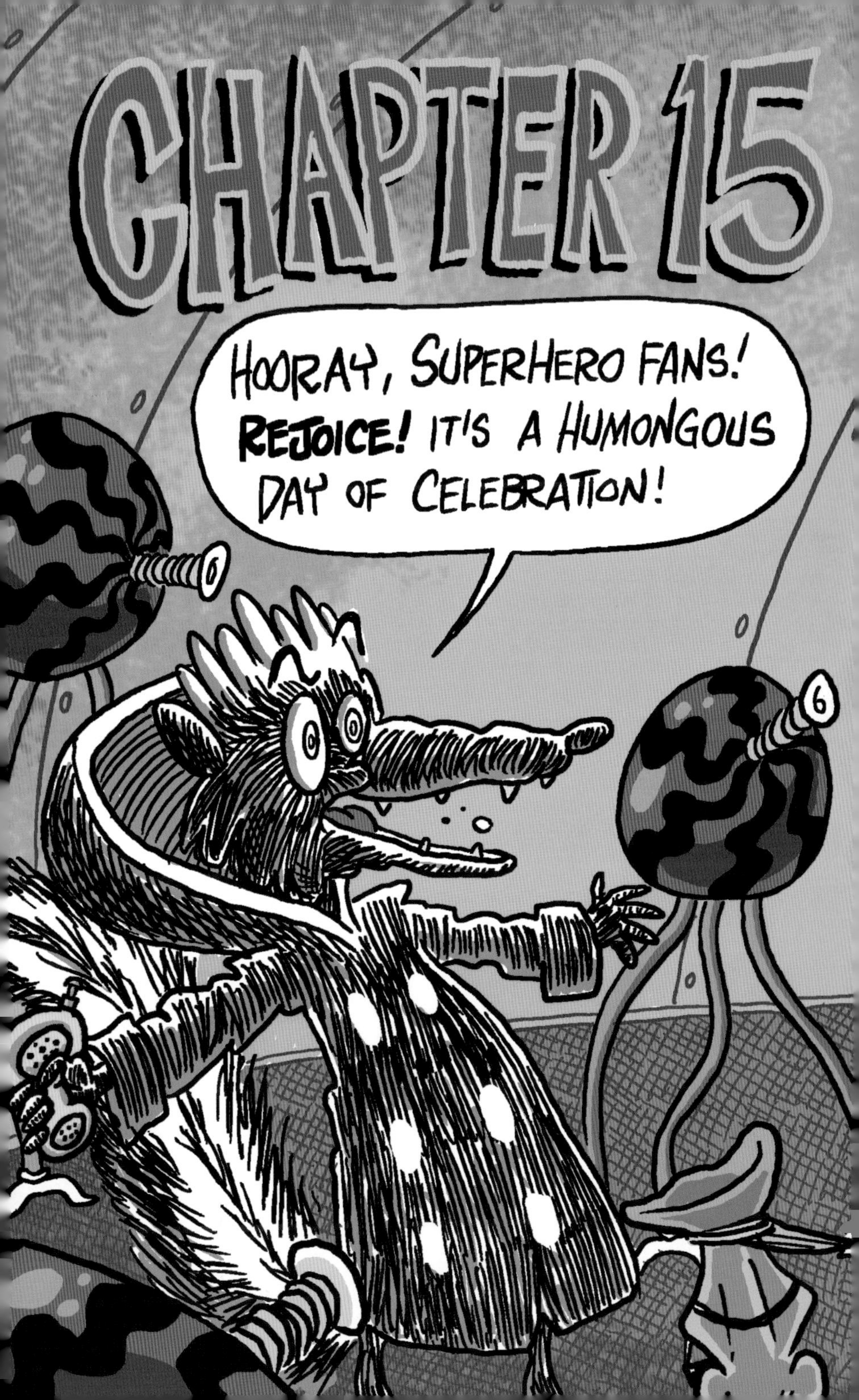
CHAPTER 15
HOORAY, SUPERHERO FANS! REJOICE! IT'S A HUMONGOUS DAY OF CELEBRATION!

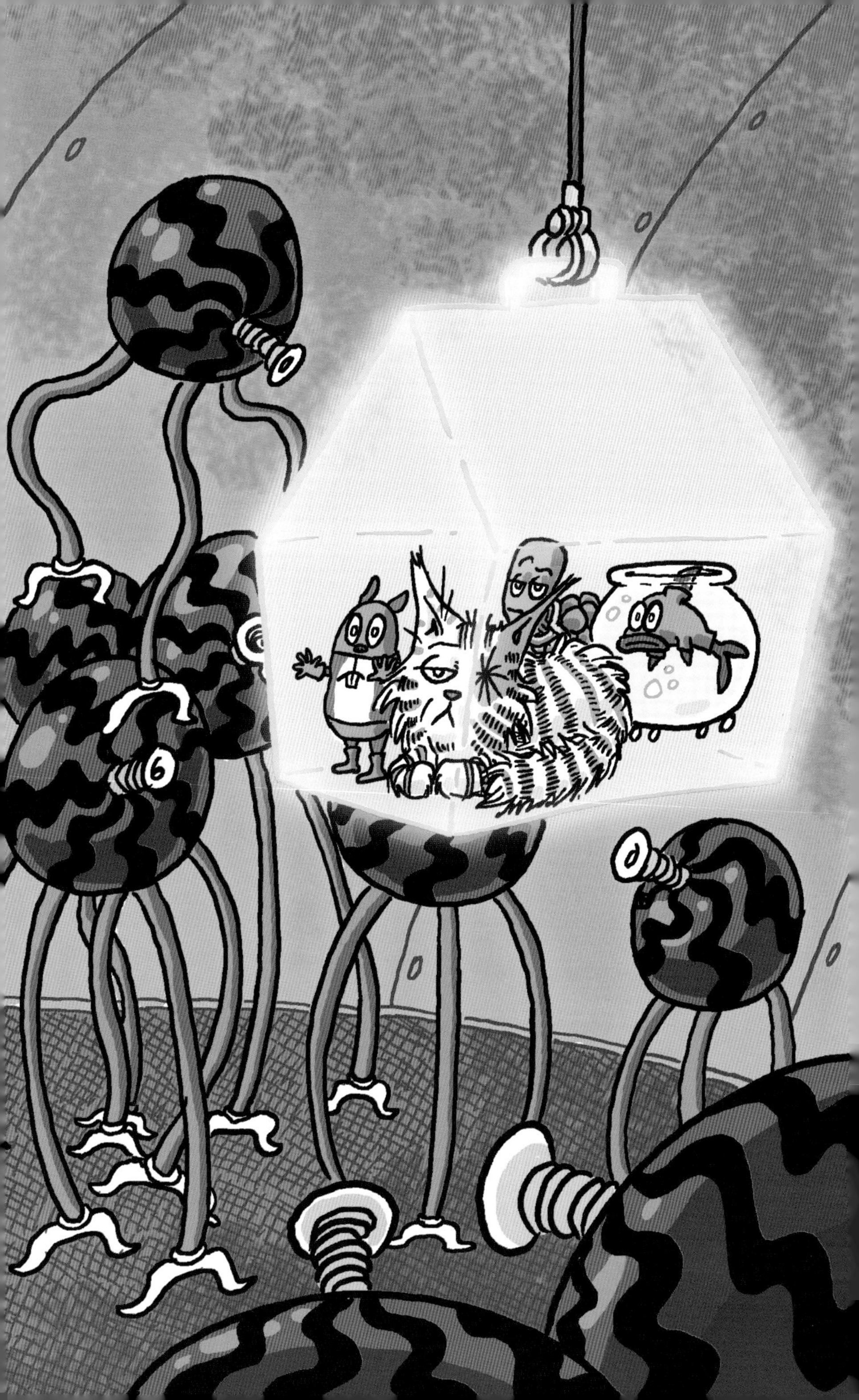

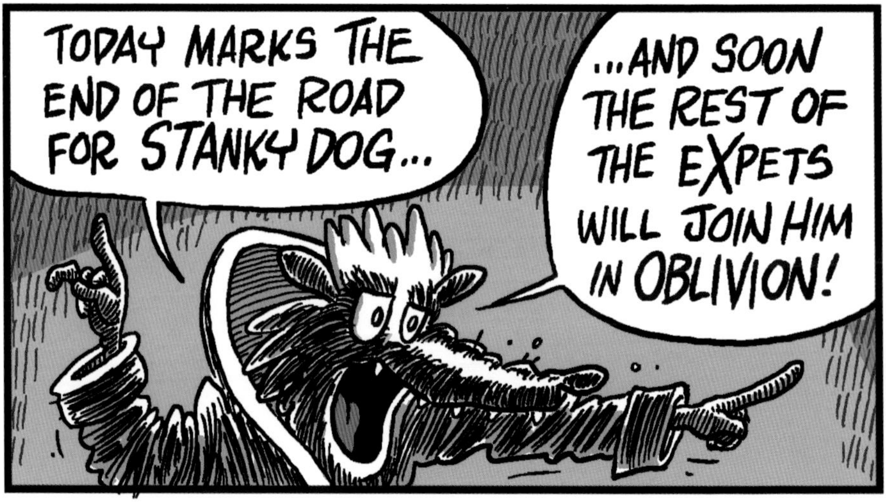
TODAY MARKS THE END OF THE ROAD FOR STANKY DOG...
...AND SOON THE REST OF THE EXPETS WILL JOIN HIM IN OBLIVION!

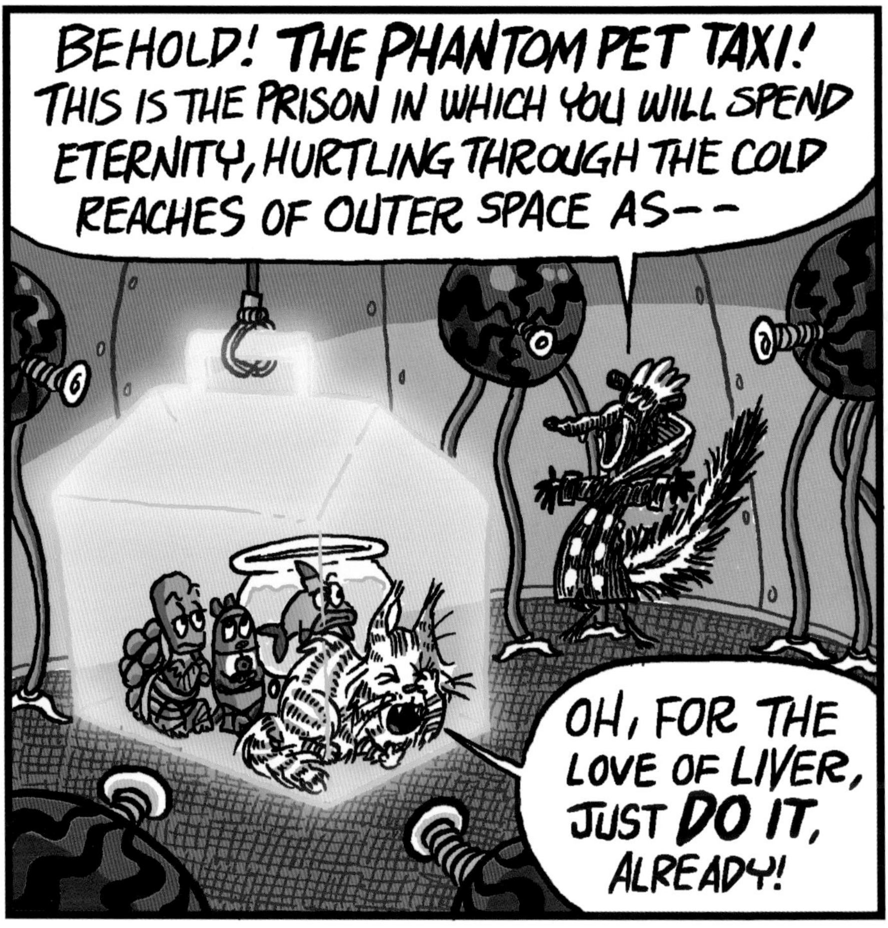
BEHOLD! THE PHANTOM PET TAXI! THIS IS THE PRISON IN WHICH YOU WILL SPEND ETERNITY, HURTLING THROUGH THE COLD REACHES OF OUTER SPACE AS--
OH, FOR THE LOVE OF LIVER, JUST DO IT, ALREADY!

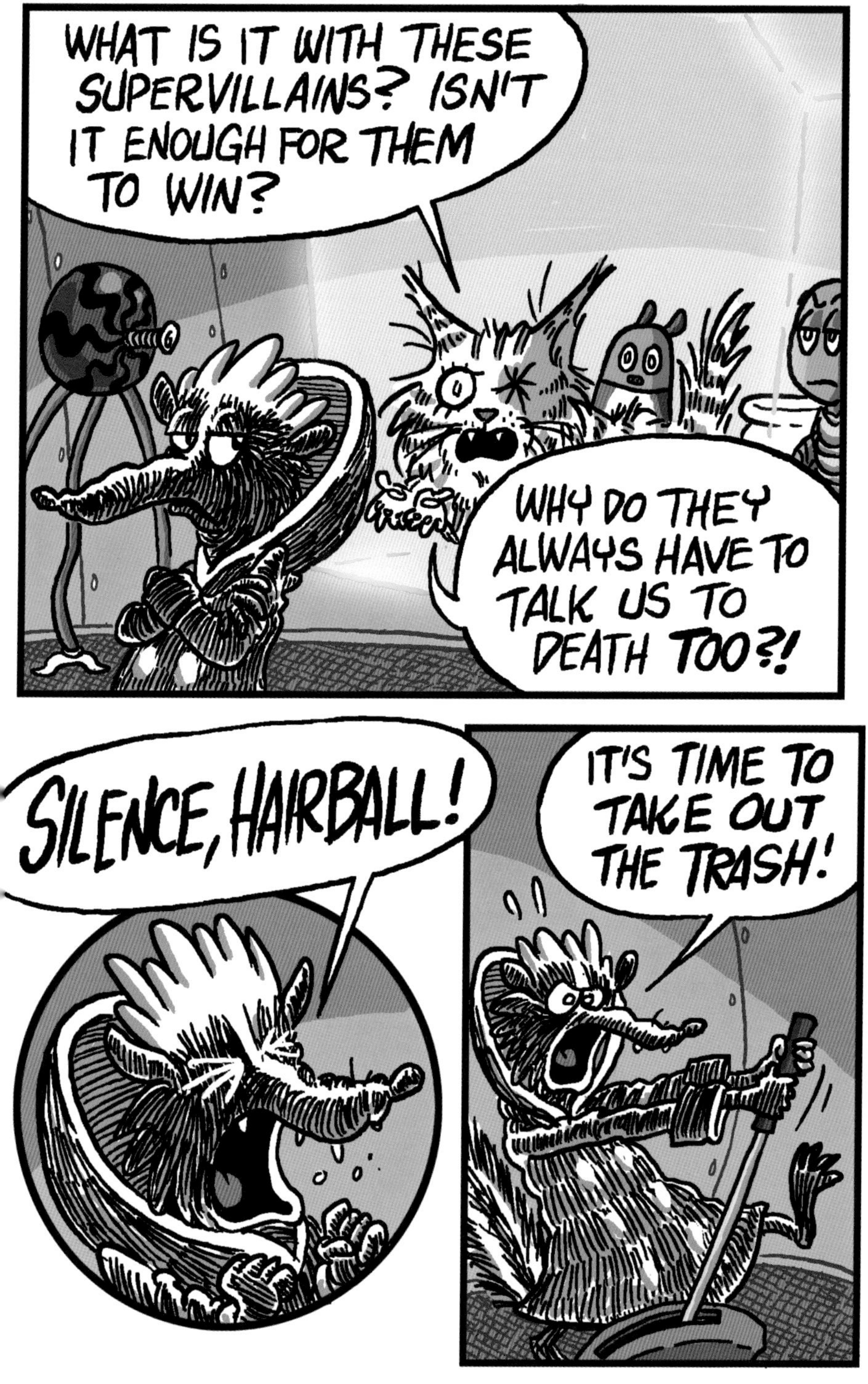
WHAT IS IT WITH THESE SUPERVILLAINS? ISN'T IT ENOUGH FOR THEM TO WIN?
WHY DO THEY ALWAYS HAVE TO TALK US TO DEATH TOO?!
SILENCE, HAIRBALL!
IT'S TIME TO TAKE OUT THE TRASH!

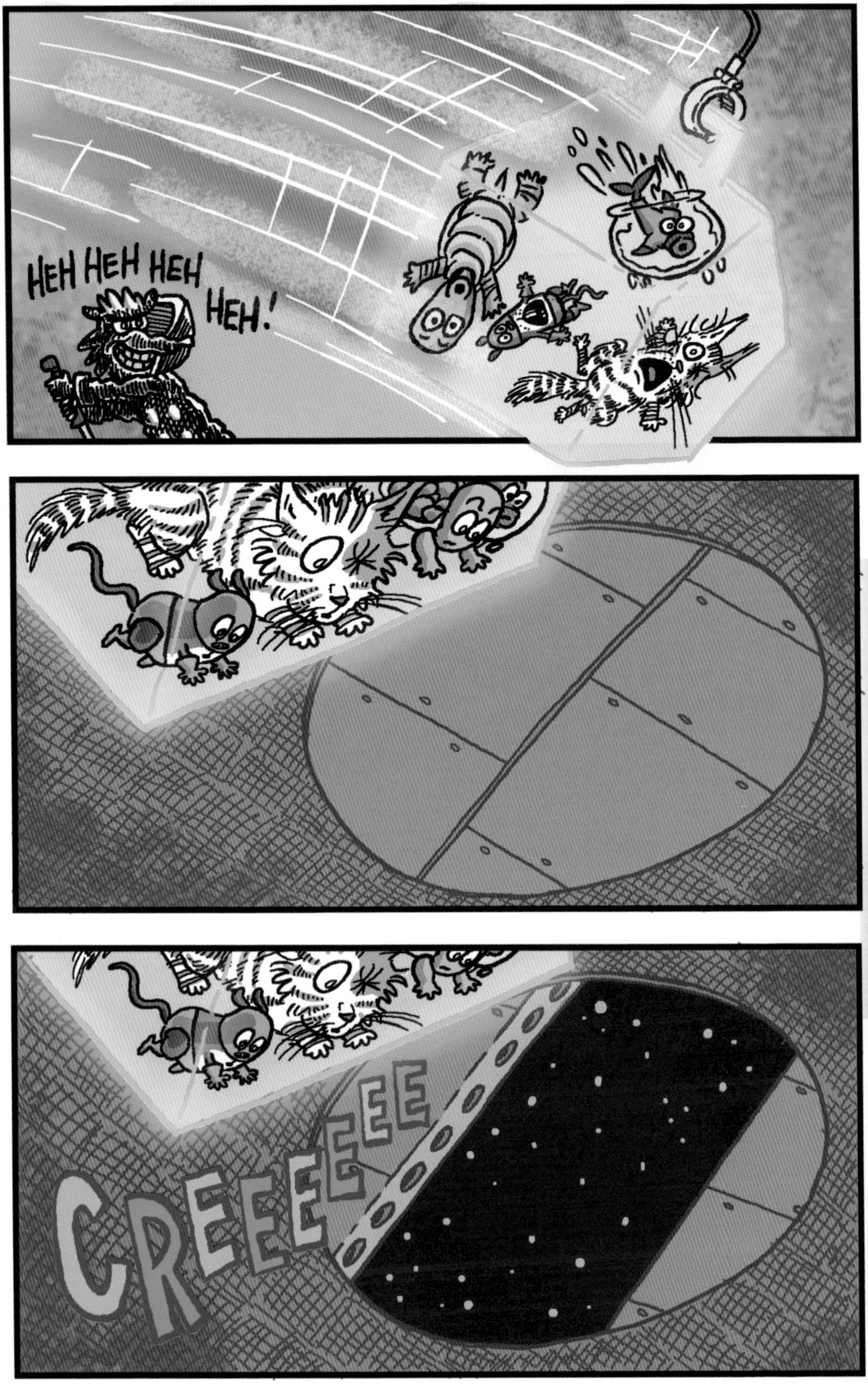
HEH HEH HEH HEH!
CREEEEEEE

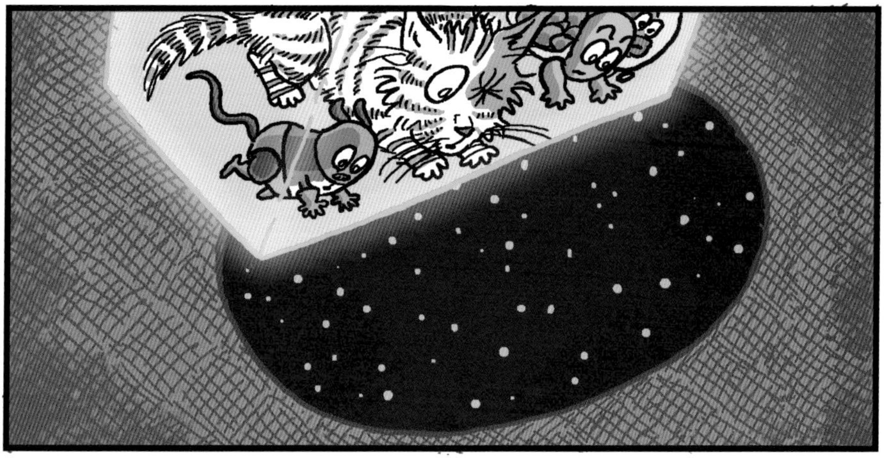

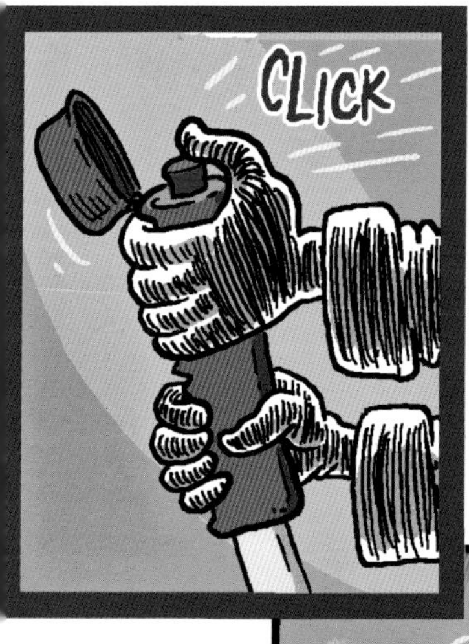
CLICK

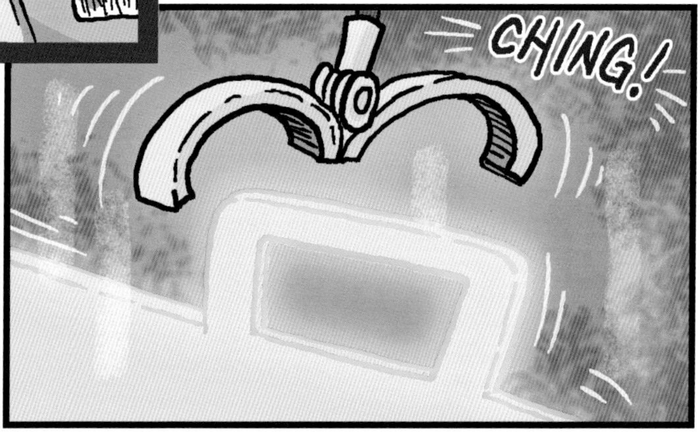
CHING!

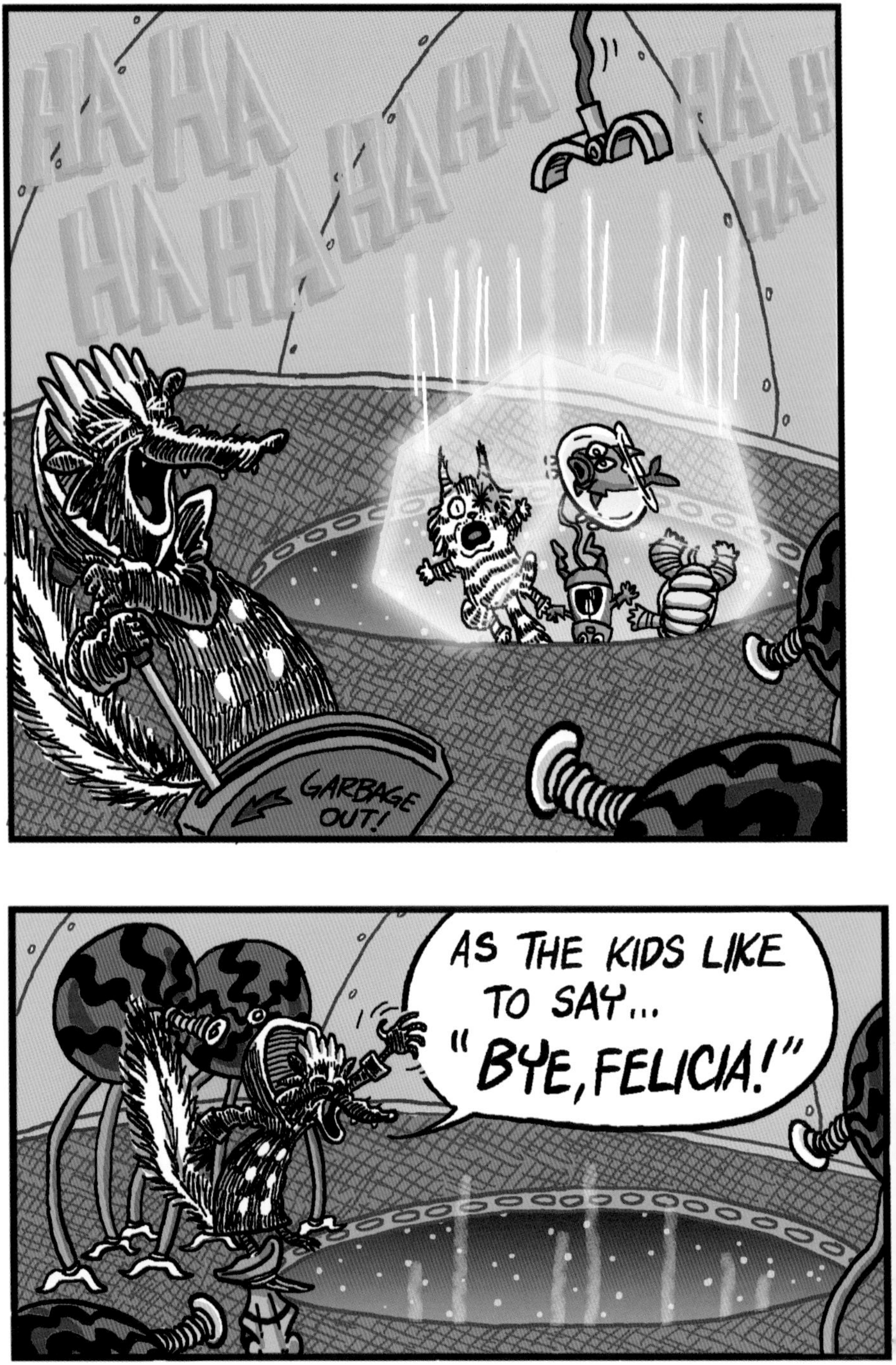
HAHA
HAHAHAHA
HAHAHA
HA
GARBAGE OUT!
AS THE KIDS LIKE TO SAY... "BYE, FELICIA!"

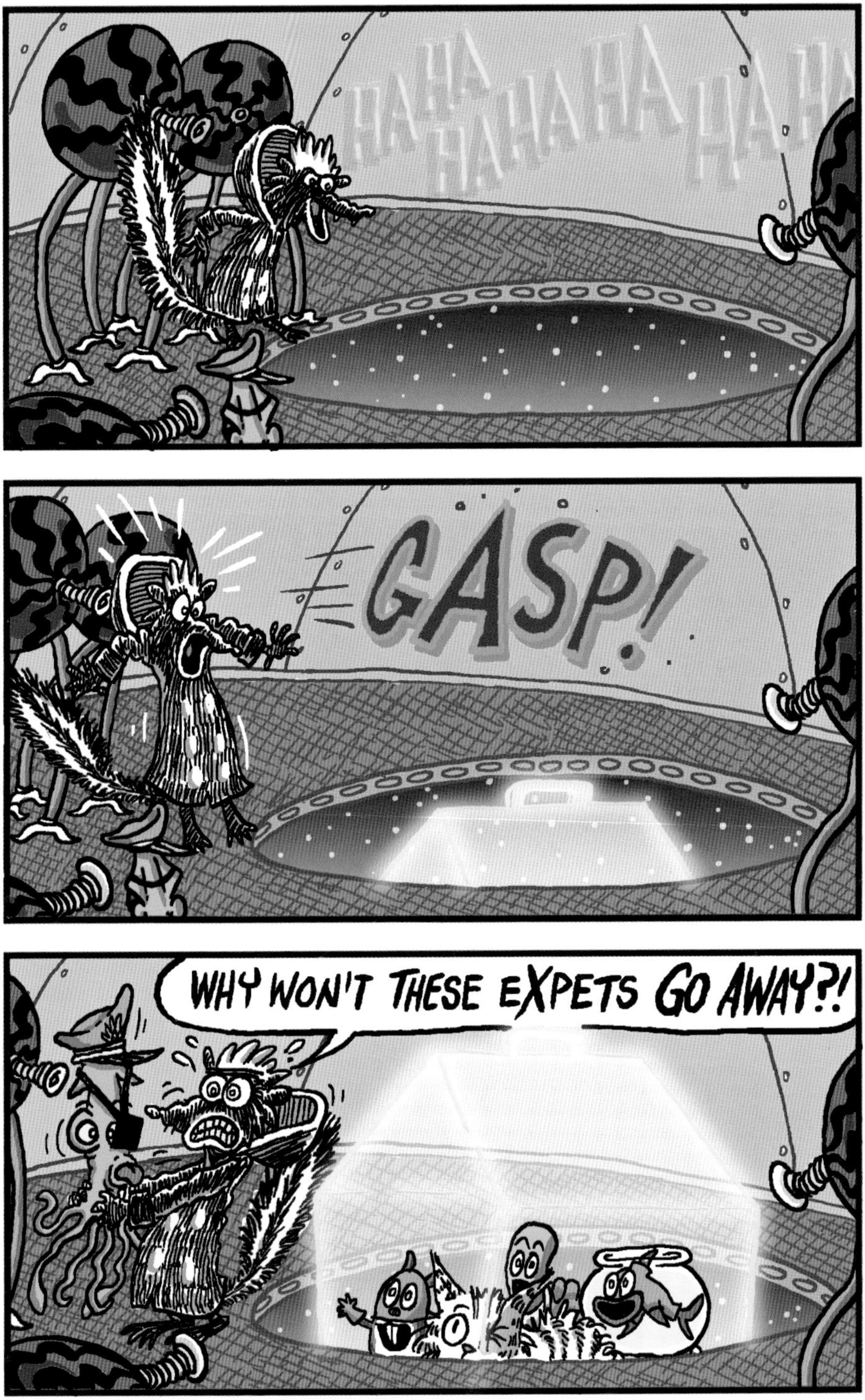
HAHA
HAHAHAHA
HAHA
GASP!
WHY WON'T THESE eXPETS GO AWAY?!

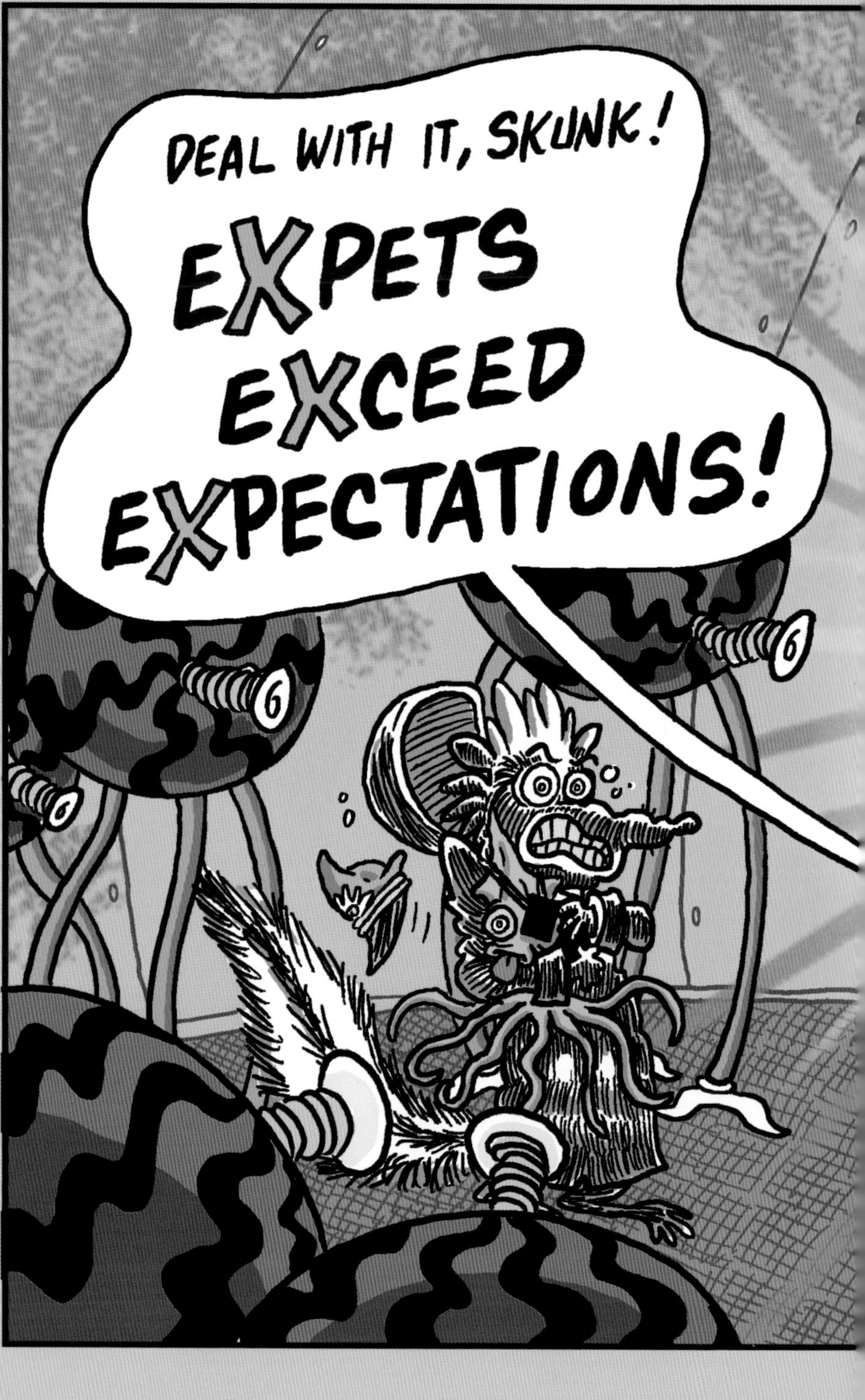
DEAL WITH IT, SKUNK!
EXPETS
EXCEED
EXPECTATIONS!

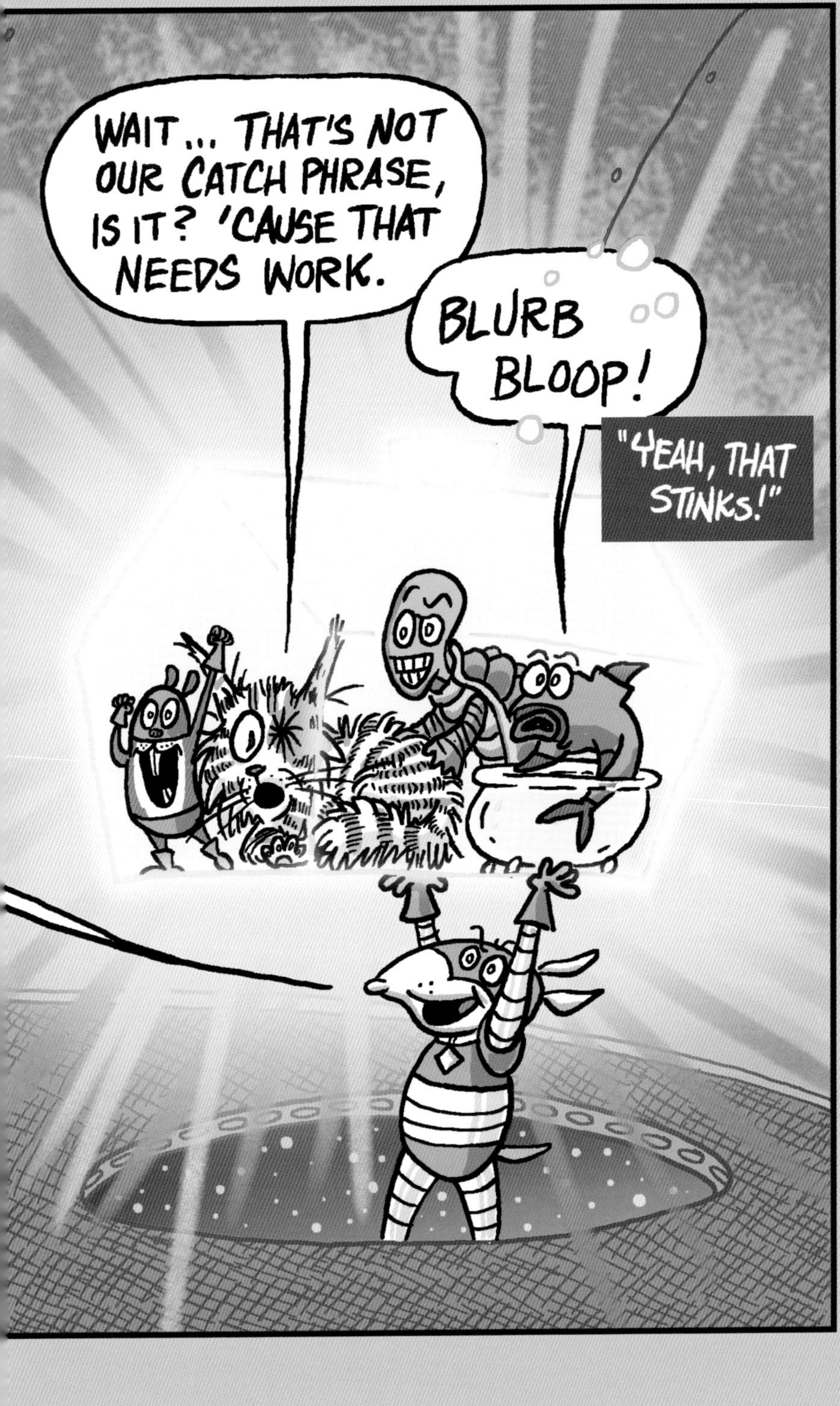
WAIT... THAT'S NOT OUR CATCH PHRASE, IS IT? 'CAUSE THAT NEEDS WORK.
BLURB BLOOP!
"YEAH, THAT STINKS!"

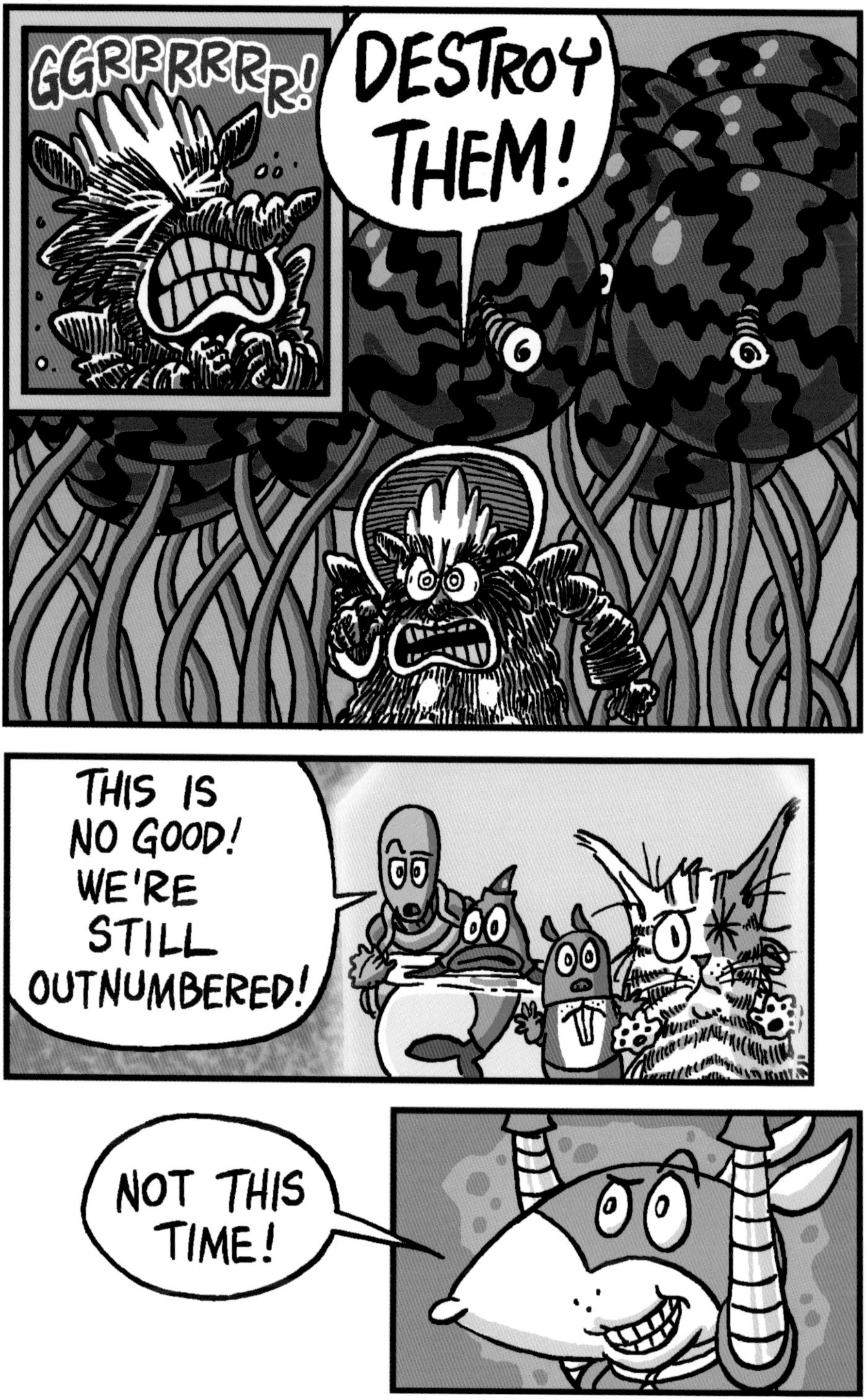
GGRRRRRRR!
DESTROY THEM!
THIS IS NO GOOD! WE'RE STILL OUTNUMBERED!
NOT THIS TIME!

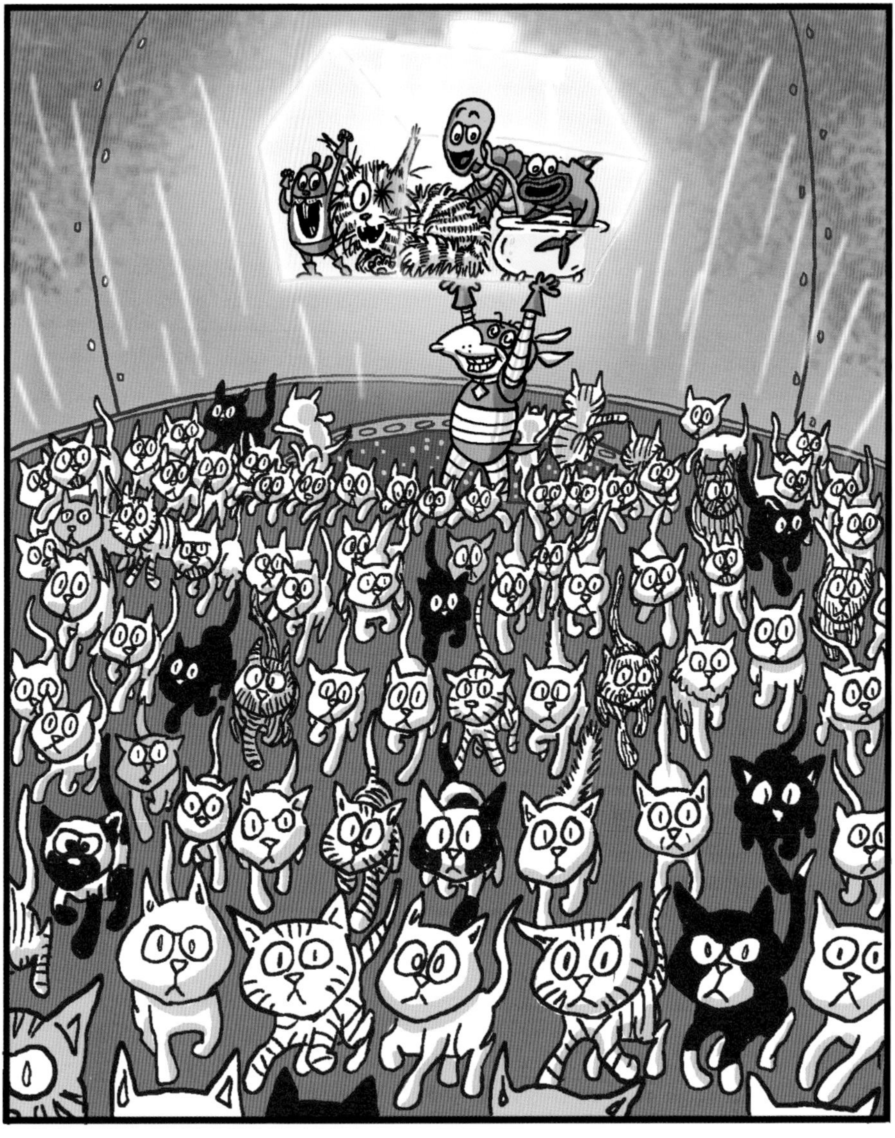

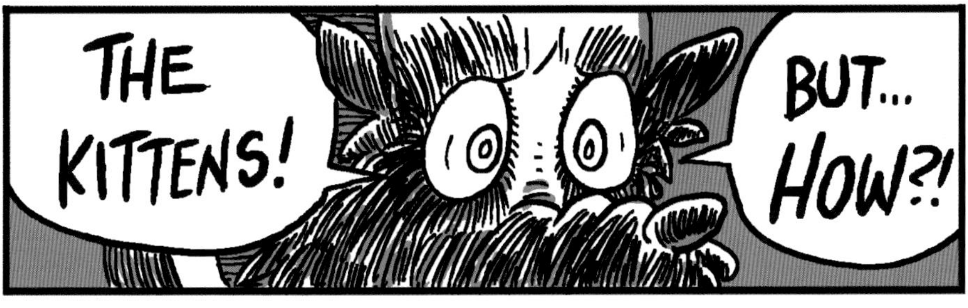
THE KITTENS!
BUT... HOW?!

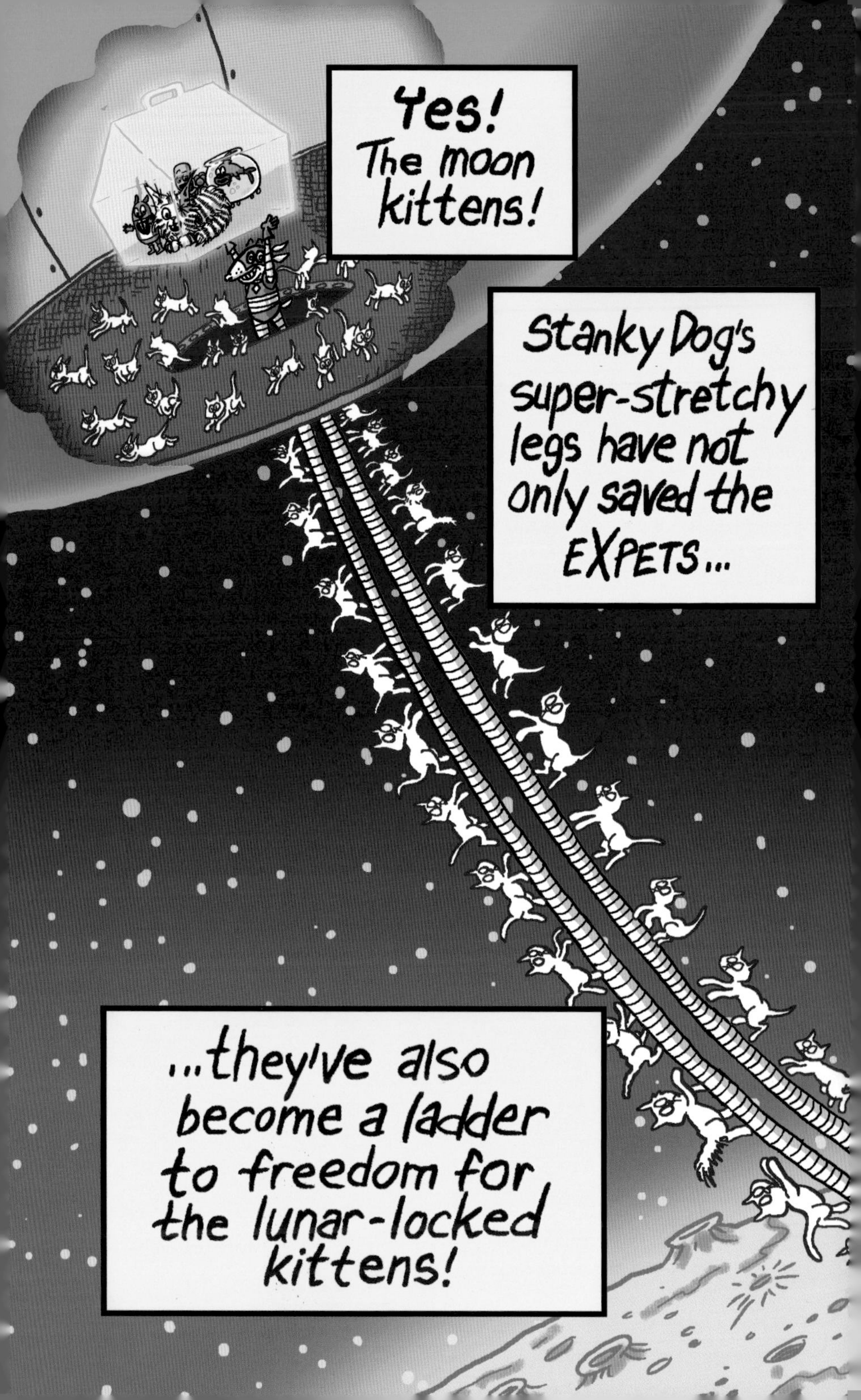
Yes! The moon kittens!
Stanky Dog's super-stretchy legs have not only saved the EXPETS...
...they've also become a ladder to freedom for the lunar-locked kittens!

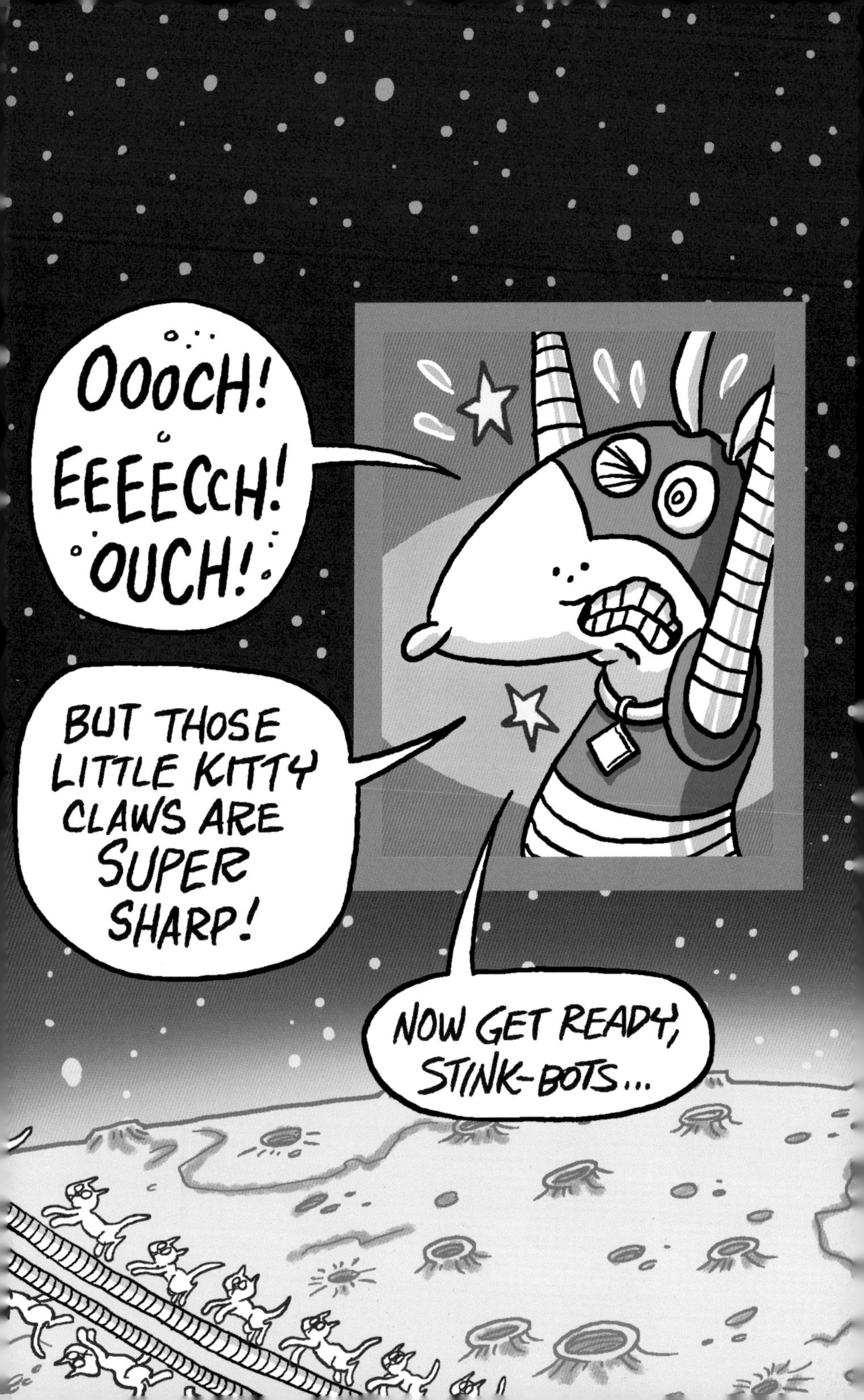
OOOCH! EEEECCH! OUCH!
BUT THOSE LITTLE KITTY CLAWS ARE SUPER SHARP!
NOW GET READY, STINK-BOTS...

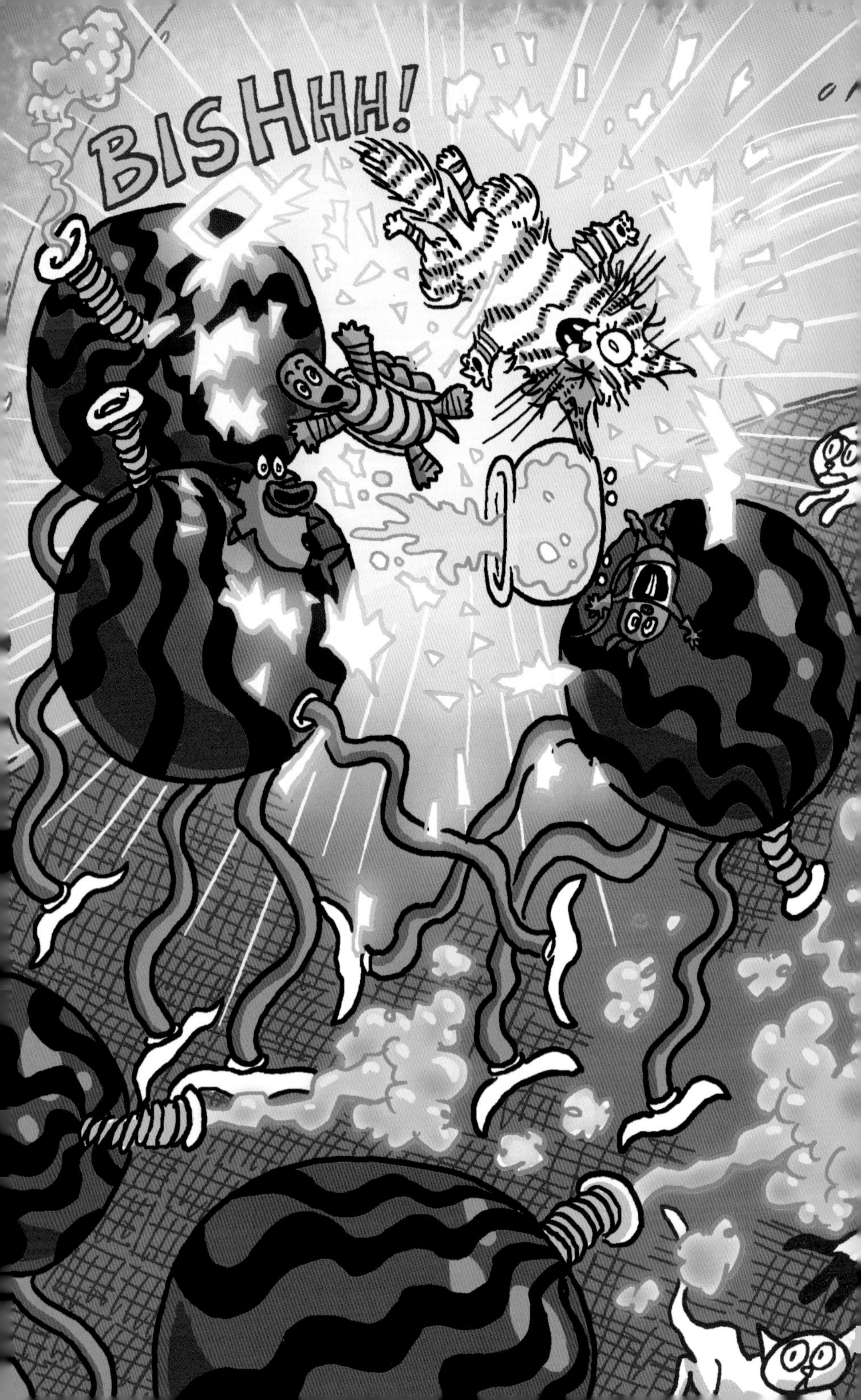
BISHHH!

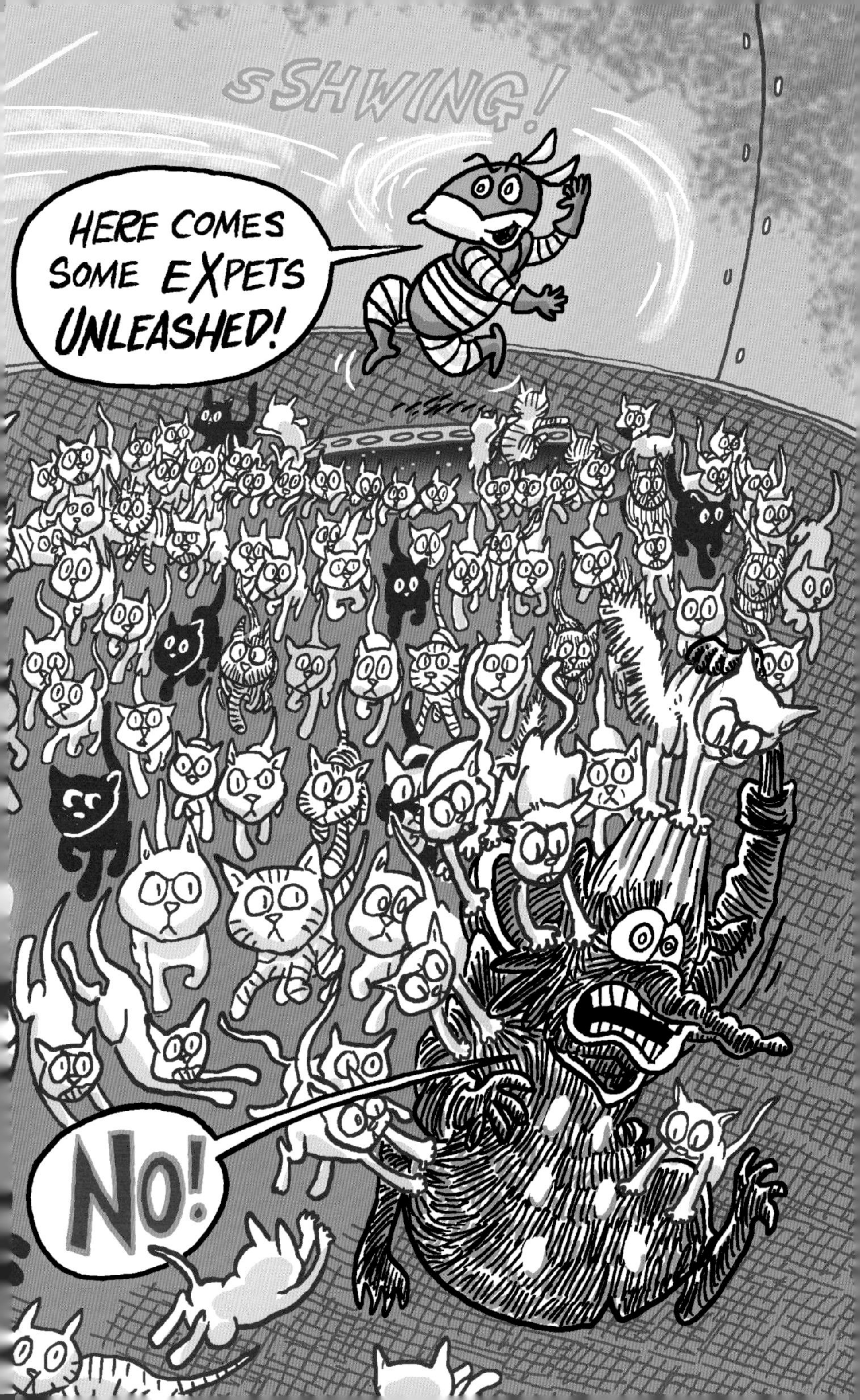
sSHWING!
HERE COMES SOME EXPETS UNLEASHED!
NO!

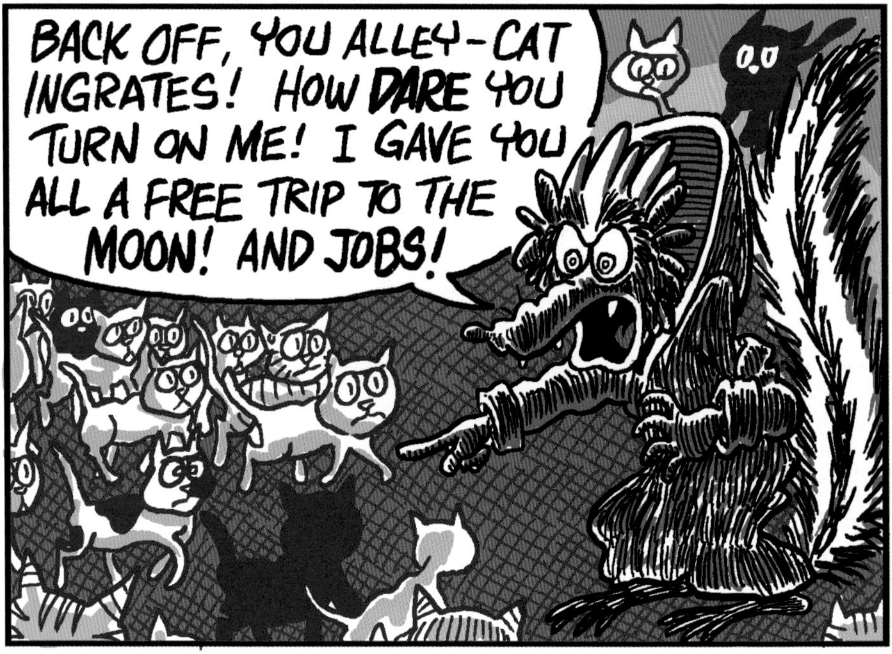
BACK OFF, YOU ALLEY-CAT INGRATES! HOW **DARE** YOU TURN ON ME! I GAVE YOU ALL A FREE TRIP TO THE MOON! AND JOBS!

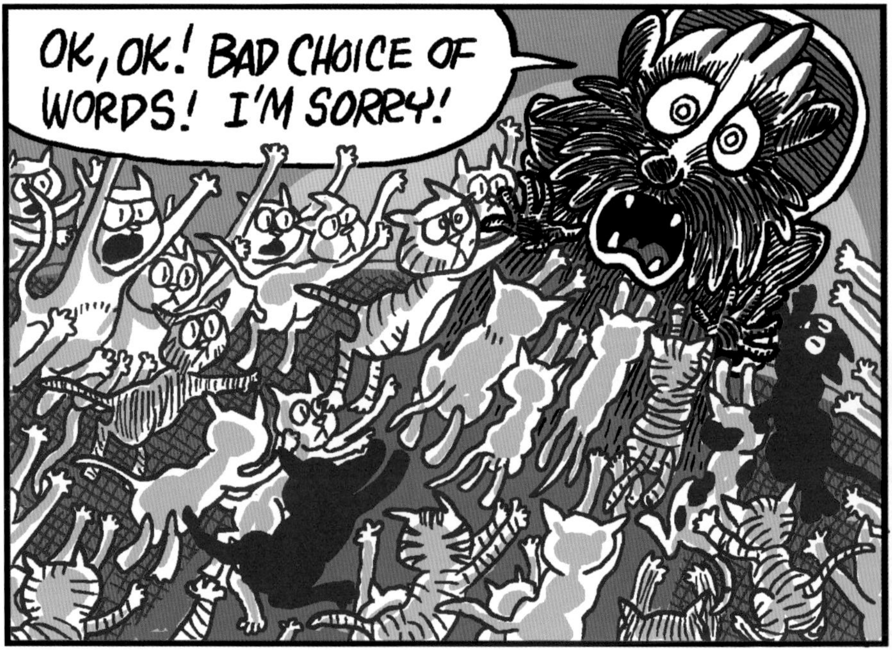
OK, OK! BAD CHOICE OF WORDS! I'M SORRY!

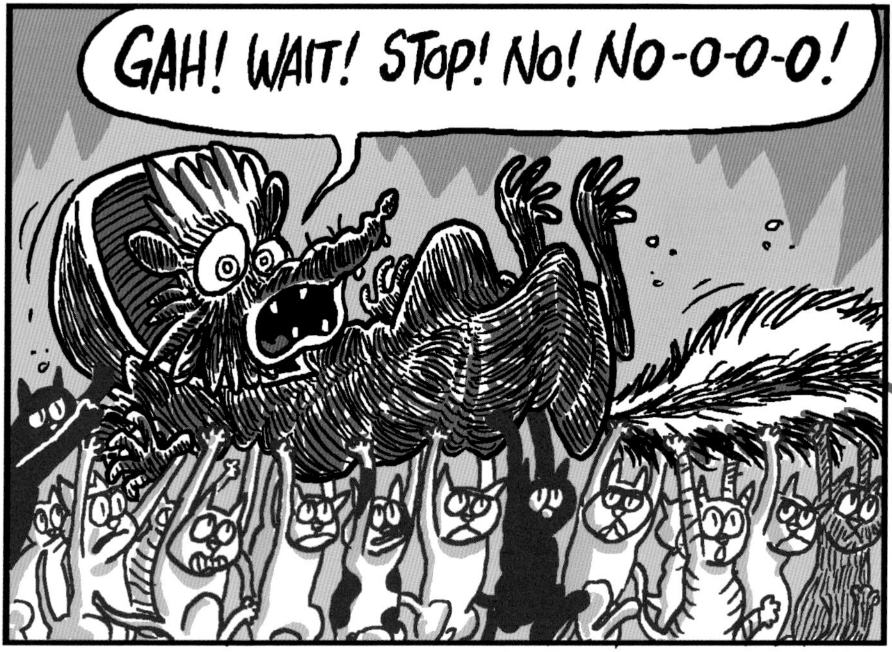
GAH! WAIT! STOP! NO! NO-O-O-O!

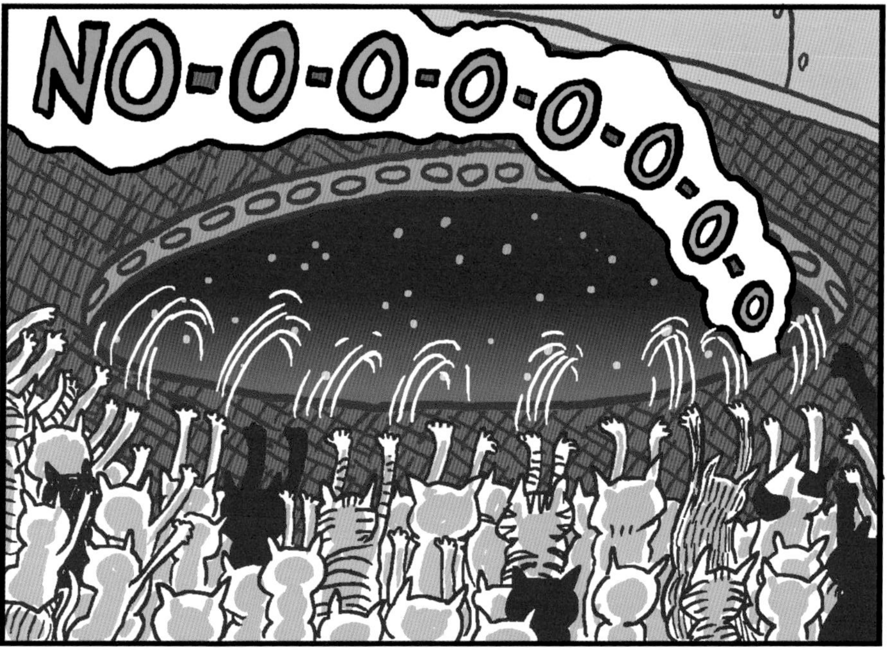
NO-O-O-O-O-O-O-O

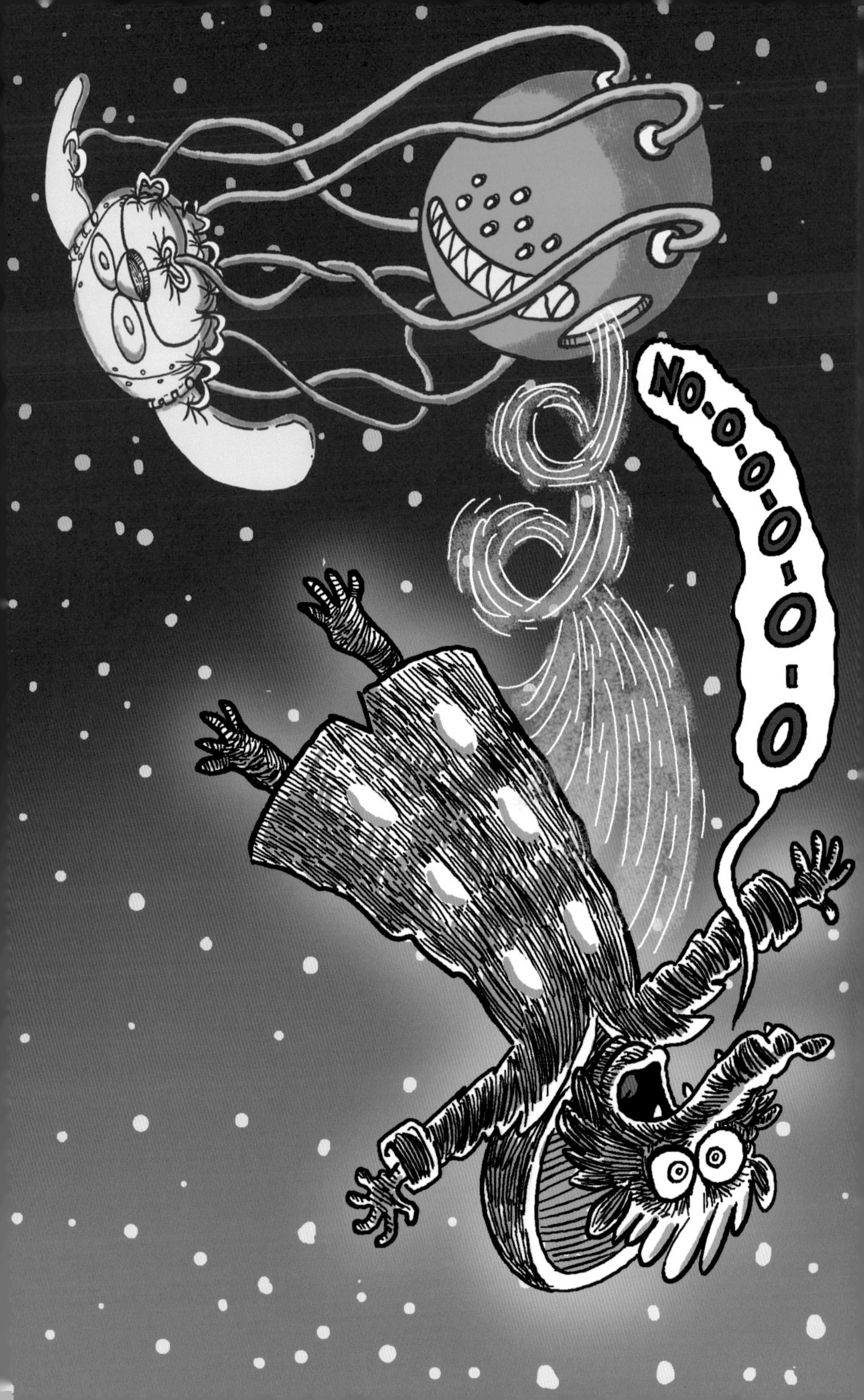
NO-O-O-O-O-O

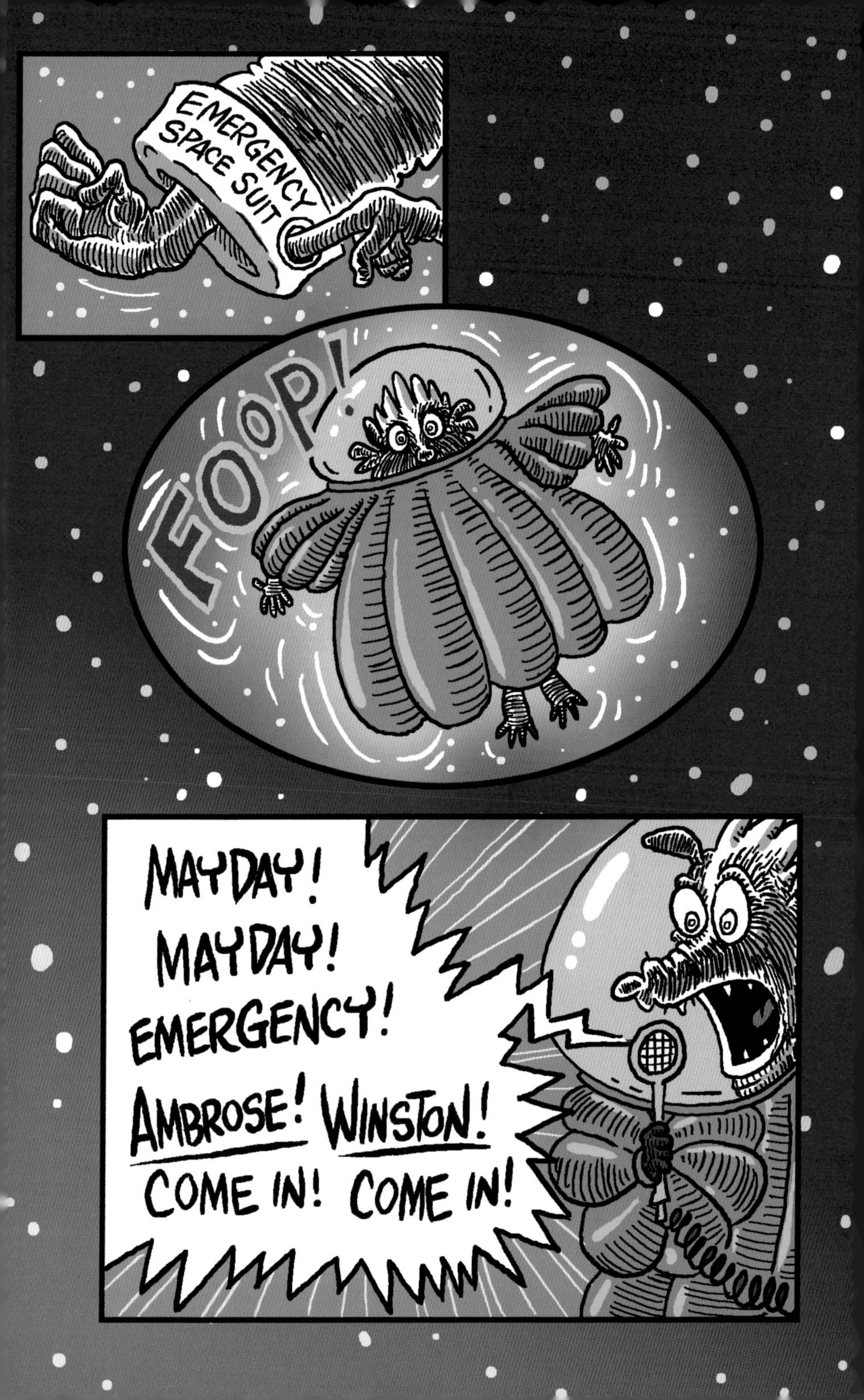
EMERGENCY SPACE SUIT
FOOP!
MAYDAY! MAYDAY! EMERGENCY! AMBROSE! WINSTON! COME IN! COME IN!

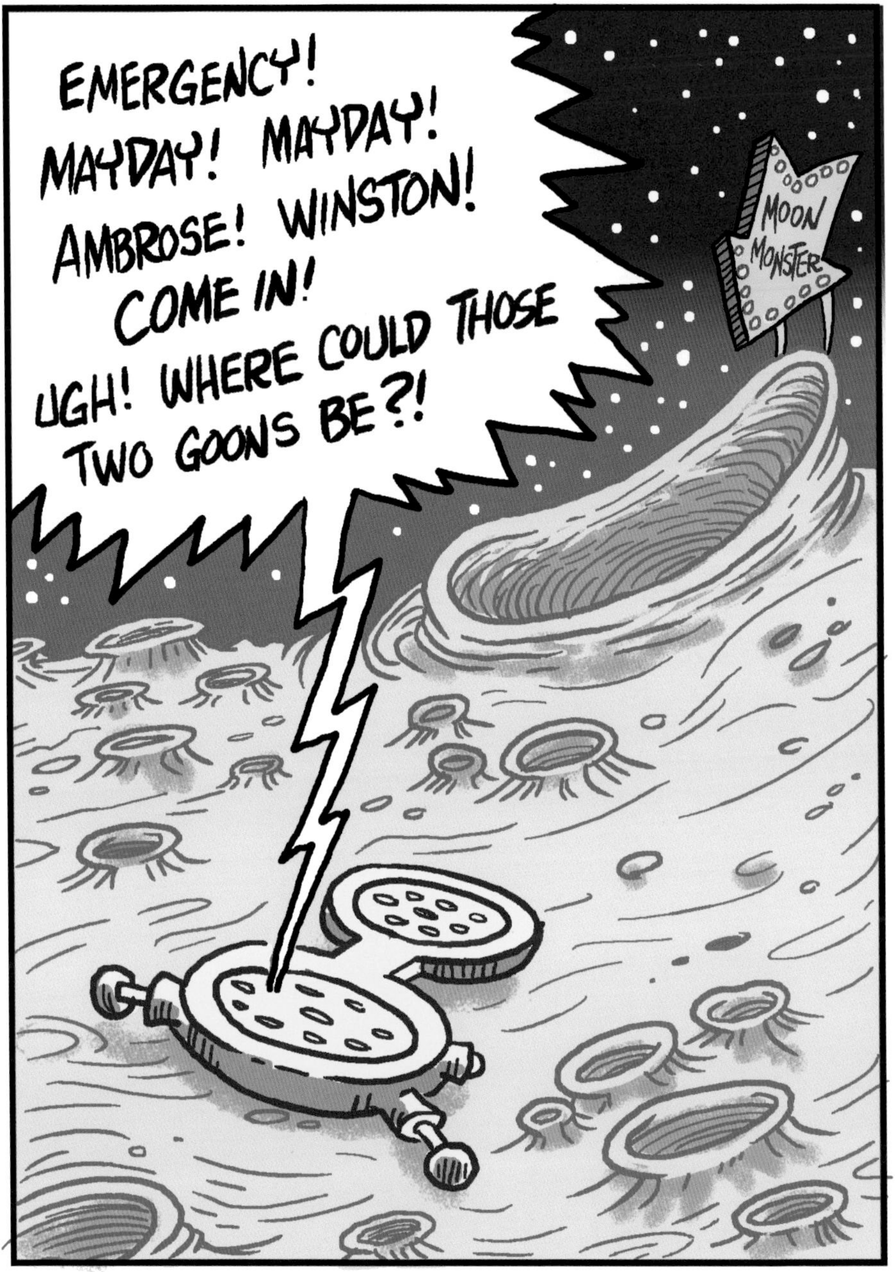
EMERGENCY! MAYDAY! MAYDAY! AMBROSE! WINSTON! COME IN! UGH! WHERE COULD THOSE TWO GOONS BE?!
MOON MONSTER

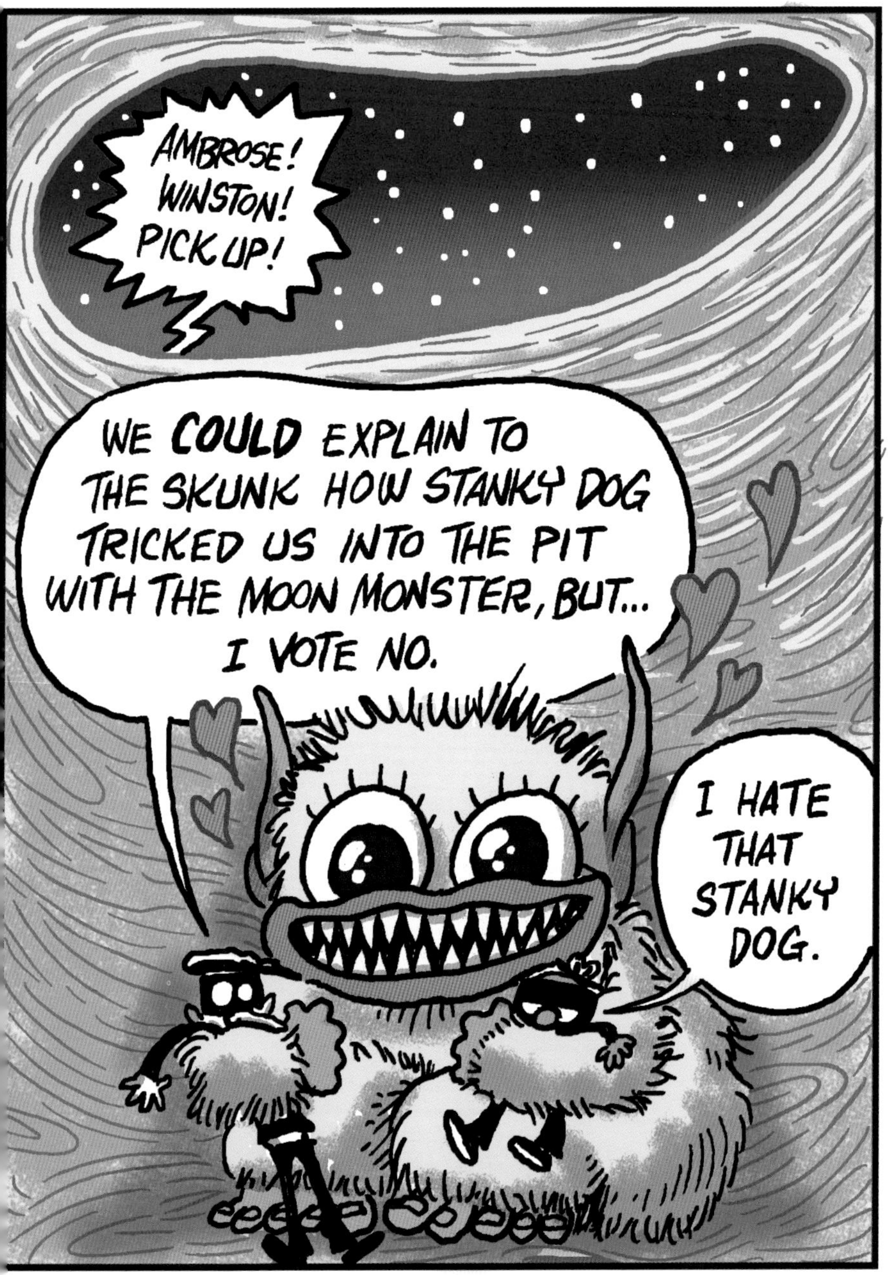
AMBROSE! WINSTON! PICK UP!
WE COULD EXPLAIN TO THE SKUNK HOW STANKY DOG TRICKED US INTO THE PIT WITH THE MOON MONSTER, BUT... I VOTE NO.
I HATE THAT STANKY DOG.

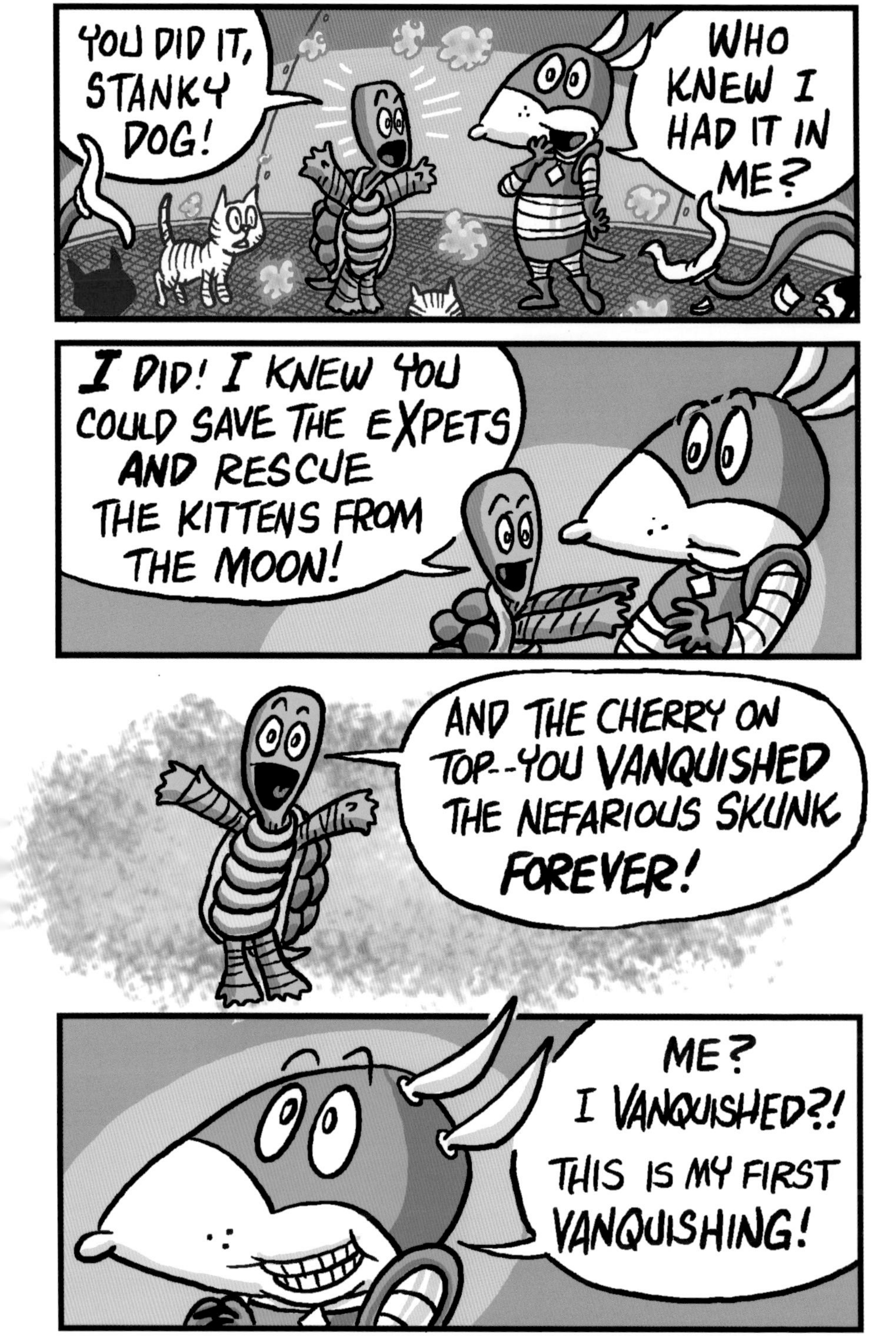
YOU DID IT, STANKY DOG!
WHO KNEW I HAD IT IN ME?
I DID! I KNEW YOU COULD SAVE THE EXPETS AND RESCUE THE KITTENS FROM THE MOON!
AND THE CHERRY ON TOP--YOU VANQUISHED THE NEFARIOUS SKUNK FOREVER!
ME? I VANQUISHED?!
THIS IS MY FIRST VANQUISHING!

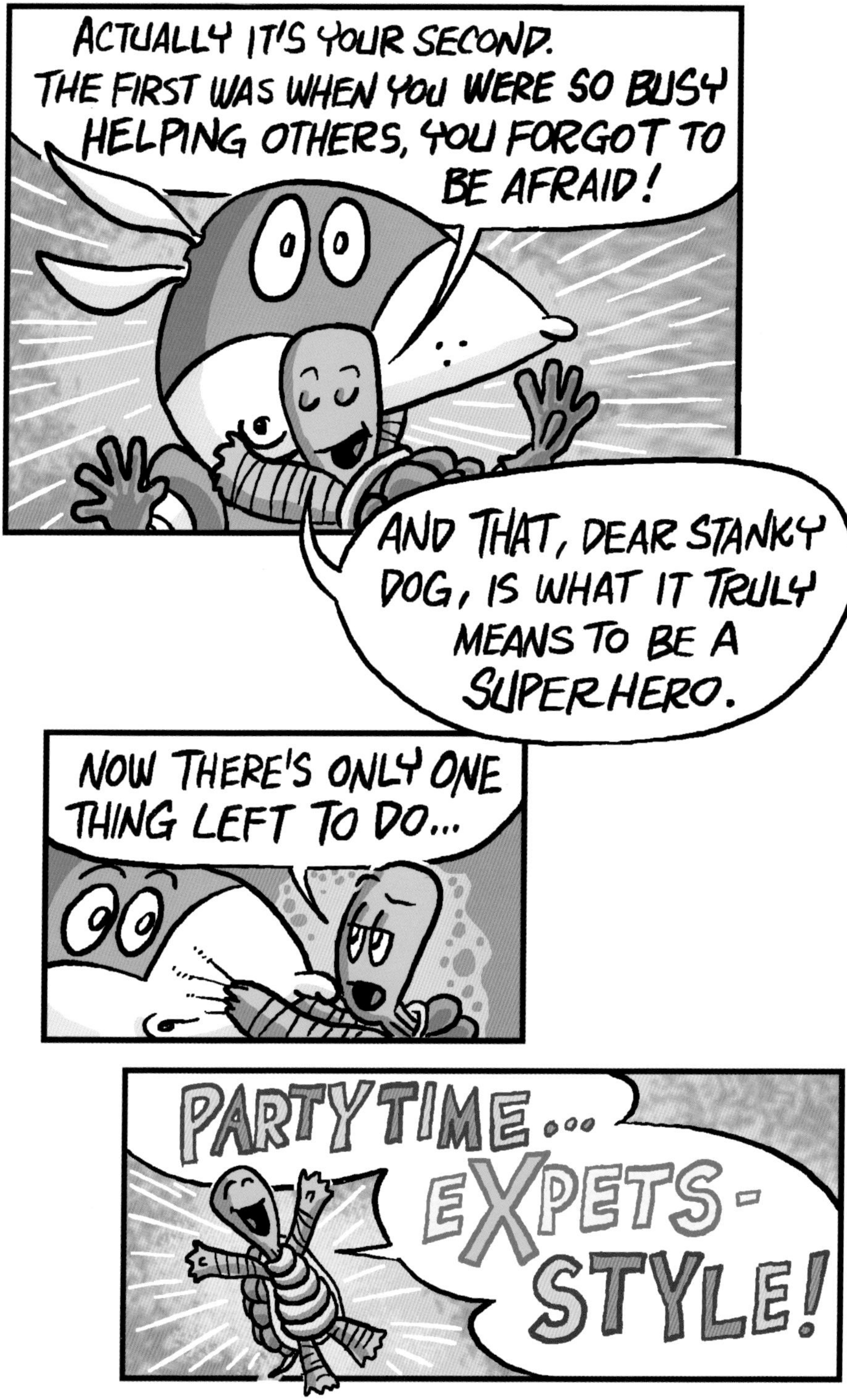
ACTUALLY IT'S YOUR SECOND. THE FIRST WAS WHEN YOU WERE SO BUSY HELPING OTHERS, YOU FORGOT TO BE AFRAID!
AND THAT, DEAR STANKY DOG, IS WHAT IT TRULY MEANS TO BE A SUPERHERO.
NOW THERE'S ONLY ONE THING LEFT TO DO...
PARTYTIME... eXPETS-STYLE!

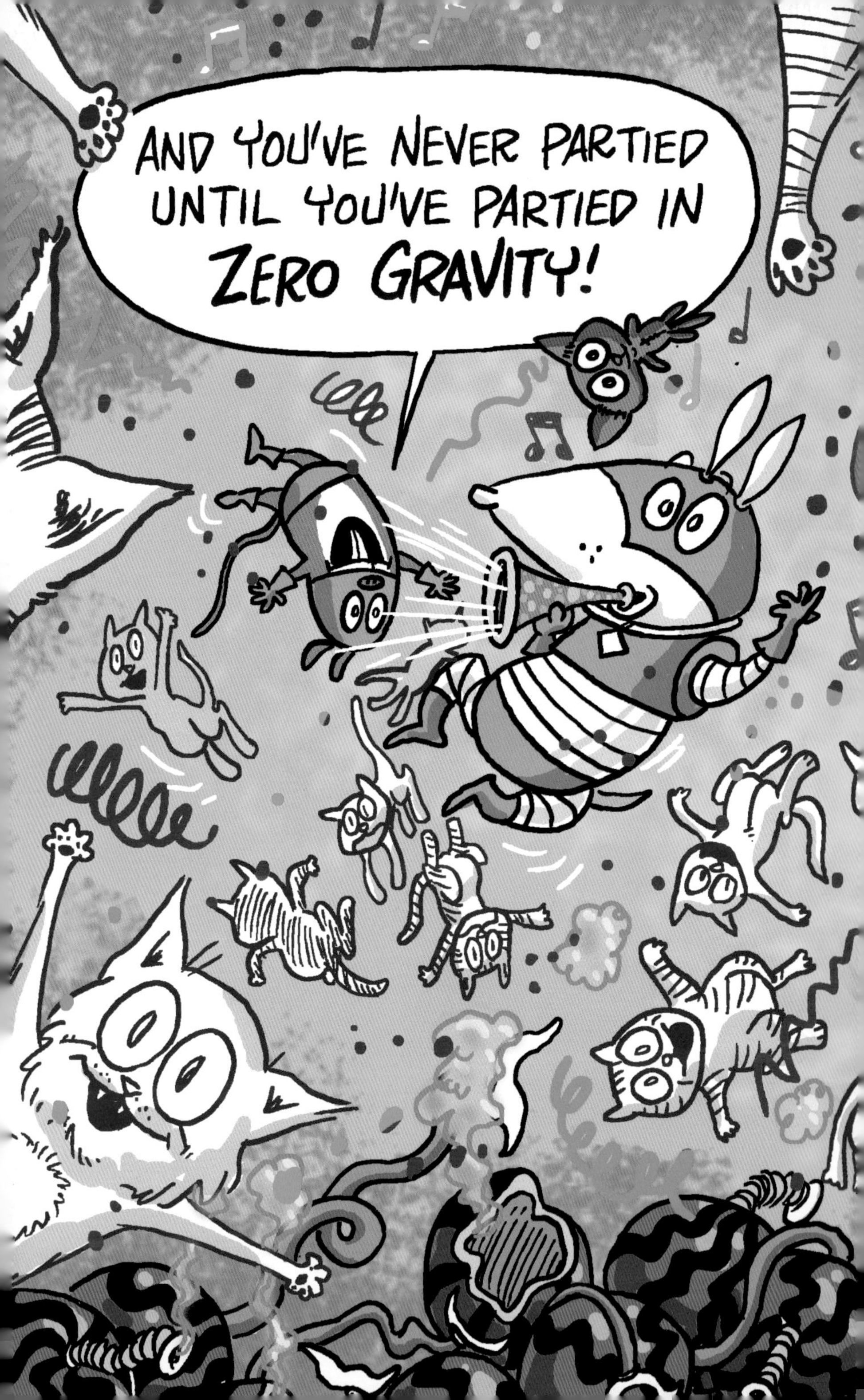
AND YOU'VE NEVER PARTIED UNTIL YOU'VE PARTIED IN ZERO GRAVITY!

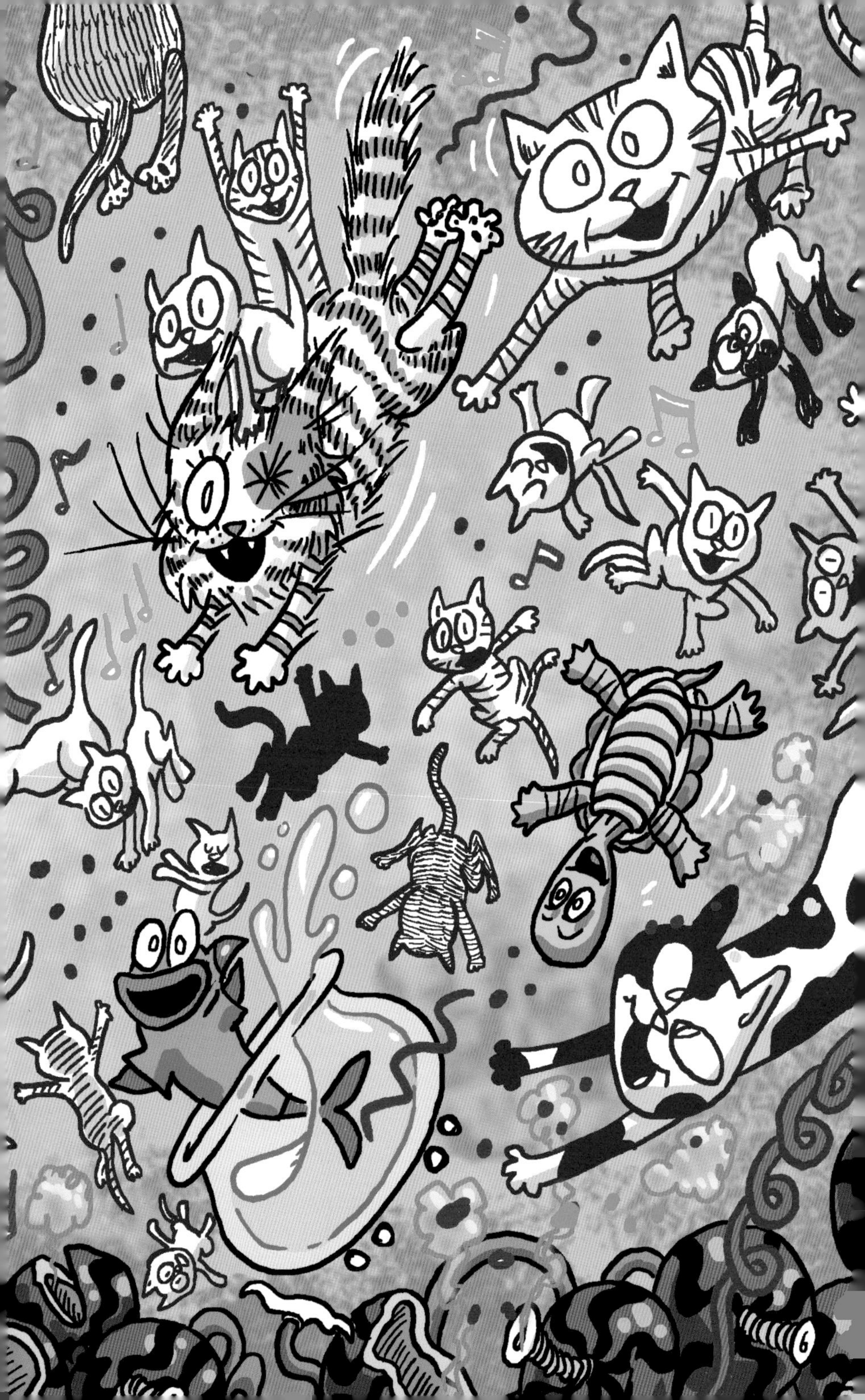

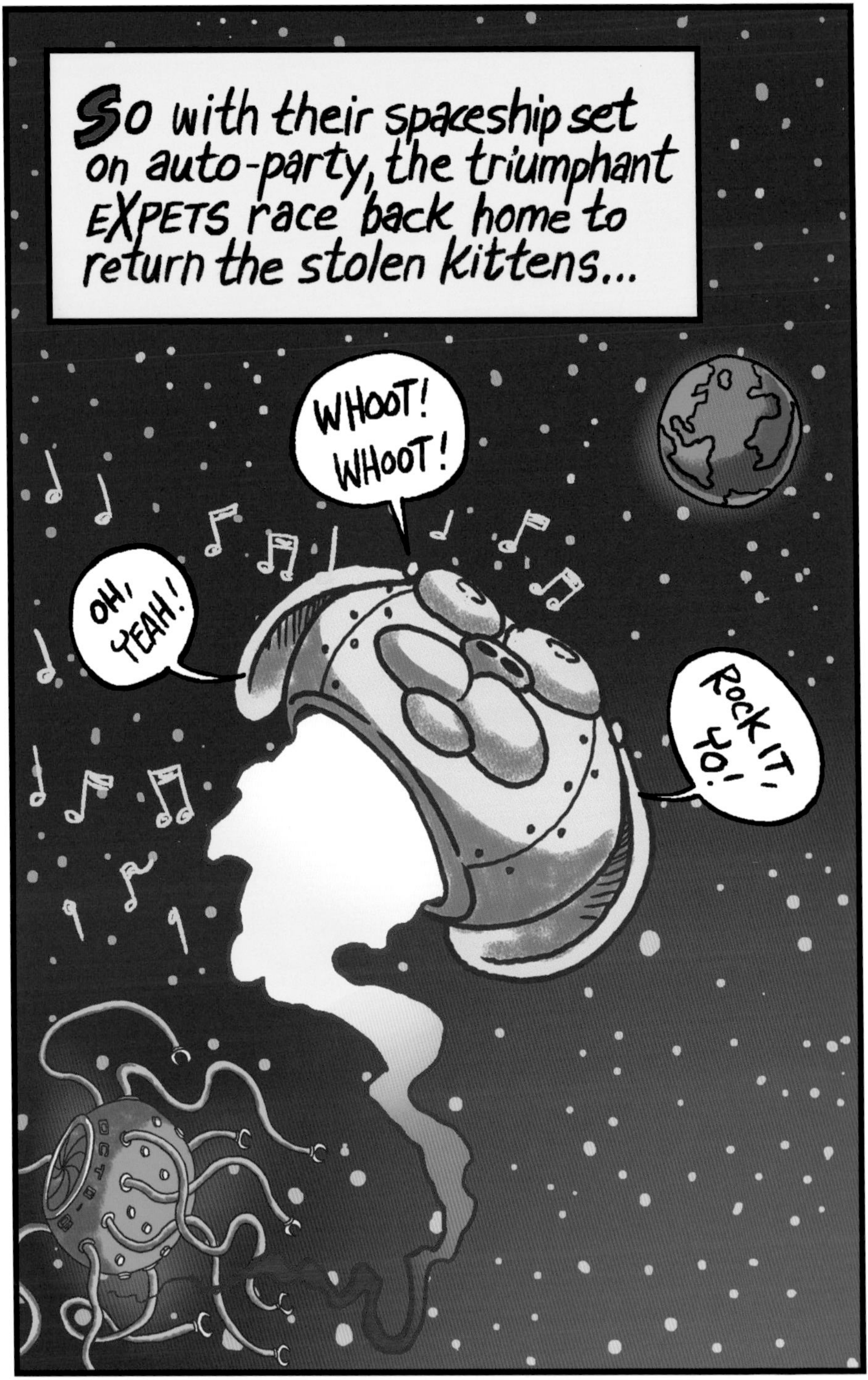
So with their spaceship set on auto-party, the triumphant EXPETS race back home to return the stolen kittens...
WHOOT! WHOOT!
OH, YEAH!
ROCK IT, YO!
OCTI-B

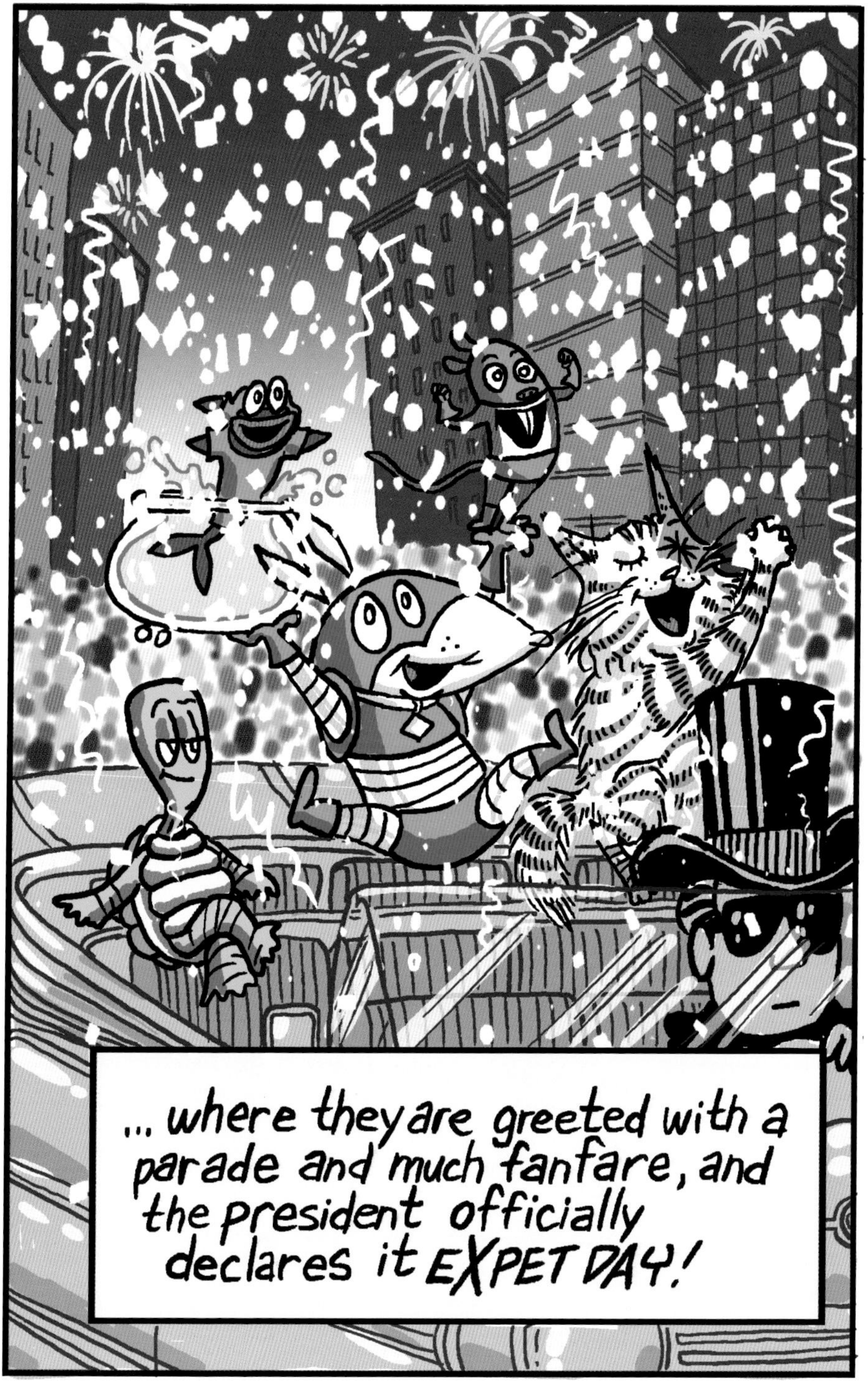
... where they are greeted with a parade and much fanfare, and the president officially declares it EXPET DAY!

But all parties must come to an end, and after receiving many medals, awards, and coupons for free ice cream, the EXPETS quietly return to their secret, everyday lives...

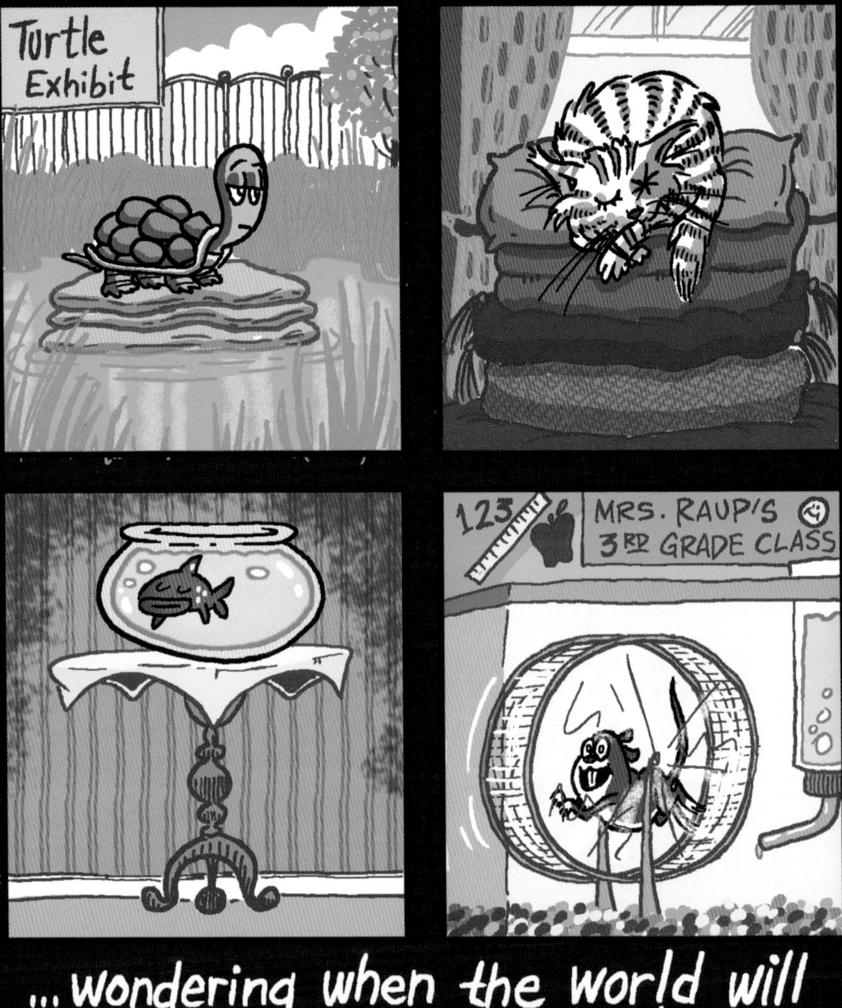
Turtle Exhibit
123
MRS. RAUP'S
3RD GRADE CLASS

...wondering when the world will again call them to action!

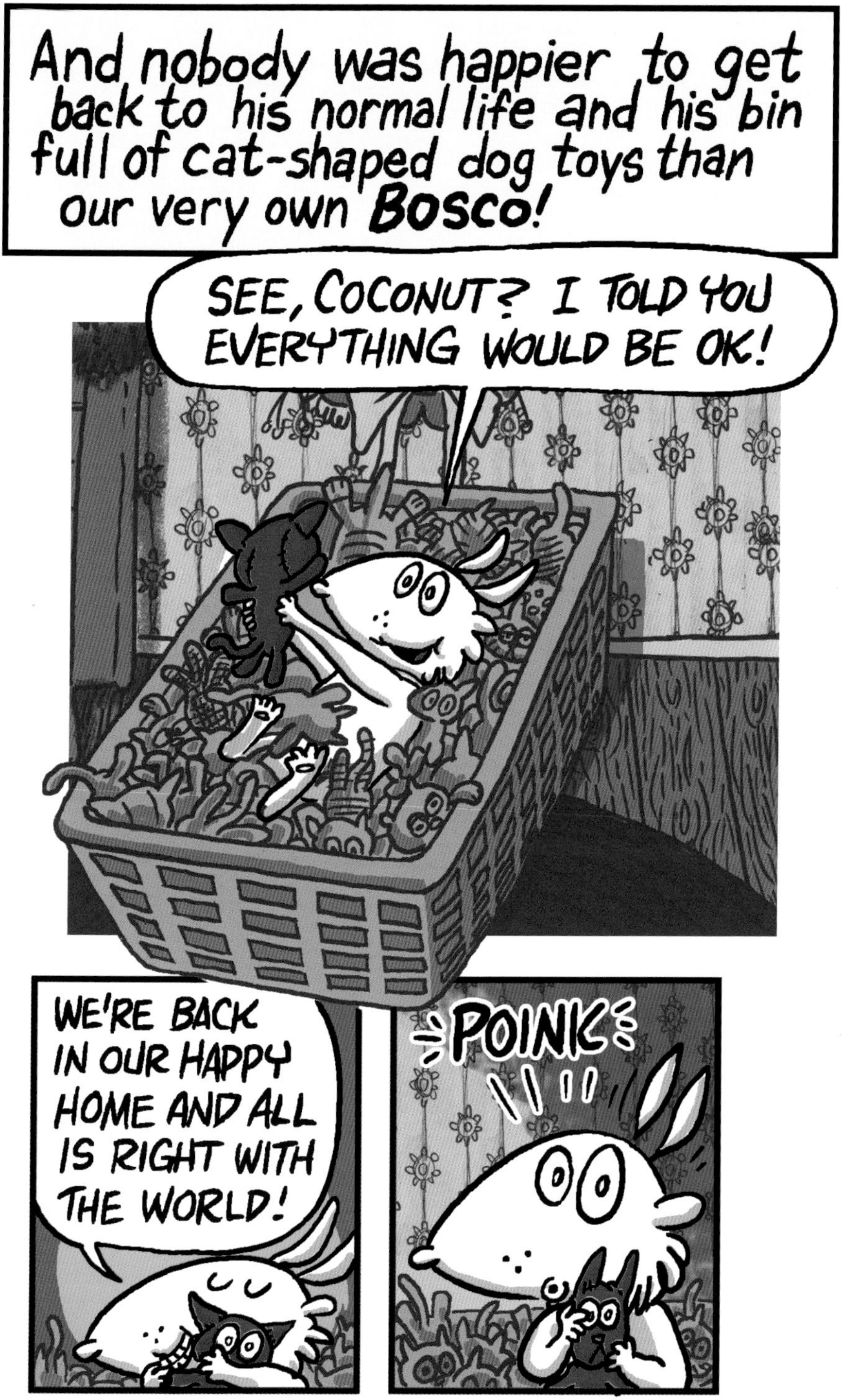
And nobody was happier to get back to his normal life and his bin full of cat-shaped dog toys than our very own **Bosco**!
SEE, COCONUT? I TOLD YOU EVERYTHING WOULD BE OK!
WE'RE BACK IN OUR HAPPY HOME AND ALL IS RIGHT WITH THE WORLD!
POINK

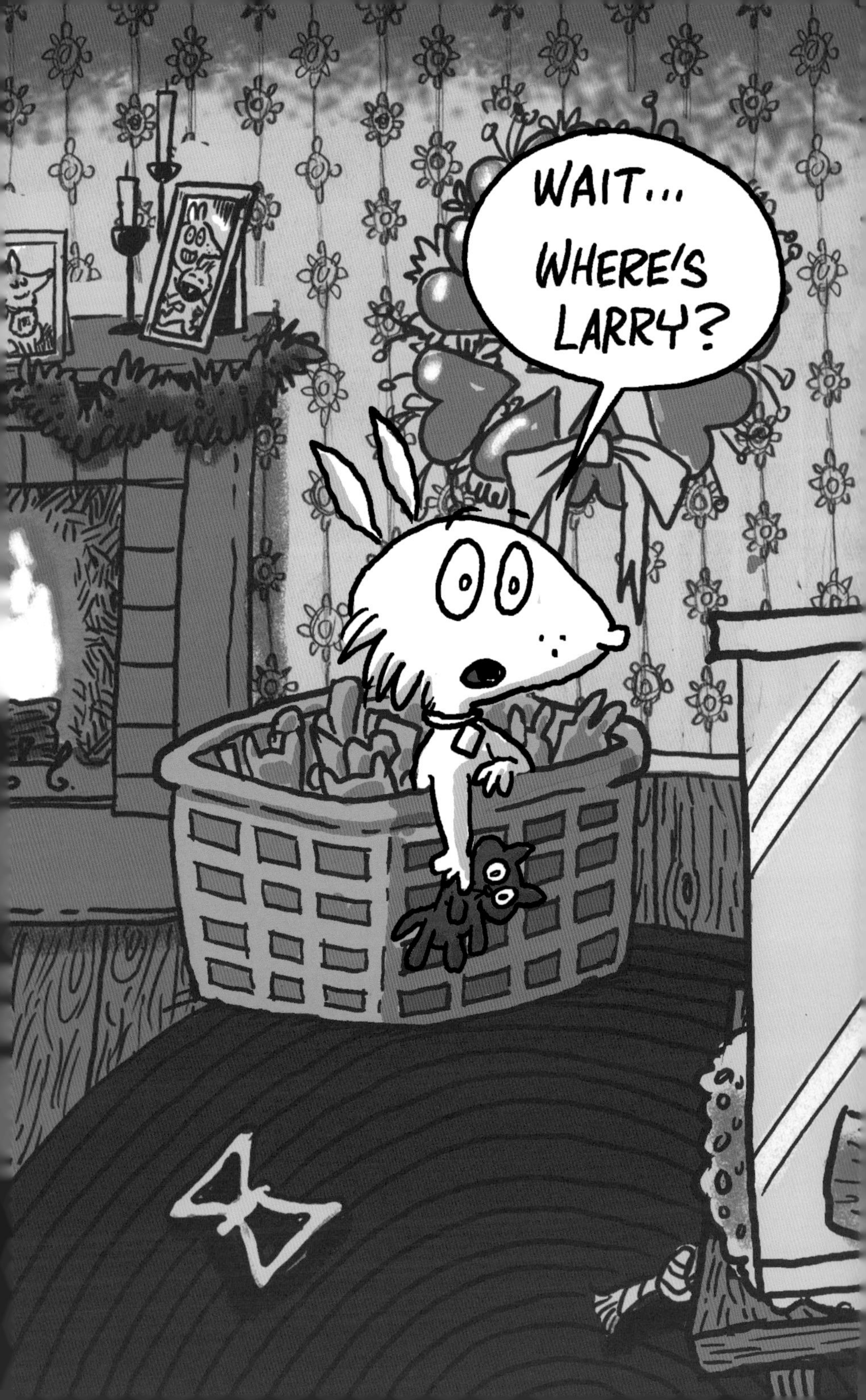
WAIT... WHERE'S LARRY?

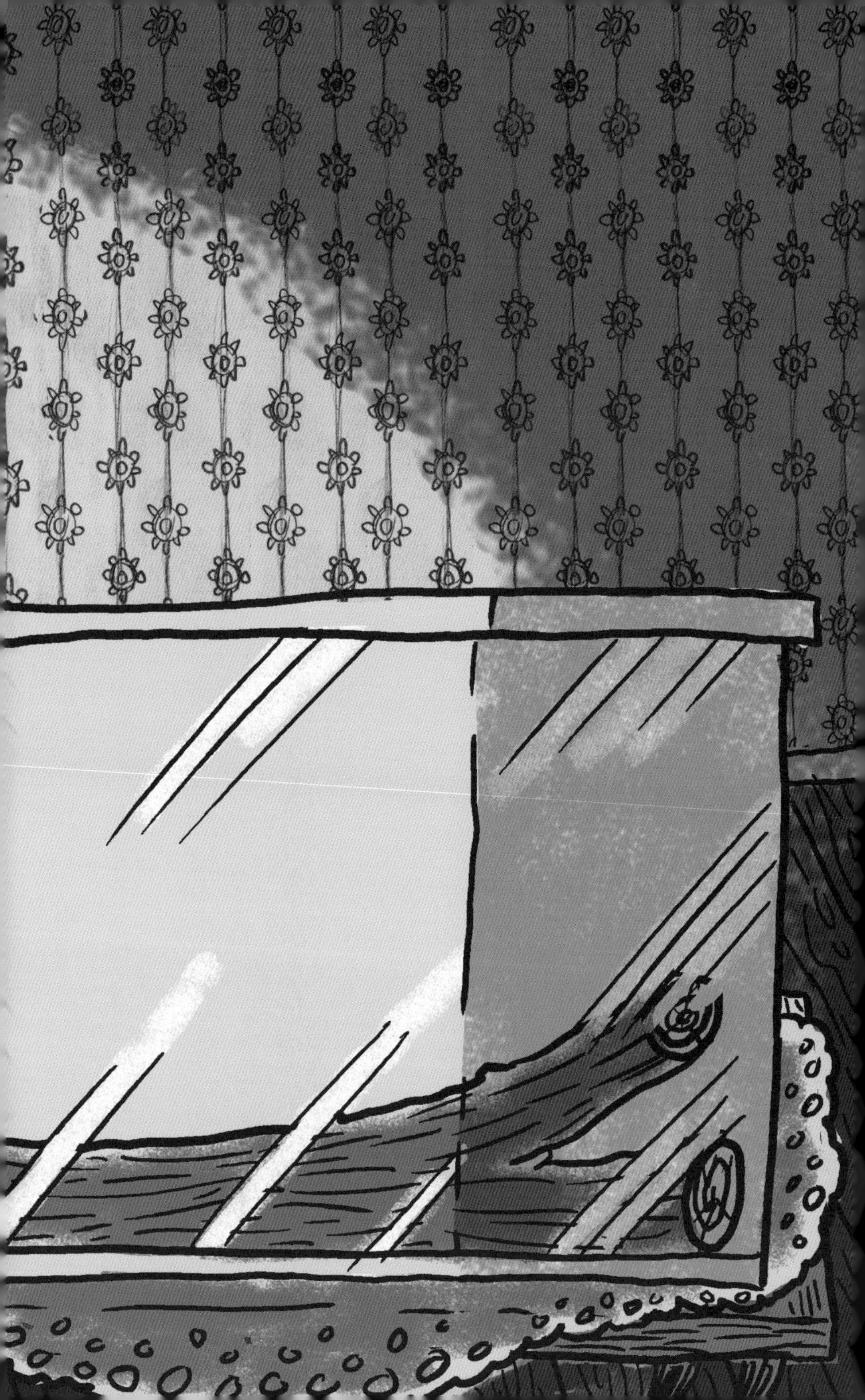

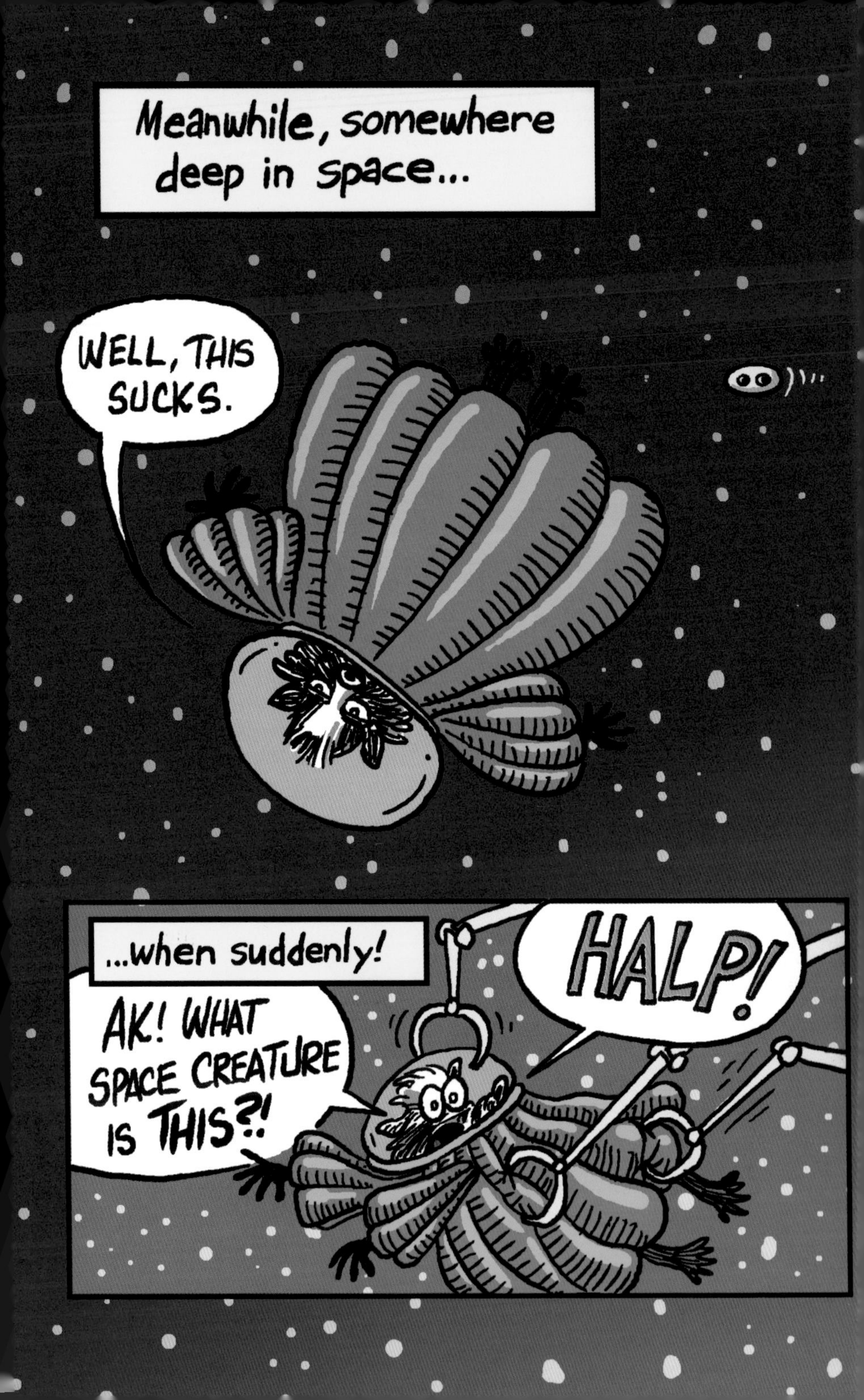

Meanwhile, somewhere deep in space...
WELL, THIS SUCKS.
...when suddenly!
AK! WHAT SPACE CREATURE IS THIS?!
HALP!

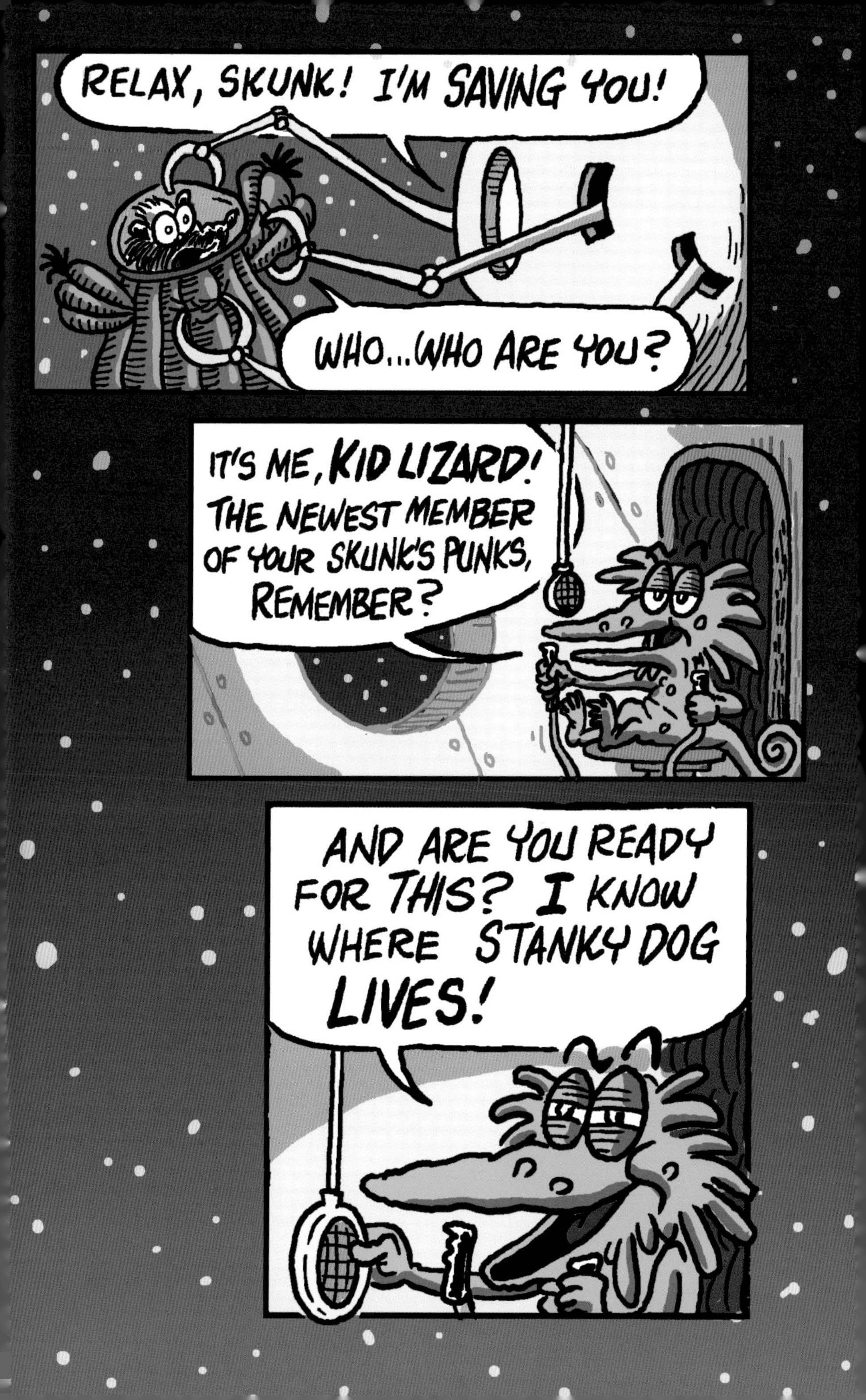
RELAX, SKUNK! I'M SAVING YOU!
WHO...WHO ARE YOU?
IT'S ME, KID LIZARD! THE NEWEST MEMBER OF YOUR SKUNK'S PUNKS, REMEMBER?
AND ARE YOU READY FOR THIS? I KNOW WHERE STANKY DOG LIVES!

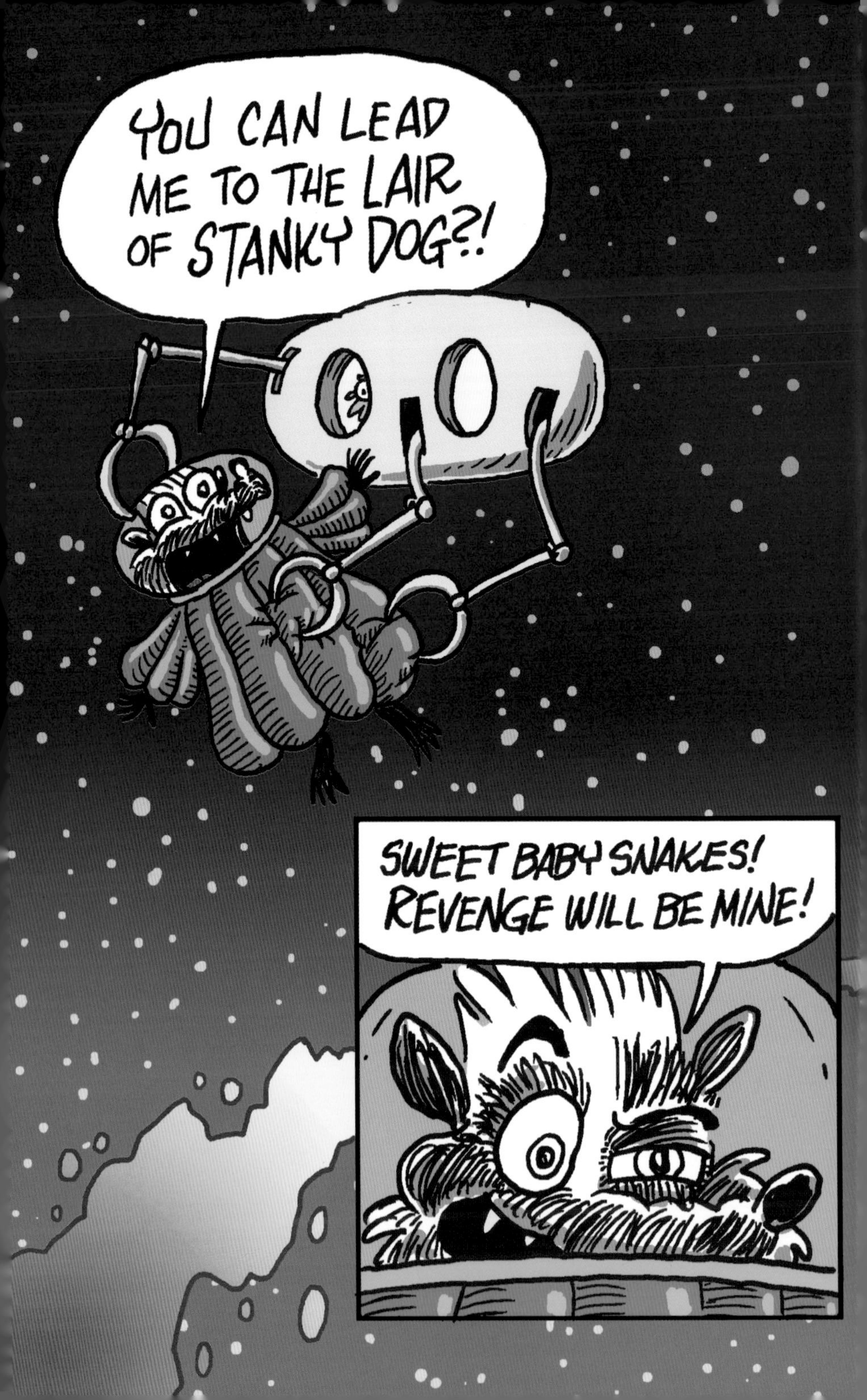
YOU CAN LEAD ME TO THE LAIR OF STANKY DOG?!
SWEET BABY SNAKES! REVENGE WILL BE MINE!

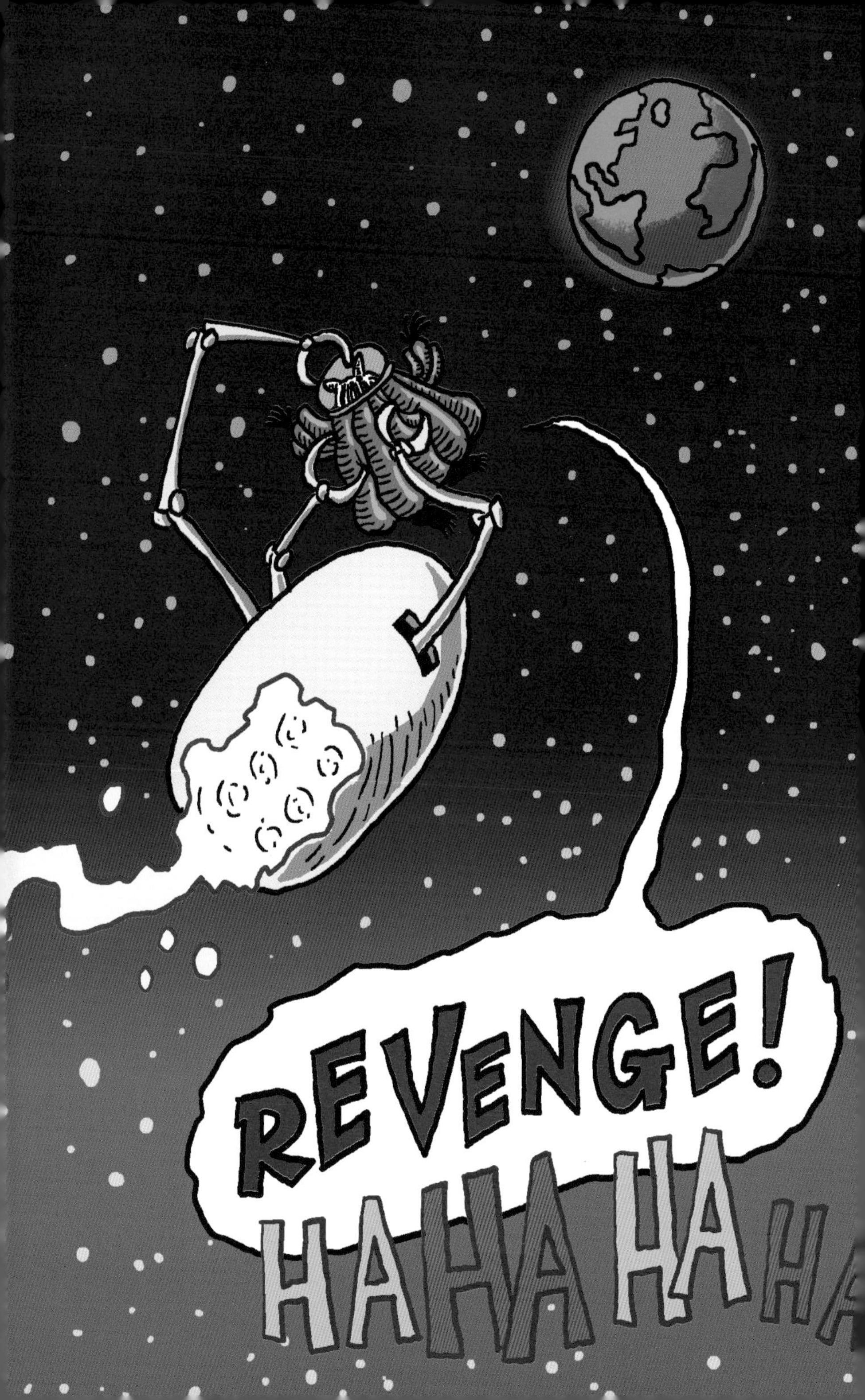
REVENGE!
HAHAHAHA

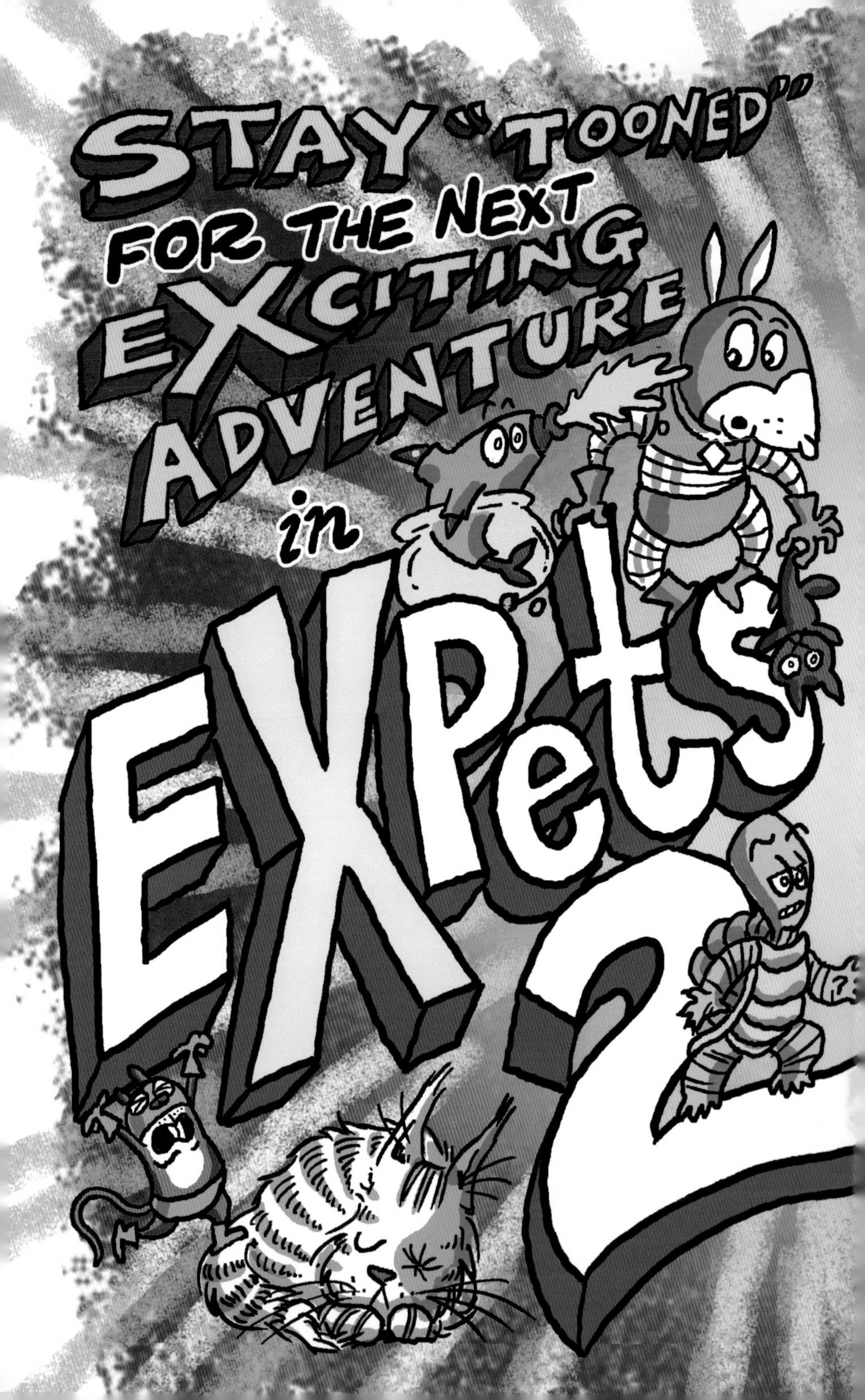
STAY "TOONED"
FOR THE NEXT
EXCITING
ADVENTURE
in
EXPets
2

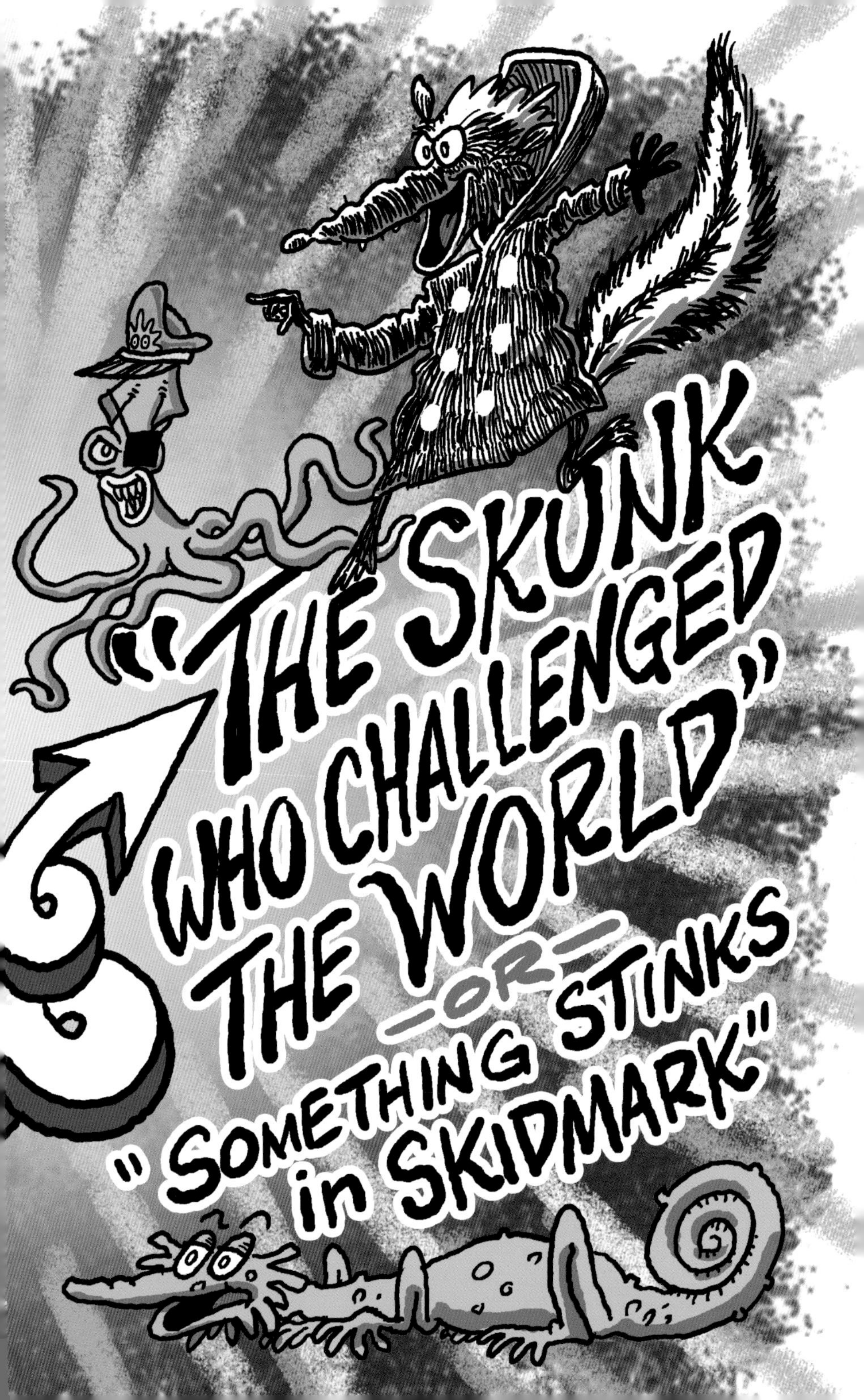
"THE SKUNK WHO CHALLENGED THE WORLD"
—OR—
"SOMETHING STINKS in SKIDMARK"

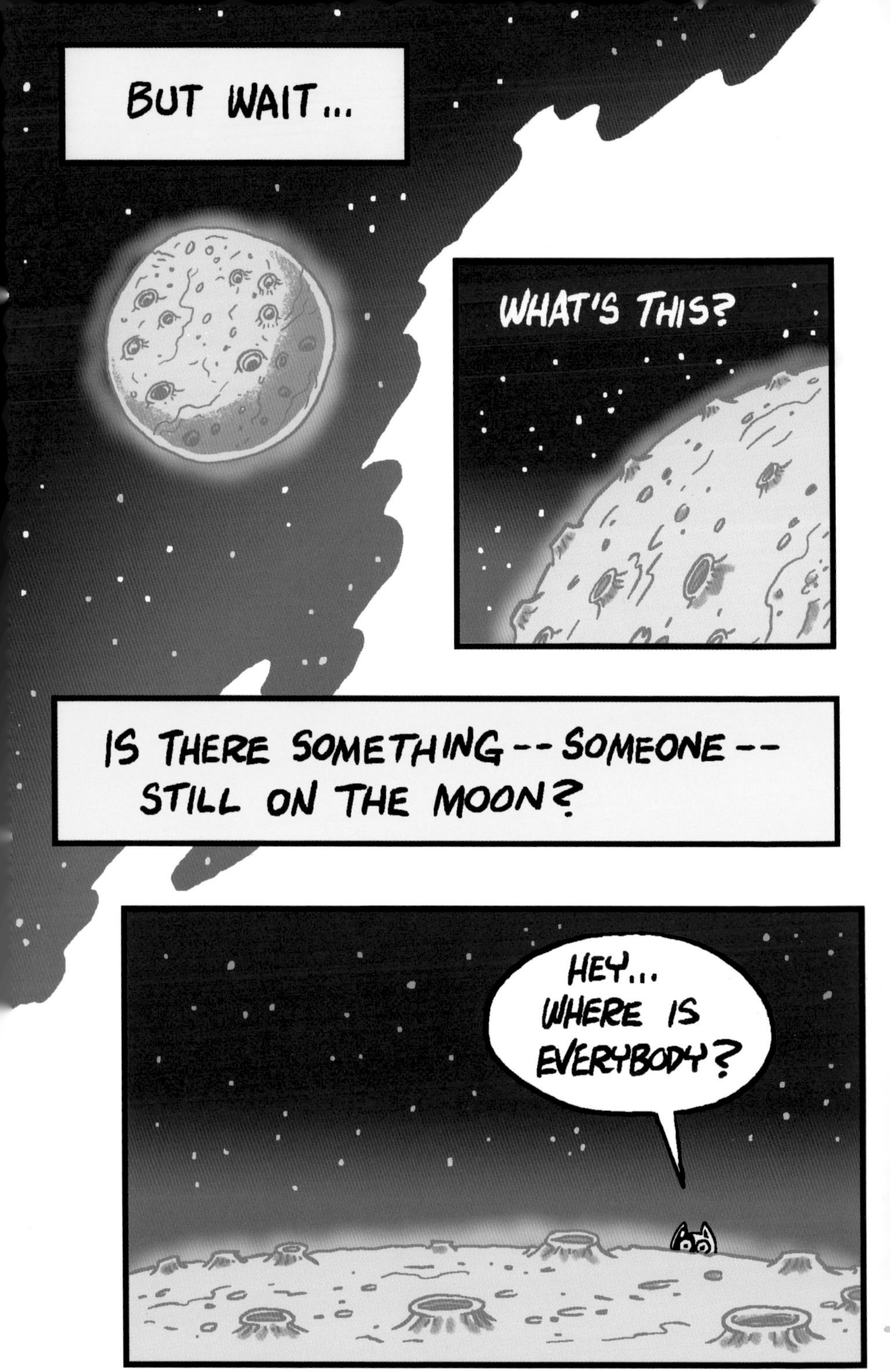
BUT WAIT...
WHAT'S THIS?
IS THERE SOMETHING--SOMEONE--STILL ON THE MOON?
HEY... WHERE IS EVERYBODY?

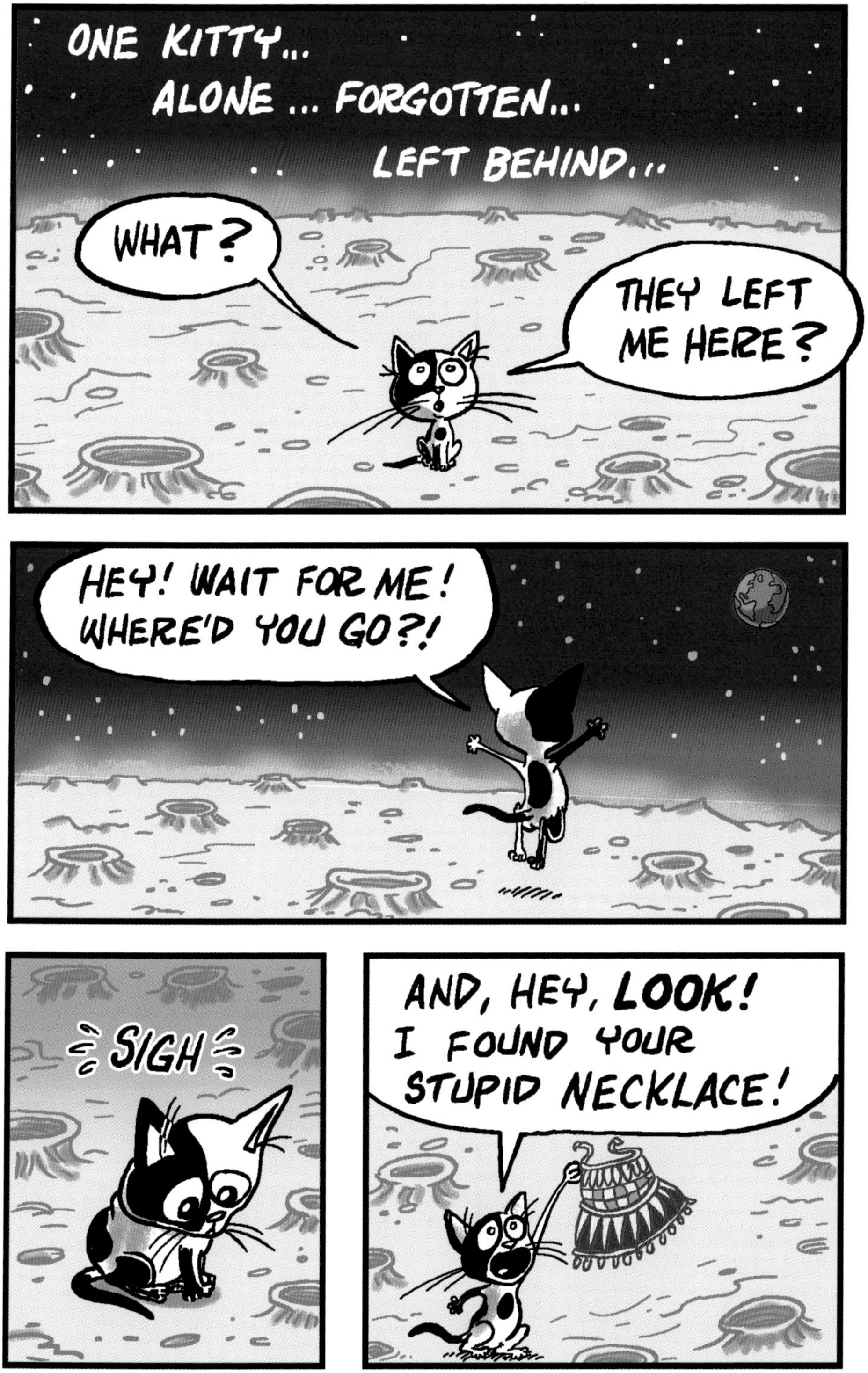
ONE KITTY... ALONE ... FORGOTTEN... LEFT BEHIND...
WHAT?
THEY LEFT ME HERE?
HEY! WAIT FOR ME! WHERE'D YOU GO?!
SIGH
AND, HEY, LOOK! I FOUND YOUR STUPID NECKLACE!

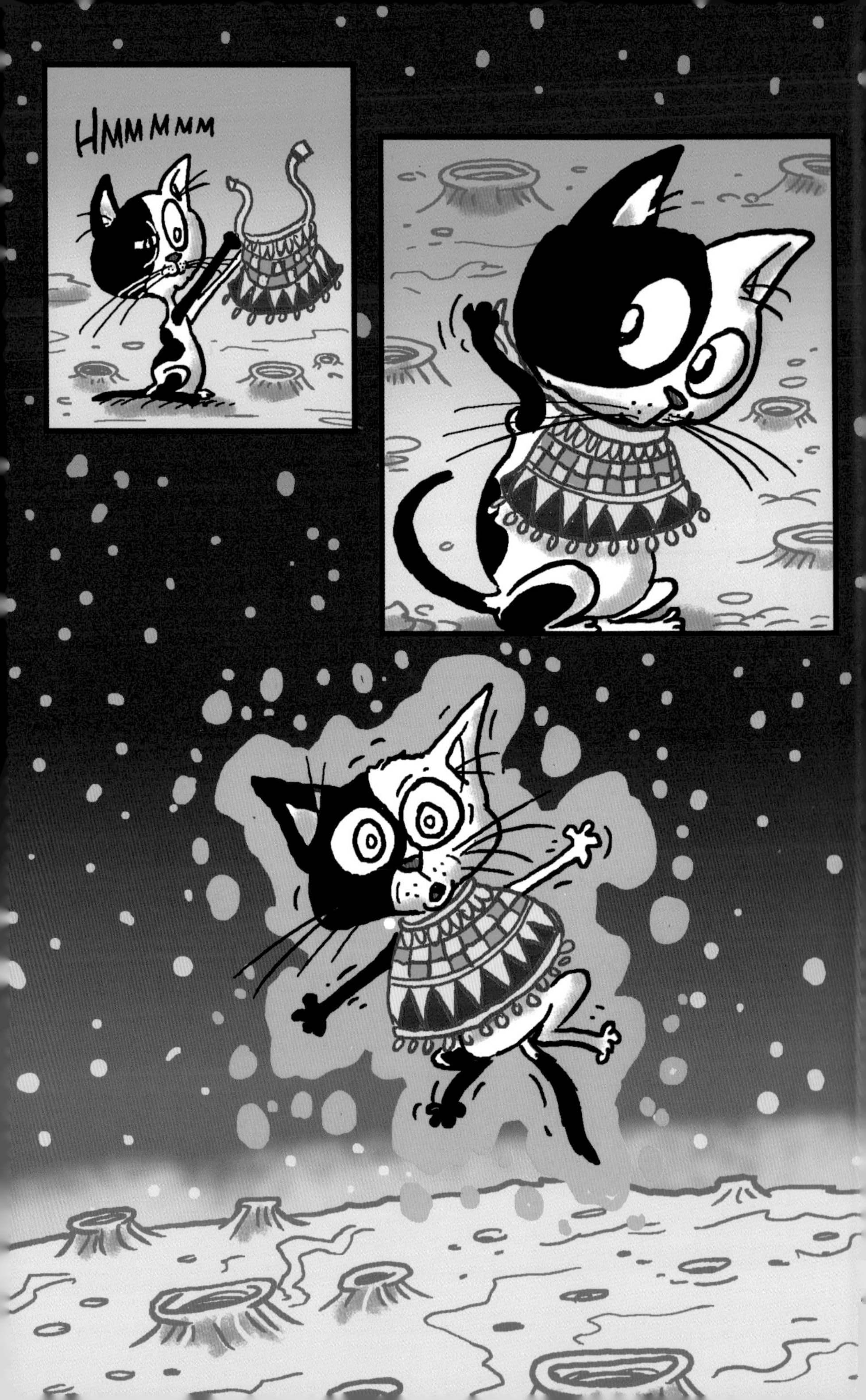
HMMMMM

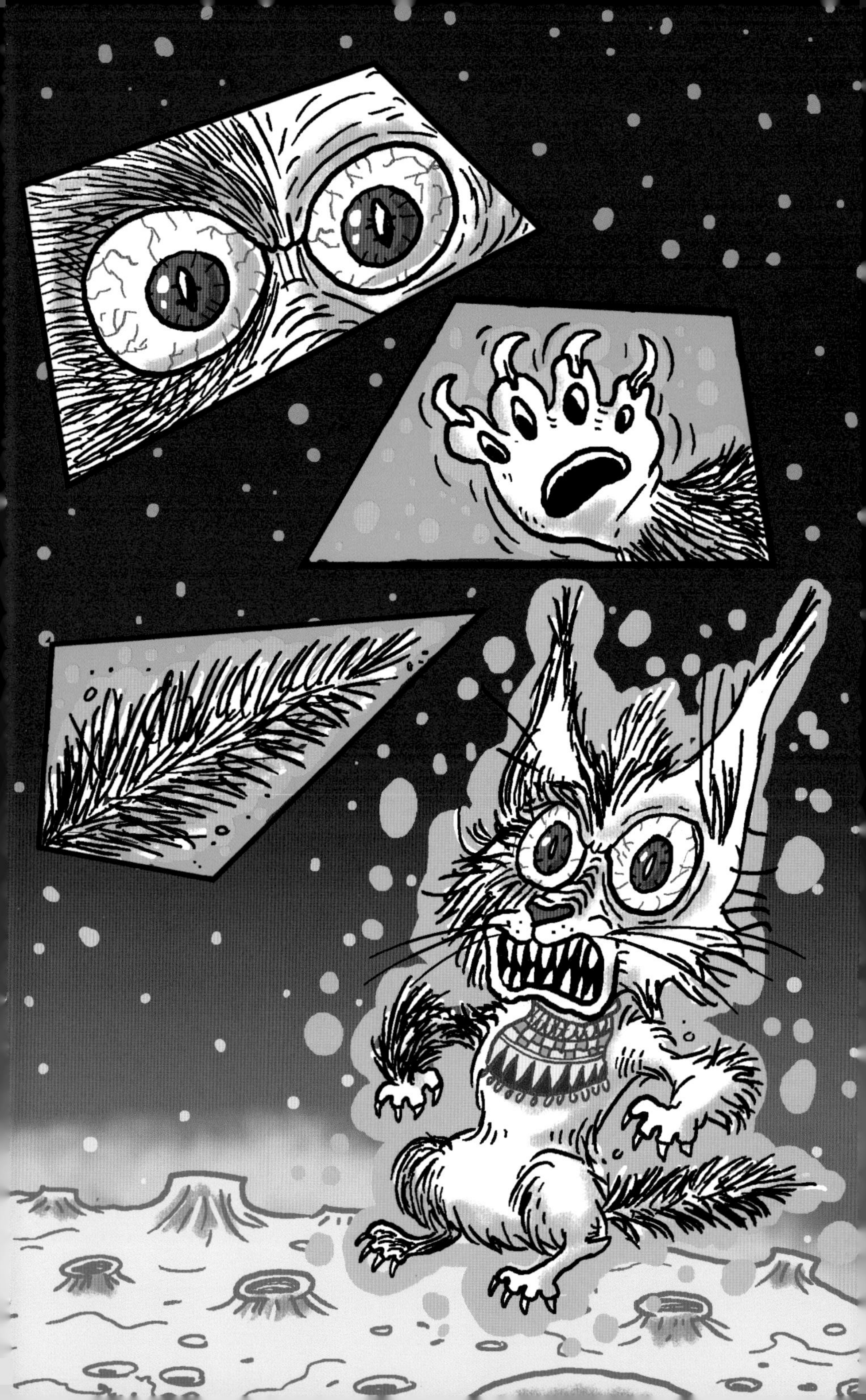

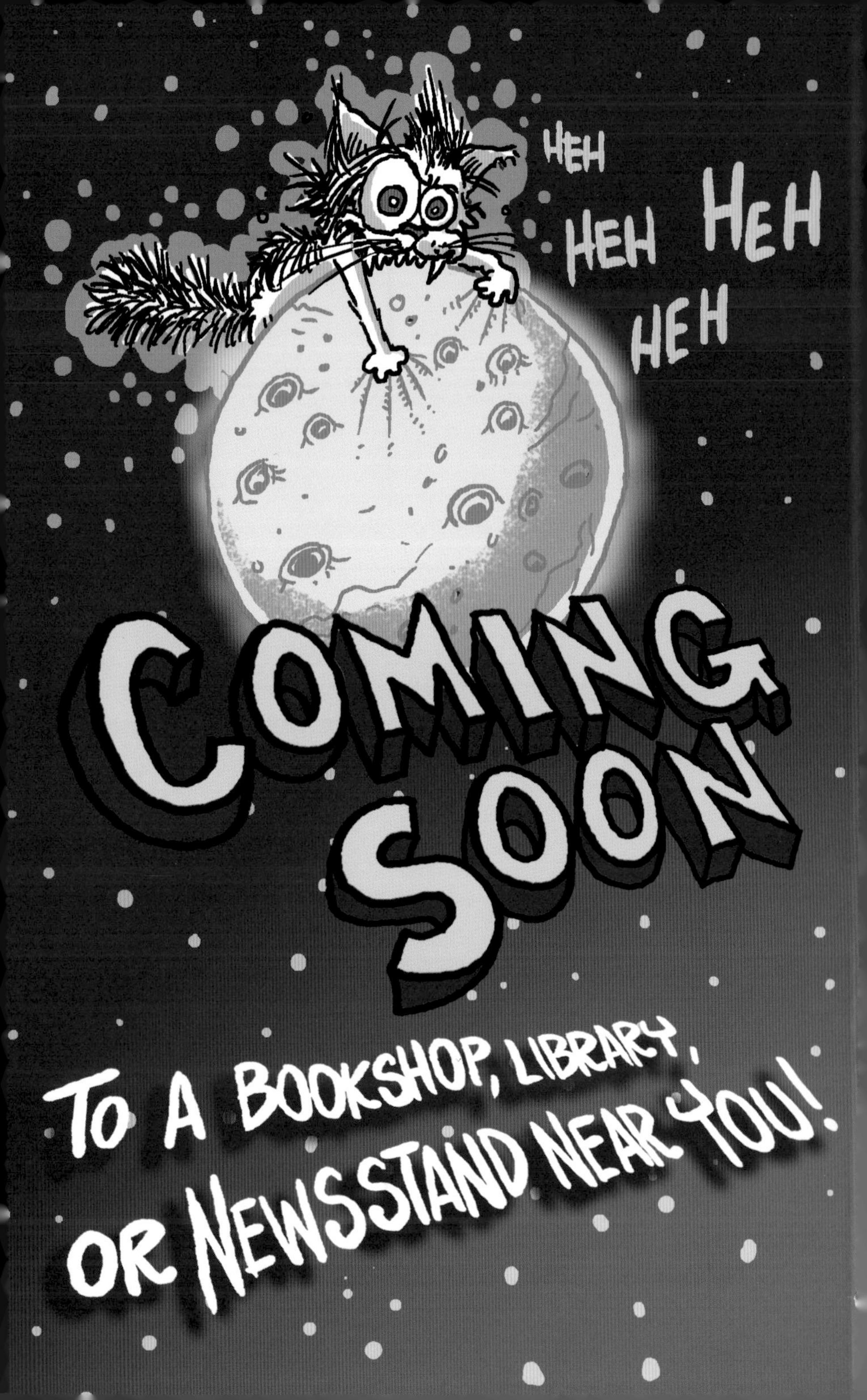
HEH
HEH HEH
HEH
COMING SOON
TO A BOOKSHOP, LIBRARY, OR NEWSSTAND NEAR YOU!

EH HEH HEH HA HA HA HA HA HA HA

Meanwhile on planet Earth,

author MARK TATULLI is hard at work battling evil deadlines to create *eXpets 2!* Though world-renown for his newspaper comic strip *Liō*, and his graphic novels *Short & Skinny*, *The Big Break*, and the Desmond Pucket series, Mark's fight to bring you the next, best episode of eXpets is real—and the clock is ticking! His three Emmys for prior work in TV, and his Best Newspaper Strip award from the National Cartoonists Society can't save him now. His only hope is to hit the art table and keep drawing! The world is waiting!

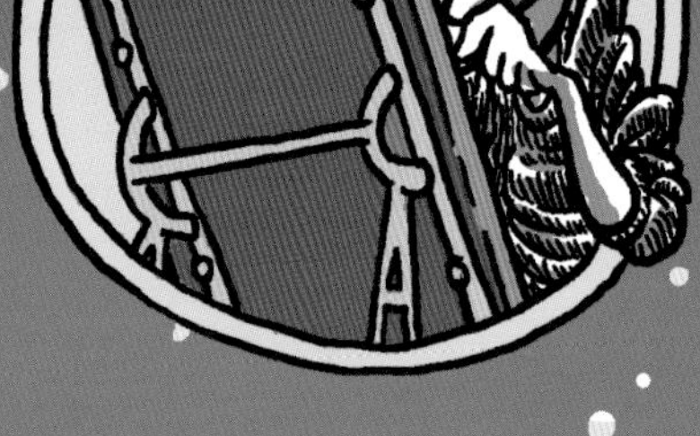

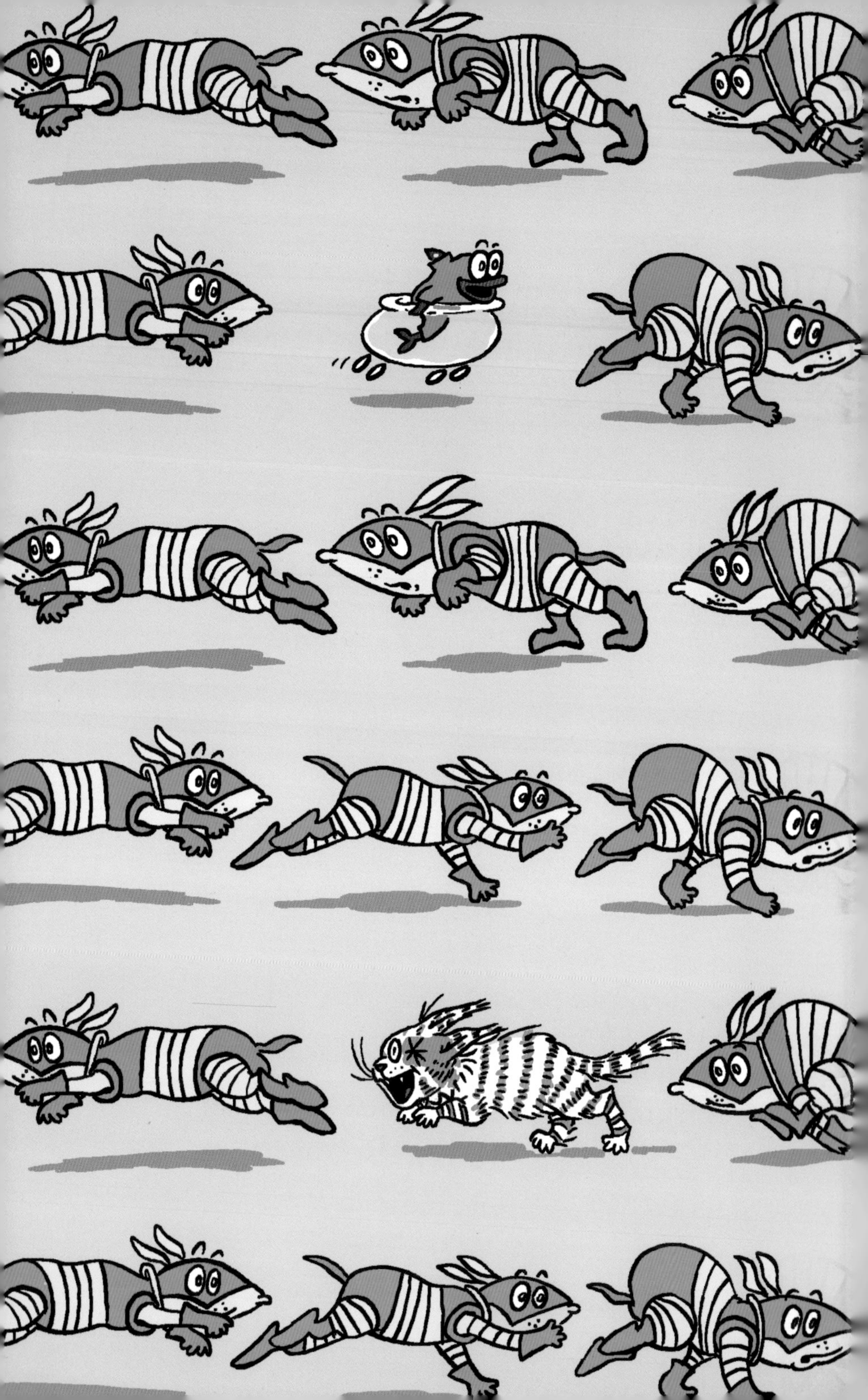

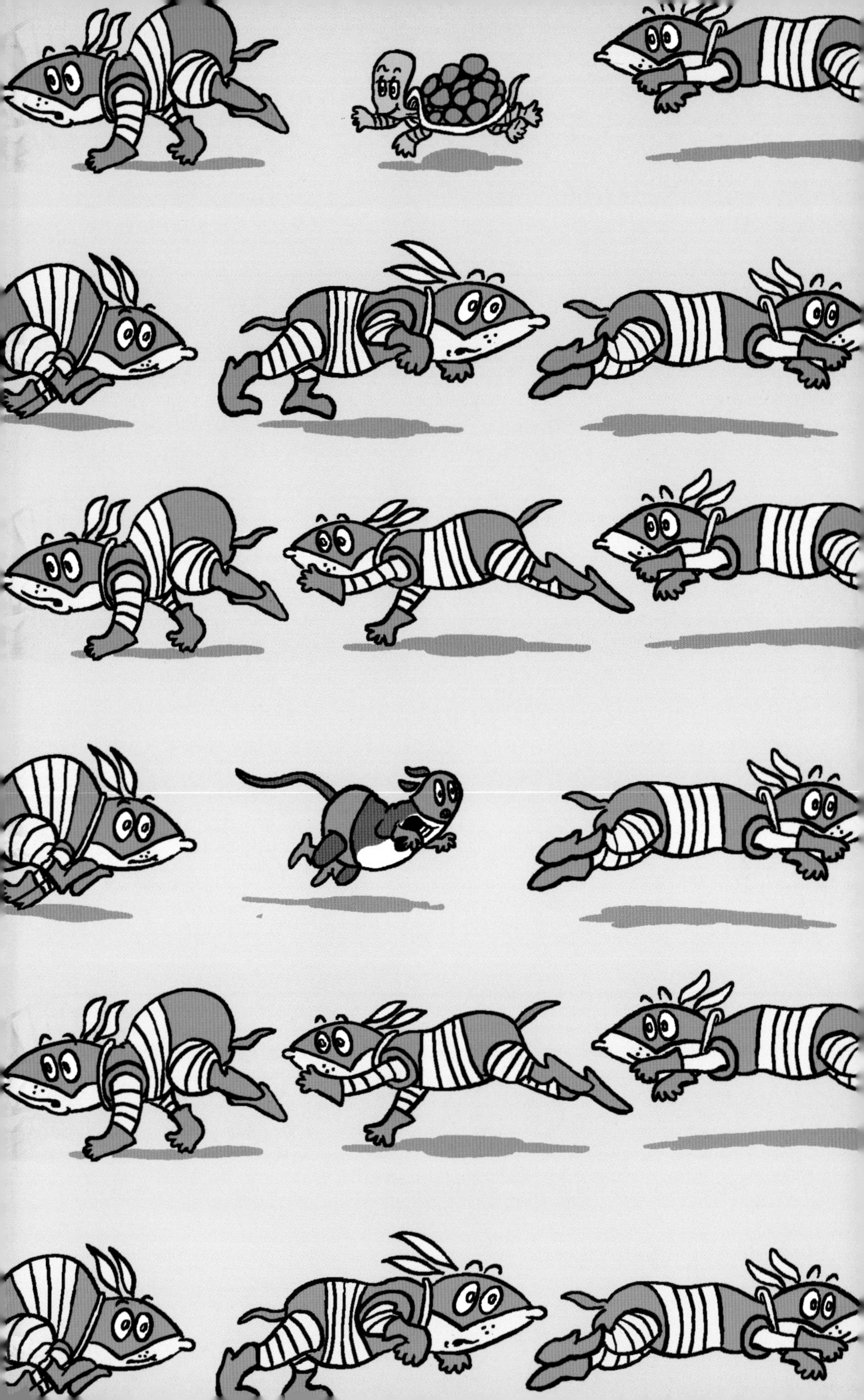